The Delicacy

James Albon

Published by Top Shelf Productions, an imprint of IDW Publishing, a division of Idea and Design Works, LLC. Offices: Top Shelf Productions, c/o Idea & Design Works, LLC, 2765 Truxtun Road, San Diego, CA 92106. Top Shelf Productions®, the Top Shelf logo, Idea and Design Works®, and the IDW logo are registered trademarks of Idea and Design Works, LLC. All Rights Reserved. With the exception of small excerpts of artwork used for review purposes, none of the contents of this publication may be reprinted without the permission of IDW Publishing.

IDW Publishing does not read or accept unsolicited submissions of ideas, stories, or artwork.

This project was completed with the generous support of the Creative Scotland Open Project Fund.

Editor-in-Chief: Chris Staros
Design by Nathan Widick

ISBN: 978-1-60309-492-4   24 23 22 21   4 3 2 1

Visit our online catalog at topshelfcomix.com.

Printed in Korea.

ALBA | CHRUTHACHAIL

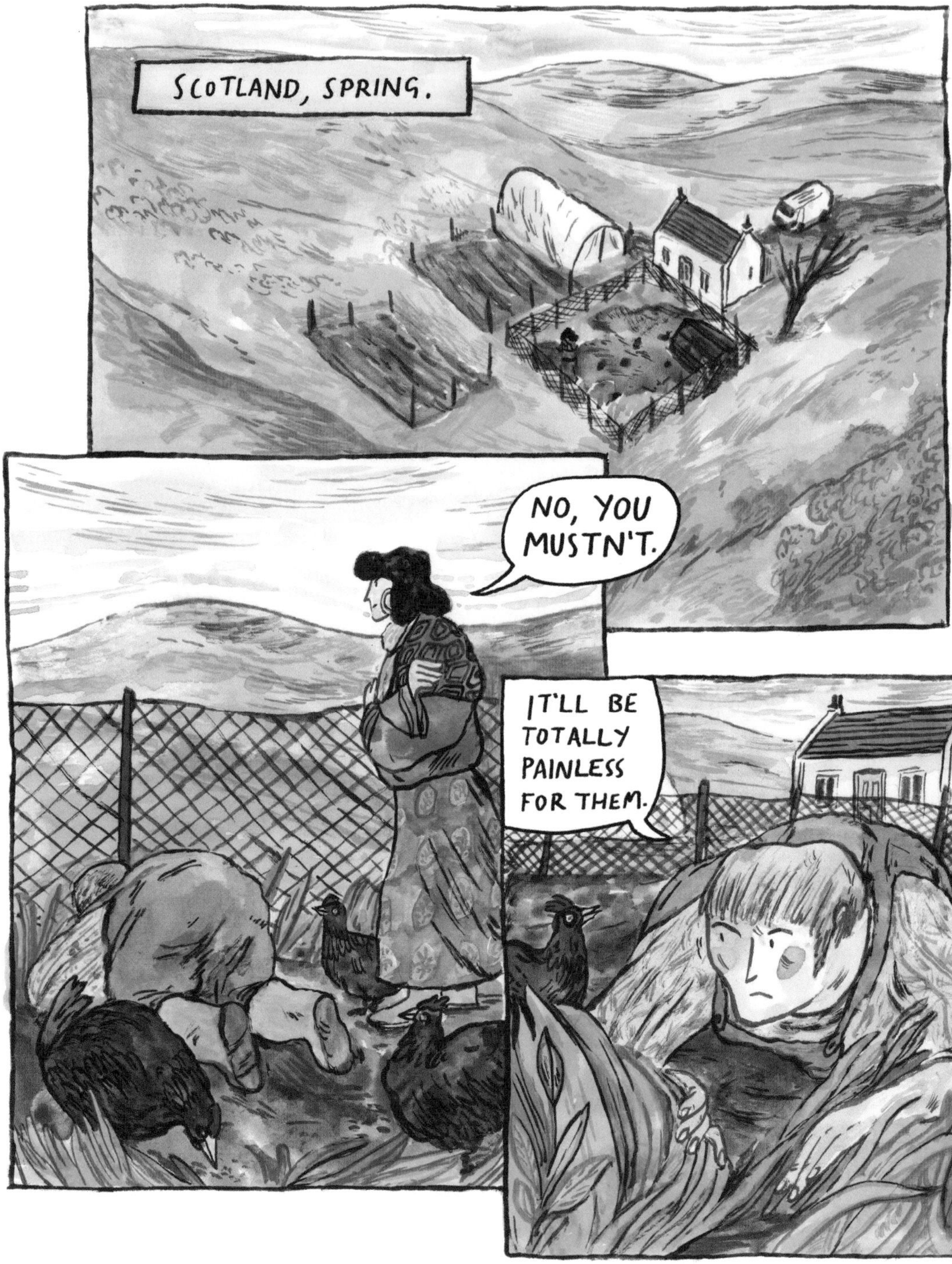
SCOTLAND, SPRING.
NO, YOU MUSTN'T.
IT'LL BE TOTALLY PAINLESS FOR THEM.

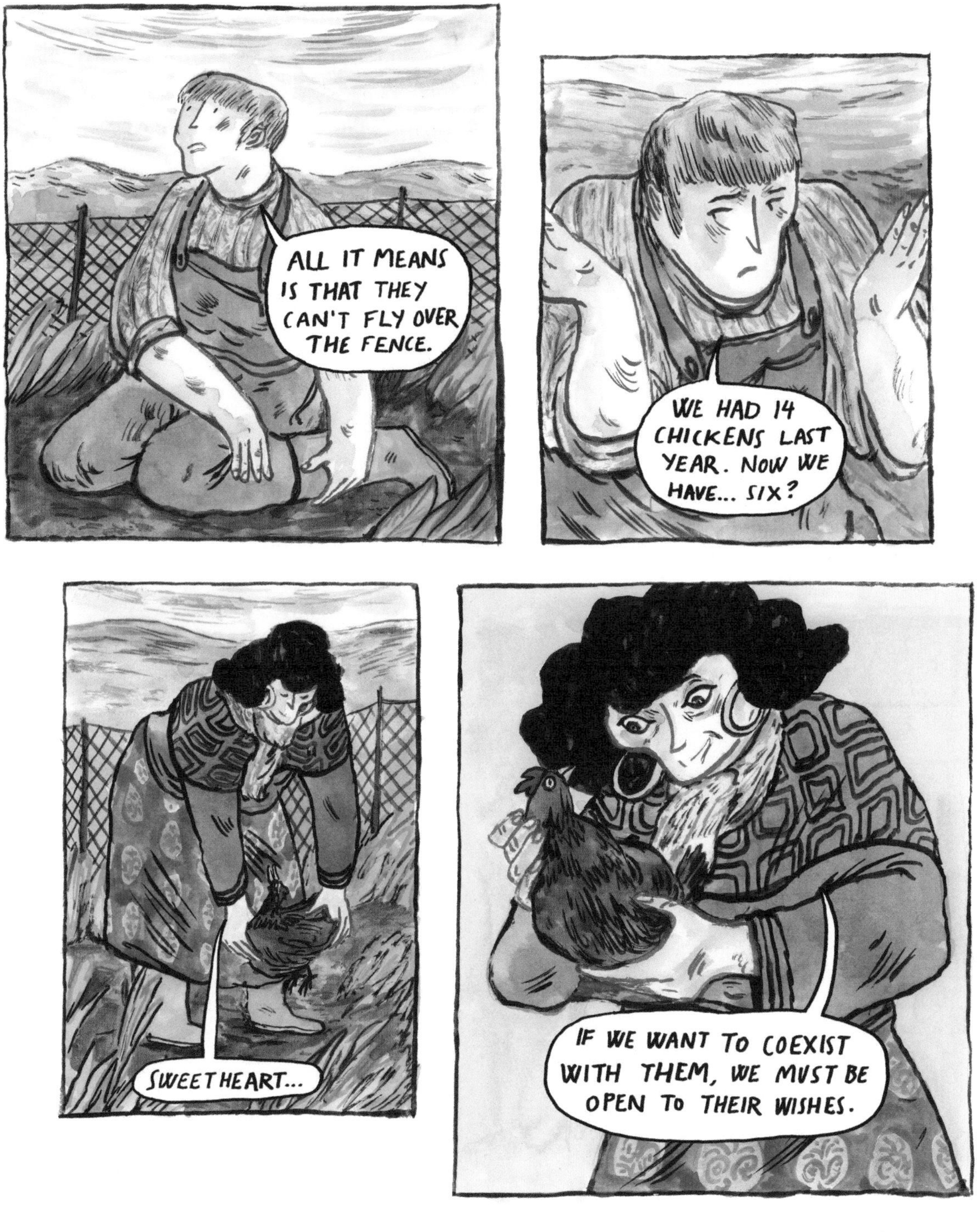
ALL IT MEANS IS THAT THEY CAN'T FLY OVER THE FENCE.
WE HAD 14 CHICKENS LAST YEAR. NOW WE HAVE... SIX?
SWEETHEART...
IF WE WANT TO COEXIST WITH THEM, WE MUST BE OPEN TO THEIR WISHES.

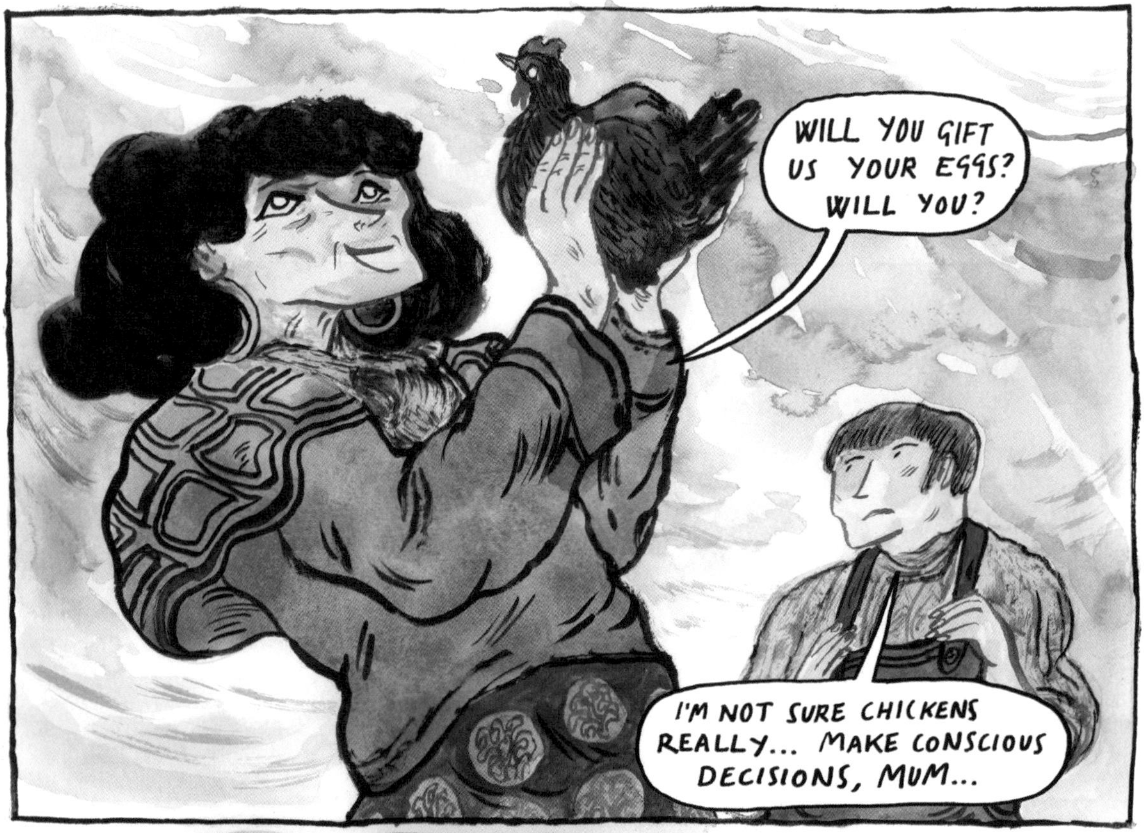
WILL YOU GIFT US YOUR EGGS? WILL YOU?
I'M NOT SURE CHICKENS REALLY... MAKE CONSCIOUS DECISIONS, MUM...

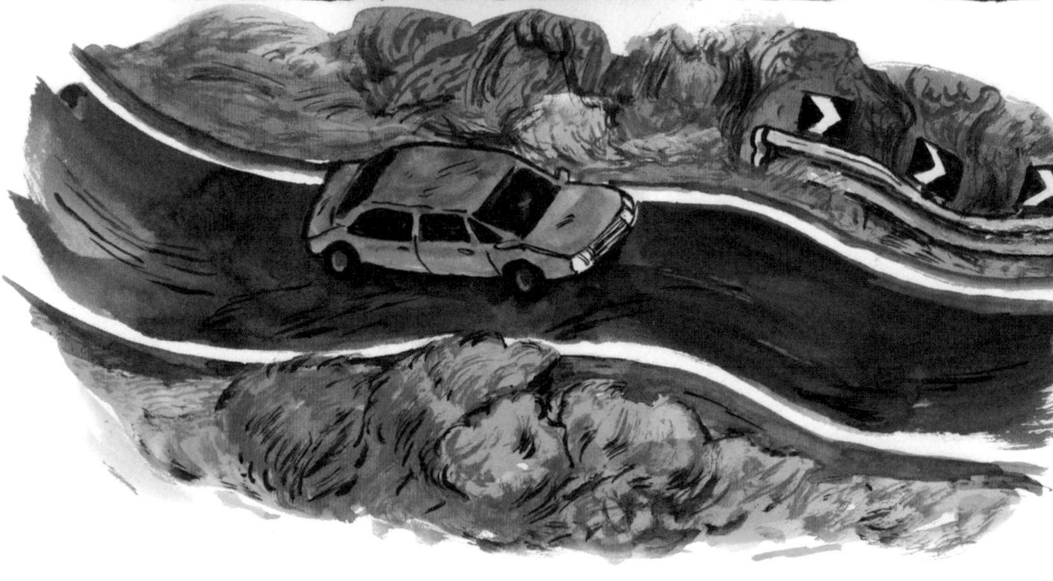

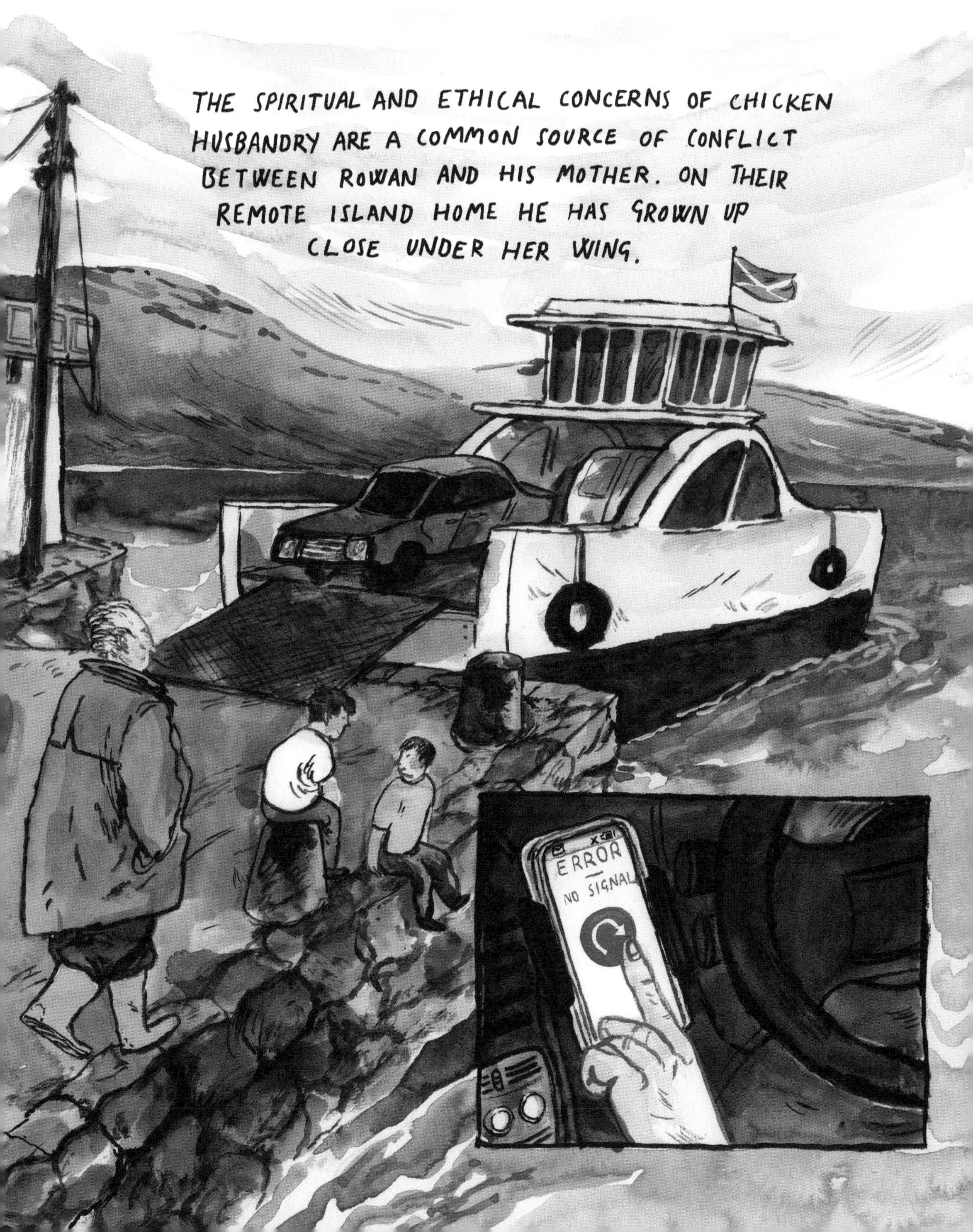
THE SPIRITUAL AND ETHICAL CONCERNS OF CHICKEN HUSBANDRY ARE A COMMON SOURCE OF CONFLICT BETWEEN ROWAN AND HIS MOTHER. ON THEIR REMOTE ISLAND HOME HE HAS GROWN UP CLOSE UNDER HER WING.
ERROR
NO SIGNAL

ROWAN LOVES FARMING. HE LOVES THE SOFT SOIL, LOVES THE SUN AND THE COOL AIR. HE LOVES HIS MOTHER. HE JUST WISHES, SOMETIMES, THAT HIS FARMING AND HIS MOTHER WEREN'T SO CLOSELY ENTWINED.

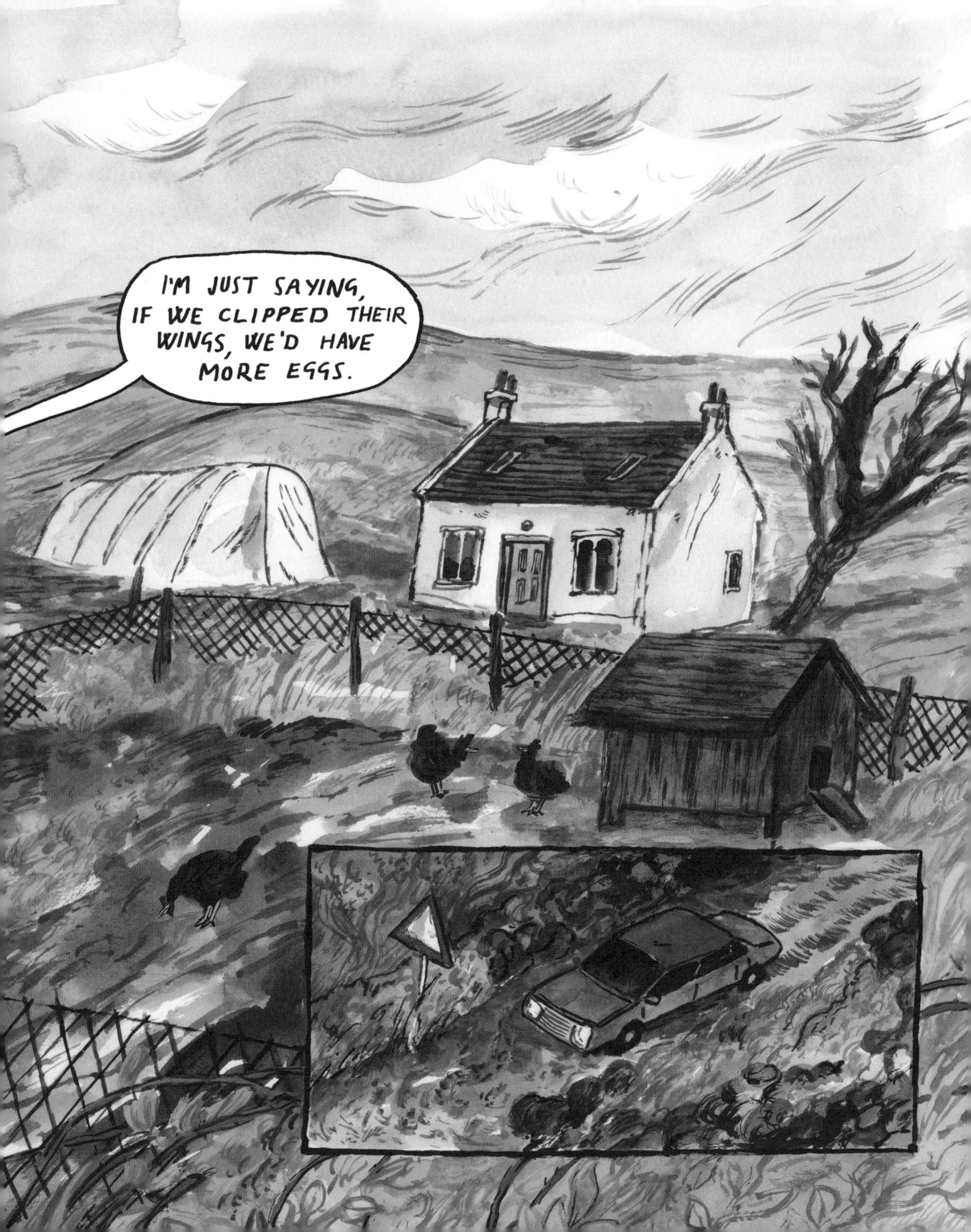
I'M JUST SAYING, IF WE CLIPPED THEIR WINGS, WE'D HAVE MORE EGGS.

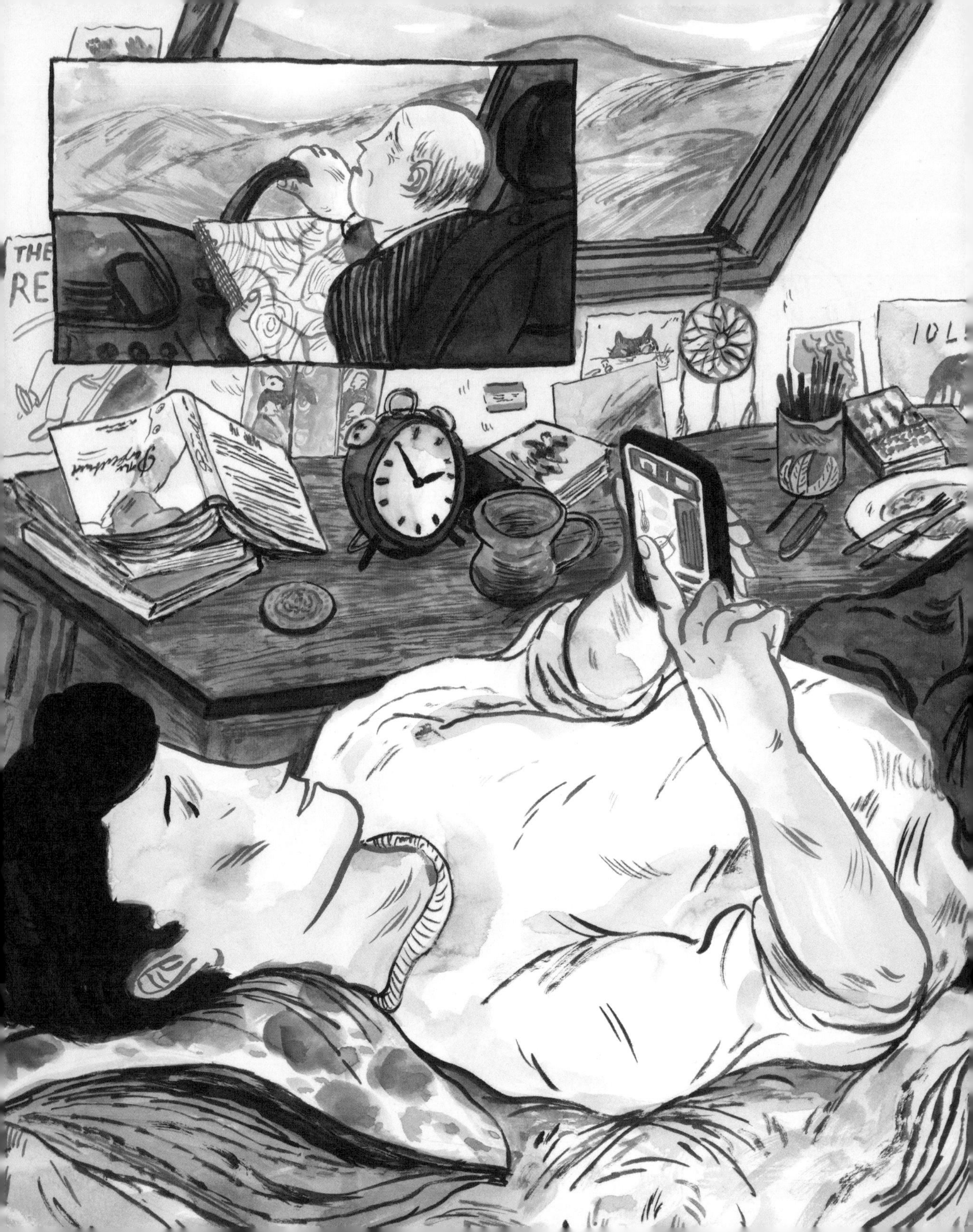

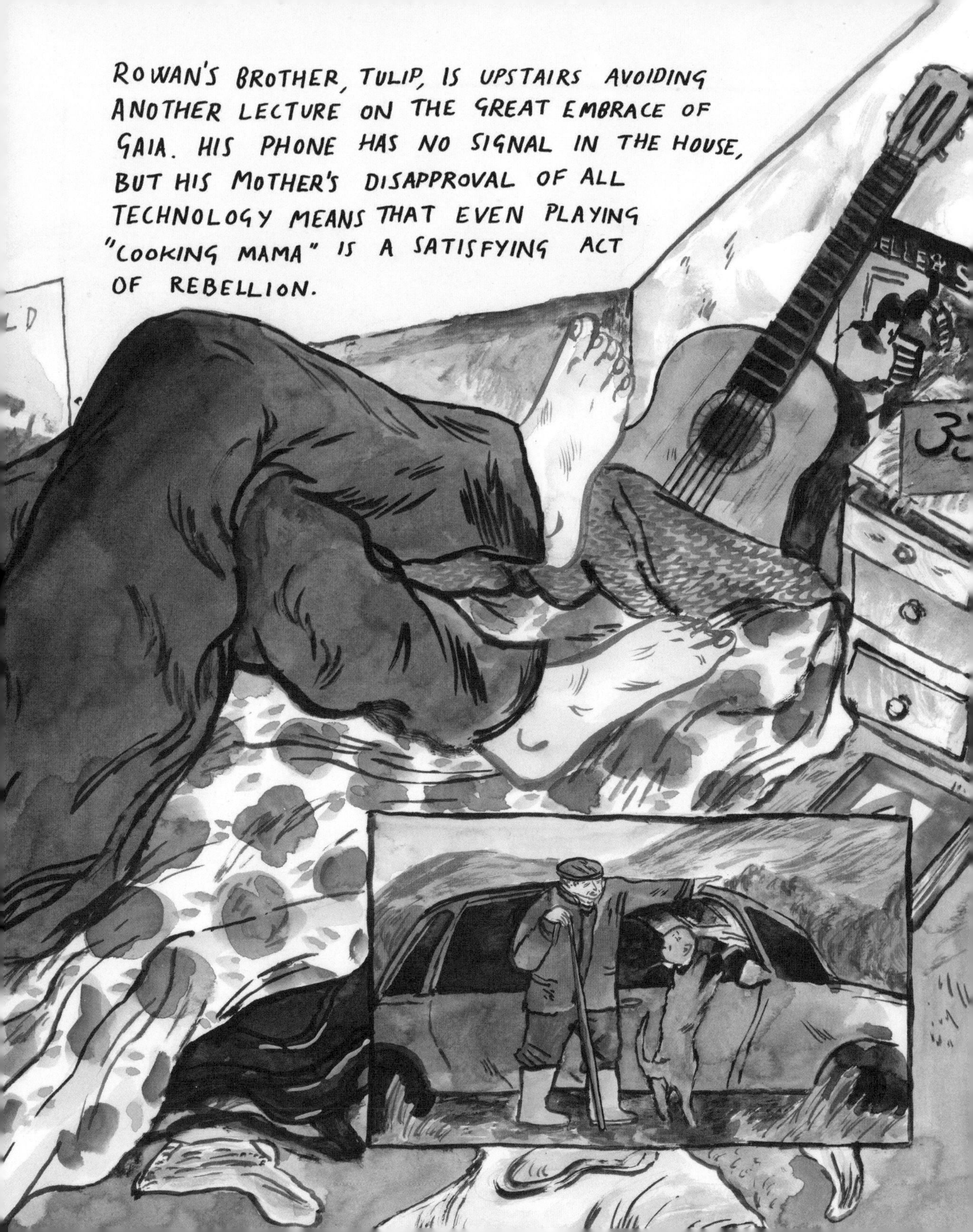
ROWAN'S BROTHER, TULIP, IS UPSTAIRS AVOIDING ANOTHER LECTURE ON THE GREAT EMBRACE OF GAIA. HIS PHONE HAS NO SIGNAL IN THE HOUSE, BUT HIS MOTHER'S DISAPPROVAL OF ALL TECHNOLOGY MEANS THAT EVEN PLAYING "COOKING MAMA" IS A SATISFYING ACT OF REBELLION.

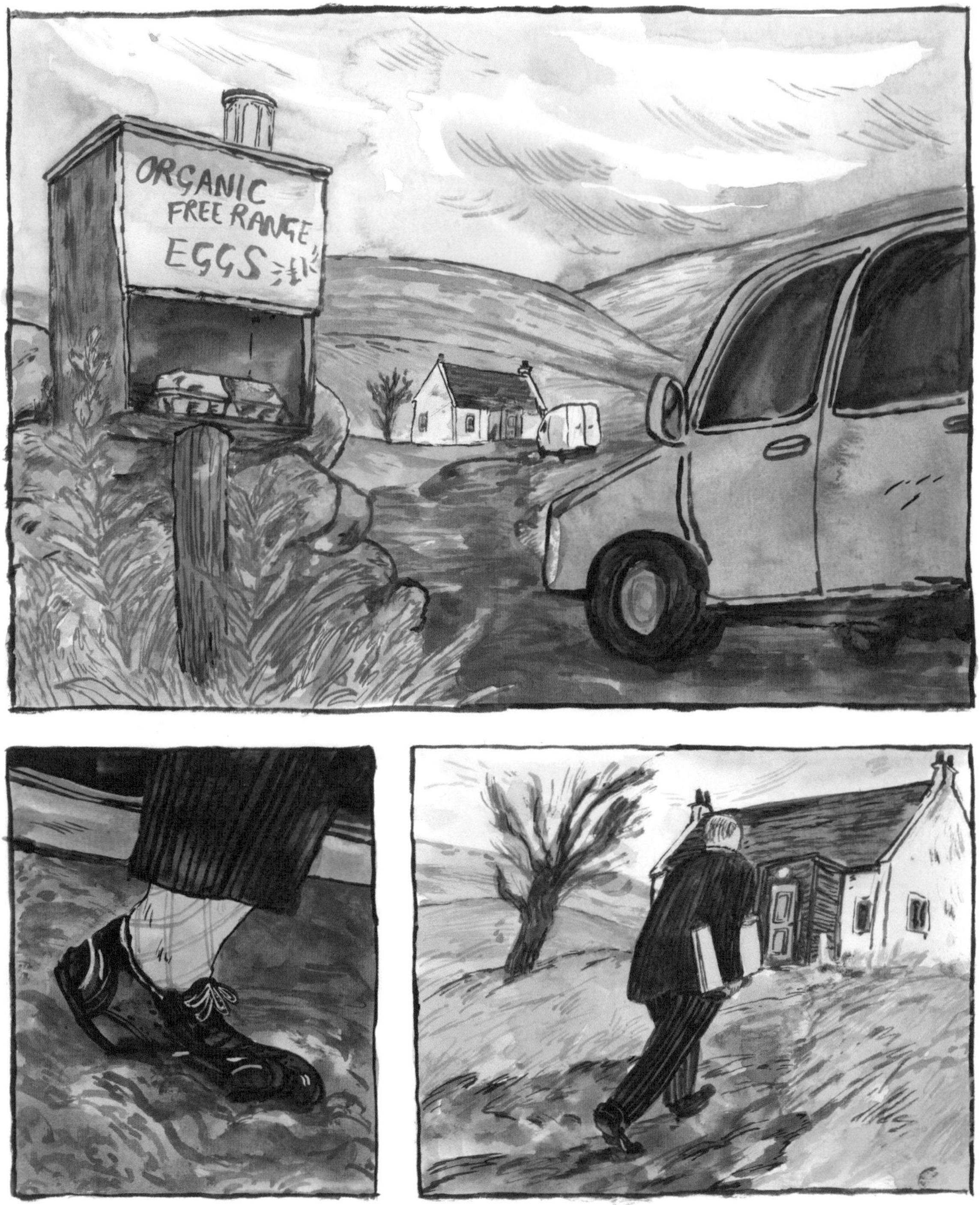
ORGANIC
FREE RANGE
EGGS

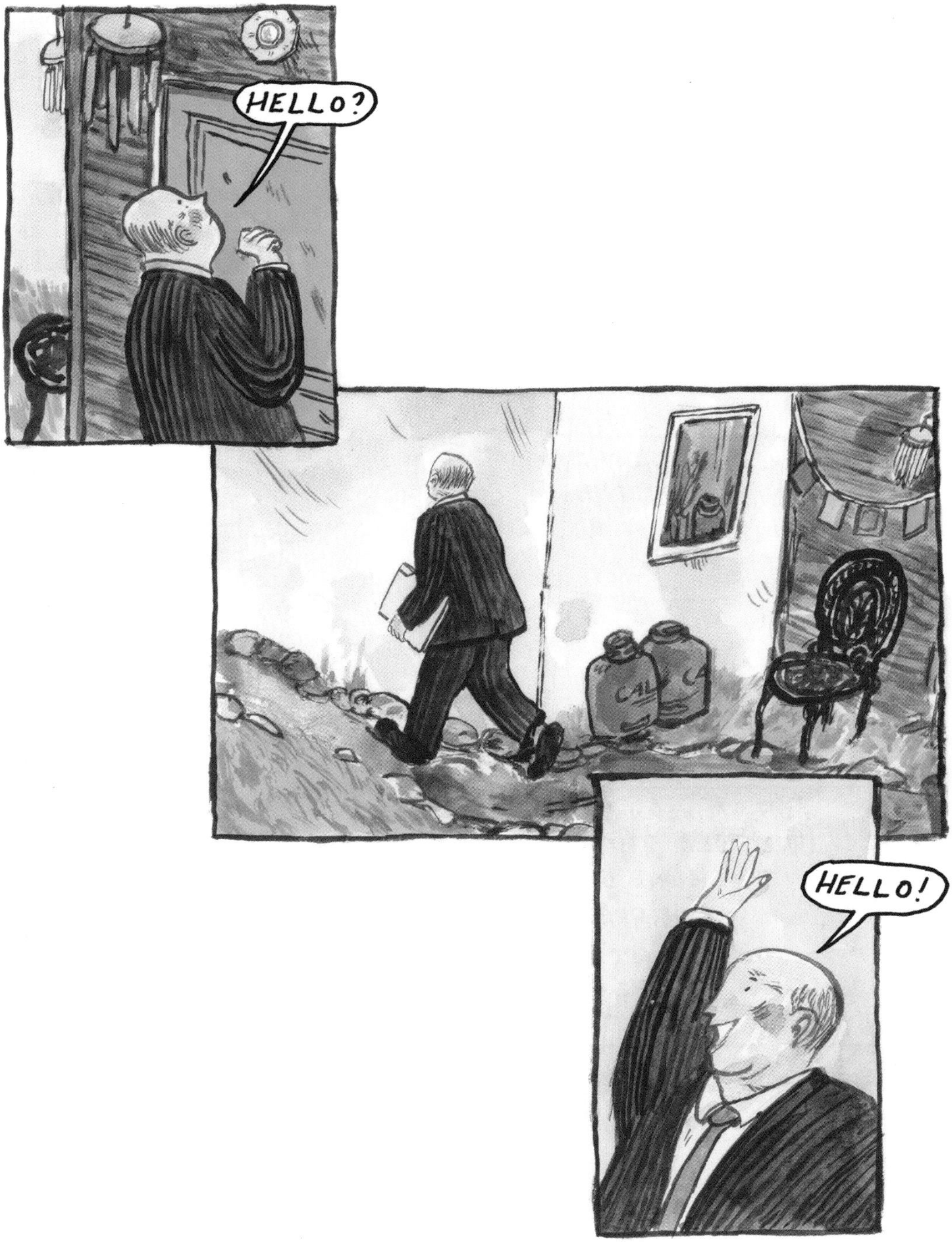
HELLO?
HELLO!

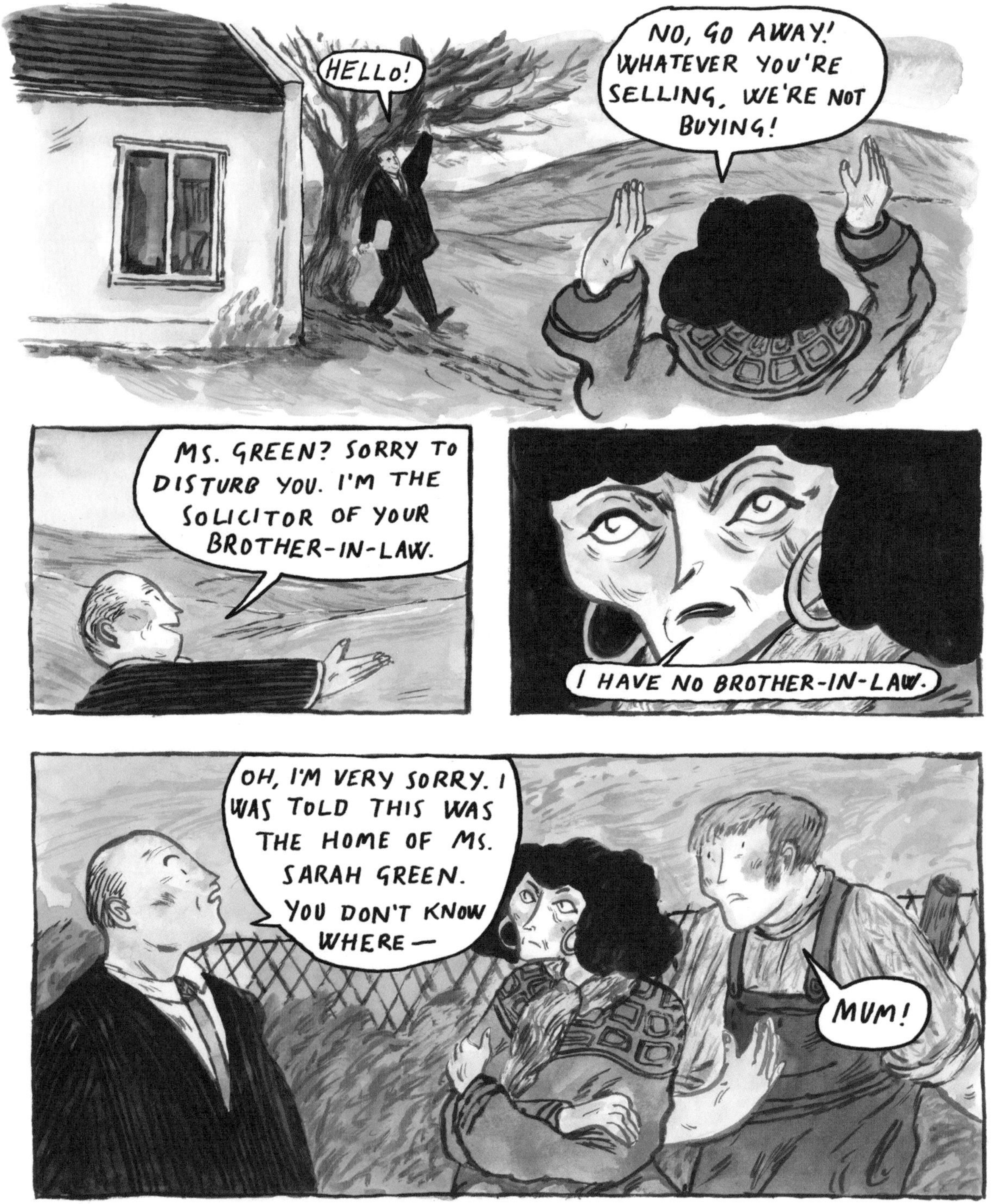
HELLO!
NO, GO AWAY! WHATEVER YOU'RE SELLING, WE'RE NOT BUYING!
MS. GREEN? SORRY TO DISTURB YOU. I'M THE SOLICITOR OF YOUR BROTHER-IN-LAW.
I HAVE NO BROTHER-IN-LAW.
OH, I'M VERY SORRY. I WAS TOLD THIS WAS THE HOME OF MS. SARAH GREEN. YOU DON'T KNOW WHERE—
MUM!

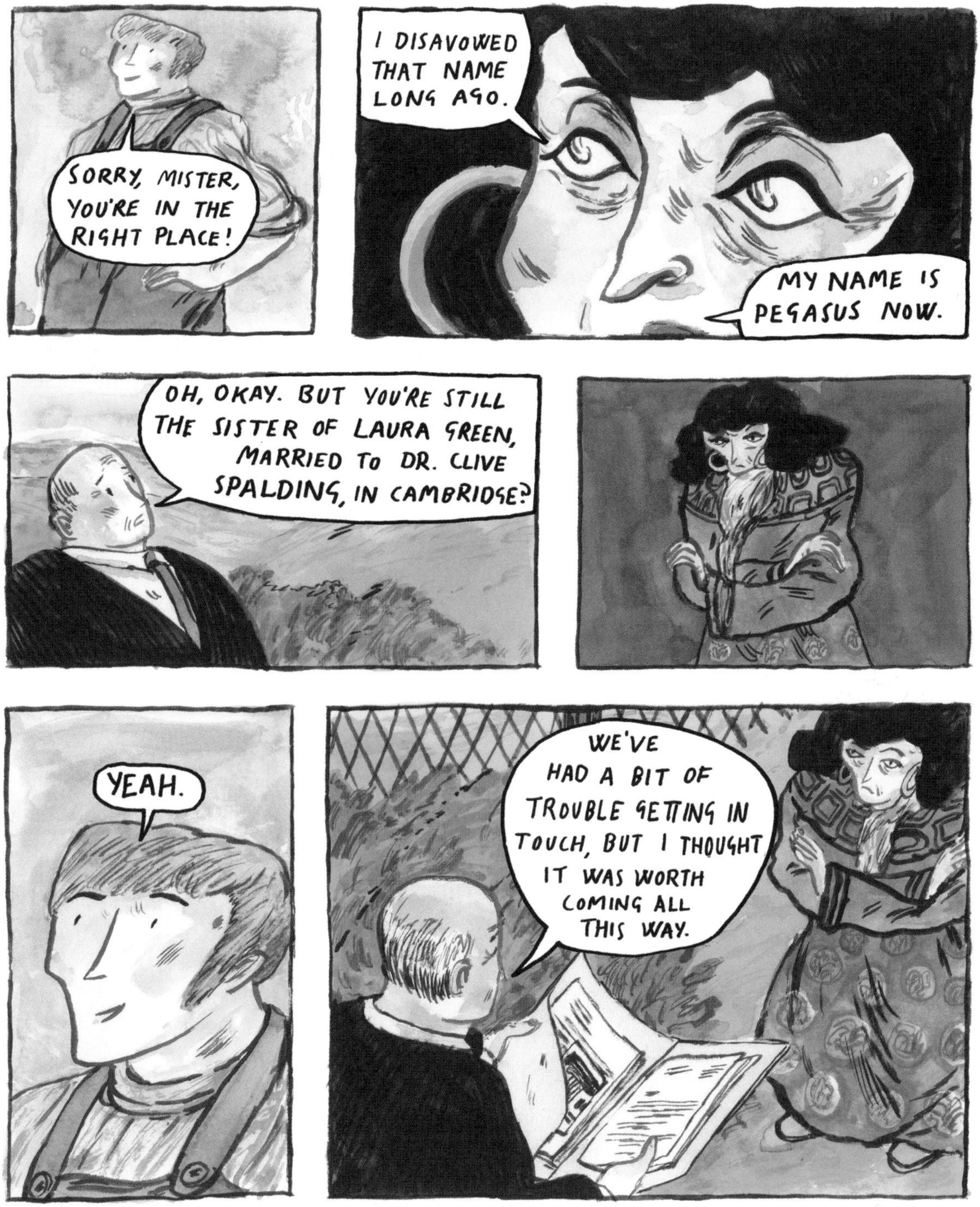
SORRY, MISTER, YOU'RE IN THE RIGHT PLACE!
I DISAVOWED THAT NAME LONG AGO.
MY NAME IS PEGASUS NOW.
OH, OKAY. BUT YOU'RE STILL THE SISTER OF LAURA GREEN, MARRIED TO DR. CLIVE SPALDING, IN CAMBRIDGE?
YEAH.
WE'VE HAD A BIT OF TROUBLE GETTING IN TOUCH, BUT I THOUGHT IT WAS WORTH COMING ALL THIS WAY.

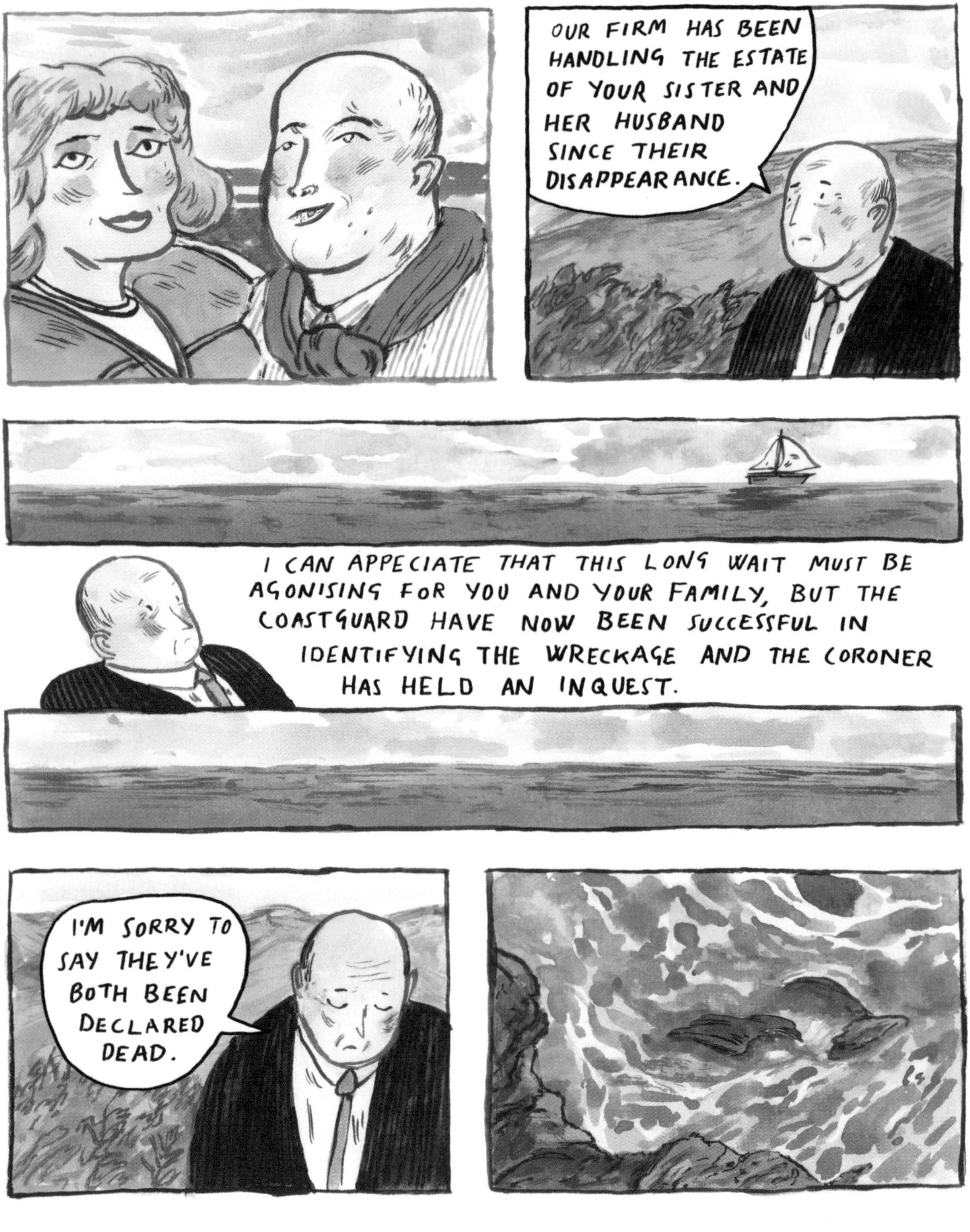
OUR FIRM HAS BEEN HANDLING THE ESTATE OF YOUR SISTER AND HER HUSBAND SINCE THEIR DISAPPEARANCE.
I CAN APPECIATE THAT THIS LONG WAIT MUST BE AGONISING FOR YOU AND YOUR FAMILY, BUT THE COASTGUARD HAVE NOW BEEN SUCCESSFUL IN IDENTIFYING THE WRECKAGE AND THE CORONER HAS HELD AN INQUEST.
I'M SORRY TO SAY THEY'VE BOTH BEEN DECLARED DEAD.

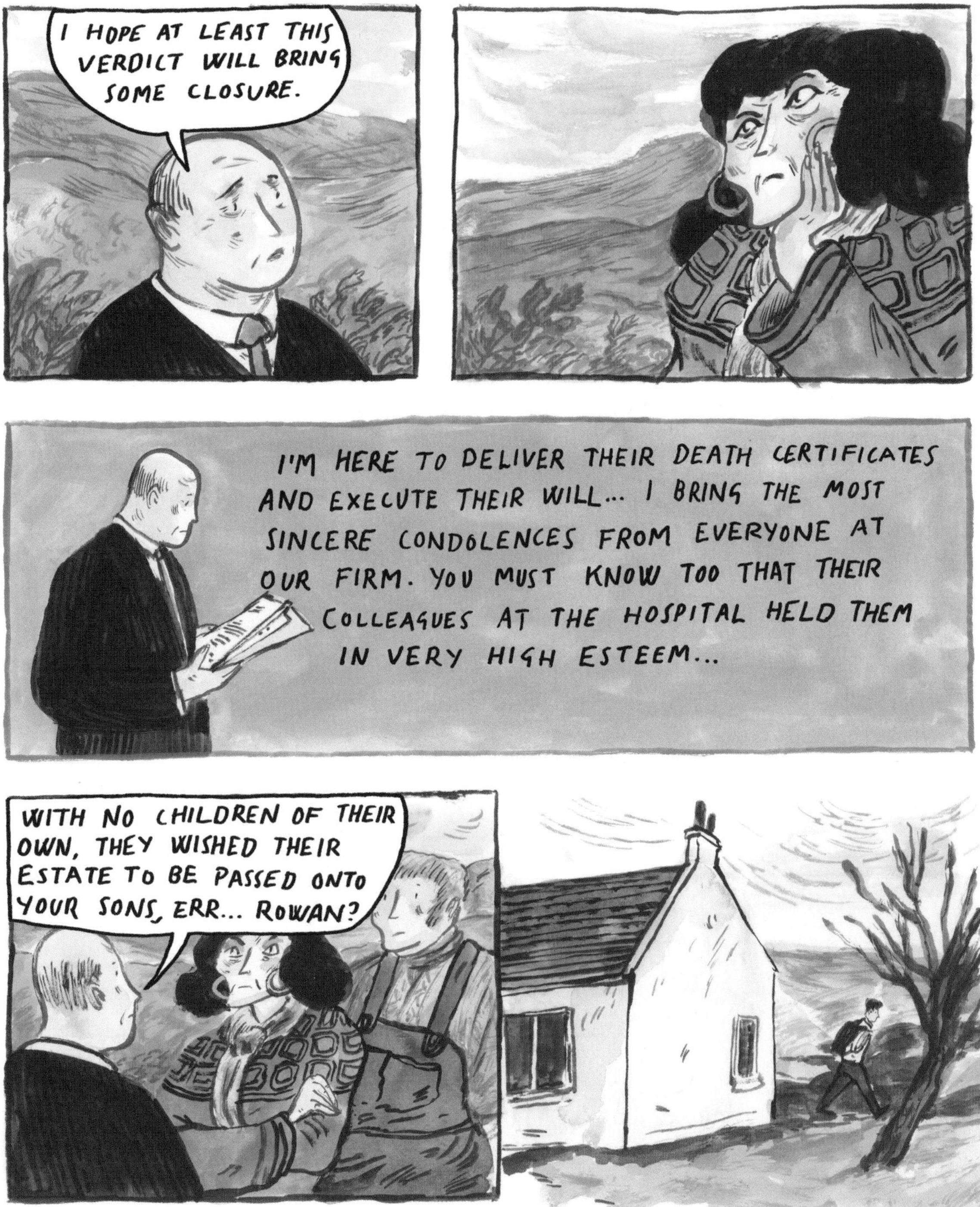

I HOPE AT LEAST THIS VERDICT WILL BRING SOME CLOSURE.
I'M HERE TO DELIVER THEIR DEATH CERTIFICATES AND EXECUTE THEIR WILL... I BRING THE MOST SINCERE CONDOLENCES FROM EVERYONE AT OUR FIRM. YOU MUST KNOW TOO THAT THEIR COLLEAGUES AT THE HOSPITAL HELD THEM IN VERY HIGH ESTEEM...
WITH NO CHILDREN OF THEIR OWN, THEY WISHED THEIR ESTATE TO BE PASSED ONTO YOUR SONS, ERR... ROWAN?

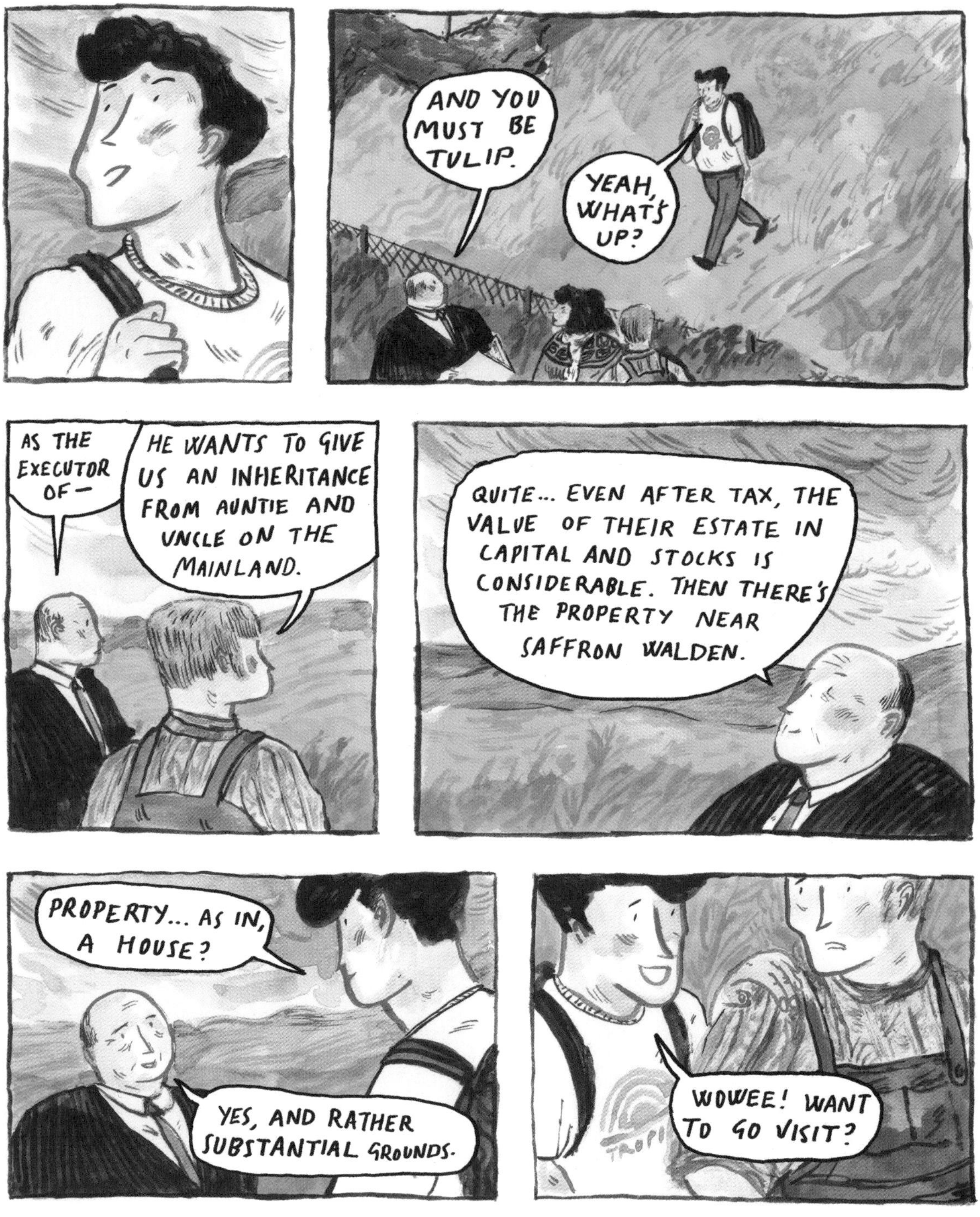
AND YOU MUST BE TULIP.
YEAH, WHAT'S UP?
AS THE EXECUTOR OF—
HE WANTS TO GIVE US AN INHERITANCE FROM AUNTIE AND UNCLE ON THE MAINLAND.
QUITE... EVEN AFTER TAX, THE VALUE OF THEIR ESTATE IN CAPITAL AND STOCKS IS CONSIDERABLE. THEN THERE'S THE PROPERTY NEAR SAFFRON WALDEN.
PROPERTY... AS IN, A HOUSE?
YES, AND RATHER SUBSTANTIAL GROUNDS.
WOWEE! WANT TO GO VISIT?

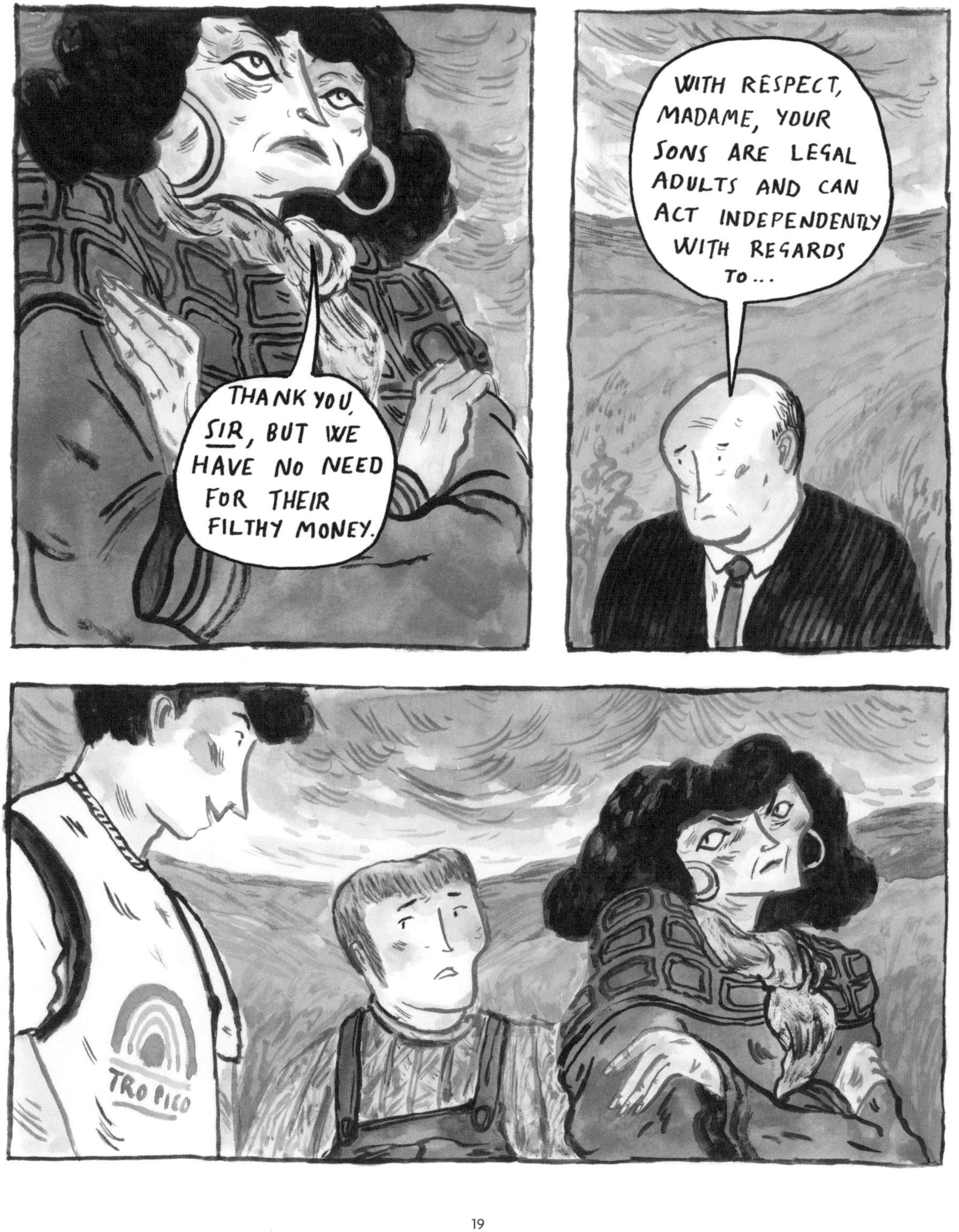
THANK YOU, SIR, BUT WE HAVE NO NEED FOR THEIR FILTHY MONEY.
WITH RESPECT, MADAME, YOUR SONS ARE LEGAL ADULTS AND CAN ACT INDEPENDENTLY WITH REGARDS TO...
TROPICO

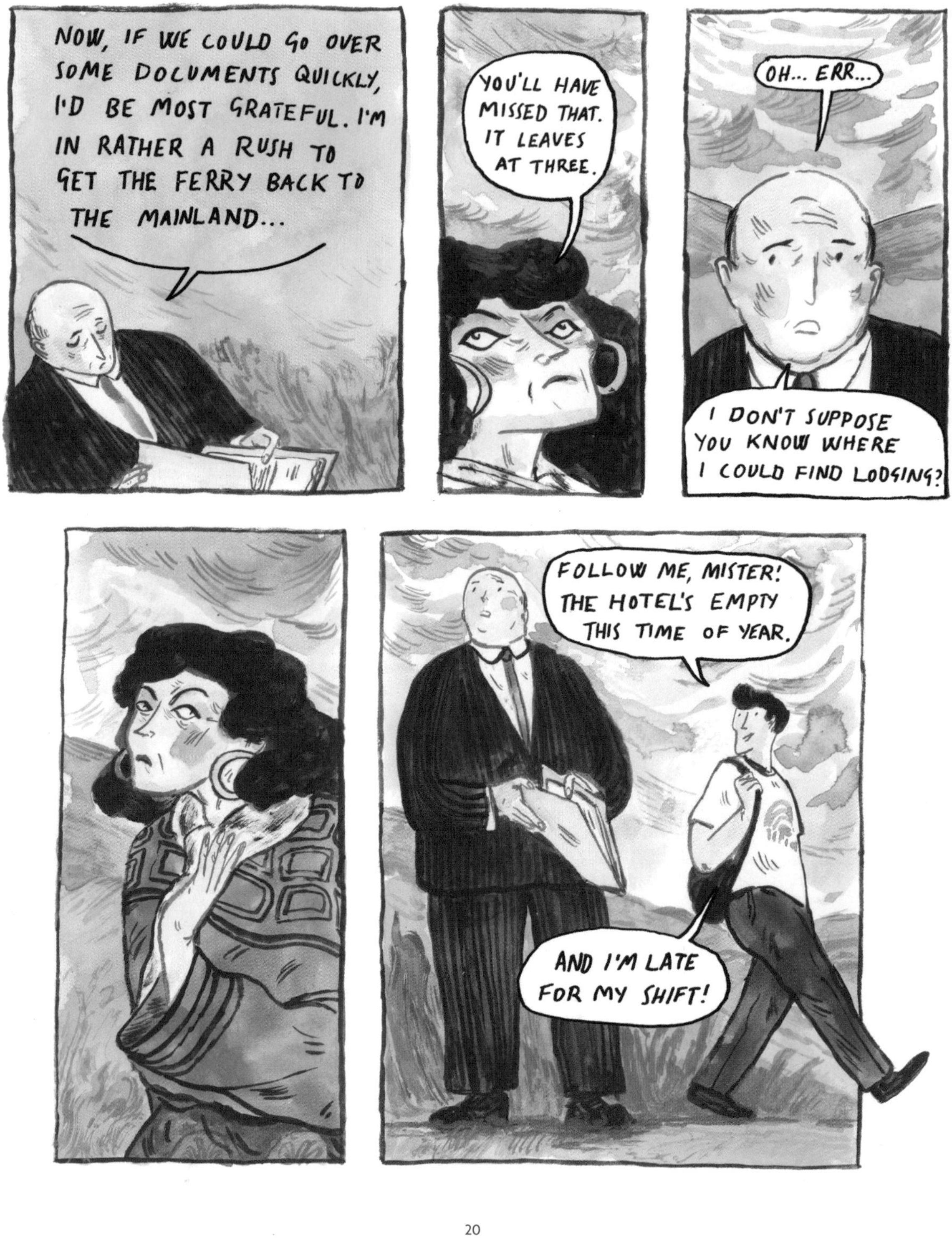
NOW, IF WE COULD GO OVER SOME DOCUMENTS QUICKLY, I'D BE MOST GRATEFUL. I'M IN RATHER A RUSH TO GET THE FERRY BACK TO THE MAINLAND...
YOU'LL HAVE MISSED THAT. IT LEAVES AT THREE.
OH... ERR...
I DON'T SUPPOSE YOU KNOW WHERE I COULD FIND LODGING?
FOLLOW ME, MISTER! THE HOTEL'S EMPTY THIS TIME OF YEAR.
AND I'M LATE FOR MY SHIFT!

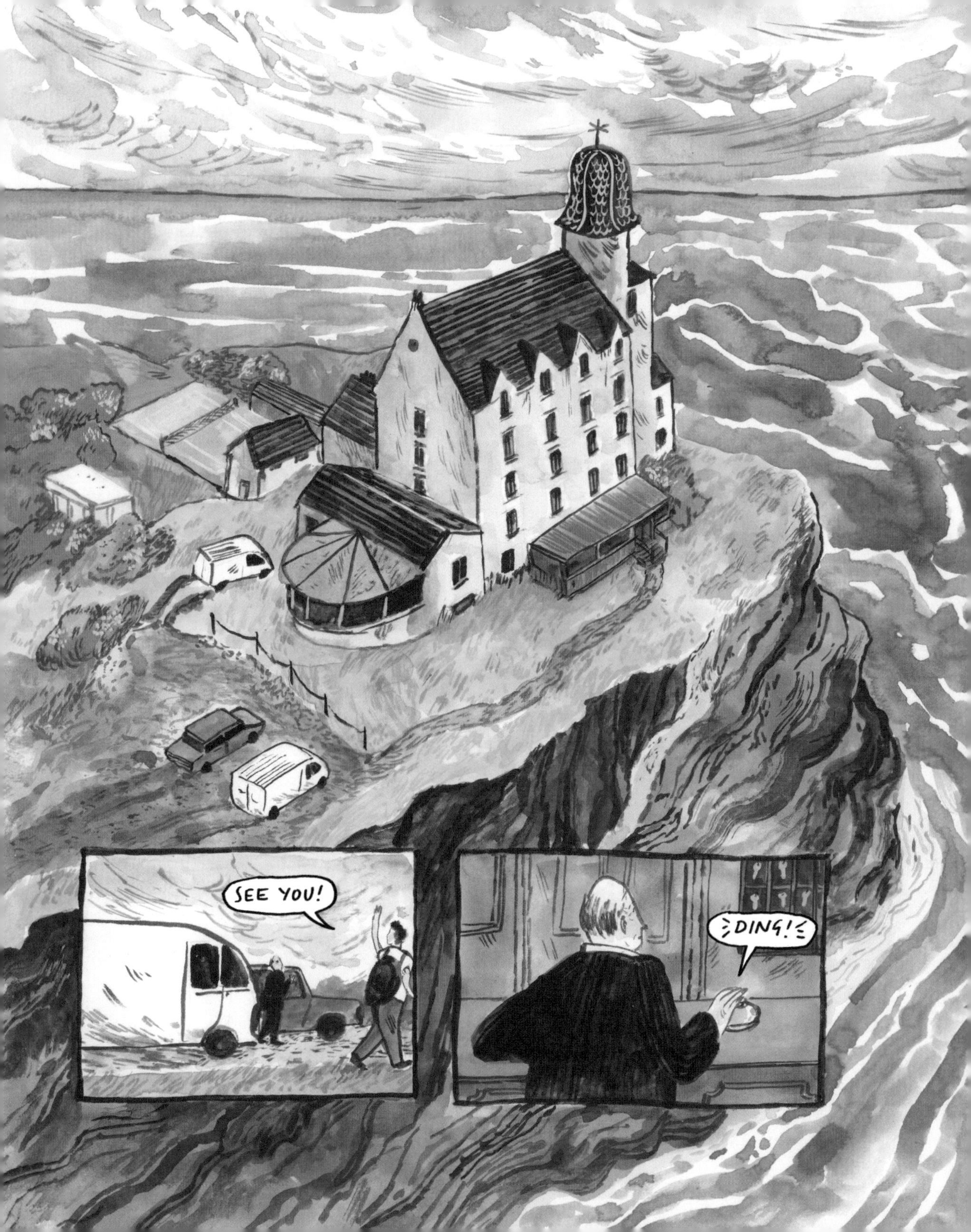
SEE YOU!
DING!

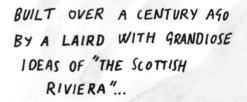

BUILT OVER A CENTURY AGO BY A LAIRD WITH GRANDIOSE IDEAS OF "THE SCOTTISH RIVIERA"...

...THE ISLAND'S HOTEL IS NOW A HUSK OF CHIPPING PAINT AND CREAKING FLOORBOARDS.

YES, TERRENCE, IT'S A DREADFUL BORE, BUT I SIMPLY DON'T SEE WHAT CAN BE DONE.

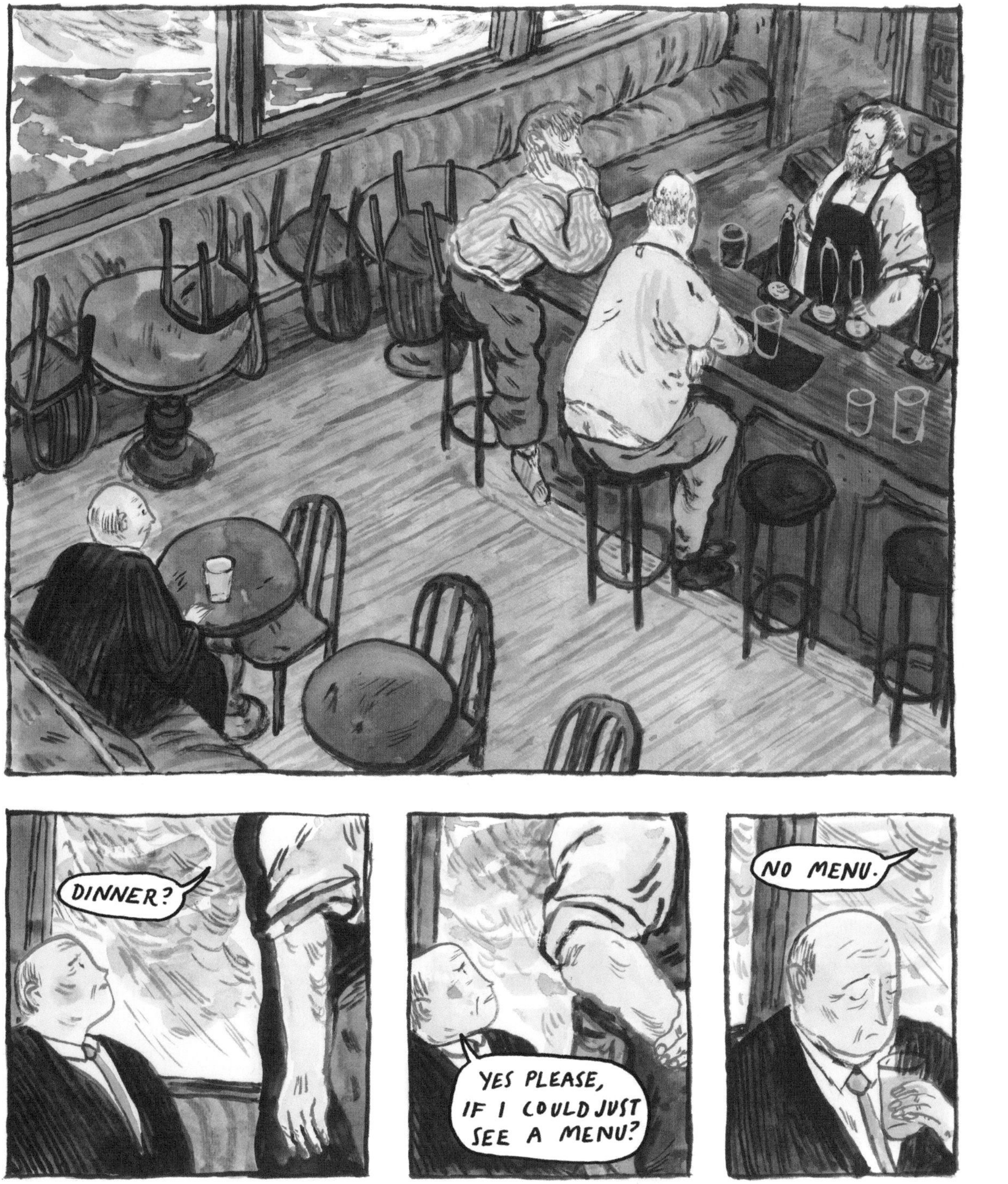
DINNER?
YES PLEASE, IF I COULD JUST SEE A MENU?
NO MENU.

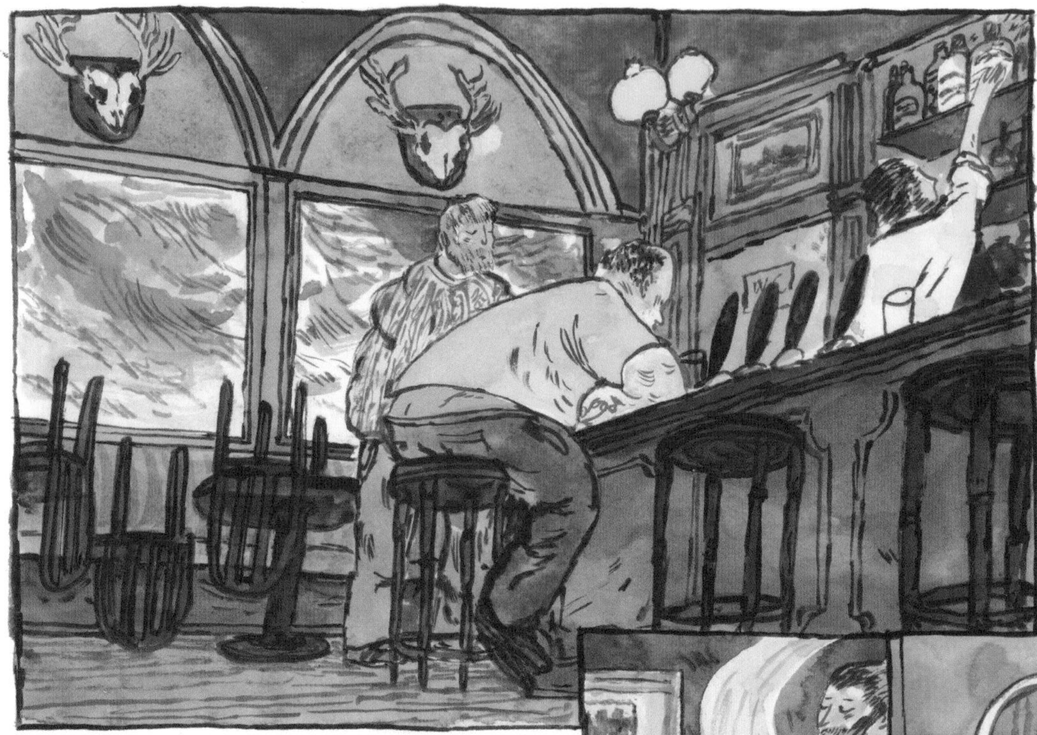

THE LAWYER SLUMPS DESPONDENTLY INTO HIS CHAIR, BUT WHEN THE FOOD ARRIVES—

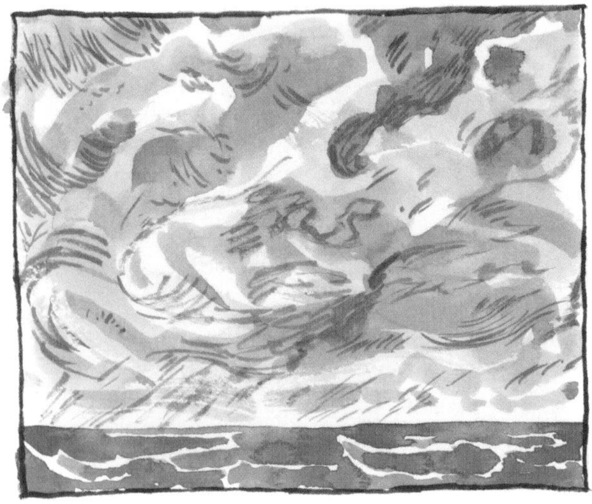

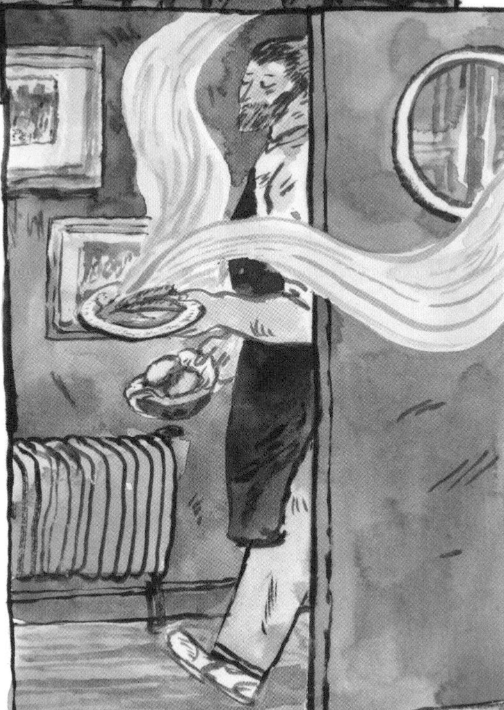

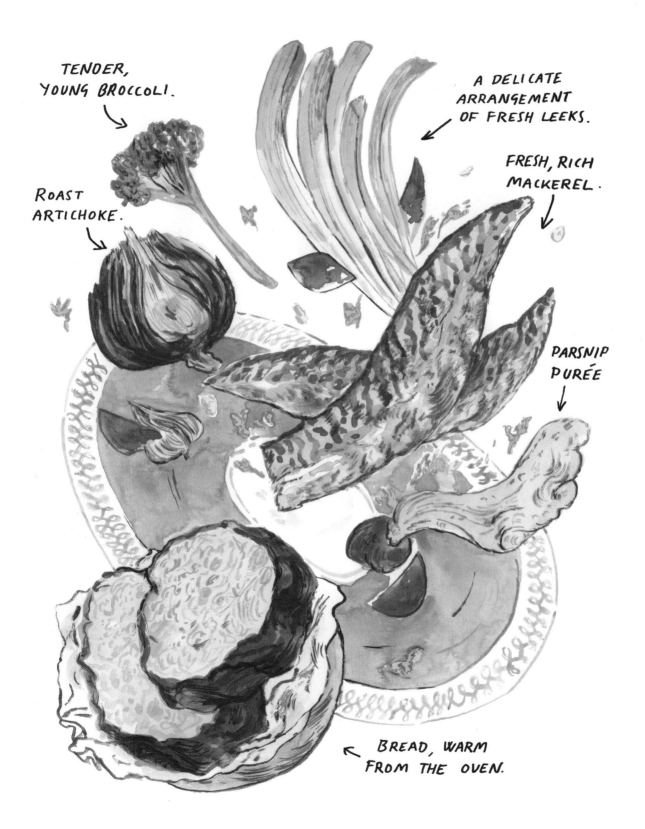

TENDER, YOUNG BROCCOLI.

A DELICATE ARRANGEMENT OF FRESH LEEKS.

FRESH, RICH MACKEREL.

ROAST ARTICHOKE.

PARSNIP PURÉE

BREAD, WARM FROM THE OVEN.

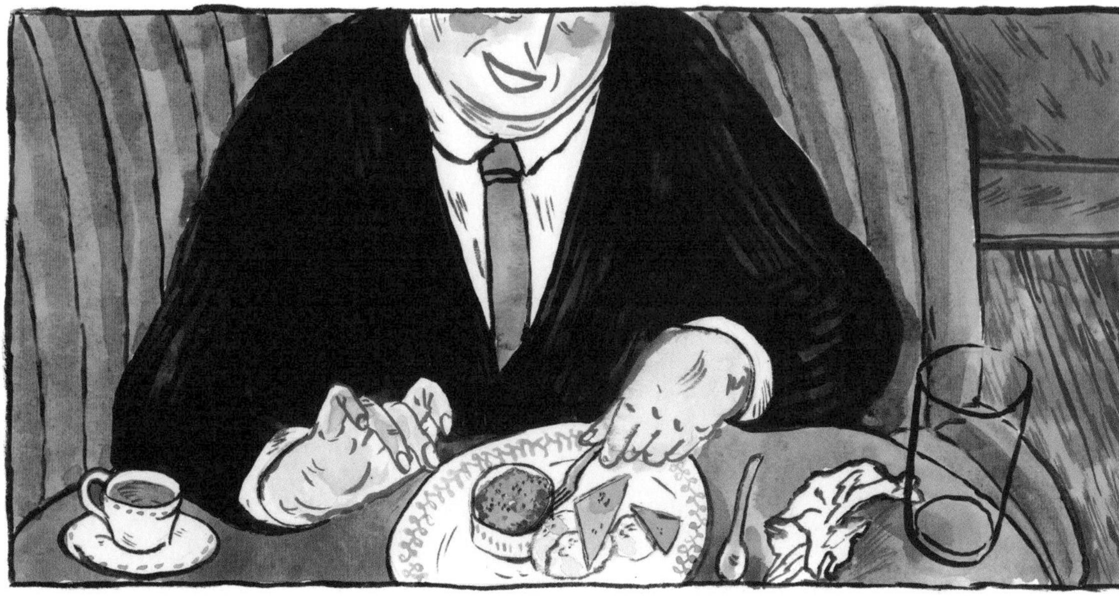

THE EVENING'S MELANCHOLY IS LIFTED. THE LAWYER IS REINVIGORATED, PREPARED TO ENDURE ANY NUMBER OF DAYS OF ISLAND PURGATORY. DESSERT ARRIVES, A WARMING, HOMELY FRUIT CRUMBLE WITH HOMEMADE ICE CREAM.

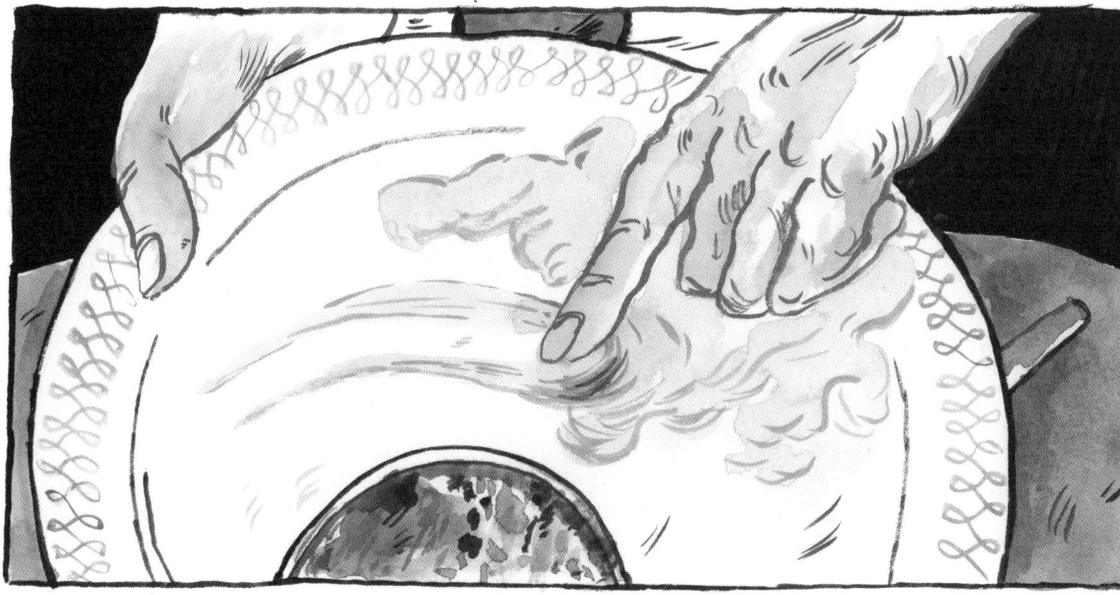

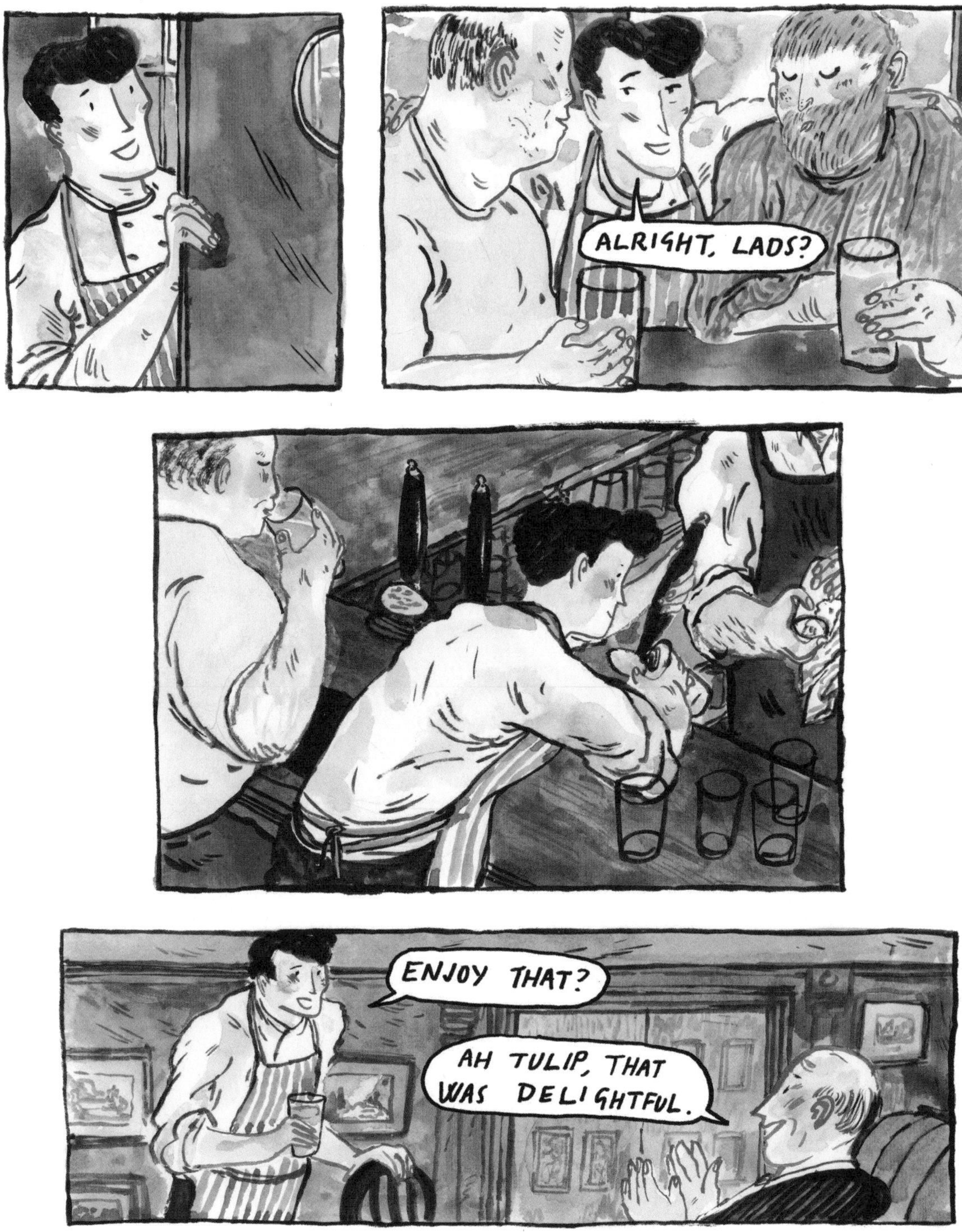
ALRIGHT, LADS?
ENJOY THAT?
AH TULIP, THAT WAS DELIGHTFUL.

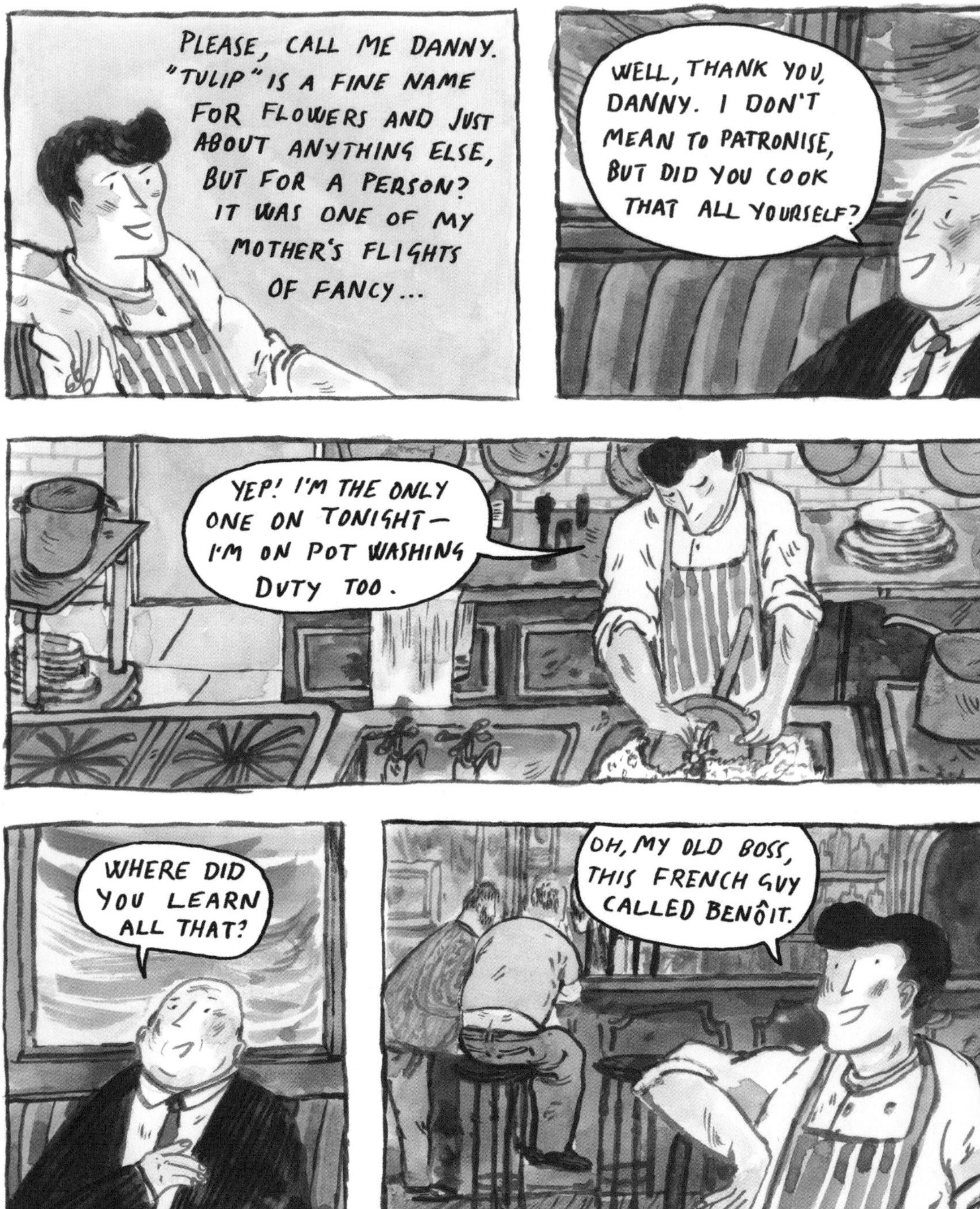
PLEASE, CALL ME DANNY. "TULIP" IS A FINE NAME FOR FLOWERS AND JUST ABOUT ANYTHING ELSE, BUT FOR A PERSON? IT WAS ONE OF MY MOTHER'S FLIGHTS OF FANCY...
WELL, THANK YOU, DANNY. I DON'T MEAN TO PATRONISE, BUT DID YOU COOK THAT ALL YOURSELF?
YEP! I'M THE ONLY ONE ON TONIGHT— I'M ON POT WASHING DUTY TOO.
WHERE DID YOU LEARN ALL THAT?
OH, MY OLD BOSS, THIS FRENCH GUY CALLED BENÔIT.

HE WAS A BIG CHEF DOWN IN LONDON, RETIRED UP HERE, THEN GOT BORED LIKE ANY SANE PERSON WOULD, AND TOOK OVER THE KITCHEN HERE. I STARTED AS A KITCHEN PORTER WHEN I WAS 15, AND HE TAUGHT ME EVERYTHING I KNOW.

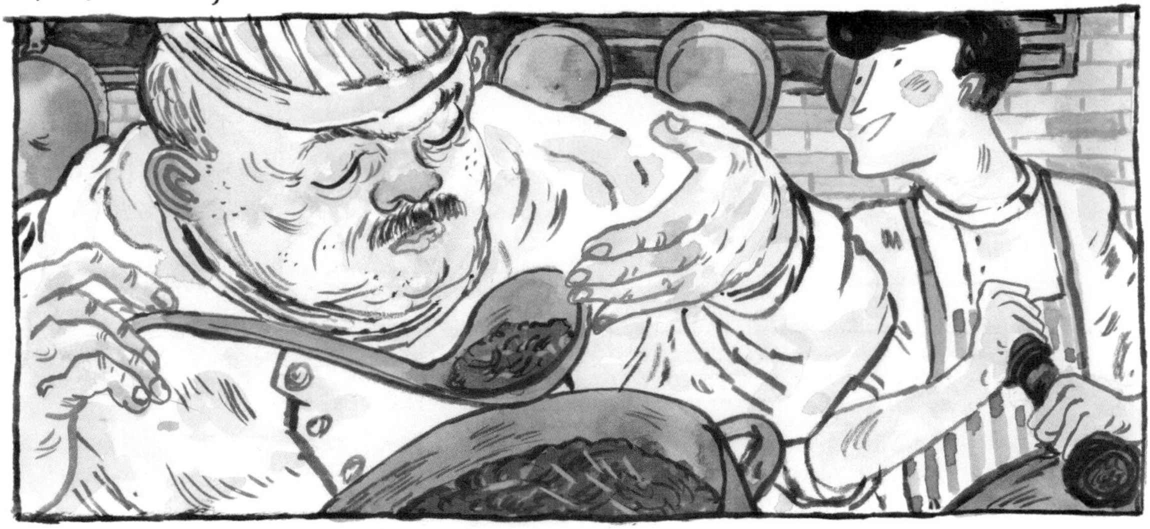

BUT NOW HE'S SUPER OLD. GOT NO TEETH.
HE MOVED BACK TO LYON TO LIVE OFF SOUP AND FOIS GRAS.

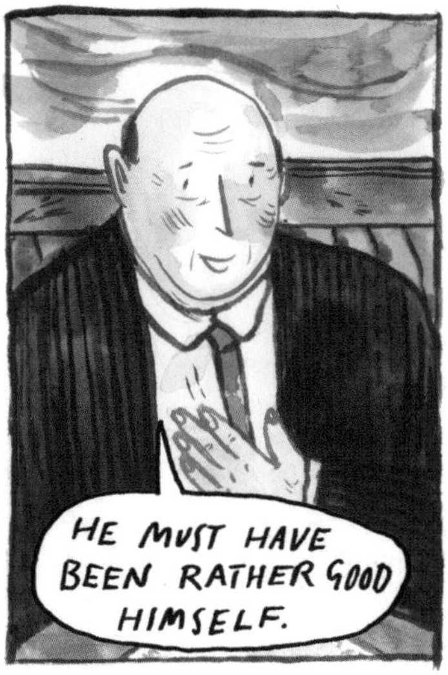
HE MUST HAVE BEEN RATHER GOOD HIMSELF.

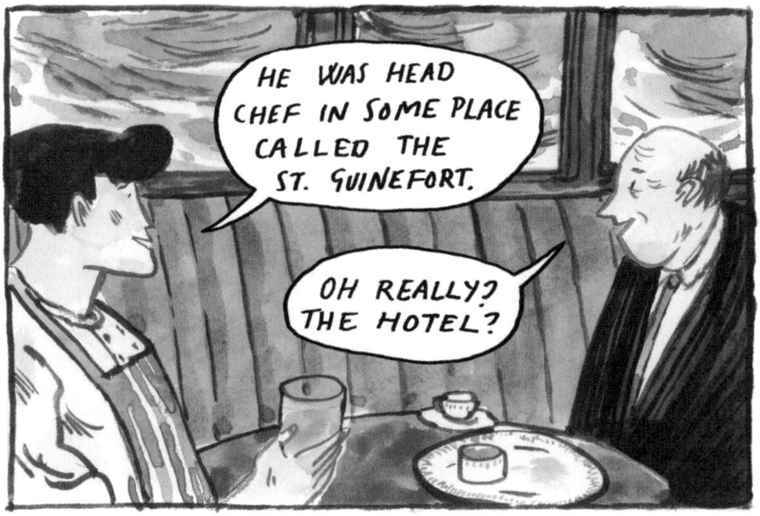
HE WAS HEAD CHEF IN SOME PLACE CALLED THE ST. GUINEFORT.
OH REALLY? THE HOTEL?

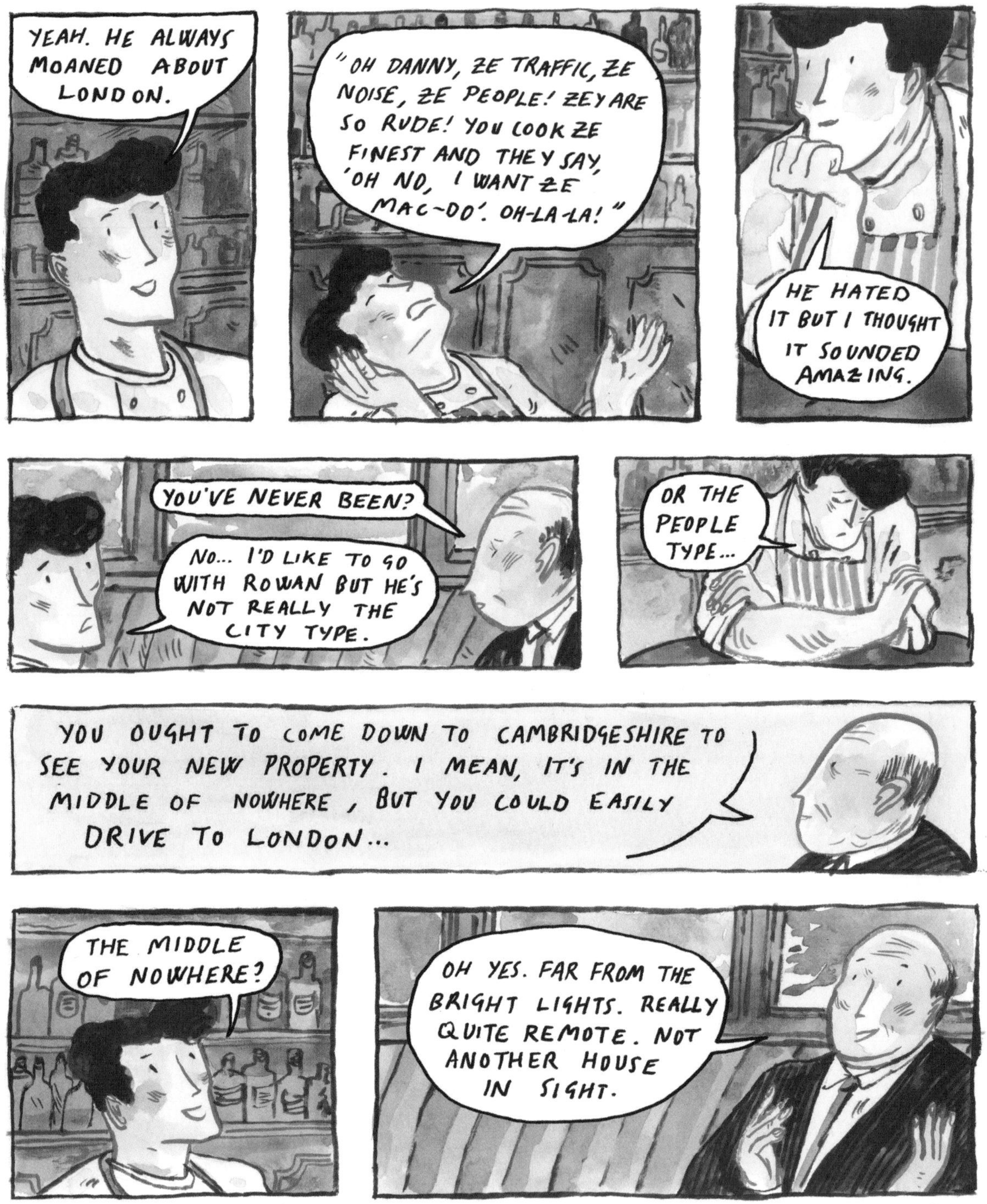
YEAH. HE ALWAYS MOANED ABOUT LONDON.
"OH DANNY, ZE TRAFFIC, ZE NOISE, ZE PEOPLE! ZEY ARE SO RUDE! YOU COOK ZE FINEST AND THEY SAY, 'OH NO, I WANT ZE MAC-DO'. OH-LA-LA!"
HE HATED IT BUT I THOUGHT IT SOUNDED AMAZING.
YOU'VE NEVER BEEN?
NO... I'D LIKE TO GO WITH ROWAN BUT HE'S NOT REALLY THE CITY TYPE.
OR THE PEOPLE TYPE...
YOU OUGHT TO COME DOWN TO CAMBRIDGESHIRE TO SEE YOUR NEW PROPERTY. I MEAN, IT'S IN THE MIDDLE OF NOWHERE, BUT YOU COULD EASILY DRIVE TO LONDON...
THE MIDDLE OF NOWHERE?
OH YES. FAR FROM THE BRIGHT LIGHTS. REALLY QUITE REMOTE. NOT ANOTHER HOUSE IN SIGHT.

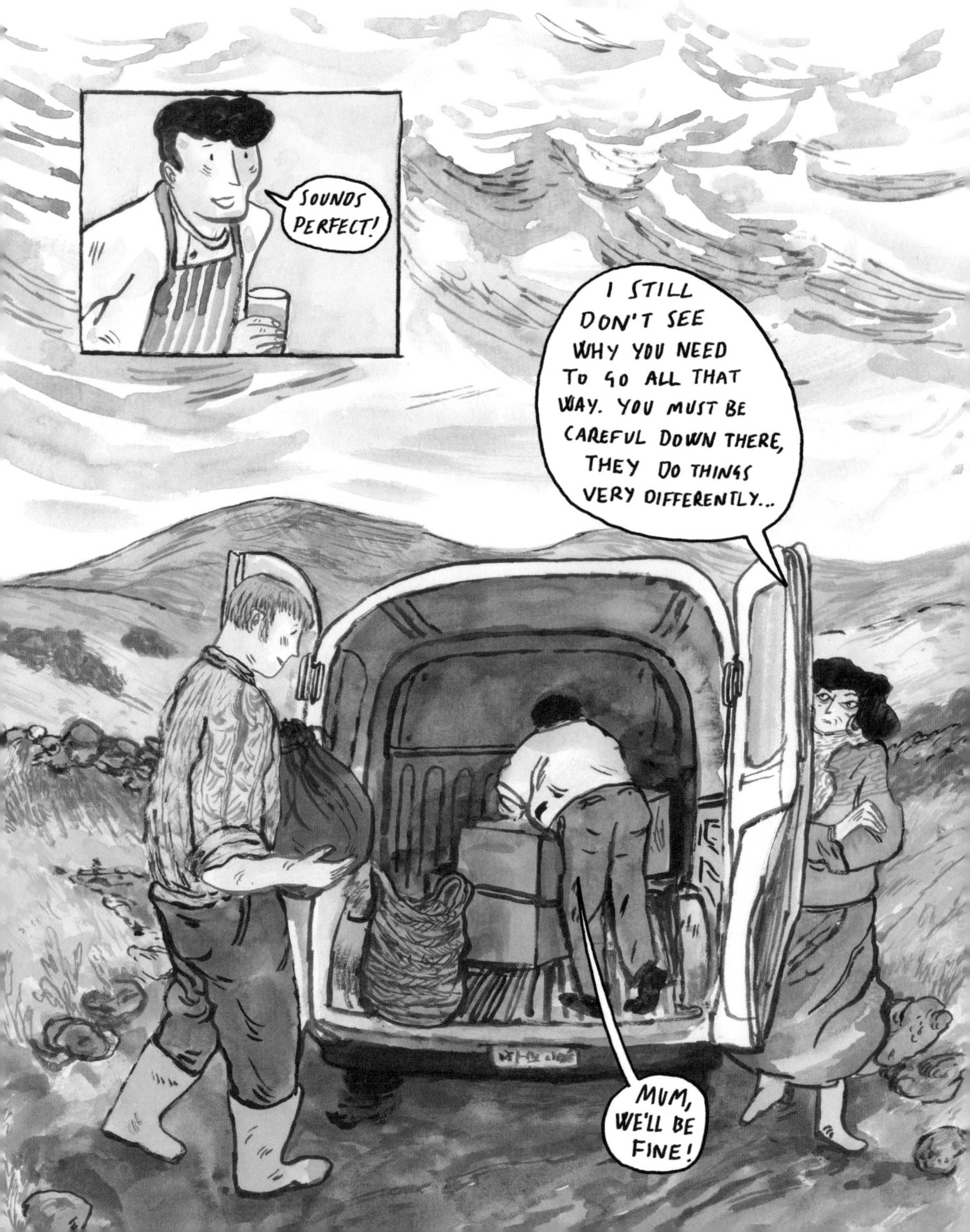
SOUNDS PERFECT!
I STILL DON'T SEE WHY YOU NEED TO GO ALL THAT WAY. YOU MUST BE CAREFUL DOWN THERE, THEY DO THINGS VERY DIFFERENTLY...
MUM, WE'LL BE FINE!

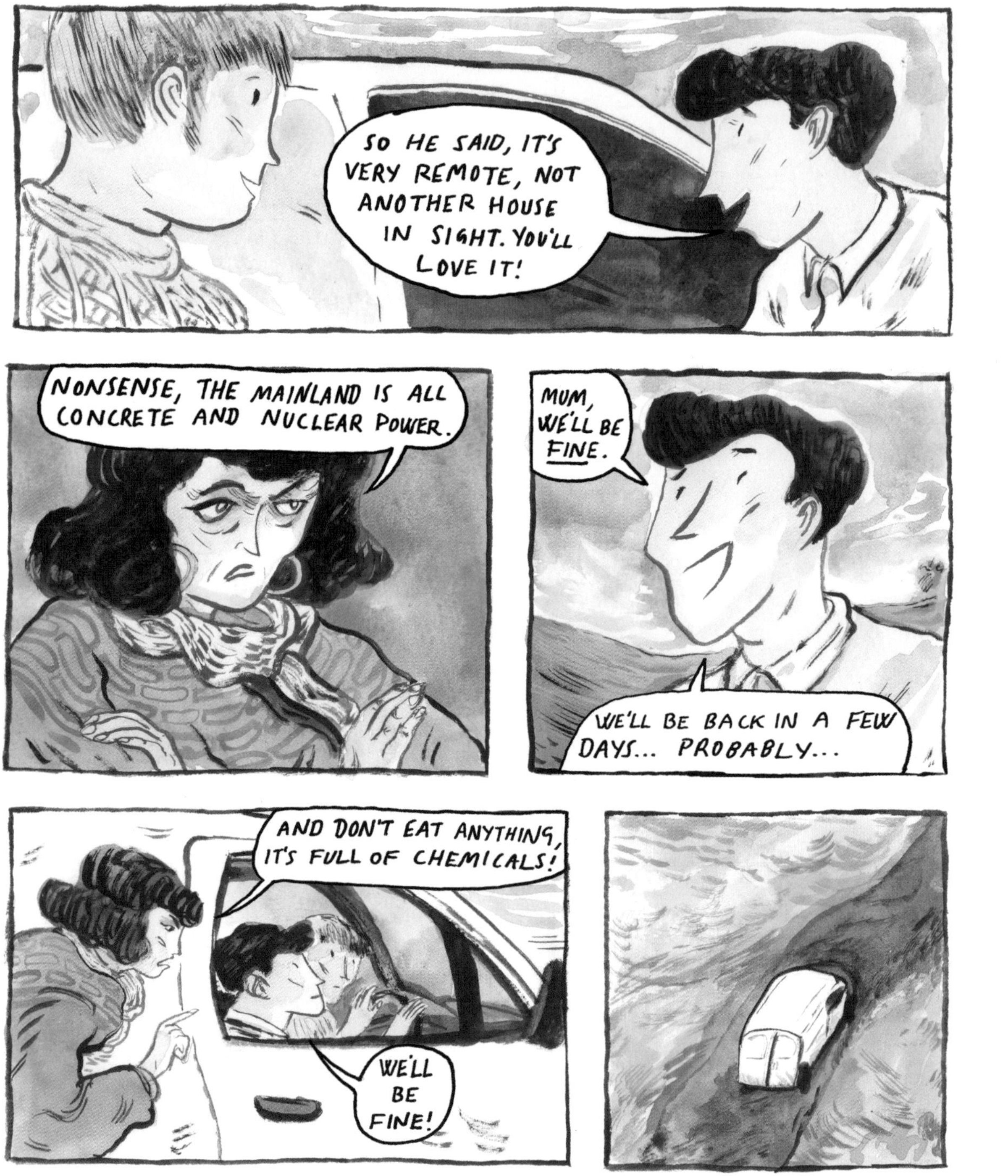
SO HE SAID, IT'S VERY REMOTE, NOT ANOTHER HOUSE IN SIGHT. YOU'LL LOVE IT!
NONSENSE, THE MAINLAND IS ALL CONCRETE AND NUCLEAR POWER.
MUM, WE'LL BE FINE.
WE'LL BE BACK IN A FEW DAYS... PROBABLY...
AND DON'T EAT ANYTHING, IT'S FULL OF CHEMICALS!
WE'LL BE FINE!

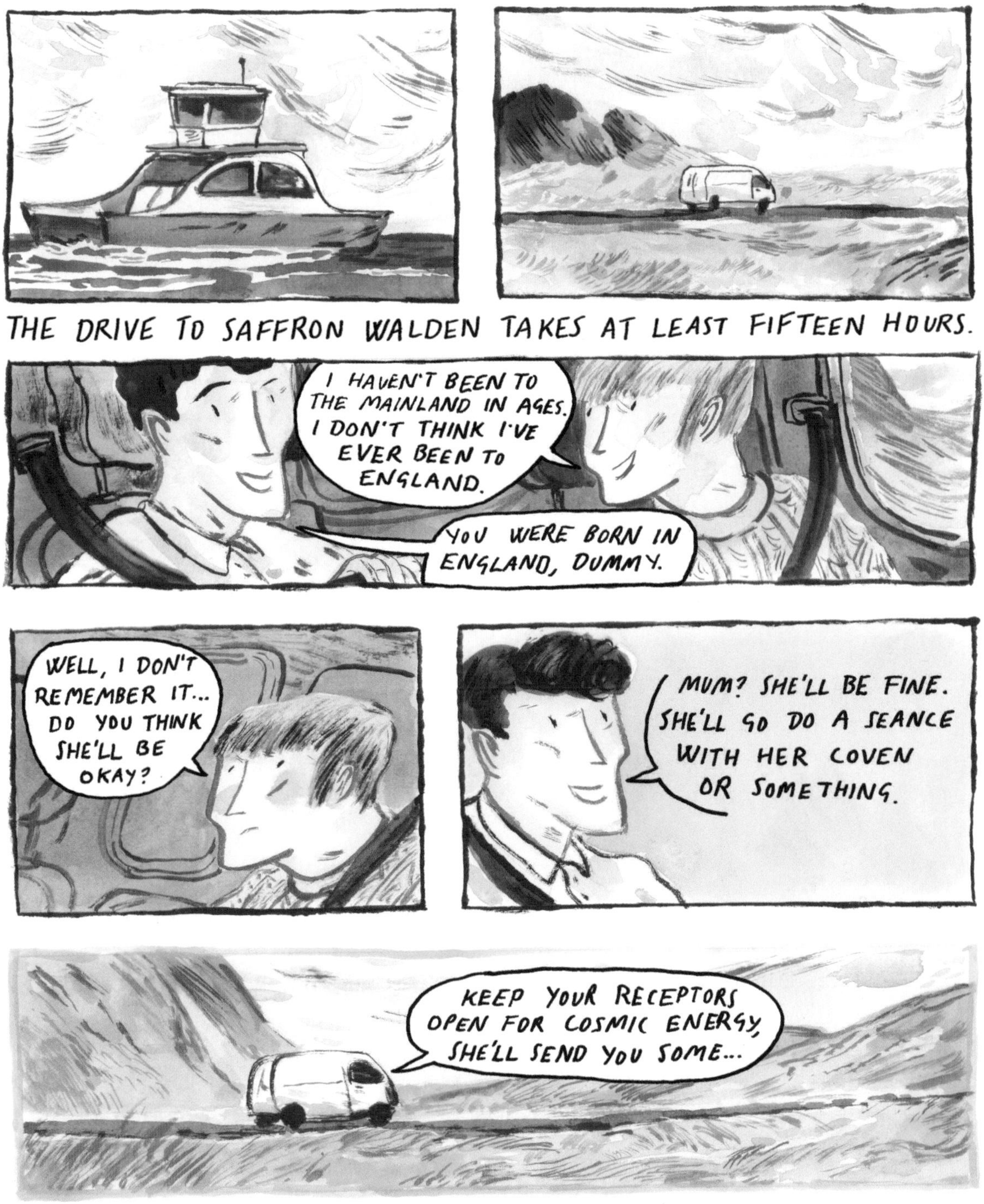
THE DRIVE TO SAFFRON WALDEN TAKES AT LEAST FIFTEEN HOURS.
I HAVEN'T BEEN TO THE MAINLAND IN AGES. I DON'T THINK I'VE EVER BEEN TO ENGLAND.
YOU WERE BORN IN ENGLAND, DUMMY.
WELL, I DON'T REMEMBER IT... DO YOU THINK SHE'LL BE OKAY?
MUM? SHE'LL BE FINE. SHE'LL GO DO A SEANCE WITH HER COVEN OR SOMETHING.
KEEP YOUR RECEPTORS OPEN FOR COSMIC ENERGY, SHE'LL SEND YOU SOME...

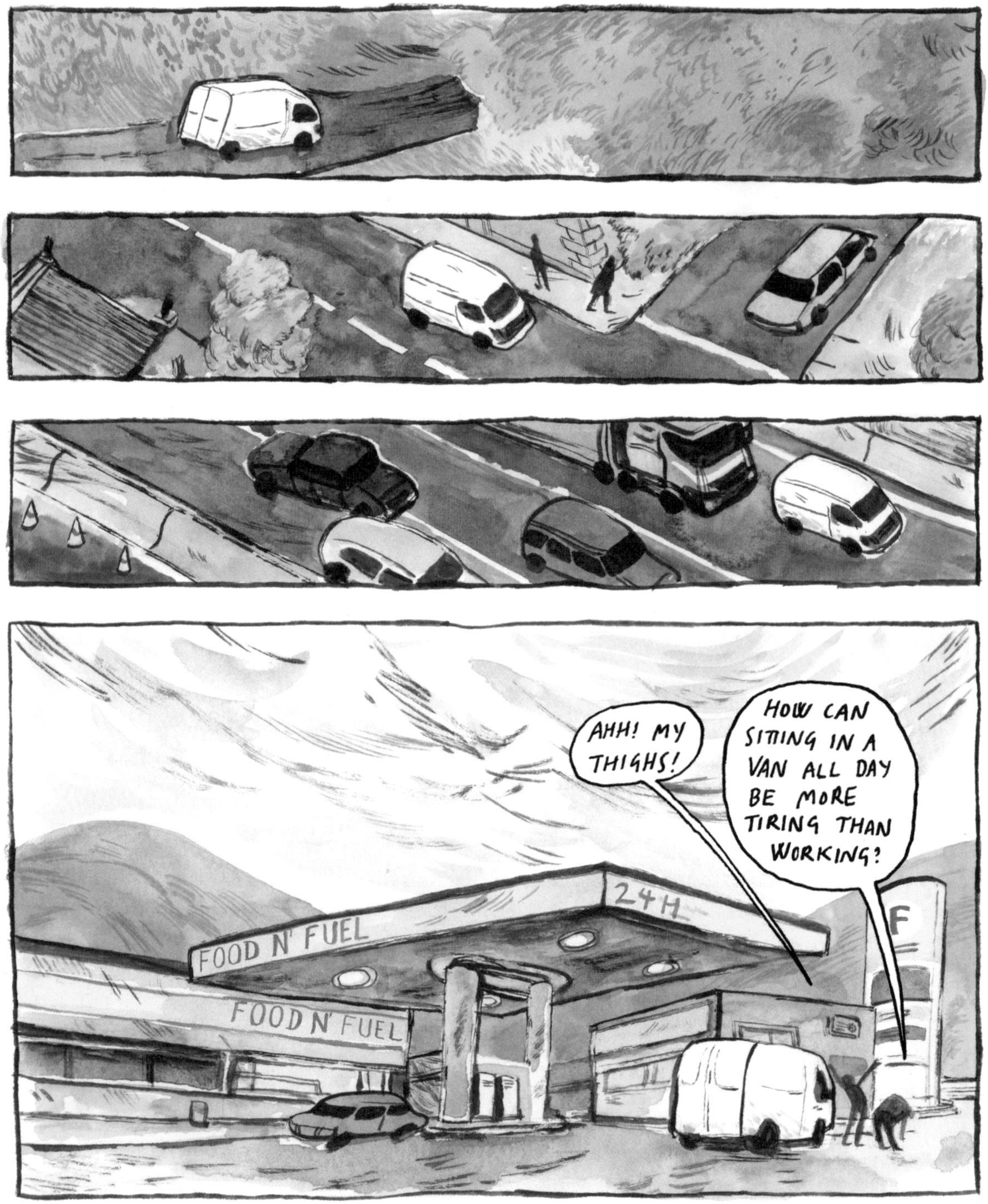
24H
FOOD N' FUEL
FOOD N' FUEL
F
AHH! MY THIGHS!
HOW CAN SITTING IN A VAN ALL DAY BE MORE TIRING THAN WORKING?

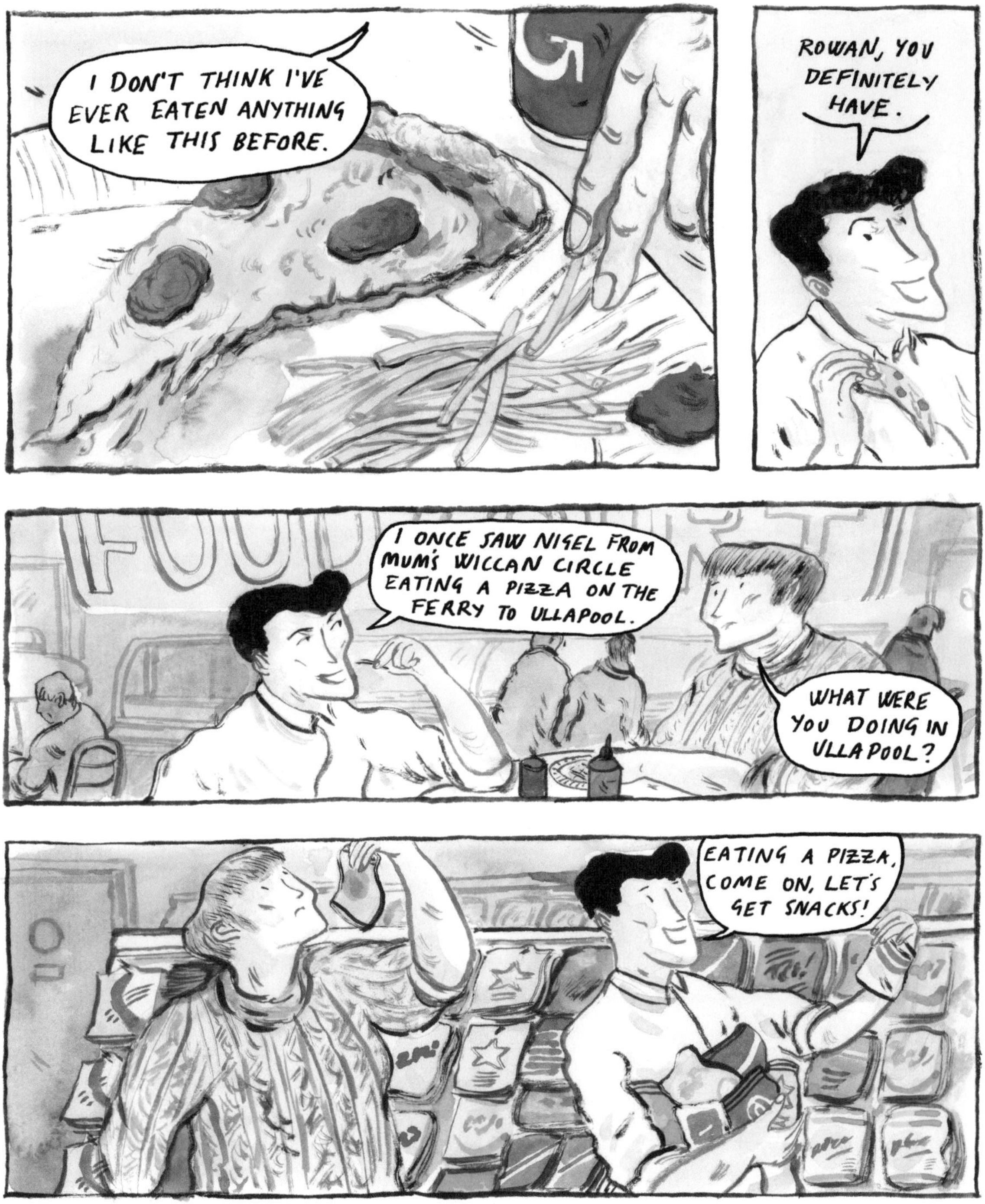
I DON'T THINK I'VE EVER EATEN ANYTHING LIKE THIS BEFORE.
ROWAN, YOU DEFINITELY HAVE.
I ONCE SAW NIGEL FROM MUM'S WICCAN CIRCLE EATING A PIZZA ON THE FERRY TO ULLAPOOL.
WHAT WERE YOU DOING IN ULLAPOOL?
EATING A PIZZA, COME ON, LET'S GET SNACKS!

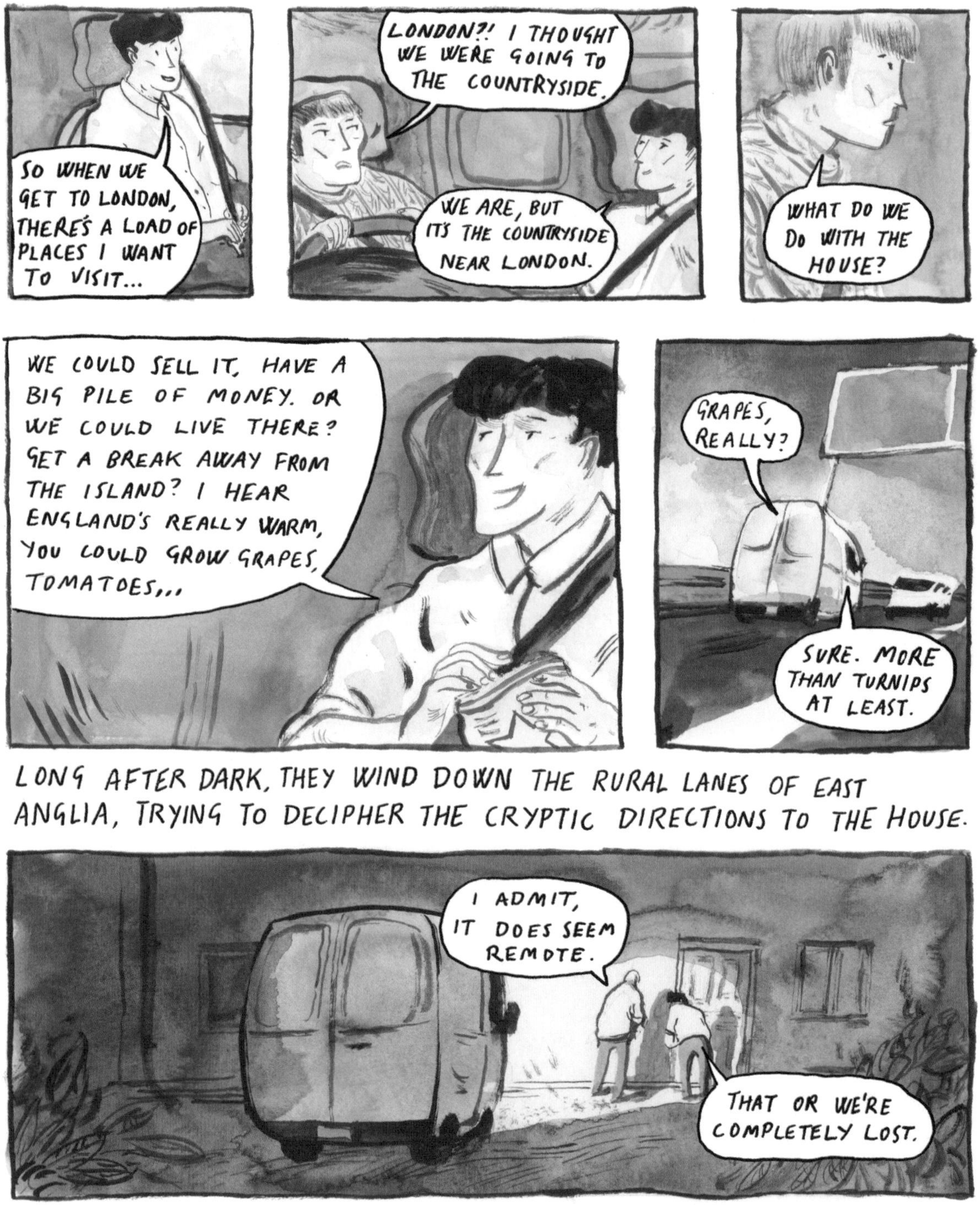
SO WHEN WE GET TO LONDON, THERE'S A LOAD OF PLACES I WANT TO VISIT...
LONDON?! I THOUGHT WE WERE GOING TO THE COUNTRYSIDE.
WE ARE, BUT IT'S THE COUNTRYSIDE NEAR LONDON.
WHAT DO WE DO WITH THE HOUSE?
WE COULD SELL IT, HAVE A BIG PILE OF MONEY. OR WE COULD LIVE THERE? GET A BREAK AWAY FROM THE ISLAND? I HEAR ENGLAND'S REALLY WARM, YOU COULD GROW GRAPES, TOMATOES,..
GRAPES, REALLY?
SURE. MORE THAN TURNIPS AT LEAST.
LONG AFTER DARK, THEY WIND DOWN THE RURAL LANES OF EAST ANGLIA, TRYING TO DECIPHER THE CRYPTIC DIRECTIONS TO THE HOUSE.
I ADMIT, IT DOES SEEM REMOTE.
THAT OR WE'RE COMPLETELY LOST.

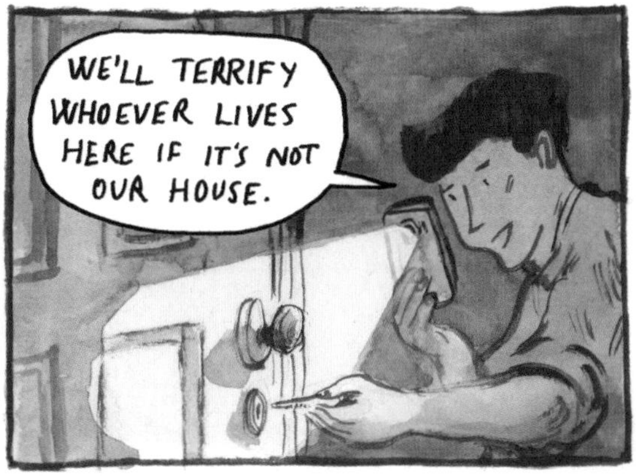
WE'LL TERRIFY WHOEVER LIVES HERE IF IT'S NOT OUR HOUSE.

BUT THE KEY TURNS IN THE LOCK. THE HOUSE IS DUSTY, STILL FILLED WITH RELICS OF ITS FORMER OWNERS. WITH THE LIGHT OF HIS PHONE, TULIP STOMPS THROUGH THE HOUSE, FUMBLING HIS WAY TO THE FUSEBOX AND WATER MAIN.

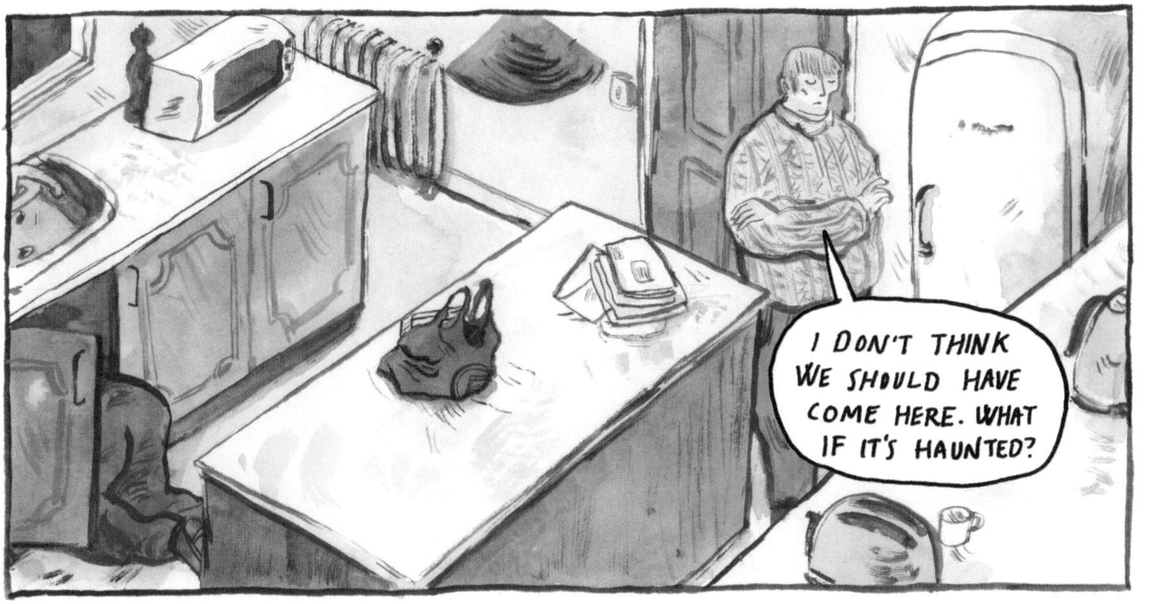
I DON'T THINK WE SHOULD HAVE COME HERE. WHAT IF IT'S HAUNTED?

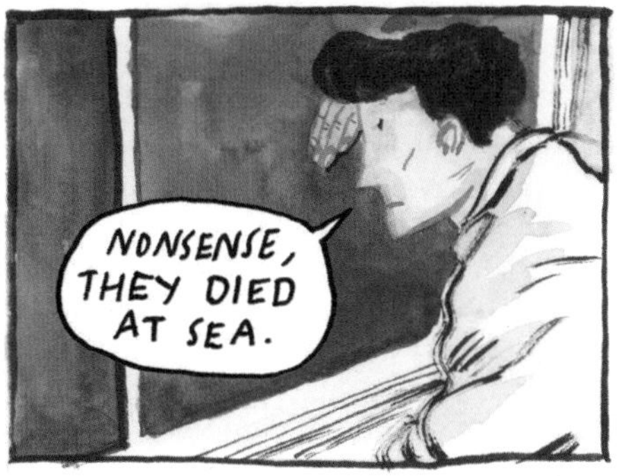
NONSENSE, THEY DIED AT SEA.

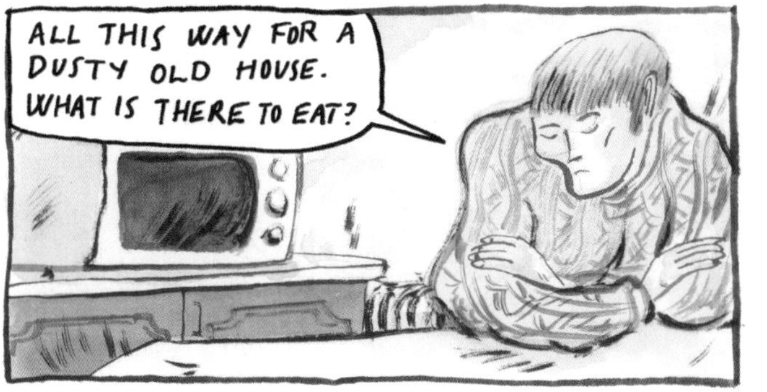
ALL THIS WAY FOR A DUSTY OLD HOUSE. WHAT IS THERE TO EAT?

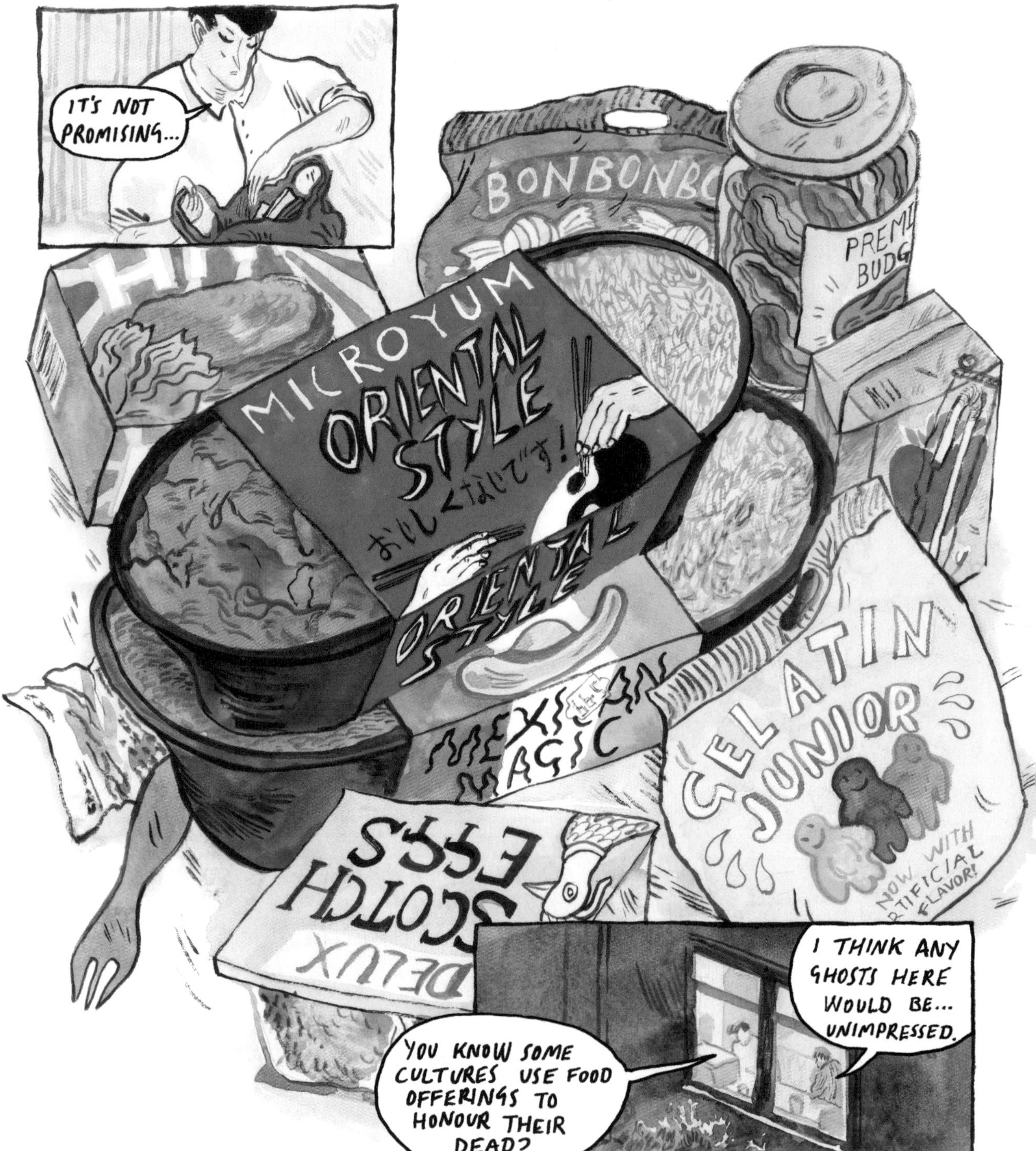
IT'S NOT PROMISING...
MICROYUM
ORIENTAL STYLE
おいしくないです!
MEXICAN MAGIC
GELATIN JUNIOR
SCOTCH EGGS
DELUX
YOU KNOW SOME CULTURES USE FOOD OFFERINGS TO HONOUR THEIR DEAD?
I THINK ANY GHOSTS HERE WOULD BE... UNIMPRESSED.

THE NEXT MORNING, TULIP WAKES TO FIND ROWAN GONE...

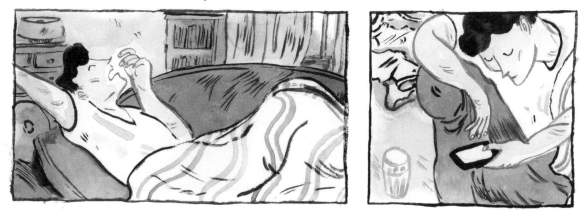

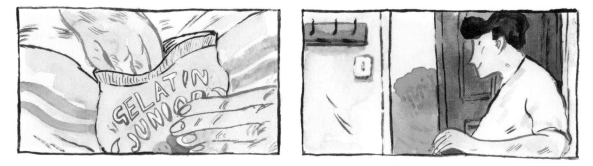

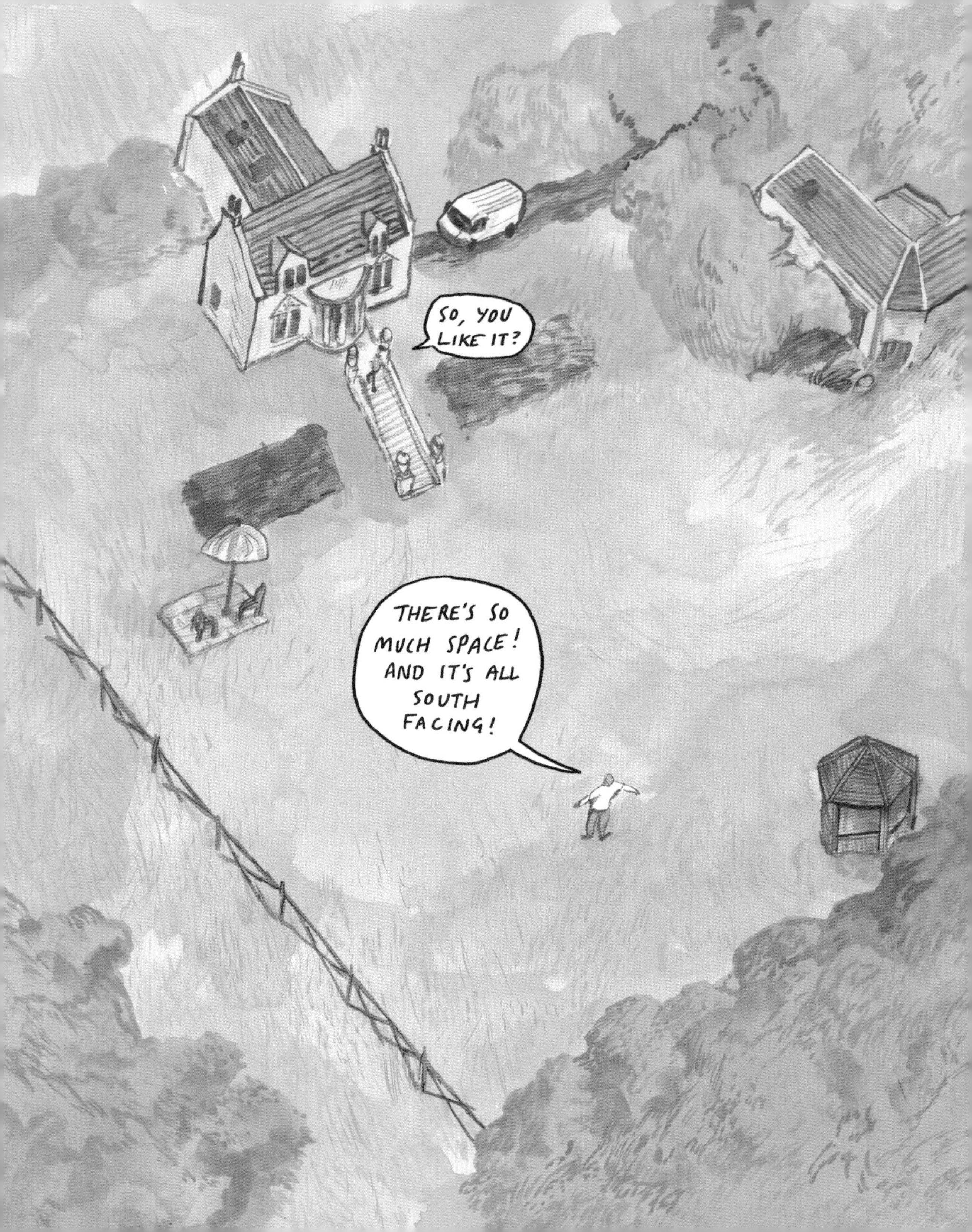
SO, YOU LIKE IT?
THERE'S SO MUCH SPACE! AND IT'S ALL SOUTH FACING!

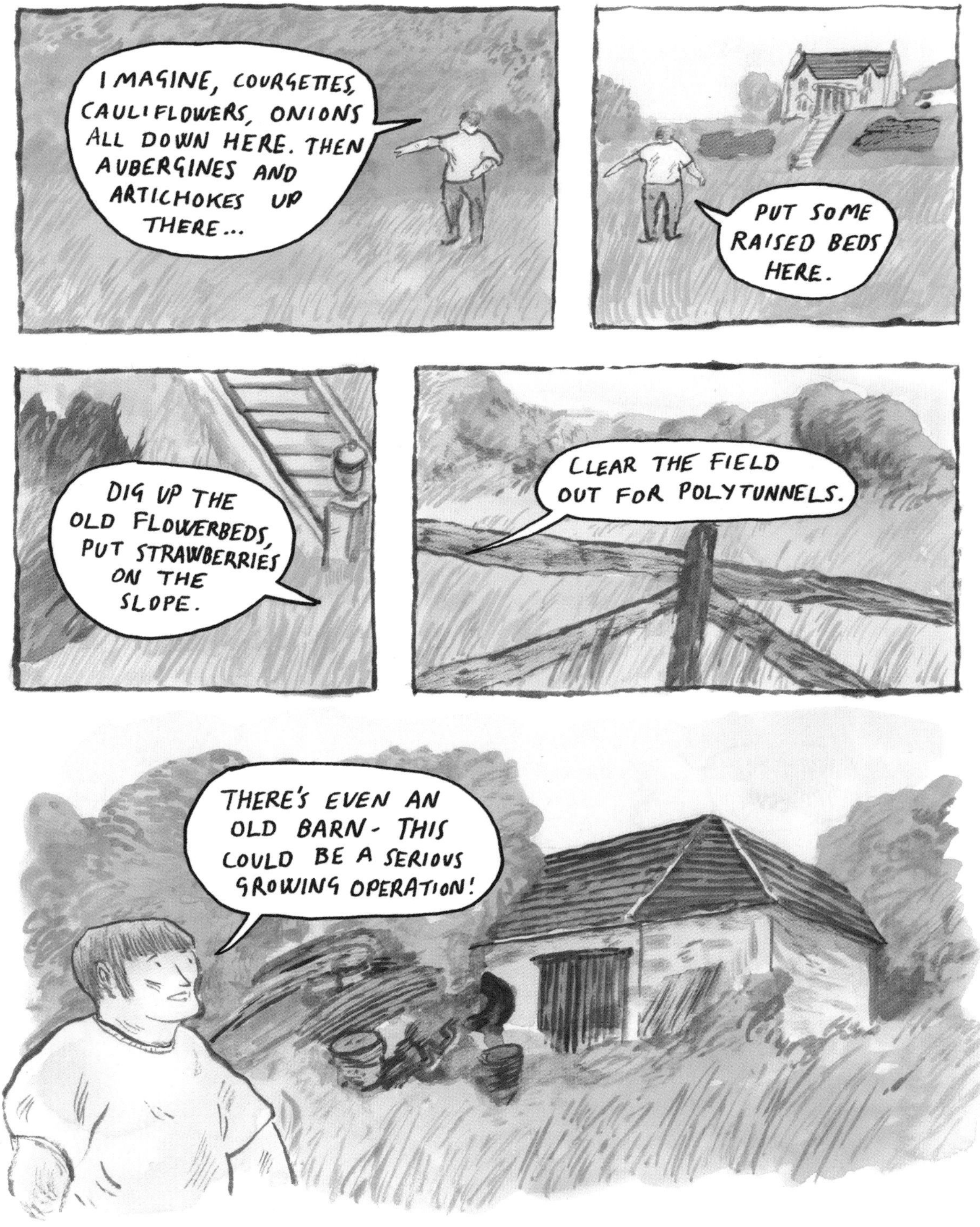
IMAGINE, COURGETTES, CAULIFLOWERS, ONIONS ALL DOWN HERE. THEN AUBERGINES AND ARTICHOKES UP THERE...
PUT SOME RAISED BEDS HERE.
DIG UP THE OLD FLOWERBEDS, PUT STRAWBERRIES ON THE SLOPE.
CLEAR THE FIELD OUT FOR POLYTUNNELS.
THERE'S EVEN AN OLD BARN - THIS COULD BE A SERIOUS GROWING OPERATION!

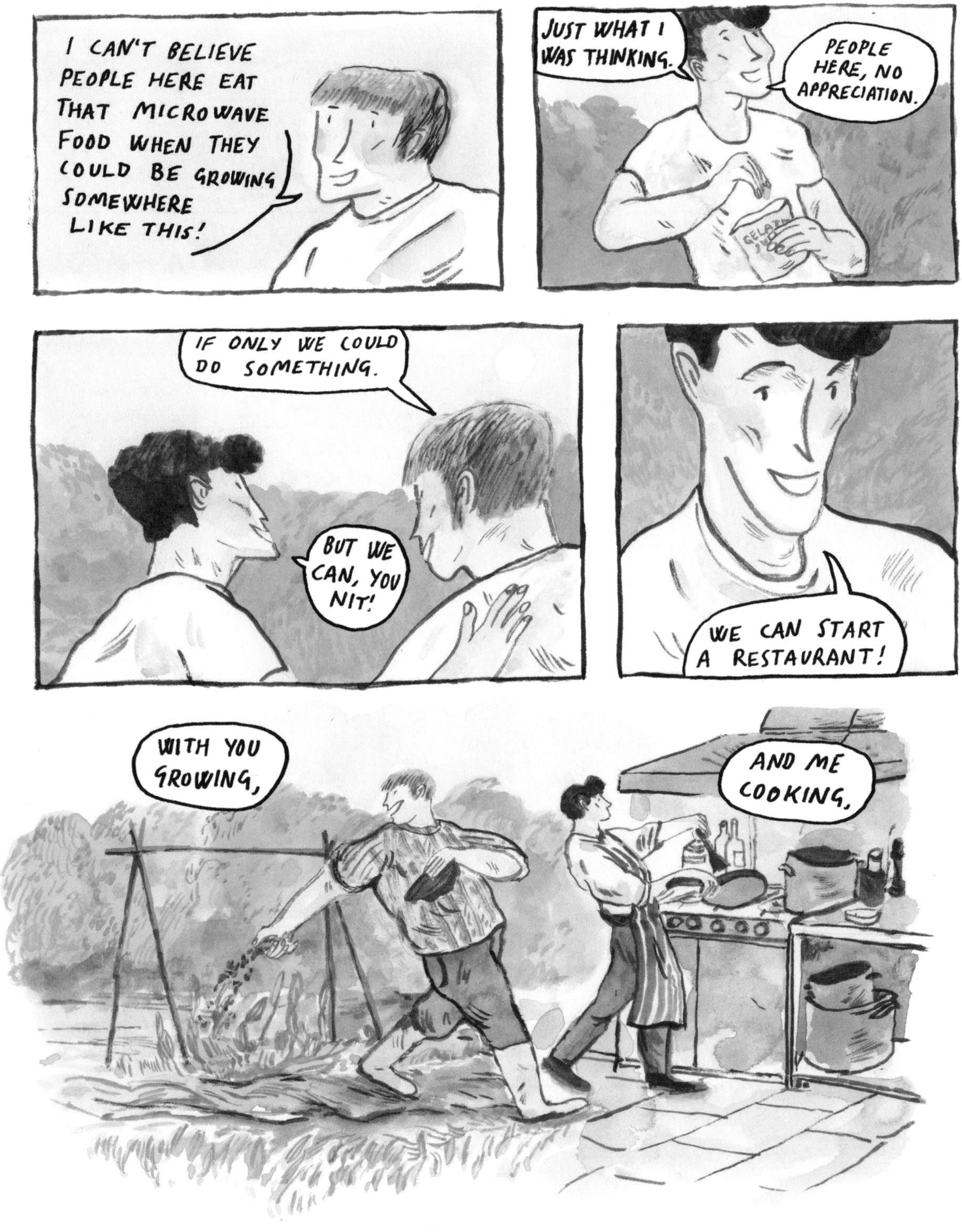
I CAN'T BELIEVE PEOPLE HERE EAT THAT MICROWAVE FOOD WHEN THEY COULD BE GROWING SOMEWHERE LIKE THIS!
JUST WHAT I WAS THINKING.
PEOPLE HERE, NO APPRECIATION.
IF ONLY WE COULD DO SOMETHING.
BUT WE CAN, YOU NIT!
WE CAN START A RESTAURANT!
WITH YOU GROWING,
AND ME COOKING.

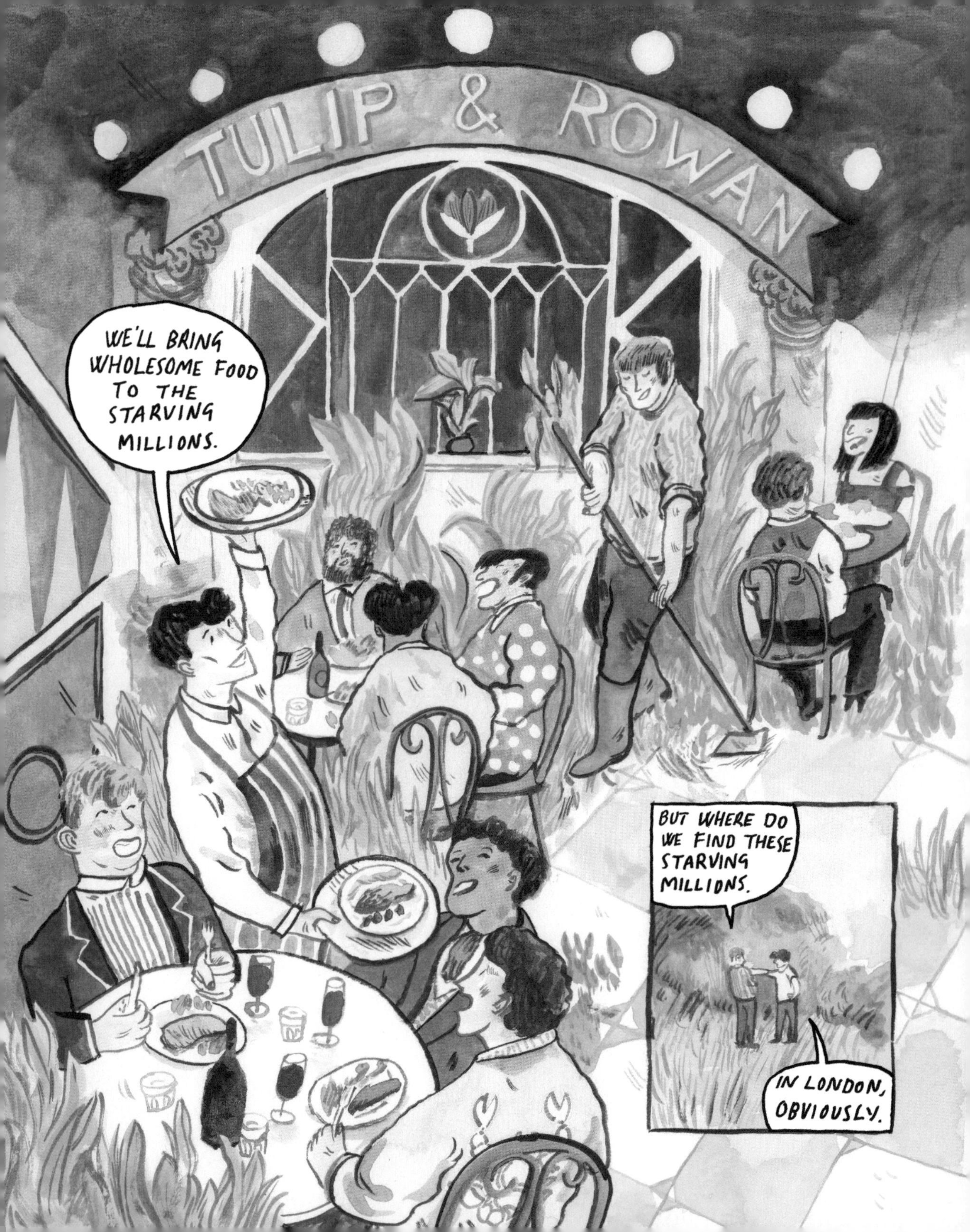
TULIP & ROWAN
WE'LL BRING WHOLESOME FOOD TO THE STARVING MILLIONS.
BUT WHERE DO WE FIND THESE STARVING MILLIONS.
IN LONDON, OBVIOUSLY.

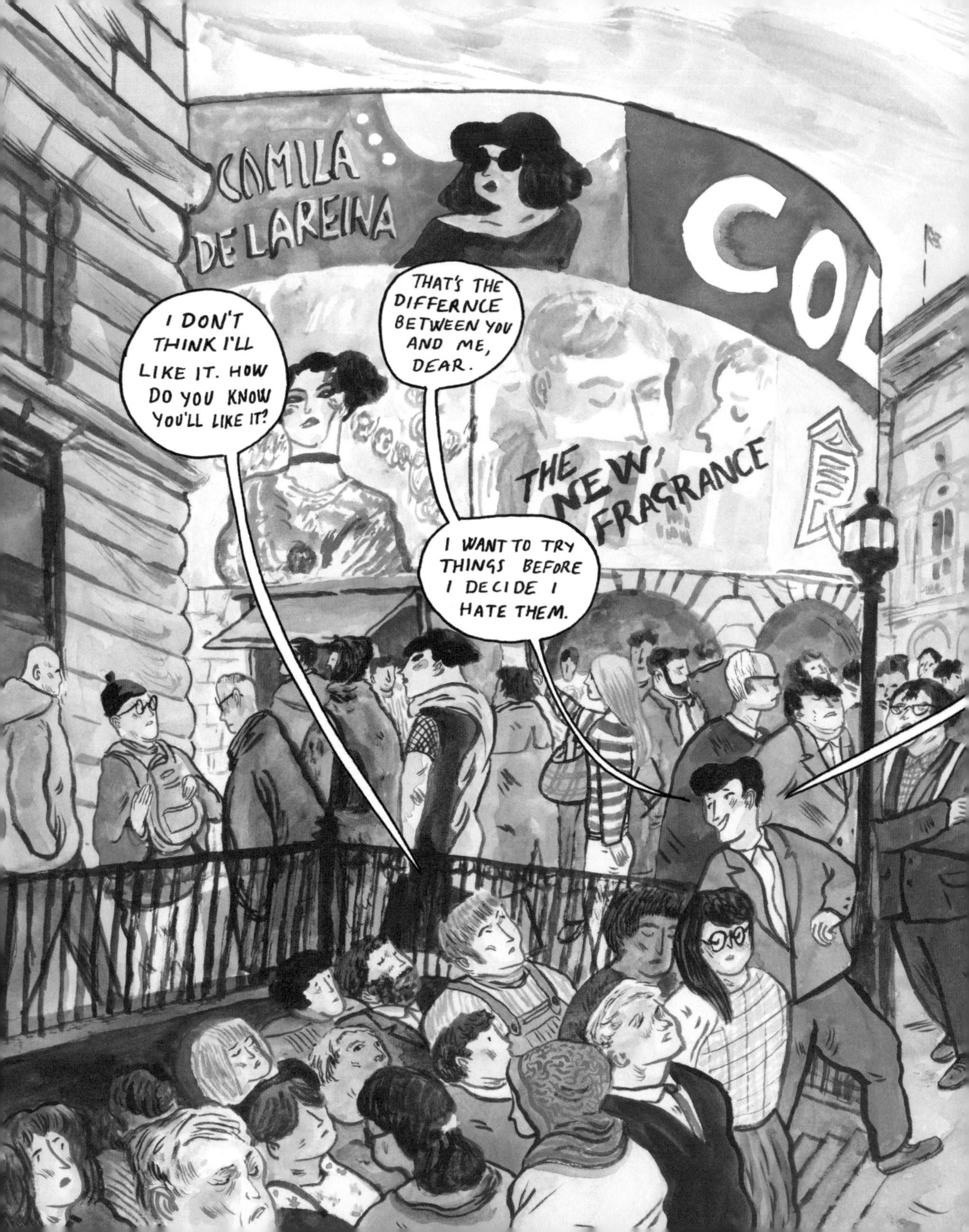

CAMILA DE LAREINA
CO
I DON'T THINK I'LL LIKE IT. HOW DO YOU KNOW YOU'LL LIKE IT?
THAT'S THE DIFFERNCE BETWEEN YOU AND ME, DEAR.
THE NEW FRAGRANCE
I WANT TO TRY THINGS BEFORE I DECIDE I HATE THEM.

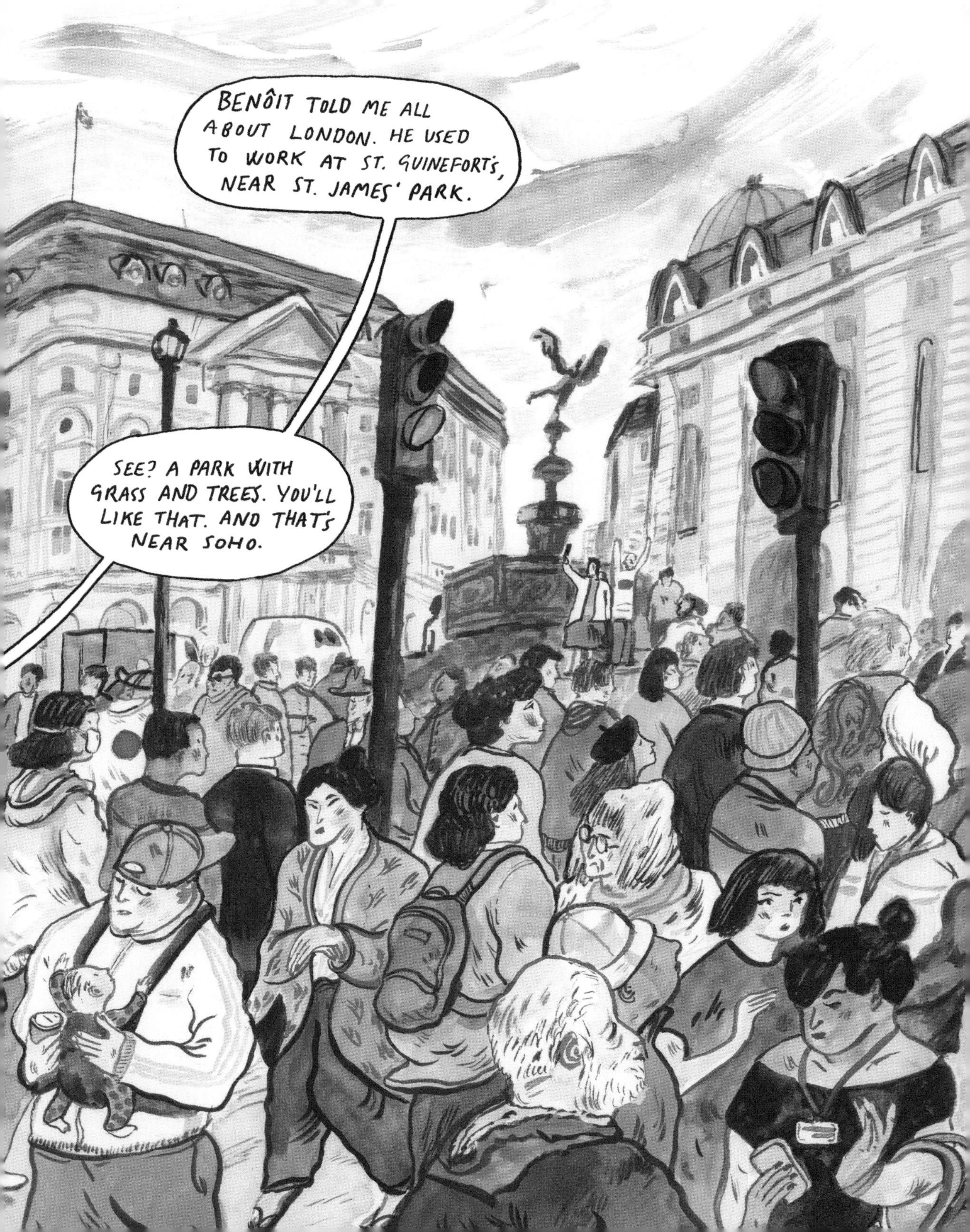
BENÔIT TOLD ME ALL ABOUT LONDON. HE USED TO WORK AT ST. GUINEFORT'S, NEAR ST. JAMES' PARK.
SEE? A PARK WITH GRASS AND TREES. YOU'LL LIKE THAT. AND THAT'S NEAR SOHO.

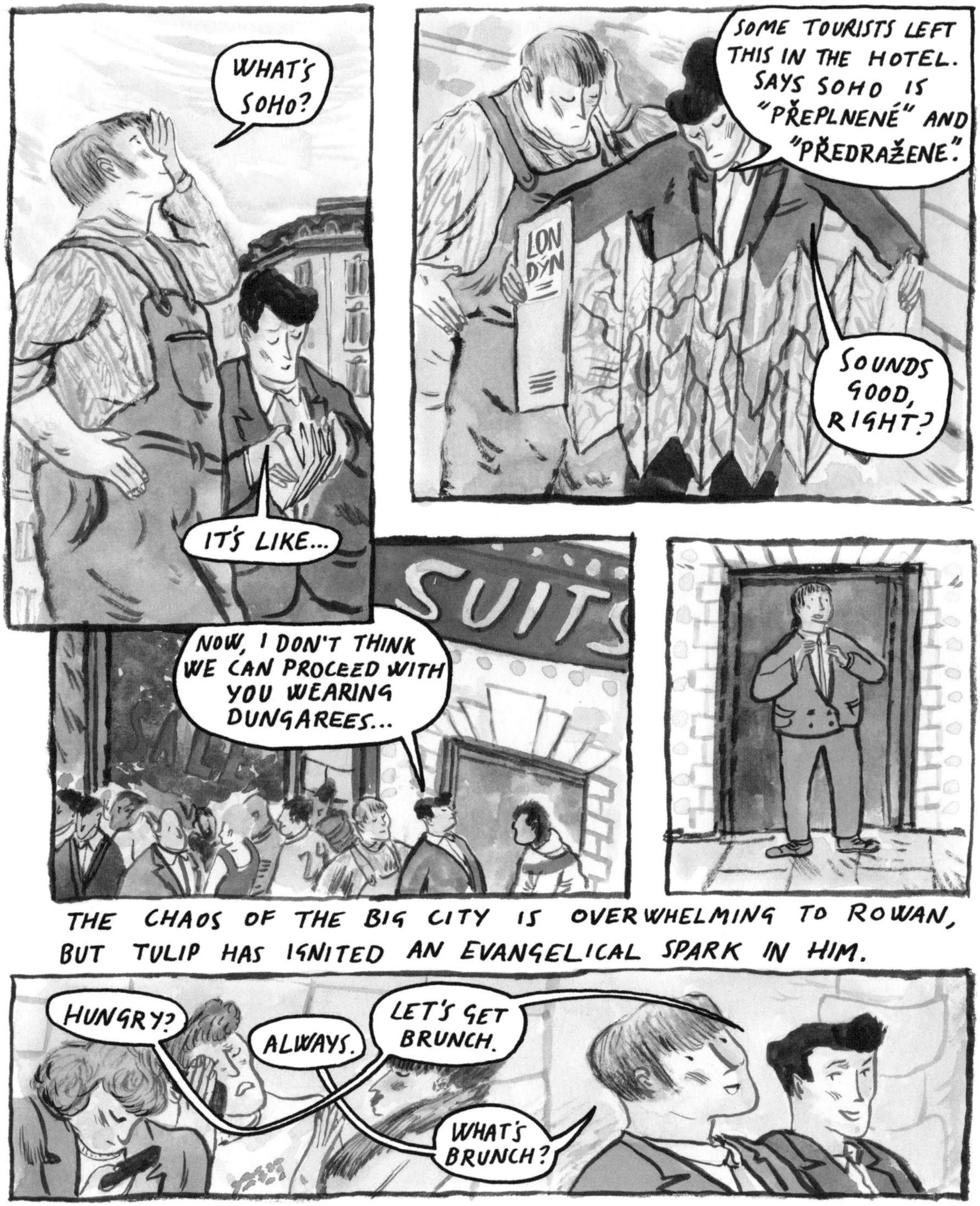
WHAT'S SOHO?
SOME TOURISTS LEFT THIS IN THE HOTEL. SAYS SOHO IS "PŘEPLNENÉ" AND "PŘEDRAŽENE".
LONDÝN
SOUNDS GOOD, RIGHT?
IT'S LIKE...
SUITS
NOW, I DON'T THINK WE CAN PROCEED WITH YOU WEARING DUNGAREES...
THE CHAOS OF THE BIG CITY IS OVERWHELMING TO ROWAN, BUT TULIP HAS IGNITED AN EVANGELICAL SPARK IN HIM.
HUNGRY?
ALWAYS.
LET'S GET BRUNCH.
WHAT'S BRUNCH?

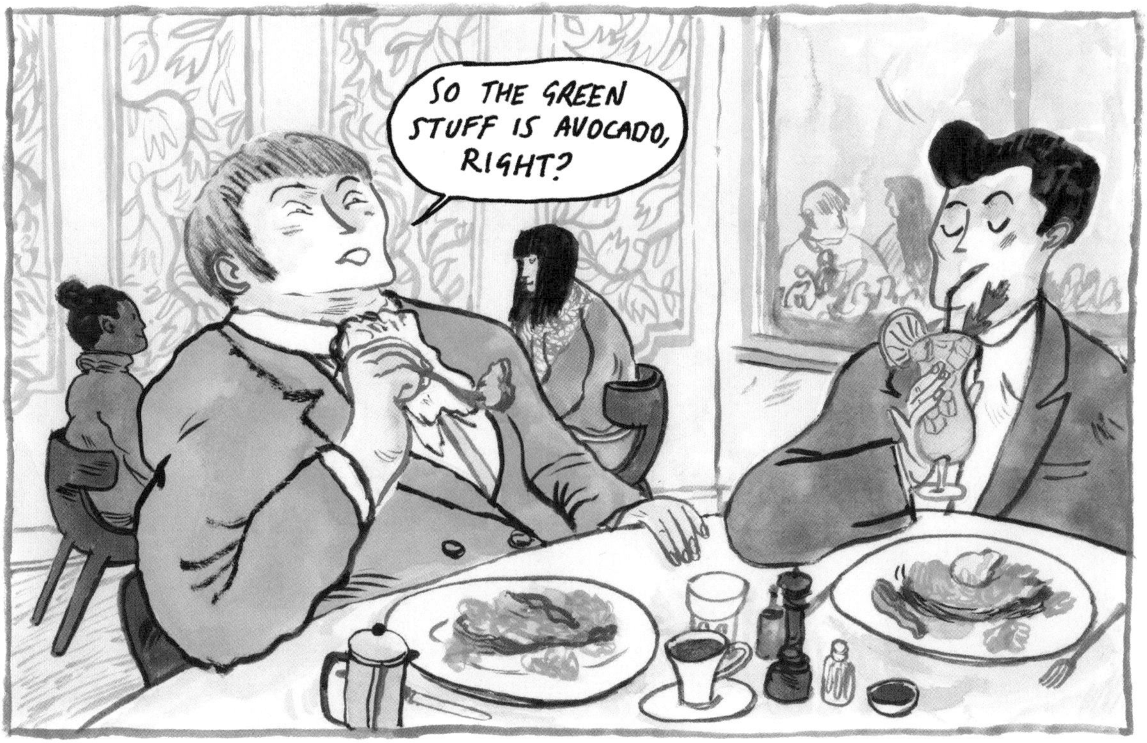
SO THE GREEN STUFF IS AVOCADO, RIGHT?

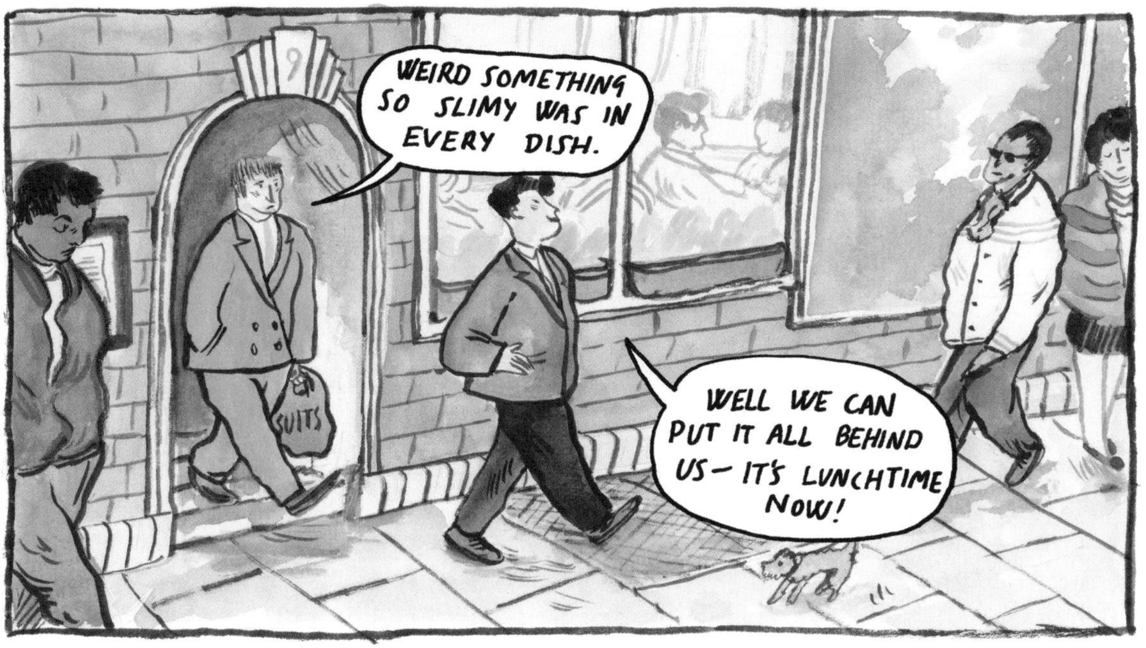
WEIRD SOMETHING SO SLIMY WAS IN EVERY DISH.
WELL WE CAN PUT IT ALL BEHIND US— IT'S LUNCHTIME NOW!
SUITS

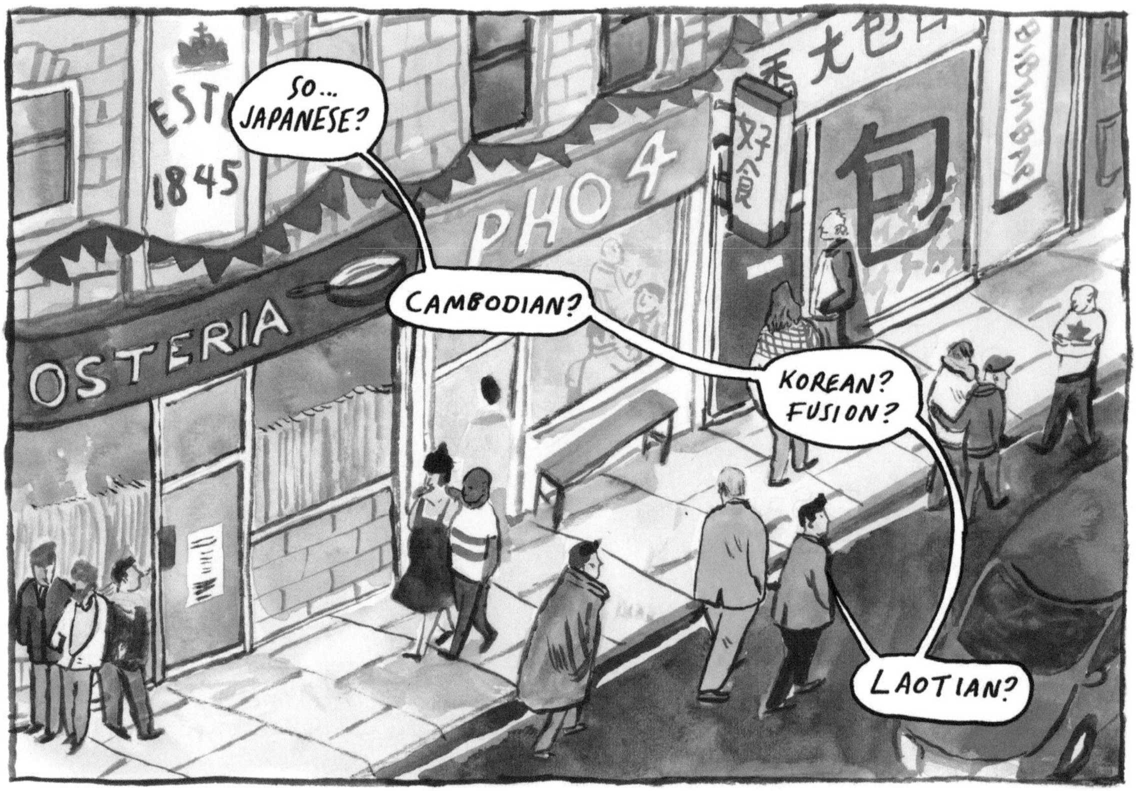
1845
OSTERIA
PHO 4
SO... JAPANESE?
CAMBODIAN?
KOREAN? FUSION?
LAOTIAN?

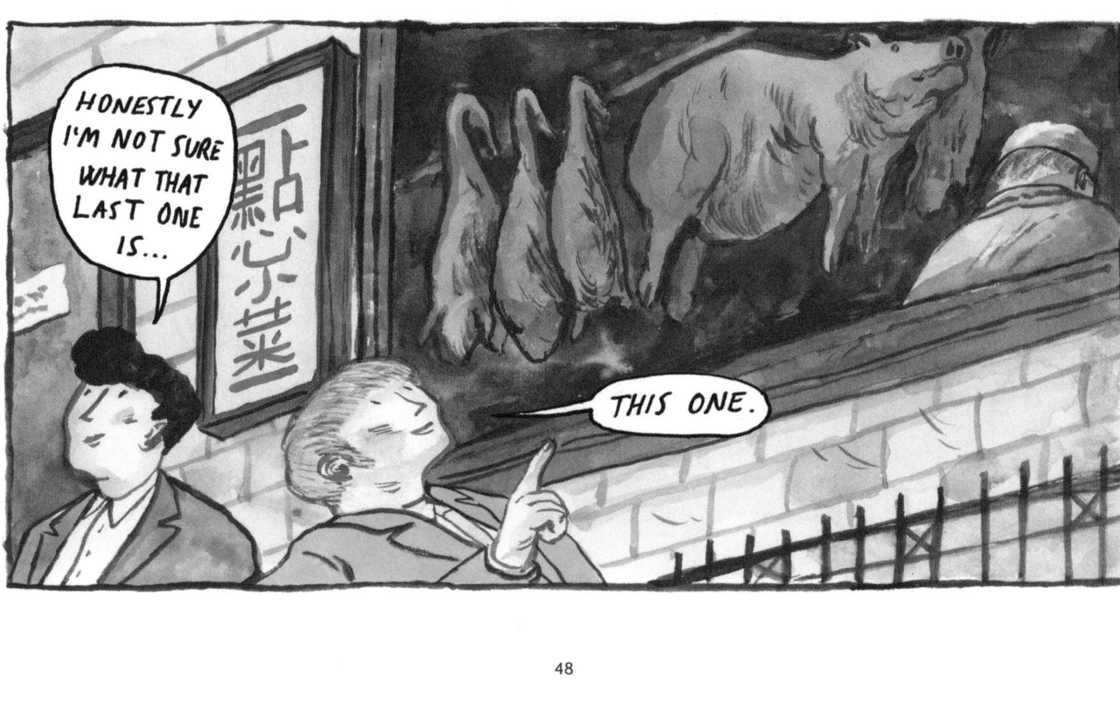
HONESTLY I'M NOT SURE WHAT THAT LAST ONE IS...
THIS ONE.

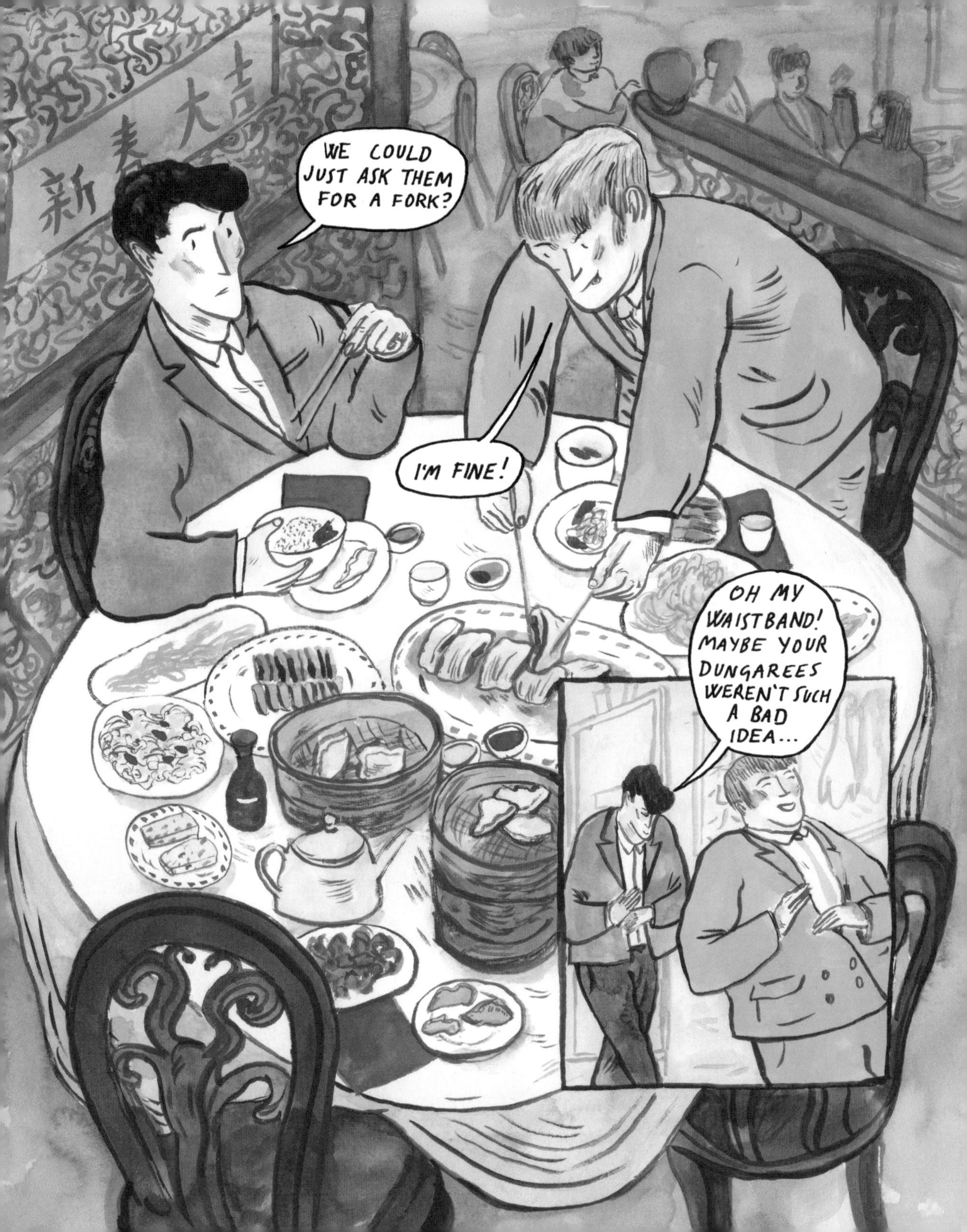
新春大吉
WE COULD JUST ASK THEM FOR A FORK?
I'M FINE!
OH MY WAISTBAND! MAYBE YOUR DUNGAREES WEREN'T SUCH A BAD IDEA...

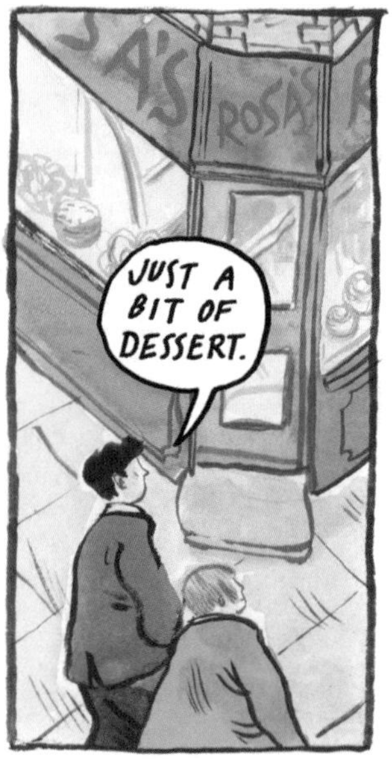
ROSA'S
JUST A BIT OF DESSERT.

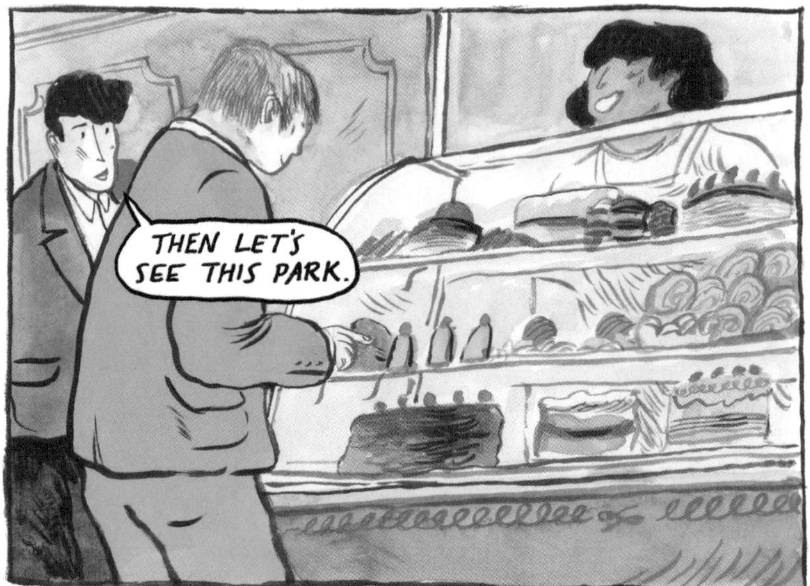
THEN LET'S SEE THIS PARK.

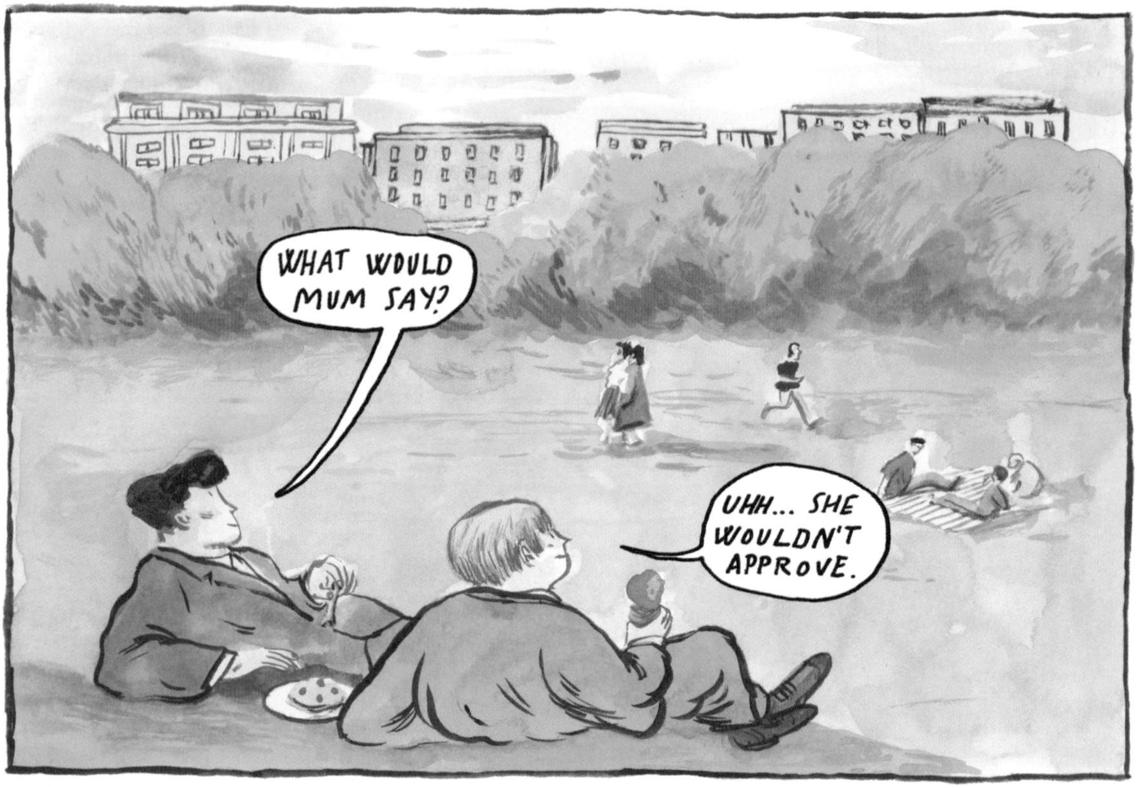
WHAT WOULD MUM SAY?
UHH... SHE WOULDN'T APPROVE.

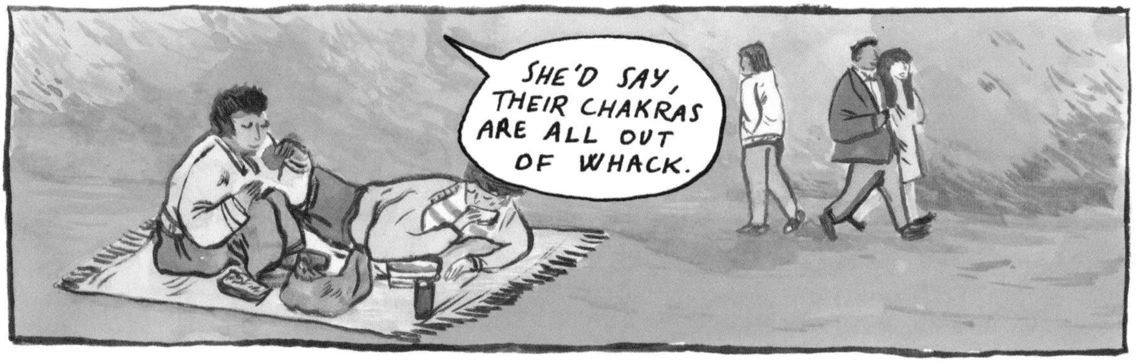
SHE'D SAY, THEIR CHAKRAS ARE ALL OUT OF WHACK.

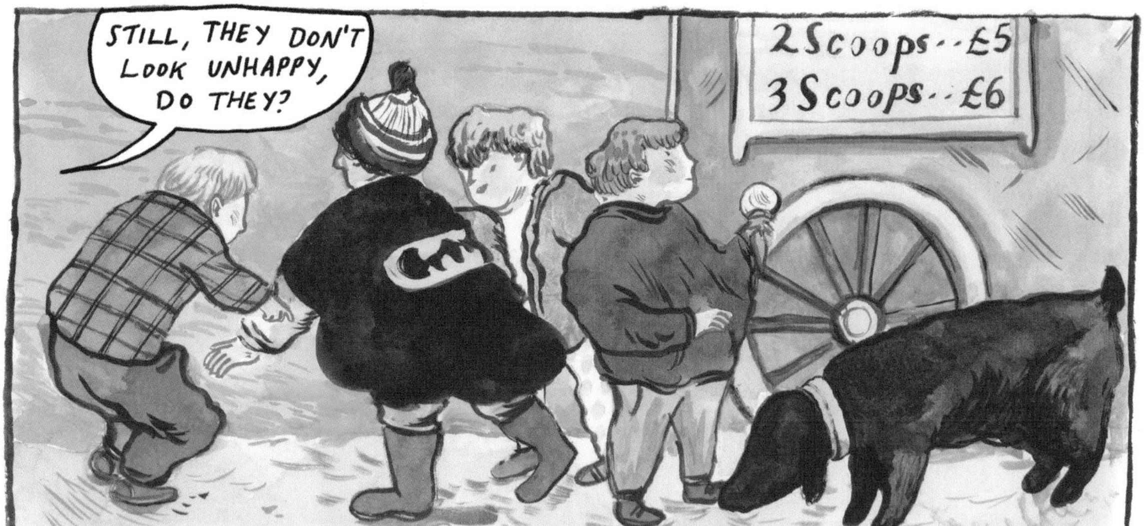
STILL, THEY DON'T LOOK UNHAPPY, DO THEY?
2 Scoops - - £5
3 Scoops - - £6

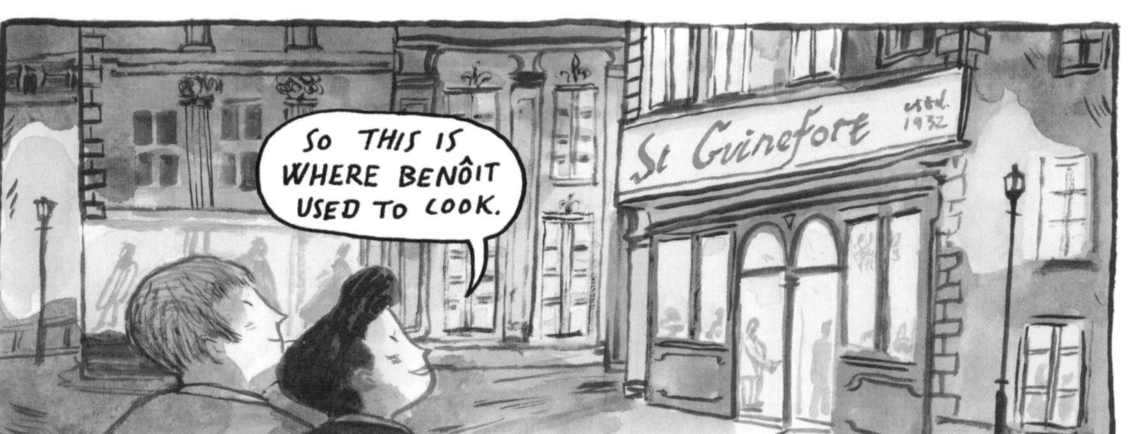
St Guinefort
estd. 1932
SO THIS IS WHERE BENÔIT USED TO COOK.

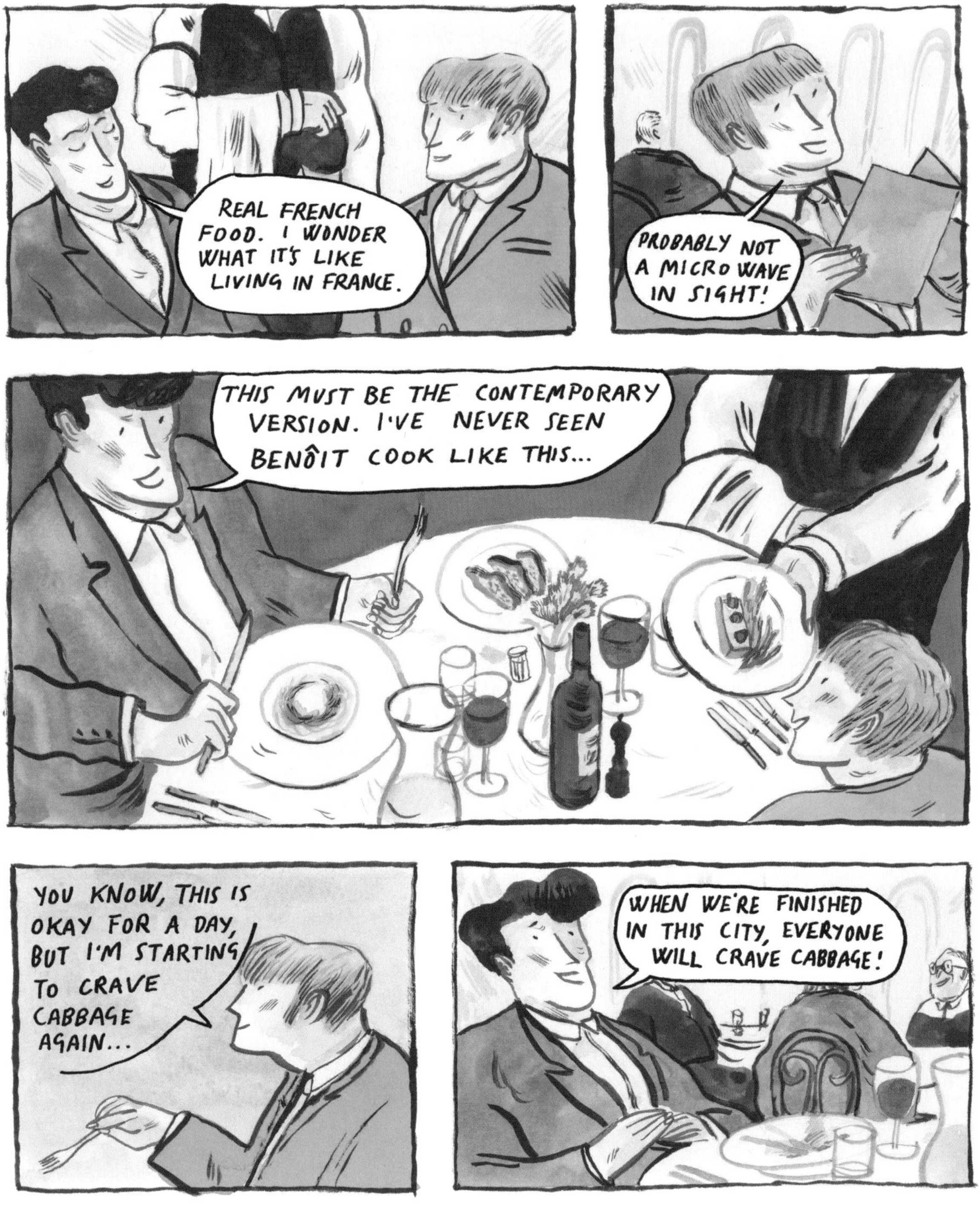
REAL FRENCH FOOD. I WONDER WHAT IT'S LIKE LIVING IN FRANCE.
PROBABLY NOT A MICRO WAVE IN SIGHT!
THIS MUST BE THE CONTEMPORARY VERSION. I'VE NEVER SEEN BENÔIT COOK LIKE THIS...
YOU KNOW, THIS IS OKAY FOR A DAY, BUT I'M STARTING TO CRAVE CABBAGE AGAIN...
WHEN WE'RE FINISHED IN THIS CITY, EVERYONE WILL CRAVE CABBAGE!

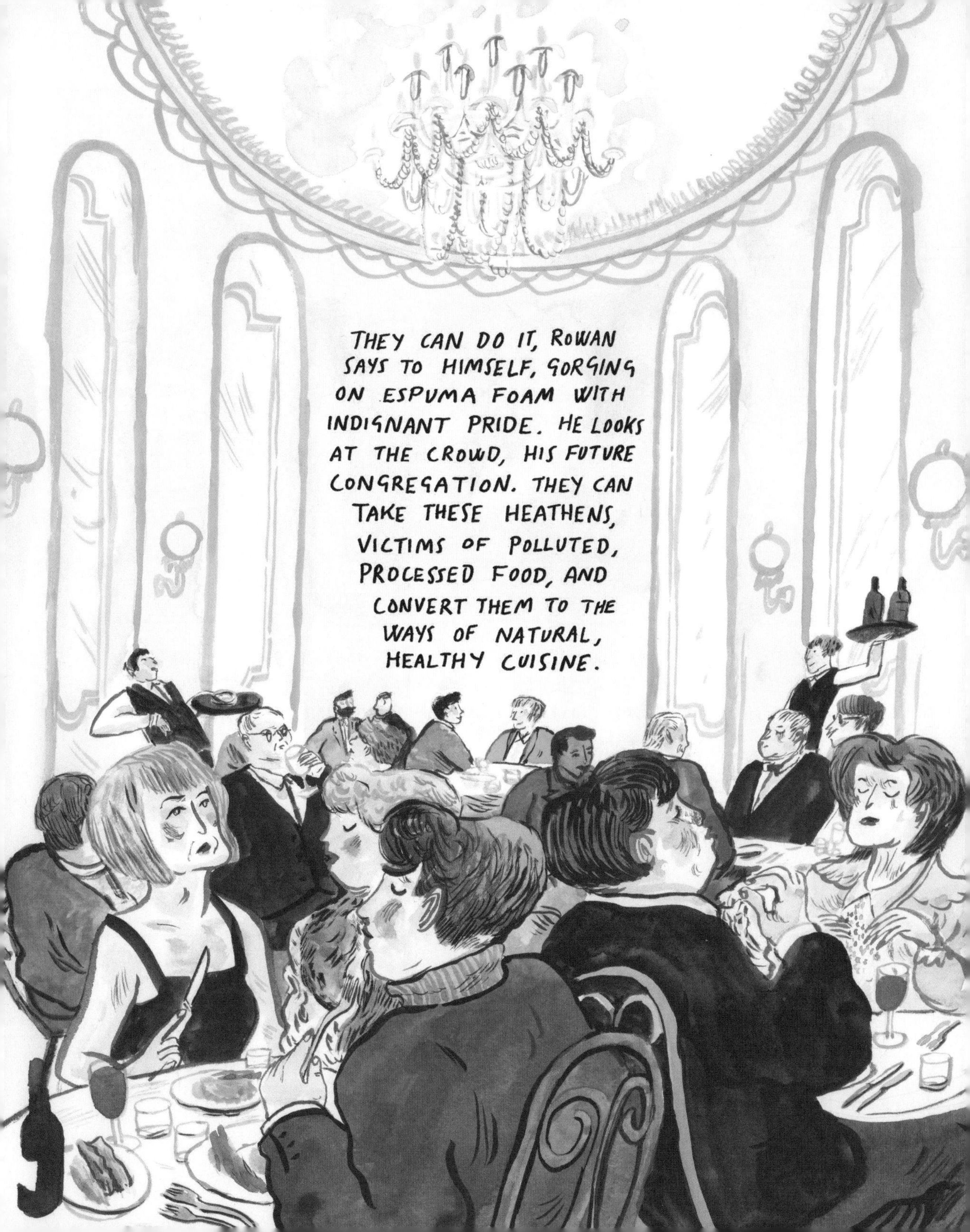
THEY CAN DO IT, ROWAN SAYS TO HIMSELF, GORGING ON ESPUMA FOAM WITH INDIGNANT PRIDE. HE LOOKS AT THE CROWD, HIS FUTURE CONGREGATION. THEY CAN TAKE THESE HEATHENS, VICTIMS OF POLLUTED, PROCESSED FOOD, AND CONVERT THEM TO THE WAYS OF NATURAL, HEALTHY CUISINE.

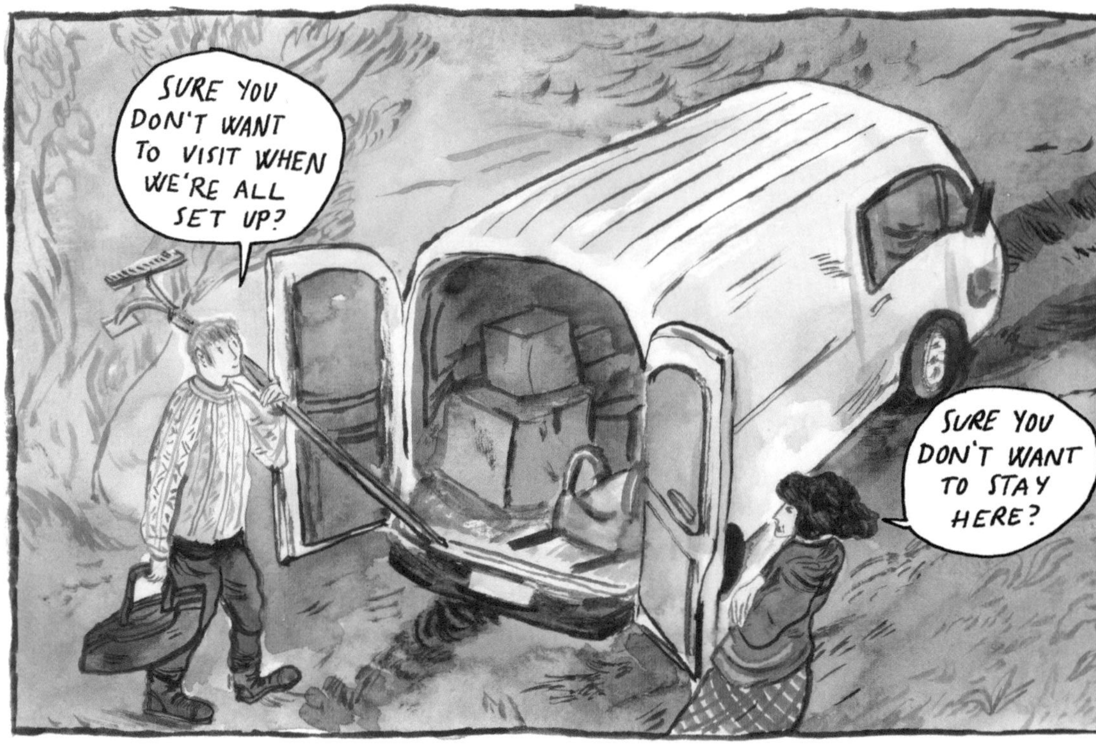
SURE YOU DON'T WANT TO VISIT WHEN WE'RE ALL SET UP?
SURE YOU DON'T WANT TO STAY HERE?

FILLED WITH INSPIRATION, ROWAN RETURNS TO SCOTLAND TO COLLECT ALL THEY NEED. HIS MOTHER MAY BE RELUCTANT TO SEE THEM GO, BUT SHE UNDERSTANDS ROWAN'S CONVICTION. TULIP STAYS IN LONDON, SEARCHING FOR A PREMISES, BUT WITHOUT HIS BROTHER, HIS BRAVADO BEGINS TO FALTER.

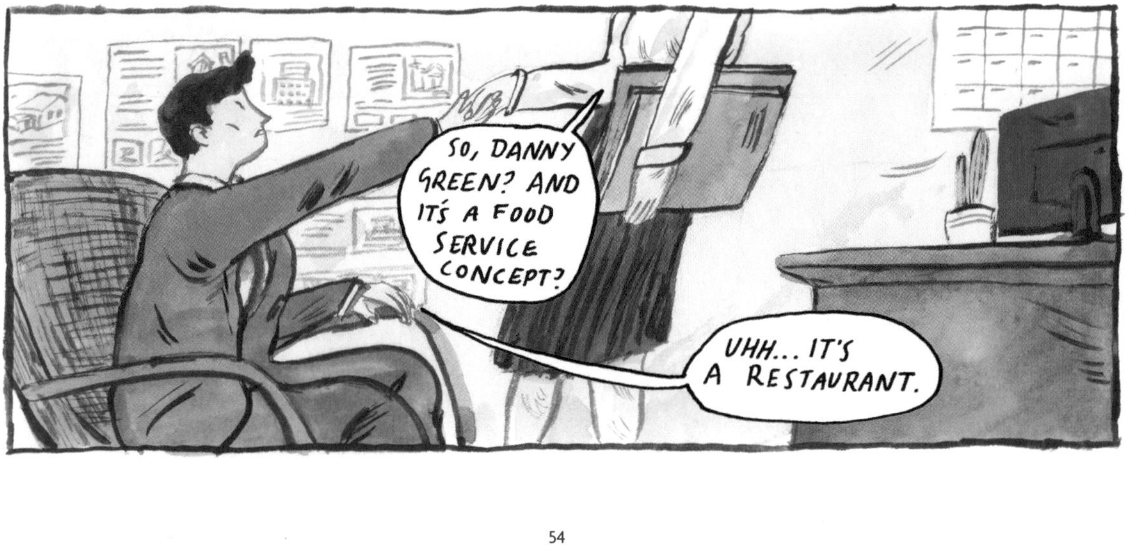
SO, DANNY GREEN? AND IT'S A FOOD SERVICE CONCEPT?
UHH... IT'S A RESTAURANT.

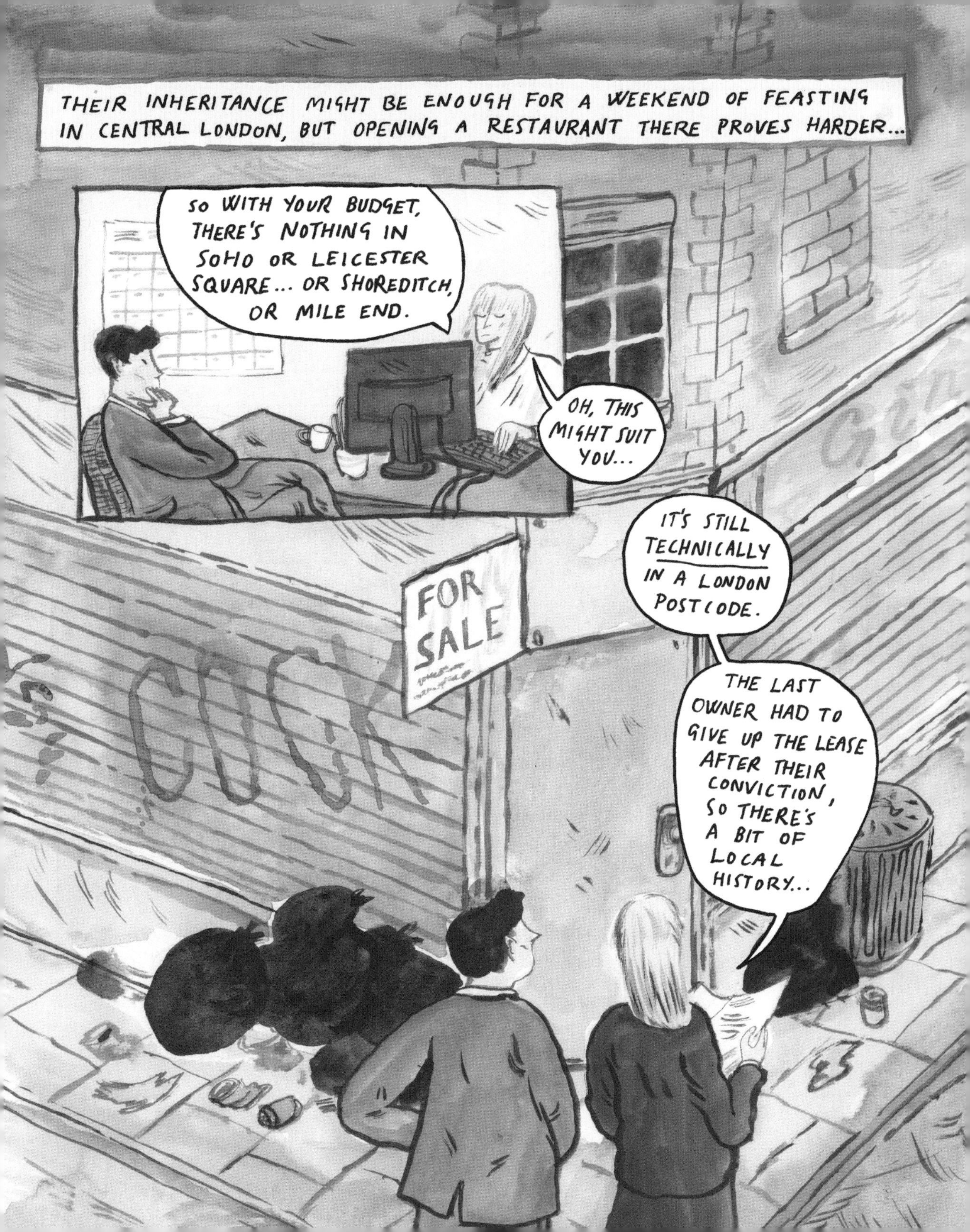
THEIR INHERITANCE MIGHT BE ENOUGH FOR A WEEKEND OF FEASTING IN CENTRAL LONDON, BUT OPENING A RESTAURANT THERE PROVES HARDER...
SO WITH YOUR BUDGET, THERE'S NOTHING IN SOHO OR LEICESTER SQUARE... OR SHOREDITCH, OR MILE END.
OH, THIS MIGHT SUIT YOU...
FOR SALE
IT'S STILL TECHNICALLY IN A LONDON POSTCODE.
THE LAST OWNER HAD TO GIVE UP THE LEASE AFTER THEIR CONVICTION, SO THERE'S A BIT OF LOCAL HISTORY...

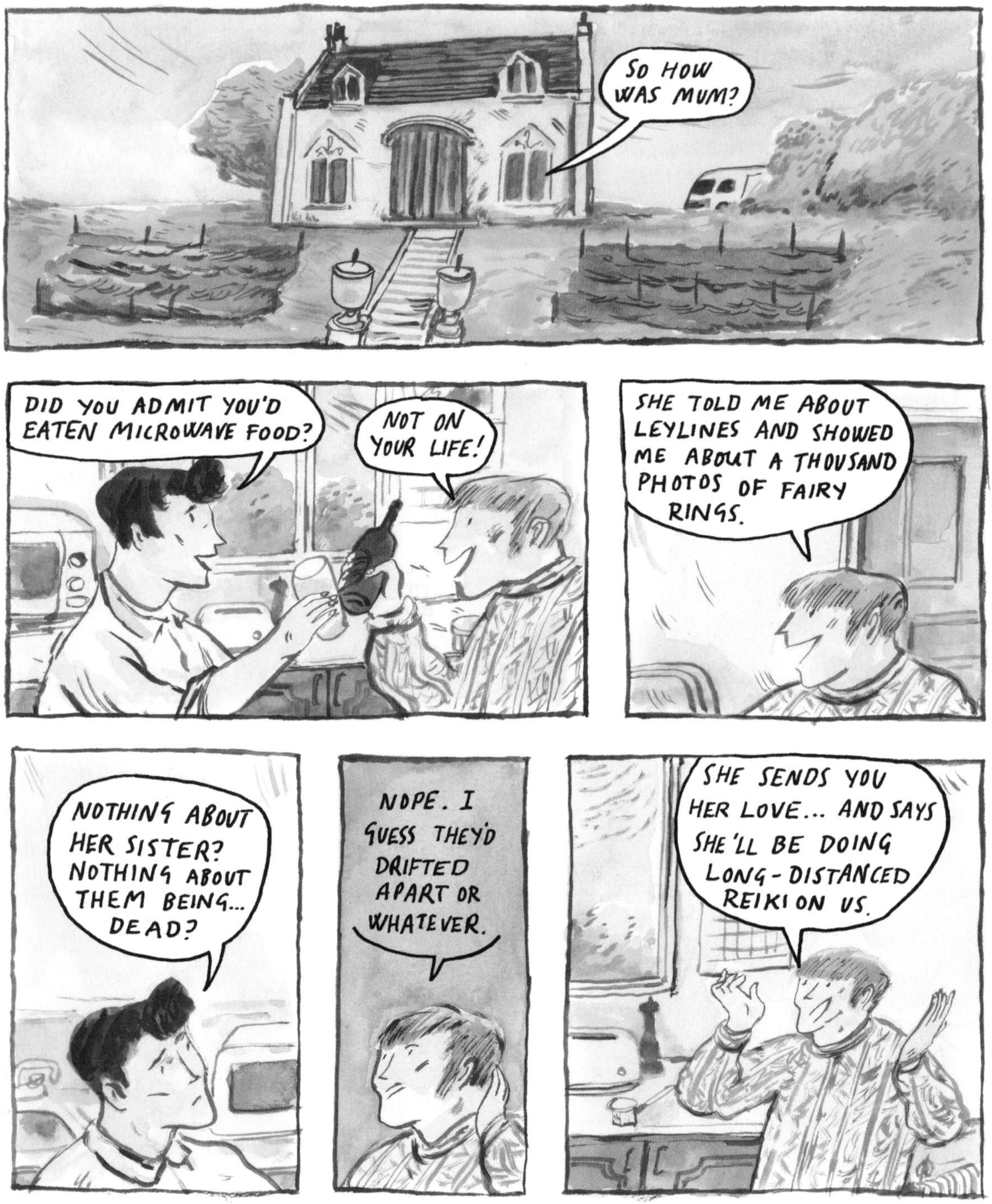
SO HOW WAS MUM?
DID YOU ADMIT YOU'D EATEN MICROWAVE FOOD?
NOT ON YOUR LIFE!
SHE TOLD ME ABOUT LEYLINES AND SHOWED ME ABOUT A THOUSAND PHOTOS OF FAIRY RINGS.
NOTHING ABOUT HER SISTER? NOTHING ABOUT THEM BEING... DEAD?
NOPE. I GUESS THEY'D DRIFTED APART OR WHATEVER.
SHE SENDS YOU HER LOVE... AND SAYS SHE'LL BE DOING LONG-DISTANCED REIKI ON US.

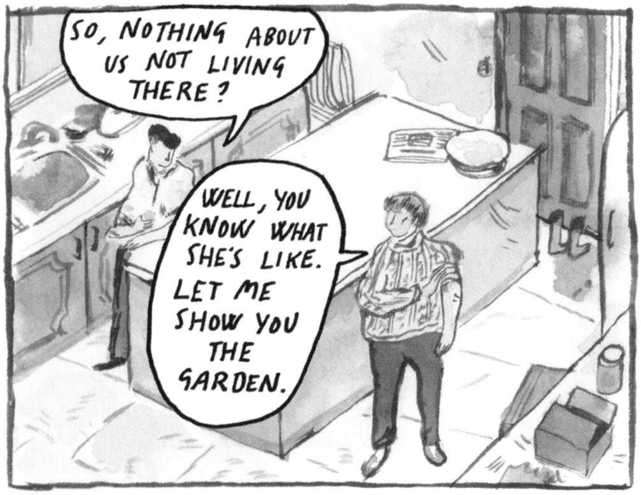
SO, NOTHING ABOUT US NOT LIVING THERE?
WELL, YOU KNOW WHAT SHE'S LIKE. LET ME SHOW YOU THE GARDEN.

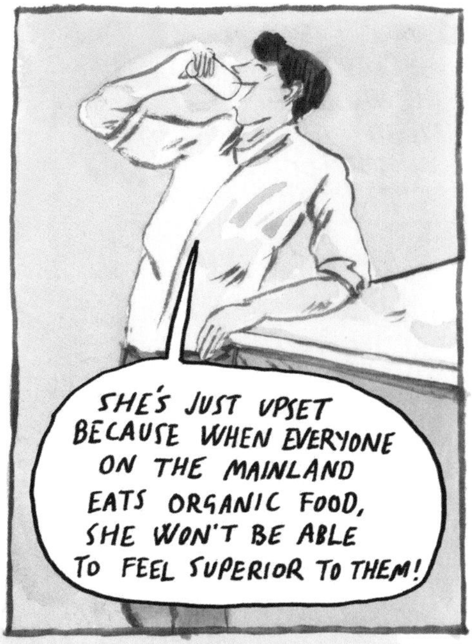
SHE'S JUST UPSET BECAUSE WHEN EVERYONE ON THE MAINLAND EATS ORGANIC FOOD, SHE WON'T BE ABLE TO FEEL SUPERIOR TO THEM!

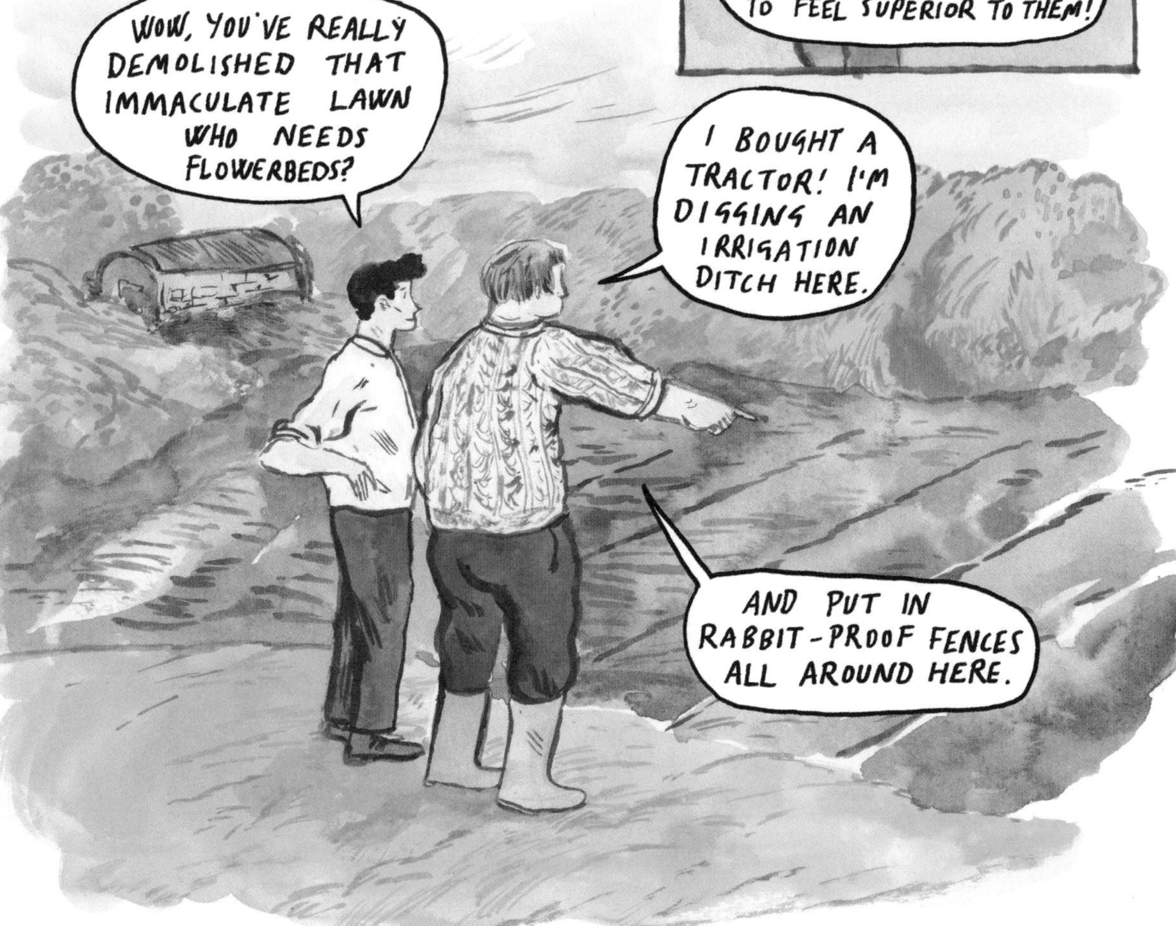
WOW, YOU'VE REALLY DEMOLISHED THAT IMMACULATE LAWN WHO NEEDS FLOWERBEDS?
I BOUGHT A TRACTOR! I'M DIGGING AN IRRIGATION DITCH HERE.
AND PUT IN RABBIT-PROOF FENCES ALL AROUND HERE.

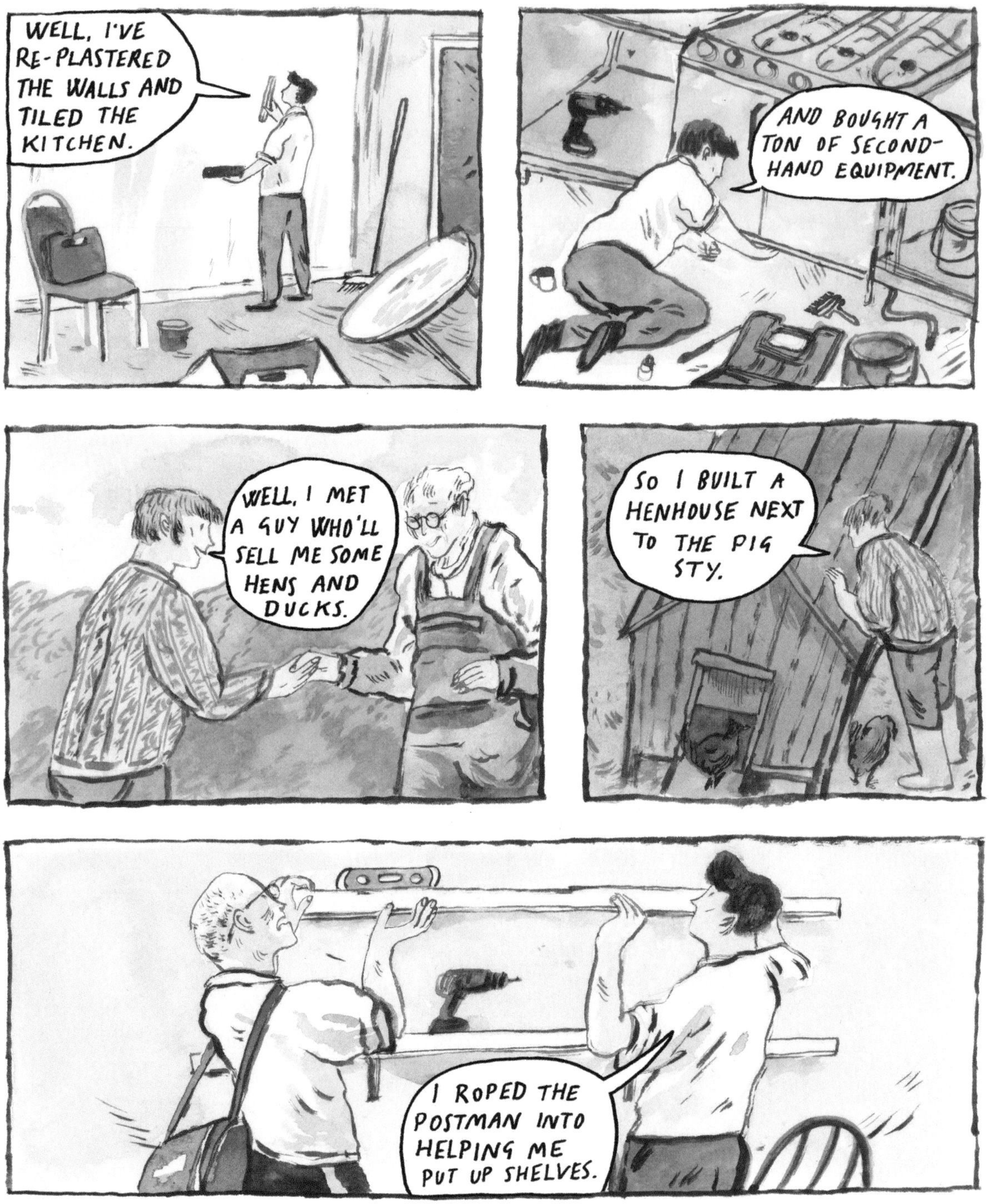
WELL, I'VE RE-PLASTERED THE WALLS AND TILED THE KITCHEN.
AND BOUGHT A TON OF SECOND-HAND EQUIPMENT.
WELL, I MET A GUY WHO'LL SELL ME SOME HENS AND DUCKS.
SO I BUILT A HENHOUSE NEXT TO THE PIG STY.
I ROPED THE POSTMAN INTO HELPING ME PUT UP SHELVES.

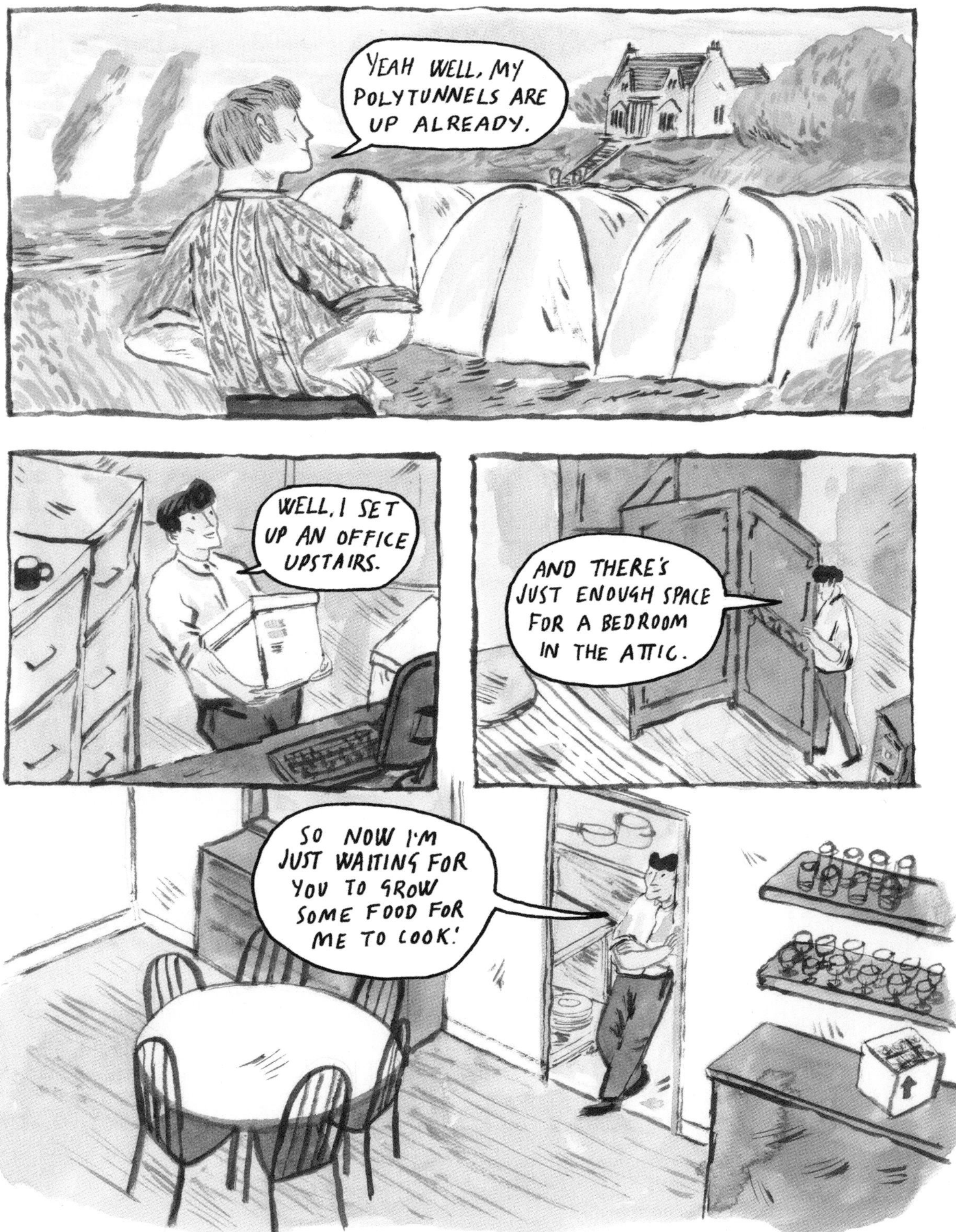
YEAH WELL, MY POLYTUNNELS ARE UP ALREADY.
WELL, I SET UP AN OFFICE UPSTAIRS.
AND THERE'S JUST ENOUGH SPACE FOR A BEDROOM IN THE ATTIC.
SO NOW I'M JUST WAITING FOR YOU TO GROW SOME FOOD FOR ME TO COOK!

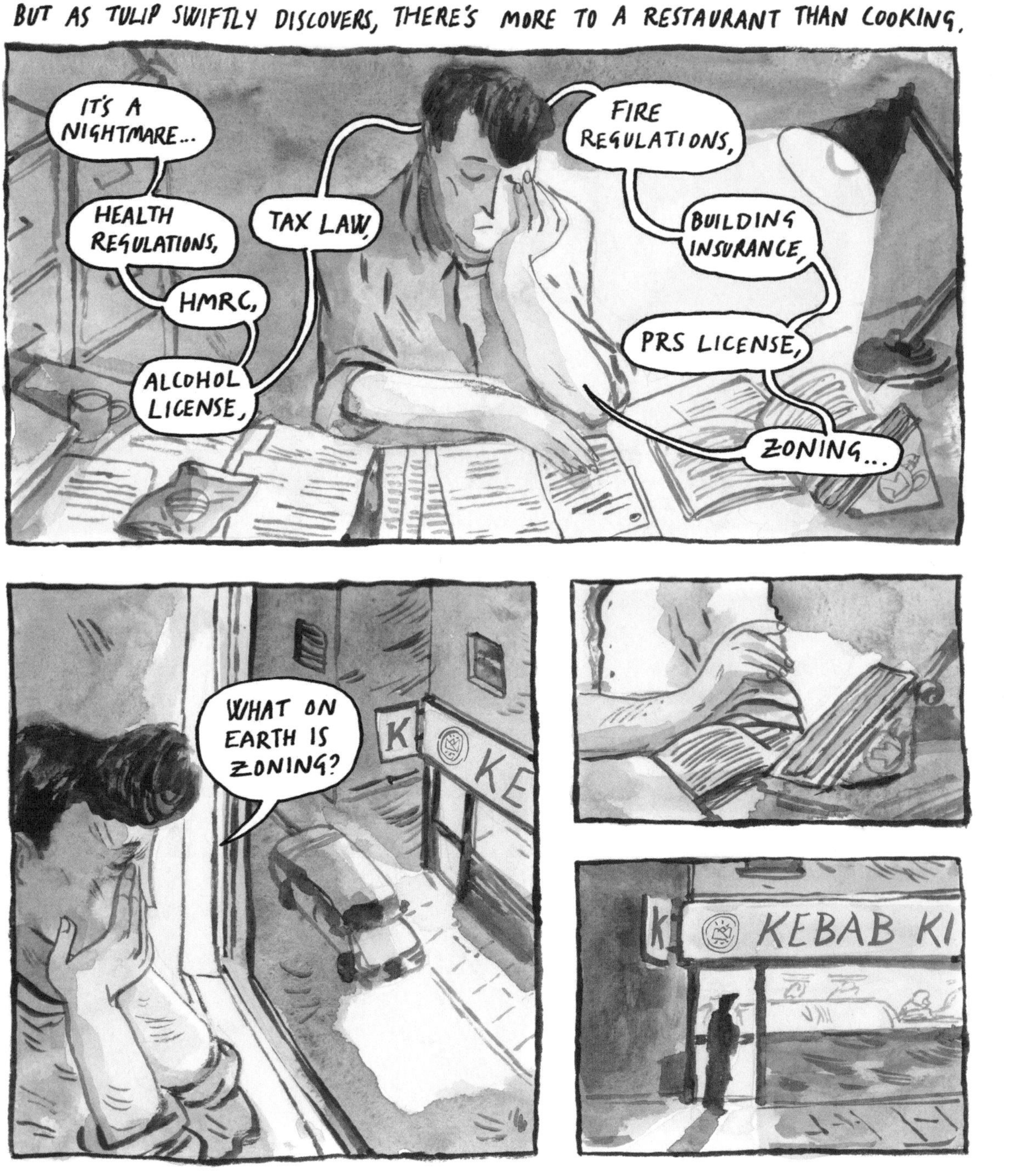
BUT AS TULIP SWIFTLY DISCOVERS, THERE'S MORE TO A RESTAURANT THAN COOKING.
IT'S A NIGHTMARE...
HEALTH REGULATIONS,
HMRC,
ALCOHOL LICENSE,
TAX LAW,
FIRE REGULATIONS,
BUILDING INSURANCE,
PRS LICENSE,
ZONING...
WHAT ON EARTH IS ZONING?
K
KE
K
KEBAB KI

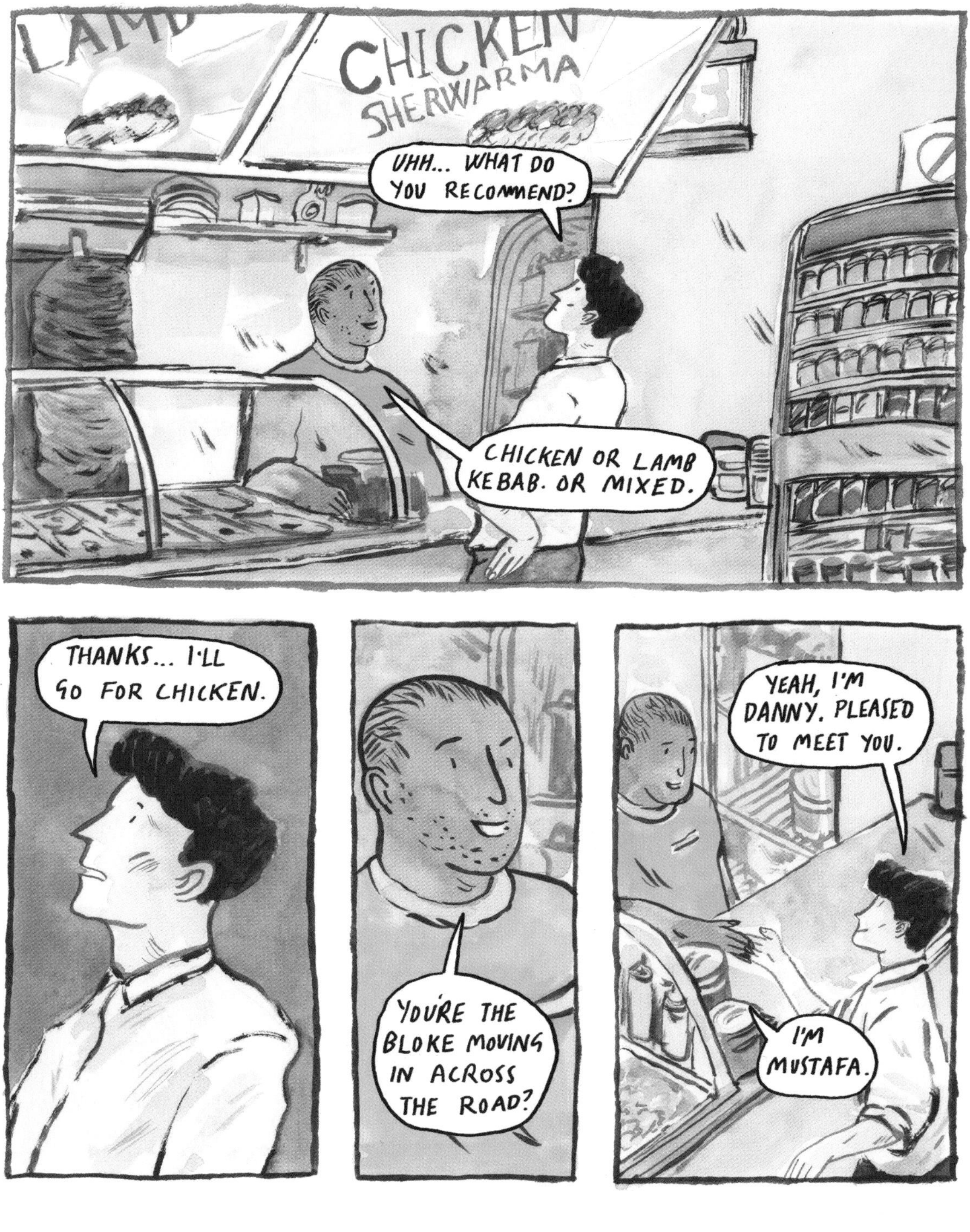
LAMB
CHICKEN SHERWARMA
UHH... WHAT DO YOU RECOMMEND?
CHICKEN OR LAMB KEBAB. OR MIXED.
THANKS... I'LL GO FOR CHICKEN.
YOU'RE THE BLOKE MOVING IN ACROSS THE ROAD?
YEAH, I'M DANNY. PLEASED TO MEET YOU.
I'M MUSTAFA.

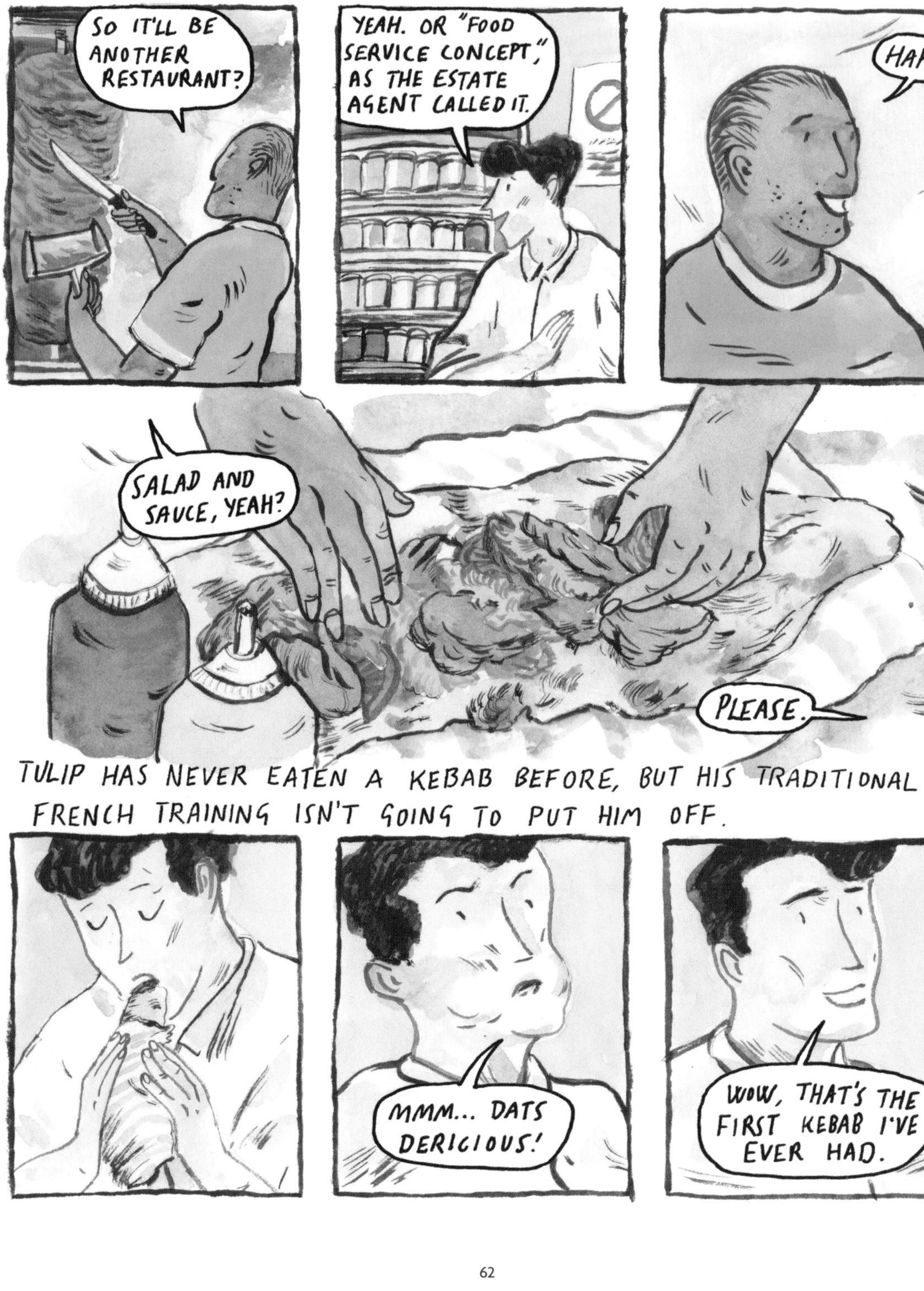
SO IT'LL BE ANOTHER RESTAURANT?
YEAH. OR "FOOD SERVICE CONCEPT," AS THE ESTATE AGENT CALLED IT.
HAH!
SALAD AND SAUCE, YEAH?
PLEASE.
TULIP HAS NEVER EATEN A KEBAB BEFORE, BUT HIS TRADITIONAL FRENCH TRAINING ISN'T GOING TO PUT HIM OFF.
MMM... DATS DERICIOUS!
WOW, THAT'S THE FIRST KEBAB I'VE EVER HAD.

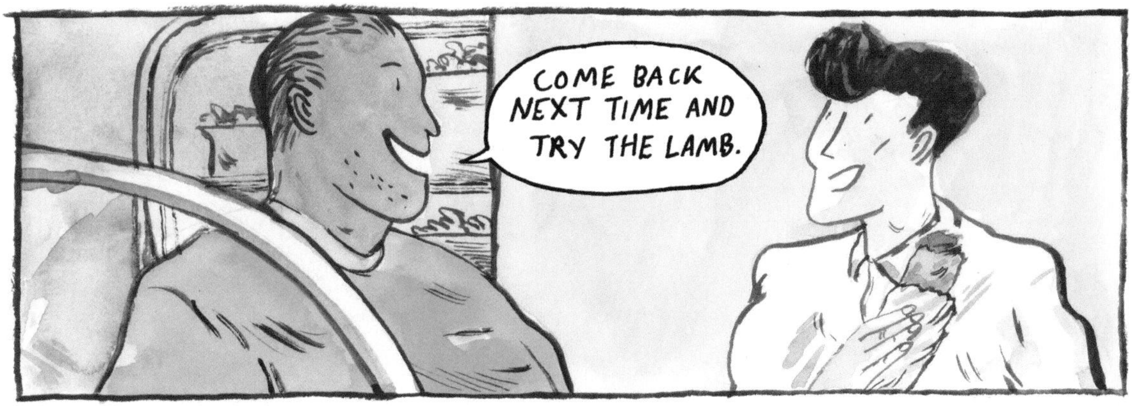
COME BACK NEXT TIME AND TRY THE LAMB.

WITH A MOSTLY FUNCTIONING KITCHEN INSTALLED, TULIP BEGINS THE DIFFICULT TASK OF STAFFING IT. HE MAY HAVE LEAPT INTO THE RESTAURANT BUSINESS WITH RIGHTEOUS ZEAL, BUT THE MEAGRE SELECTION OF APPLICANTS SEEM TO RANGE FROM THE MERCENARY TO THE WOEFULLY UNDERWHELMING.

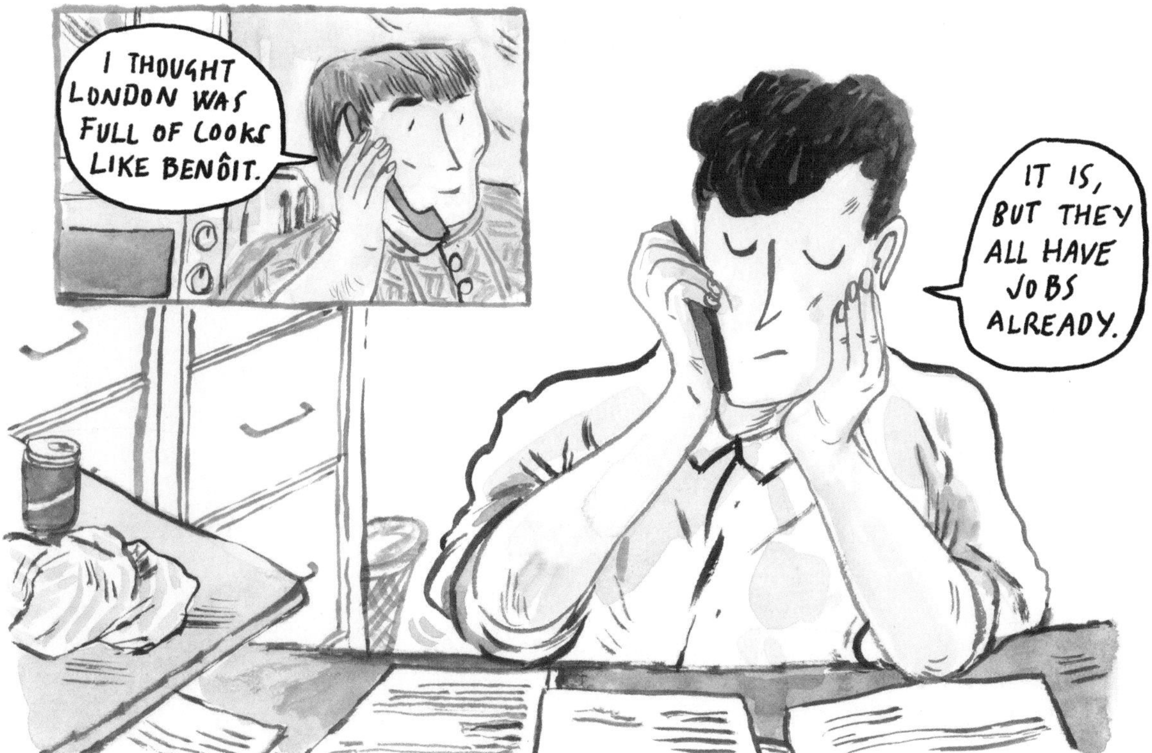
I THOUGHT LONDON WAS FULL OF COOKS LIKE BENÔIT.
IT IS, BUT THEY ALL HAVE JOBS ALREADY.

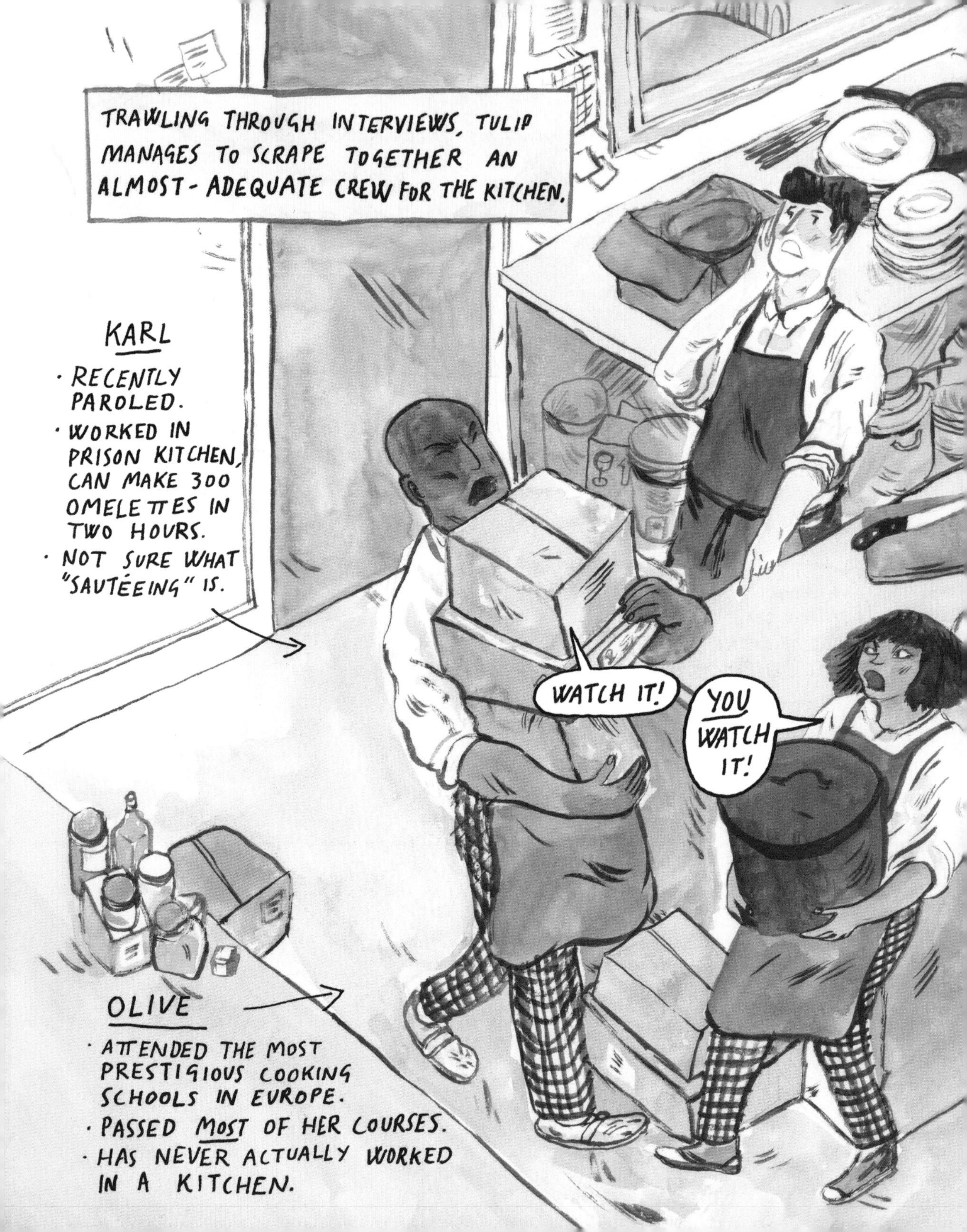
TRAWLING THROUGH INTERVIEWS, TULIP MANAGES TO SCRAPE TOGETHER AN ALMOST-ADEQUATE CREW FOR THE KITCHEN.
KARL
· RECENTLY PAROLED.
· WORKED IN PRISON KITCHEN, CAN MAKE 300 OMELETTES IN TWO HOURS.
· NOT SURE WHAT "SAUTÉEING" IS.
WATCH IT!
YOU WATCH IT!
OLIVE
· ATTENDED THE MOST PRESTIGIOUS COOKING SCHOOLS IN EUROPE.
· PASSED MOST OF HER COURSES.
· HAS NEVER ACTUALLY WORKED IN A KITCHEN.

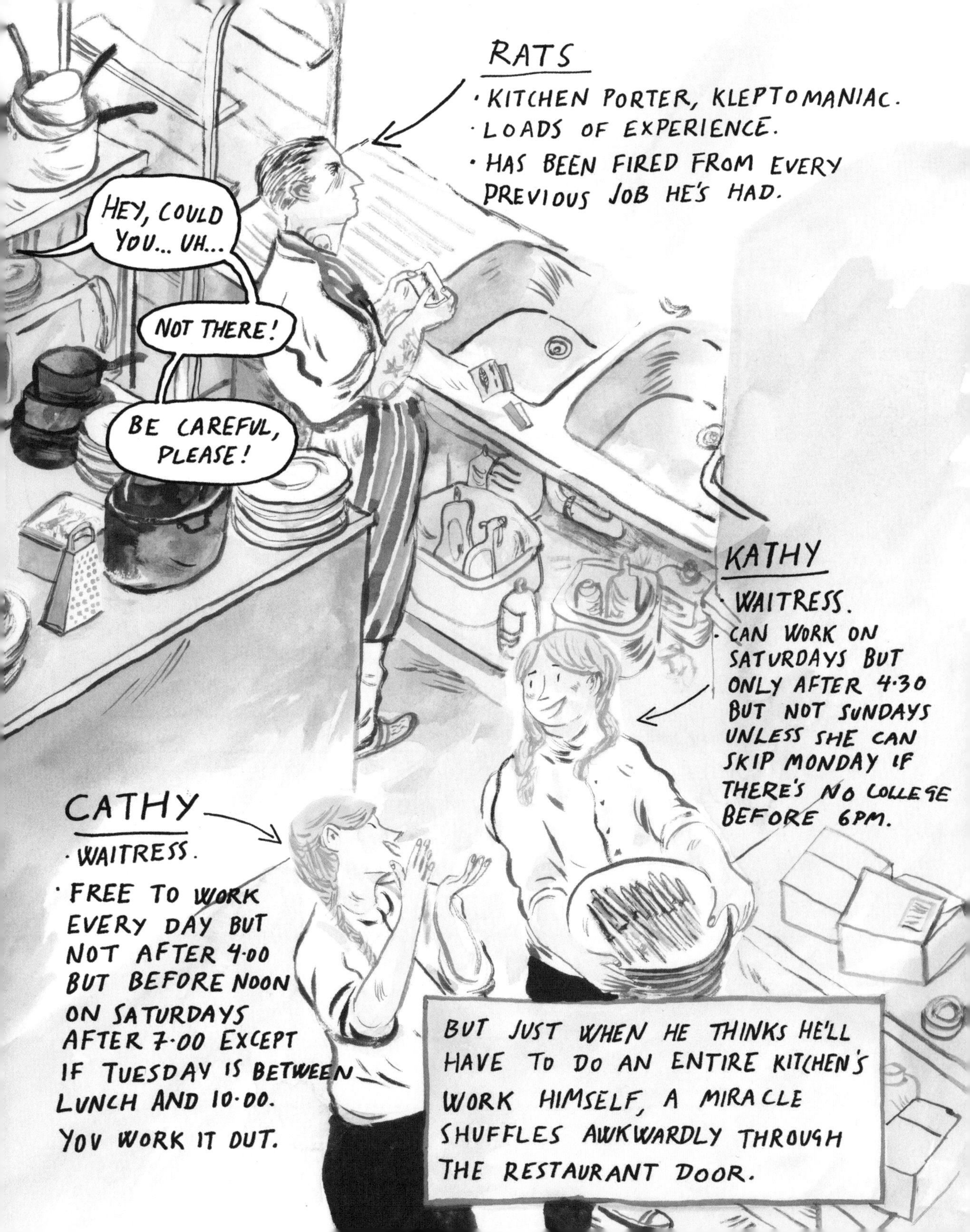
RATS
· KITCHEN PORTER, KLEPTOMANIAC.
· LOADS OF EXPERIENCE.
· HAS BEEN FIRED FROM EVERY PREVIOUS JOB HE'S HAD.
HEY, COULD YOU... UH...
NOT THERE!
BE CAREFUL, PLEASE!
KATHY
· WAITRESS.
· CAN WORK ON SATURDAYS BUT ONLY AFTER 4·30 BUT NOT SUNDAYS UNLESS SHE CAN SKIP MONDAY IF THERE'S NO COLLEGE BEFORE 6PM.
CATHY
· WAITRESS.
· FREE TO WORK EVERY DAY BUT NOT AFTER 4·00 BUT BEFORE NOON ON SATURDAYS AFTER 7·00 EXCEPT IF TUESDAY IS BETWEEN LUNCH AND 10·00.
YOU WORK IT OUT.
BUT JUST WHEN HE THINKS HE'LL HAVE TO DO AN ENTIRE KITCHEN'S WORK HIMSELF, A MIRACLE SHUFFLES AWKWARDLY THROUGH THE RESTAURANT DOOR.

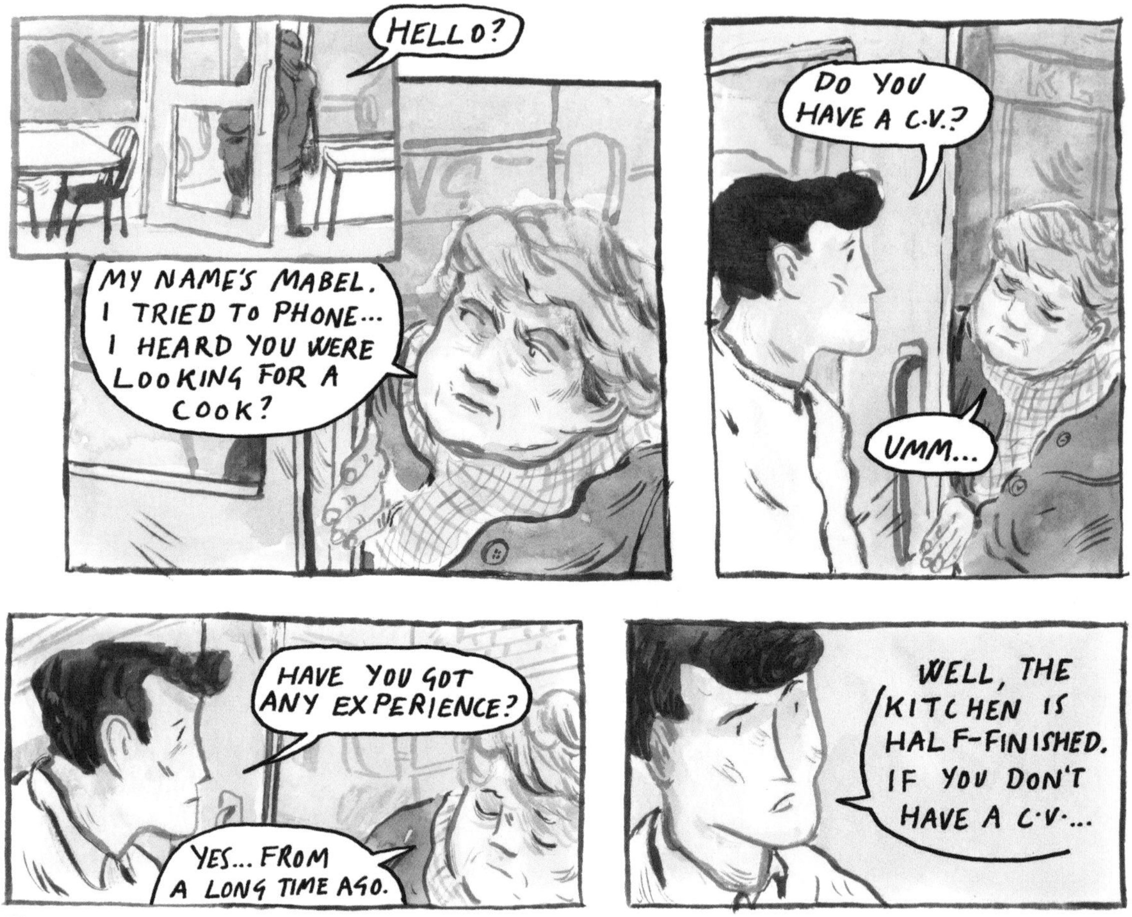
HELLO?
MY NAME'S MABEL. I TRIED TO PHONE... I HEARD YOU WERE LOOKING FOR A COOK?
DO YOU HAVE A C.V.?
UMM...
HAVE YOU GOT ANY EXPERIENCE?
YES... FROM A LONG TIME AGO.
WELL, THE KITCHEN IS HALF-FINISHED. IF YOU DON'T HAVE A C.V....

TOO EMBARRASSED TO DISMISS THE TIMID WOMAN, TULIP INVITES HER IN. RESTAURANT WORK IS NOT FOR THE FAINT-HEARTED. THE BODY NEEDS THE STRENGTH TO RUN UP STAIRS, CARRY HEAVY POTS, AND BEND INTO LOW REACH-INS ONE HUNDRED TIMES A DAY.

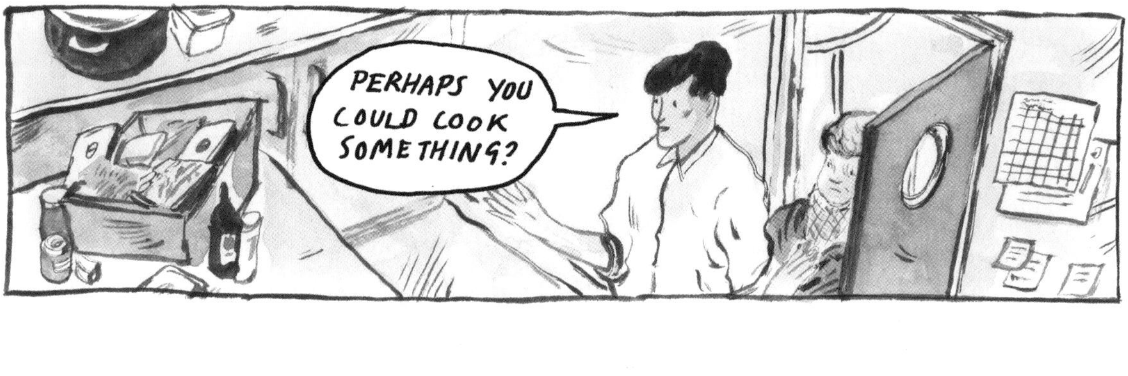
PERHAPS YOU COULD COOK SOMETHING?

TULIP LOOKS WITH PITY AS SHE CLUMSILY DEPOSITS HER BAG AND COAT AND SURVEYS THE MEAGRE INGREDIENTS ON THE COUNTER.

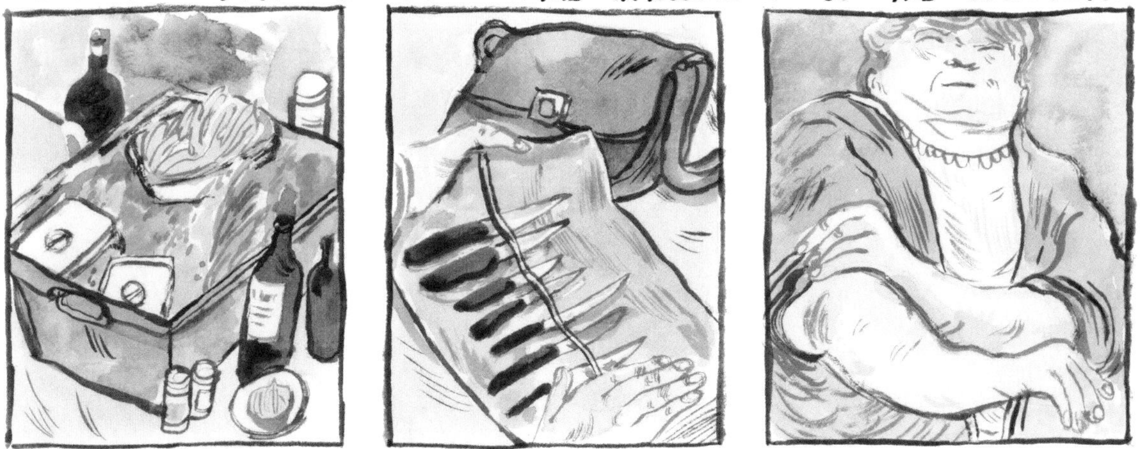

BUT HIS ATTENTION IS PIQUED AS SHE PRODUCES A ROLL OF EXPENSIVE KNIVES. HE SEES A FAMILIAR, CONFIDENT GRIP ON THE PAN. IN A FLASH, A SHALLOT IS JULIENNED. A LEMON IS JUICED WITH ONE HAND WHILE GARLIC IS REDUCED TO A FINE PASTE.

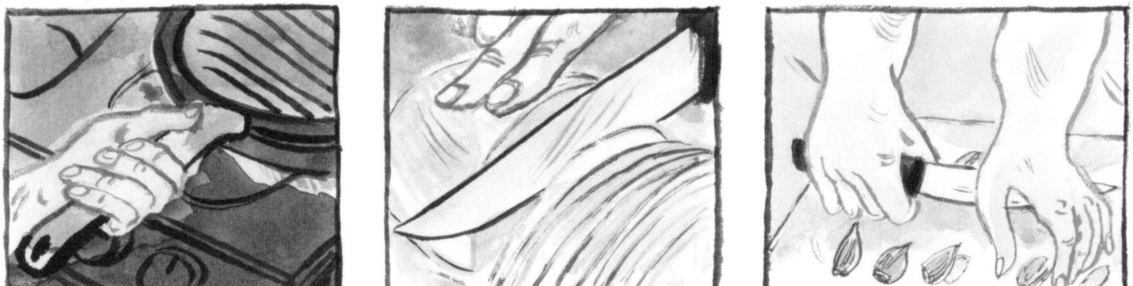

POTATOES ARE PURÉED, HERBS MIXED FASTER THAN TULIP CAN KEEP TRACK OF, CHICKEN WINGS ARE BONED, SEASONED, AND SAUTÉED.

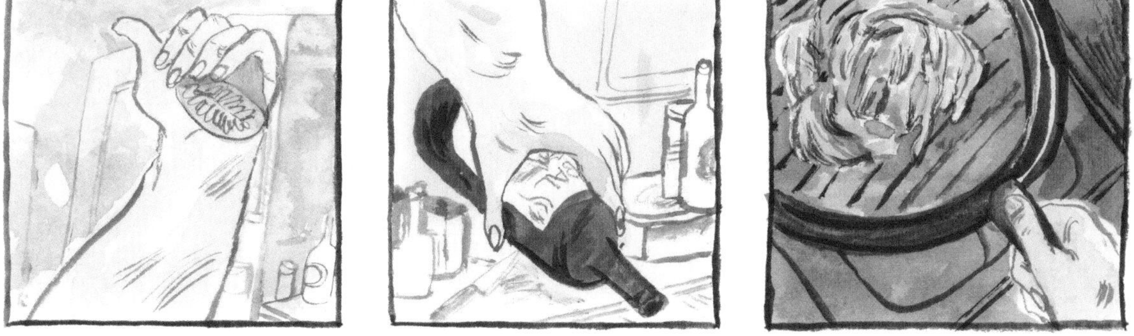

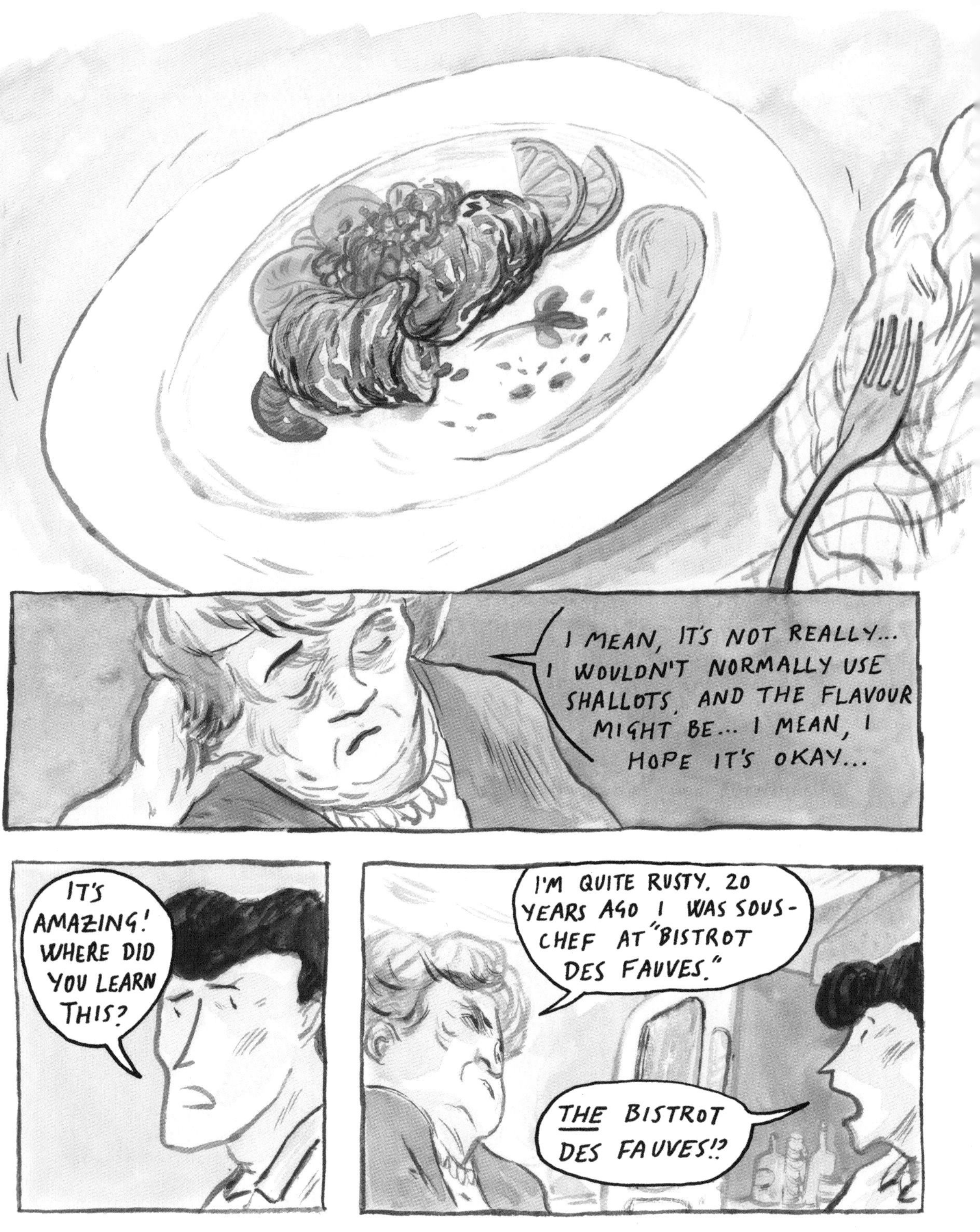
I MEAN, IT'S NOT REALLY... I WOULDN'T NORMALLY USE SHALLOTS, AND THE FLAVOUR MIGHT BE... I MEAN, I HOPE IT'S OKAY...
IT'S AMAZING! WHERE DID YOU LEARN THIS?
I'M QUITE RUSTY. 20 YEARS AGO I WAS SOUS-CHEF AT "BISTROT DES FAUVES."
THE BISTROT DES FAUVES!?

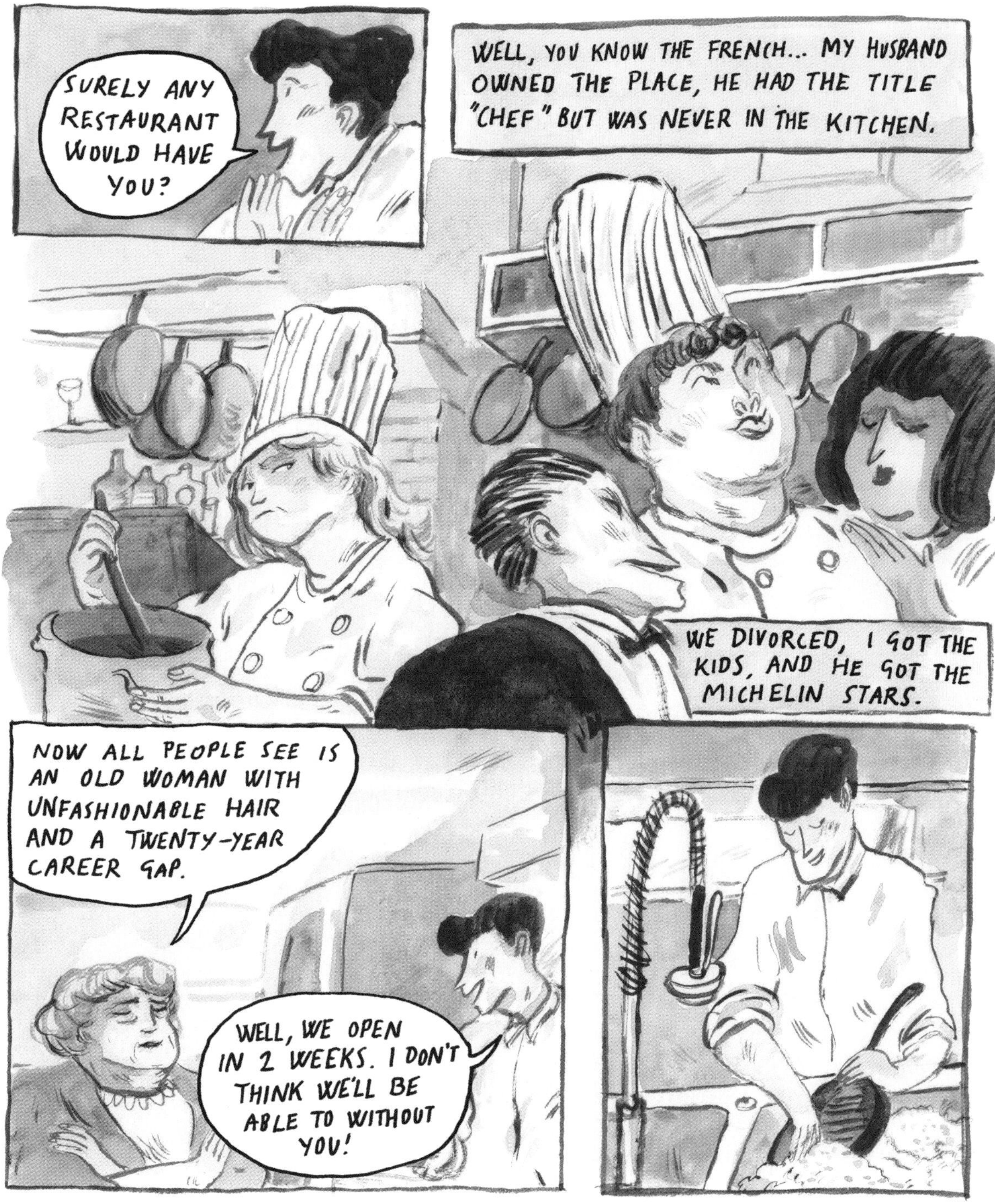
SURELY ANY RESTAURANT WOULD HAVE YOU?
WELL, YOU KNOW THE FRENCH... MY HUSBAND OWNED THE PLACE, HE HAD THE TITLE "CHEF" BUT WAS NEVER IN THE KITCHEN.
WE DIVORCED, I GOT THE KIDS, AND HE GOT THE MICHELIN STARS.
NOW ALL PEOPLE SEE IS AN OLD WOMAN WITH UNFASHIONABLE HAIR AND A TWENTY-YEAR CAREER GAP.
WELL, WE OPEN IN 2 WEEKS. I DON'T THINK WE'LL BE ABLE TO WITHOUT YOU!

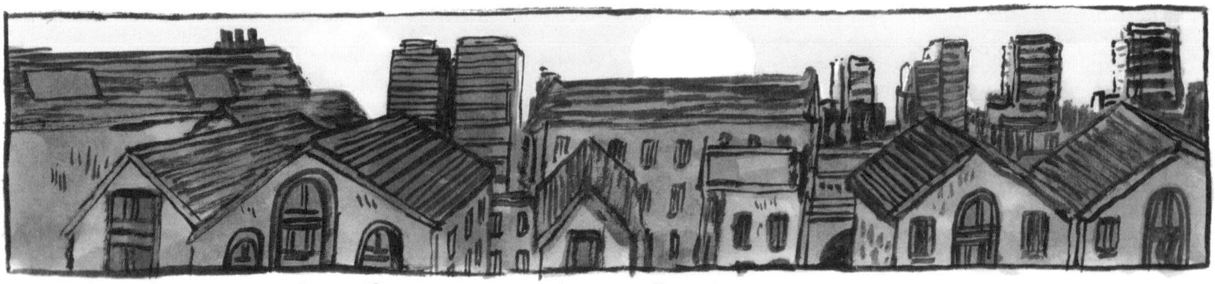

SWEAT, SUN AND AIR POLLUTION. SUMMER IN LONDON.
TULIP HAS OPENED HIS RESTAURANT!

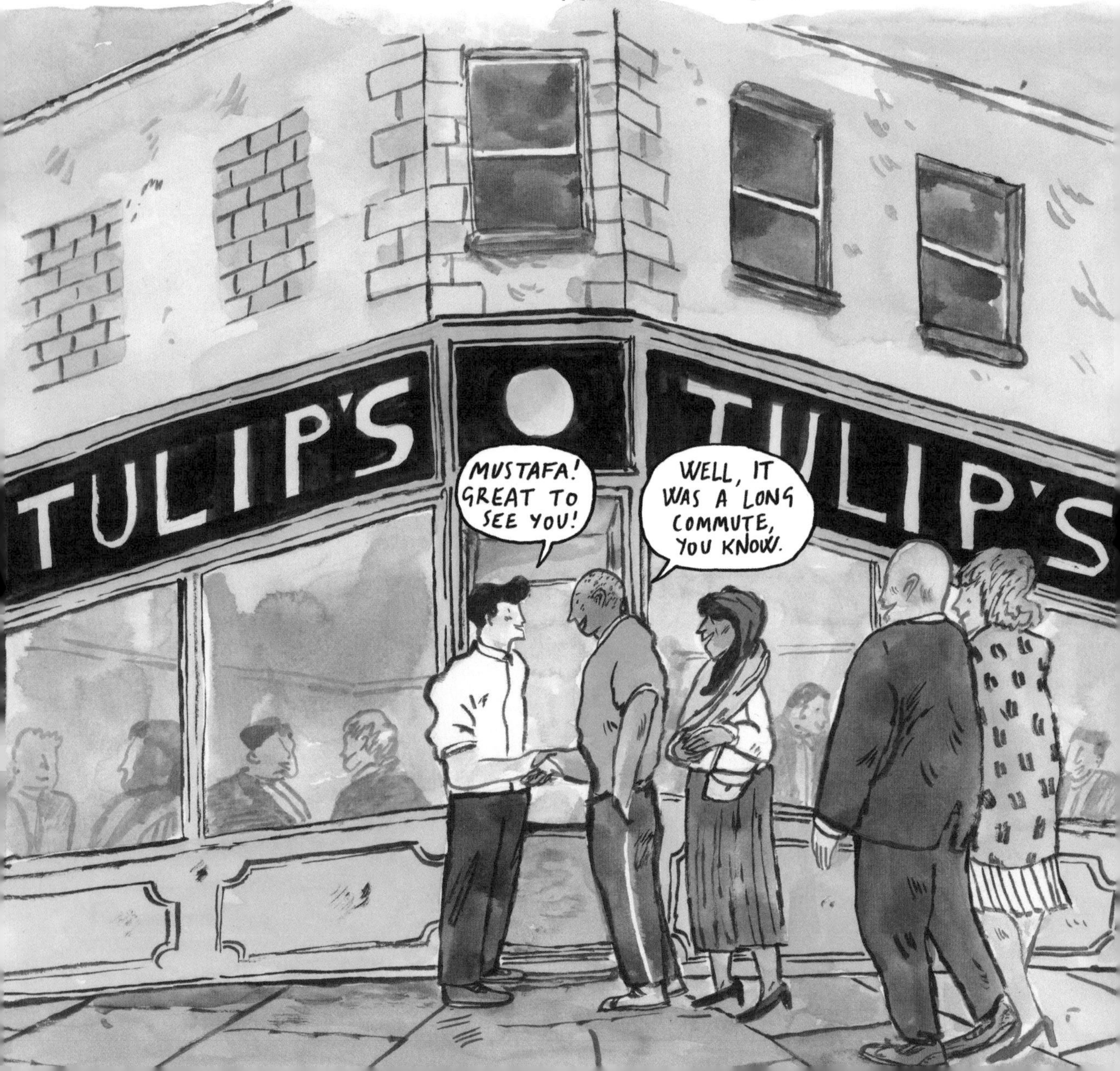
TULIP'S
TULIP'S
MUSTAFA! GREAT TO SEE YOU!
WELL, IT WAS A LONG COMMUTE, YOU KNOW.

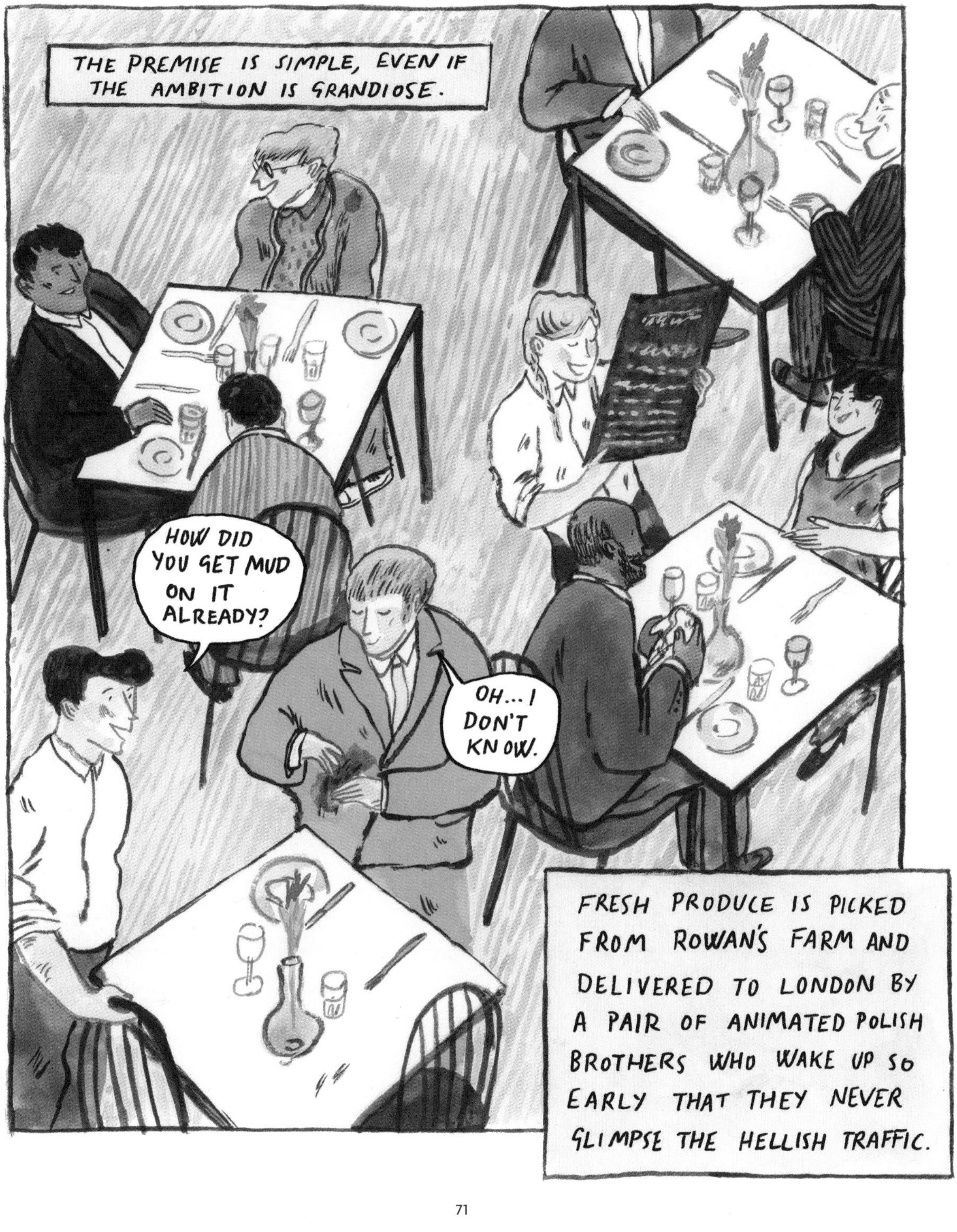
THE PREMISE IS SIMPLE, EVEN IF THE AMBITION IS GRANDIOSE.
HOW DID YOU GET MUD ON IT ALREADY?
OH... I DON'T KNOW.
FRESH PRODUCE IS PICKED FROM ROWAN'S FARM AND DELIVERED TO LONDON BY A PAIR OF ANIMATED POLISH BROTHERS WHO WAKE UP SO EARLY THAT THEY NEVER GLIMPSE THE HELLISH TRAFFIC.

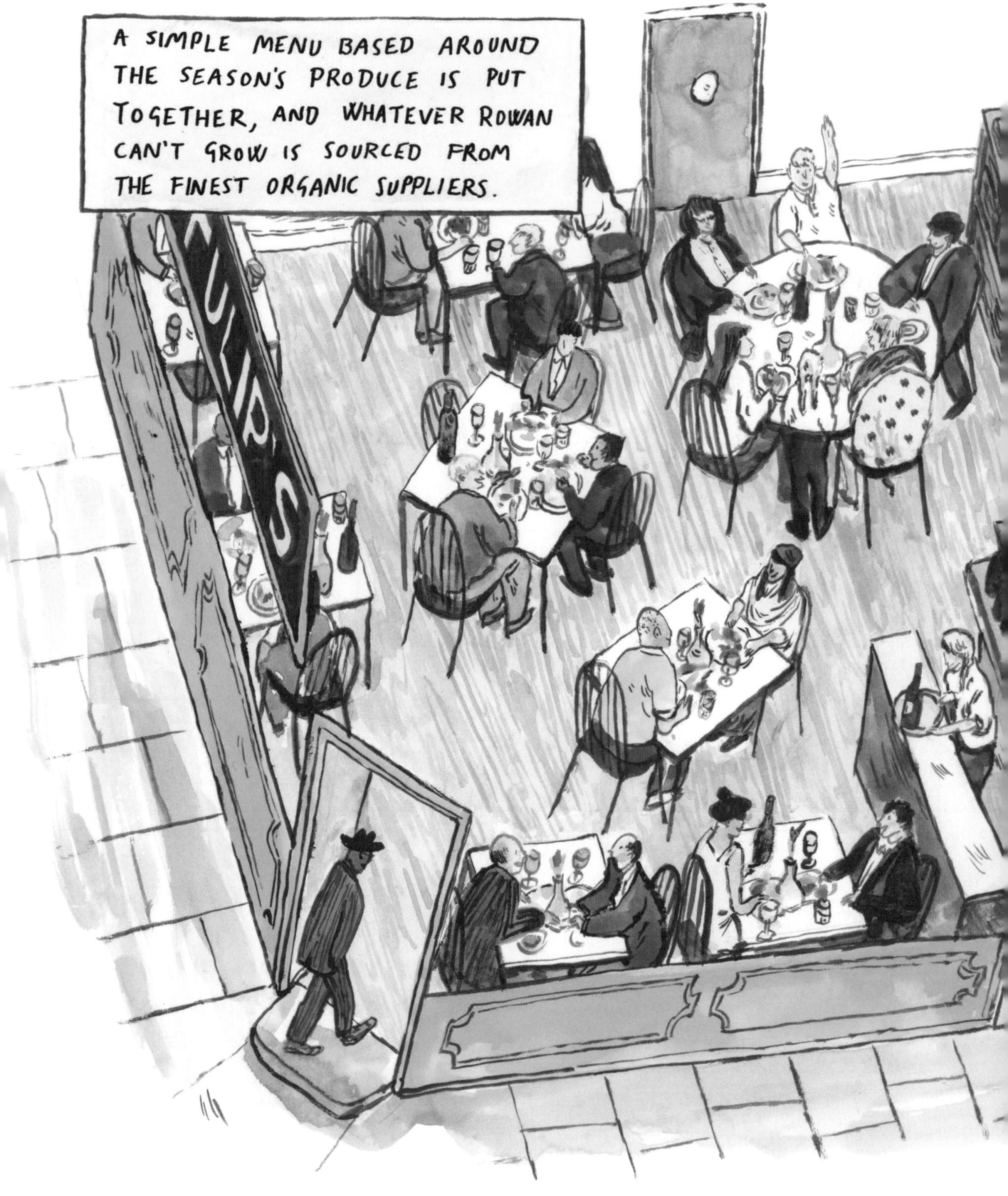
A SIMPLE MENU BASED AROUND THE SEASON'S PRODUCE IS PUT TOGETHER, AND WHATEVER ROWAN CAN'T GROW IS SOURCED FROM THE FINEST ORGANIC SUPPLIERS.

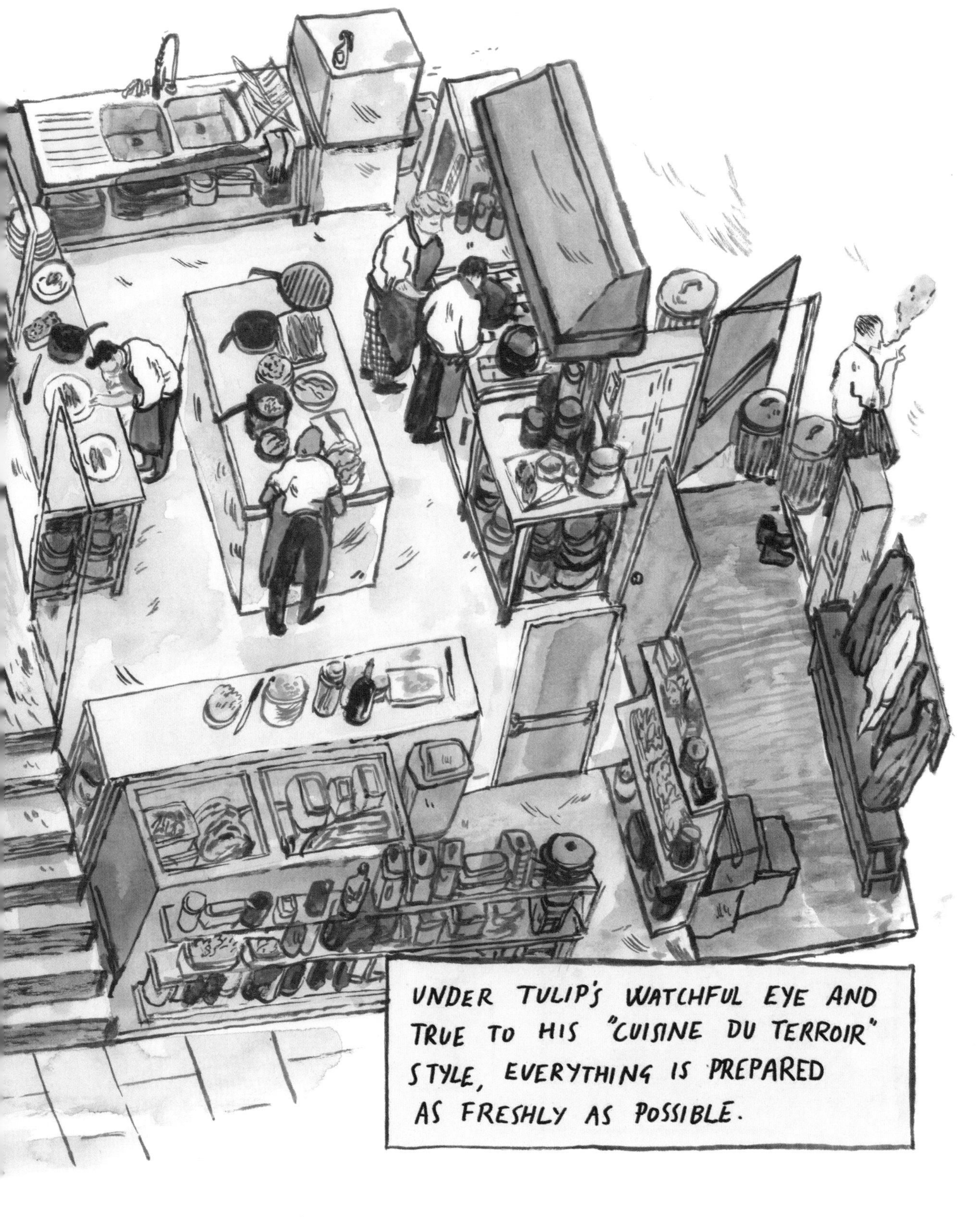
UNDER TULIP'S WATCHFUL EYE AND TRUE TO HIS "CUISINE DU TERROIR" STYLE, EVERYTHING IS PREPARED AS FRESHLY AS POSSIBLE.

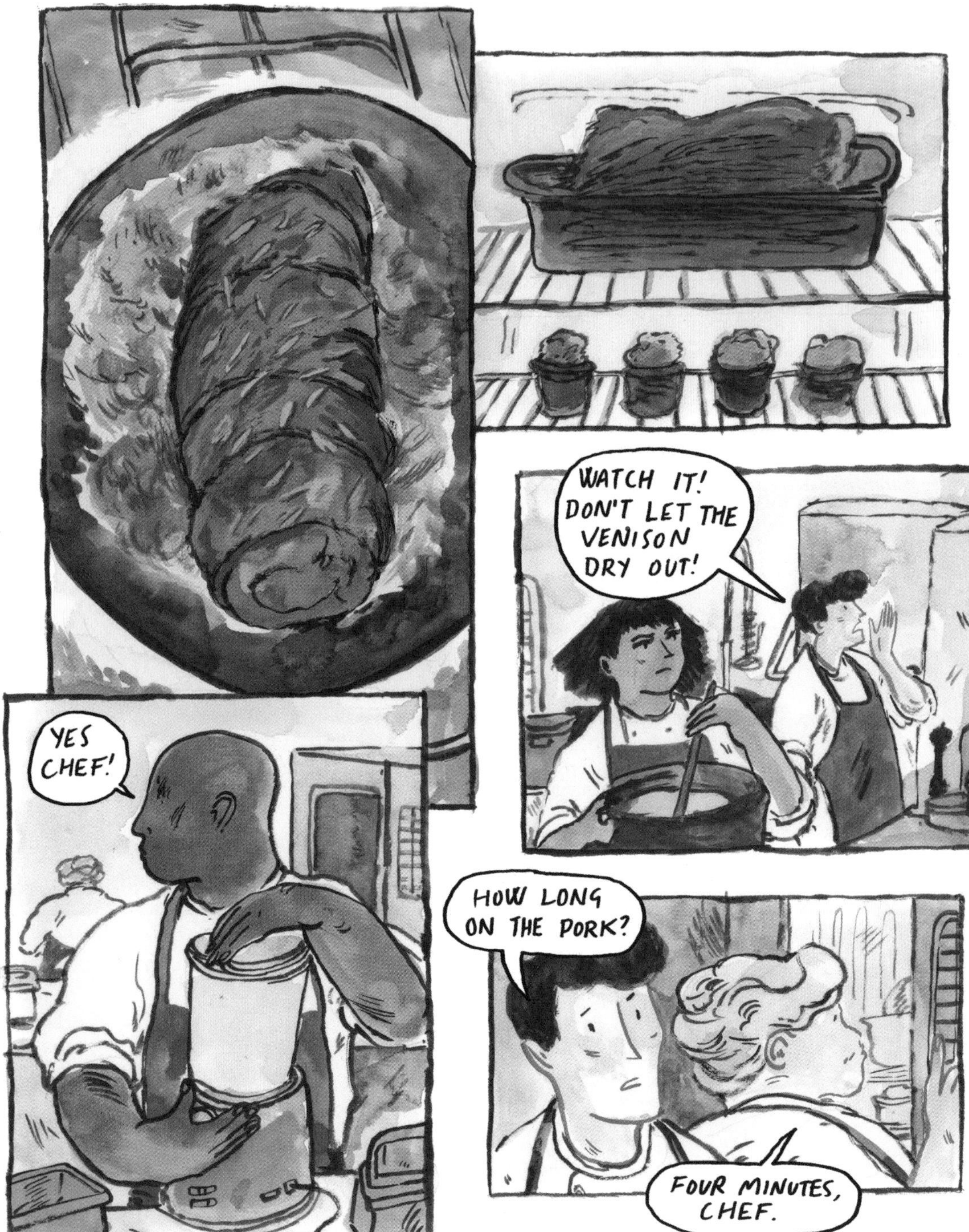
WATCH IT! DON'T LET THE VENISON DRY OUT!
YES CHEF!
HOW LONG ON THE PORK?
FOUR MINUTES, CHEF.

THE SUPERLATIVE FRESHNESS OF THE PRODUCE RADIATES HEALTH.

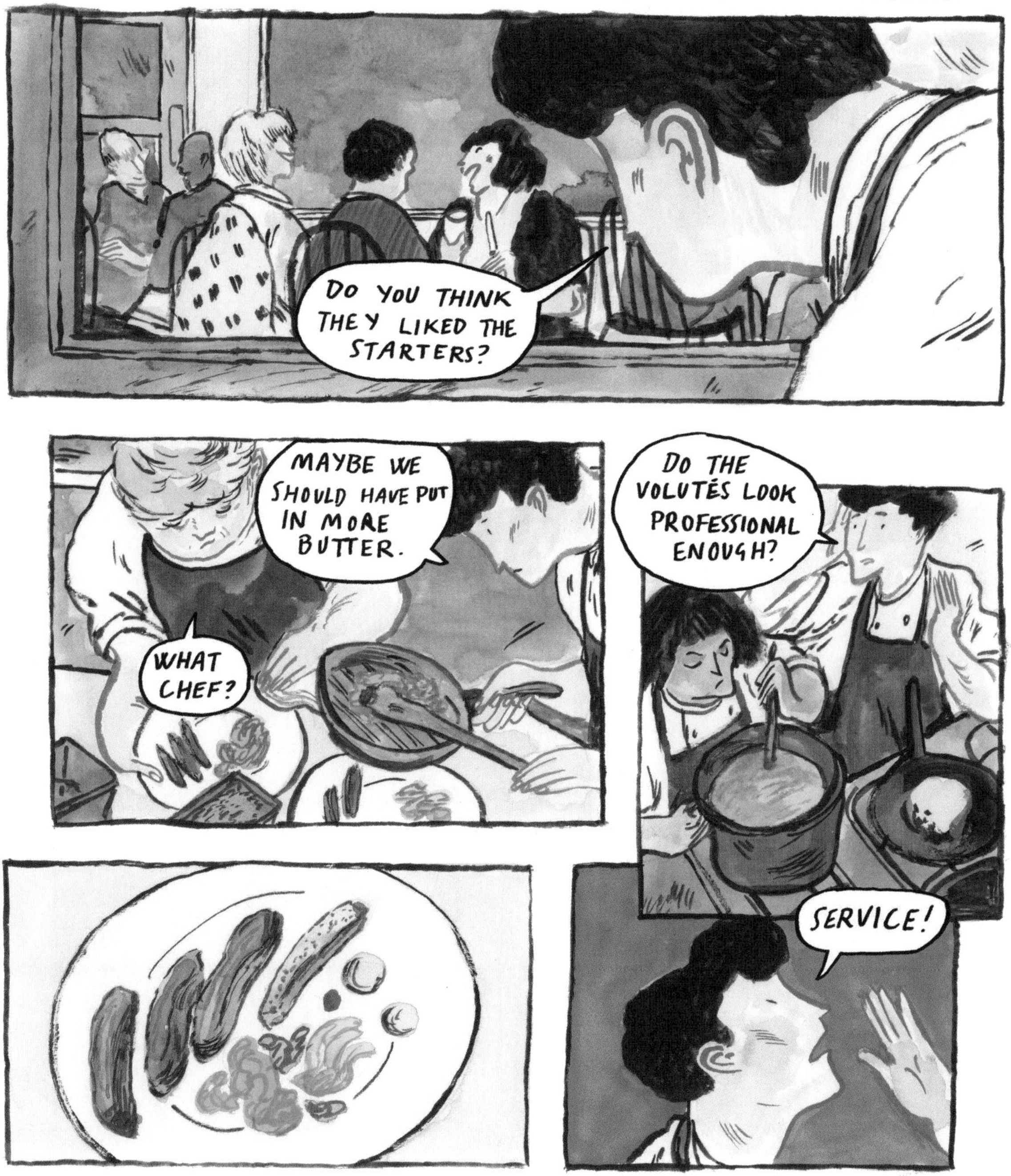
DO YOU THINK THEY LIKED THE STARTERS?
MAYBE WE SHOULD HAVE PUT IN MORE BUTTER.
WHAT CHEF?
DO THE VOLUTÉS LOOK PROFESSIONAL ENOUGH?
SERVICE!

HE CAN FINALLY CALL HIMSELF A REAL LONDON RESTAURATEUR.

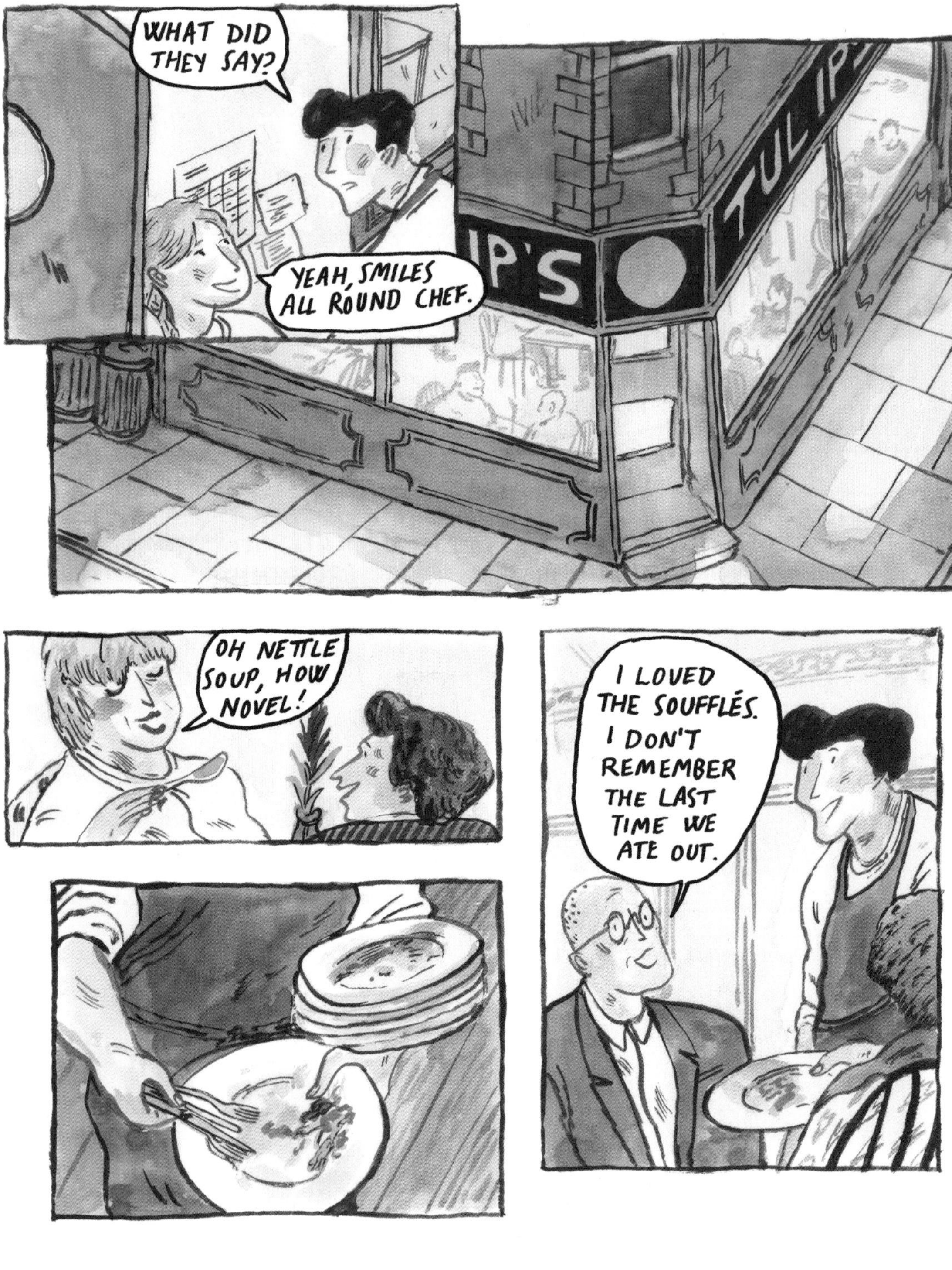
WHAT DID THEY SAY?
YEAH, SMILES ALL ROUND CHEF.
TULIP'S
OH NETTLE SOUP, HOW NOVEL!
I LOVED THE SOUFFLÉS. I DON'T REMEMBER THE LAST TIME WE ATE OUT.

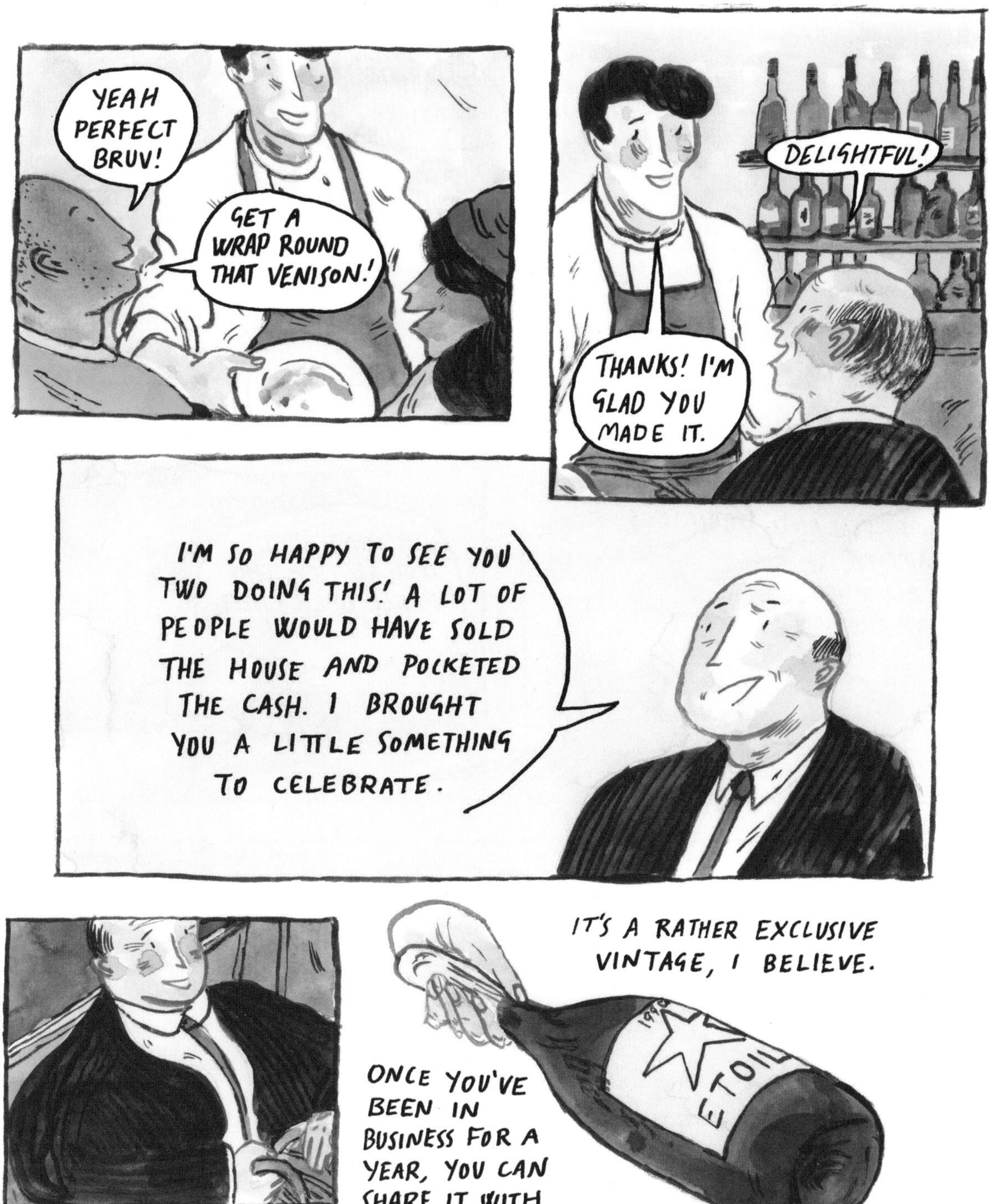
YEAH PERFECT BRUV!
GET A WRAP ROUND THAT VENISON!
DELIGHTFUL!
THANKS! I'M GLAD YOU MADE IT.
I'M SO HAPPY TO SEE YOU TWO DOING THIS! A LOT OF PEOPLE WOULD HAVE SOLD THE HOUSE AND POCKETED THE CASH. I BROUGHT YOU A LITTLE SOMETHING TO CELEBRATE.
IT'S A RATHER EXCLUSIVE VINTAGE, I BELIEVE.
ETOIL
ONCE YOU'VE BEEN IN BUSINESS FOR A YEAR, YOU CAN SHARE IT WITH YOUR BROTHER.

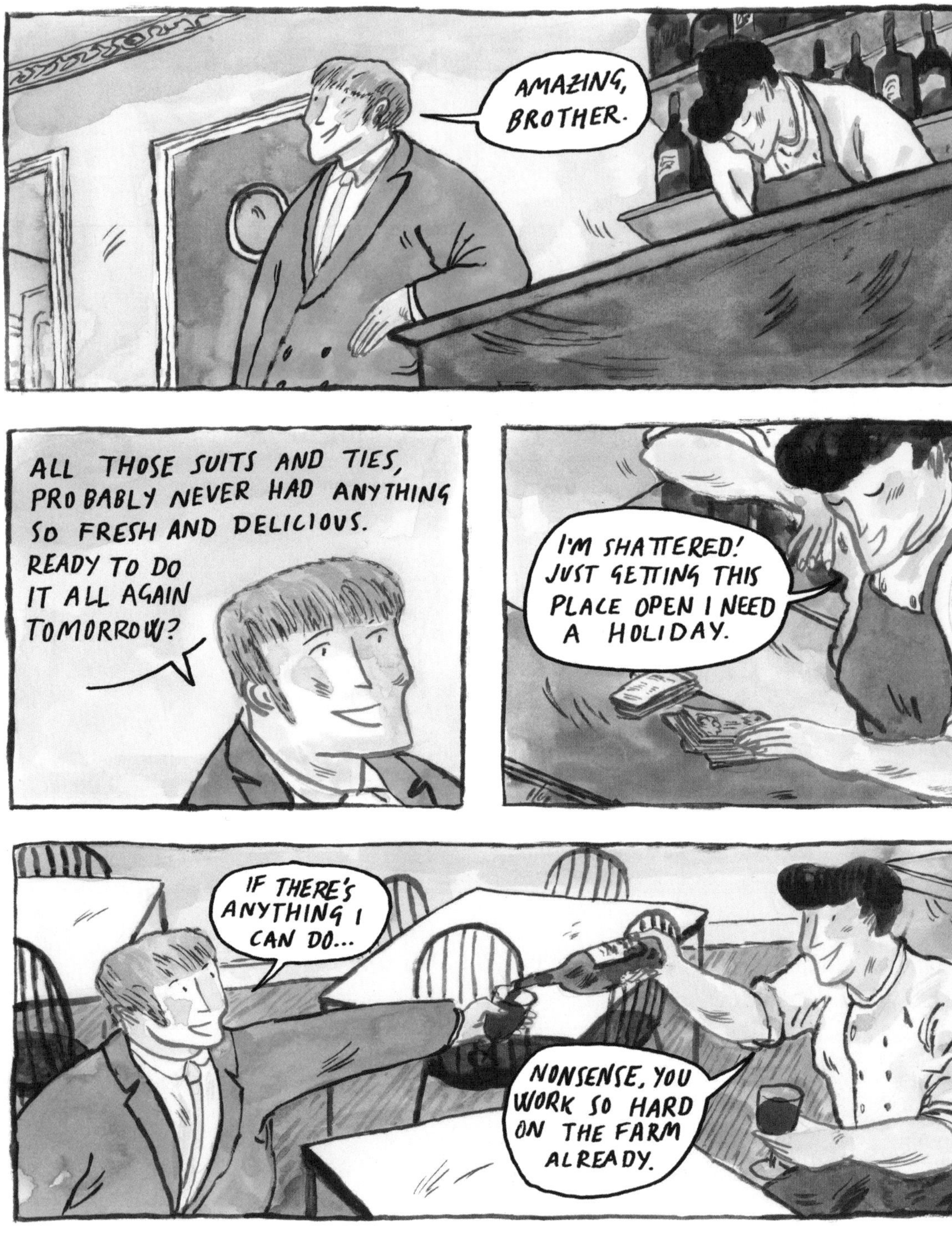
AMAZING, BROTHER.
ALL THOSE SUITS AND TIES, PROBABLY NEVER HAD ANYTHING SO FRESH AND DELICIOUS.
READY TO DO IT ALL AGAIN TOMORROW?
I'M SHATTERED! JUST GETTING THIS PLACE OPEN I NEED A HOLIDAY.
IF THERE'S ANYTHING I CAN DO...
NONSENSE, YOU WORK SO HARD ON THE FARM ALREADY.

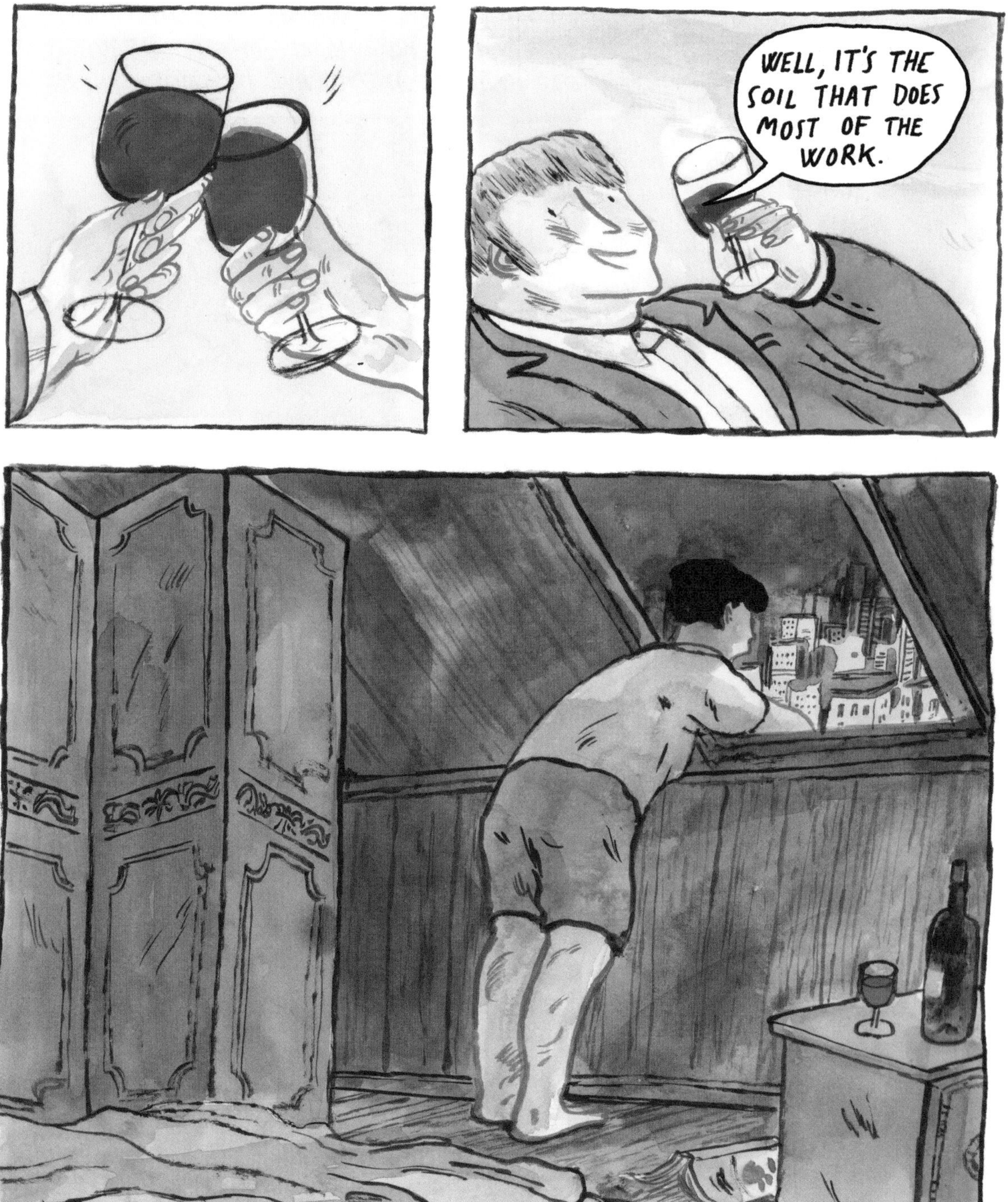
WELL, IT'S THE SOIL THAT DOES MOST OF THE WORK.

BUT UNLIKE ROWAN'S RICH SOIL, THE FICKLE WHIMS OF THE PUBLIC ARE IMPOSSIBLE TO PREDICT. A DOZEN LONDONERS MIGHT BRAVE THE POURING RAIN TO VISIT TULIP'S ONE NIGHT, AND LEAVE IT EMPTY THE NEXT.

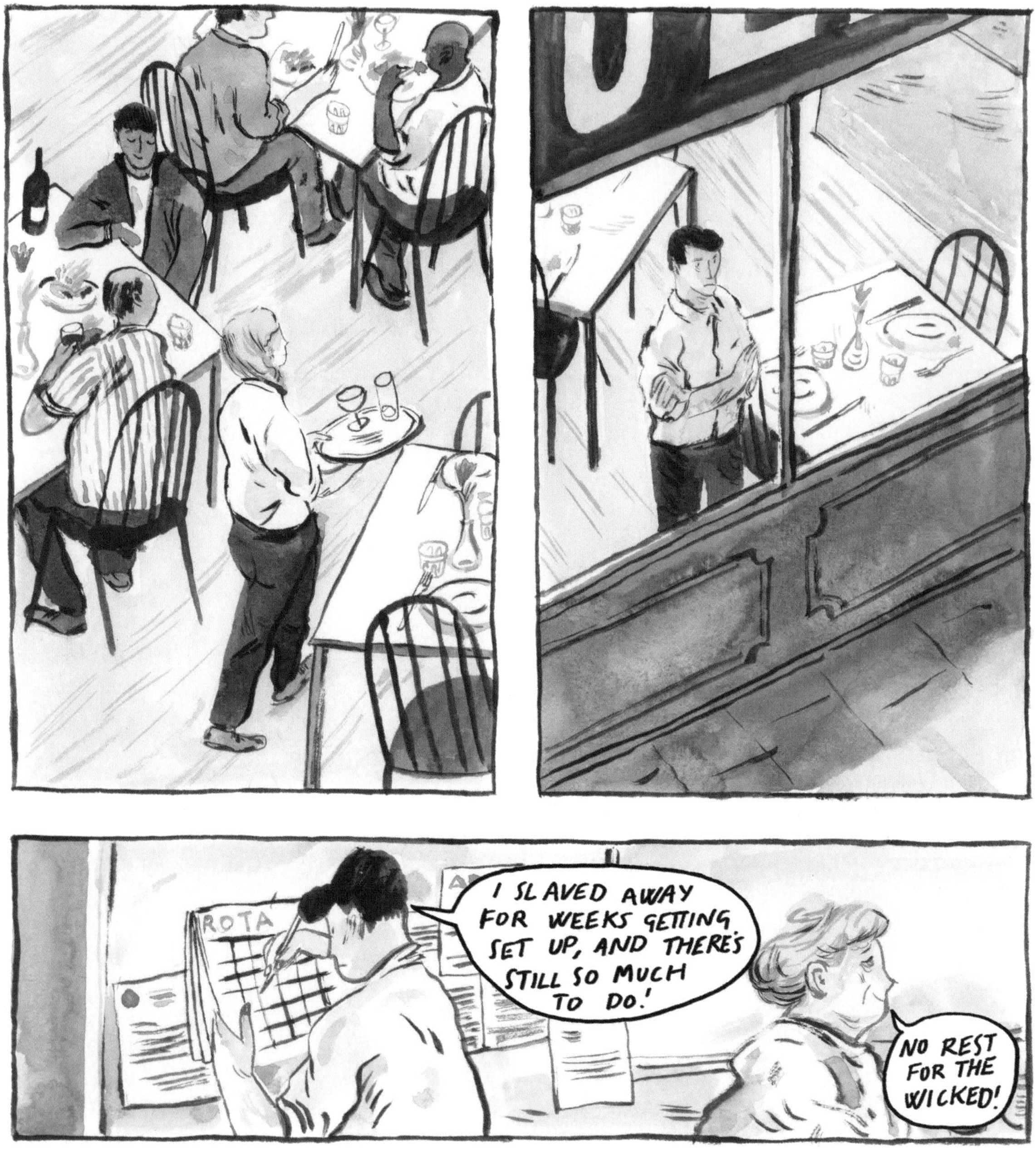
ROTA
I SLAVED AWAY FOR WEEKS GETTING SET UP, AND THERE'S STILL SO MUCH TO DO!
NO REST FOR THE WICKED!

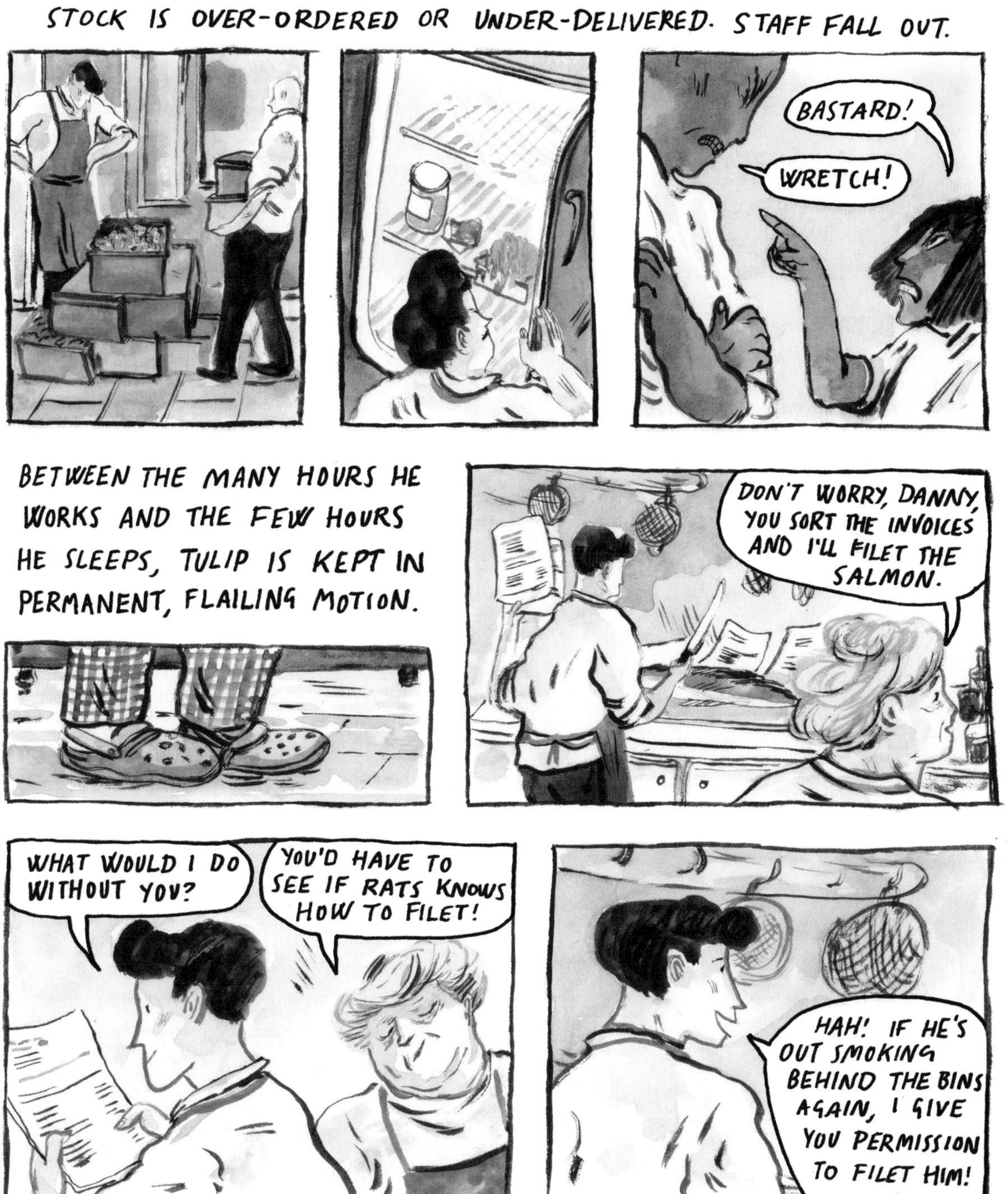
STOCK IS OVER-ORDERED OR UNDER-DELIVERED. STAFF FALL OUT.
BASTARD!
WRETCH!
BETWEEN THE MANY HOURS HE WORKS AND THE FEW HOURS HE SLEEPS, TULIP IS KEPT IN PERMANENT, FLAILING MOTION.
DON'T WORRY, DANNY, YOU SORT THE INVOICES AND I'LL FILET THE SALMON.
WHAT WOULD I DO WITHOUT YOU?
YOU'D HAVE TO SEE IF RATS KNOWS HOW TO FILET!
HAH! IF HE'S OUT SMOKING BEHIND THE BINS AGAIN, I GIVE YOU PERMISSION TO FILET HIM!

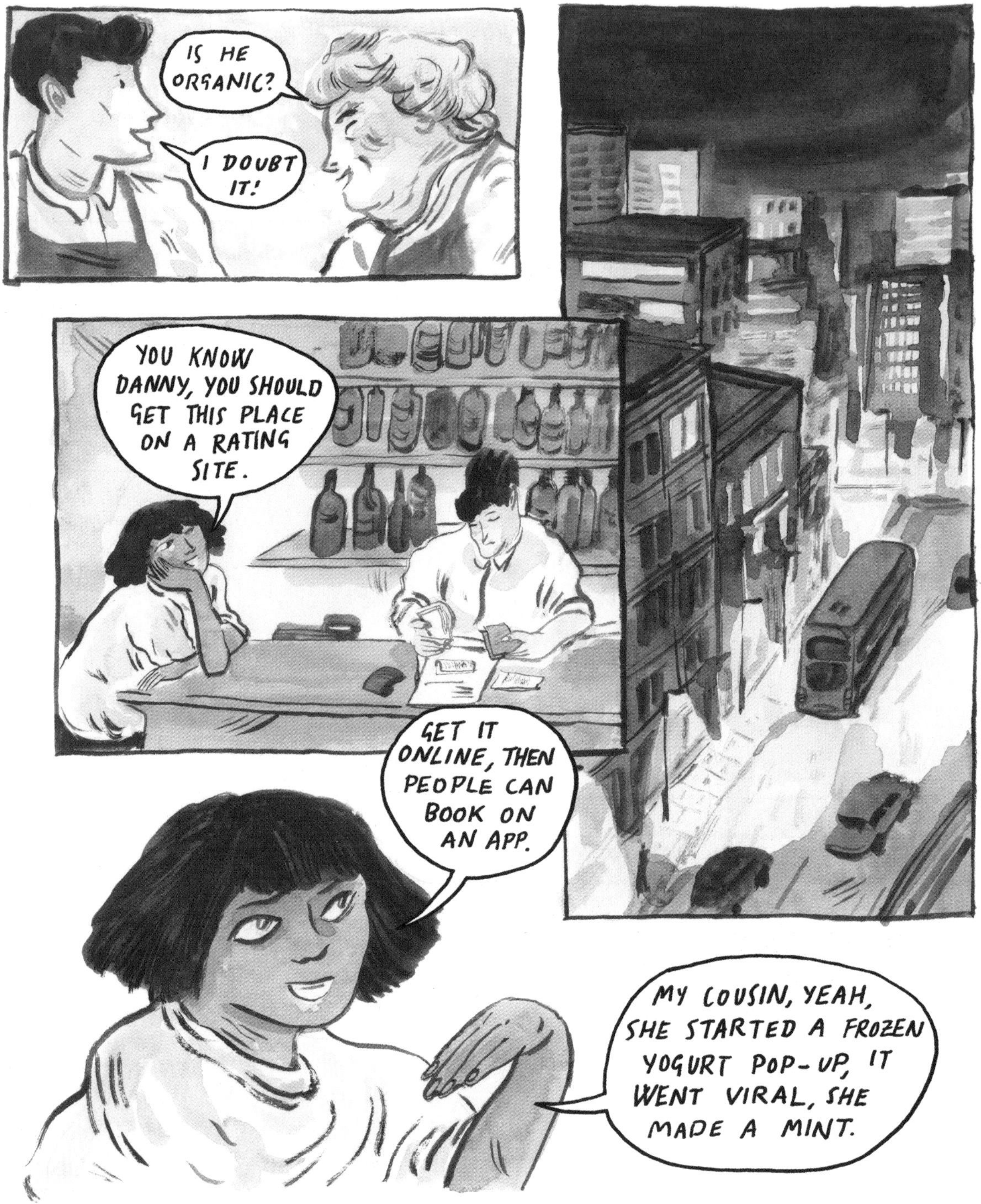
IS HE ORGANIC?
I DOUBT IT!
YOU KNOW DANNY, YOU SHOULD GET THIS PLACE ON A RATING SITE.
GET IT ONLINE, THEN PEOPLE CAN BOOK ON AN APP.
MY COUSIN, YEAH, SHE STARTED A FROZEN YOGURT POP-UP, IT WENT VIRAL, SHE MADE A MINT.

TULIP WAS HOMESCHOOLED AND NEVER VACCINATED. OLIVE'S WORDS MEAN NOTHING TO HIM, AND THE THOUGHT OF ANYTHING GOING VIRAL FILLS HIM WITH DREAD.

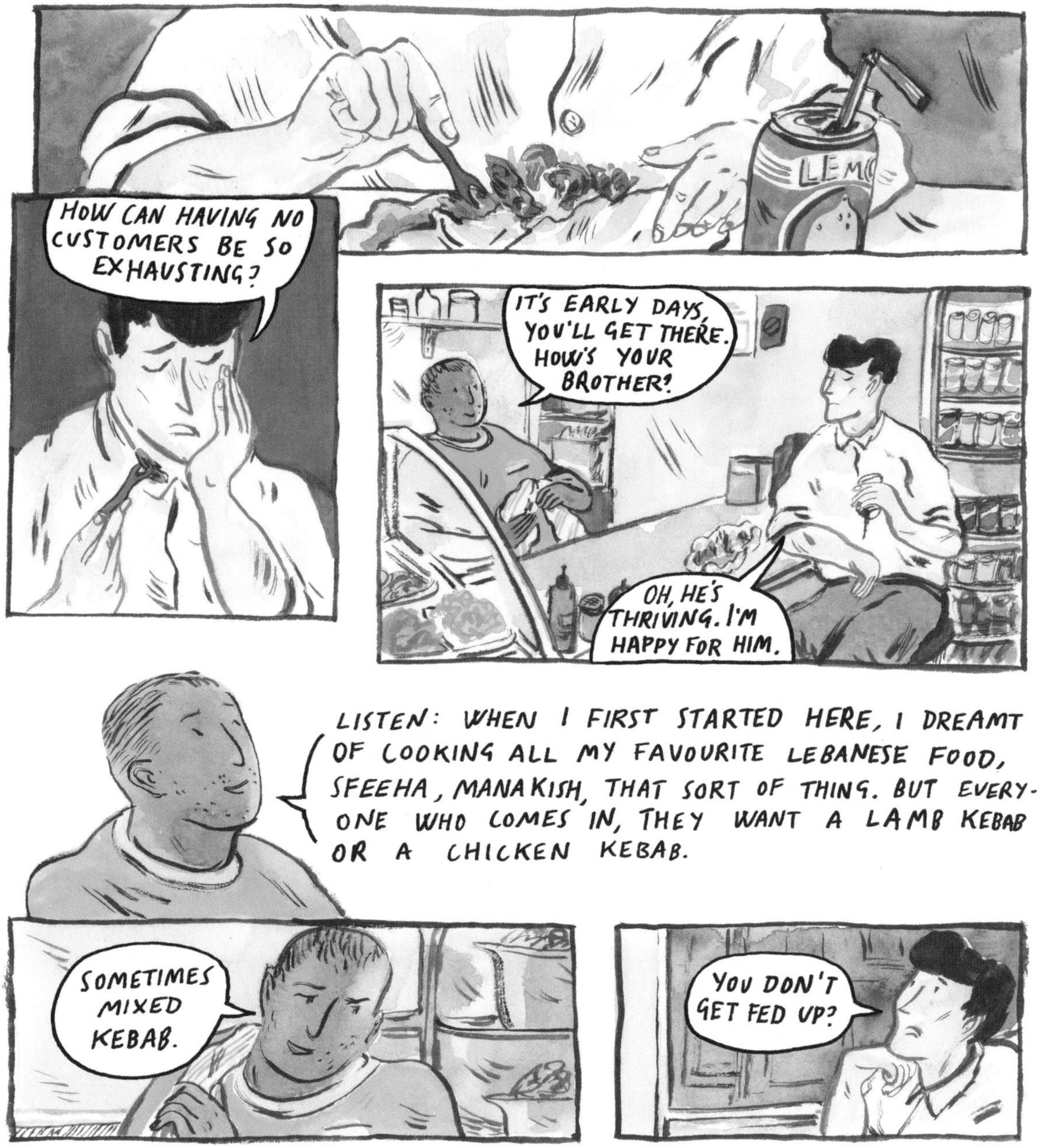
HOW CAN HAVING NO CUSTOMERS BE SO EXHAUSTING?
IT'S EARLY DAYS, YOU'LL GET THERE. HOW'S YOUR BROTHER?
OH, HE'S THRIVING. I'M HAPPY FOR HIM.
LISTEN: WHEN I FIRST STARTED HERE, I DREAMT OF COOKING ALL MY FAVOURITE LEBANESE FOOD, SFEEHA, MANAKISH, THAT SORT OF THING. BUT EVERY-ONE WHO COMES IN, THEY WANT A LAMB KEBAB OR A CHICKEN KEBAB.
SOMETIMES MIXED KEBAB.
YOU DON'T GET FED UP?

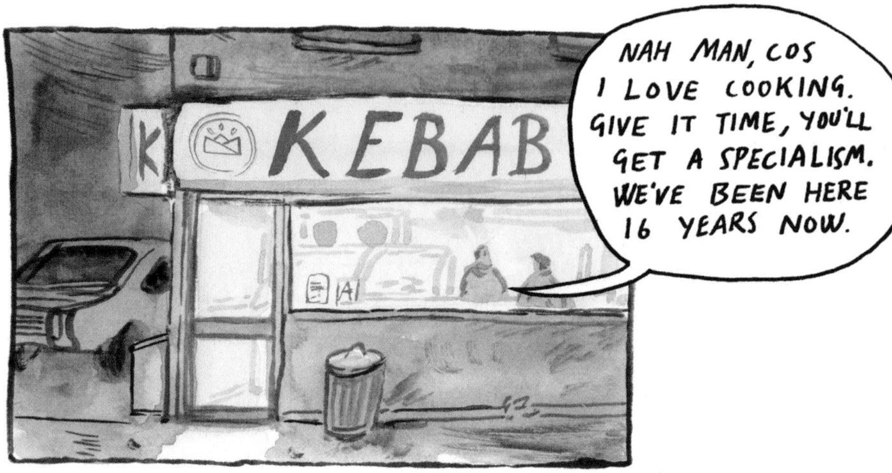
KEBAB
NAH MAN, COS I LOVE COOKING. GIVE IT TIME, YOU'LL GET A SPECIALISM. WE'VE BEEN HERE 16 YEARS NOW.

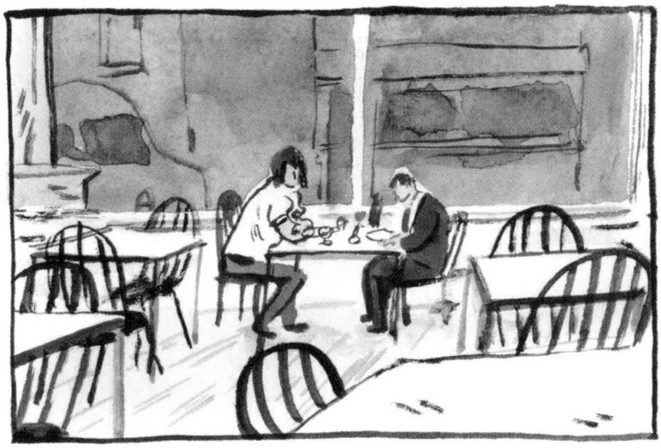

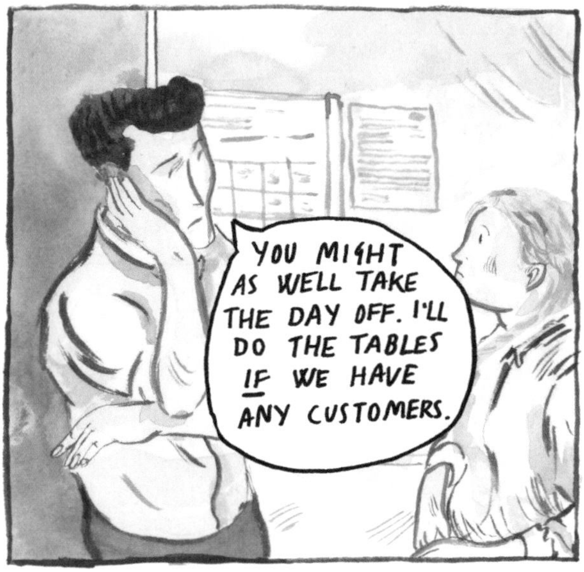
YOU MIGHT AS WELL TAKE THE DAY OFF. I'LL DO THE TABLES IF WE HAVE ANY CUSTOMERS.

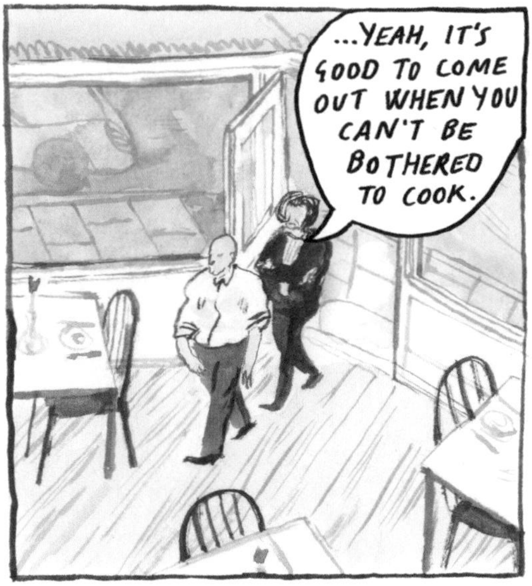
...YEAH, IT'S GOOD TO COME OUT WHEN YOU CAN'T BE BOTHERED TO COOK.

CONTRARY TO ROWAN'S EVANGELICAL DREAM, LOCAL ORGANIC FOOD IS NOTHING NEW. WHAT TULIP THOUGHT WOULD BE EXCITING AND FRESH IS ALREADY ECLIPSED BY HEALTH FOOD FADS, DETOX DIETS FROM CALIFORNIA AND "PURIFYING" BERRIES FROM SOUTHEAST ASIA.

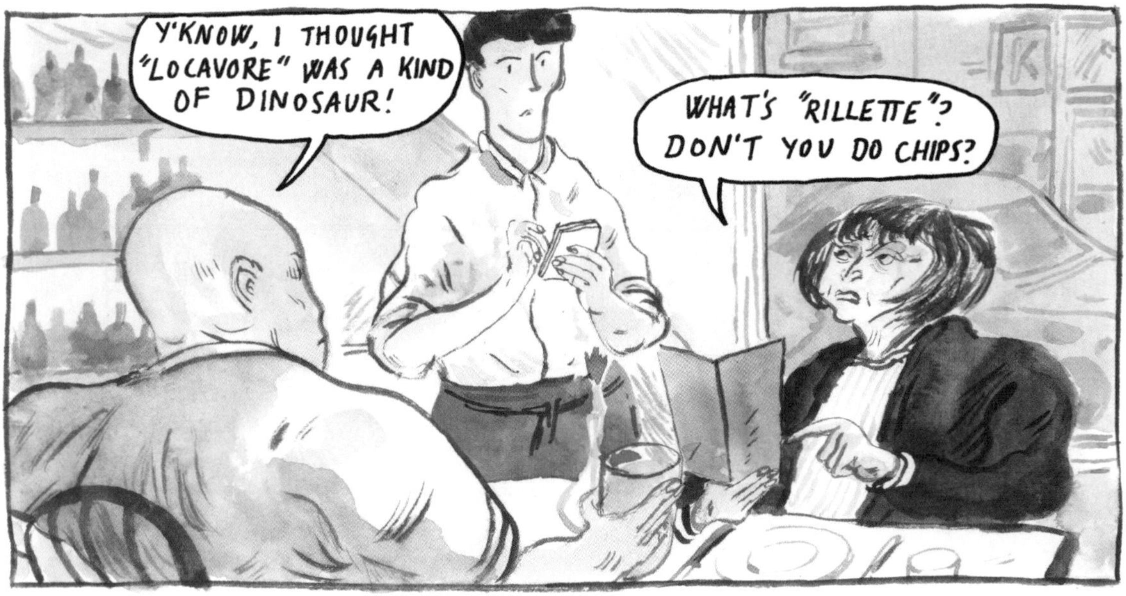
Y'KNOW, I THOUGHT "LOCAVORE" WAS A KIND OF DINOSAUR!
WHAT'S "RILLETTE"? DON'T YOU DO CHIPS?

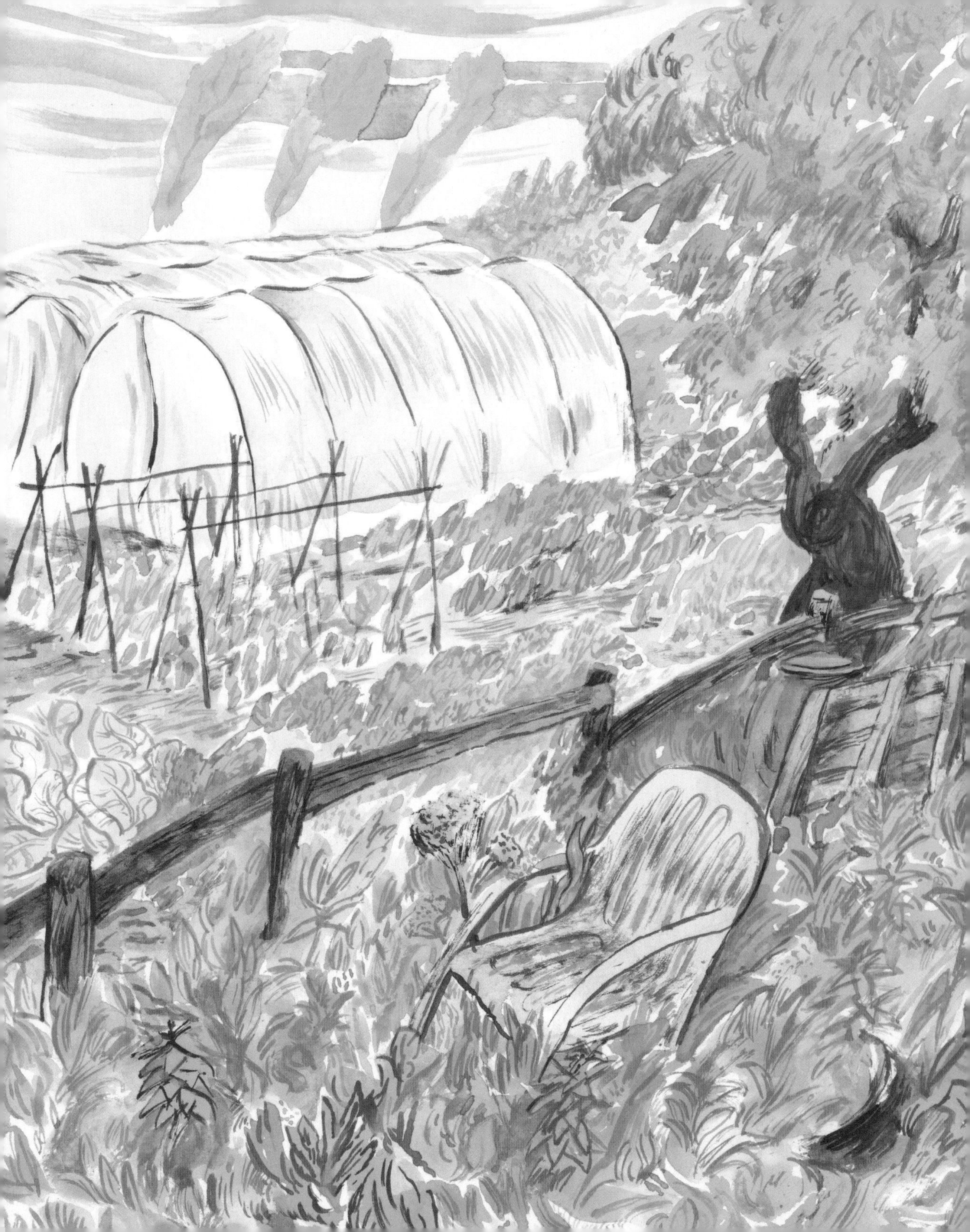

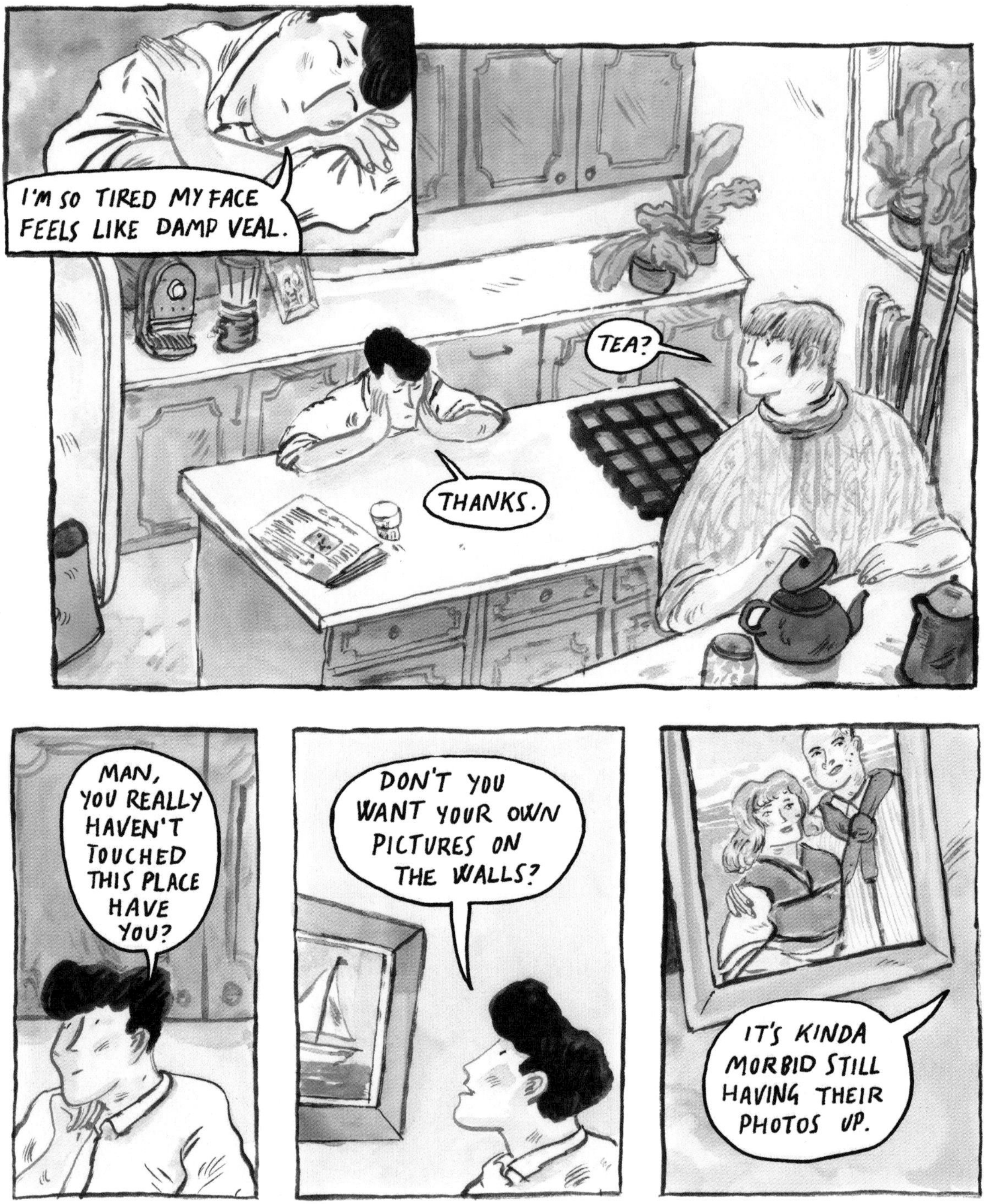
I'M SO TIRED MY FACE FEELS LIKE DAMP VEAL.
TEA?
THANKS.
MAN, YOU REALLY HAVEN'T TOUCHED THIS PLACE HAVE YOU?
DON'T YOU WANT YOUR OWN PICTURES ON THE WALLS?
IT'S KINDA MORBID STILL HAVING THEIR PHOTOS UP.

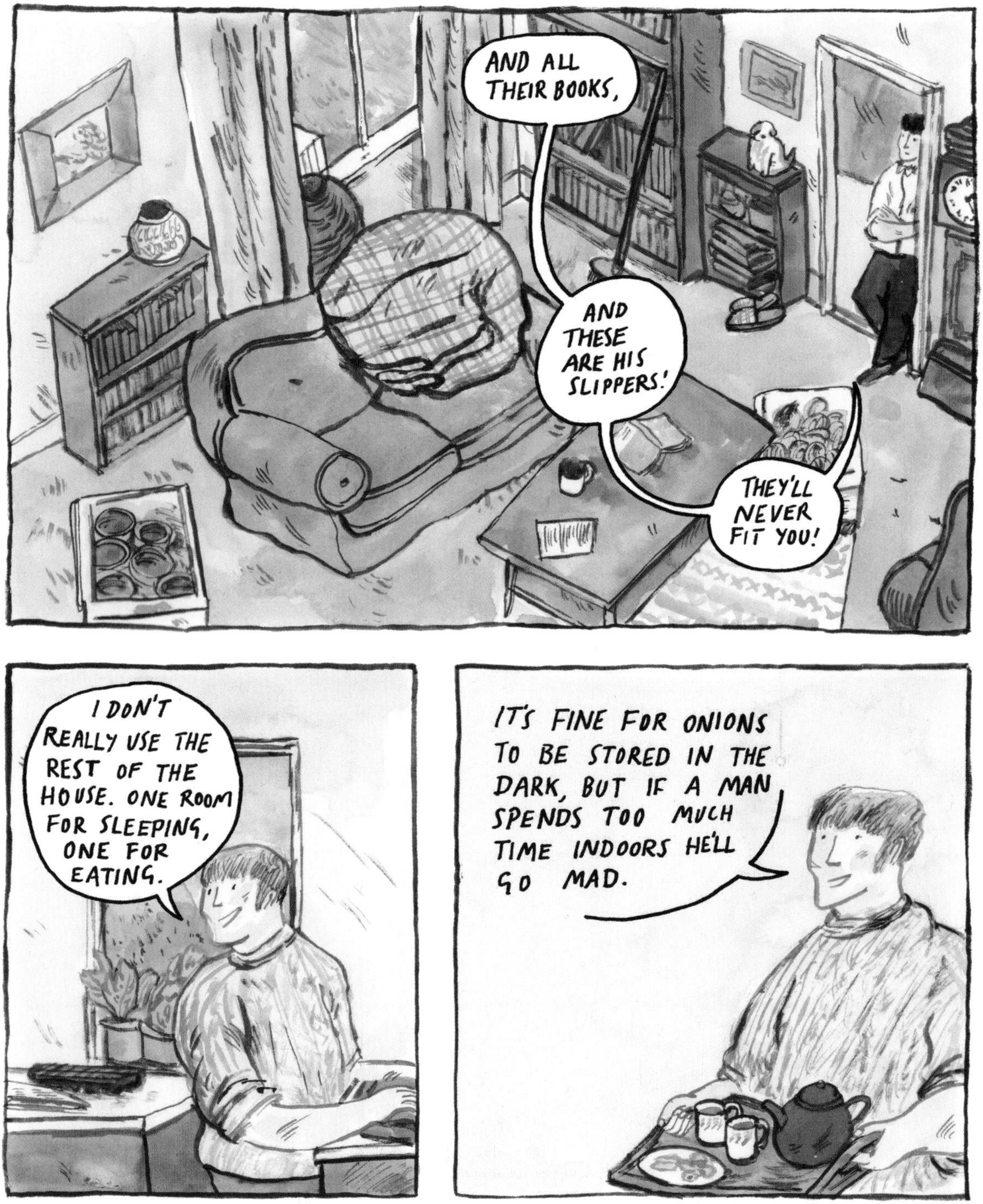
AND ALL THEIR BOOKS,
AND THESE ARE HIS SLIPPERS!
THEY'LL NEVER FIT YOU!
I DON'T REALLY USE THE REST OF THE HOUSE. ONE ROOM FOR SLEEPING, ONE FOR EATING.
IT'S FINE FOR ONIONS TO BE STORED IN THE DARK, BUT IF A MAN SPENDS TOO MUCH TIME INDOORS HE'LL GO MAD.

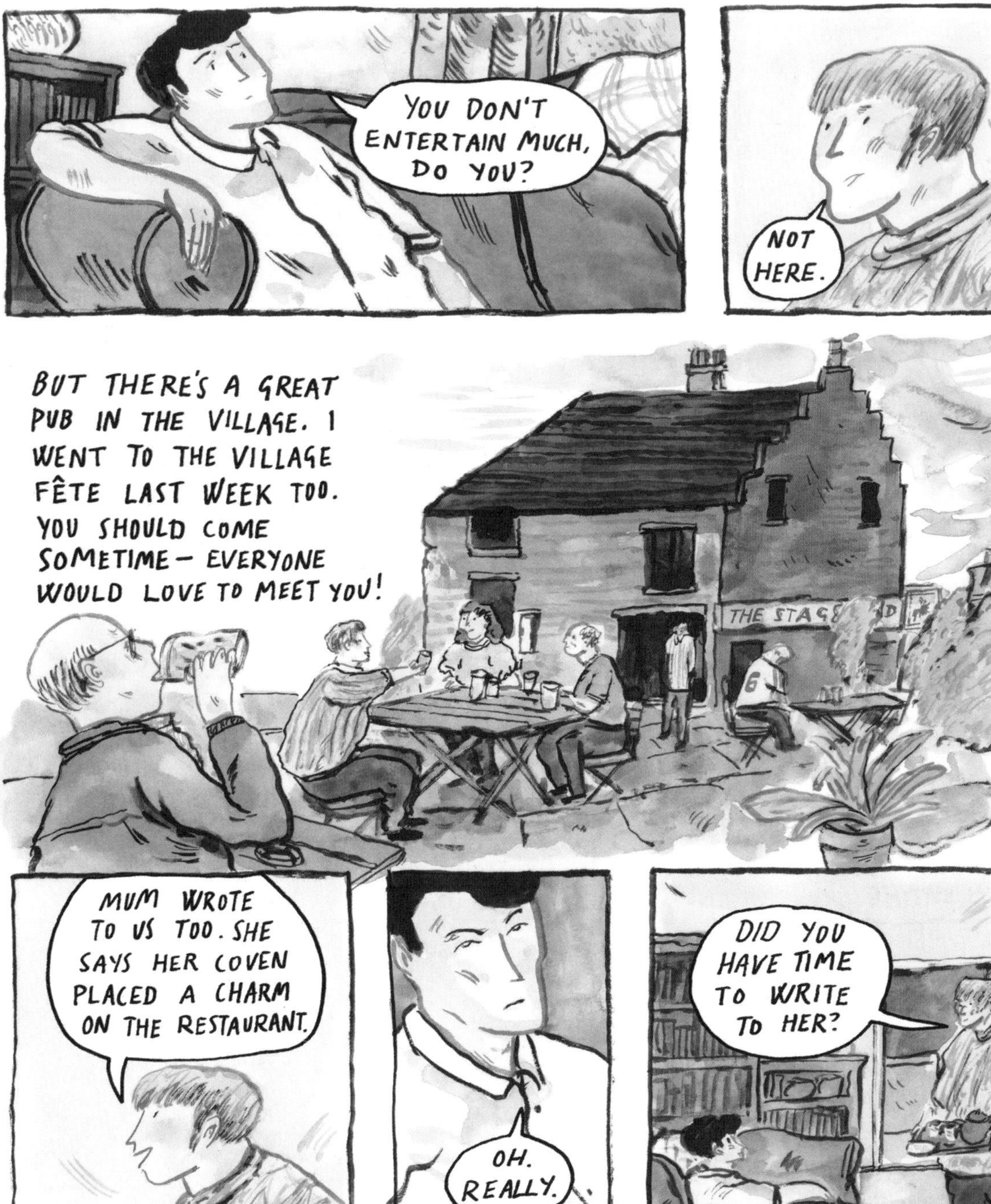
YOU DON'T ENTERTAIN MUCH, DO YOU?
NOT HERE.
BUT THERE'S A GREAT PUB IN THE VILLAGE. I WENT TO THE VILLAGE FÊTE LAST WEEK TOO. YOU SHOULD COME SOMETIME – EVERYONE WOULD LOVE TO MEET YOU!
THE STAG
MUM WROTE TO US TOO. SHE SAYS HER COVEN PLACED A CHARM ON THE RESTAURANT.
OH. REALLY.
DID YOU HAVE TIME TO WRITE TO HER?

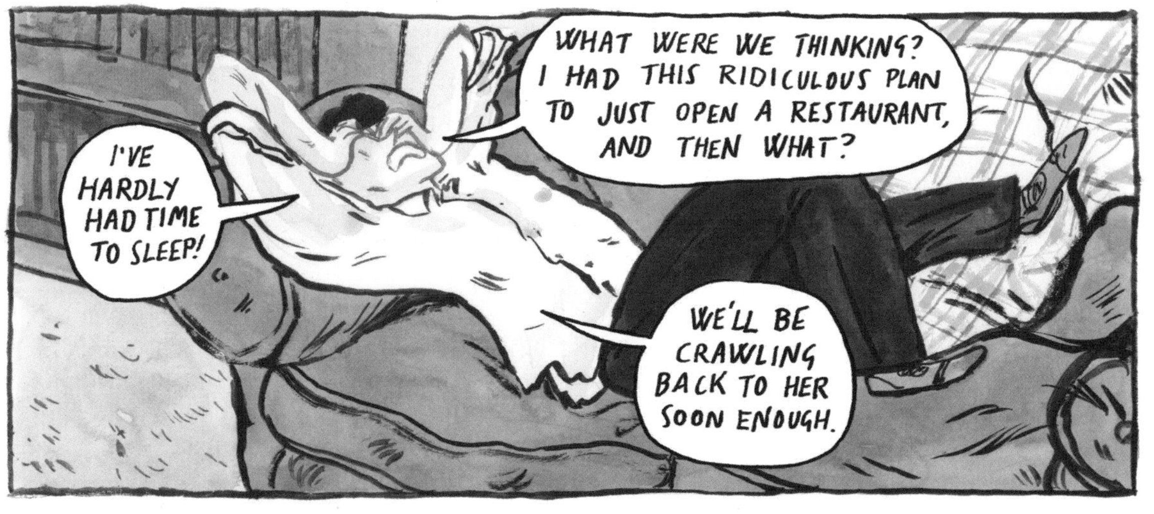
WHAT WERE WE THINKING? I HAD THIS RIDICULOUS PLAN TO JUST OPEN A RESTAURANT, AND THEN WHAT?
I'VE HARDLY HAD TIME TO SLEEP!
WE'LL BE CRAWLING BACK TO HER SOON ENOUGH.

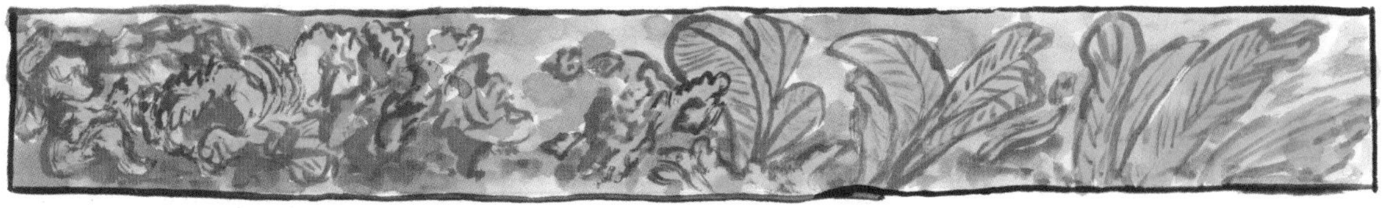

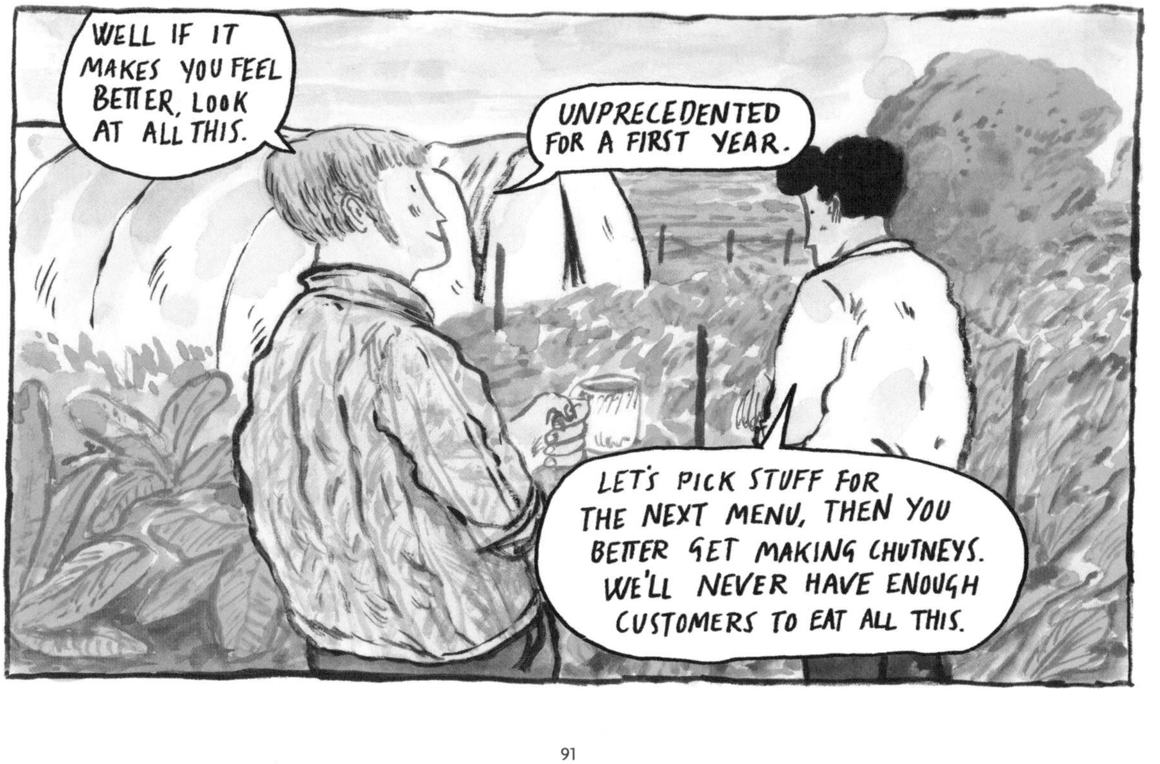
WELL IF IT MAKES YOU FEEL BETTER, LOOK AT ALL THIS.
UNPRECEDENTED FOR A FIRST YEAR.
LET'S PICK STUFF FOR THE NEXT MENU, THEN YOU BETTER GET MAKING CHUTNEYS. WE'LL NEVER HAVE ENOUGH CUSTOMERS TO EAT ALL THIS.

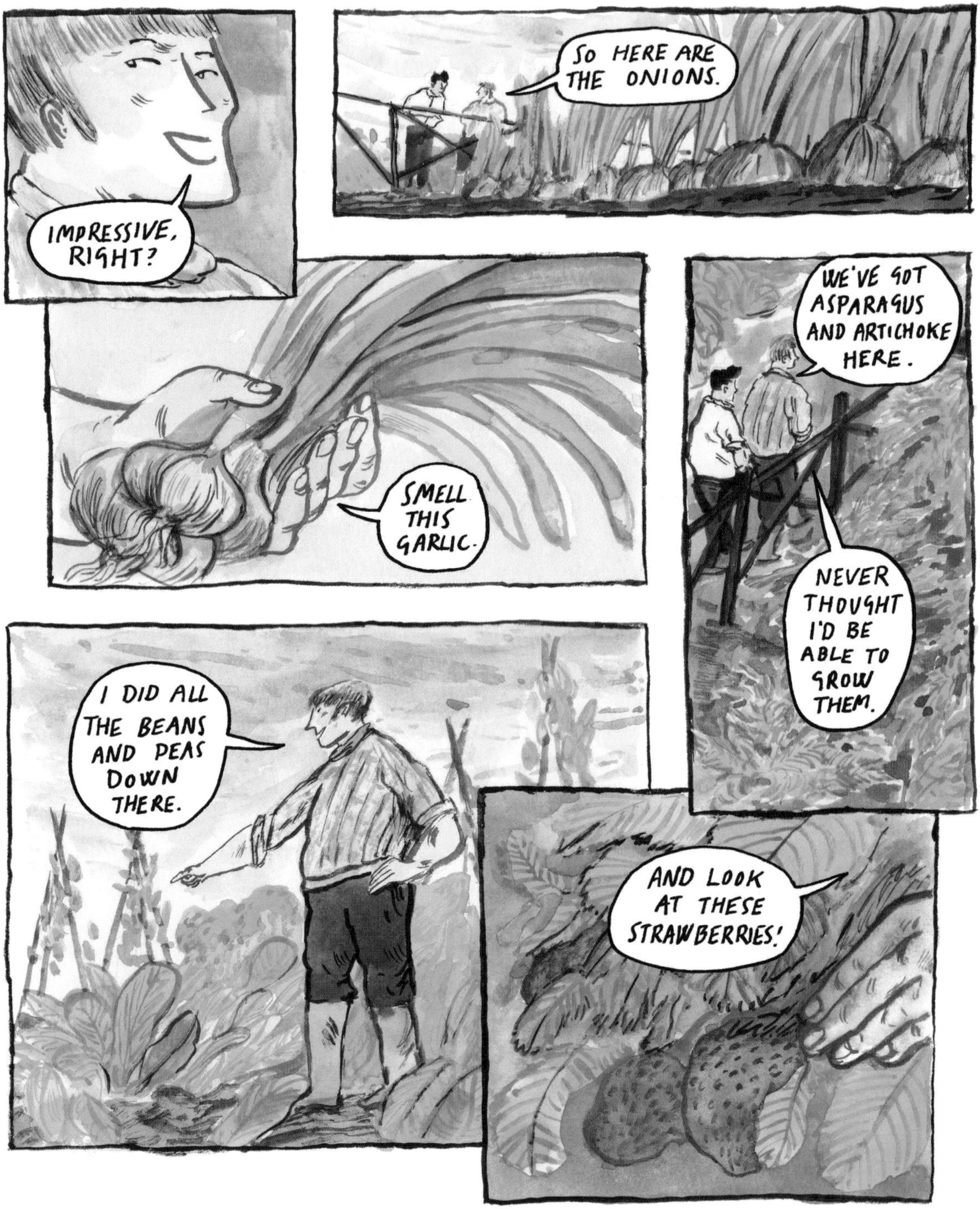
IMPRESSIVE, RIGHT?
SO HERE ARE THE ONIONS.
SMELL THIS GARLIC.
WE'VE GOT ASPARAGUS AND ARTICHOKE HERE.
NEVER THOUGHT I'D BE ABLE TO GROW THEM.
I DID ALL THE BEANS AND PEAS DOWN THERE.
AND LOOK AT THESE STRAWBERRIES!

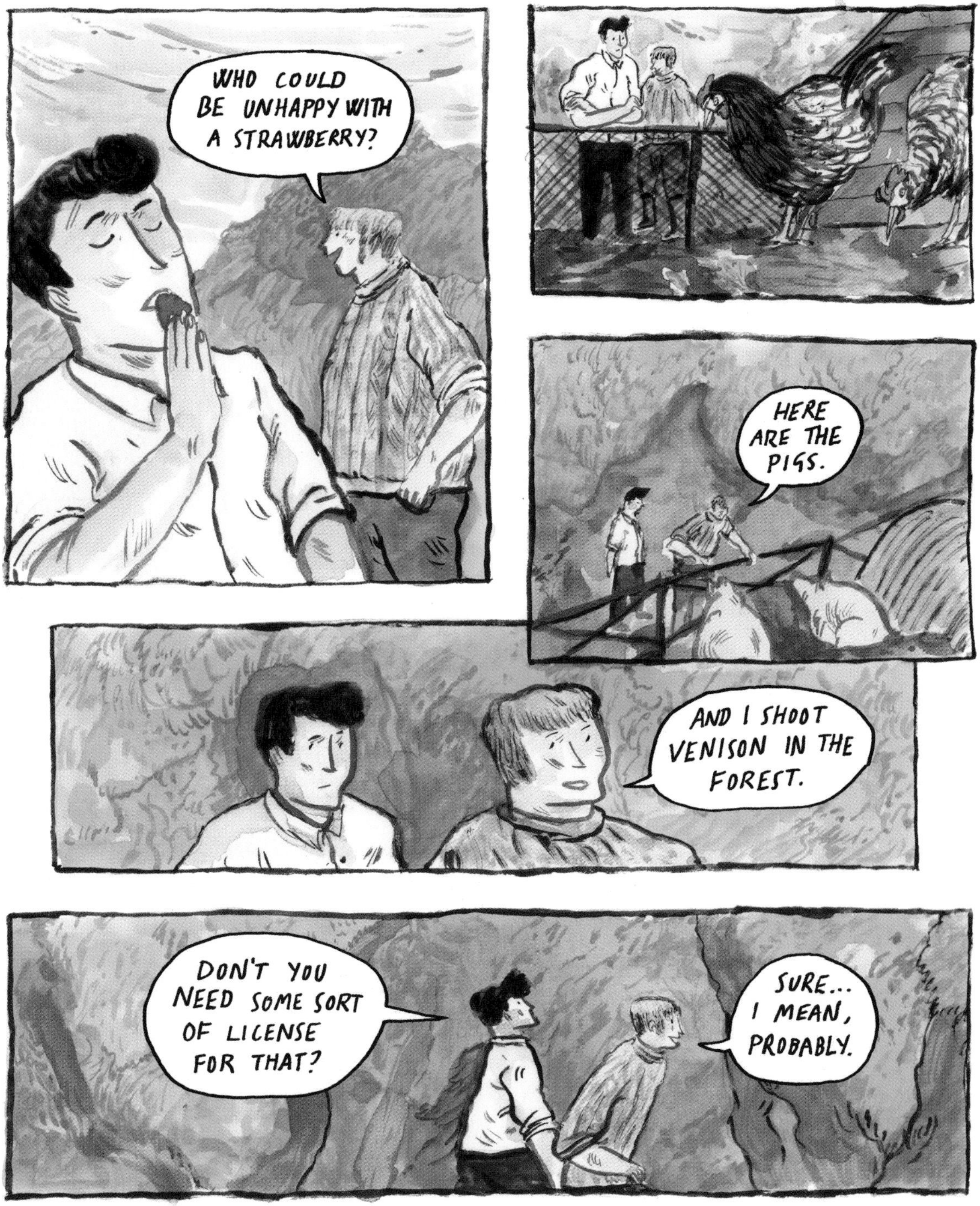
WHO COULD BE UNHAPPY WITH A STRAWBERRY?
HERE ARE THE PIGS.
AND I SHOOT VENISON IN THE FOREST.
DON'T YOU NEED SOME SORT OF LICENSE FOR THAT?
SURE... I MEAN, PROBABLY.

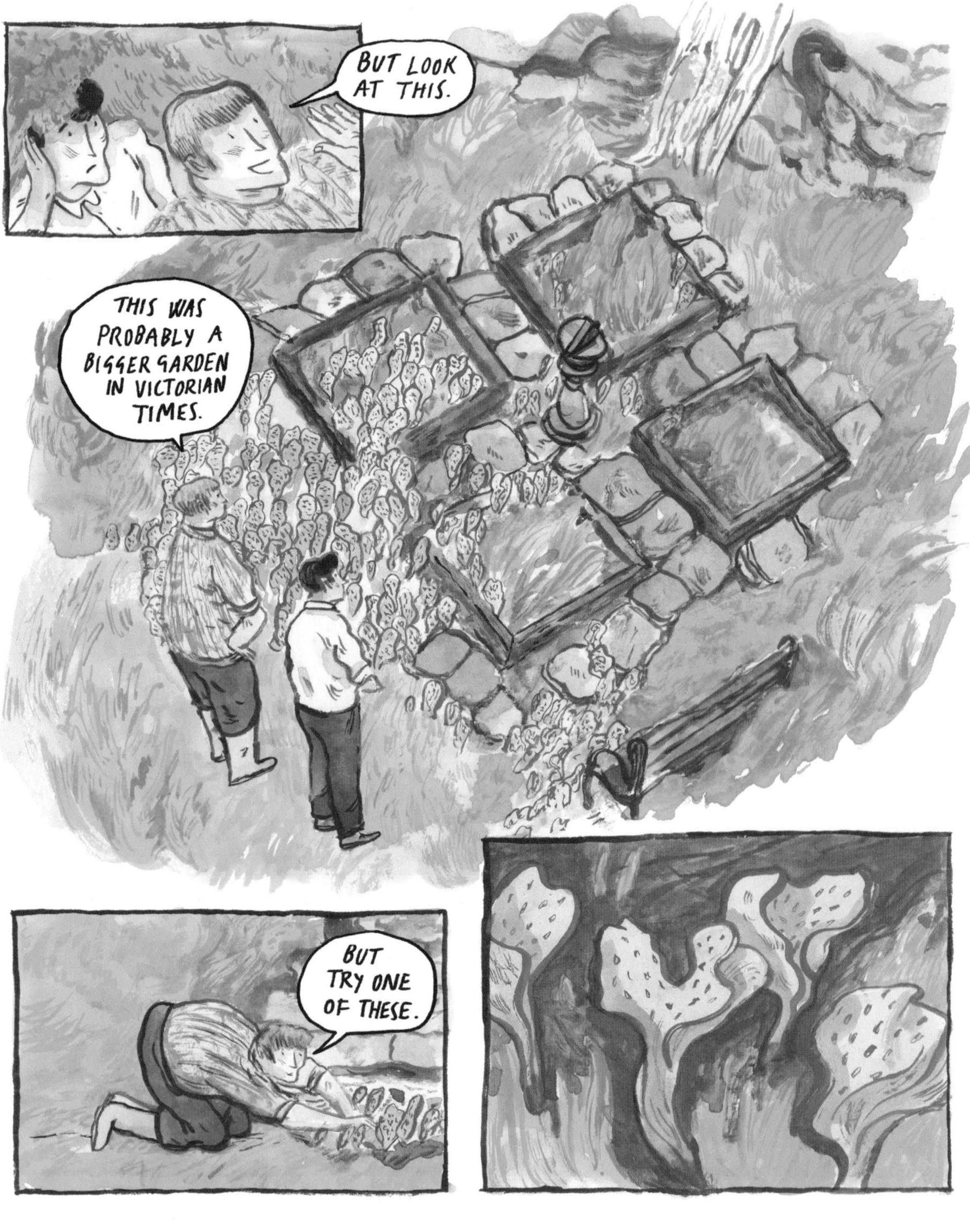
BUT LOOK AT THIS.
THIS WAS PROBABLY A BIGGER GARDEN IN VICTORIAN TIMES.
BUT TRY ONE OF THESE.

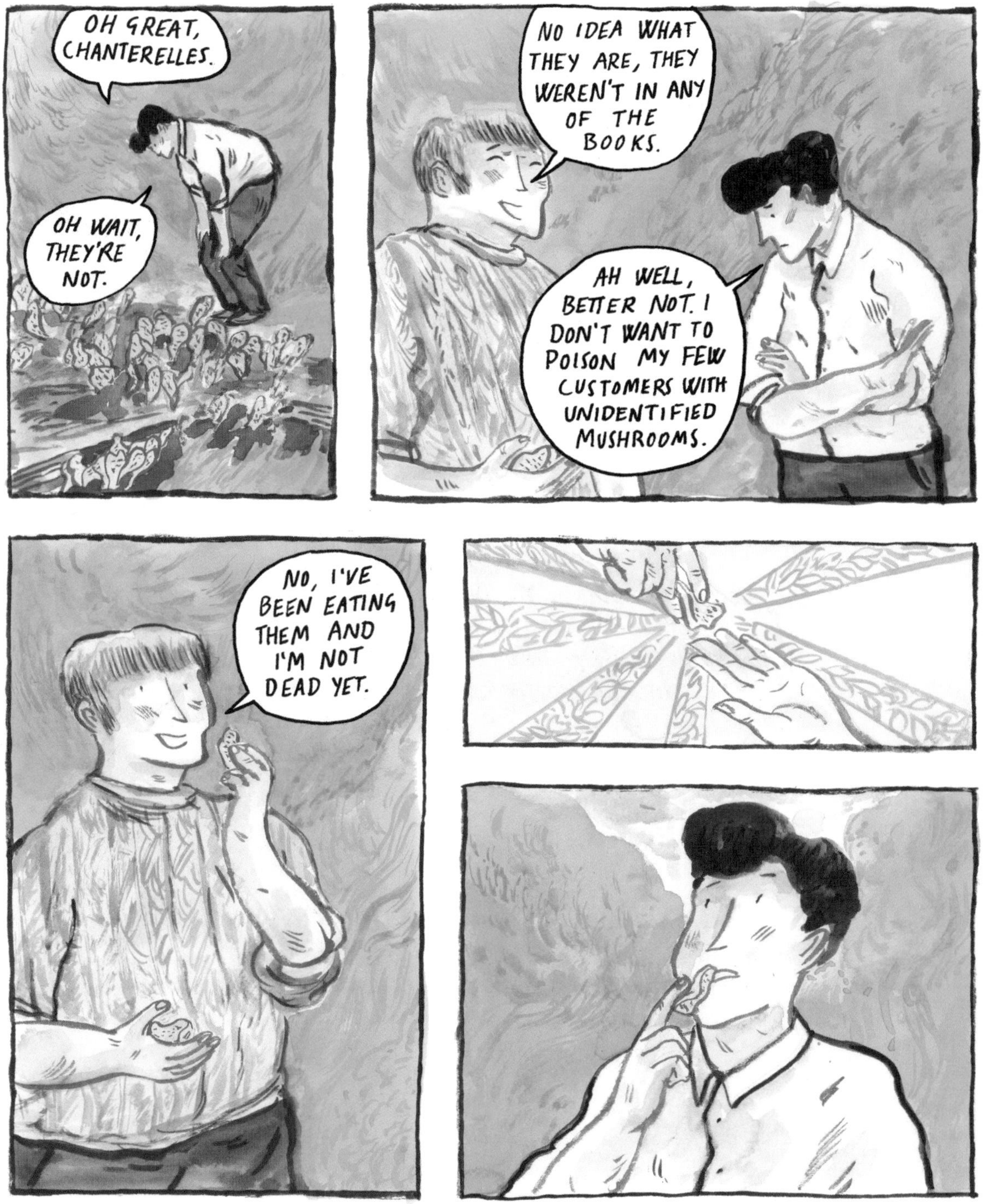
OH GREAT, CHANTERELLES.
OH WAIT, THEY'RE NOT.
NO IDEA WHAT THEY ARE, THEY WEREN'T IN ANY OF THE BOOKS.
AH WELL, BETTER NOT. I DON'T WANT TO POISON MY FEW CUSTOMERS WITH UNIDENTIFIED MUSHROOMS.
NO, I'VE BEEN EATING THEM AND I'M NOT DEAD YET.

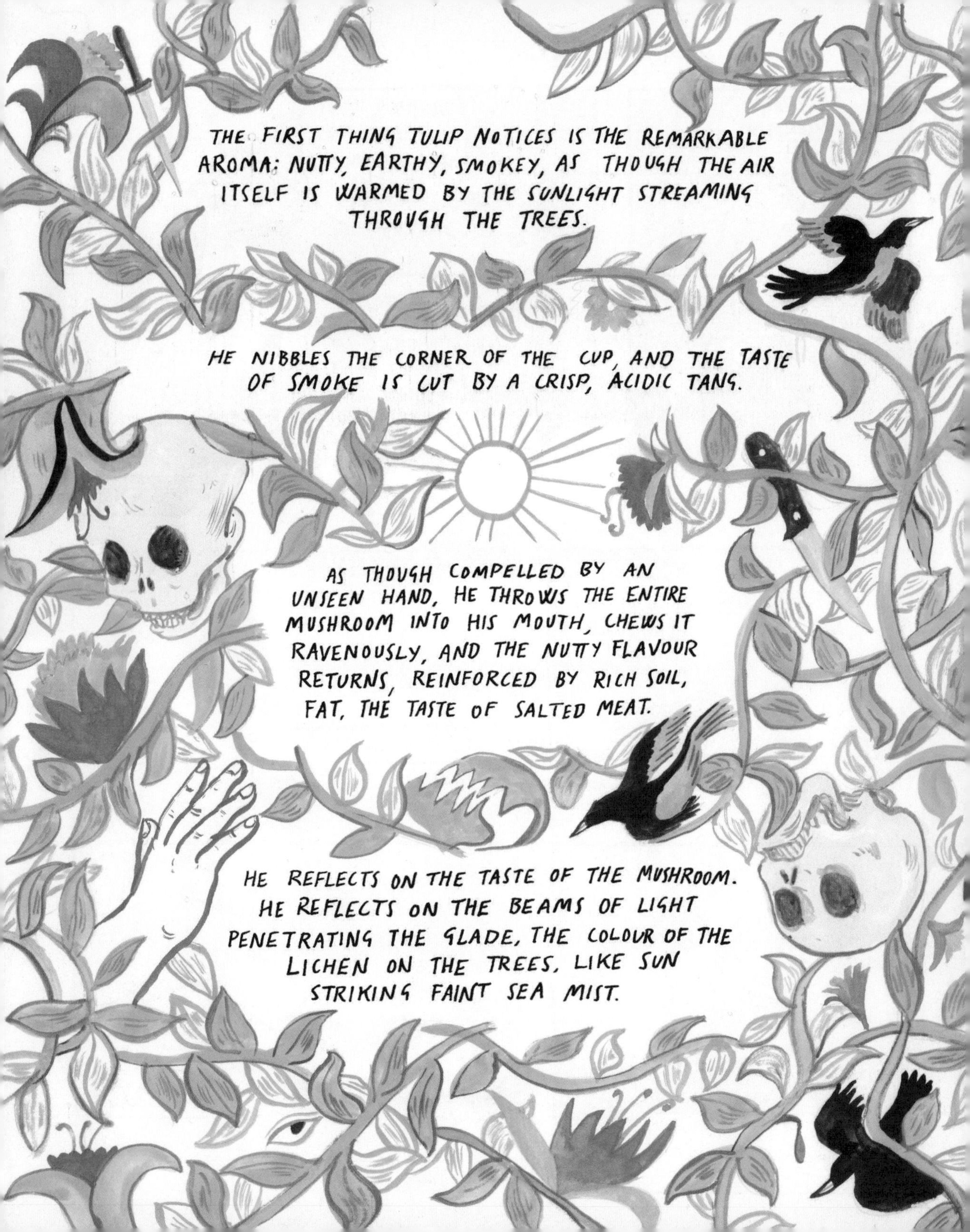
THE FIRST THING TULIP NOTICES IS THE REMARKABLE AROMA: NUTTY, EARTHY, SMOKEY, AS THOUGH THE AIR ITSELF IS WARMED BY THE SUNLIGHT STREAMING THROUGH THE TREES.
HE NIBBLES THE CORNER OF THE CUP, AND THE TASTE OF SMOKE IS CUT BY A CRISP, ACIDIC TANG.
AS THOUGH COMPELLED BY AN UNSEEN HAND, HE THROWS THE ENTIRE MUSHROOM INTO HIS MOUTH, CHEWS IT RAVENOUSLY, AND THE NUTTY FLAVOUR RETURNS, REINFORCED BY RICH SOIL, FAT, THE TASTE OF SALTED MEAT.
HE REFLECTS ON THE TASTE OF THE MUSHROOM. HE REFLECTS ON THE BEAMS OF LIGHT PENETRATING THE GLADE, THE COLOUR OF THE LICHEN ON THE TREES, LIKE SUN STRIKING FAINT SEA MIST.

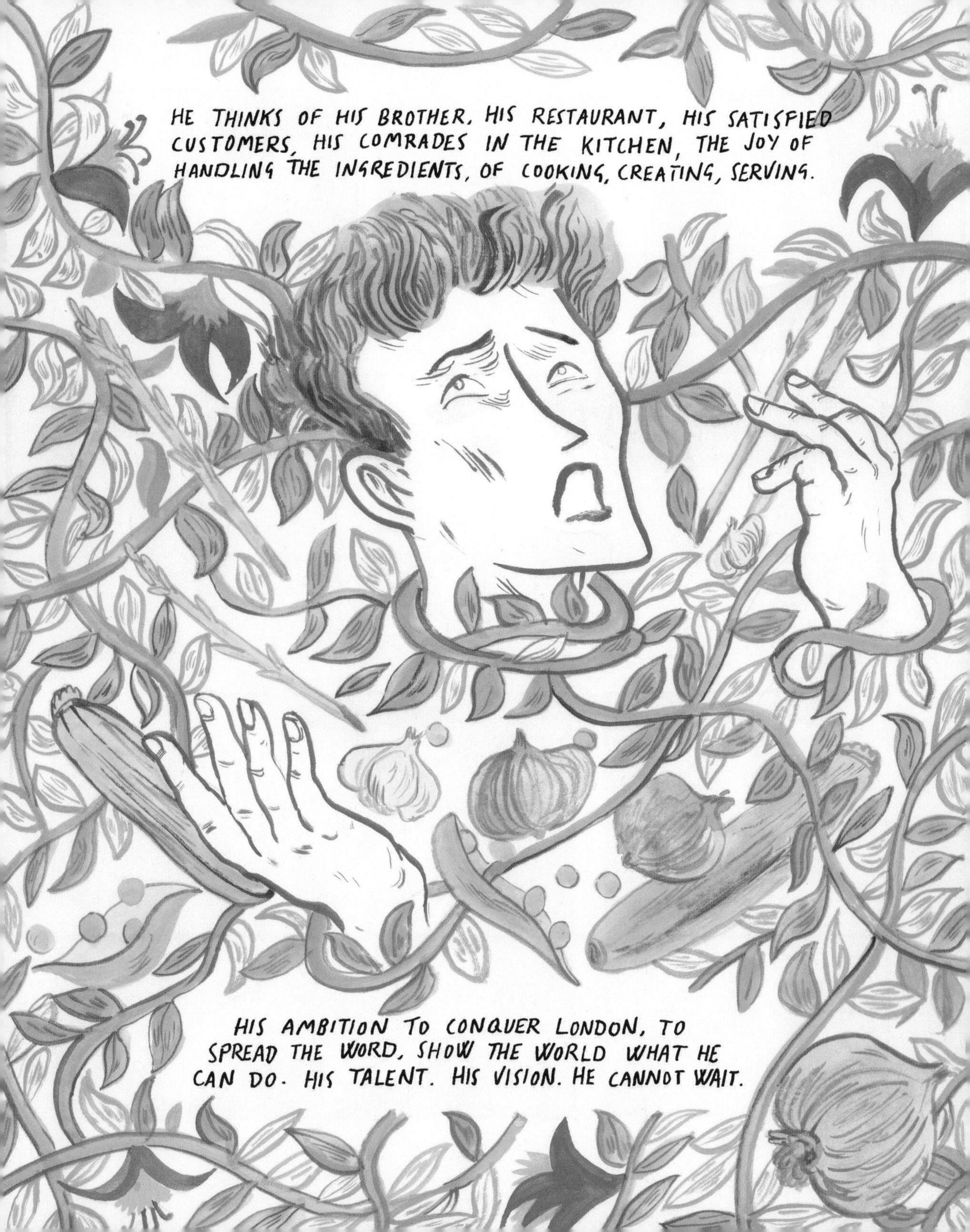
HE THINKS OF HIS BROTHER, HIS RESTAURANT, HIS SATISFIED CUSTOMERS, HIS COMRADES IN THE KITCHEN, THE JOY OF HANDLING THE INGREDIENTS, OF COOKING, CREATING, SERVING.
HIS AMBITION TO CONQUER LONDON, TO SPREAD THE WORD, SHOW THE WORLD WHAT HE CAN DO. HIS TALENT. HIS VISION. HE CANNOT WAIT.

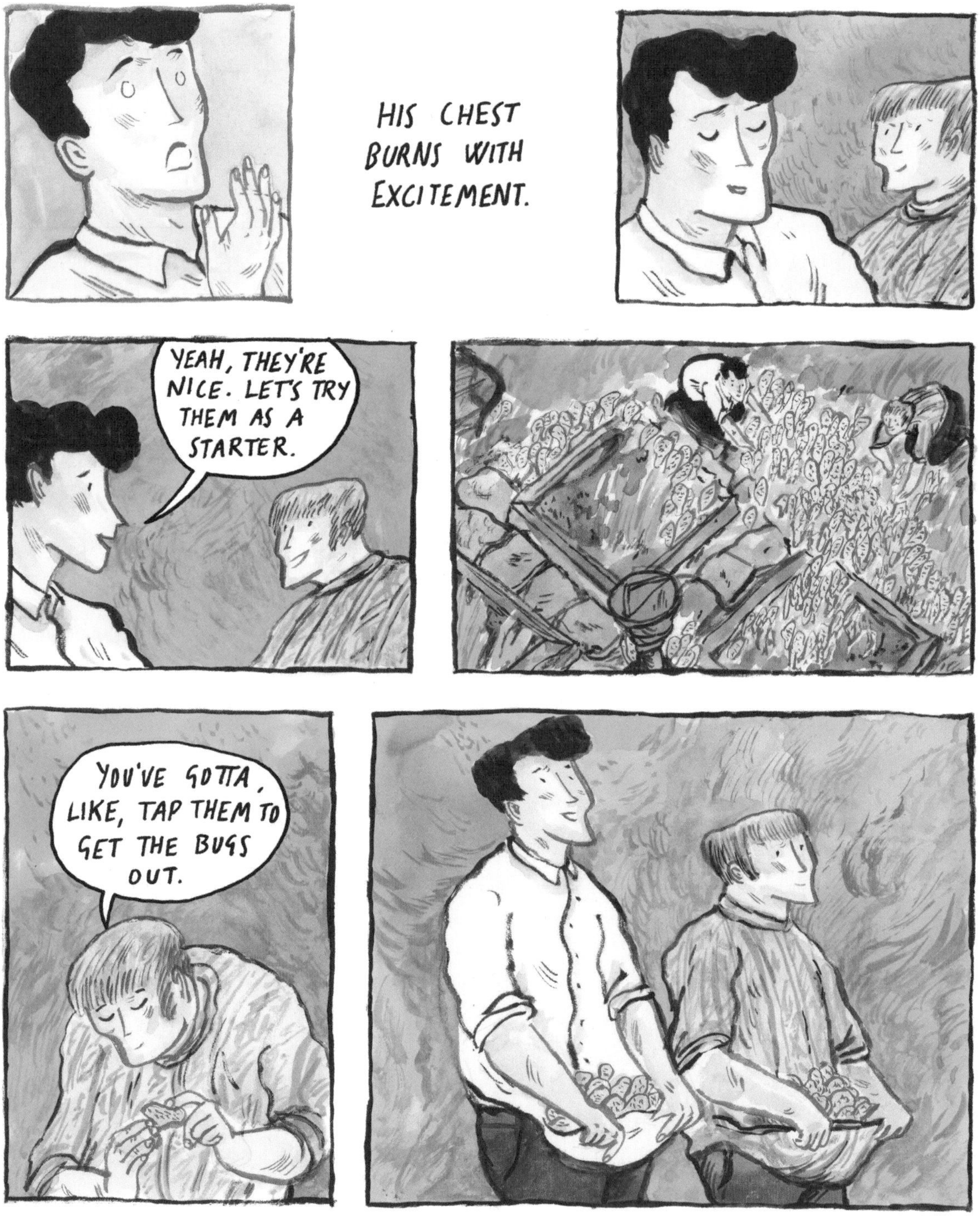
HIS CHEST BURNS WITH EXCITEMENT.
YEAH, THEY'RE NICE. LET'S TRY THEM AS A STARTER.
YOU'VE GOTTA, LIKE, TAP THEM TO GET THE BUGS OUT.

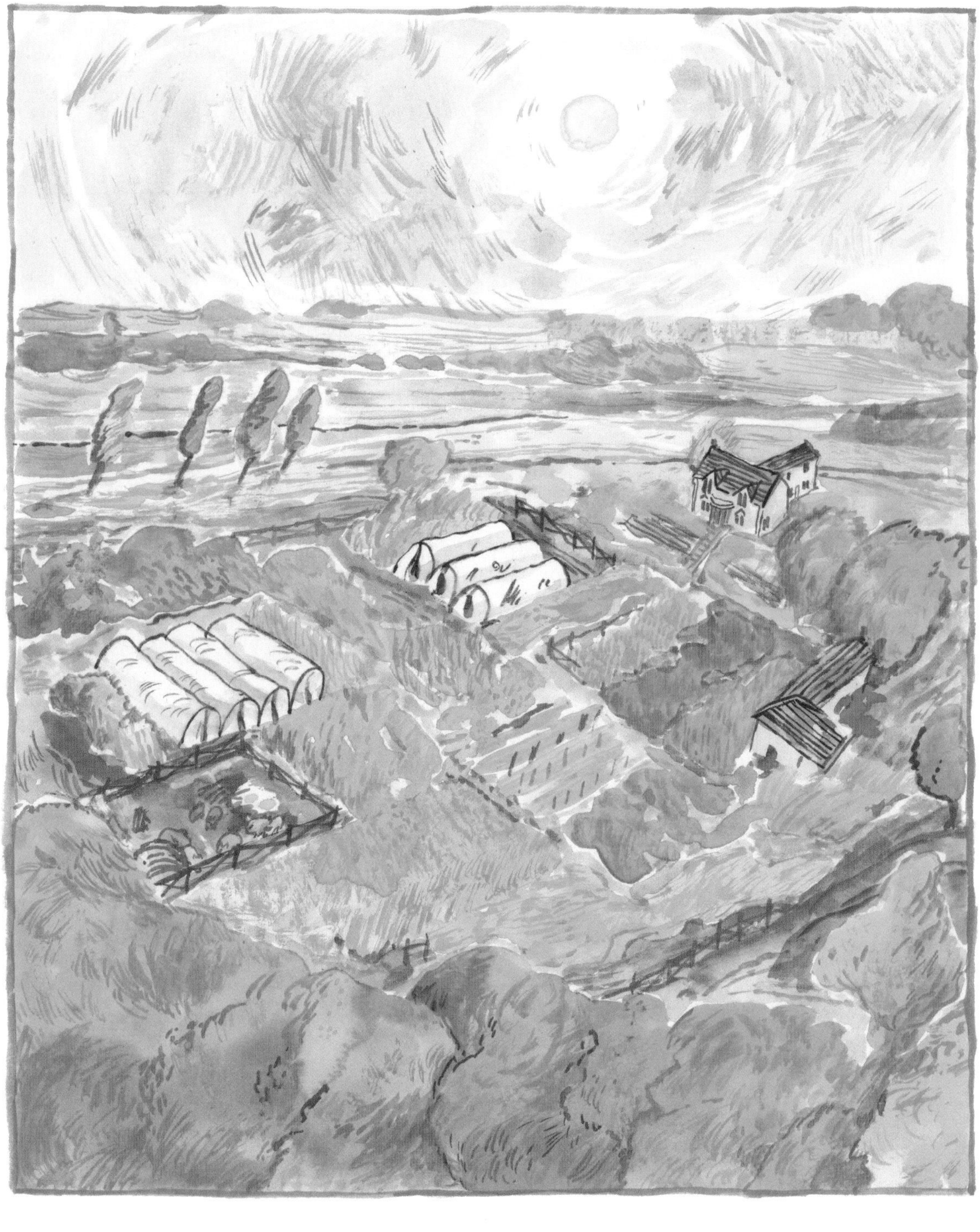

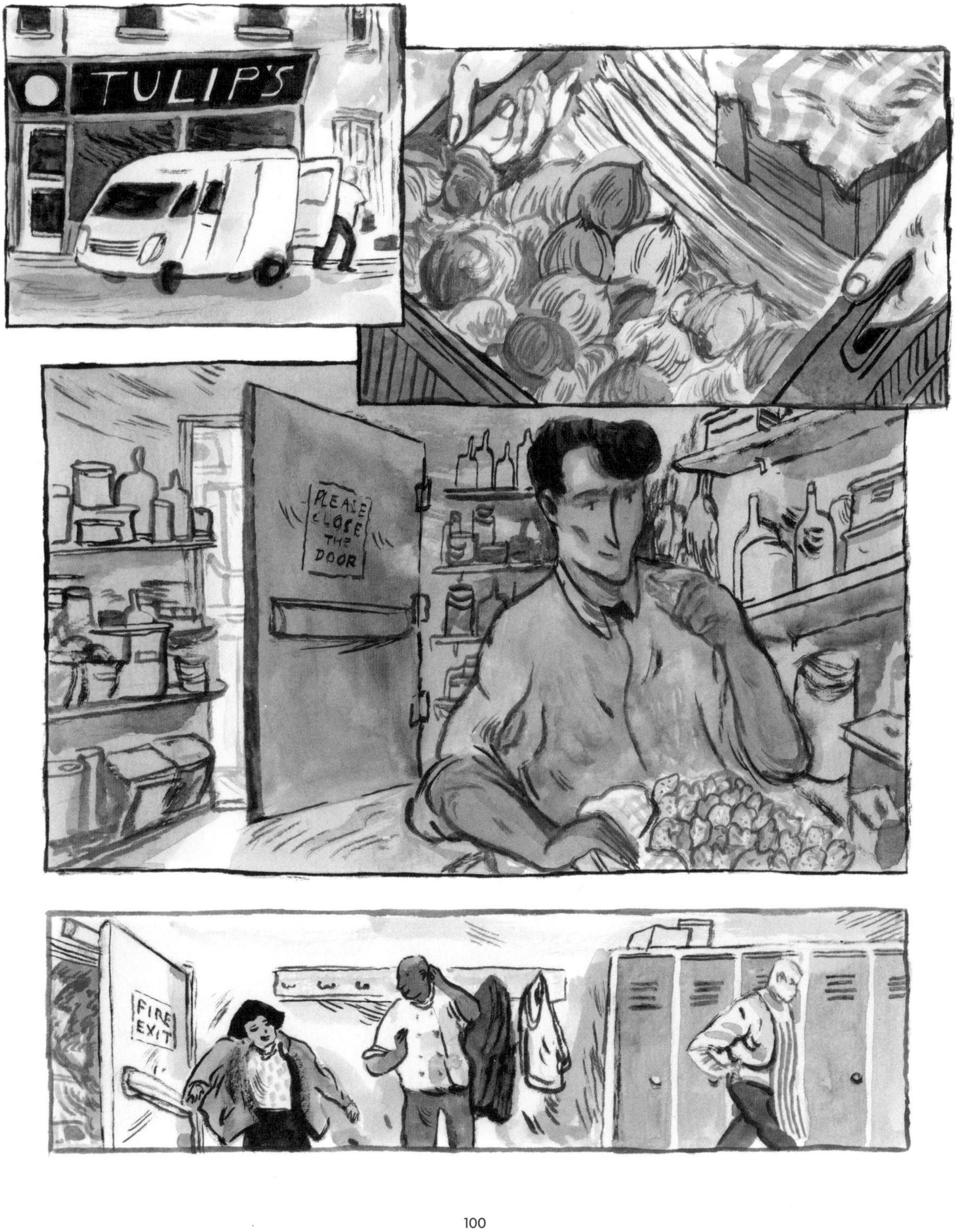
TULIP'S
PLEASE CLOSE THE DOOR
FIRE EXIT

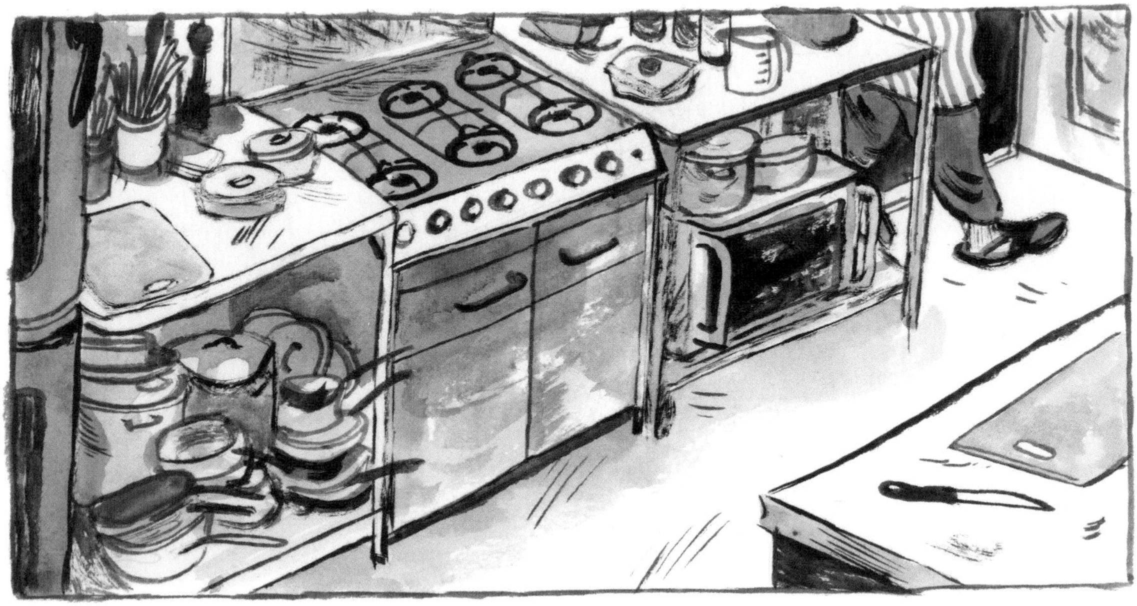
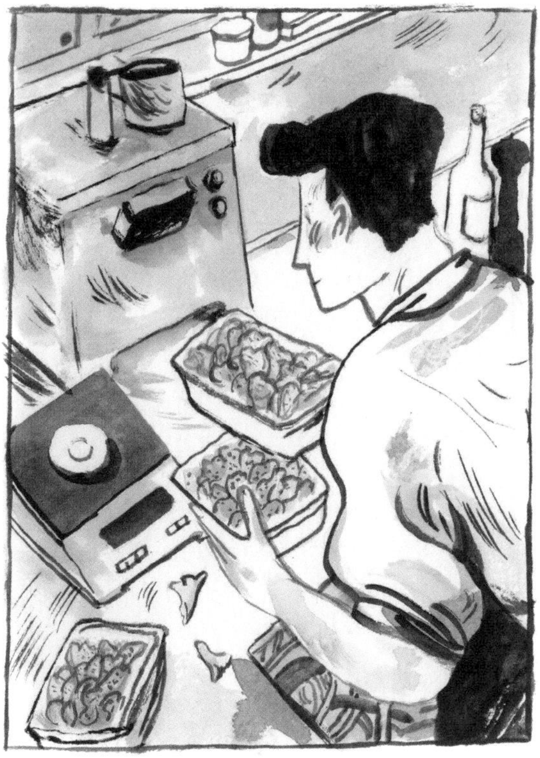
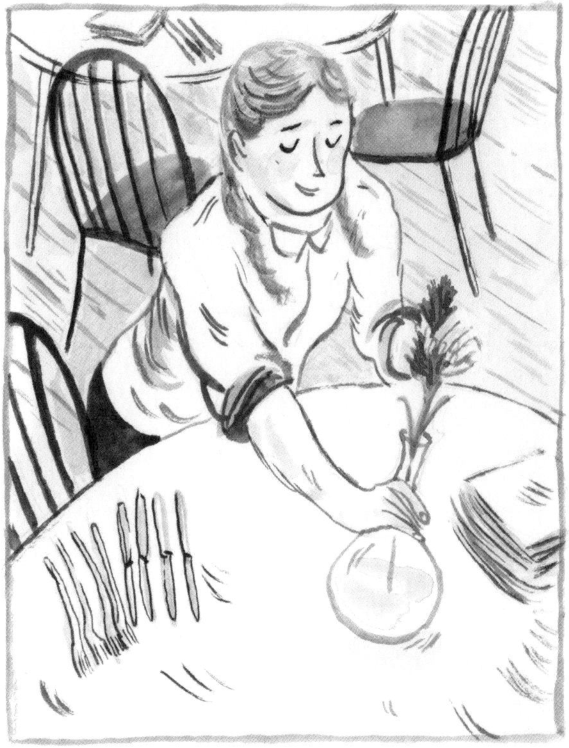

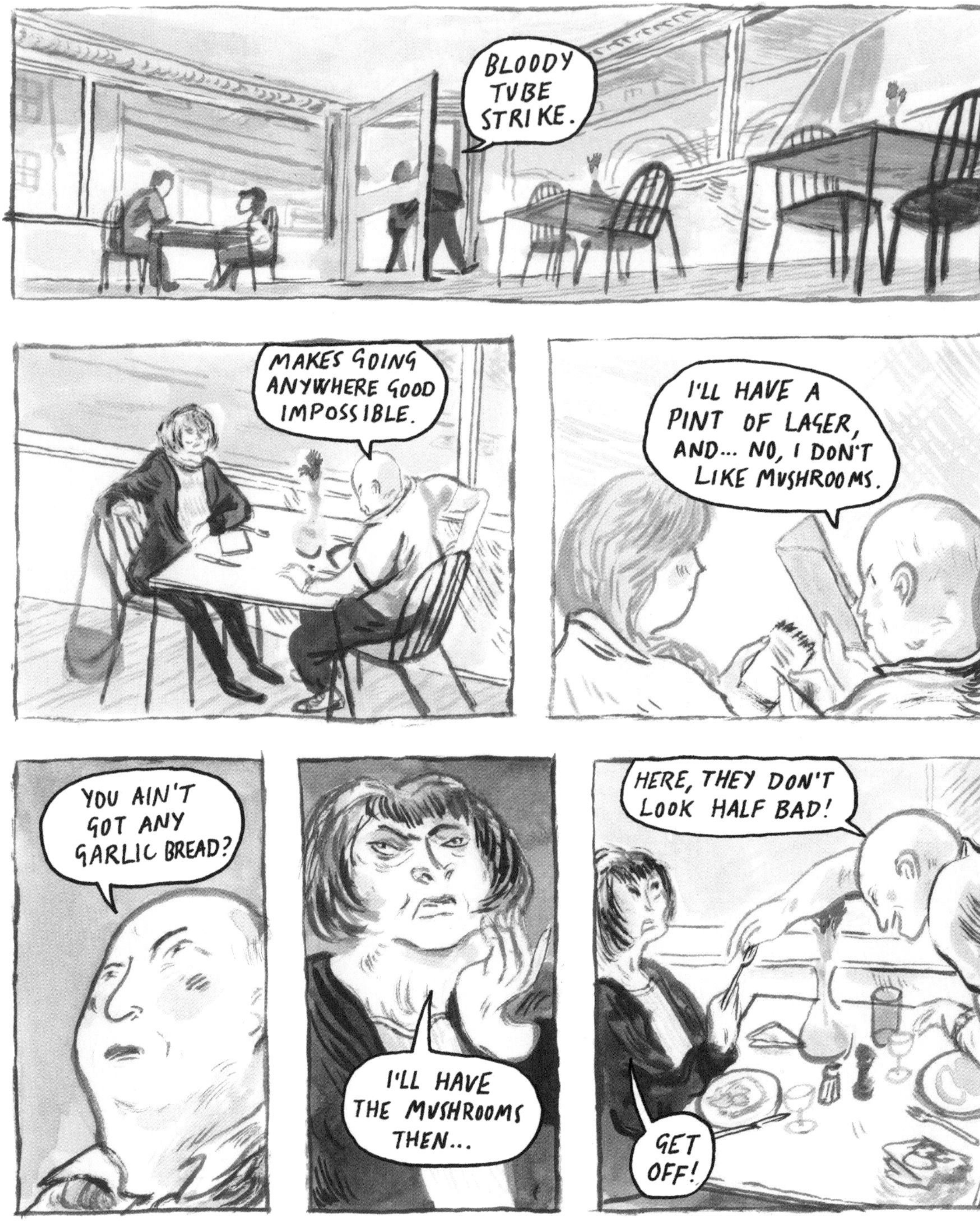
BLOODY TUBE STRIKE.
MAKES GOING ANYWHERE GOOD IMPOSSIBLE.
I'LL HAVE A PINT OF LAGER, AND... NO, I DON'T LIKE MUSHROOMS.
YOU AIN'T GOT ANY GARLIC BREAD?
I'LL HAVE THE MUSHROOMS THEN...
HERE, THEY DON'T LOOK HALF BAD!
GET OFF!

FOR ONCE, THE COUPLE LEAVE SMILING, AND TO TULIP'S SURPRISE, THEY RETURN THE NEXT DAY.

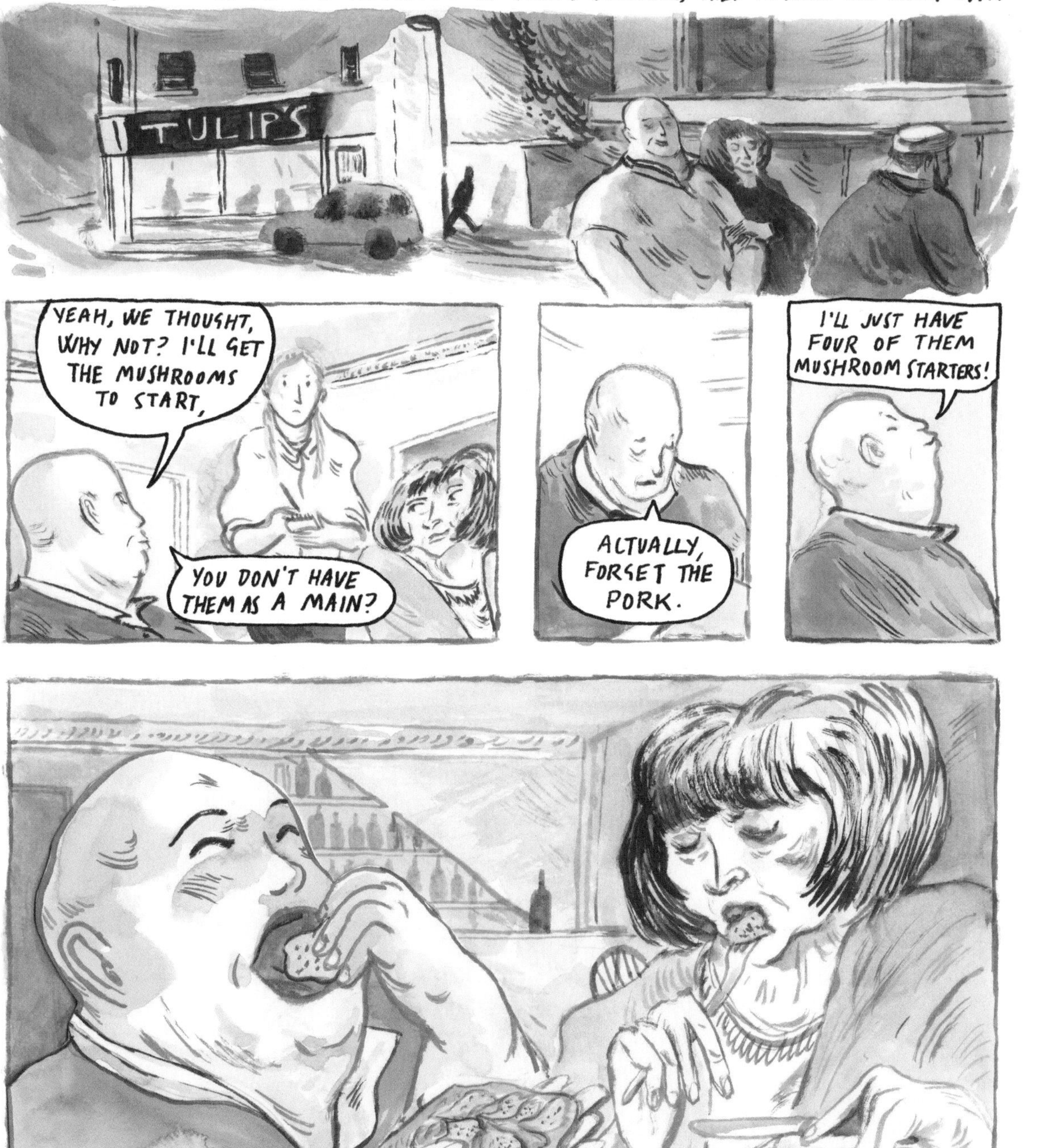
TULIP'S
YEAH, WE THOUGHT, WHY NOT? I'LL GET THE MUSHROOMS TO START,
YOU DON'T HAVE THEM AS A MAIN?
ACTUALLY, FORGET THE PORK.
I'LL JUST HAVE FOUR OF THEM MUSHROOM STARTERS!

BUOYED BY THE FEEDBACK, TULIP ASKS ROWAN FOR MORE MUSHROOMS.

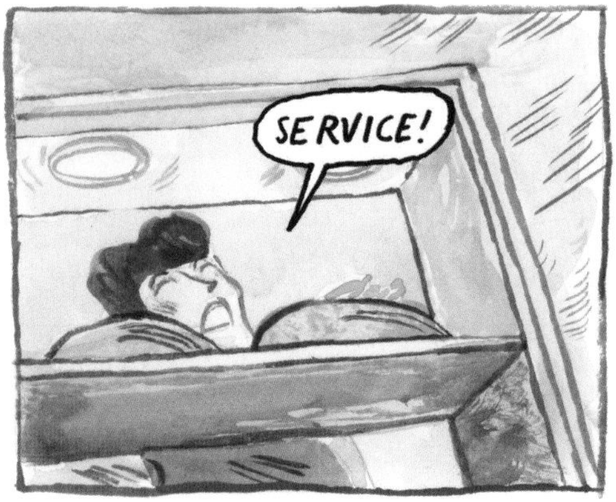
SERVICE!

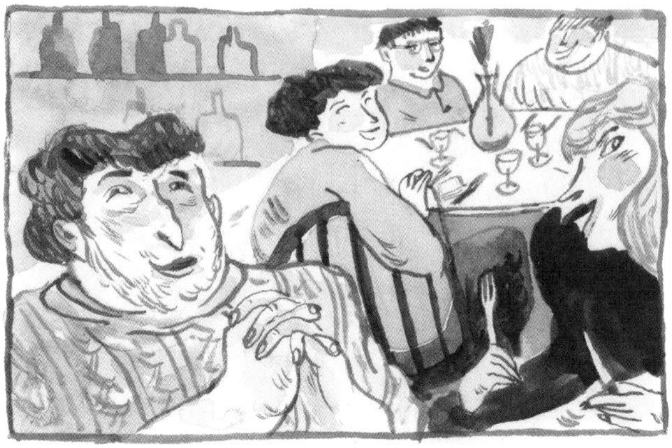

DINERS ARE STRUCK NOT ONLY BY THE MUSHROOMS' DELICIOUS FLAVOUR, BUT BY THE SAME OVERWHELMING FEELINGS OF JOY, VIVACITY AND ENERGY.

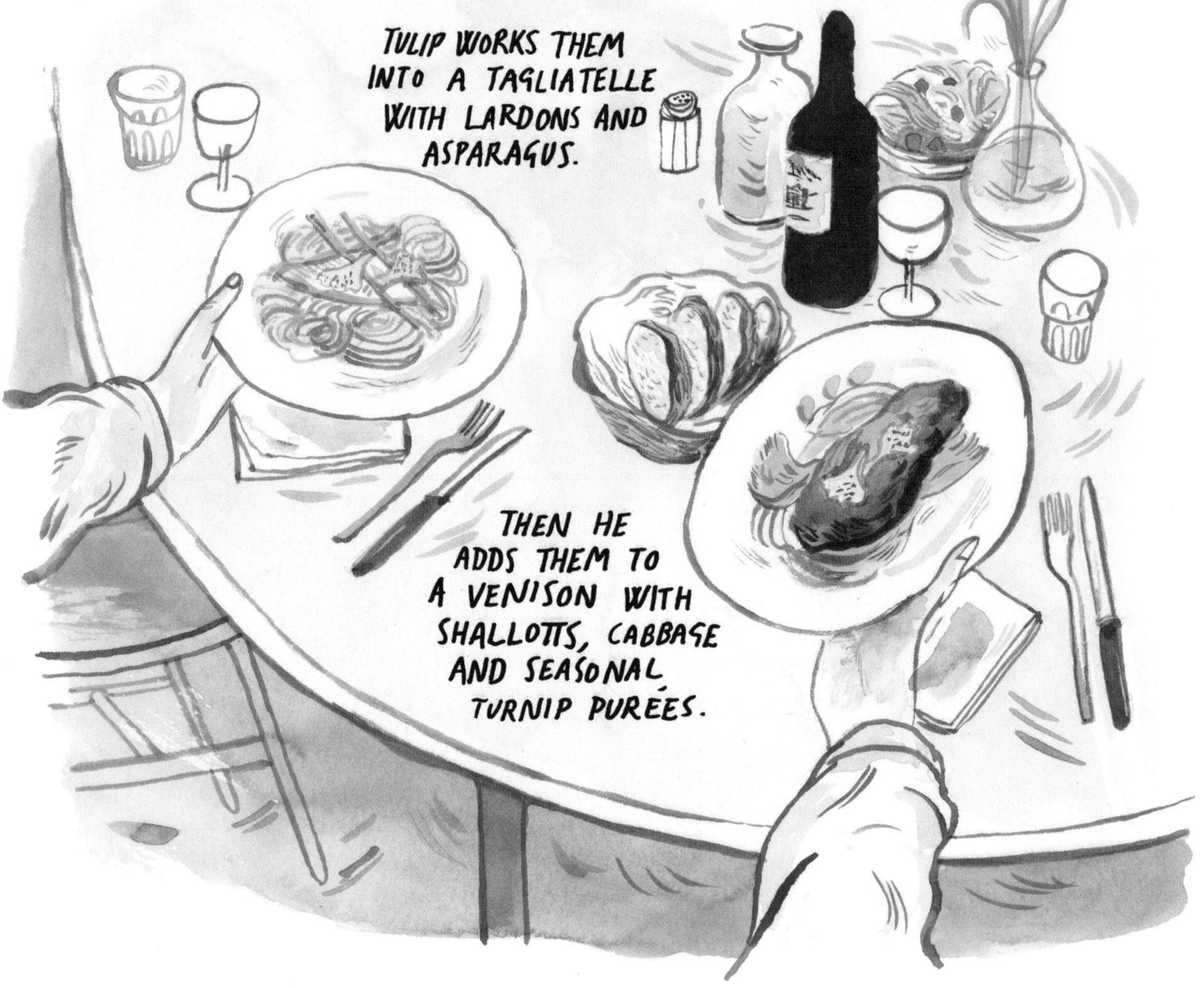
TULIP WORKS THEM INTO A TAGLIATELLE WITH LARDONS AND ASPARAGUS.
THEN HE ADDS THEM TO A VENISON WITH SHALLOTTS, CABBAGE AND SEASONAL TURNIP PURÉES.

EXHAUSTED COMMUTERS ARRIVE SLUMPING AT THEIR TABLES AND LEAVE READY TO FACE THE WORLD.

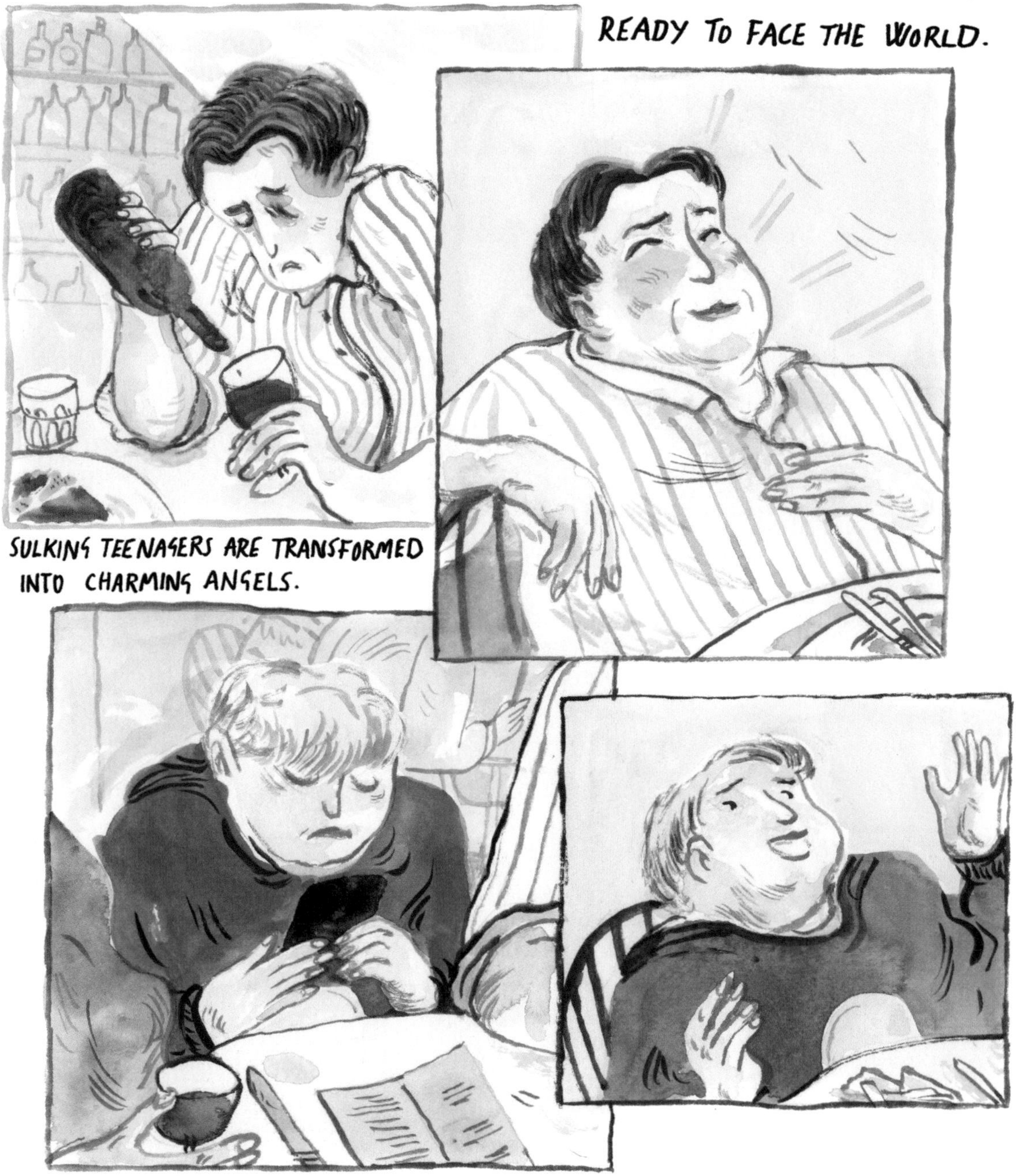
SULKING TEENAGERS ARE TRANSFORMED INTO CHARMING ANGELS.

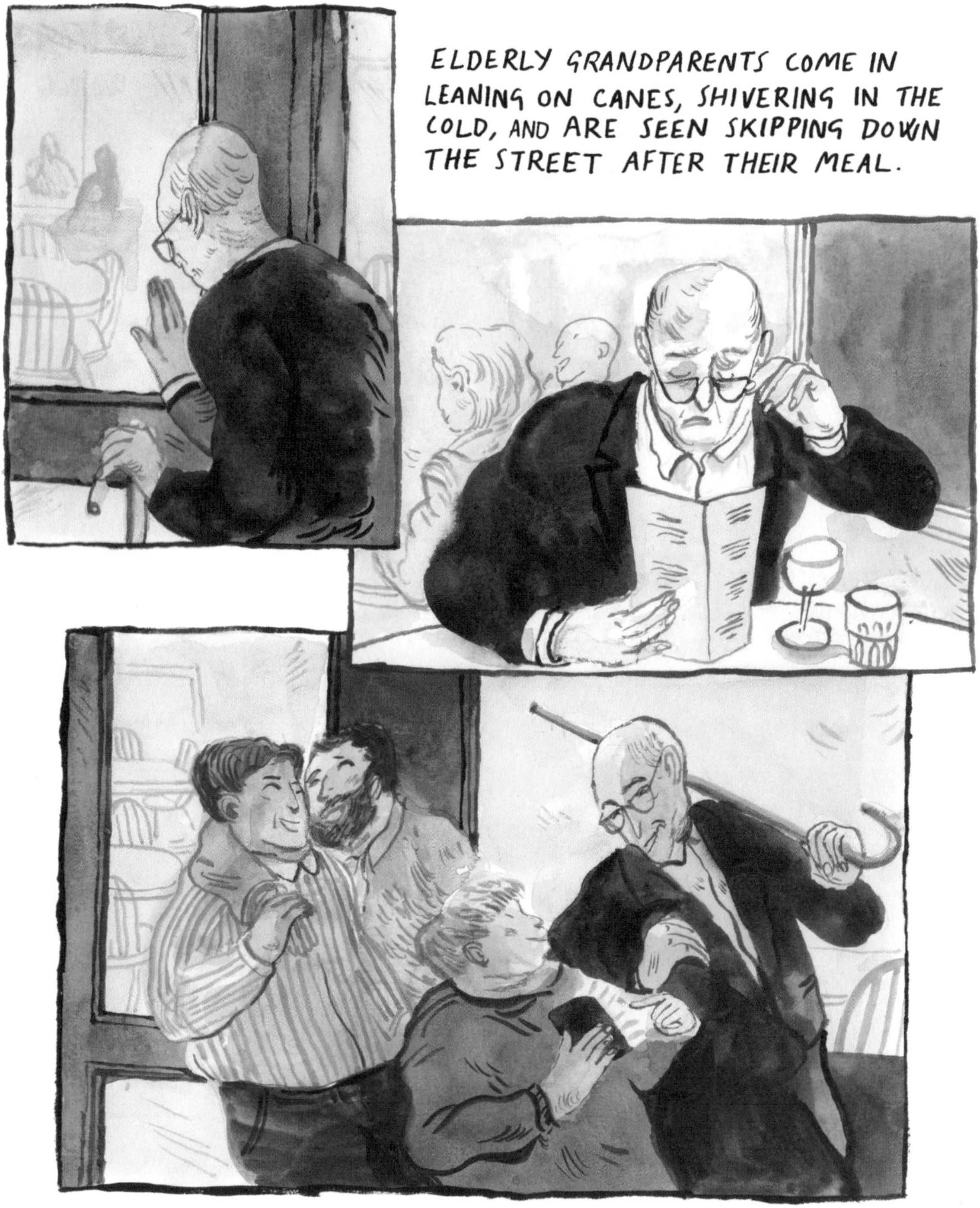
ELDERLY GRANDPARENTS COME IN LEANING ON CANES, SHIVERING IN THE COLD, AND ARE SEEN SKIPPING DOWN THE STREET AFTER THEIR MEAL.

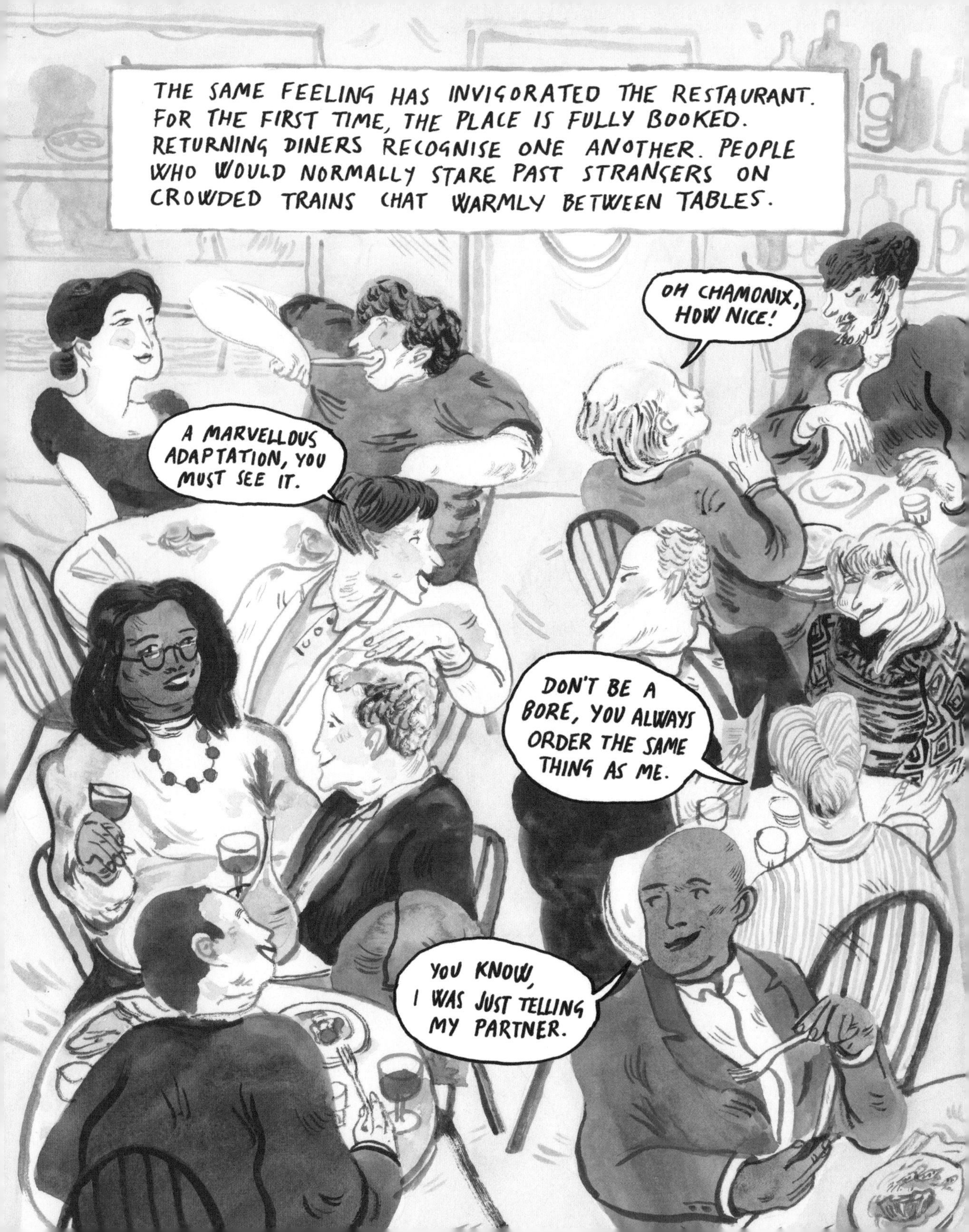
THE SAME FEELING HAS INVIGORATED THE RESTAURANT. FOR THE FIRST TIME, THE PLACE IS FULLY BOOKED. RETURNING DINERS RECOGNISE ONE ANOTHER. PEOPLE WHO WOULD NORMALLY STARE PAST STRANGERS ON CROWDED TRAINS CHAT WARMLY BETWEEN TABLES.
OH CHAMONIX, HOW NICE!
A MARVELLOUS ADAPTATION, YOU MUST SEE IT.
DON'T BE A BORE, YOU ALWAYS ORDER THE SAME THING AS ME.
YOU KNOW, I WAS JUST TELLING MY PARTNER.

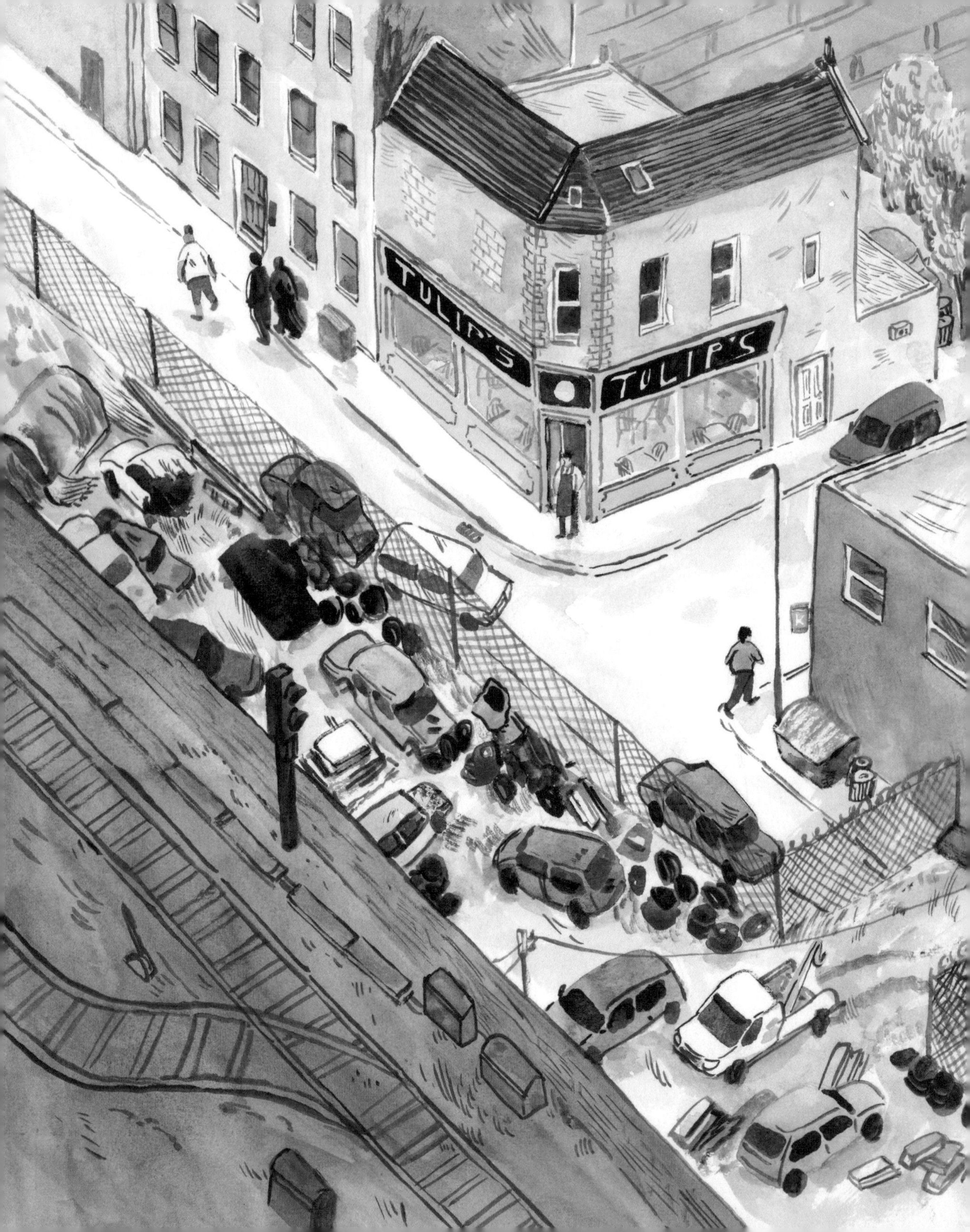
TULIP'S
TULIP'S

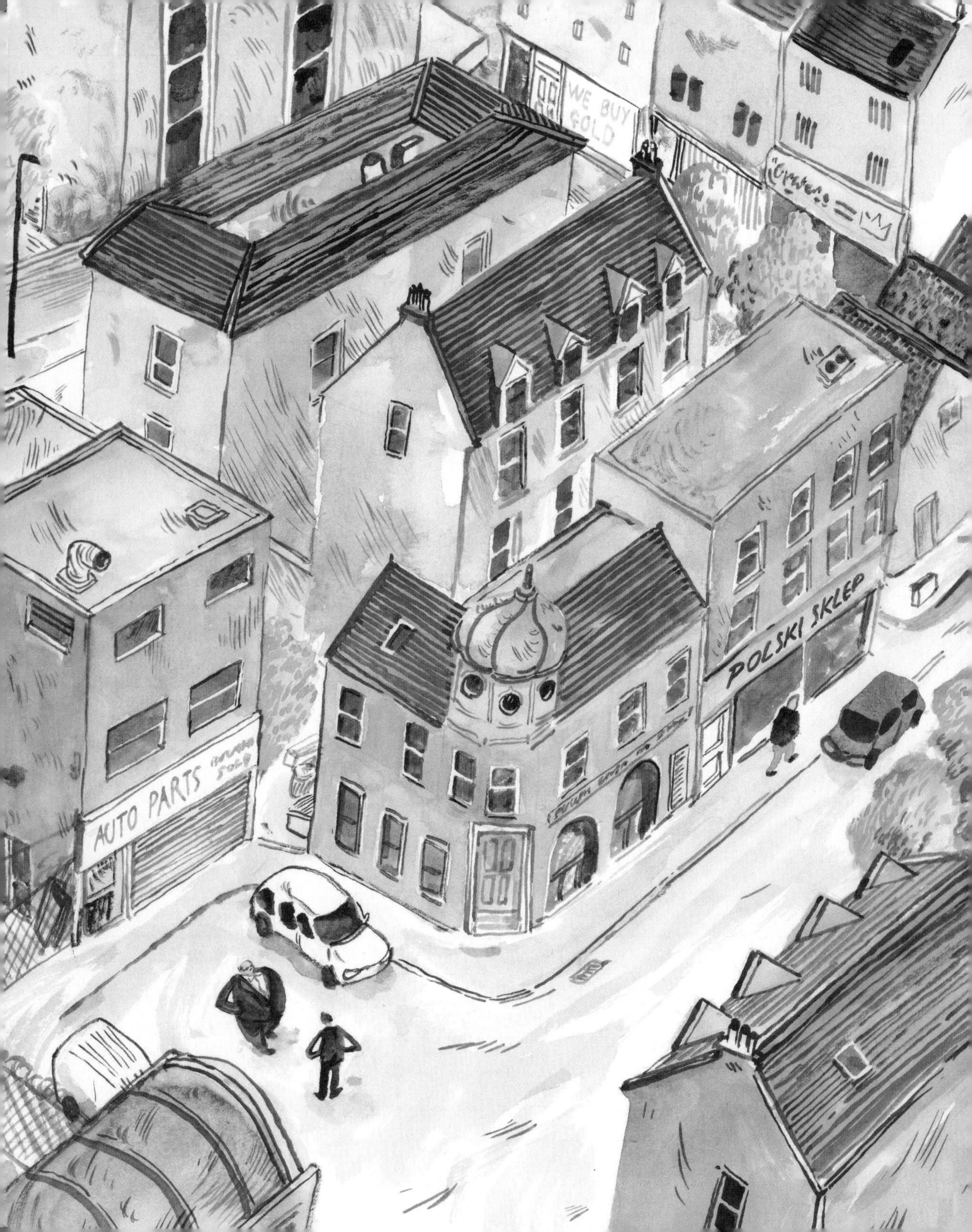
WE BUY GOLD
AUTO PARTS
POLSKI SKLEP

THE REWARD FOR GOOD WORK IS MORE WORK. TULIP IS ABLE TO HIRE MORE STAFF AND START OPENING AT LUNCHTIMES.

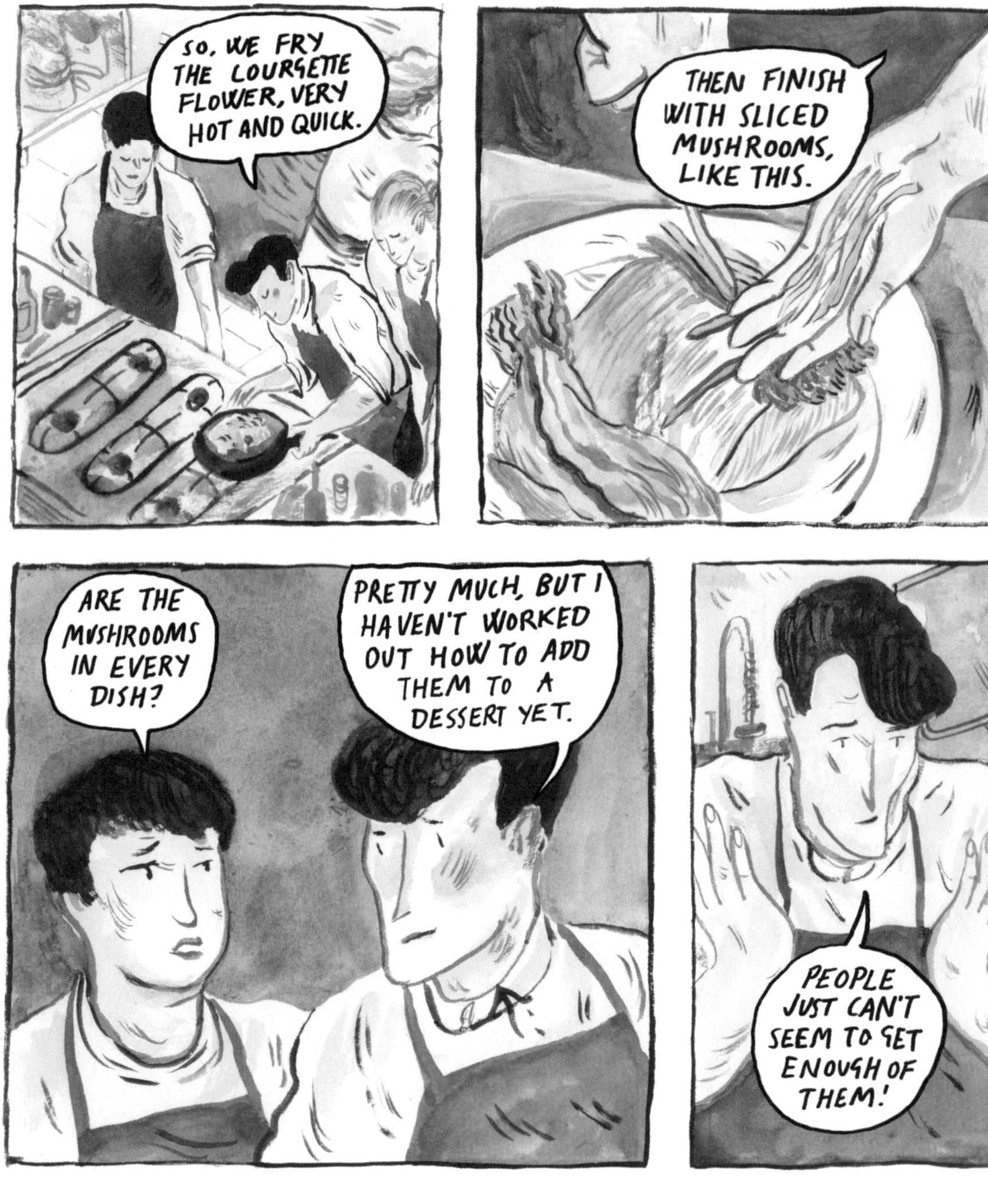
SO, WE FRY THE COURGETTE FLOWER, VERY HOT AND QUICK.
THEN FINISH WITH SLICED MUSHROOMS, LIKE THIS.
ARE THE MUSHROOMS IN EVERY DISH?
PRETTY MUCH, BUT I HAVEN'T WORKED OUT HOW TO ADD THEM TO A DESSERT YET.
PEOPLE JUST CAN'T SEEM TO GET ENOUGH OF THEM!

WHAT'S MORE, HE'S ABLE TO LEAVE HIS TINY ATTIC AND MOVE INTO A REAL FLAT.

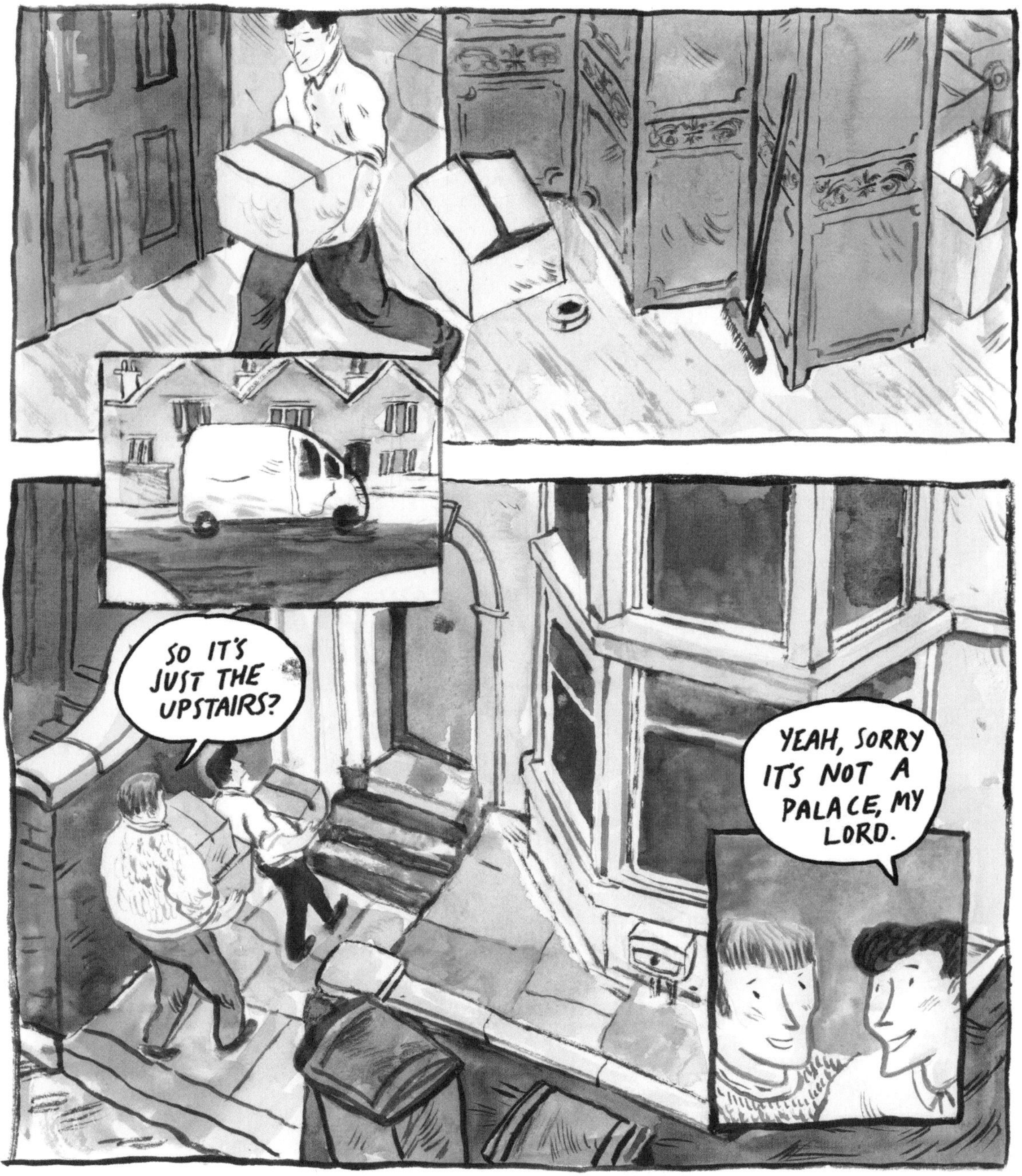
SO IT'S JUST THE UPSTAIRS?
YEAH, SORRY IT'S NOT A PALACE, MY LORD.

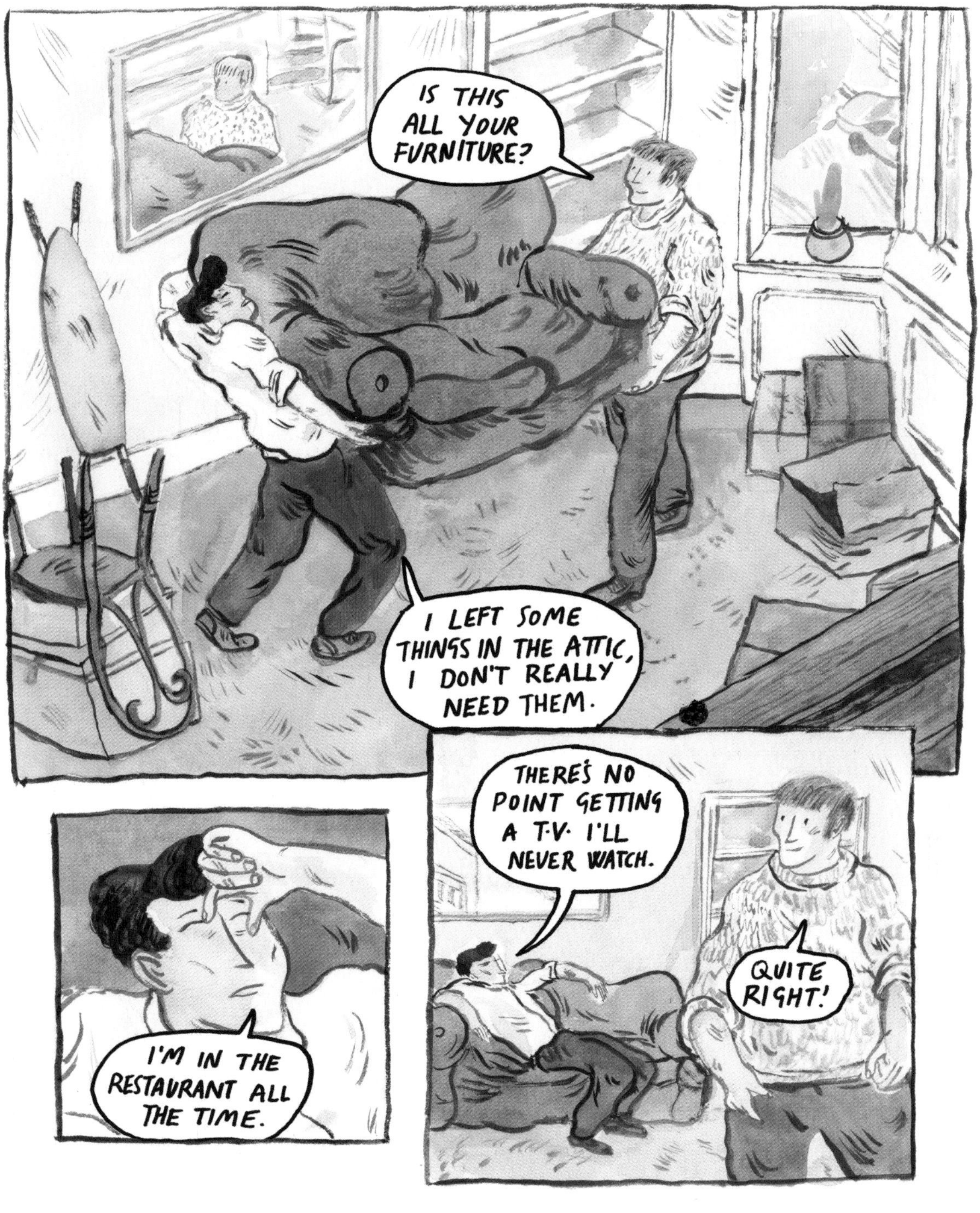
IS THIS ALL YOUR FURNITURE?
I LEFT SOME THINGS IN THE ATTIC, I DON'T REALLY NEED THEM.
I'M IN THE RESTAURANT ALL THE TIME.
THERE'S NO POINT GETTING A T.V. I'LL NEVER WATCH.
QUITE RIGHT!

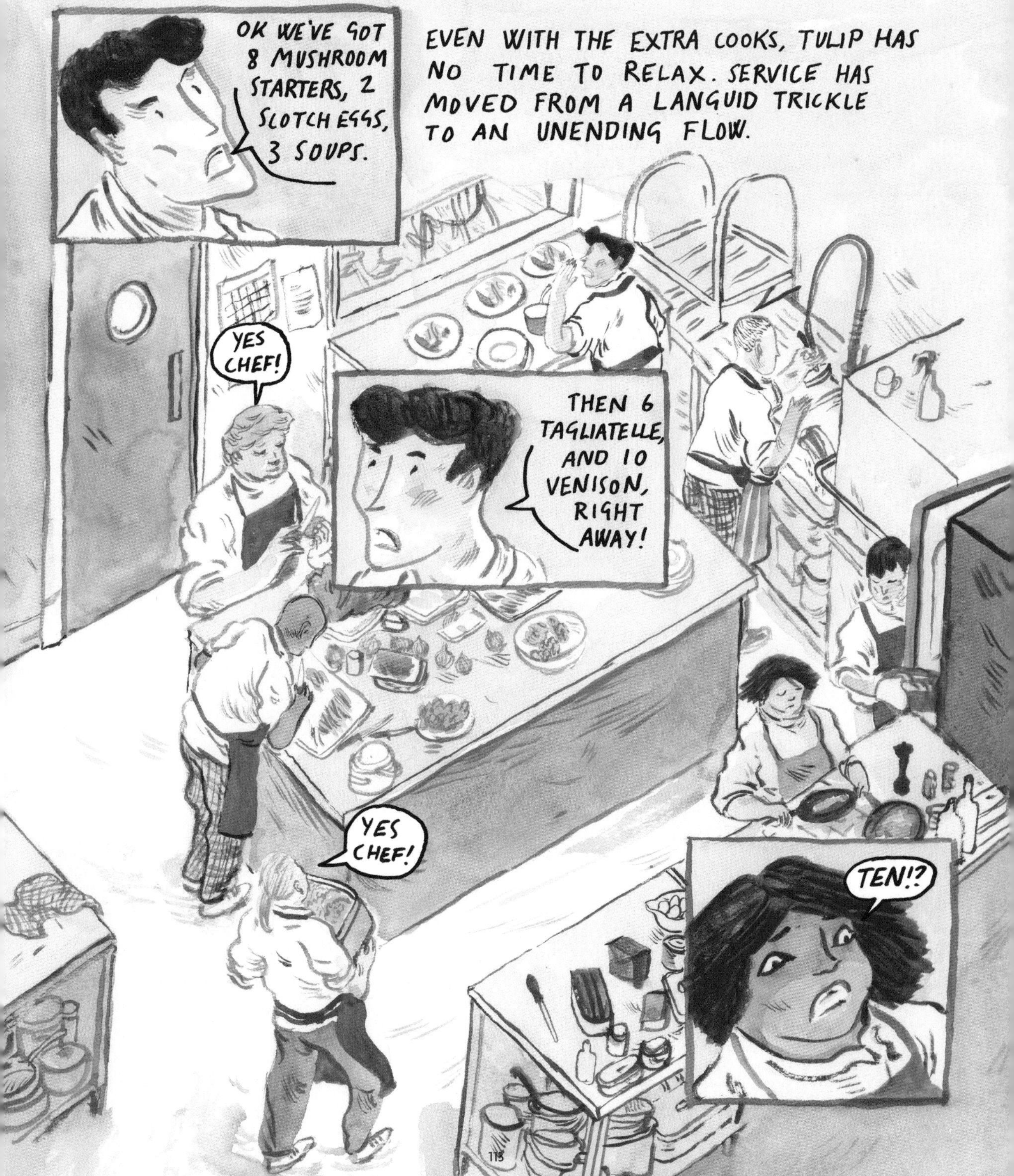
OK WE'VE GOT 8 MUSHROOM STARTERS, 2 SCOTCH EGGS, 3 SOUPS.
EVEN WITH THE EXTRA COOKS, TULIP HAS NO TIME TO RELAX. SERVICE HAS MOVED FROM A LANGUID TRICKLE TO AN UNENDING FLOW.
YES CHEF!
THEN 6 TAGLIATELLE, AND 10 VENISON, RIGHT AWAY!
YES CHEF!
TEN!?

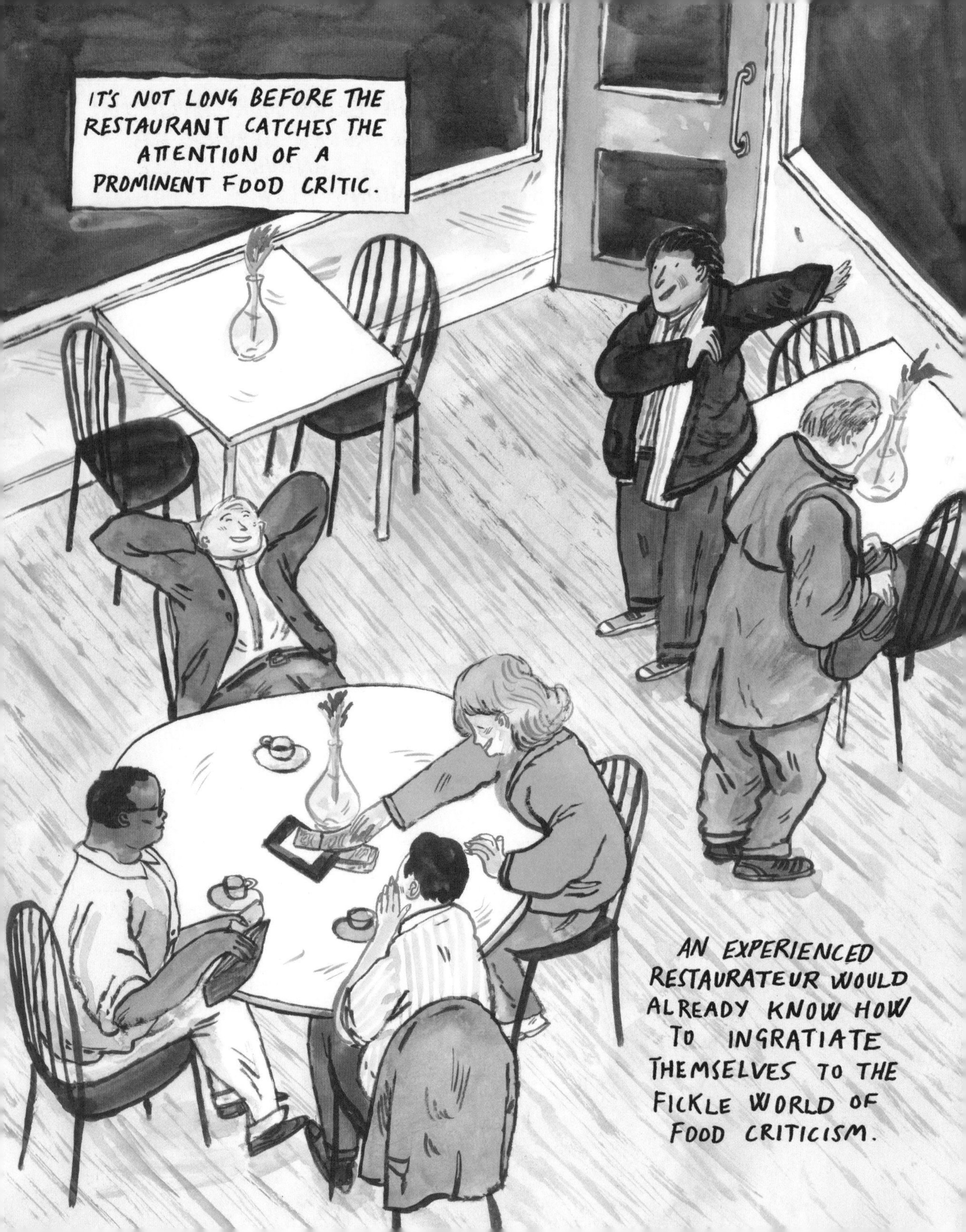
IT'S NOT LONG BEFORE THE RESTAURANT CATCHES THE ATTENTION OF A PROMINENT FOOD CRITIC.
AN EXPERIENCED RESTAURATEUR WOULD ALREADY KNOW HOW TO INGRATIATE THEMSELVES TO THE FICKLE WORLD OF FOOD CRITICISM.

FOR ALL OF HIS HARD WORK AND TALENT, THE REVIEW IS A GENUINE SURPRISE.

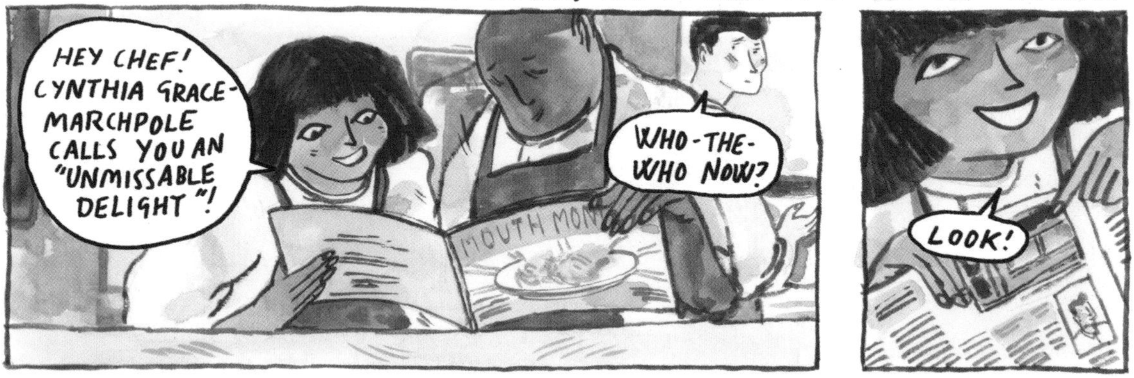
HEY CHEF! CYNTHIA GRACE-MARCHPOLE CALLS YOU AN "UNMISSABLE DELIGHT"!
WHO-THE-WHO NOW?
MOUTH MO
LOOK!

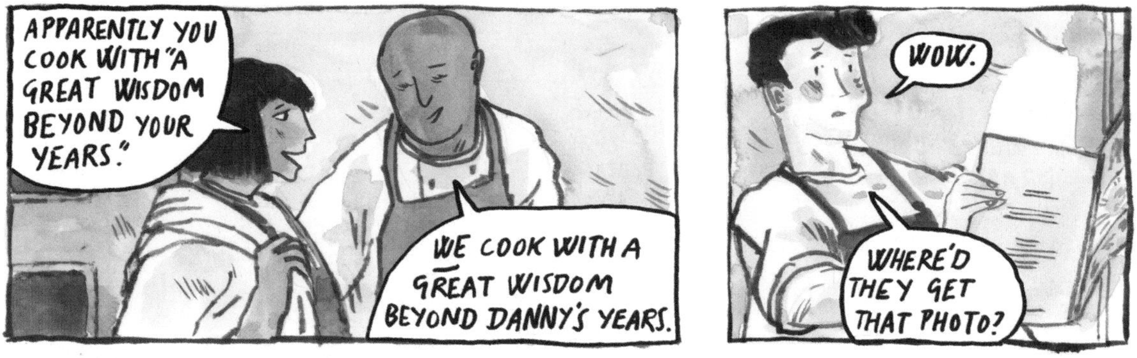
APPARENTLY YOU COOK WITH "A GREAT WISDOM BEYOND YOUR YEARS."
WE COOK WITH A GREAT WISDOM BEYOND DANNY'S YEARS.
WOW.
WHERE'D THEY GET THAT PHOTO?

SPURRED BY THE RECOMMENDATION, INTREPID FOODIES BEGIN TO LEAVE THE COMFORTS OF ISLINGTON AND STOKE NEWINGTON, AND MAKE A PILGRIMAGE TO DINE AT TULIP'S.

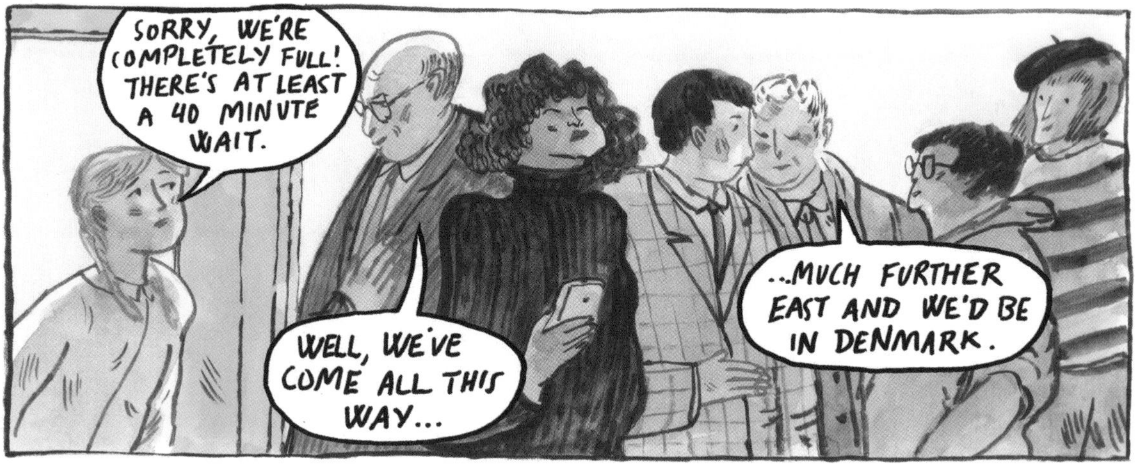
SORRY, WE'RE COMPLETELY FULL! THERE'S AT LEAST A 40 MINUTE WAIT.
WELL, WE'VE COME ALL THIS WAY...
...MUCH FURTHER EAST AND WE'D BE IN DENMARK.

NOW AS EACH EXHAUSTING SHIFT ENDS, TULIP AND HIS TEAM HAVE SOMETHING TO CELEBRATE.

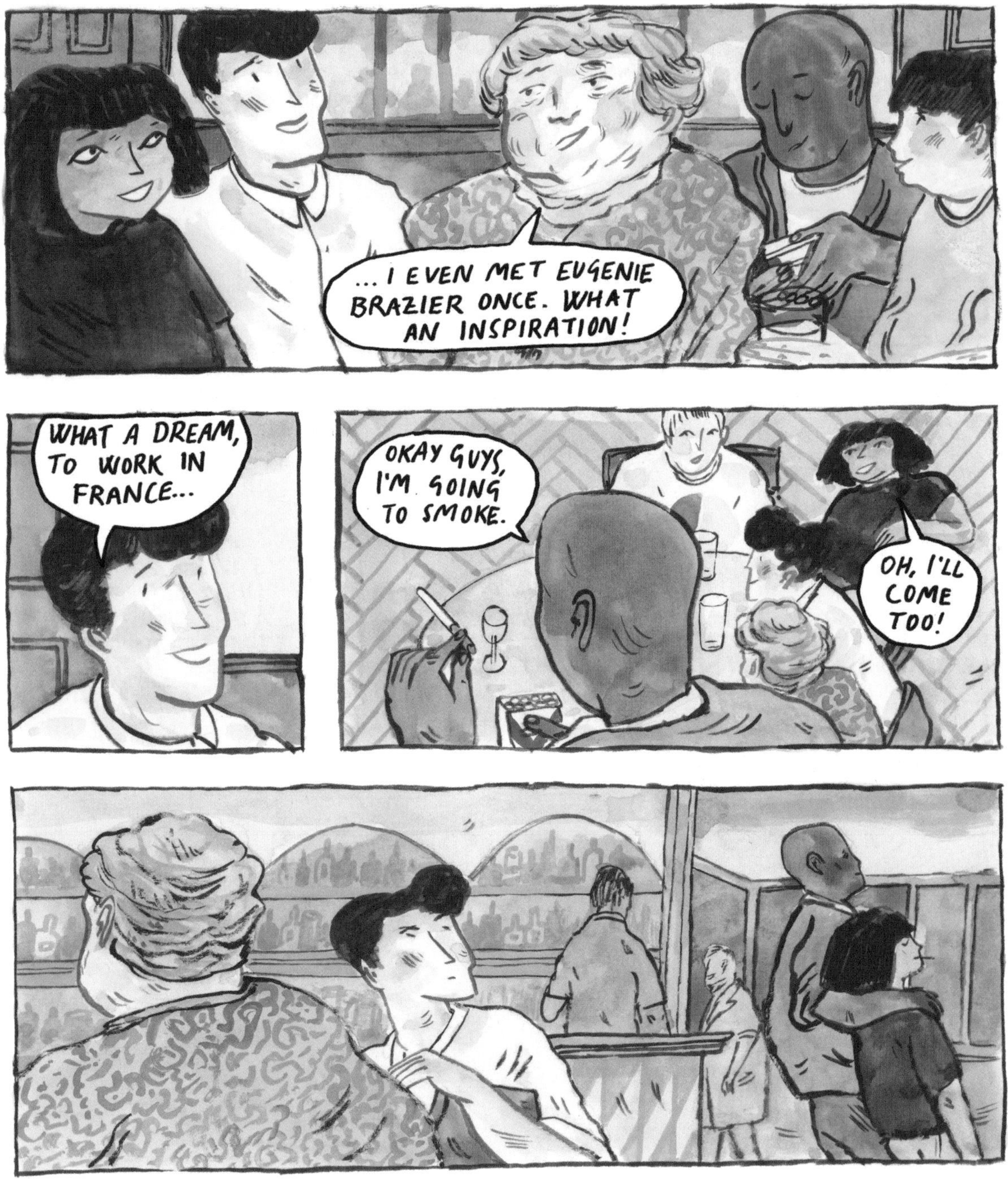
...I EVEN MET EUGENIE BRAZIER ONCE. WHAT AN INSPIRATION!
WHAT A DREAM, TO WORK IN FRANCE...
OKAY GUYS, I'M GOING TO SMOKE.
OH, I'LL COME TOO!

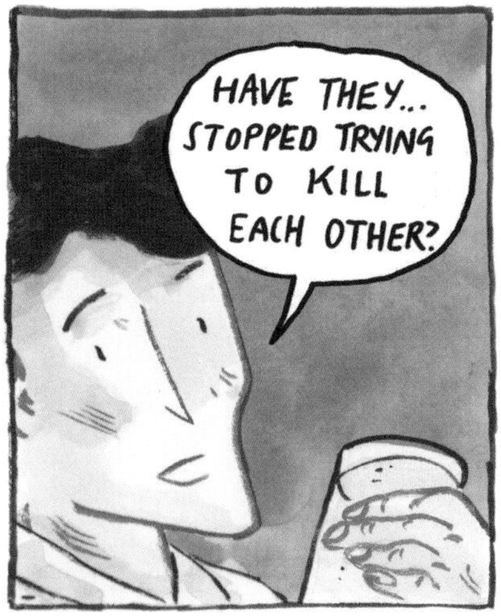
HAVE THEY... STOPPED TRYING TO KILL EACH OTHER?

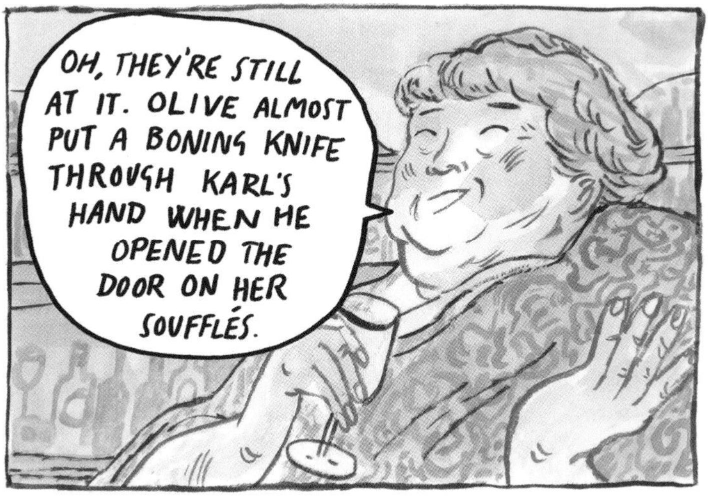
OH, THEY'RE STILL AT IT. OLIVE ALMOST PUT A BONING KNIFE THROUGH KARL'S HAND WHEN HE OPENED THE DOOR ON HER SOUFFLÉS.

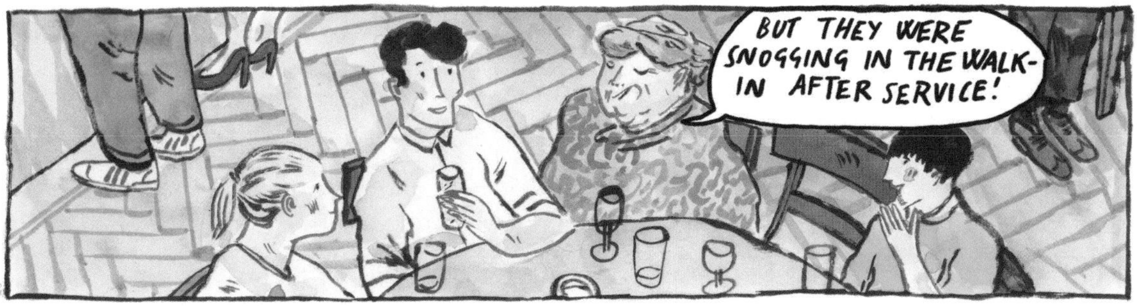
BUT THEY WERE SNOGGING IN THE WALK-IN AFTER SERVICE!

TULIP STARTS TO DEVELOP A TASTE FOR LONDON NIGHTLIFE.

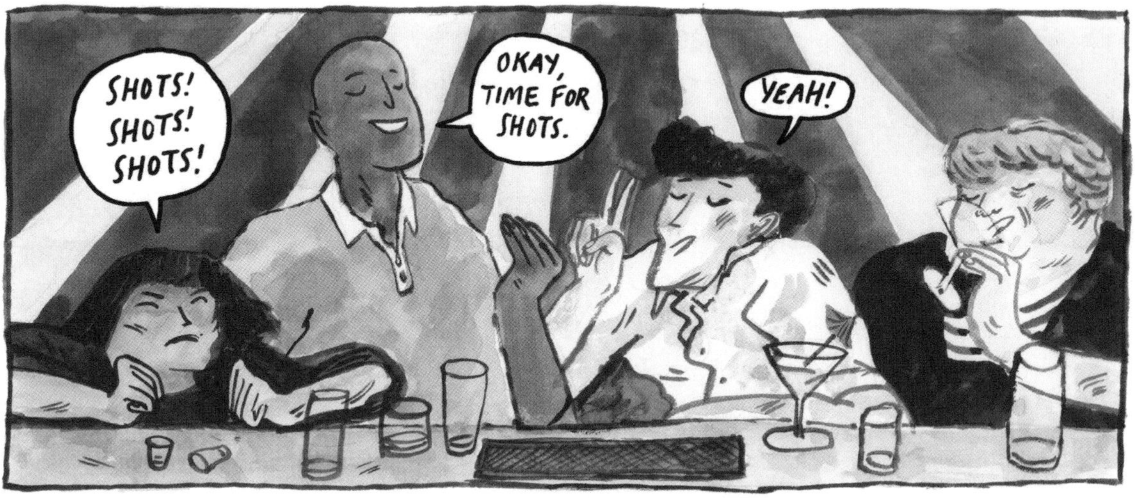
SHOTS! SHOTS! SHOTS!
OKAY, TIME FOR SHOTS.
YEAH!

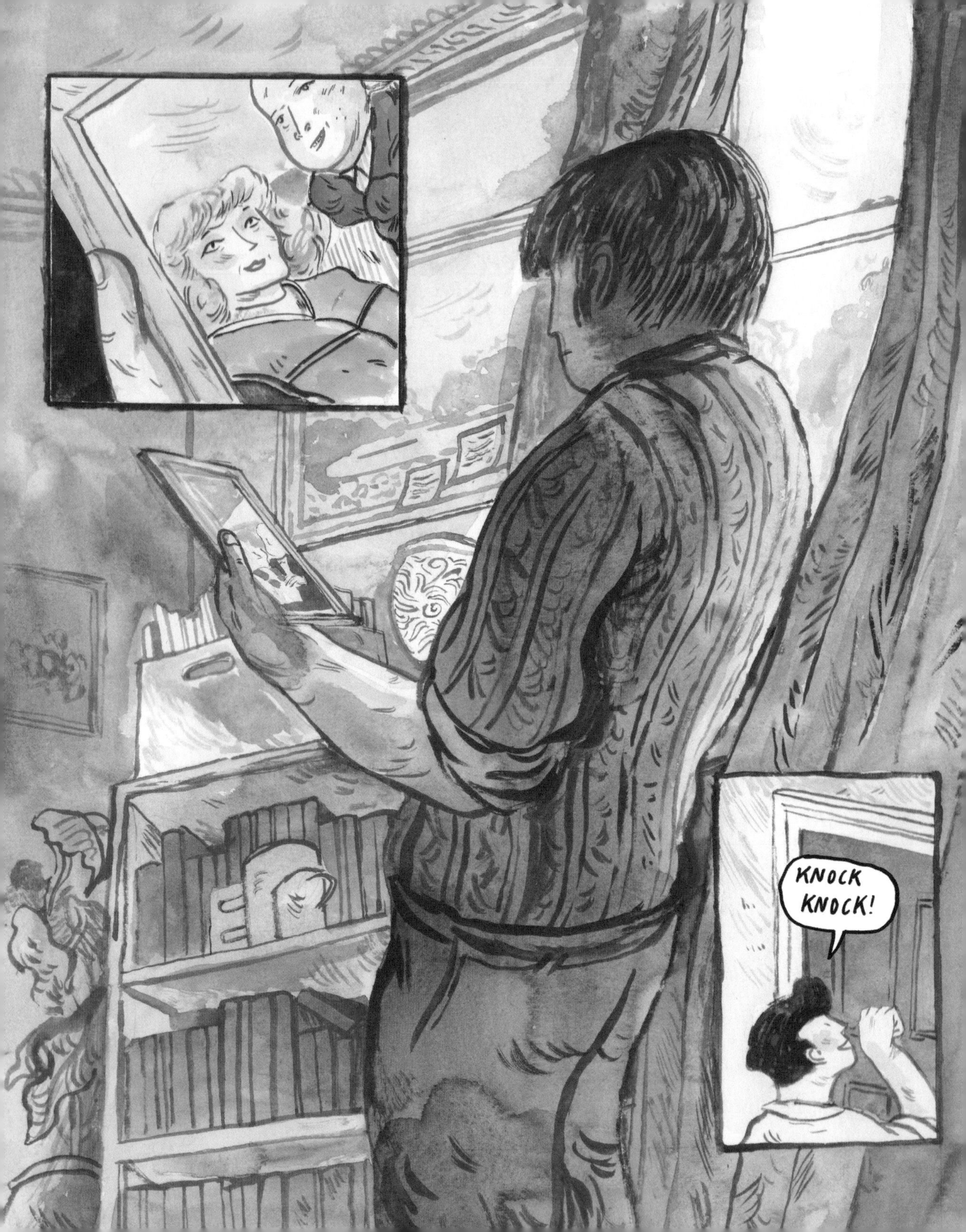
KNOCK KNOCK!

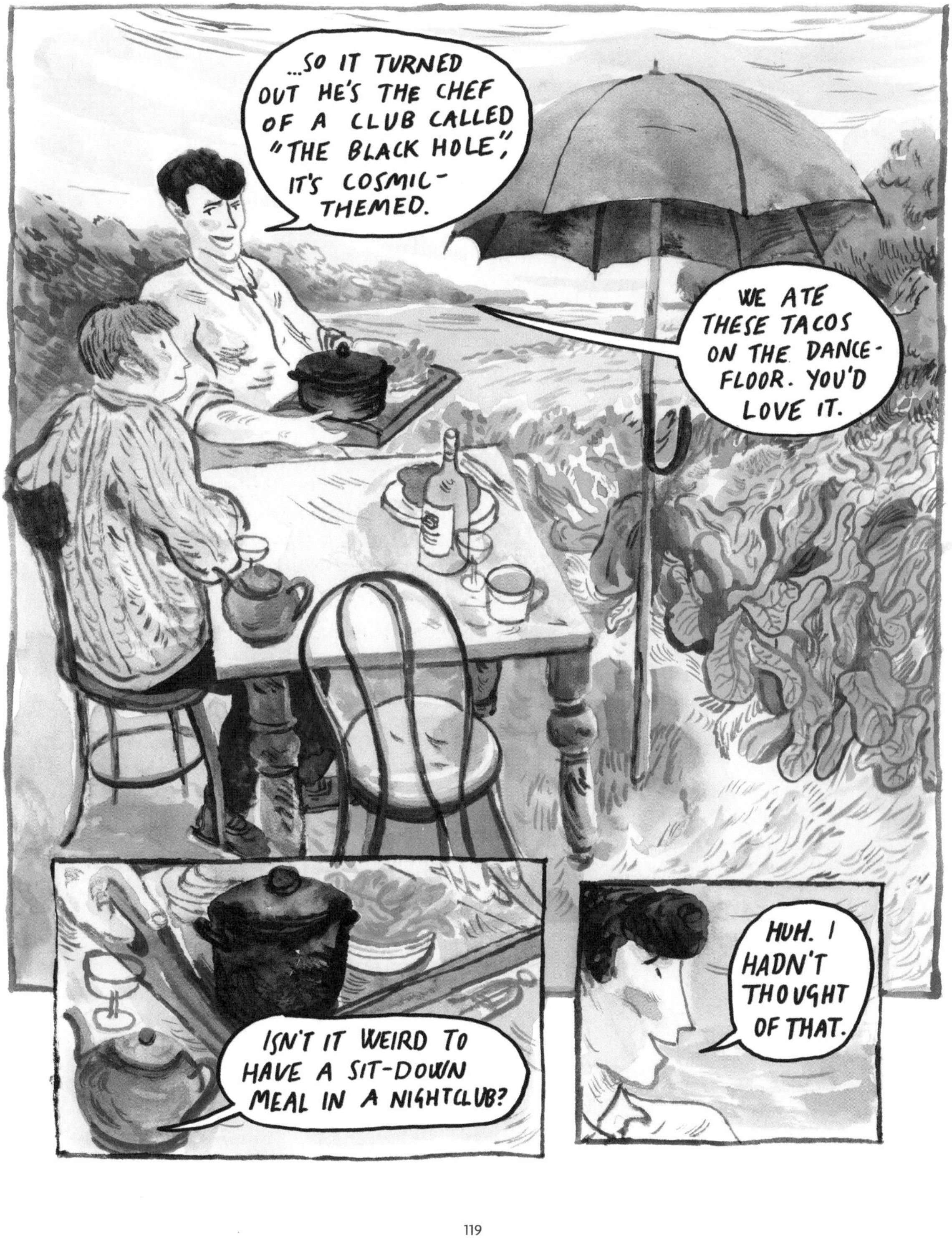
...SO IT TURNED OUT HE'S THE CHEF OF A CLUB CALLED "THE BLACK HOLE", IT'S COSMIC-THEMED.
WE ATE THESE TACOS ON THE DANCE-FLOOR. YOU'D LOVE IT.
ISN'T IT WEIRD TO HAVE A SIT-DOWN MEAL IN A NIGHTCLUB?
HUH. I HADN'T THOUGHT OF THAT.

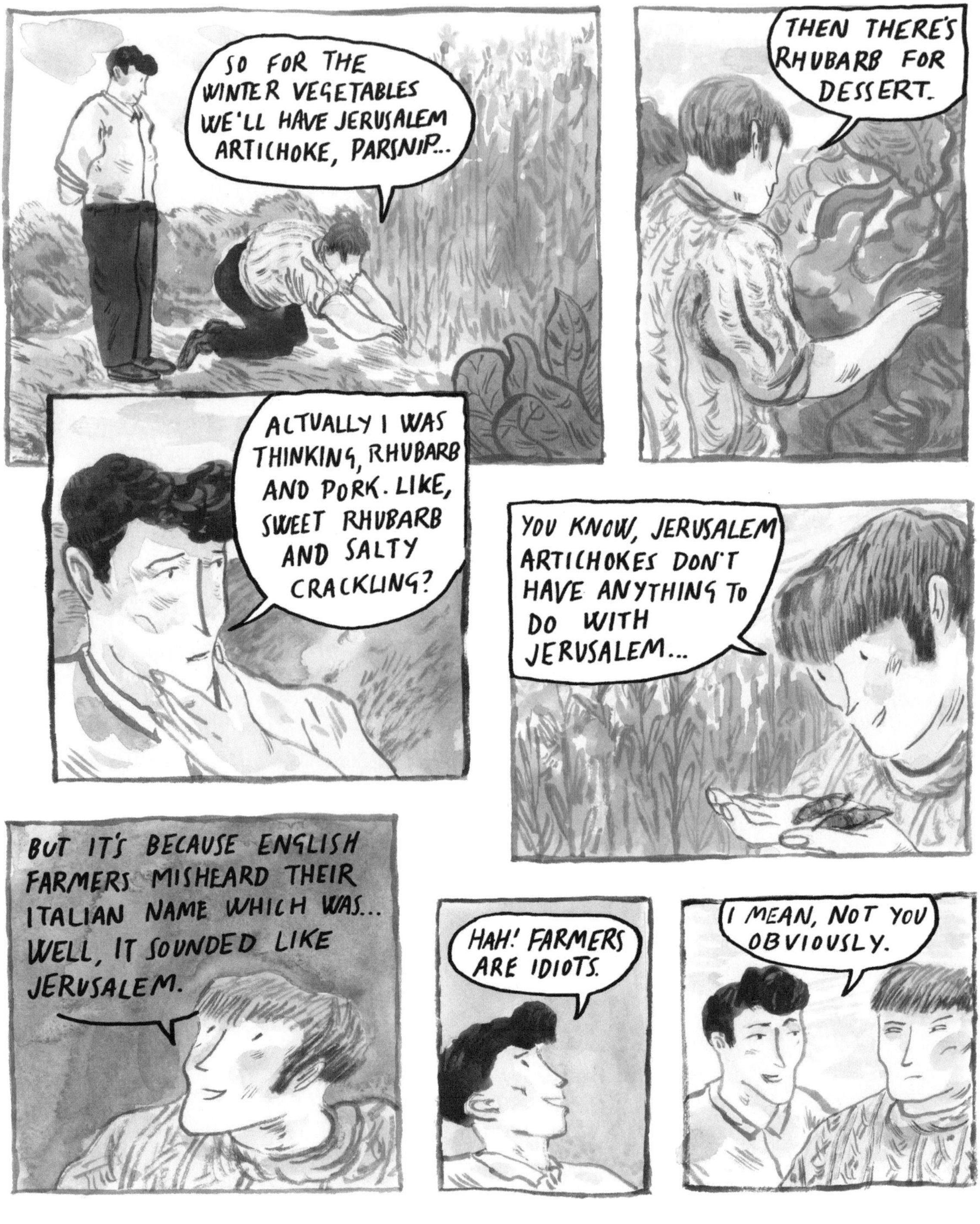
SO FOR THE WINTER VEGETABLES WE'LL HAVE JERUSALEM ARTICHOKE, PARSNIP...
THEN THERE'S RHUBARB FOR DESSERT.
ACTUALLY I WAS THINKING, RHUBARB AND PORK. LIKE, SWEET RHUBARB AND SALTY CRACKLING?
YOU KNOW, JERUSALEM ARTICHOKES DON'T HAVE ANYTHING TO DO WITH JERUSALEM...
BUT IT'S BECAUSE ENGLISH FARMERS MISHEARD THEIR ITALIAN NAME WHICH WAS... WELL, IT SOUNDED LIKE JERUSALEM.
HAH! FARMERS ARE IDIOTS.
I MEAN, NOT YOU OBVIOUSLY.

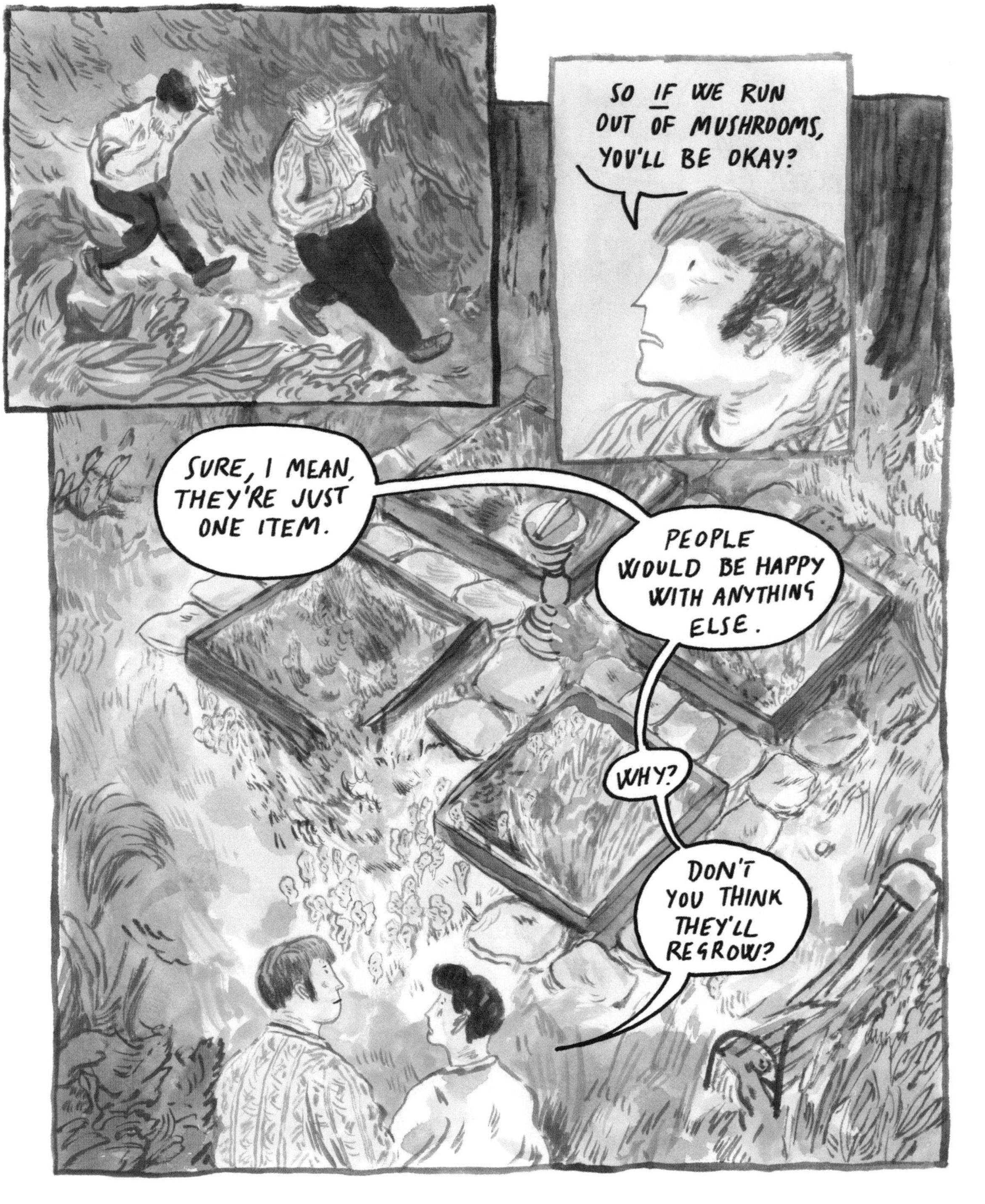
SO IF WE RUN OUT OF MUSHROOMS, YOU'LL BE OKAY?
SURE, I MEAN, THEY'RE JUST ONE ITEM.
PEOPLE WOULD BE HAPPY WITH ANYTHING ELSE.
WHY?
DON'T YOU THINK THEY'LL REGROW?

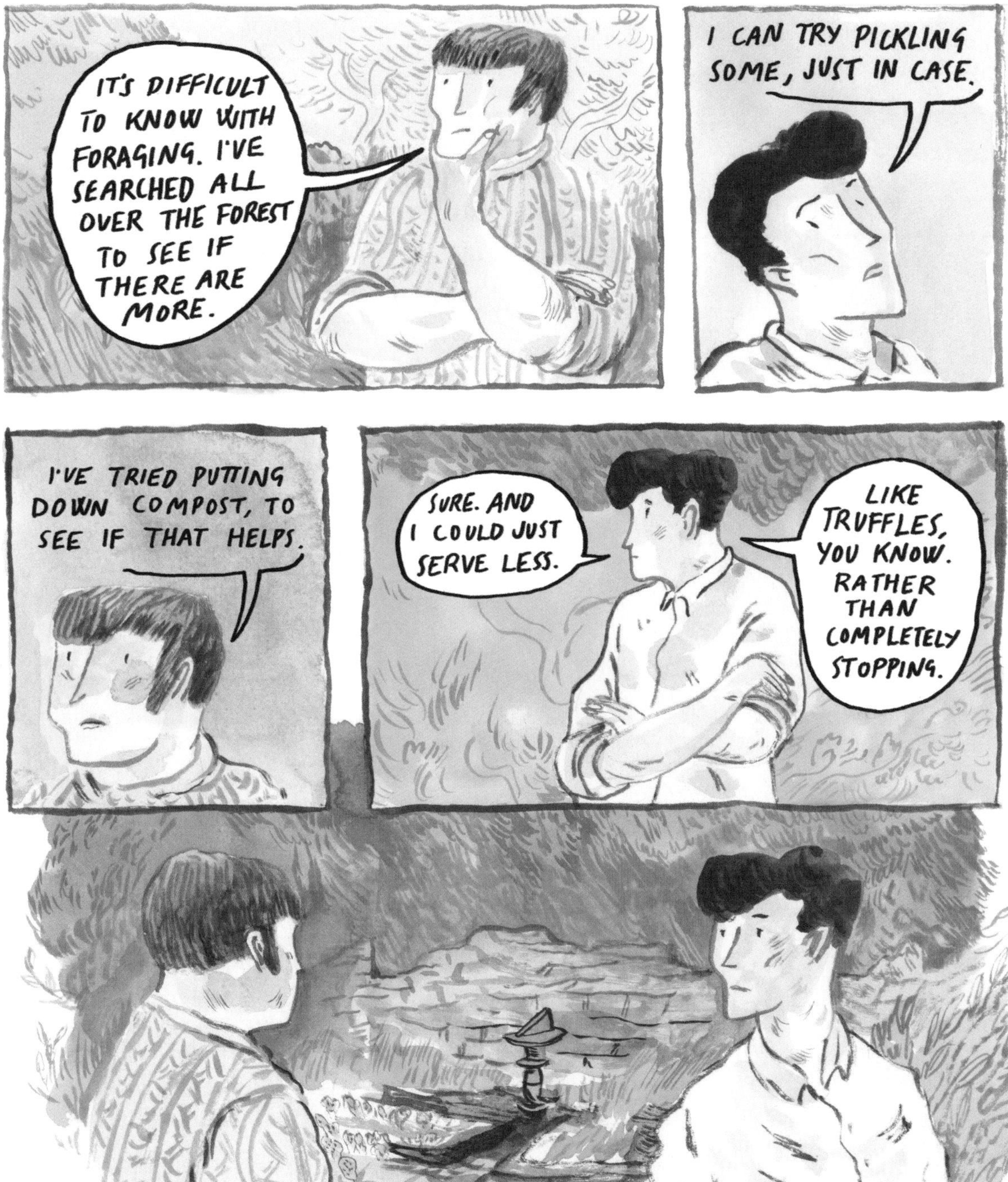
IT'S DIFFICULT TO KNOW WITH FORAGING. I'VE SEARCHED ALL OVER THE FOREST TO SEE IF THERE ARE MORE.
I CAN TRY PICKLING SOME, JUST IN CASE.
I'VE TRIED PUTTING DOWN COMPOST, TO SEE IF THAT HELPS.
SURE. AND I COULD JUST SERVE LESS.
LIKE TRUFFLES, YOU KNOW. RATHER THAN COMPLETELY STOPPING.

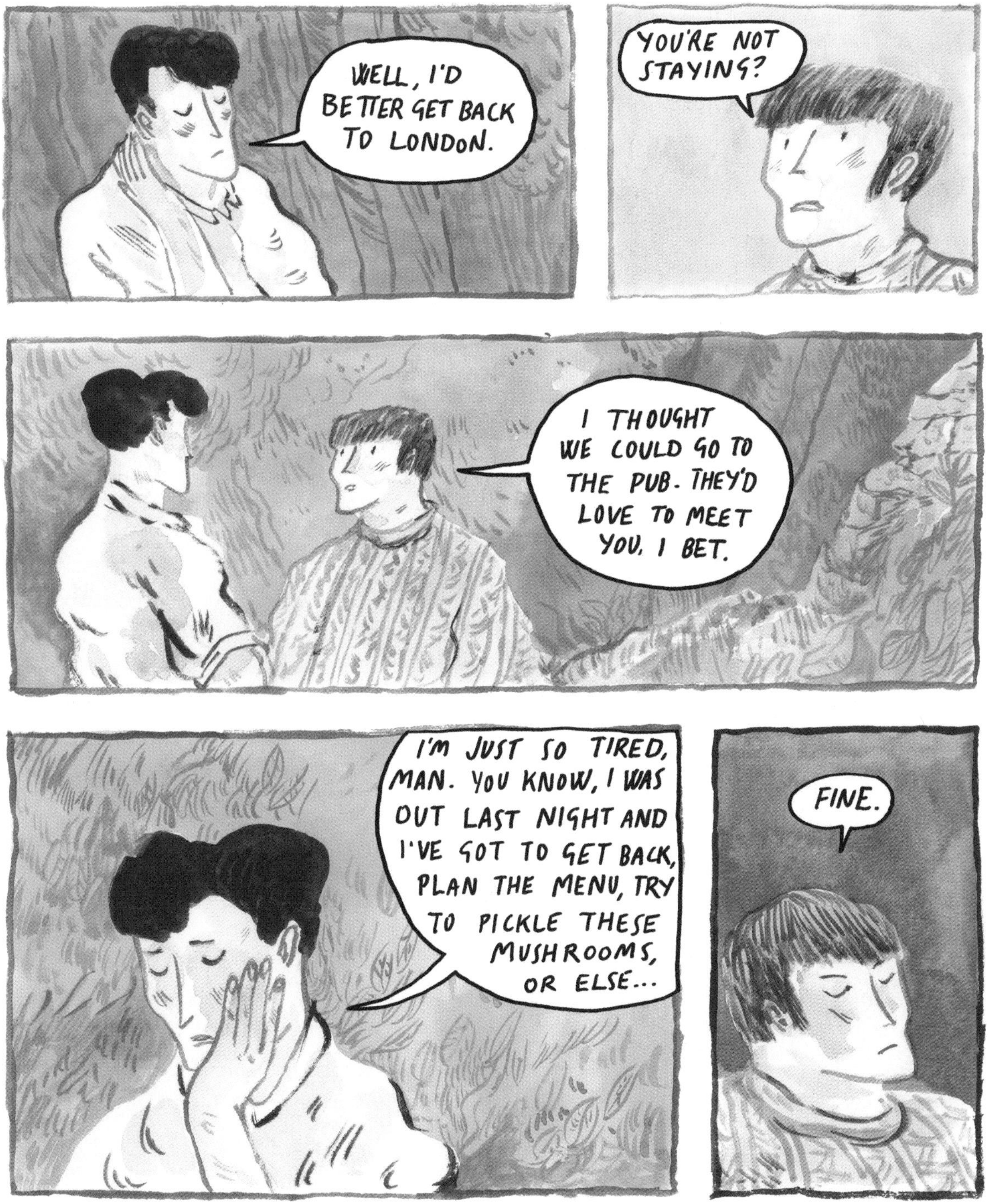
WELL, I'D BETTER GET BACK TO LONDON.
YOU'RE NOT STAYING?
I THOUGHT WE COULD GO TO THE PUB. THEY'D LOVE TO MEET YOU, I BET.
I'M JUST SO TIRED, MAN. YOU KNOW, I WAS OUT LAST NIGHT AND I'VE GOT TO GET BACK, PLAN THE MENU, TRY TO PICKLE THESE MUSHROOMS, OR ELSE...
FINE.

THE LACK OF MUSHROOMS HAS TULIP ON EDGE AGAIN. WORRY RETURNS LIKE HUNGER. HIS SUCCESS, HIS CUSTOMERS, HIS REVIEWS MIGHT BE SOOTHING FOR NOW, BUT HE STRUGGLES TO HIDE HIS GROWING NEED FOR VALIDATION, GNAWING SOMEWHERE BEYOND HIS STOMACH.

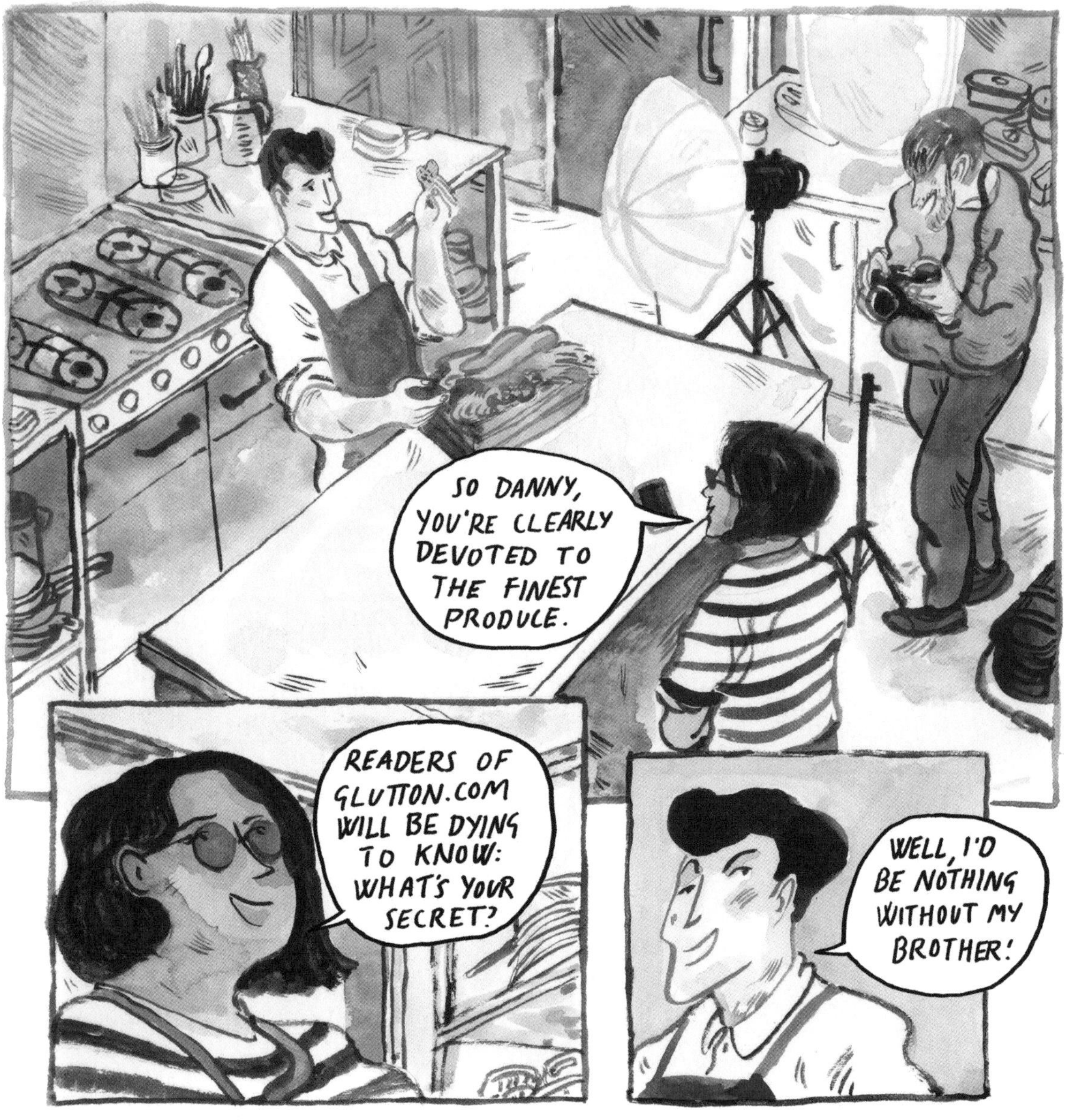
SO DANNY, YOU'RE CLEARLY DEVOTED TO THE FINEST PRODUCE.
READERS OF GLUTTON.COM WILL BE DYING TO KNOW: WHAT'S YOUR SECRET?
WELL, I'D BE NOTHING WITHOUT MY BROTHER!

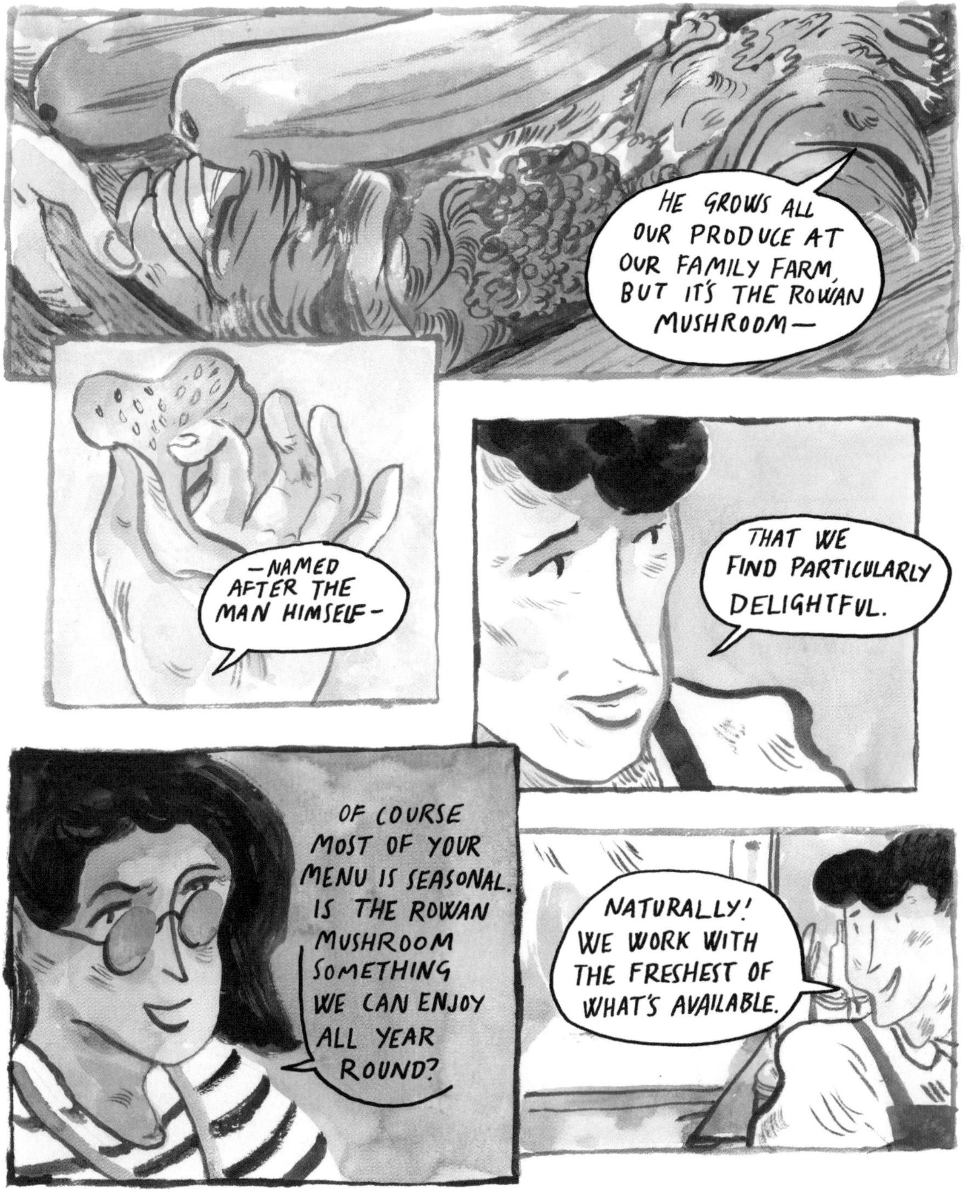
HE GROWS ALL OUR PRODUCE AT OUR FAMILY FARM, BUT IT'S THE ROWAN MUSHROOM—
—NAMED AFTER THE MAN HIMSELF—
THAT WE FIND PARTICULARLY DELIGHTFUL.
OF COURSE MOST OF YOUR MENU IS SEASONAL. IS THE ROWAN MUSHROOM SOMETHING WE CAN ENJOY ALL YEAR ROUND?
NATURALLY! WE WORK WITH THE FRESHEST OF WHAT'S AVAILABLE.

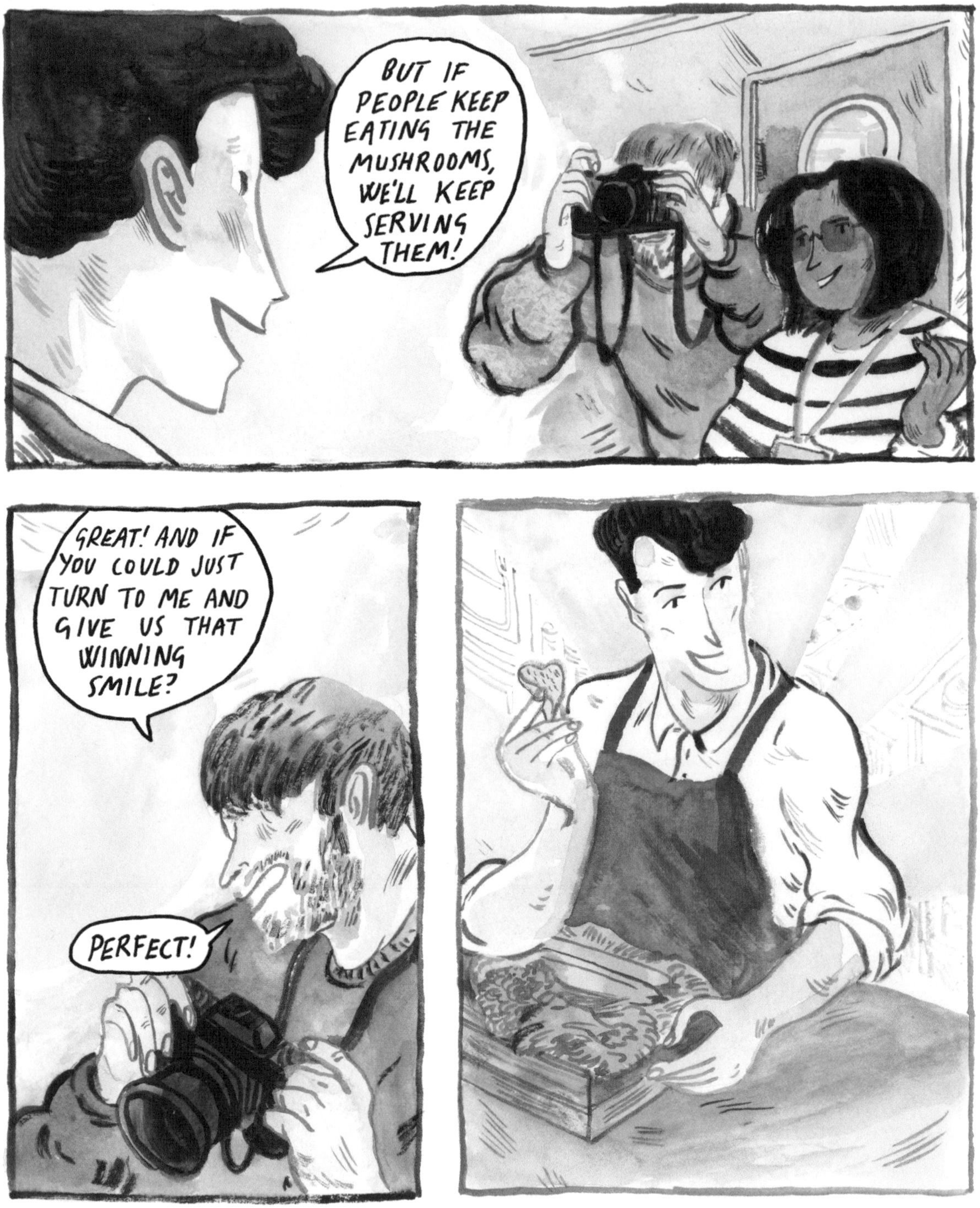
BUT IF PEOPLE KEEP EATING THE MUSHROOMS, WE'LL KEEP SERVING THEM!
GREAT! AND IF YOU COULD JUST TURN TO ME AND GIVE US THAT WINNING SMILE?
PERFECT!

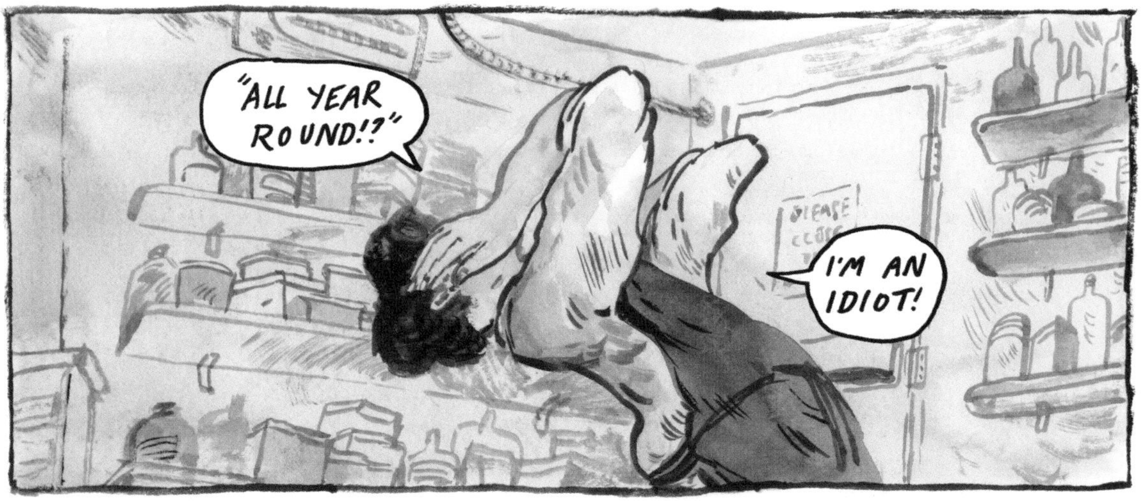
"ALL YEAR ROUND!?"
I'M AN IDIOT!

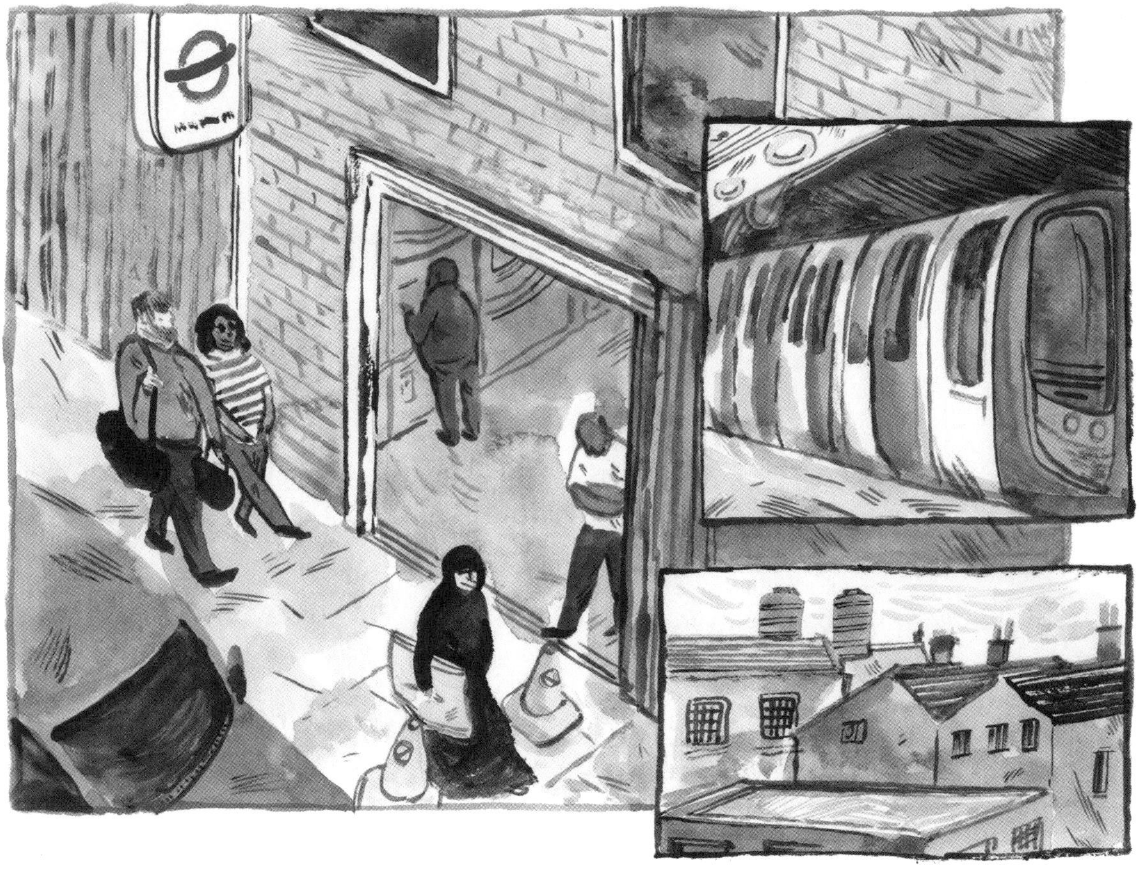

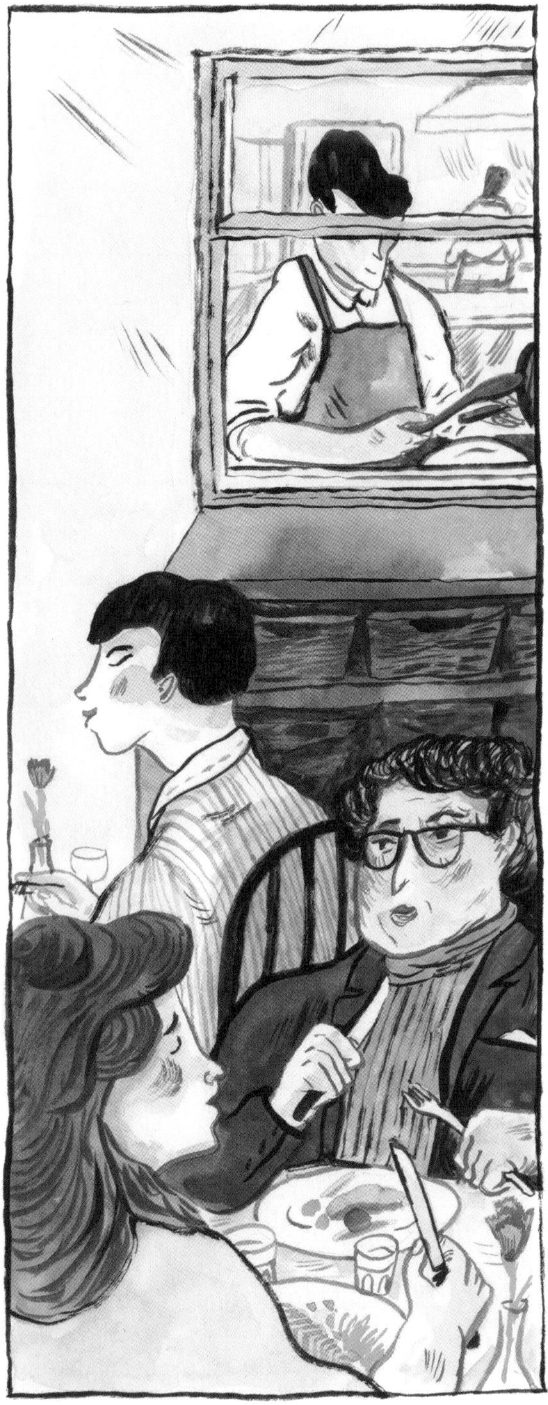
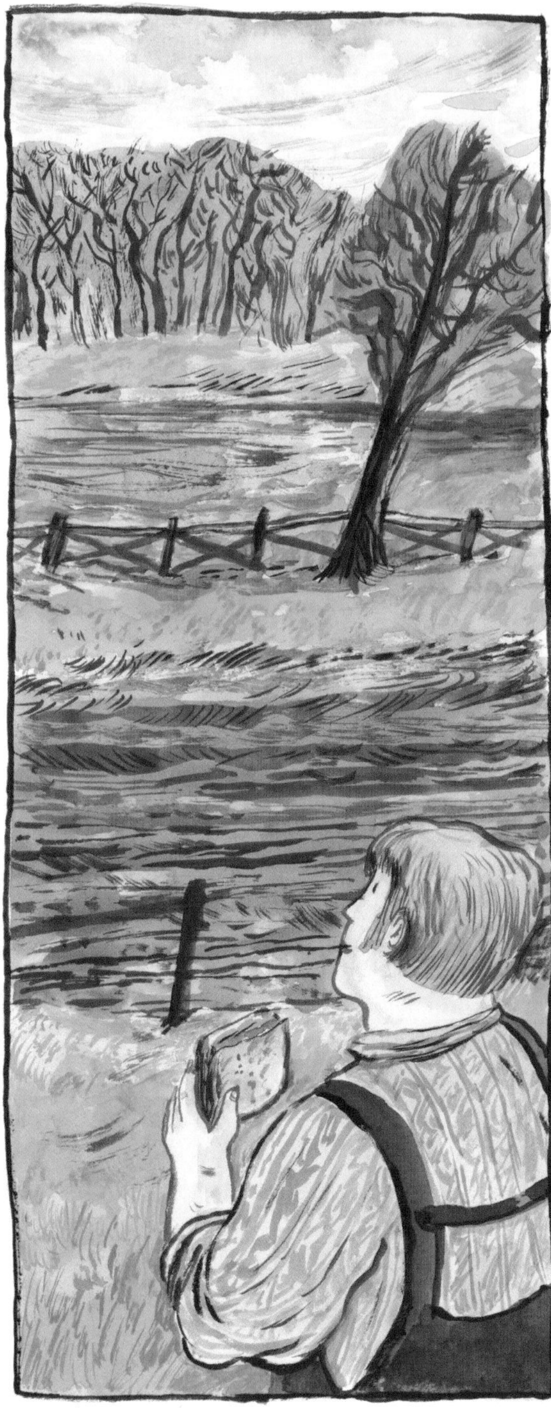

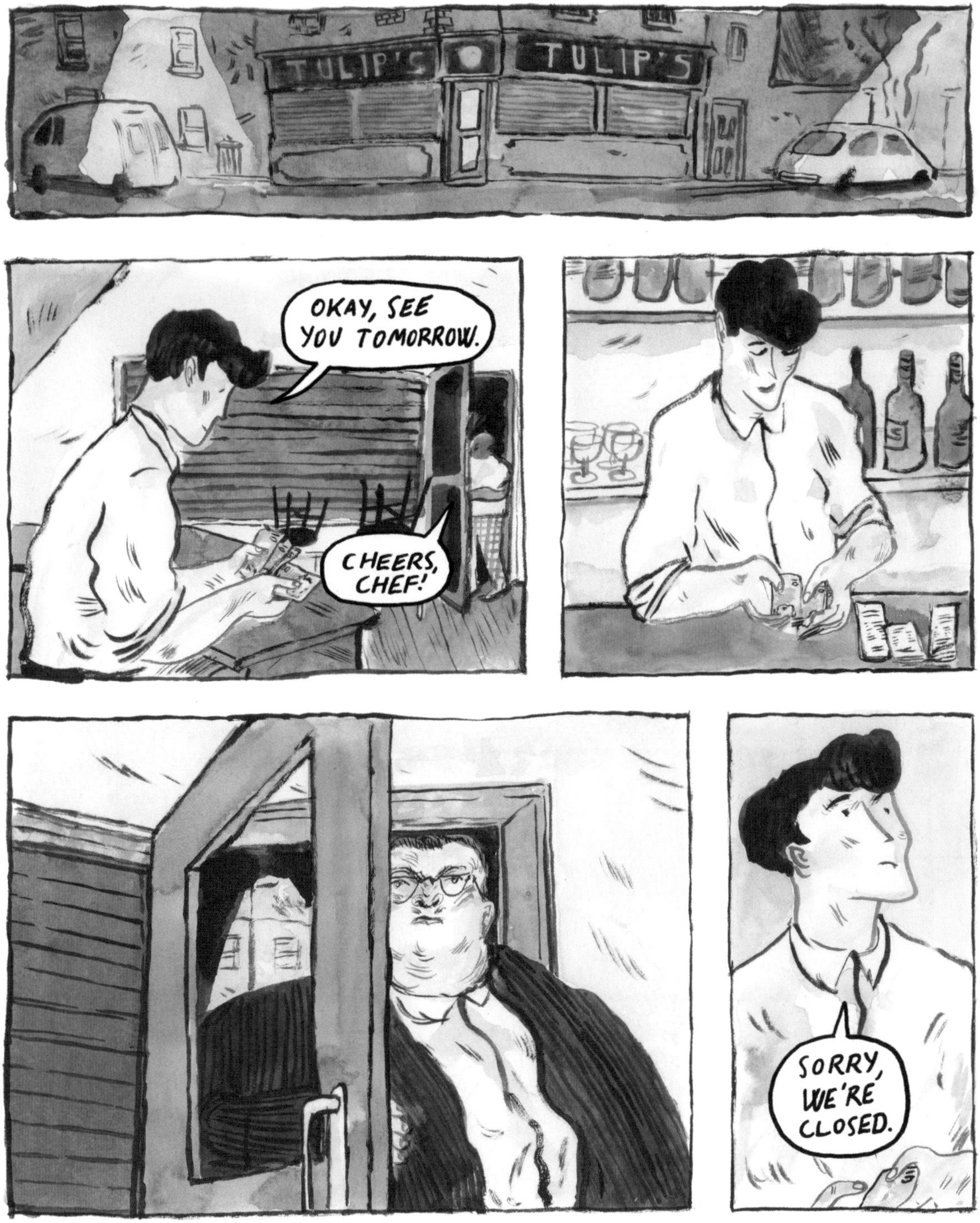
TULIP'S
TULIP'S
OKAY, SEE YOU TOMORROW.
CHEERS, CHEF!
SORRY, WE'RE CLOSED.

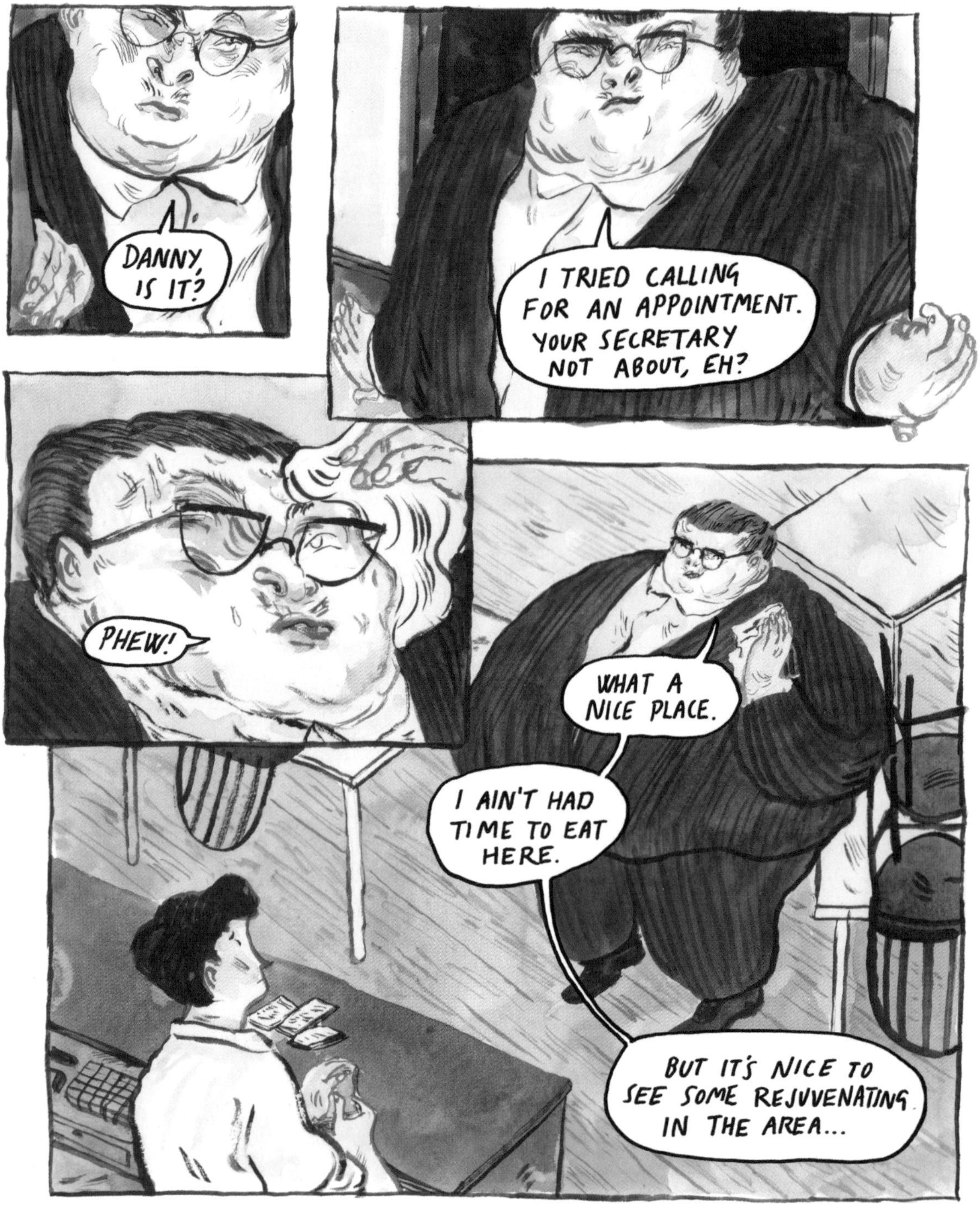
DANNY, IS IT?
I TRIED CALLING FOR AN APPOINTMENT. YOUR SECRETARY NOT ABOUT, EH?
PHEW!
WHAT A NICE PLACE.
I AIN'T HAD TIME TO EAT HERE.
BUT IT'S NICE TO SEE SOME REJUVENATING IN THE AREA...

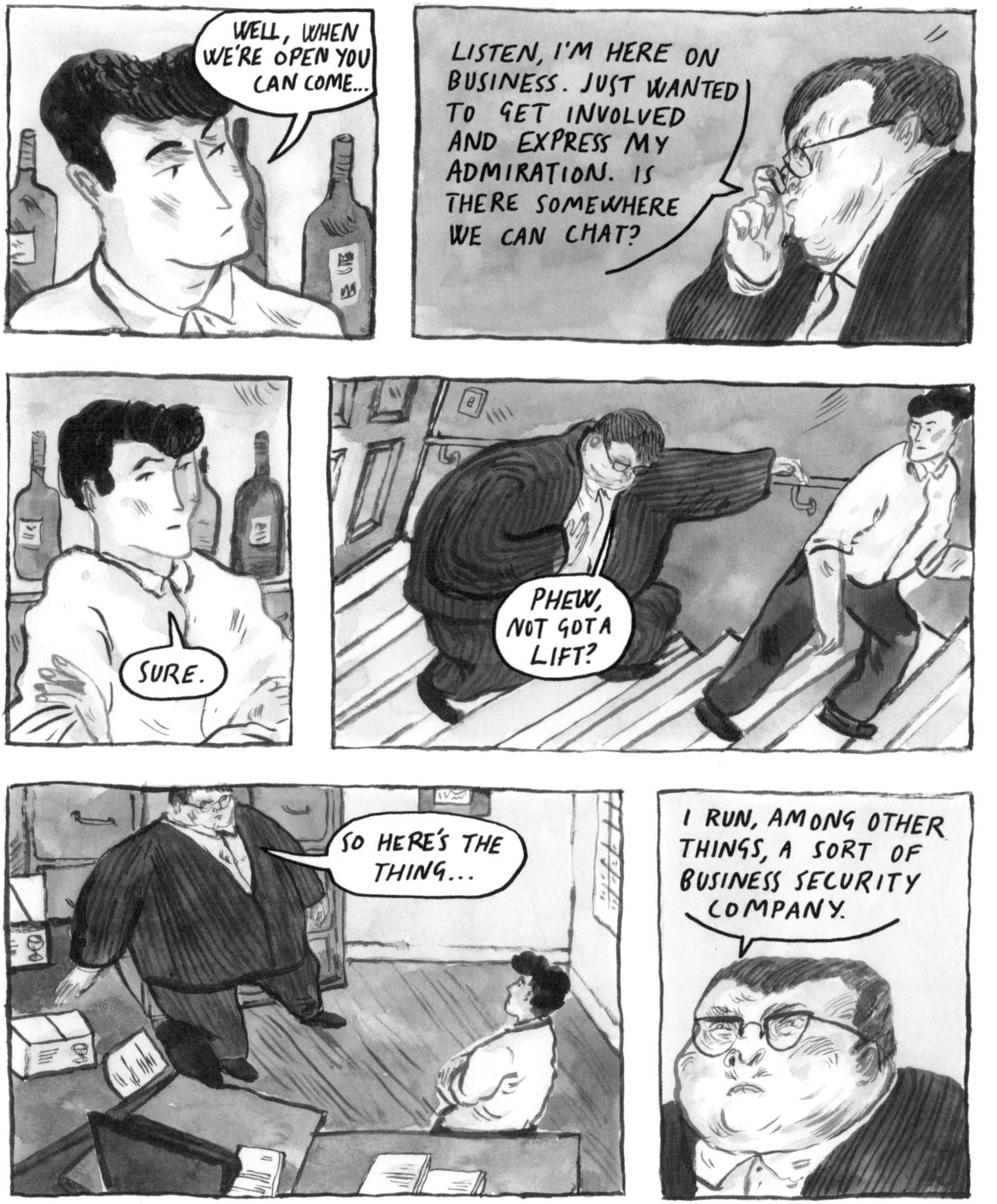
WELL, WHEN WE'RE OPEN YOU CAN COME...
LISTEN, I'M HERE ON BUSINESS. JUST WANTED TO GET INVOLVED AND EXPRESS MY ADMIRATION. IS THERE SOMEWHERE WE CAN CHAT?
SURE.
PHEW, NOT GOT A LIFT?
SO HERE'S THE THING...
I RUN, AMONG OTHER THINGS, A SORT OF BUSINESS SECURITY COMPANY.

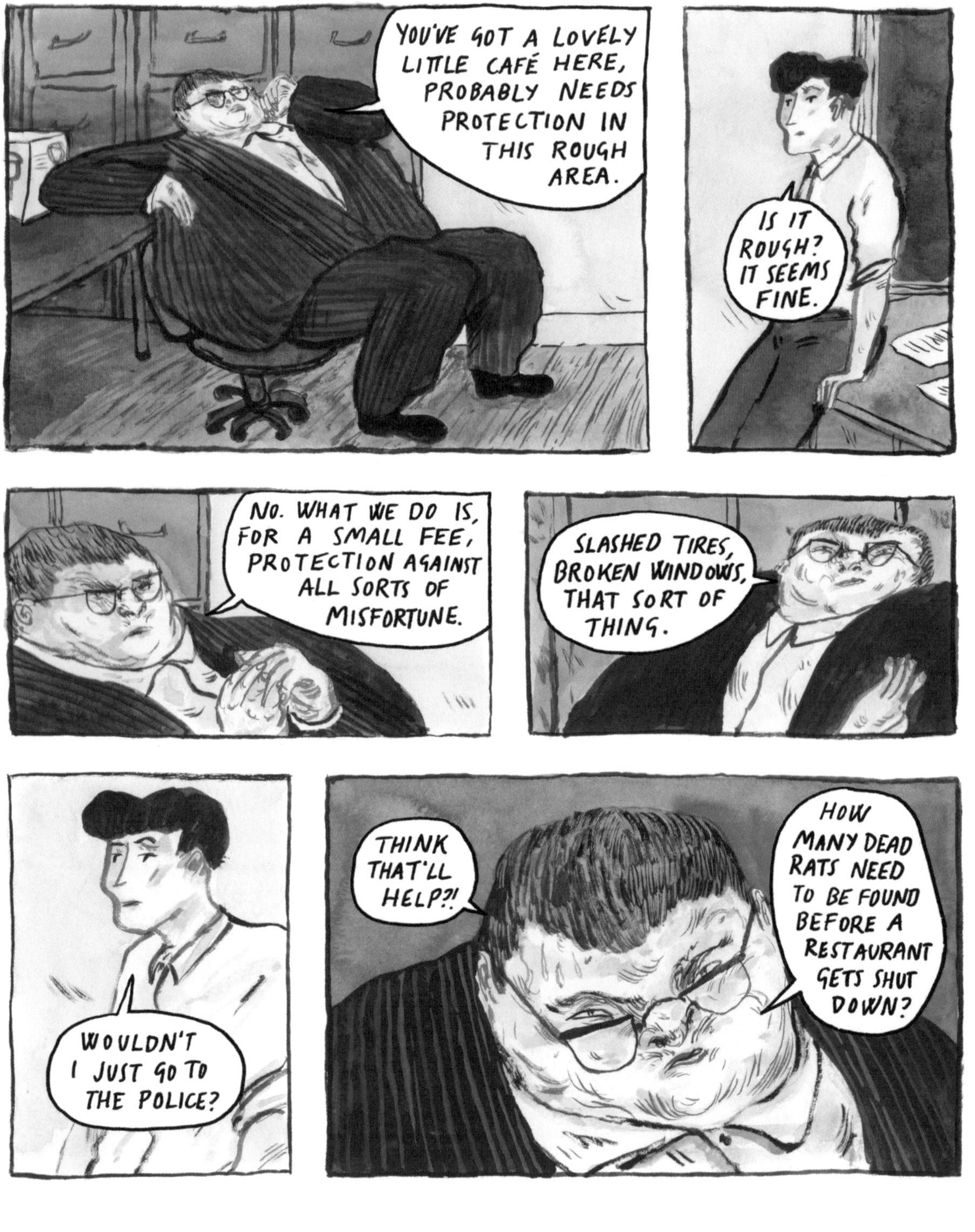
YOU'VE GOT A LOVELY LITTLE CAFÉ HERE, PROBABLY NEEDS PROTECTION IN THIS ROUGH AREA.
IS IT ROUGH? IT SEEMS FINE.
NO. WHAT WE DO IS, FOR A SMALL FEE, PROTECTION AGAINST ALL SORTS OF MISFORTUNE.
SLASHED TIRES, BROKEN WINDOWS, THAT SORT OF THING.
WOULDN'T I JUST GO TO THE POLICE?
THINK THAT'LL HELP?!
HOW MANY DEAD RATS NEED TO BE FOUND BEFORE A RESTAURANT GETS SHUT DOWN?

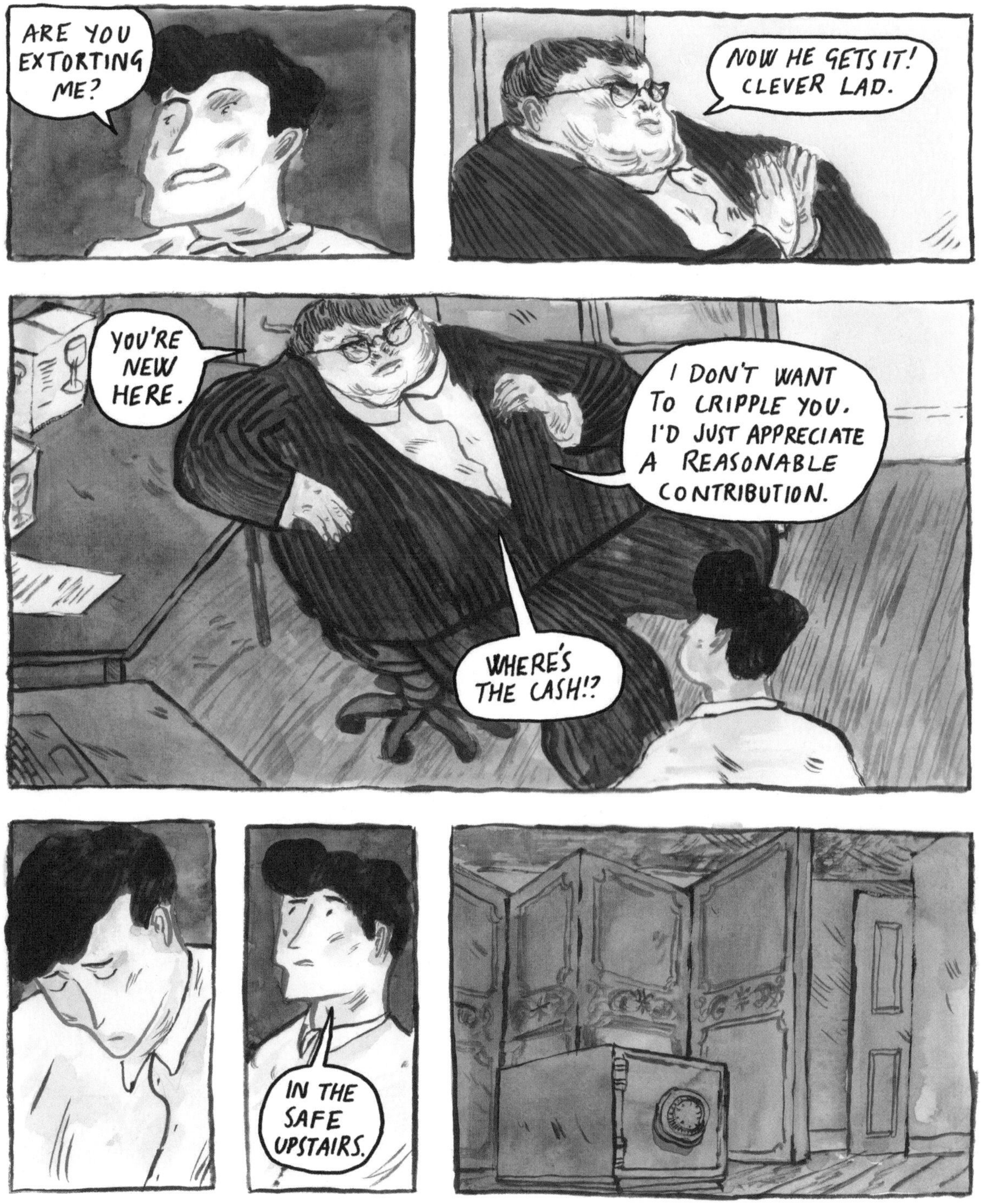
ARE YOU EXTORTING ME?
NOW HE GETS IT! CLEVER LAD.
YOU'RE NEW HERE.
I DON'T WANT TO CRIPPLE YOU. I'D JUST APPRECIATE A REASONABLE CONTRIBUTION.
WHERE'S THE CASH!?
IN THE SAFE UPSTAIRS.

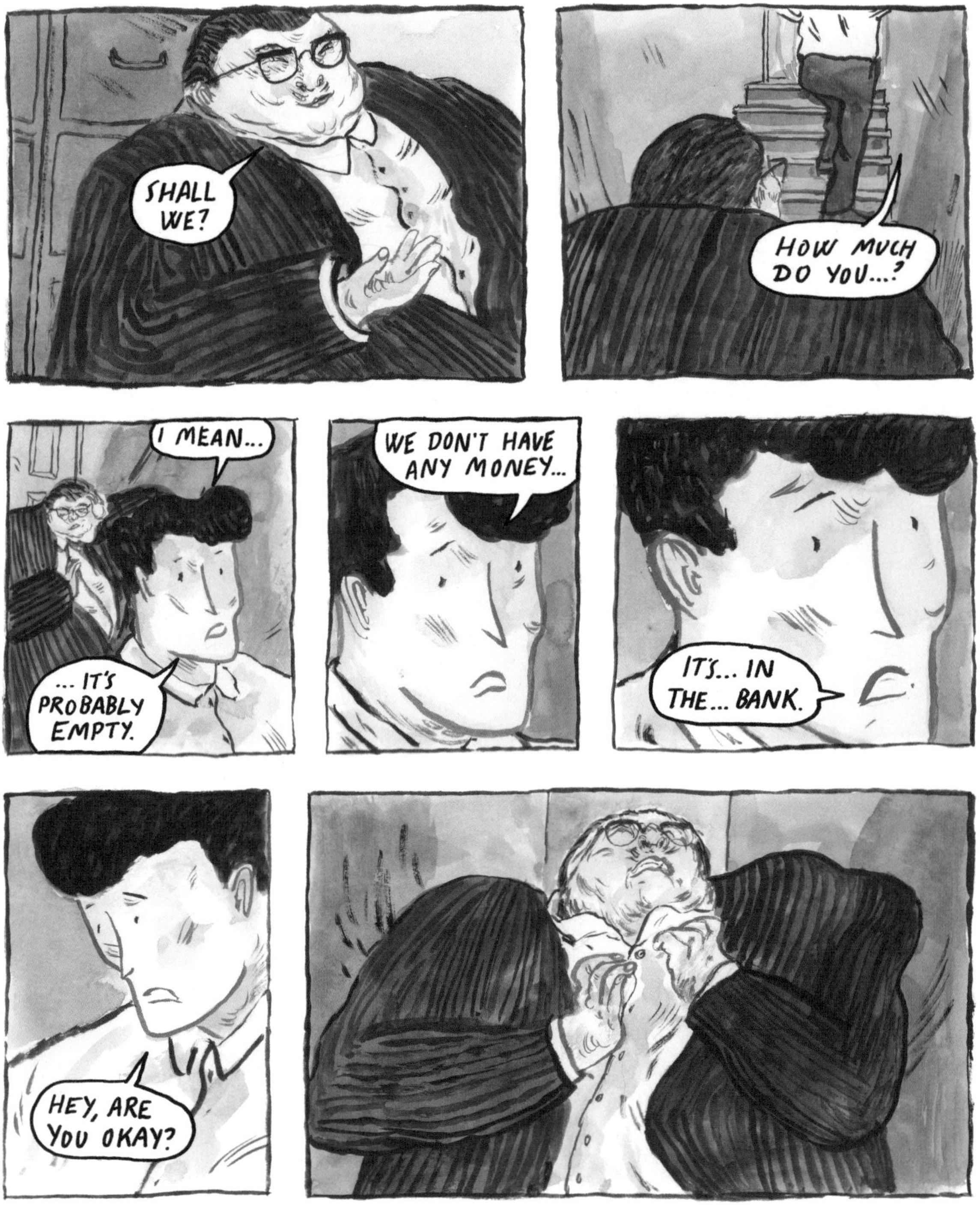
SHALL WE?
HOW MUCH DO YOU...?
I MEAN...
... IT'S PROBABLY EMPTY.
WE DON'T HAVE ANY MONEY...
IT'S... IN THE... BANK.
HEY, ARE YOU OKAY?

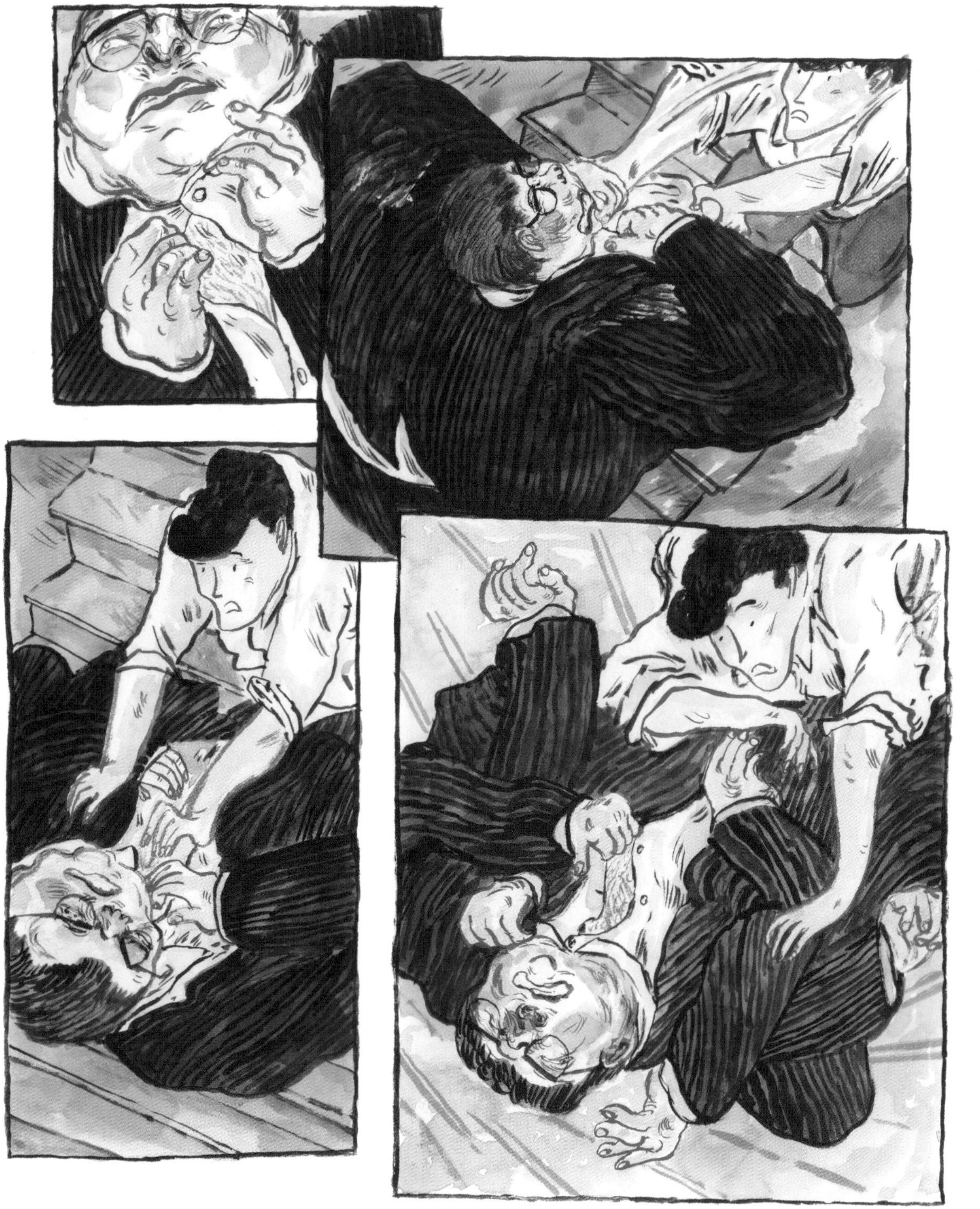

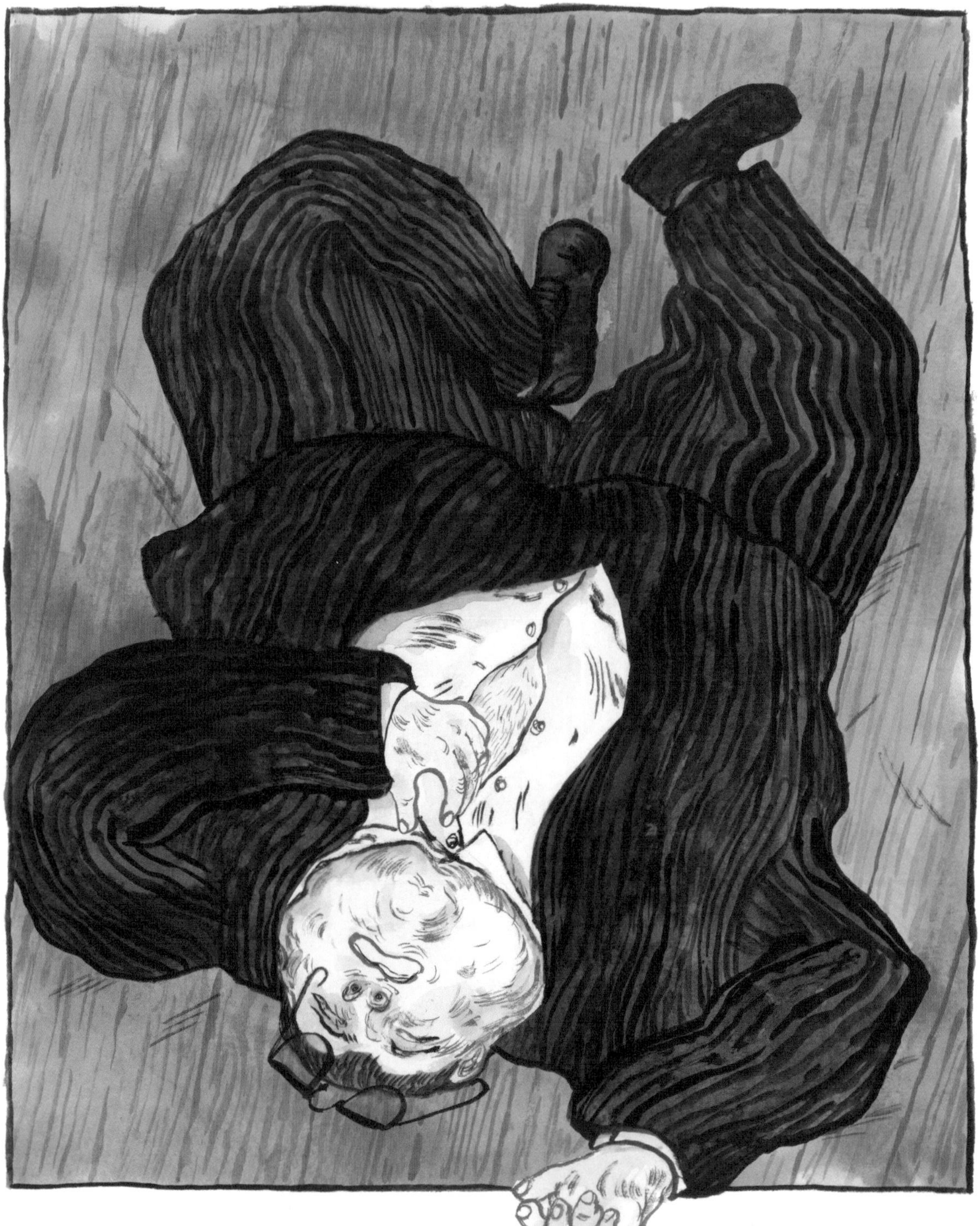

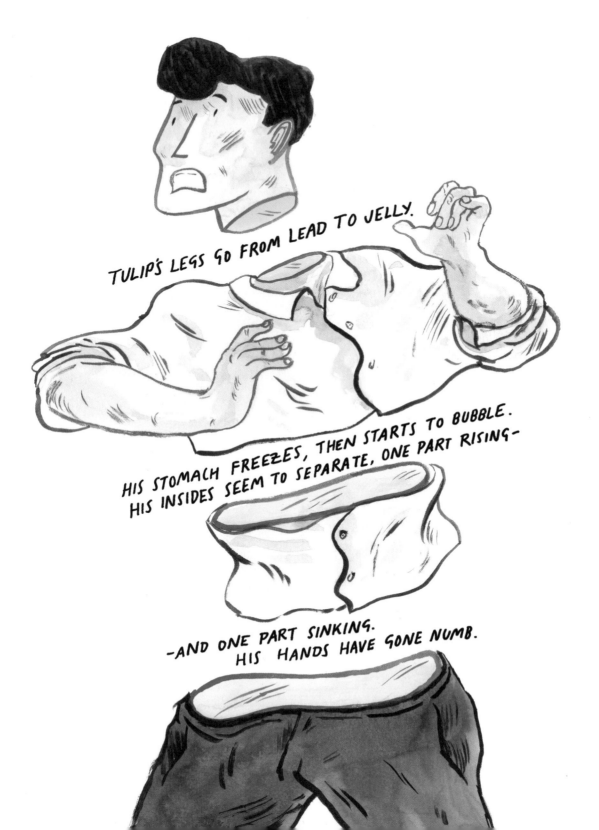

TULIP'S LEGS GO FROM LEAD TO JELLY.

HIS STOMACH FREEZES, THEN STARTS TO BUBBLE.
HIS INSIDES SEEM TO SEPARATE, ONE PART RISING—

—AND ONE PART SINKING.
HIS HANDS HAVE GONE NUMB.

HE THINKS OF CALLING THE POLICE, THEN IMAGINES THE CONSEQUENCES: THOUSANDS OF GANGSTERS ENACTING VIOLENT AND ANATOMICALLY PERVERSE REVENGE, BEYOND THE IMAGINATION OF THE FINEST SUSHI CHEF.

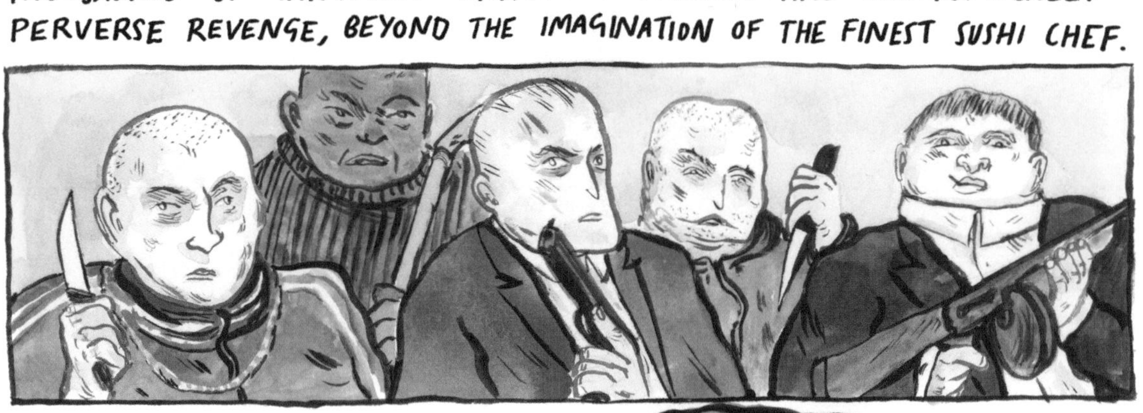

HE THINKS OF DISPOSING OF THE BODY.

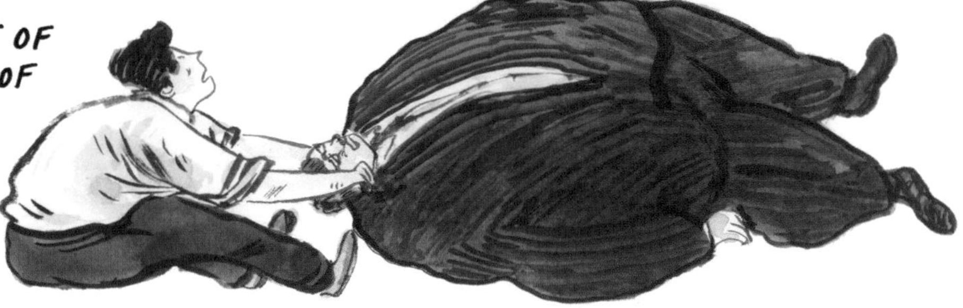

CHOPPING IT UP.

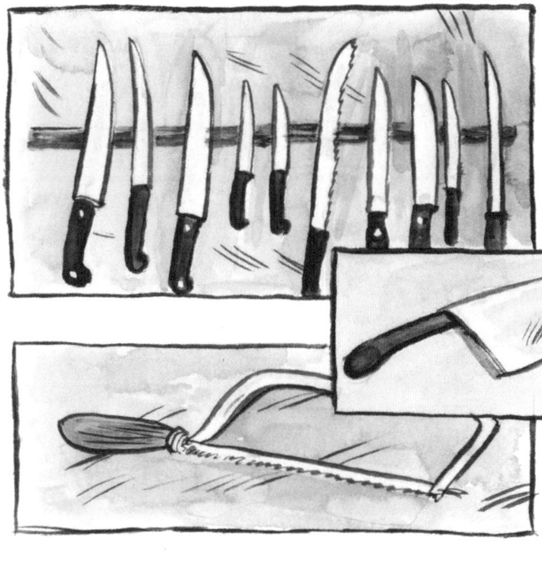

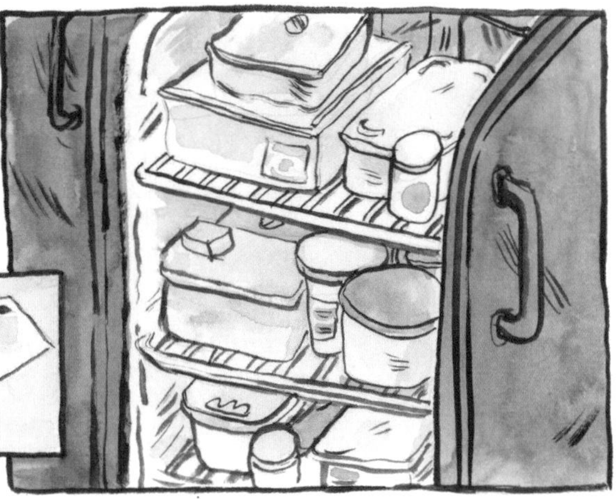

HE LOOKS DOUBTFULLY AT THE SIZE OF HIS FREEZER.

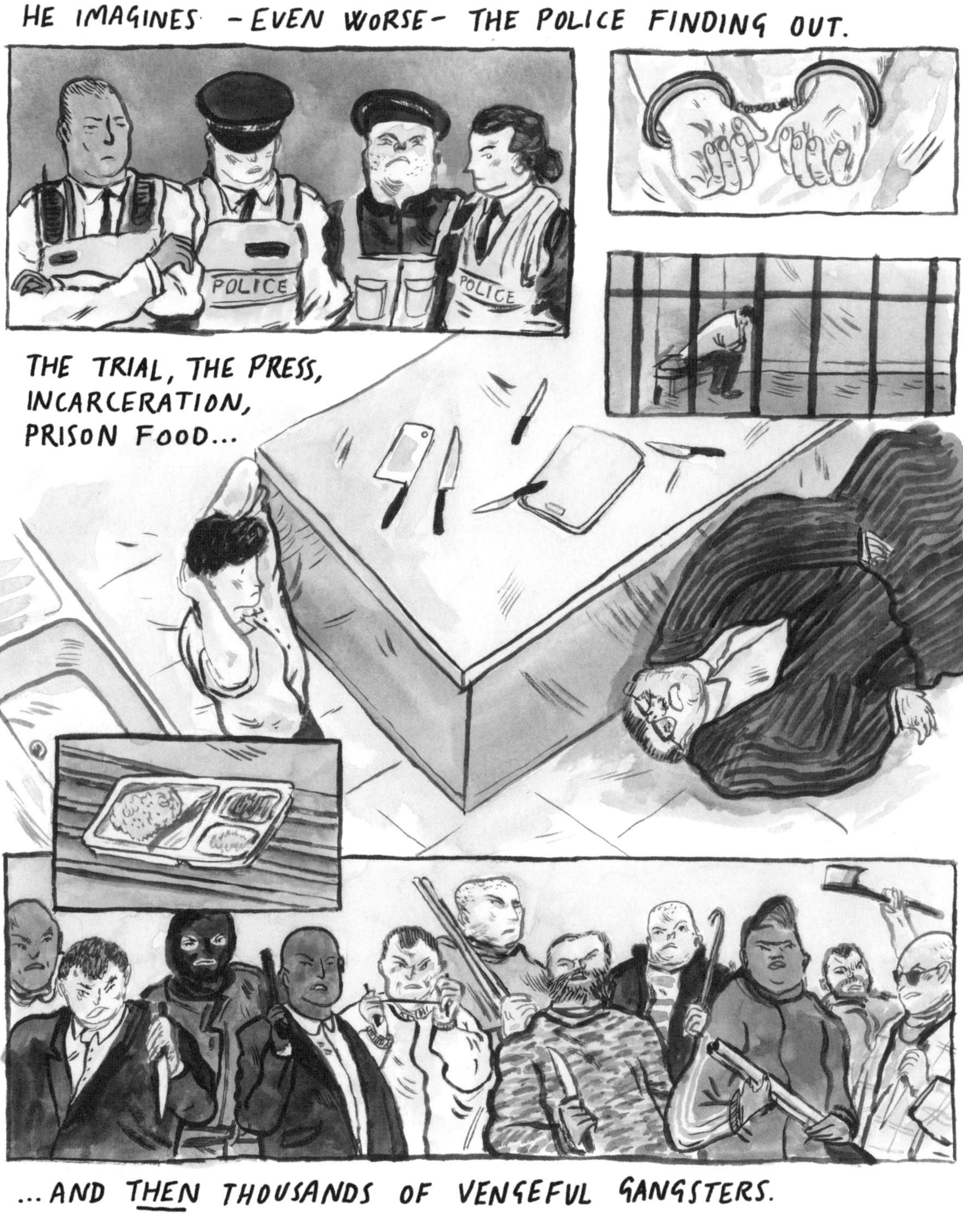
HE IMAGINES -EVEN WORSE- THE POLICE FINDING OUT.
POLICE
POLICE
THE TRIAL, THE PRESS, INCARCERATION, PRISON FOOD...
...AND THEN THOUSANDS OF VENGEFUL GANGSTERS.

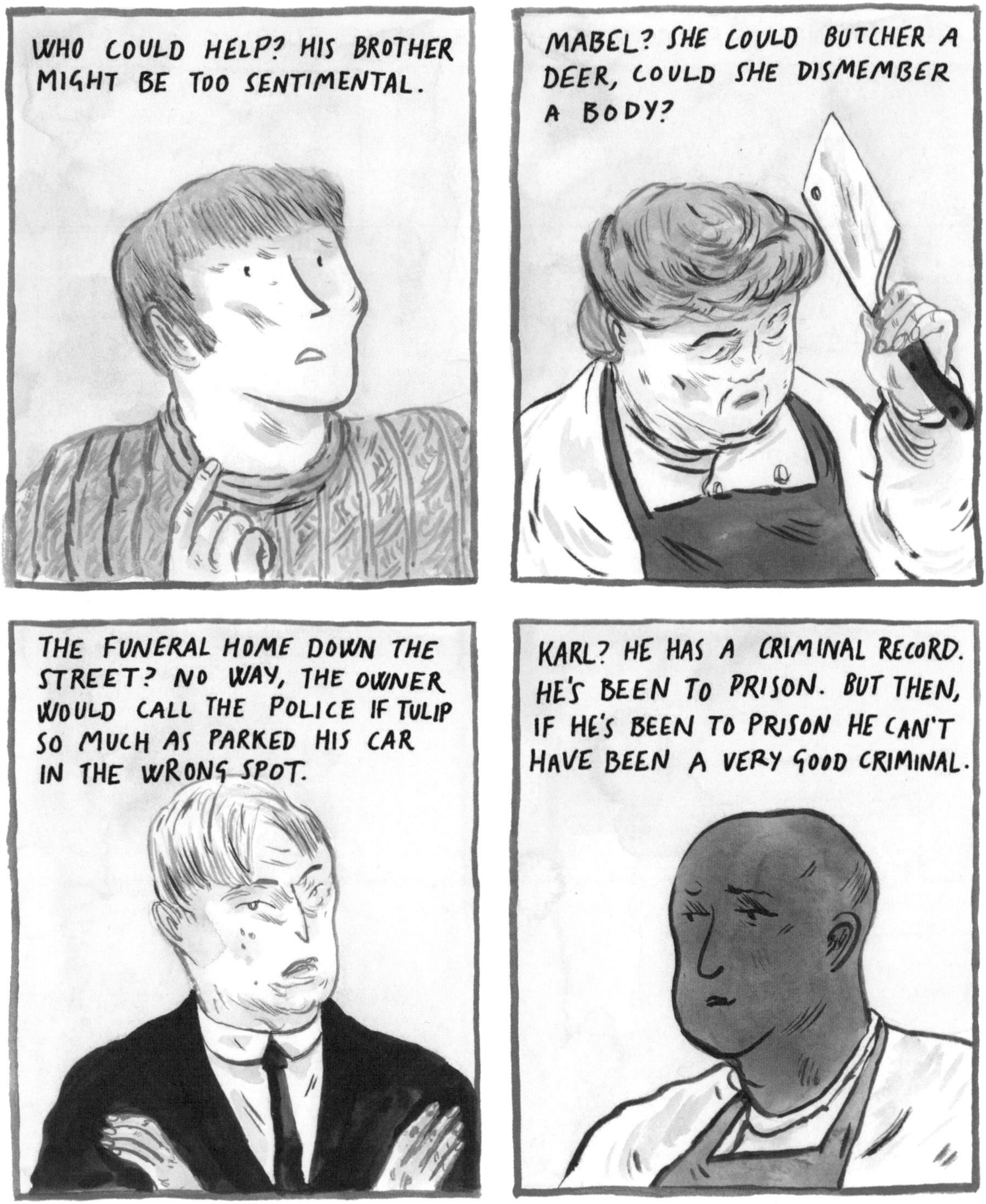
WHO COULD HELP? HIS BROTHER MIGHT BE TOO SENTIMENTAL.
MABEL? SHE COULD BUTCHER A DEER, COULD SHE DISMEMBER A BODY?
THE FUNERAL HOME DOWN THE STREET? NO WAY, THE OWNER WOULD CALL THE POLICE IF TULIP SO MUCH AS PARKED HIS CAR IN THE WRONG SPOT.
KARL? HE HAS A CRIMINAL RECORD. HE'S BEEN TO PRISON. BUT THEN, IF HE'S BEEN TO PRISON HE CAN'T HAVE BEEN A VERY GOOD CRIMINAL.

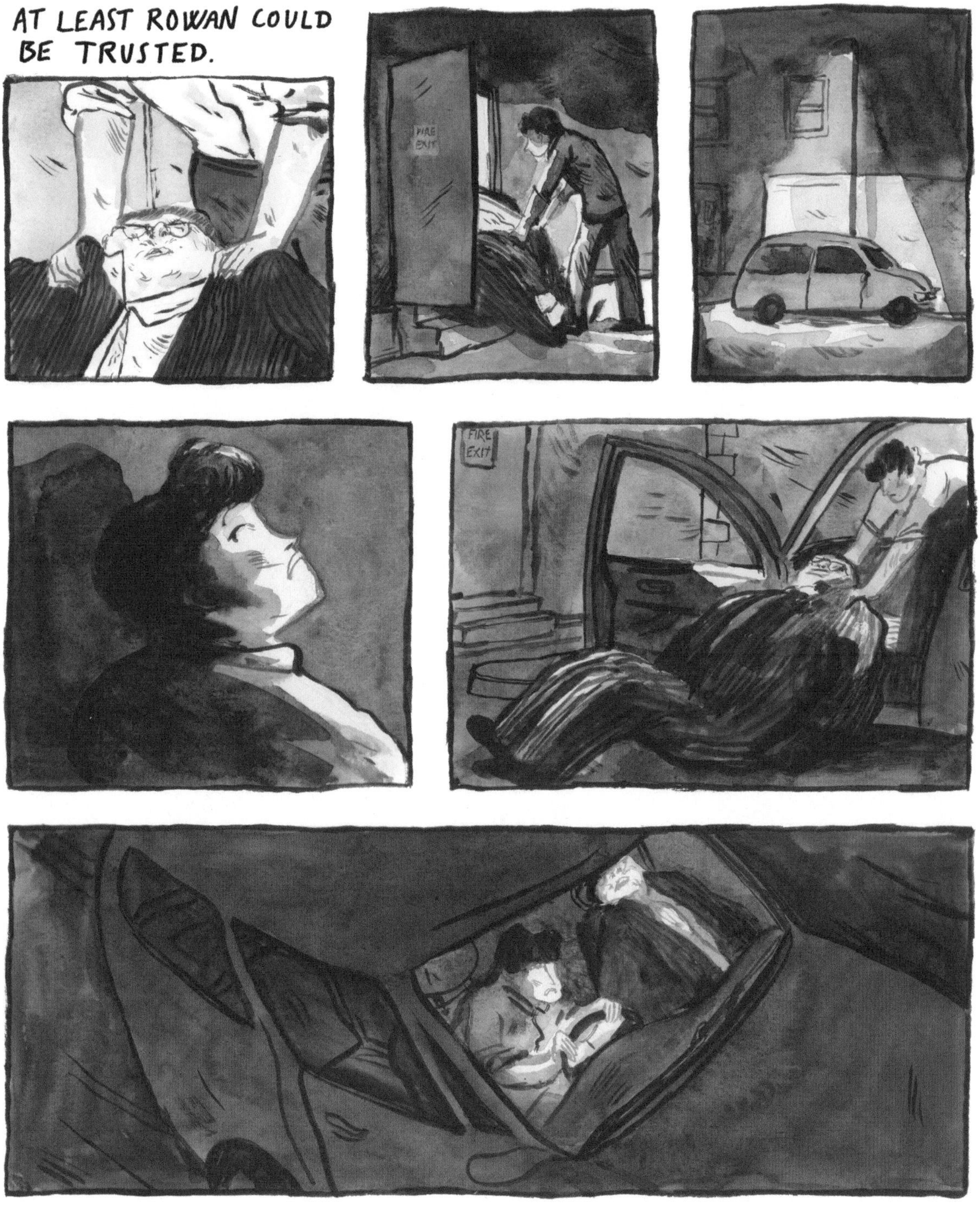
AT LEAST ROWAN COULD BE TRUSTED.
FIRE EXIT
FIRE EXIT

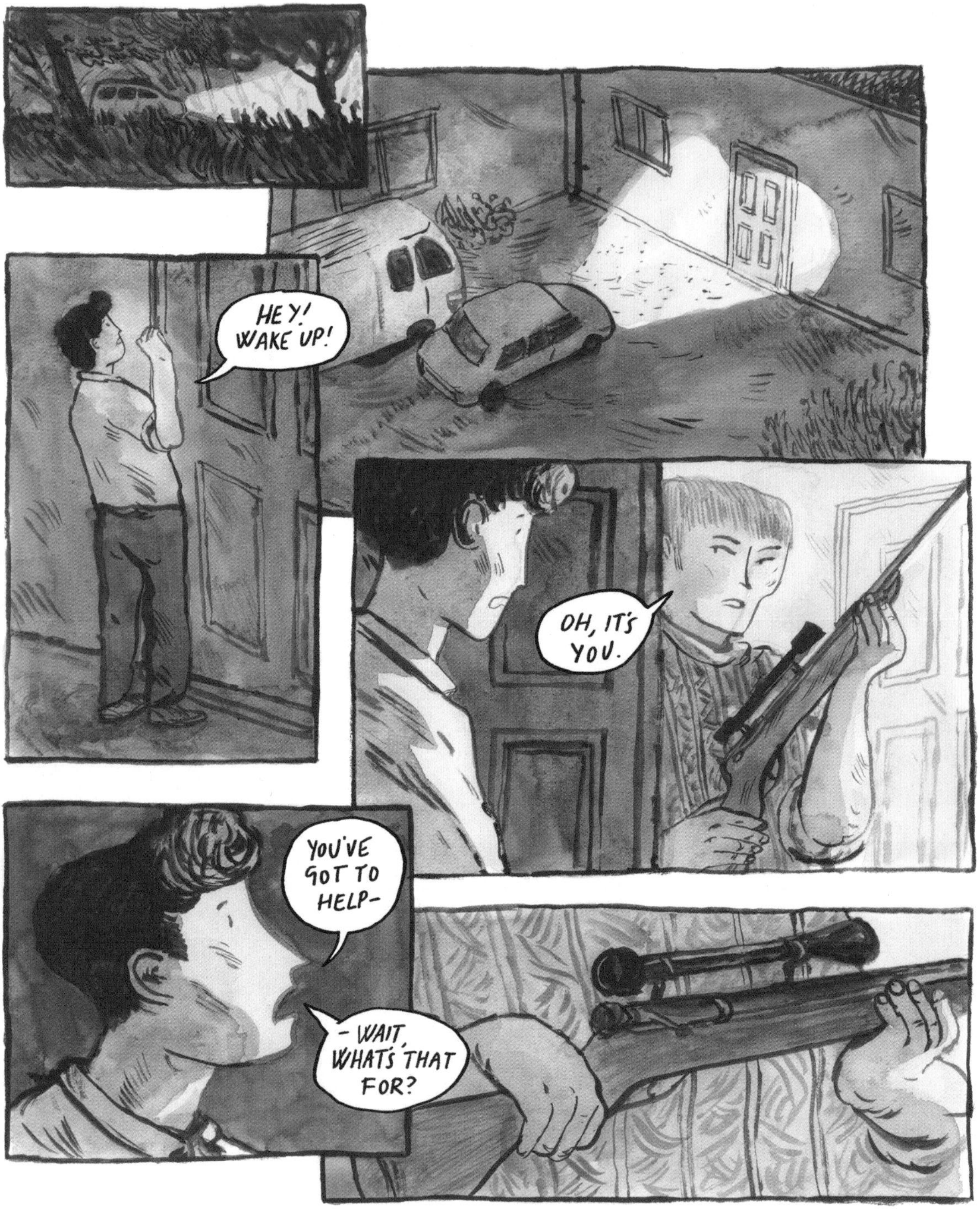
HEY! WAKE UP!
OH, IT'S YOU.
YOU'VE GOT TO HELP-
-WAIT, WHAT'S THAT FOR?

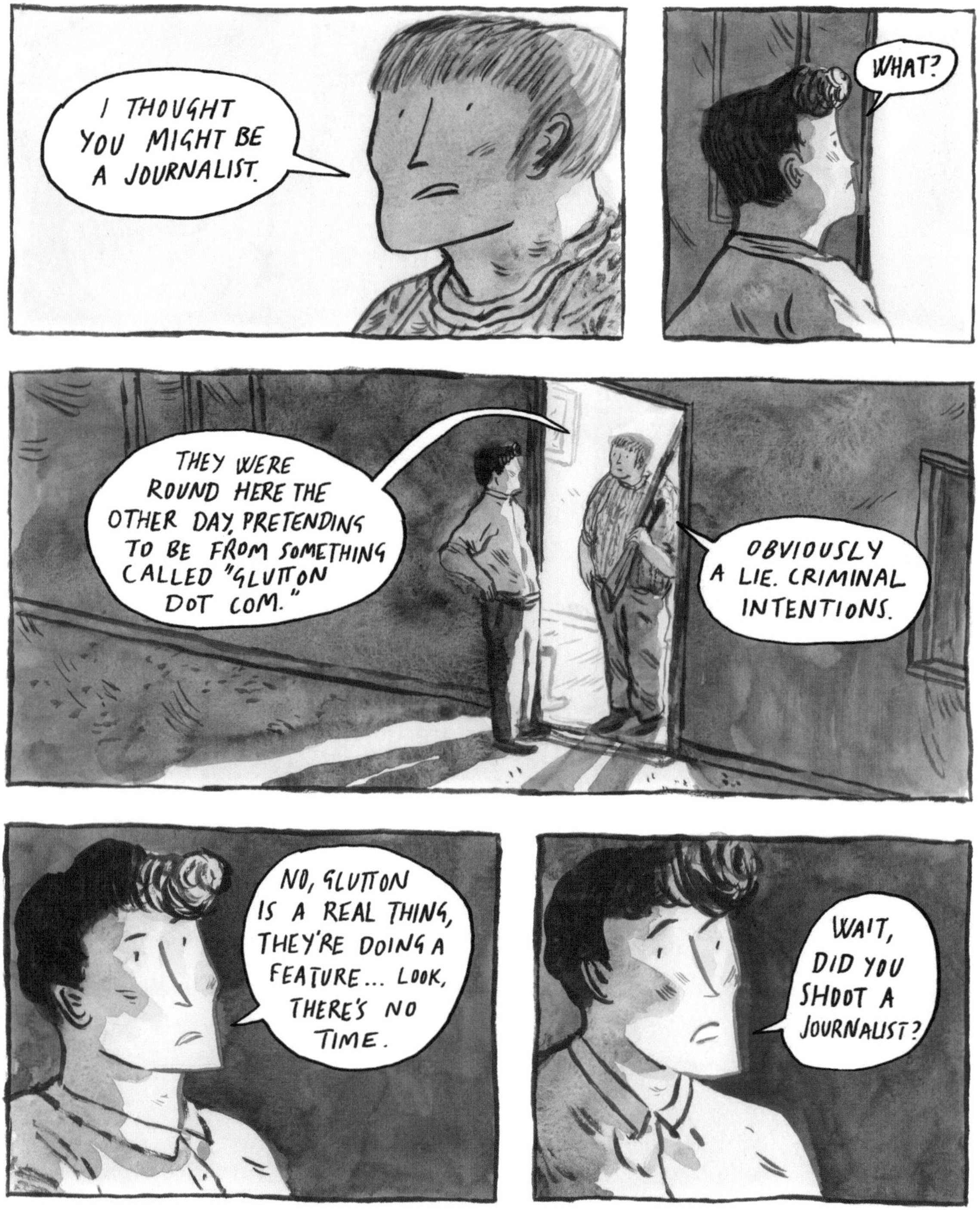
I THOUGHT YOU MIGHT BE A JOURNALIST.
WHAT?
THEY WERE ROUND HERE THE OTHER DAY, PRETENDING TO BE FROM SOMETHING CALLED "GLUTTON DOT COM."
OBVIOUSLY A LIE. CRIMINAL INTENTIONS.
NO, GLUTTON IS A REAL THING, THEY'RE DOING A FEATURE... LOOK, THERE'S NO TIME.
WAIT, DID YOU SHOOT A JOURNALIST?

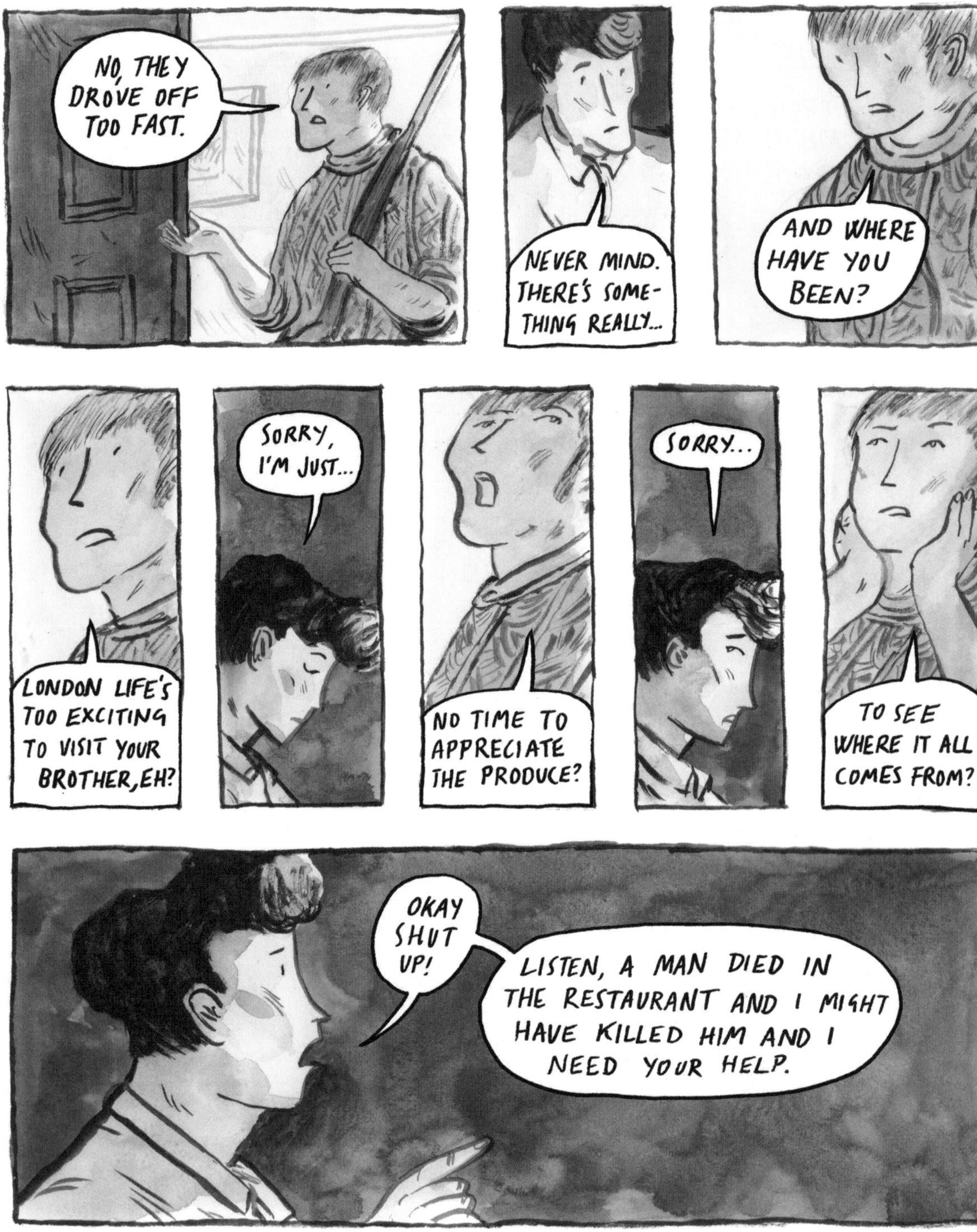
NO, THEY DROVE OFF TOO FAST.
NEVER MIND. THERE'S SOME-THING REALLY...
AND WHERE HAVE YOU BEEN?
LONDON LIFE'S TOO EXCITING TO VISIT YOUR BROTHER, EH?
SORRY, I'M JUST...
NO TIME TO APPRECIATE THE PRODUCE?
SORRY...
TO SEE WHERE IT ALL COMES FROM?
OKAY SHUT UP!
LISTEN, A MAN DIED IN THE RESTAURANT AND I MIGHT HAVE KILLED HIM AND I NEED YOUR HELP.

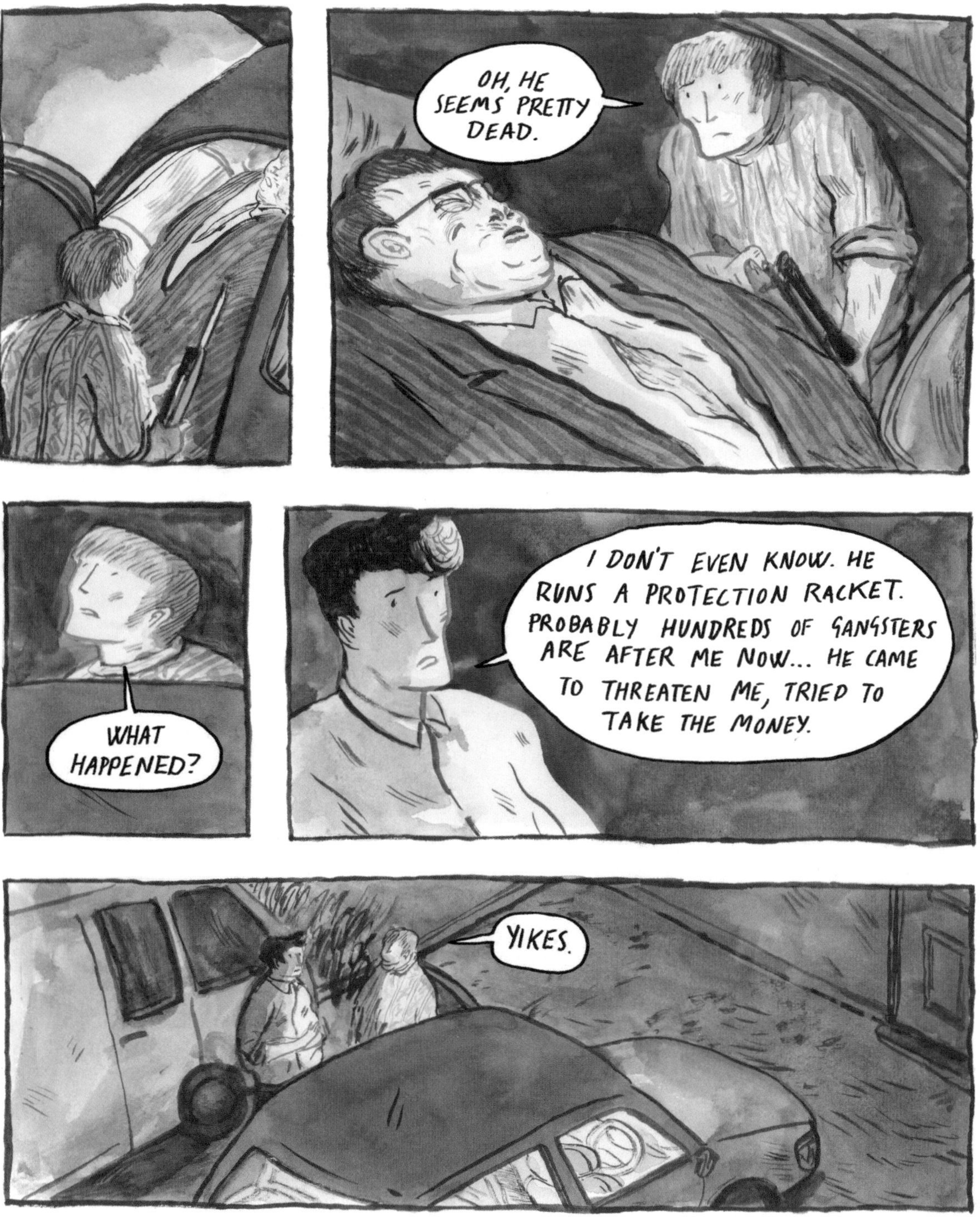
OH, HE SEEMS PRETTY DEAD.
WHAT HAPPENED?
I DON'T EVEN KNOW. HE RUNS A PROTECTION RACKET. PROBABLY HUNDREDS OF GANGSTERS ARE AFTER ME NOW... HE CAME TO THREATEN ME, TRIED TO TAKE THE MONEY.
YIKES.

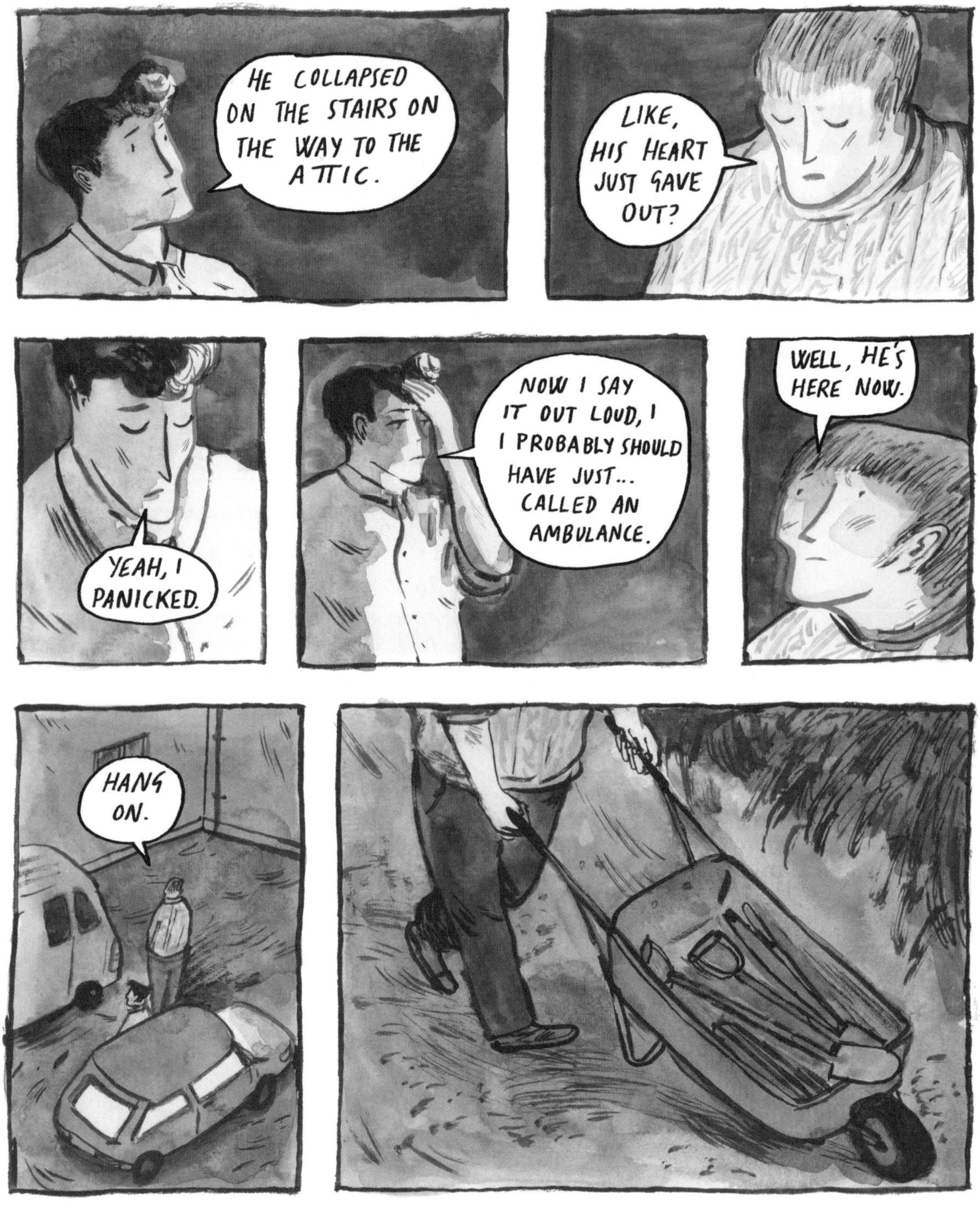
HE COLLAPSED ON THE STAIRS ON THE WAY TO THE ATTIC.
LIKE, HIS HEART JUST GAVE OUT?
YEAH, I PANICKED.
NOW I SAY IT OUT LOUD, I I PROBABLY SHOULD HAVE JUST... CALLED AN AMBULANCE.
WELL, HE'S HERE NOW.
HANG ON.

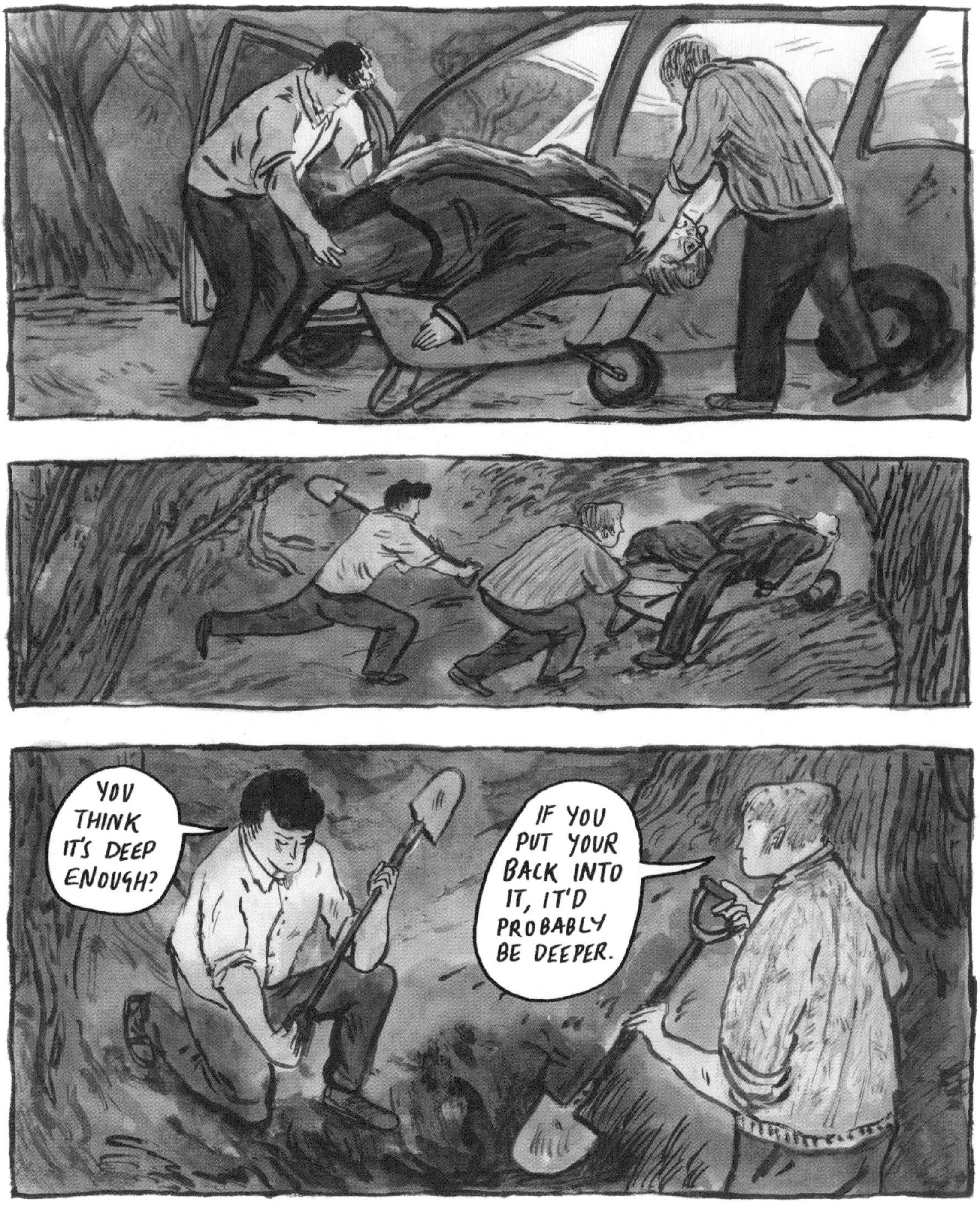
YOU THINK IT'S DEEP ENOUGH?
IF YOU PUT YOUR BACK INTO IT, IT'D PROBABLY BE DEEPER.

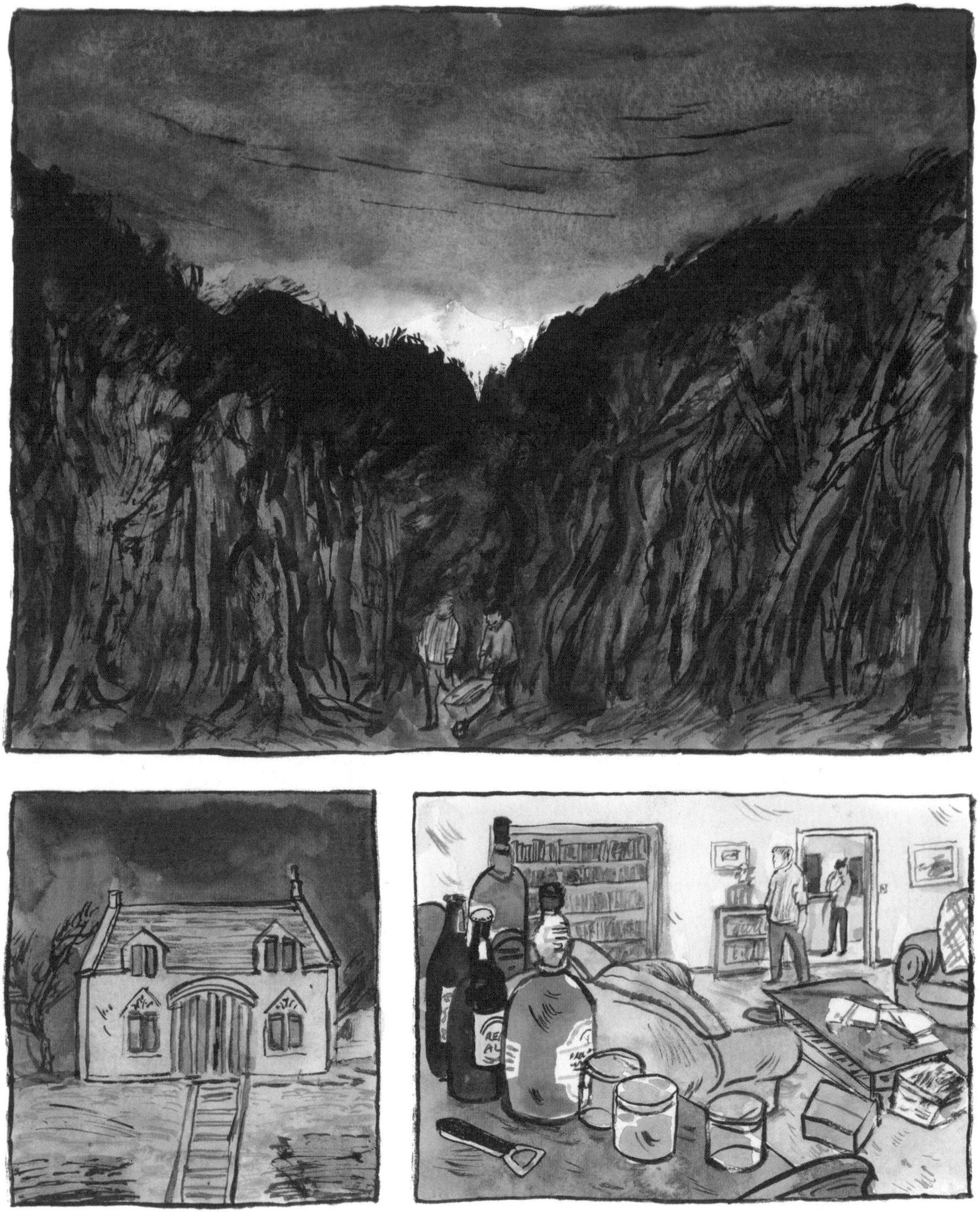

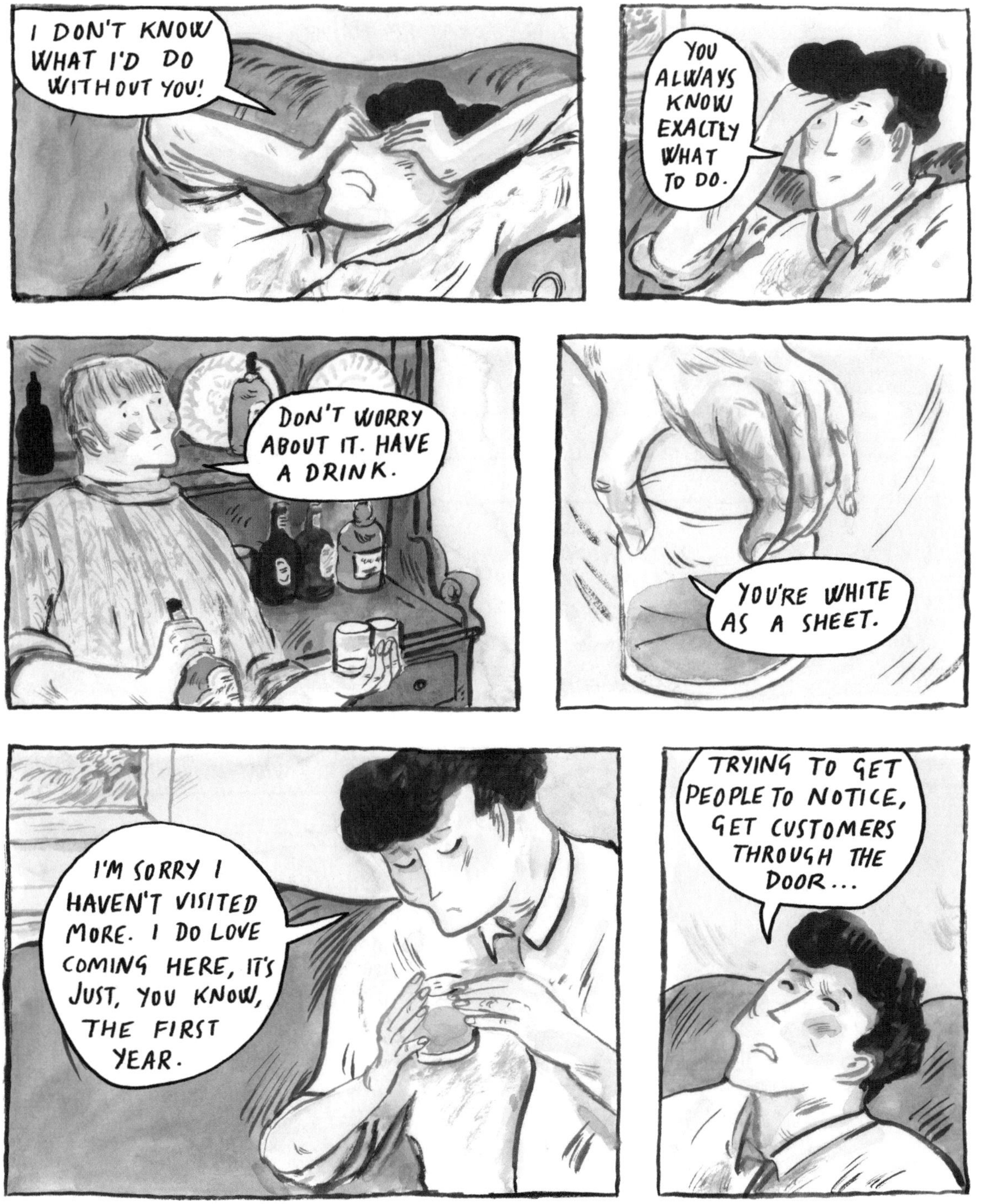
I DON'T KNOW WHAT I'D DO WITHOUT YOU!
YOU ALWAYS KNOW EXACTLY WHAT TO DO.
DON'T WORRY ABOUT IT. HAVE A DRINK.
YOU'RE WHITE AS A SHEET.
I'M SORRY I HAVEN'T VISITED MORE. I DO LOVE COMING HERE, IT'S JUST, YOU KNOW, THE FIRST YEAR.
TRYING TO GET PEOPLE TO NOTICE, GET CUSTOMERS THROUGH THE DOOR...

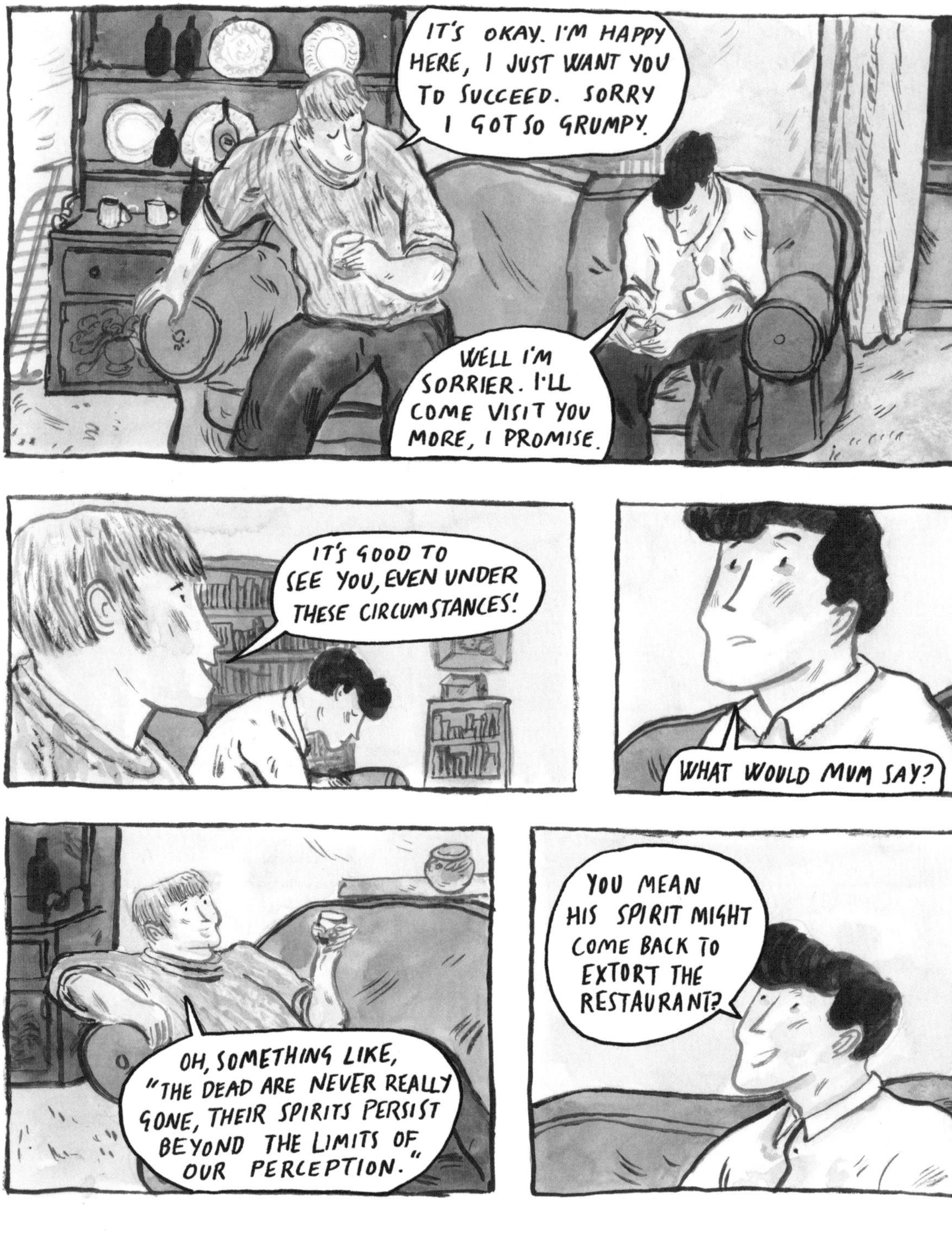
IT'S OKAY. I'M HAPPY HERE, I JUST WANT YOU TO SUCCEED. SORRY I GOT SO GRUMPY.
WELL I'M SORRIER. I'LL COME VISIT YOU MORE, I PROMISE.
IT'S GOOD TO SEE YOU, EVEN UNDER THESE CIRCUMSTANCES!
WHAT WOULD MUM SAY?
OH, SOMETHING LIKE, "THE DEAD ARE NEVER REALLY GONE, THEIR SPIRITS PERSIST BEYOND THE LIMITS OF OUR PERCEPTION."
YOU MEAN HIS SPIRIT MIGHT COME BACK TO EXTORT THE RESTAURANT?

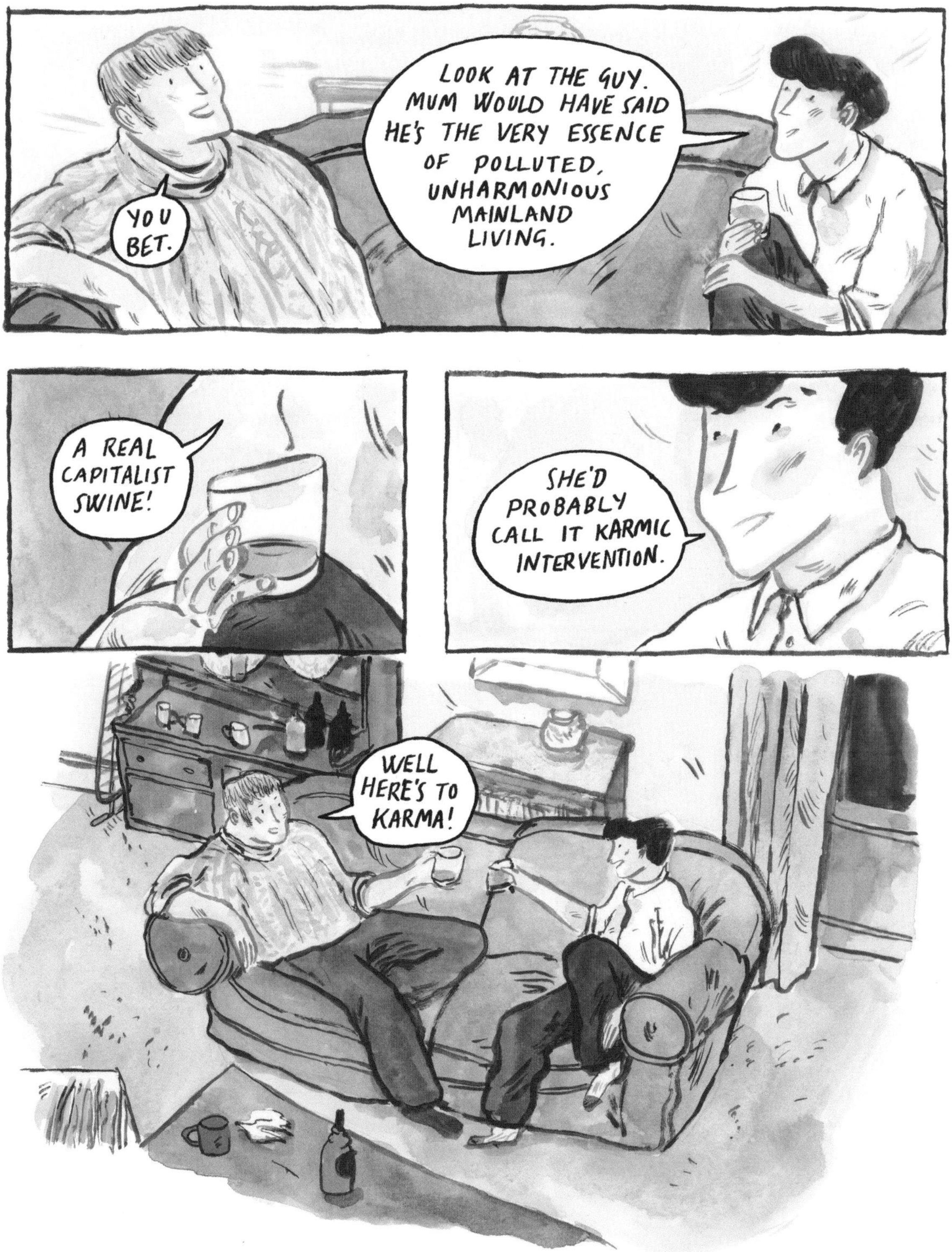
LOOK AT THE GUY. MUM WOULD HAVE SAID HE'S THE VERY ESSENCE OF POLLUTED, UNHARMONIOUS MAINLAND LIVING.
YOU BET.
A REAL CAPITALIST SWINE!
SHE'D PROBABLY CALL IT KARMIC INTERVENTION.
WELL HERE'S TO KARMA!

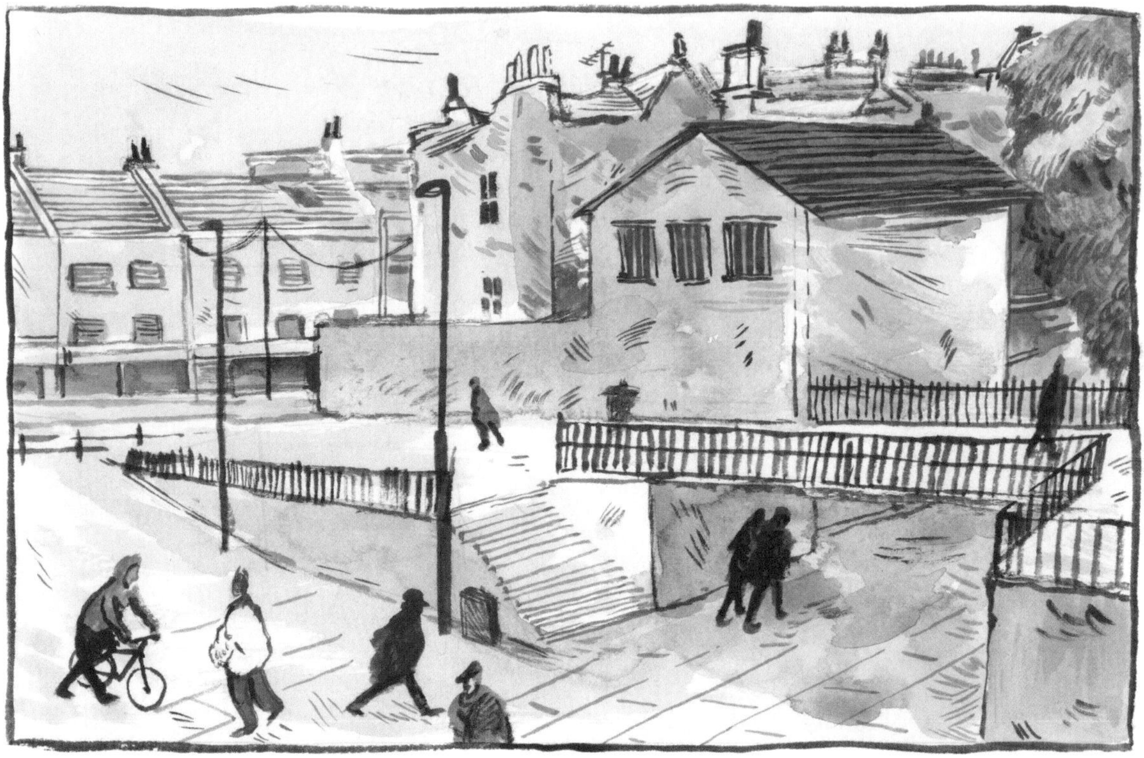

TULIP RETURNS TO LONDON, TRYING TO ACT LIKE NOTHING HAS HAPPENED.

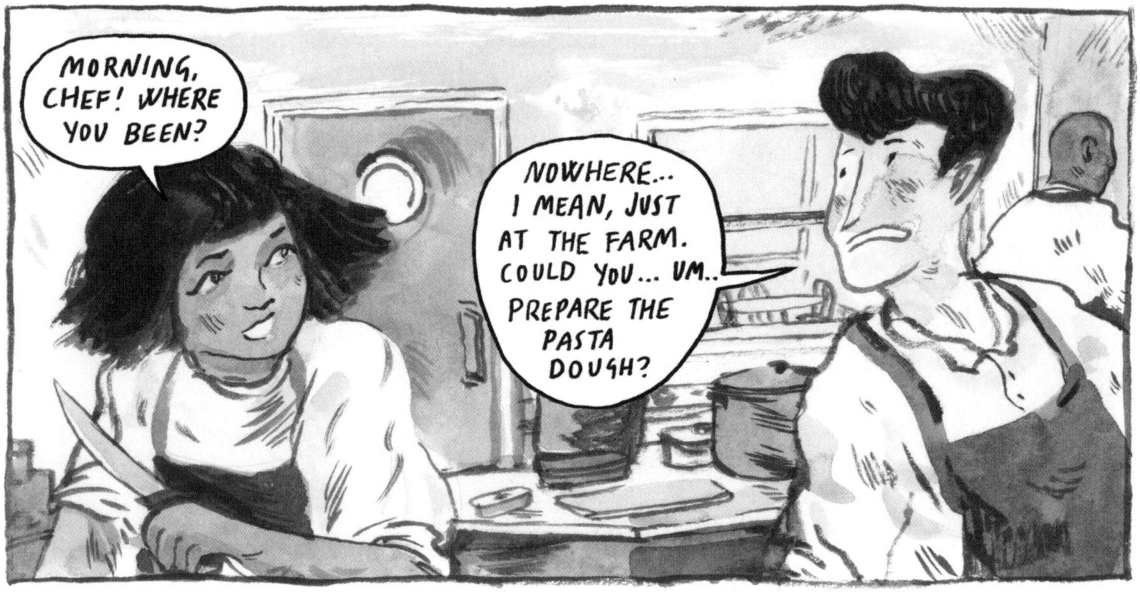
MORNING, CHEF! WHERE YOU BEEN?
NOWHERE... I MEAN, JUST AT THE FARM. COULD YOU... UM.. PREPARE THE PASTA DOUGH?

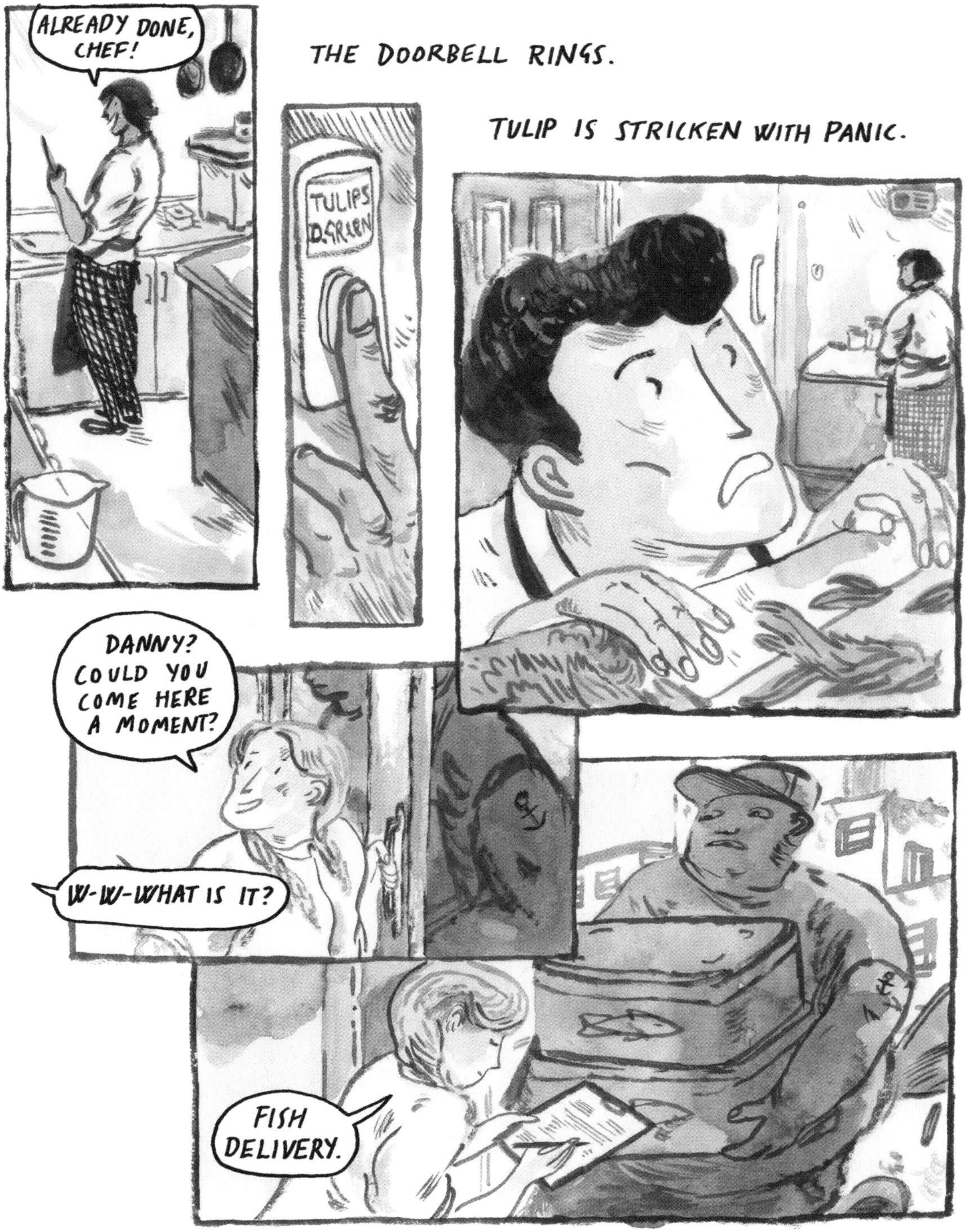
ALREADY DONE, CHEF!
THE DOORBELL RINGS.
TULIP IS STRICKEN WITH PANIC.
DANNY? COULD YOU COME HERE A MOMENT?
W-W-WHAT IS IT?
FISH DELIVERY.

TULIP SWAGGERS OFF WITH FEIGNED RELAXATION, THEN NEARLY LEAPS OUT OF HIS SKIN TO HEAR A FIST POUNDING ON THE BACK DOOR.

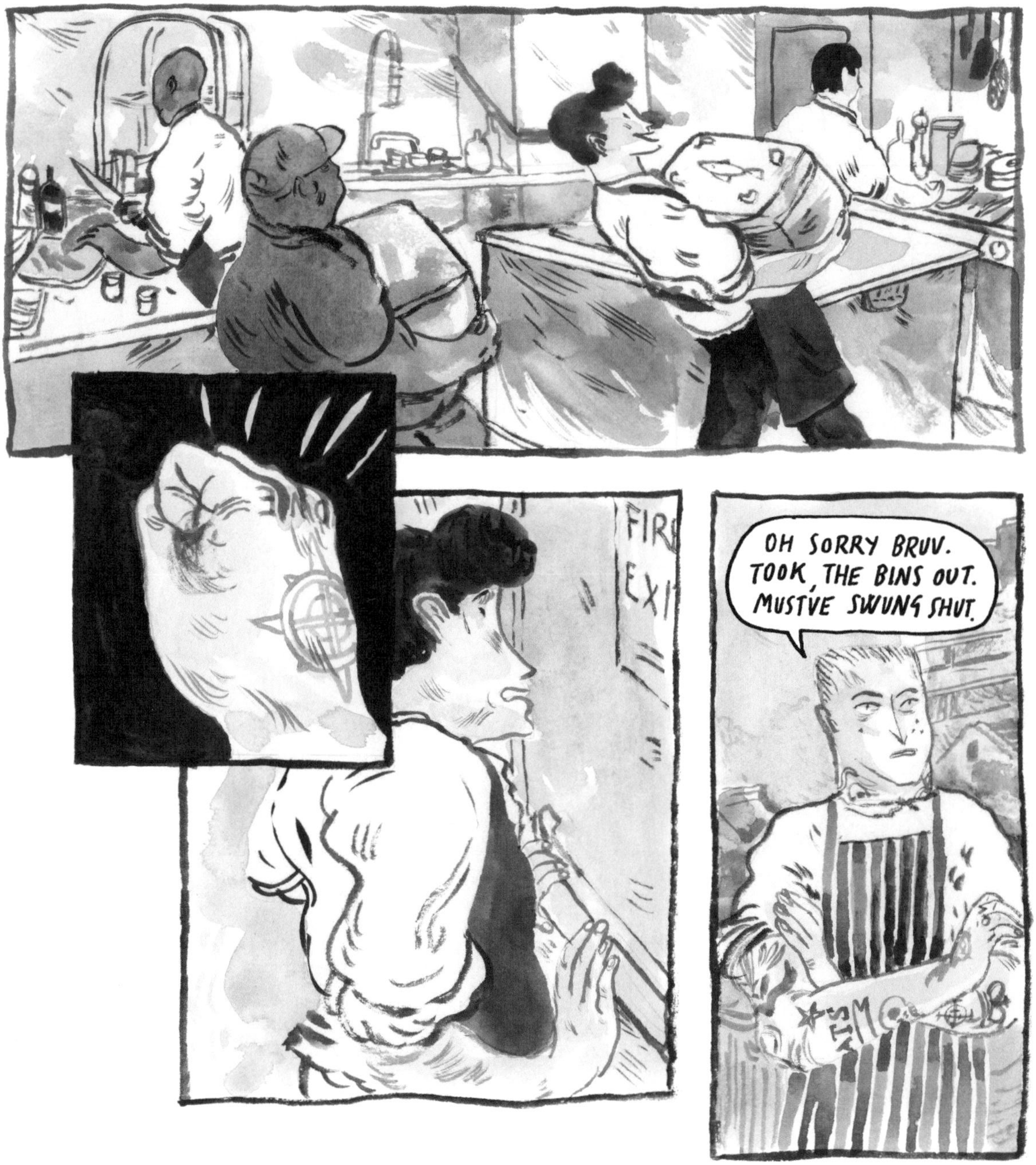
OH SORRY BRUV. TOOK THE BINS OUT. MUSTVE SWUNG SHUT.

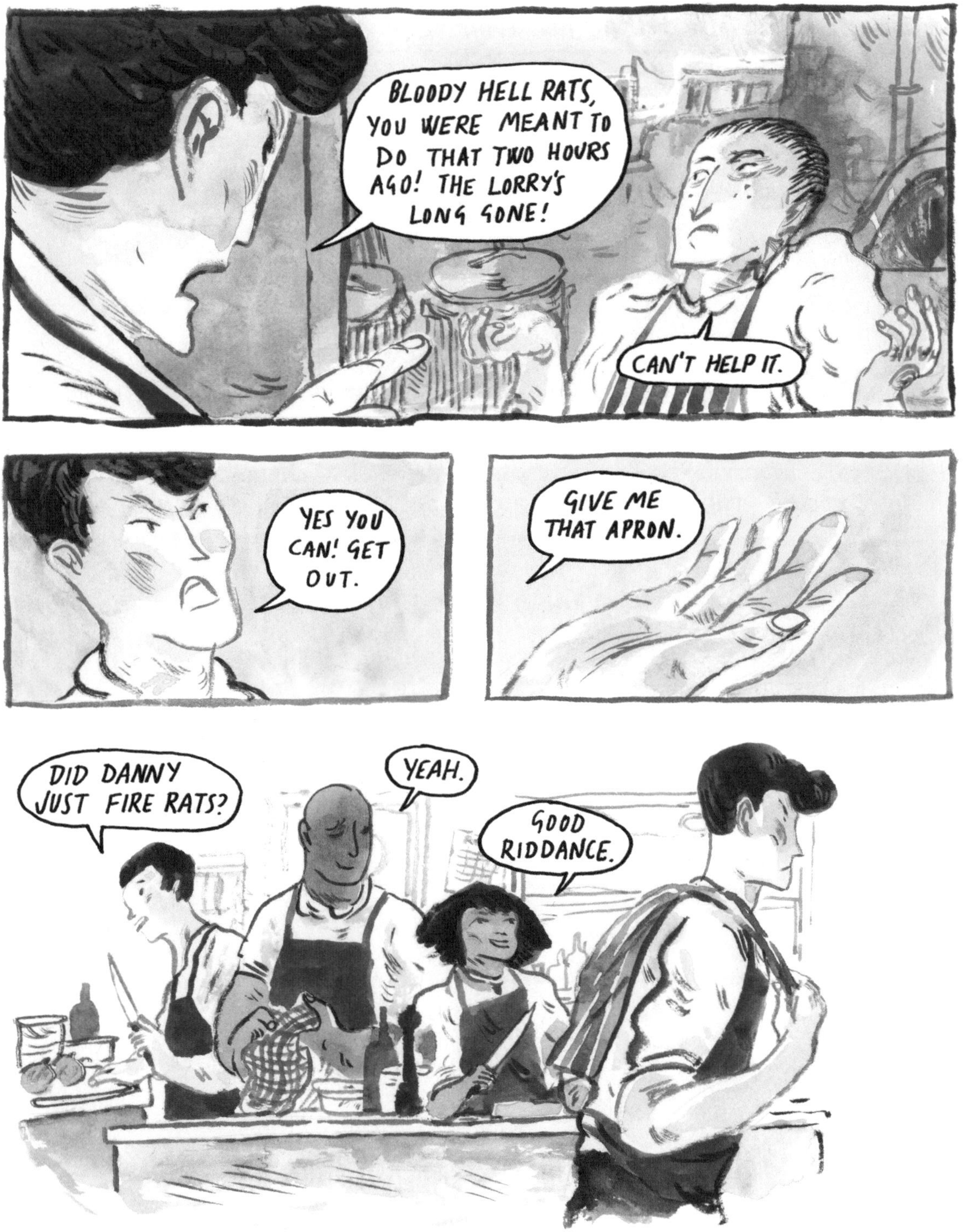
BLOODY HELL RATS, YOU WERE MEANT TO DO THAT TWO HOURS AGO! THE LORRY'S LONG GONE!
CAN'T HELP IT.
YES YOU CAN! GET OUT.
GIVE ME THAT APRON.
DID DANNY JUST FIRE RATS?
YEAH.
GOOD RIDDANCE.

LUNCH BEGINS WITH PARANOIA. TULIP GLARES AT DINERS WITH SUSPICION.

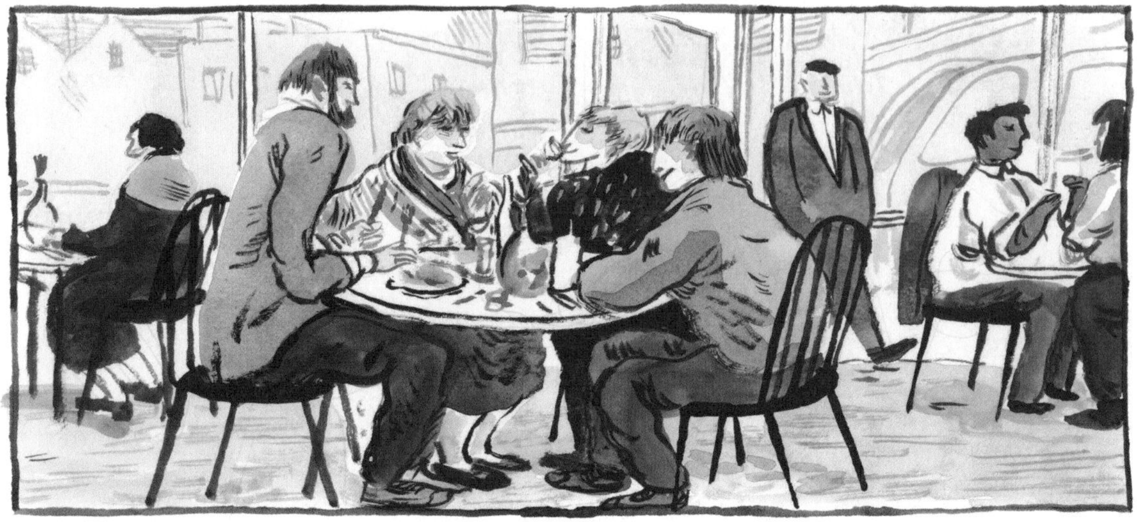

HE EXPECTS THE POLICE TO ARRIVE, OR GANGSTERS TO BURST IN.

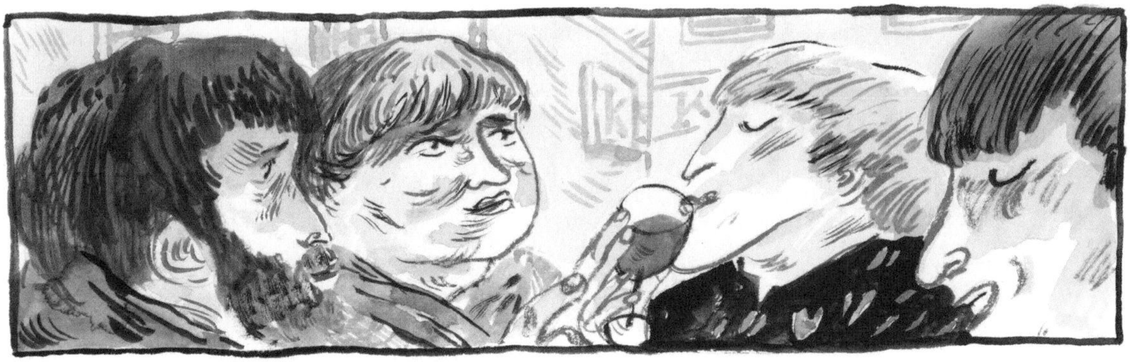

BUT THE HORROR AND GUILT BEGIN TO BE BURIED BY THE PROSAIC DEMANDS OF SERVICE.

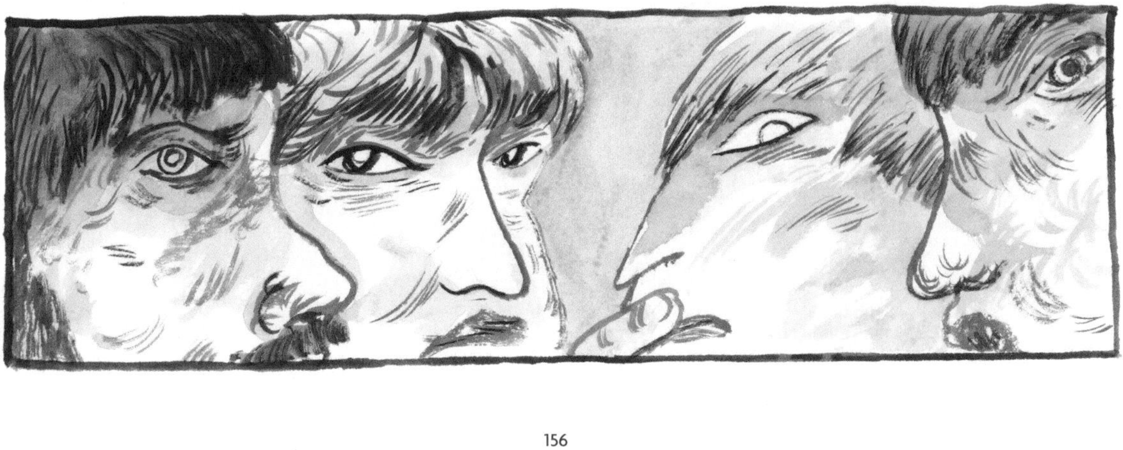

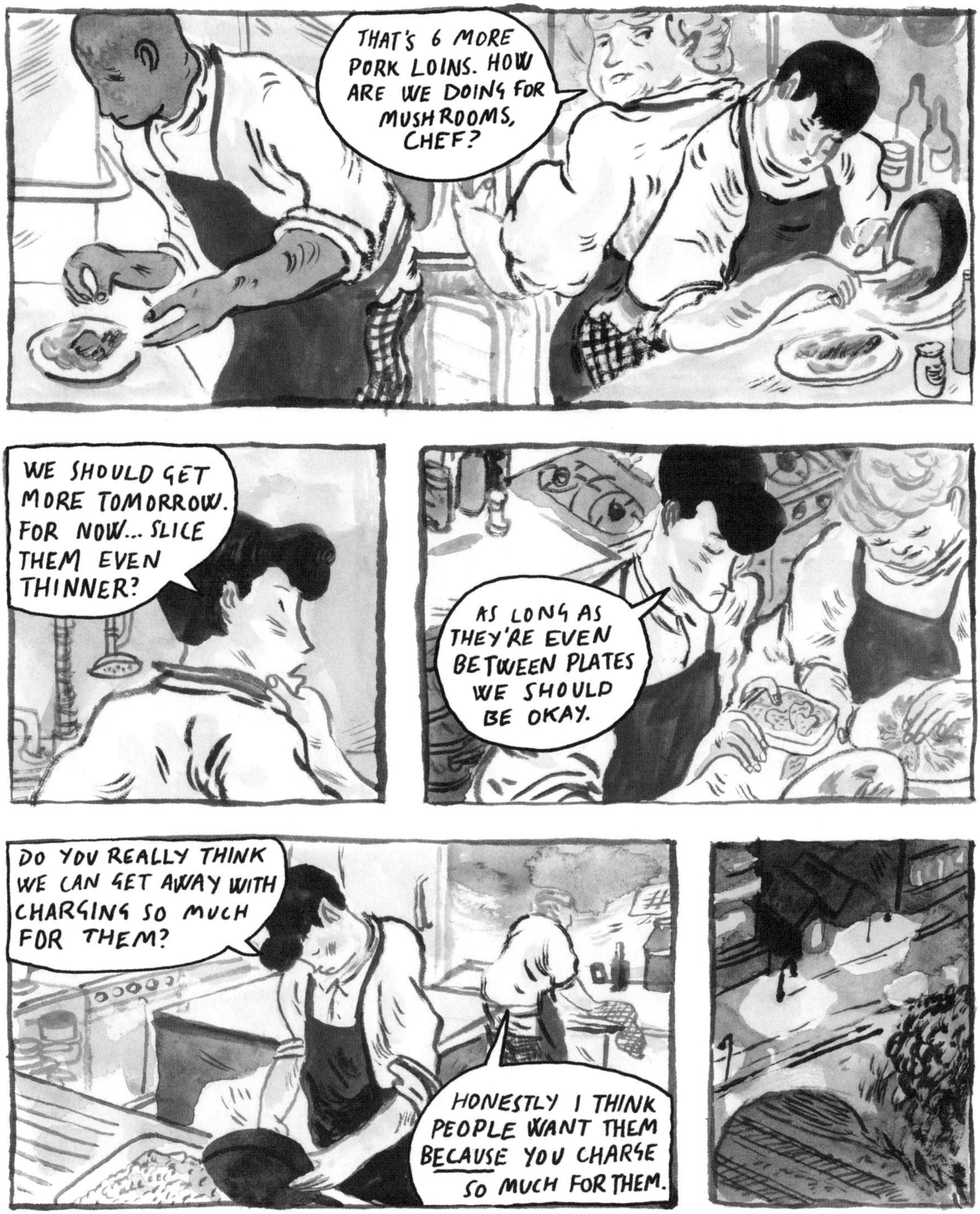
THAT'S 6 MORE PORK LOINS. HOW ARE WE DOING FOR MUSHROOMS, CHEF?
WE SHOULD GET MORE TOMORROW. FOR NOW... SLICE THEM EVEN THINNER?
AS LONG AS THEY'RE EVEN BETWEEN PLATES WE SHOULD BE OKAY.
DO YOU REALLY THINK WE CAN GET AWAY WITH CHARGING SO MUCH FOR THEM?
HONESTLY I THINK PEOPLE WANT THEM BECAUSE YOU CHARGE SO MUCH FOR THEM.

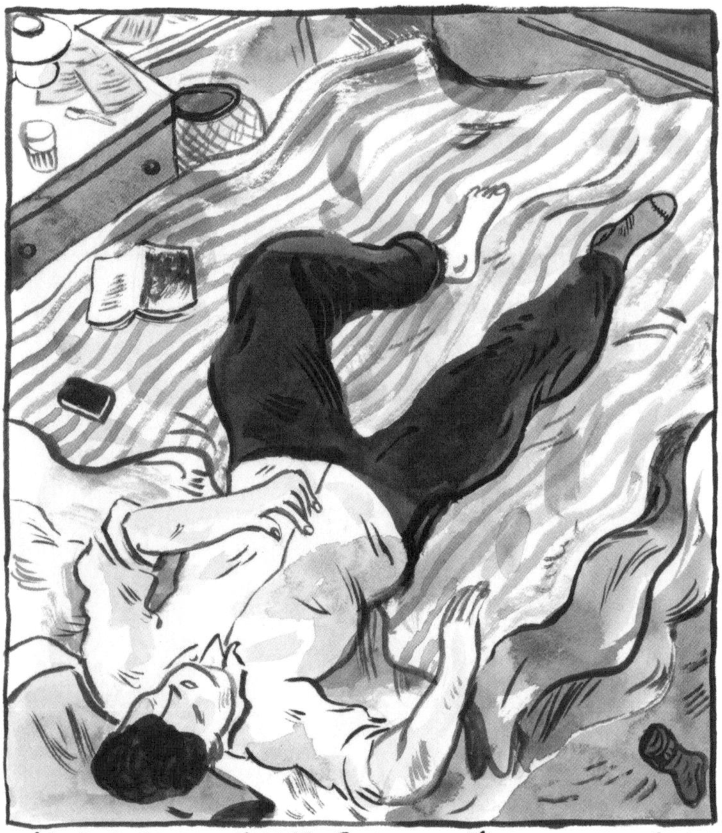

MABEL IS RIGHT, TULIP REFLECTS, AS HE COLLAPSES FULLY CLOTHED INTO BED.

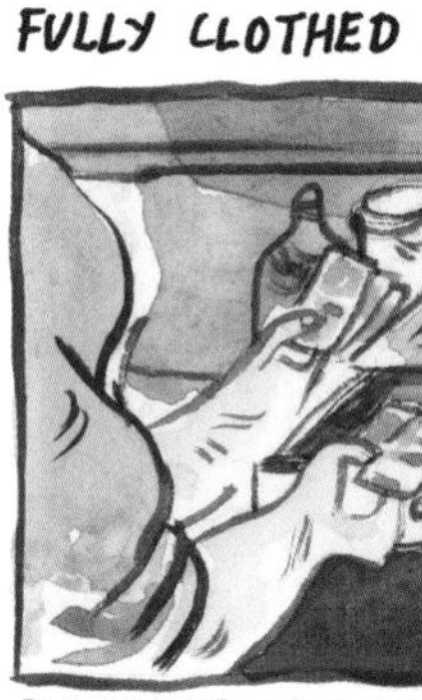

DESPITE HIS ANXIETIES OVER MUSHROOM SUPPLY, HE GROWS RICHER WITH EVERY WEEK.

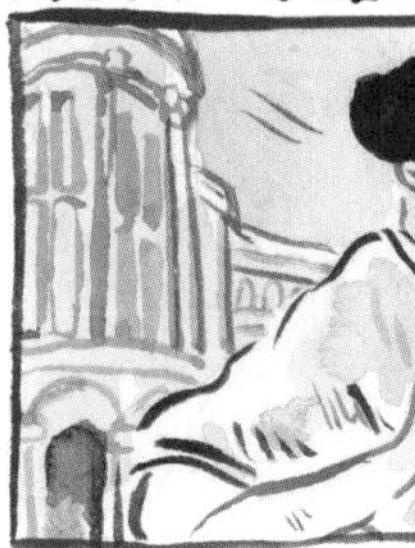

HE DISTRACTS HIMSELF FROM WORRY AND GUILT BY WILDLY SPLASHING OUT, DETERMINED TO SPEND HIS WAY INTO THE SOCIAL CIRCLES OF OTHER PRESTIGIOUS CHEFS.

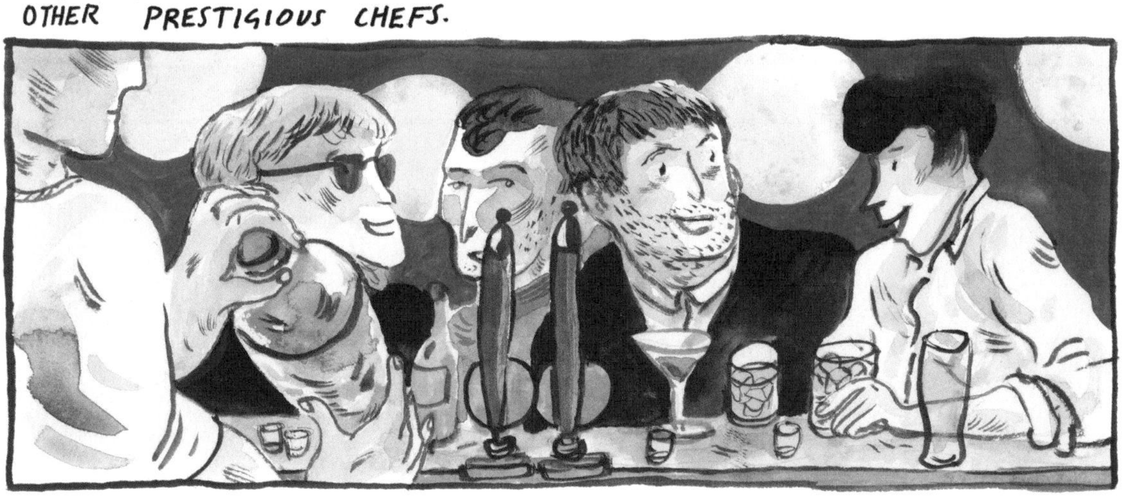

ROUNDS OF COCKTAILS, EXPENSIVE SUITS, FLASHY GADGETS.

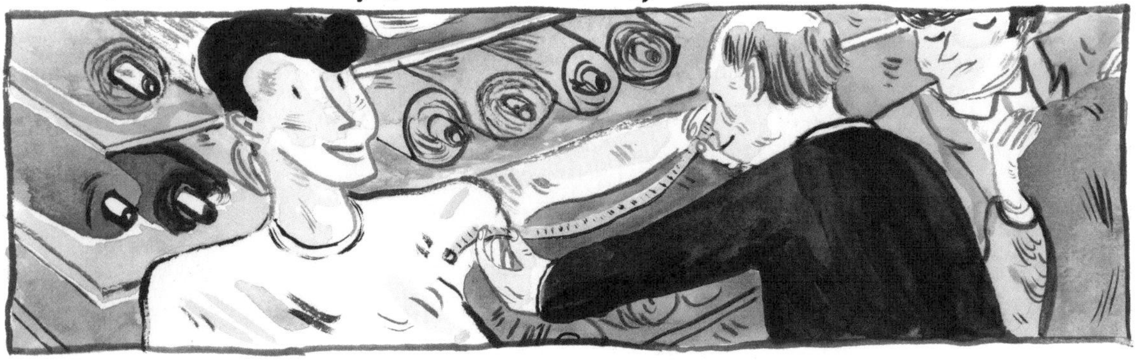

A GIANT T.V. FOR HIS HOME, WHICH HE NEVER FINDS TIME TO WATCH.

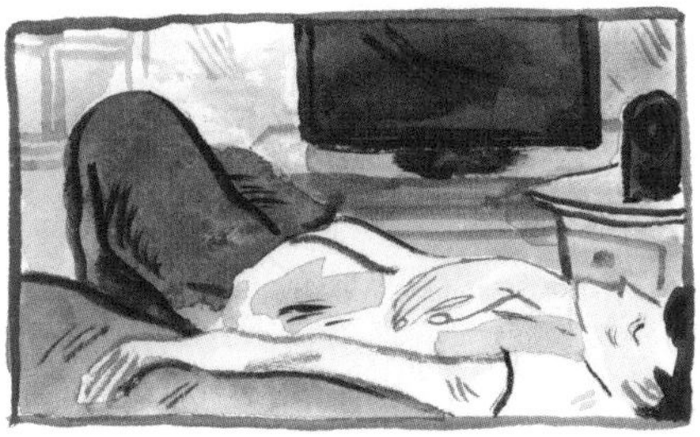

ON HIS RARE VISITS TO ROWAN HE'S EXHAUSTED, BUT AT LEAST, HE THINKS, HE LOOKS LIKE A REAL LONDON RESTAURATEUR.

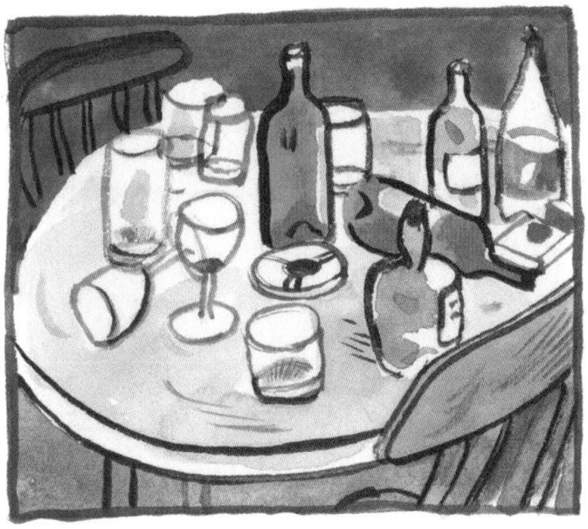

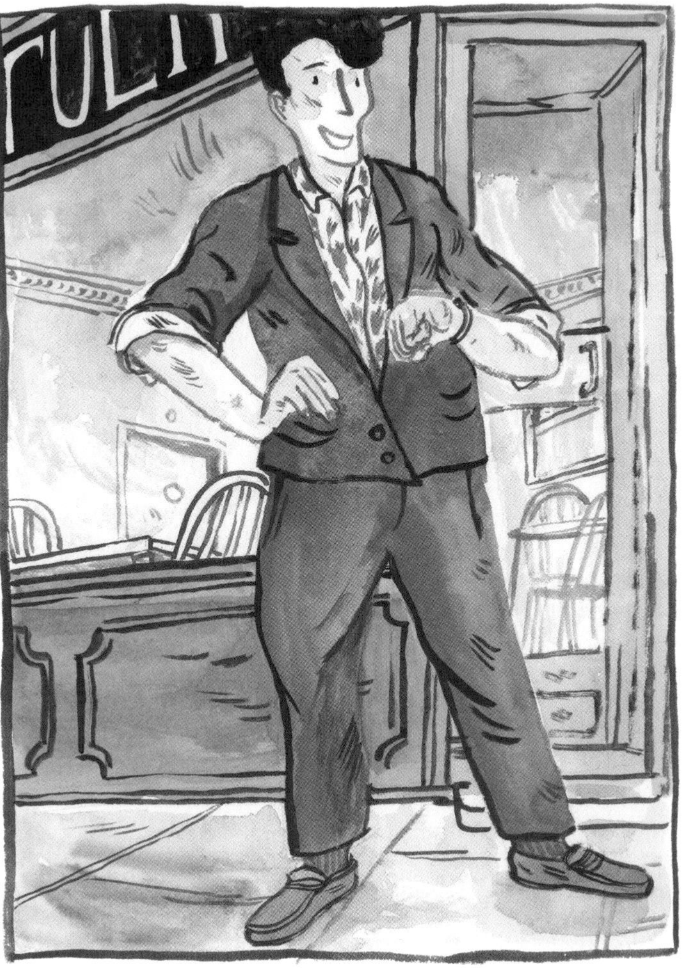

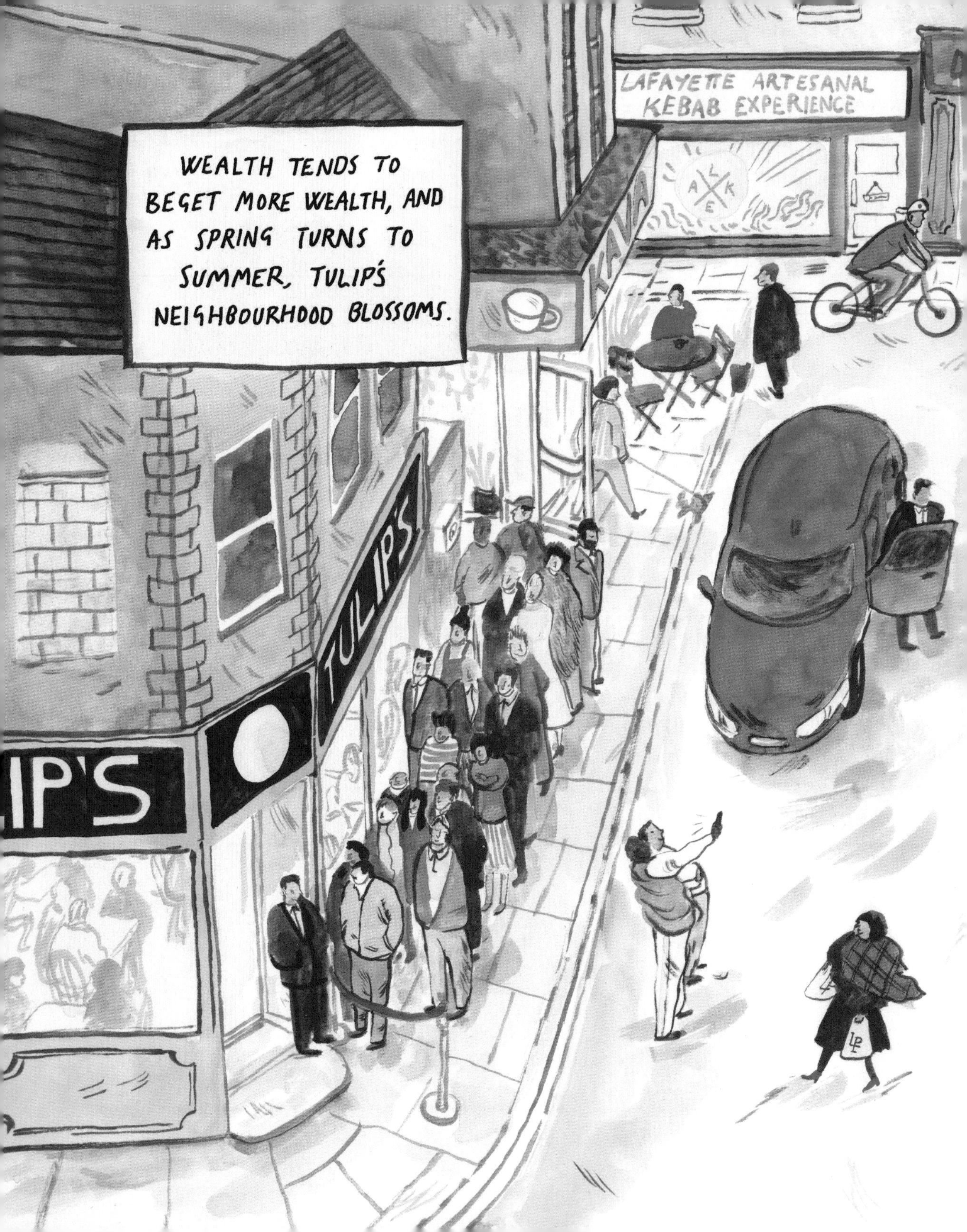
WEALTH TENDS TO BEGET MORE WEALTH, AND AS SPRING TURNS TO SUMMER, TULIP'S NEIGHBOURHOOD BLOSSOMS.
LAFAYETTE ARTESANAL KEBAB EXPERIENCE
KAVA
TULIP'S
IP'S

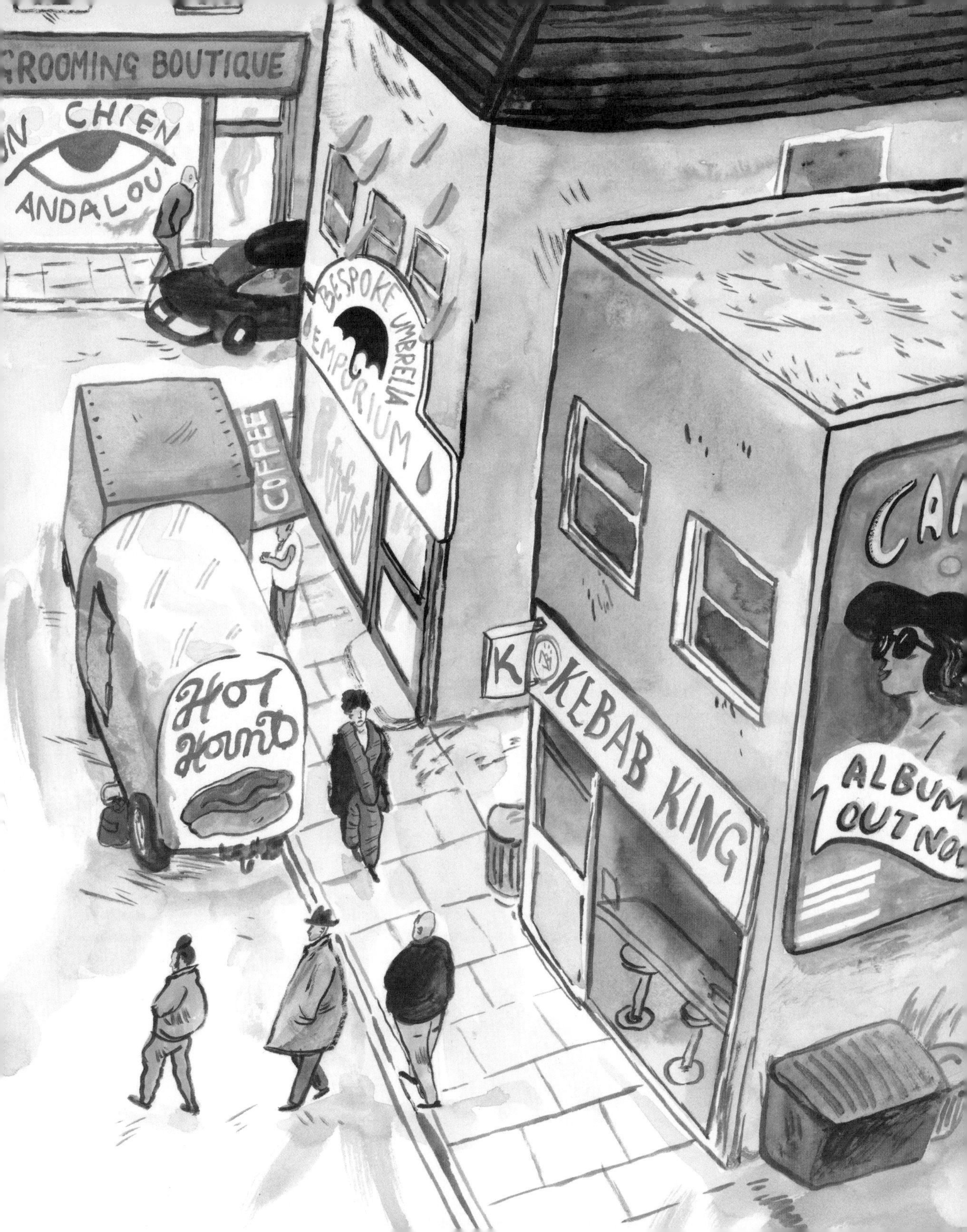

GROOMING BOUTIQUE
CHIEN
ANDALOU
BESPOKE UMBRELLA EMPORIUM
COFFEE
Hot Hound
K
KEBAB KING
ALBUM
OUT NO

TULIP SPENDS LESS AND LESS TIME IN THE KITCHEN AND MORE TIME PLANNING, BALANCING NUMBERS, LOOKING FOR NEW WAYS TO INSINUATE HIMSELF INTO THE GASTRONOMIC ELITE.

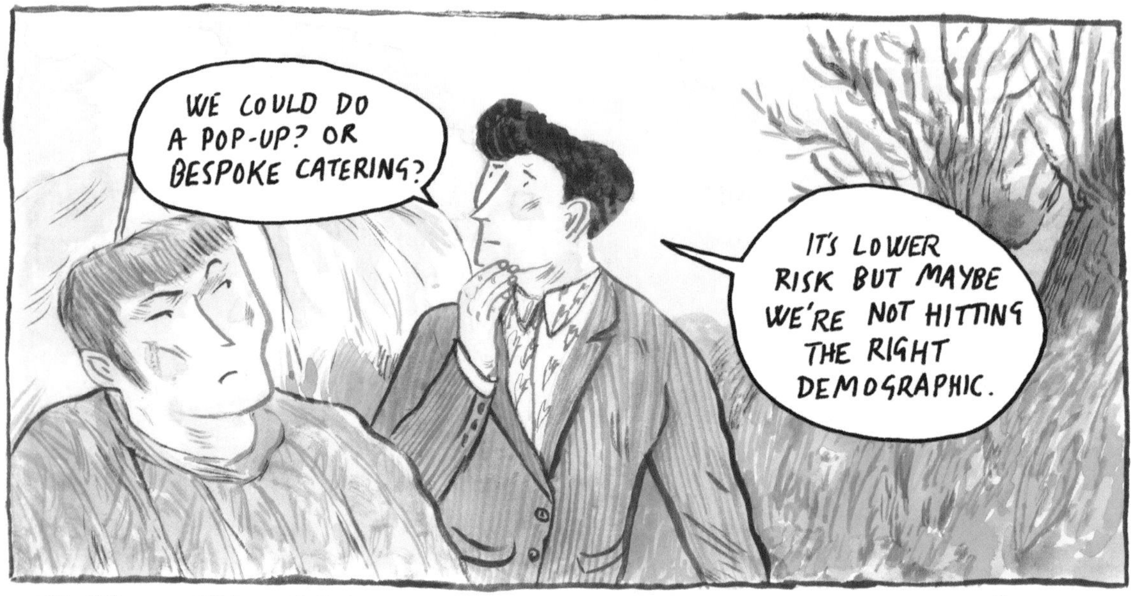
WE COULD DO A POP-UP? OR BESPOKE CATERING?
IT'S LOWER RISK BUT MAYBE WE'RE NOT HITTING THE RIGHT DEMOGRAPHIC.

HE PROMOTES MABEL TO CHEF DE CUISINE, A TASK SHE TAKES TO WITH RELISH, TRAINING THE YOUNGER COOKS AND TERRORISING THE WAITERS AND KITCHEN PORTERS.

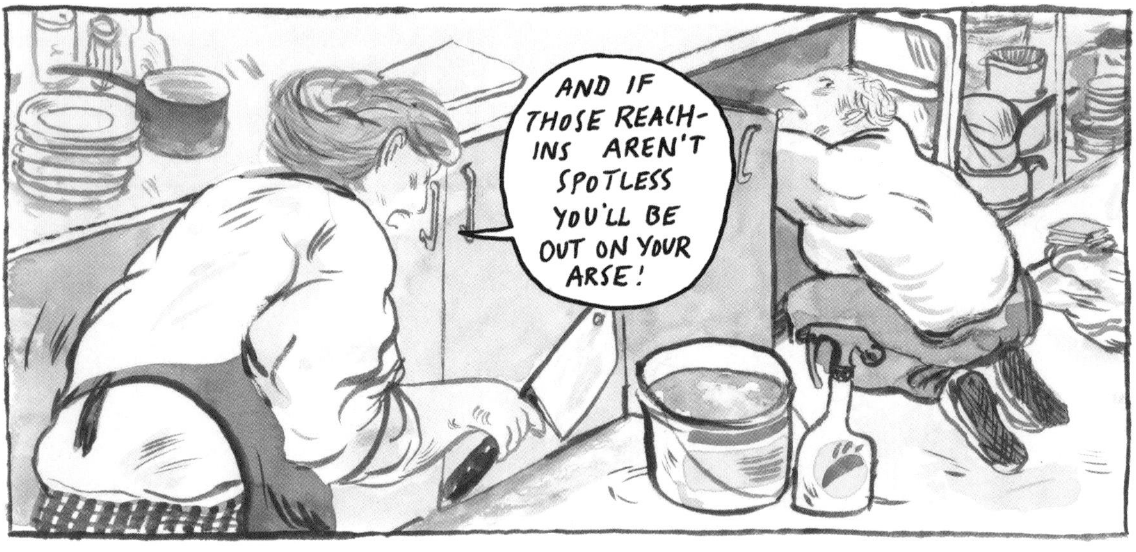
AND IF THOSE REACH-INS AREN'T SPOTLESS YOU'LL BE OUT ON YOUR ARSE!

TULIP ALSO HIRES A MUCH-NEEDED MAÎTRE D', A MAN CALLING HIMSELF MARCEL. HE'S PERFECT, BRINGING AN IMPRESSIVE RÉSUMÉ, A WORLD-CLASS SNEER, AND AFFECTING AN OBSEQUIOUS FRENCH ACCENT WHICH RECALLS SOME FORGOTTEN ERA OF FINE-DINING.

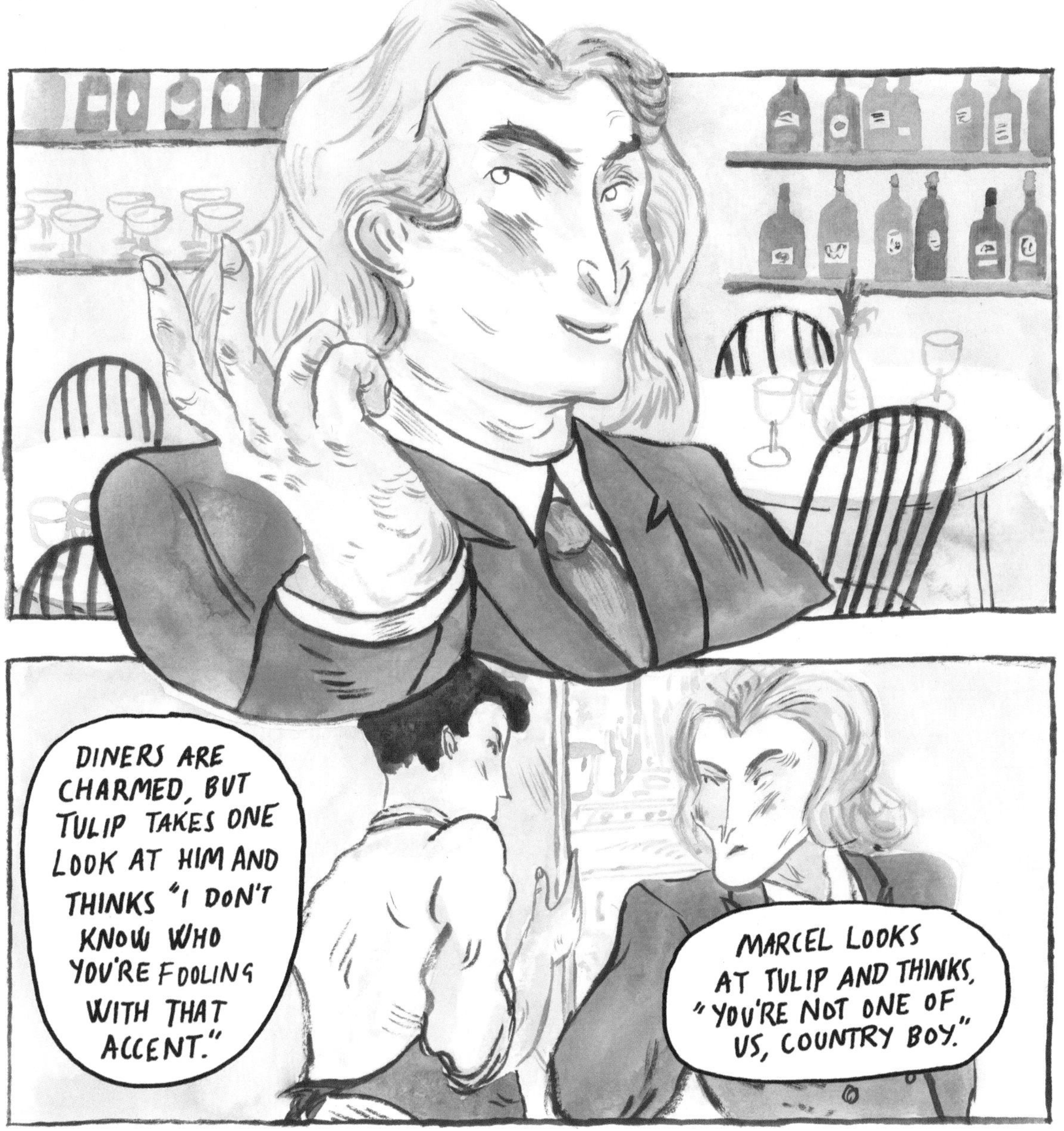

DINERS ARE CHARMED, BUT TULIP TAKES ONE LOOK AT HIM AND THINKS "I DON'T KNOW WHO YOU'RE FOOLING WITH THAT ACCENT."
MARCEL LOOKS AT TULIP AND THINKS, "YOU'RE NOT ONE OF US, COUNTRY BOY."

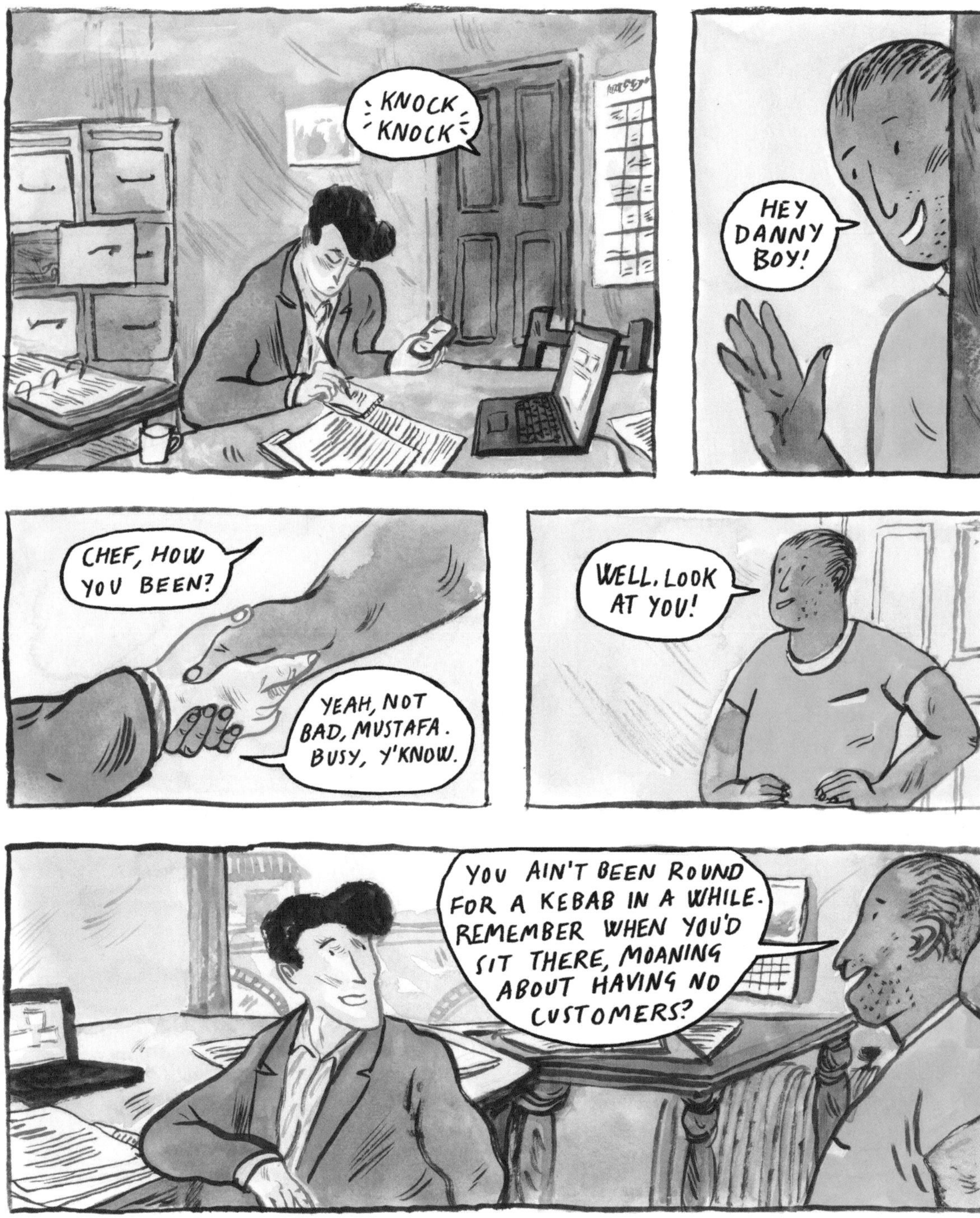
KNOCK KNOCK
HEY DANNY BOY!
CHEF, HOW YOU BEEN?
YEAH, NOT BAD, MUSTAFA. BUSY, Y'KNOW.
WELL, LOOK AT YOU!
YOU AIN'T BEEN ROUND FOR A KEBAB IN A WHILE. REMEMBER WHEN YOU'D SIT THERE, MOANING ABOUT HAVING NO CUSTOMERS?

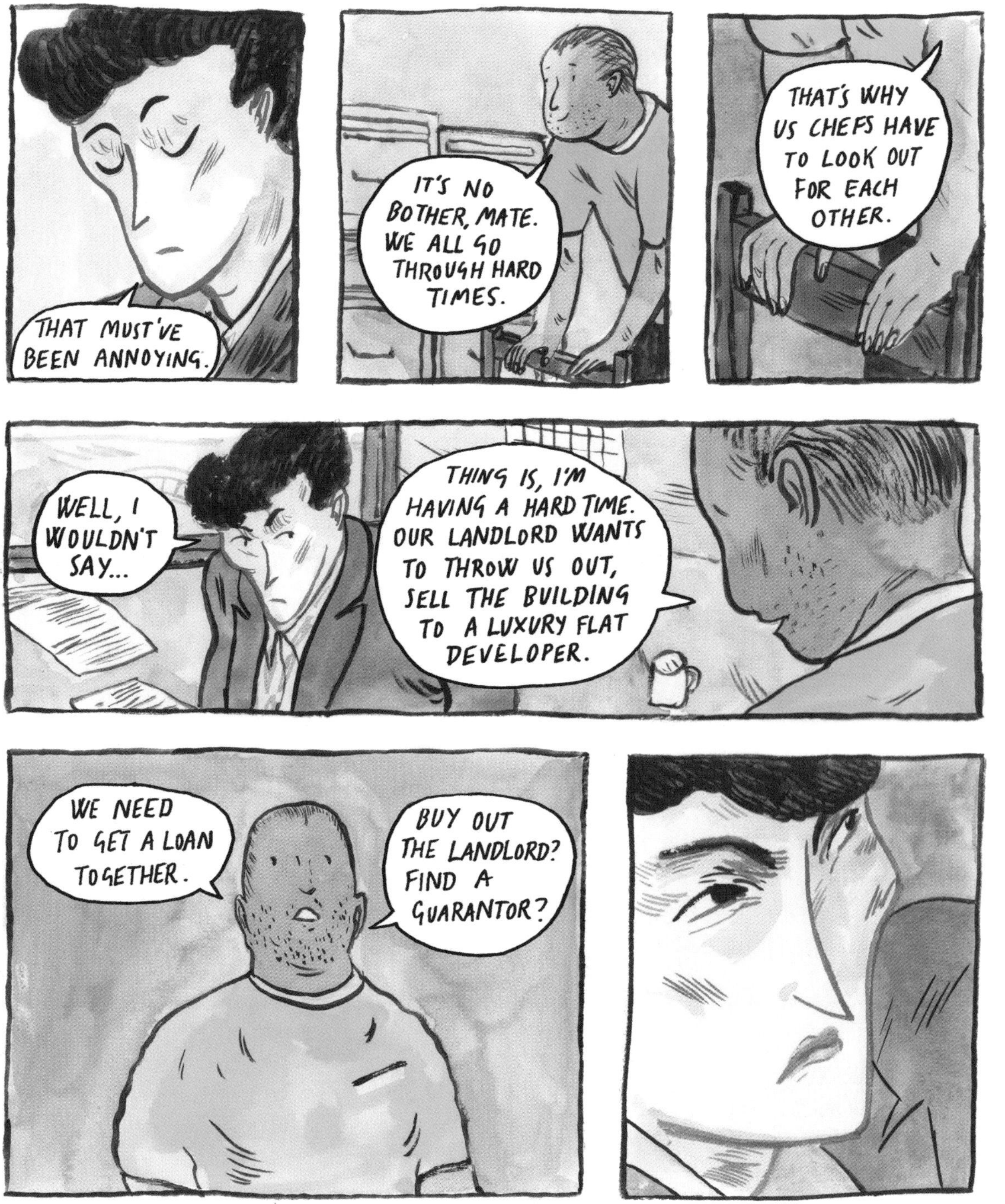
THAT MUST'VE BEEN ANNOYING.
IT'S NO BOTHER, MATE. WE ALL GO THROUGH HARD TIMES.
THAT'S WHY US CHEFS HAVE TO LOOK OUT FOR EACH OTHER.
WELL, I WOULDN'T SAY...
THING IS, I'M HAVING A HARD TIME. OUR LANDLORD WANTS TO THROW US OUT, SELL THE BUILDING TO A LUXURY FLAT DEVELOPER.
WE NEED TO GET A LOAN TOGETHER.
BUY OUT THE LANDLORD? FIND A GUARANTOR?

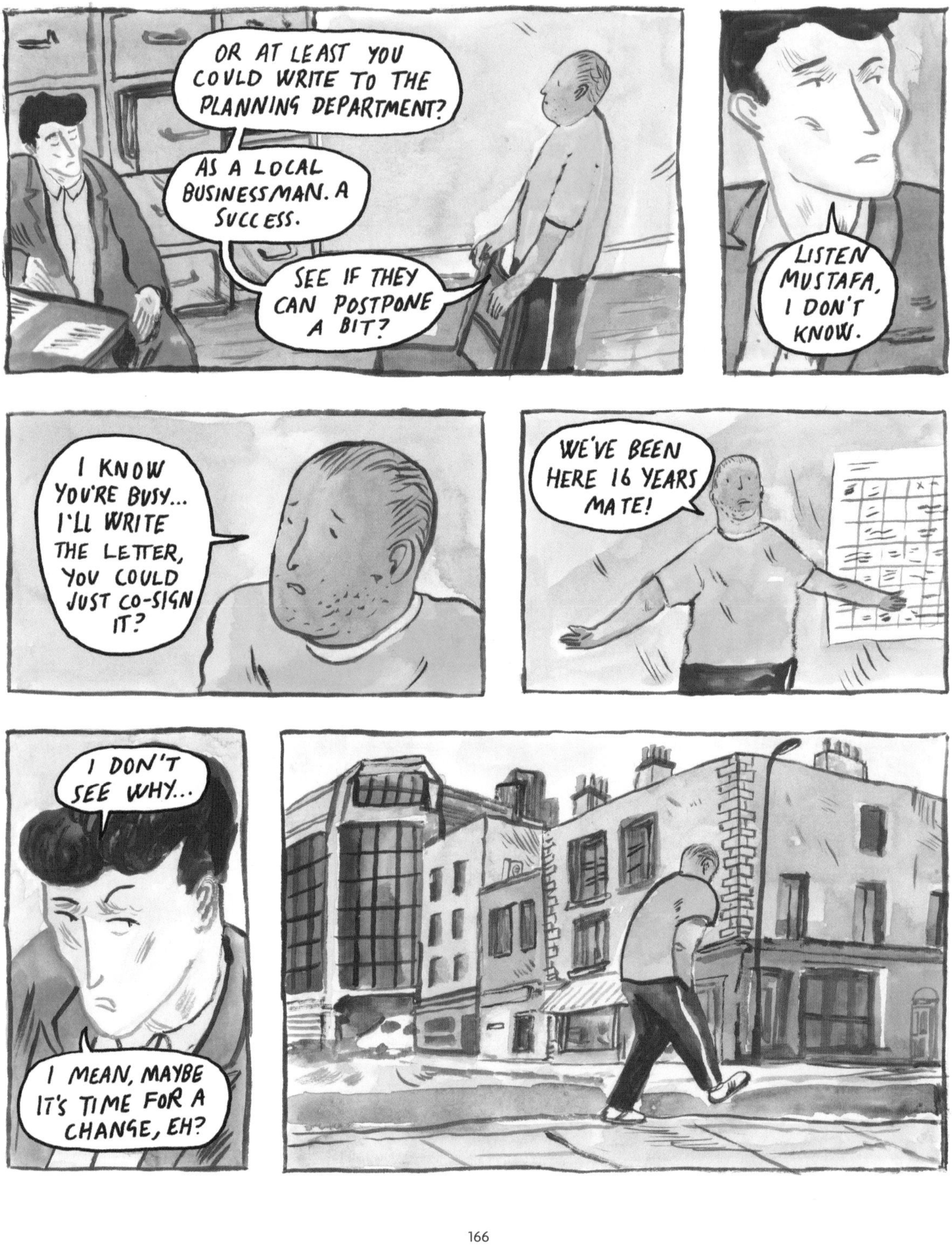
OR AT LEAST YOU COULD WRITE TO THE PLANNING DEPARTMENT?
AS A LOCAL BUSINESSMAN. A SUCCESS.
SEE IF THEY CAN POSTPONE A BIT?
LISTEN MUSTAFA, I DON'T KNOW.
I KNOW YOU'RE BUSY... I'LL WRITE THE LETTER, YOU COULD JUST CO-SIGN IT?
WE'VE BEEN HERE 16 YEARS MATE!
I DON'T SEE WHY...
I MEAN, MAYBE IT'S TIME FOR A CHANGE, EH?

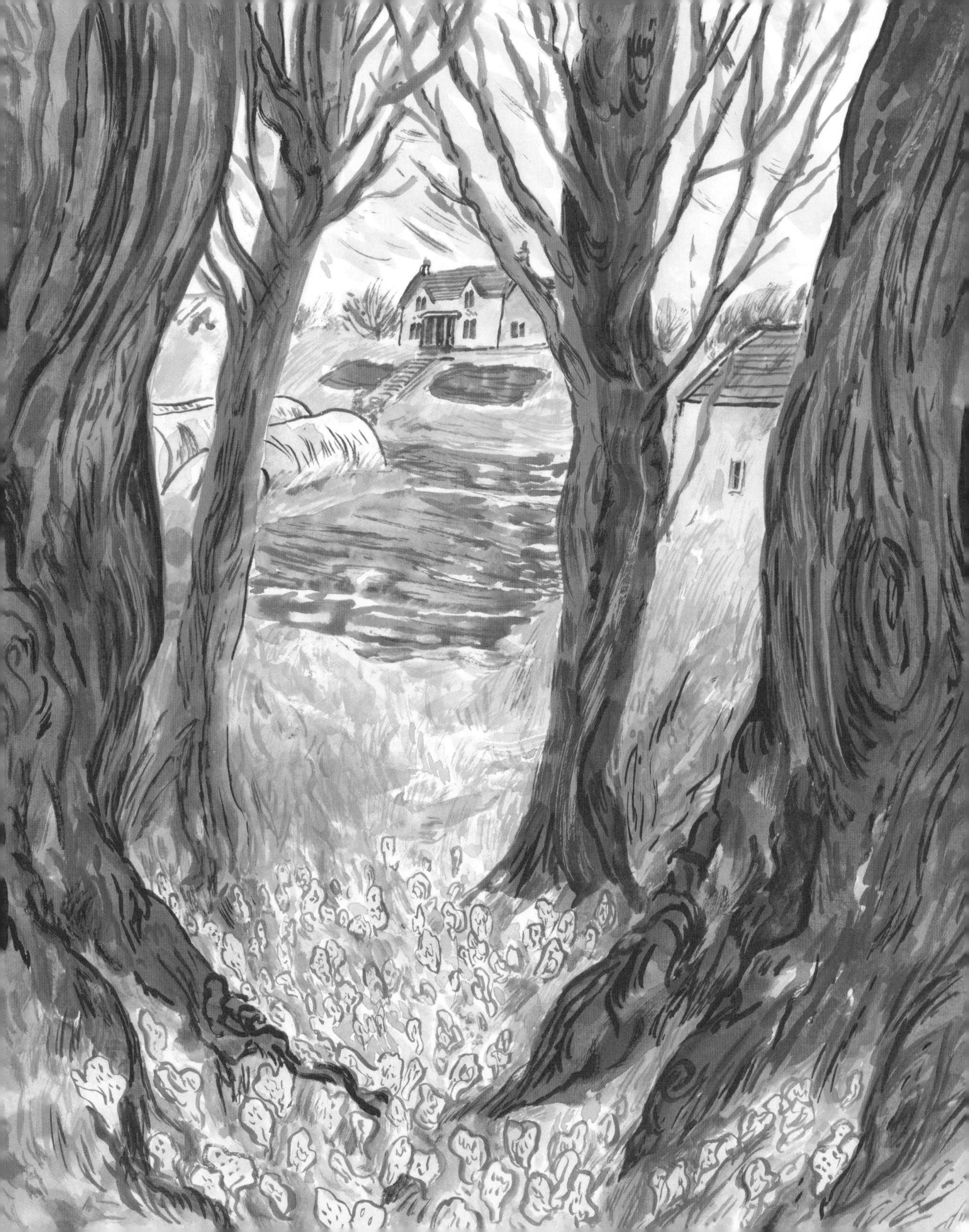

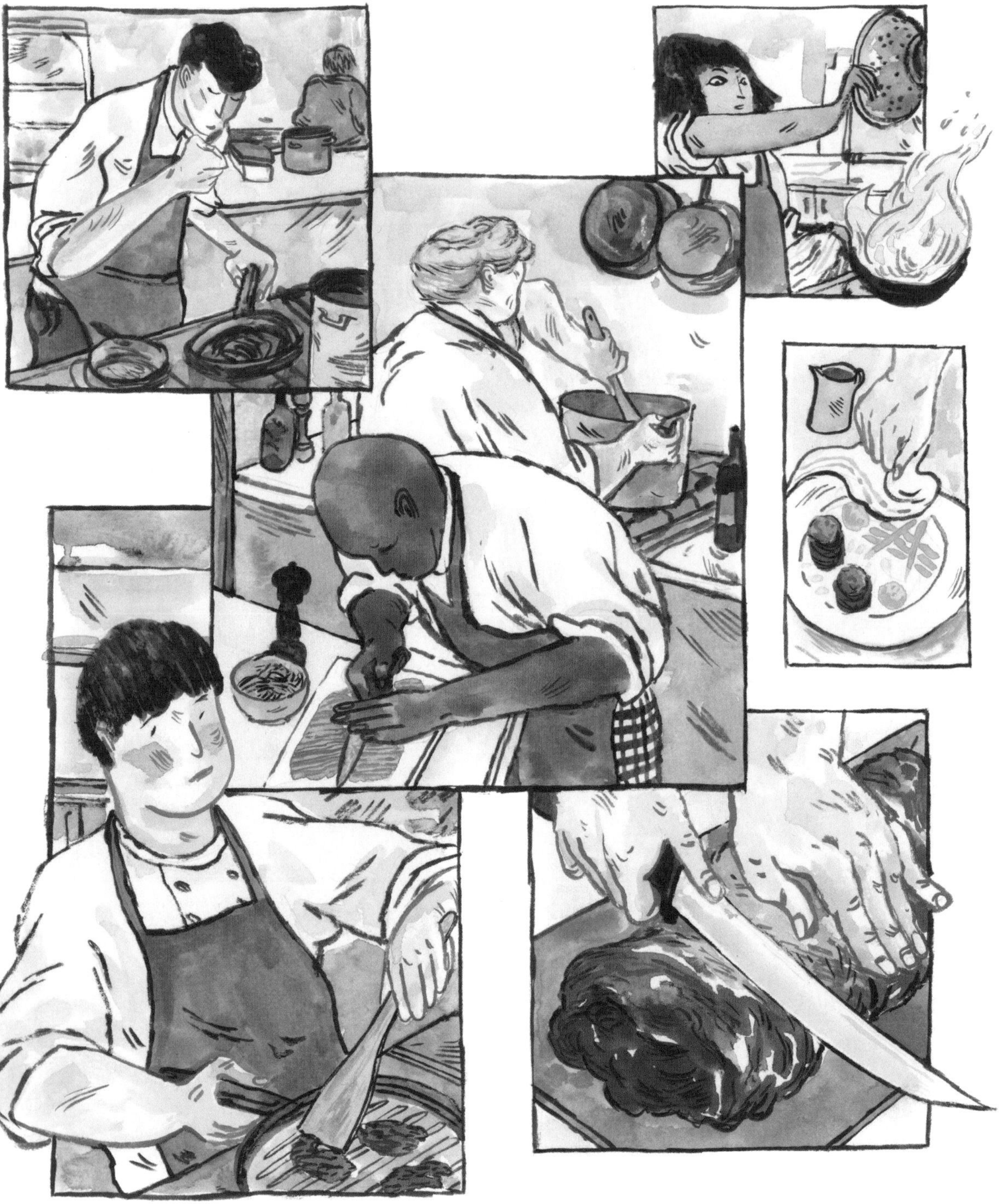

IT'S FRIDAY NIGHT AND THE RESTAURANT IS FRANTICALLY BUSY. TULIP WORKS FURIOUSLY IN THE KITCHEN WHILE MARCEL GLIDES AROUND THE DINING ROOM...

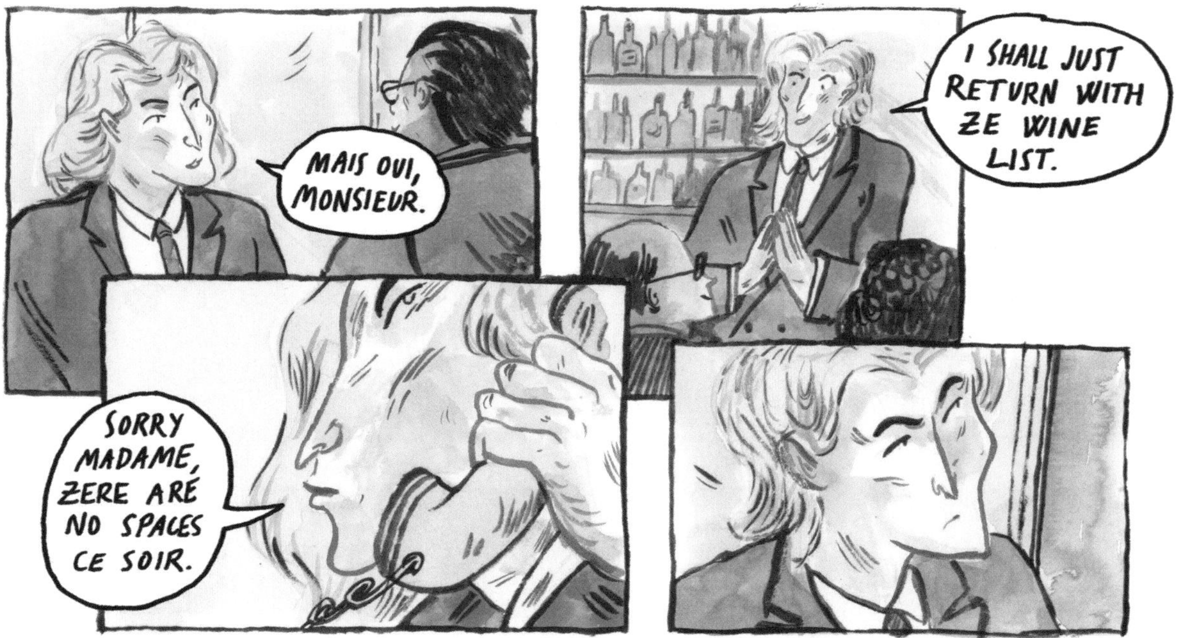
MAIS OUI, MONSIEUR.
I SHALL JUST RETURN WITH ZE WINE LIST.
SORRY MADAME, ZERE ARE NO SPACES CE SOIR.

...AND SO IS THE FIRST TO NOTICE THE ENORMOUS LIMOUSINE, STRUGGLING TO REVERSE DOWN THEIR NARROW STREET.

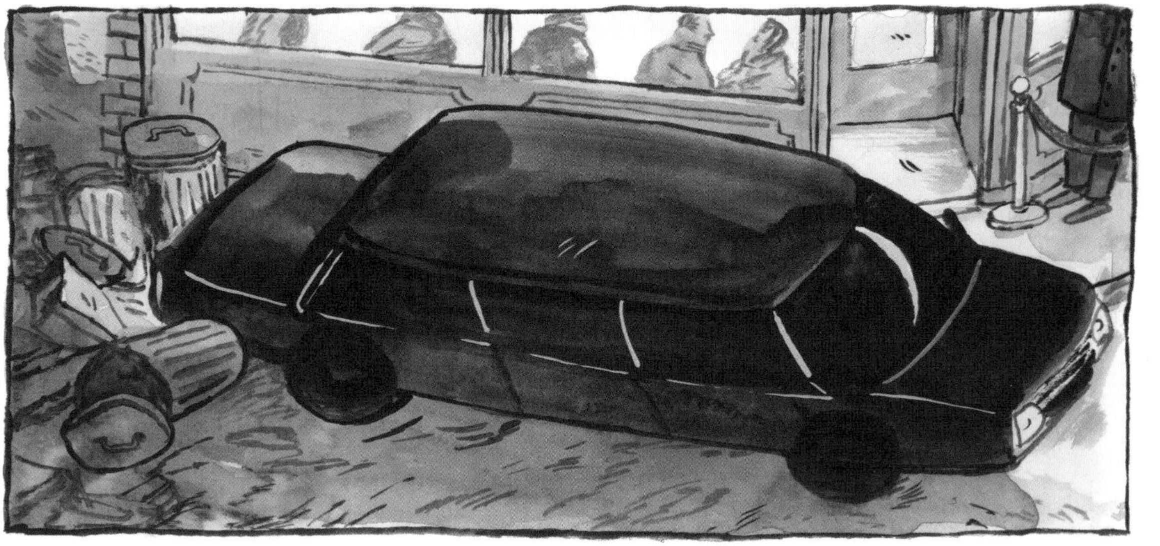

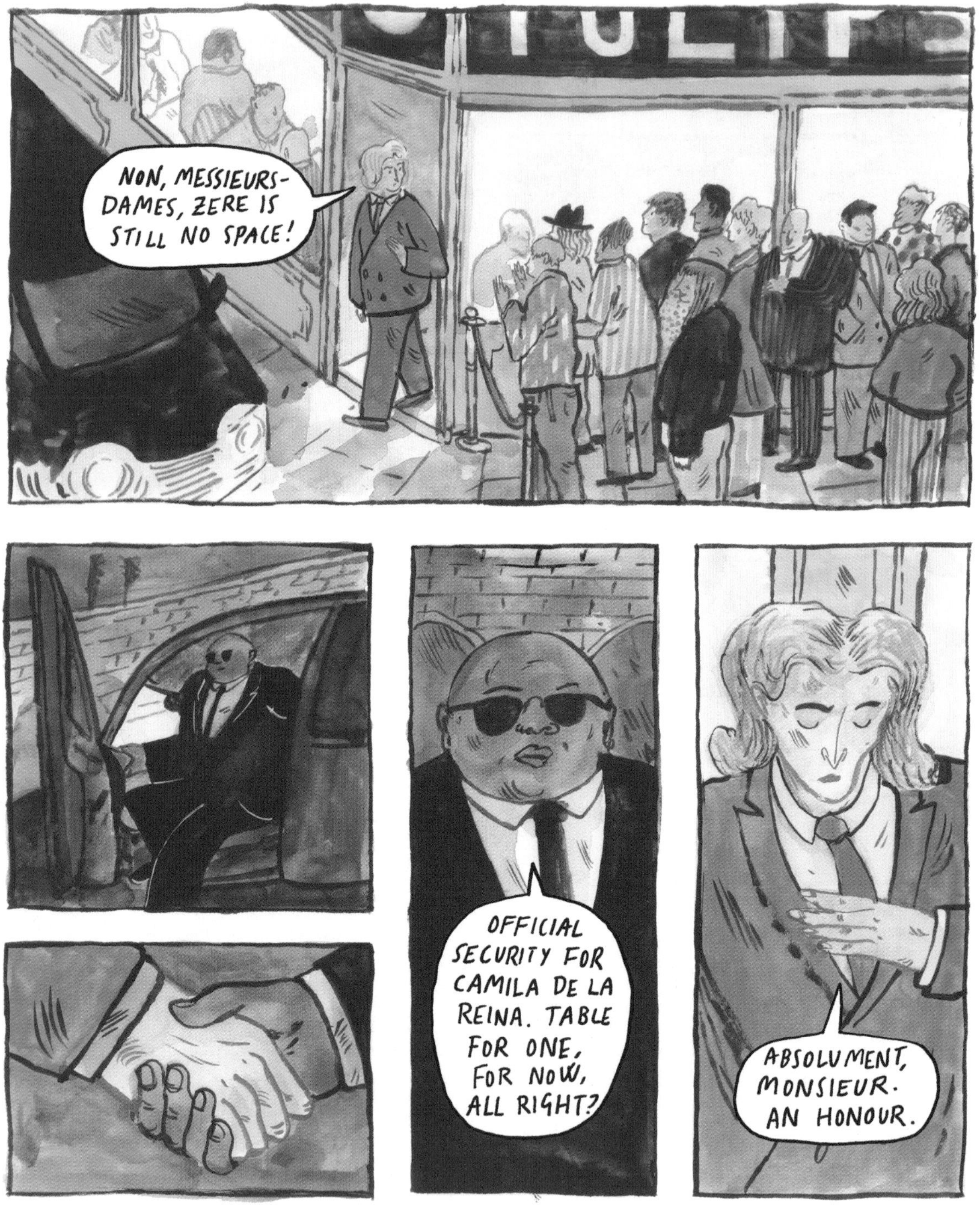
NON, MESSIEURS-DAMES, ZERE IS STILL NO SPACE!
OFFICIAL SECURITY FOR CAMILA DE LA REINA. TABLE FOR ONE, FOR NOW, ALL RIGHT?
ABSOLUMENT, MONSIEUR. AN HONOUR.

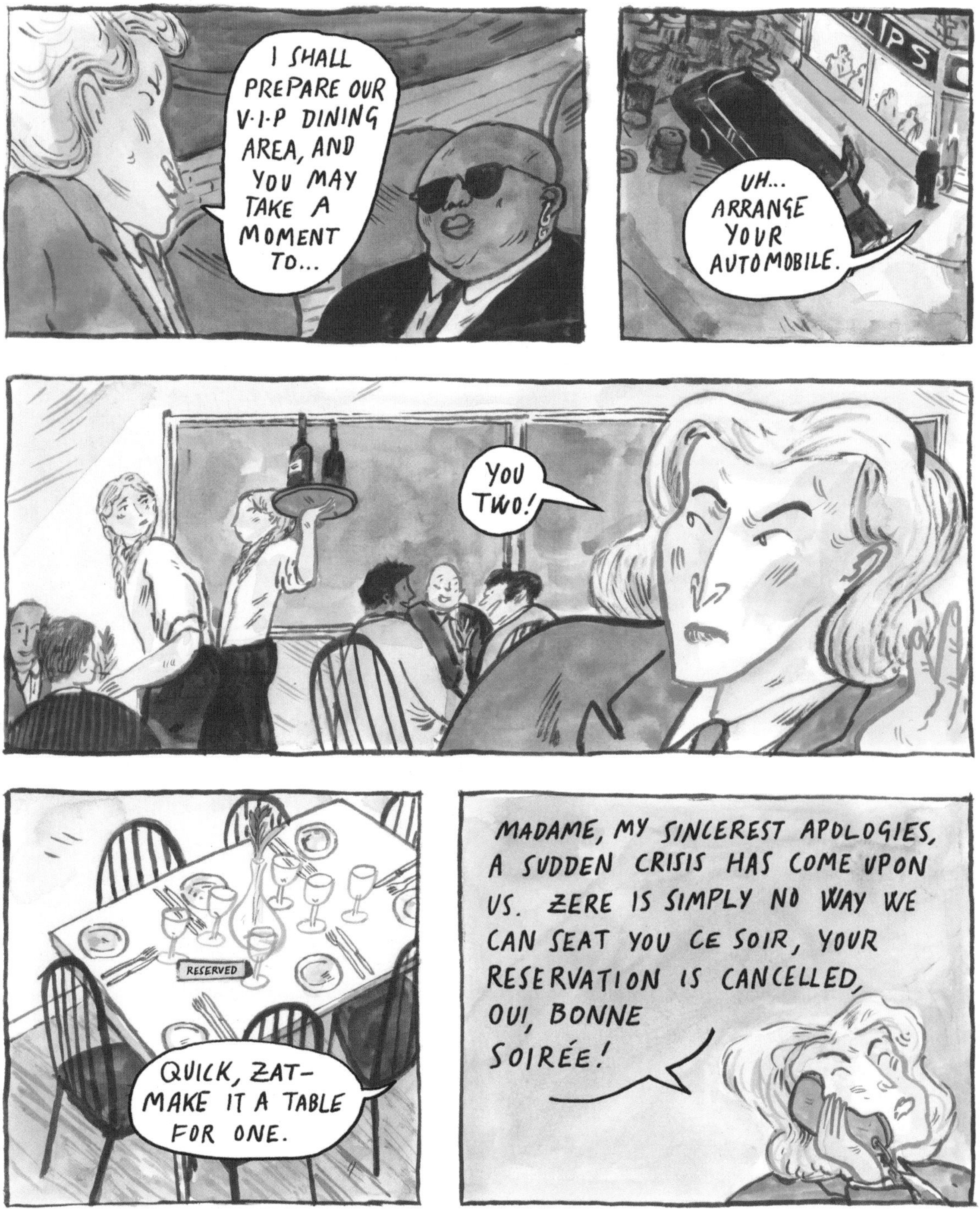
I SHALL PREPARE OUR V·I·P DINING AREA, AND YOU MAY TAKE A MOMENT TO...
UH... ARRANGE YOUR AUTOMOBILE.
YOU TWO!
RESERVED
QUICK, ZAT- MAKE IT A TABLE FOR ONE.
MADAME, MY SINCEREST APOLOGIES, A SUDDEN CRISIS HAS COME UPON US. ZERE IS SIMPLY NO WAY WE CAN SEAT YOU CE SOIR, YOUR RESERVATION IS CANCELLED, OUI, BONNE SOIRÉE!

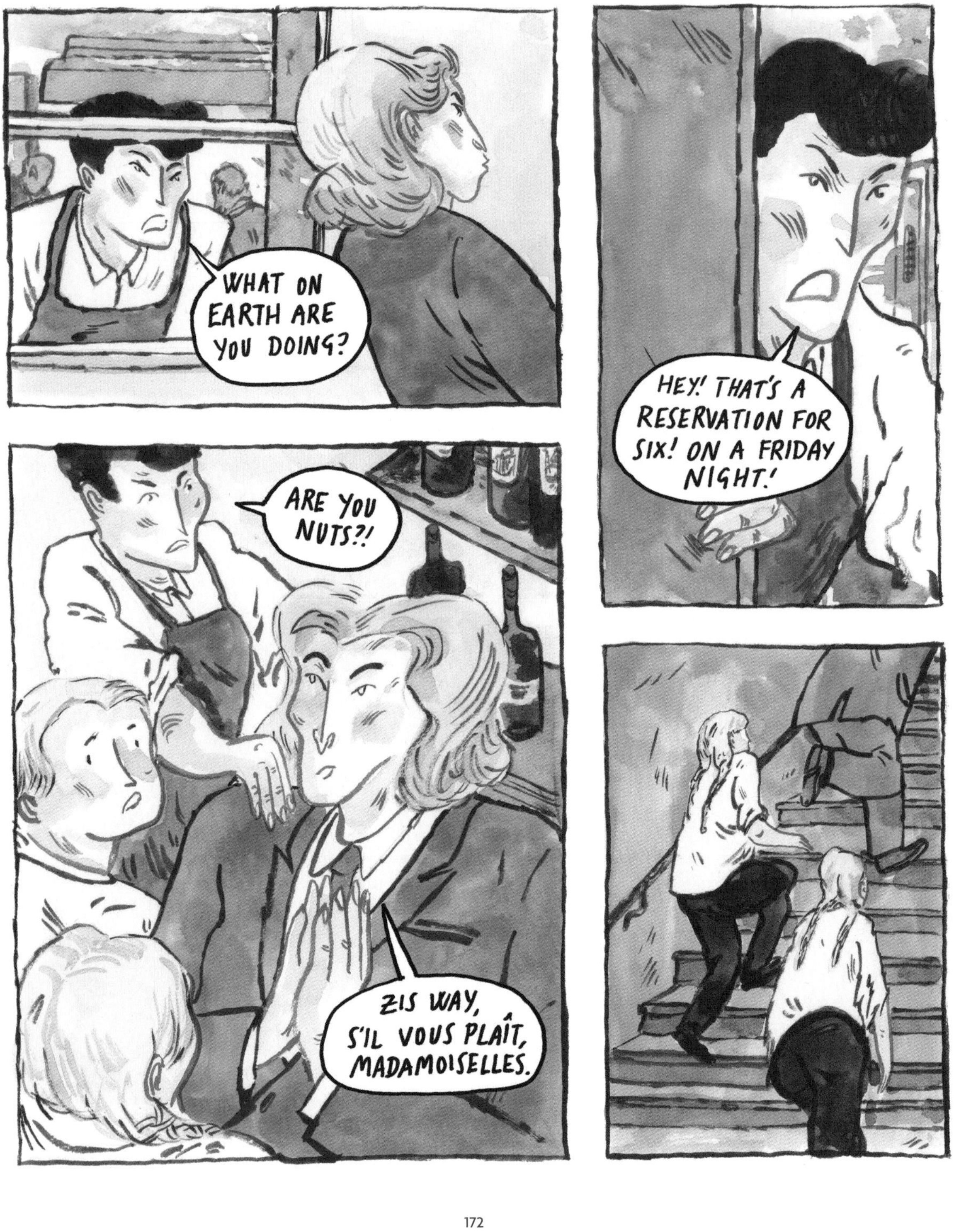
WHAT ON EARTH ARE YOU DOING?
HEY! THAT'S A RESERVATION FOR SIX! ON A FRIDAY NIGHT!
ARE YOU NUTS?!
ZIS WAY, S'IL VOUS PLAÎT, MADAMOISELLES.

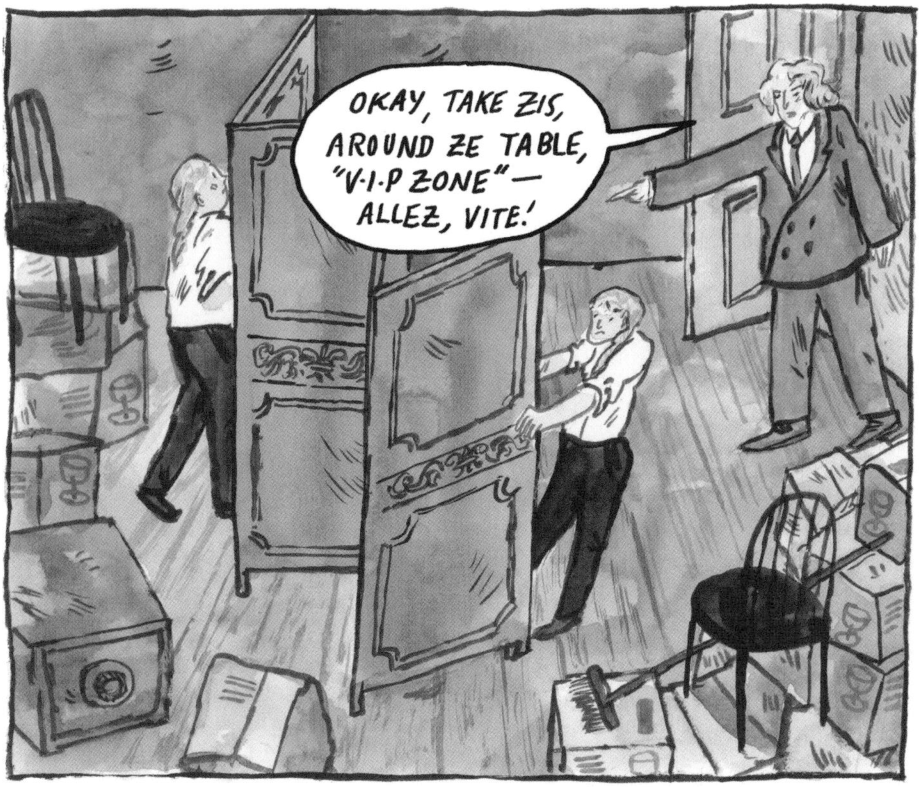
OKAY, TAKE ZIS, AROUND ZE TABLE, "V·I·P ZONE"— ALLEZ, VITE!

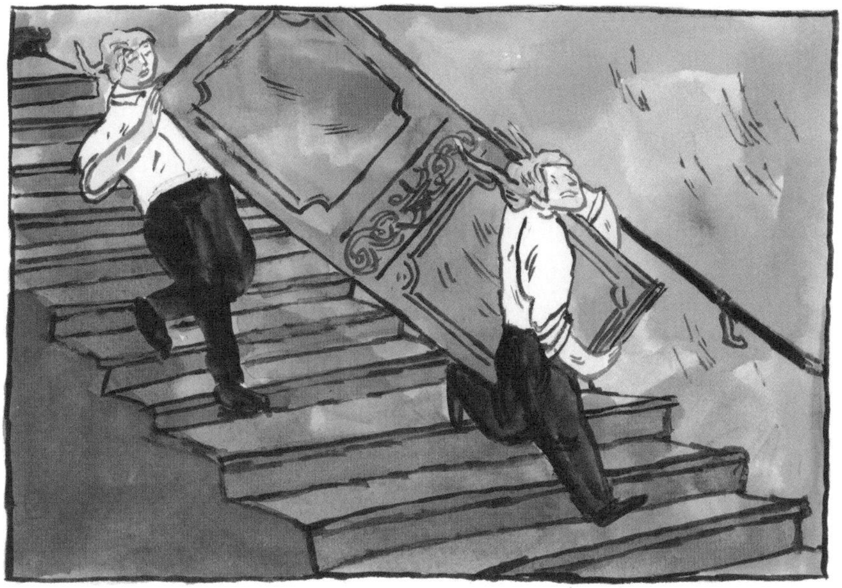

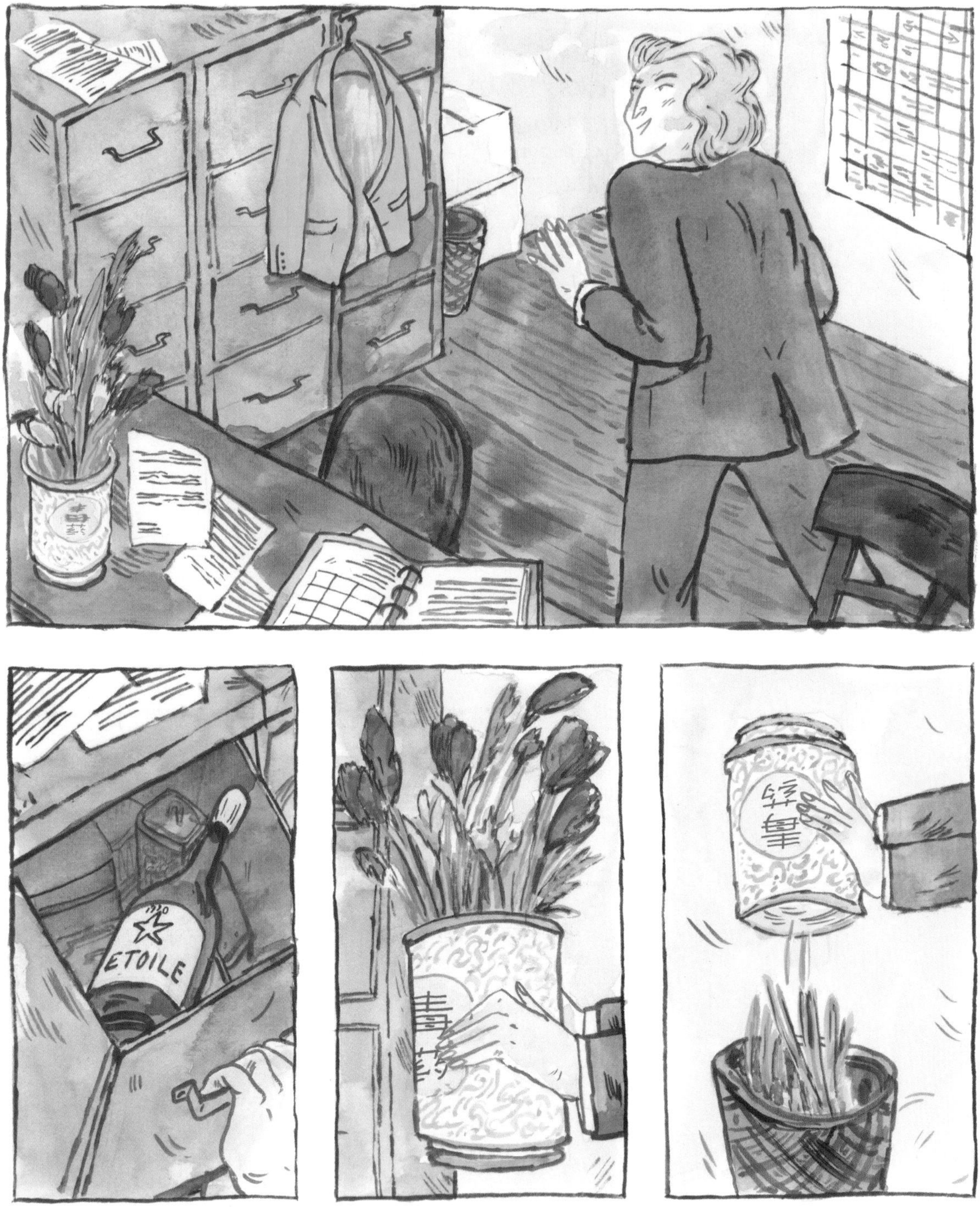
ETOILE

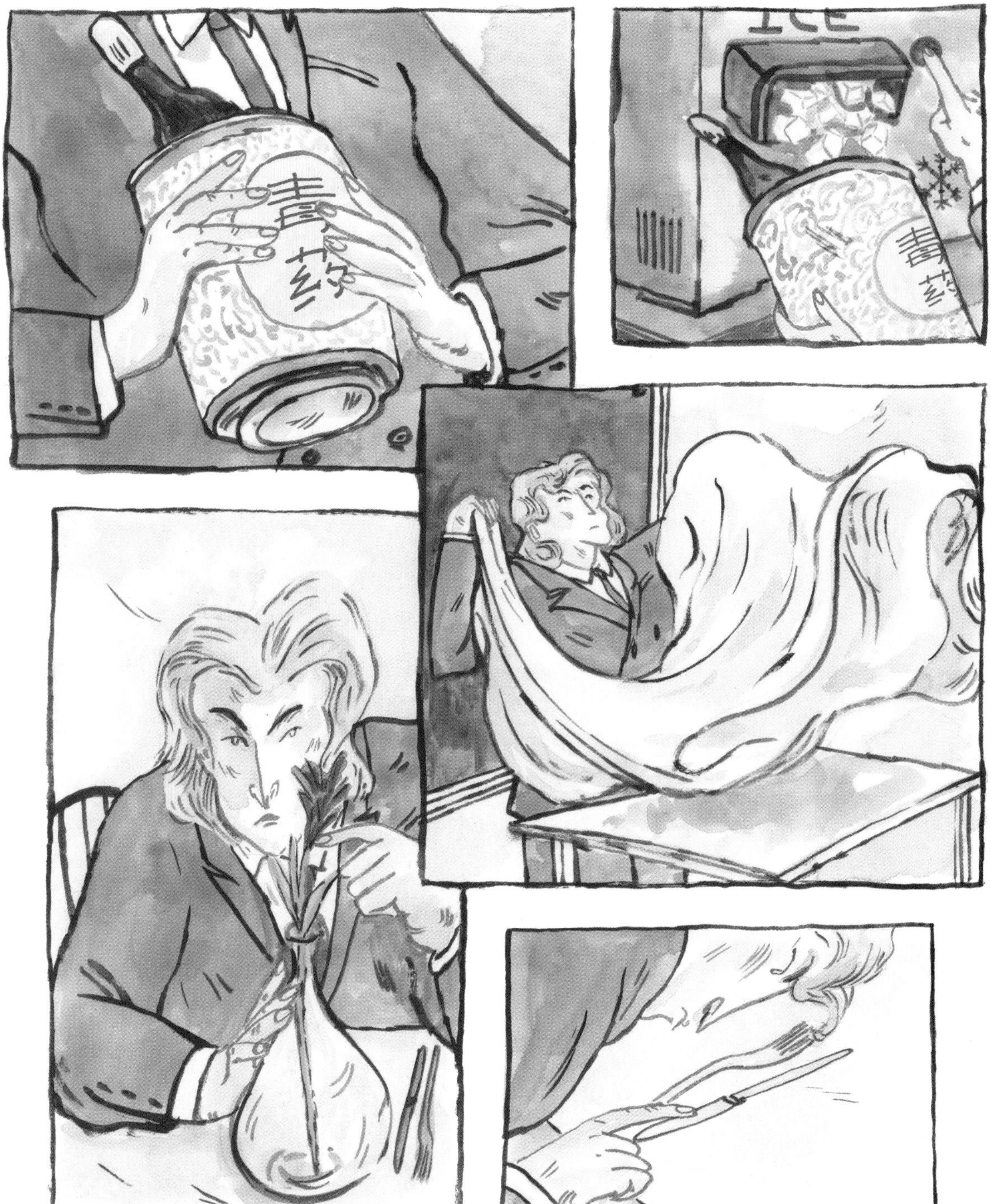
ICE

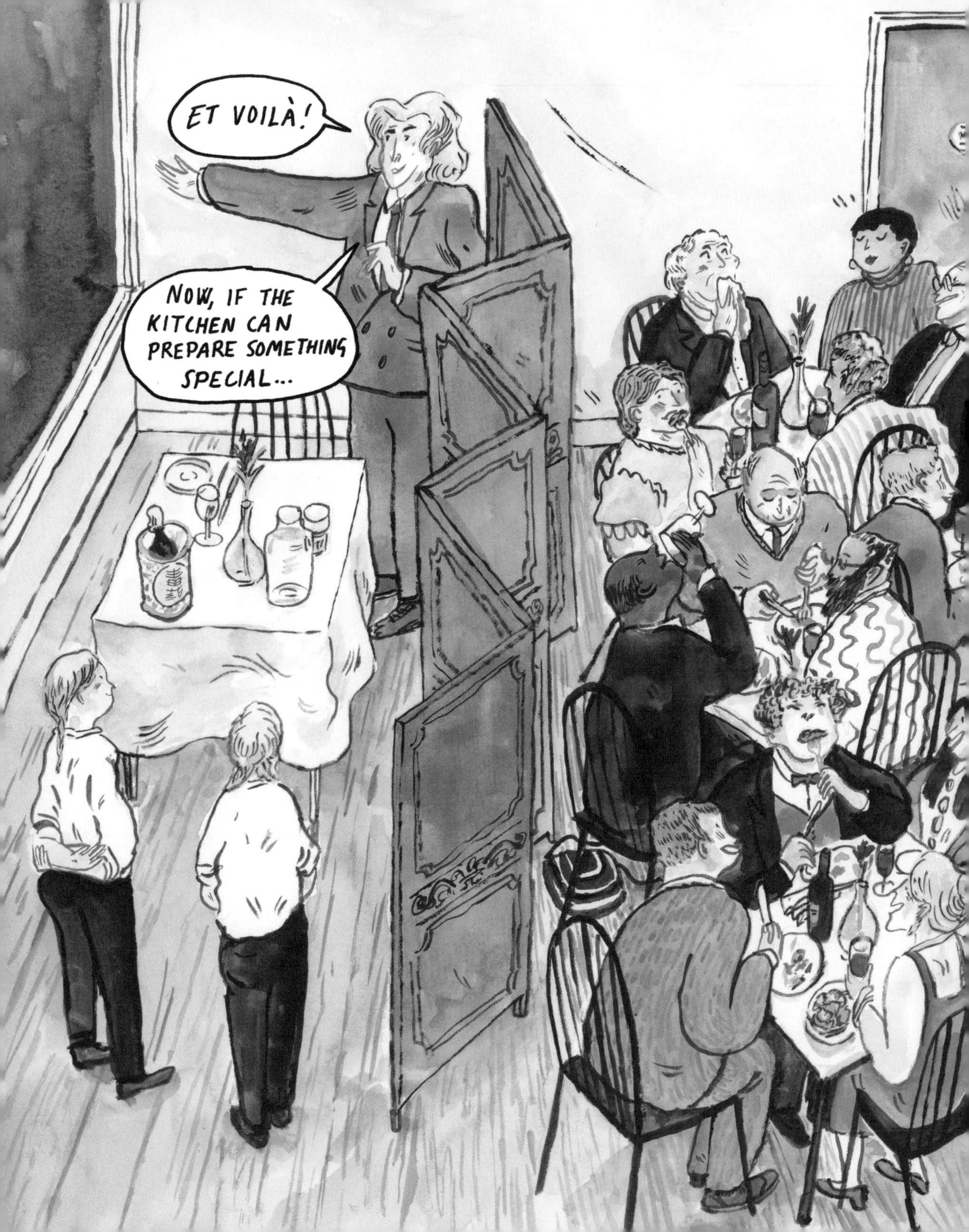
ET VOILÀ!
NOW, IF THE KITCHEN CAN PREPARE SOMETHING SPECIAL...

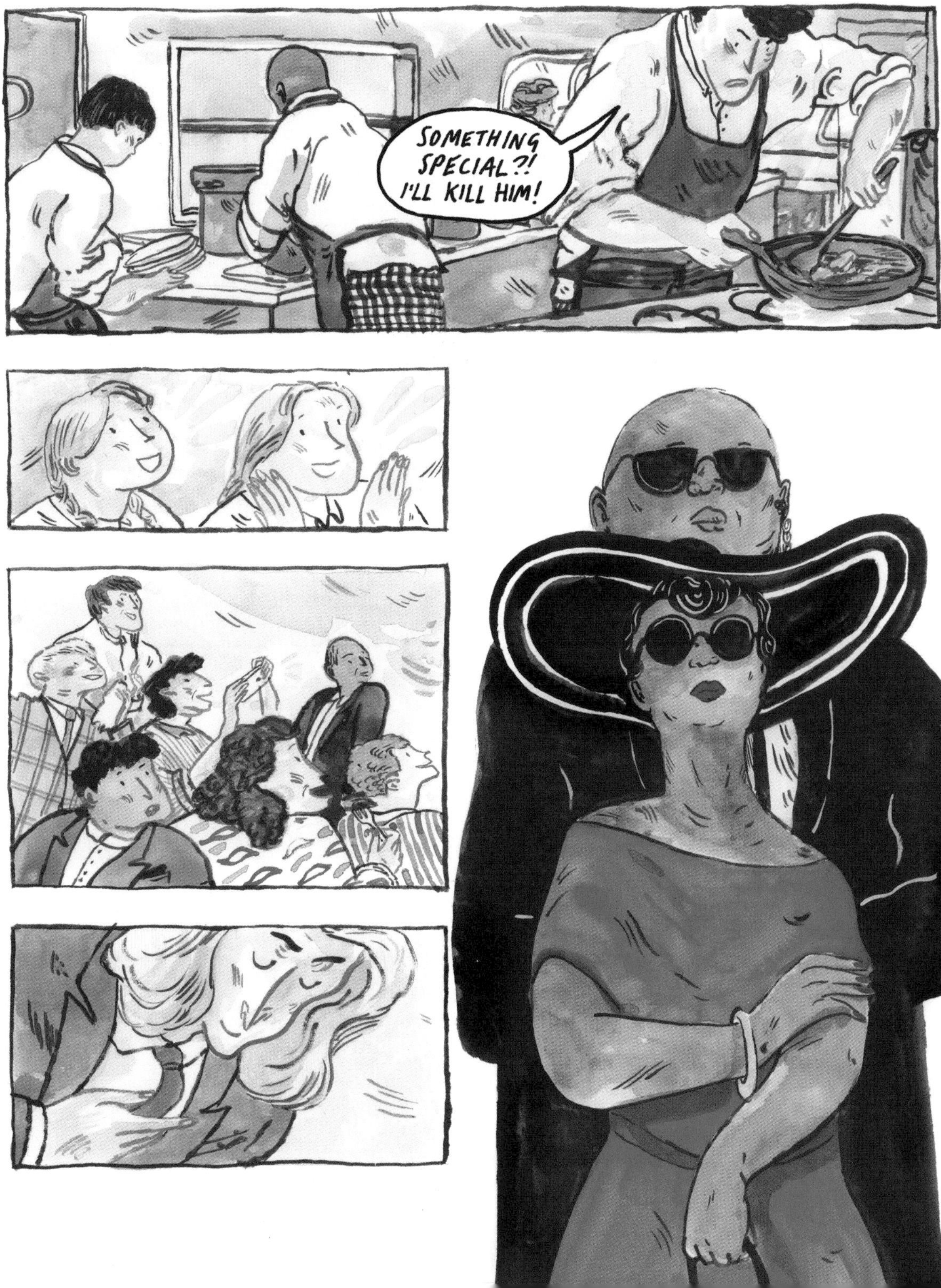
SOMETHING SPECIAL?! I'LL KILL HIM!

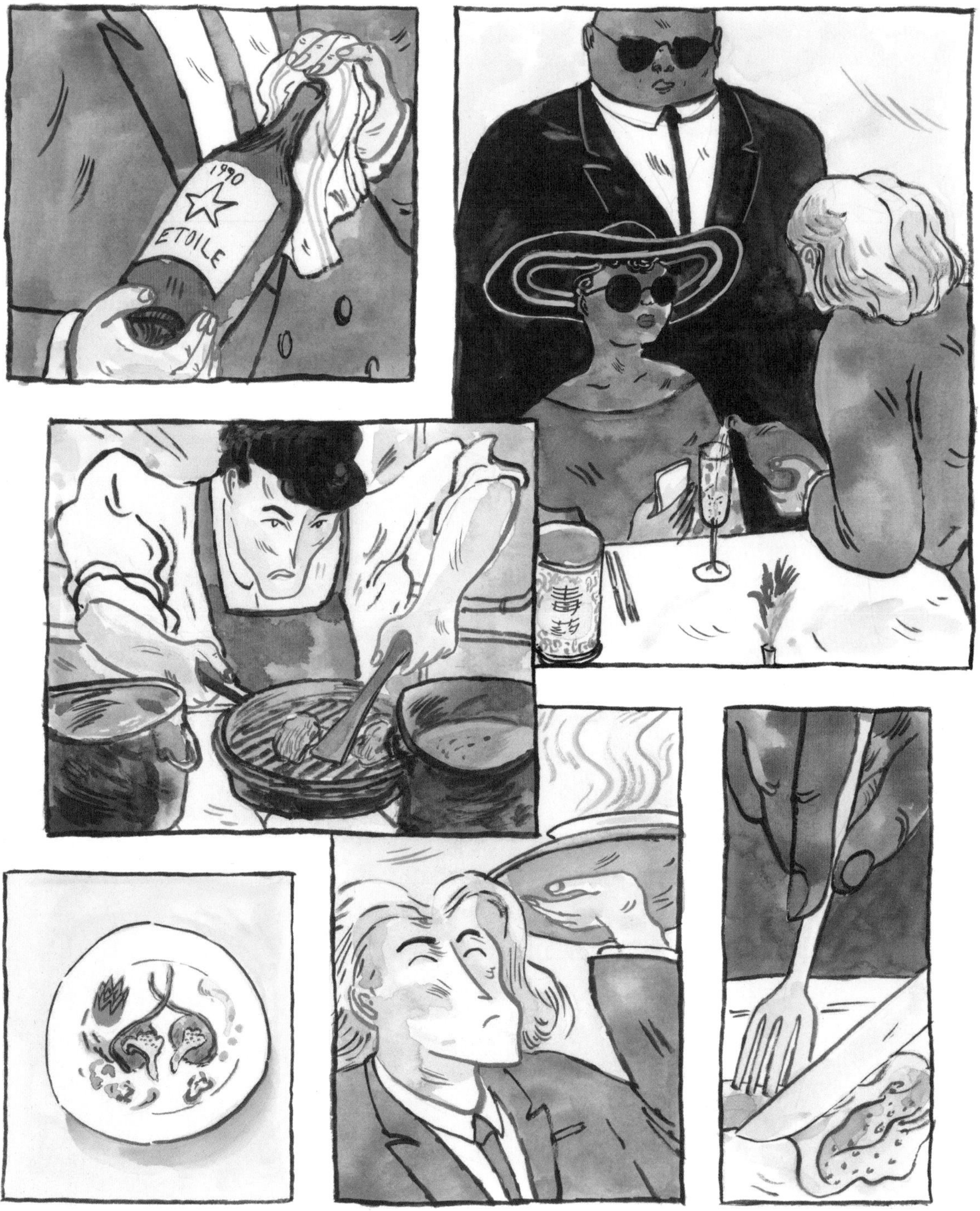
1990
ETOILE

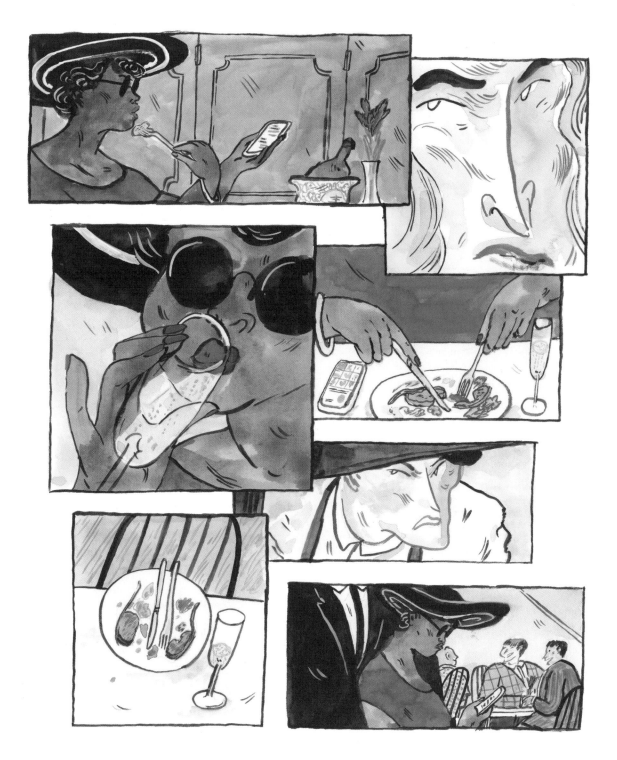

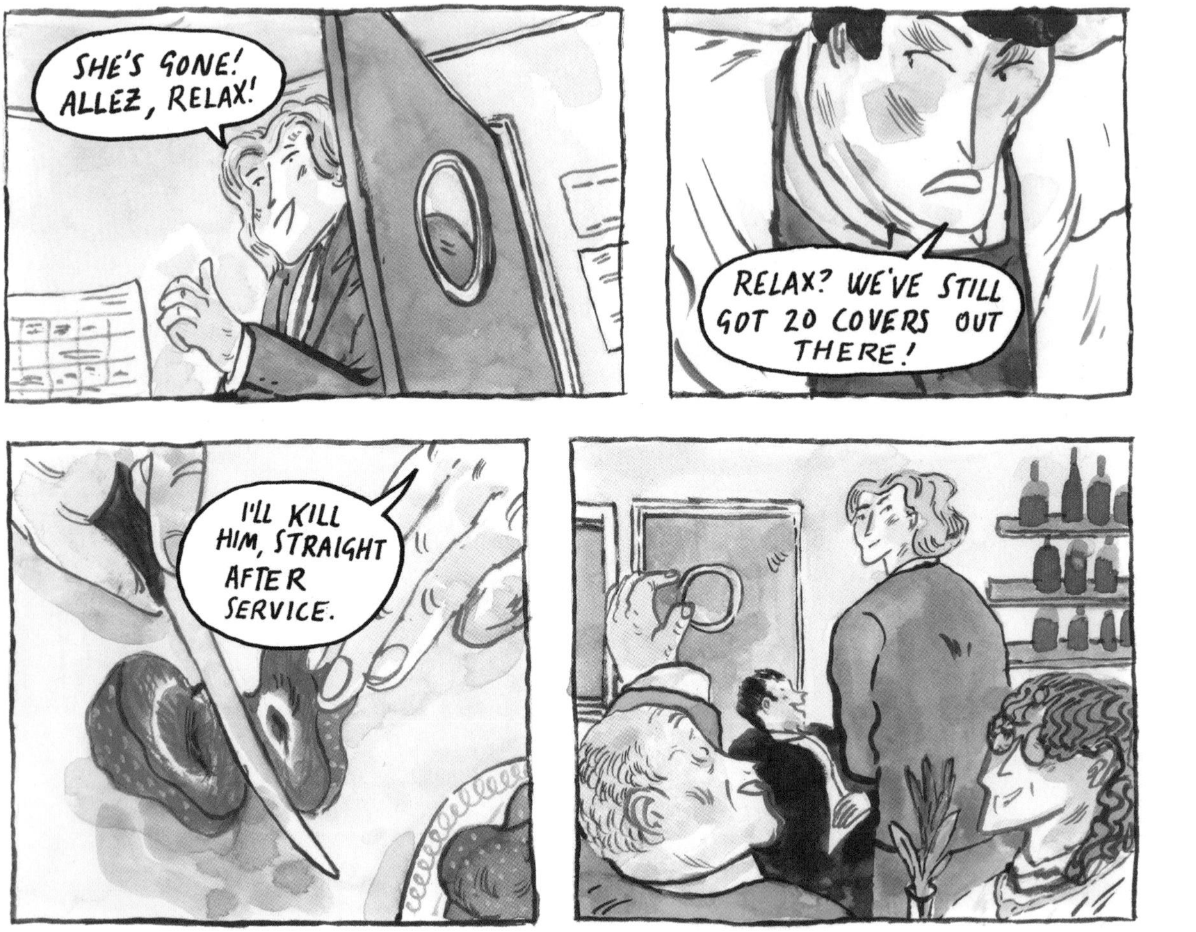
SHE'S GONE! ALLEZ, RELAX!
RELAX? WE'VE STILL GOT 20 COVERS OUT THERE!
I'LL KILL HIM, STRAIGHT AFTER SERVICE.

BUT AS SERVICE WINDS DOWN, THE PHONE RINGS. IT RINGS AGAIN AND AGAIN.

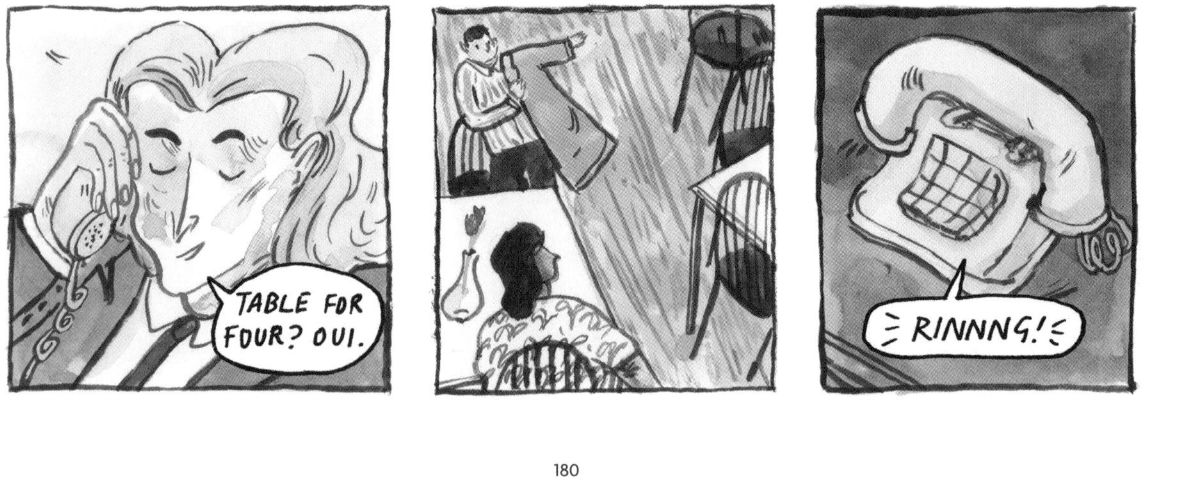
TABLE FOR FOUR? OUI.
RINNNG!

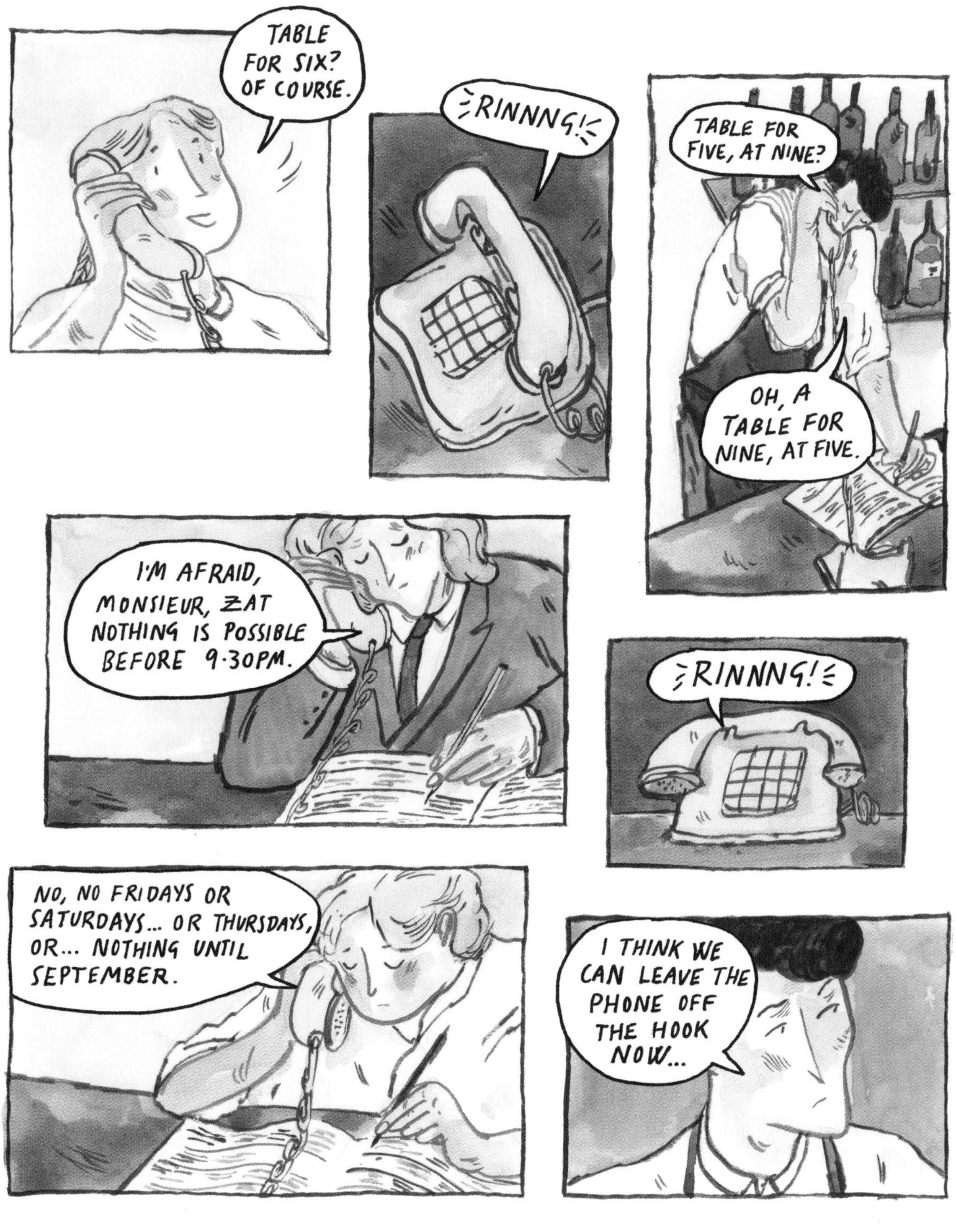
TABLE FOR SIX? OF COURSE.
RINNNG!
TABLE FOR FIVE, AT NINE?
OH, A TABLE FOR NINE, AT FIVE.
I'M AFRAID, MONSIEUR, ZAT NOTHING IS POSSIBLE BEFORE 9:30PM.
RINNNG!
NO, NO FRIDAYS OR SATURDAYS... OR THURSDAYS, OR... NOTHING UNTIL SEPTEMBER.
I THINK WE CAN LEAVE THE PHONE OFF THE HOOK NOW...

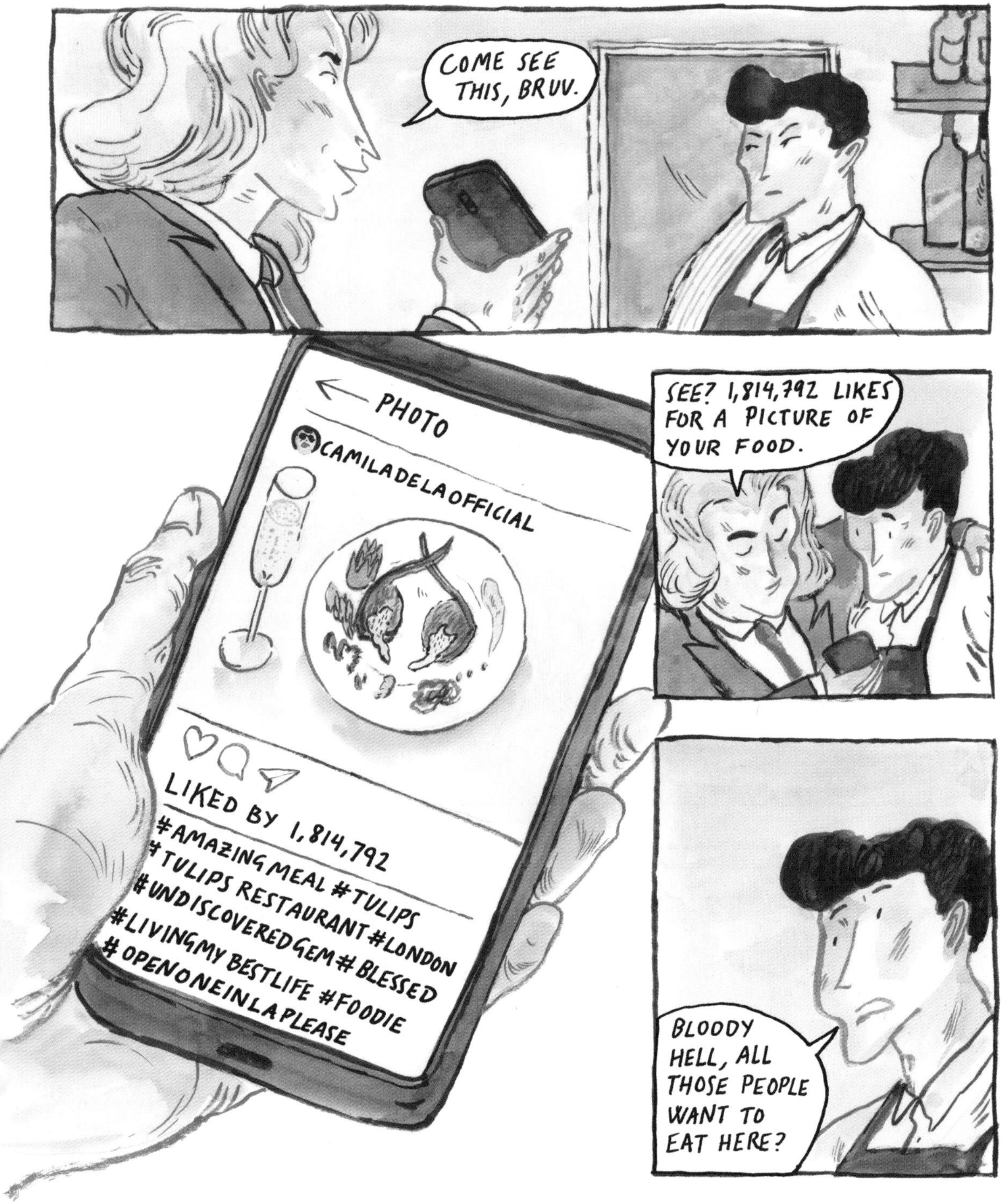
COME SEE THIS, BRUV.
PHOTO
CAMILADELAOFFICIAL
LIKED BY 1,814,792
#AMAZINGMEAL #TULIPS #TULIPSRESTAURANT #LONDON #UNDISCOVEREDGEM #BLESSED #LIVINGMYBESTLIFE #FOODIE #OPENONEINLAPLEASE
SEE? 1,814,792 LIKES FOR A PICTURE OF YOUR FOOD.
BLOODY HELL, ALL THOSE PEOPLE WANT TO EAT HERE?

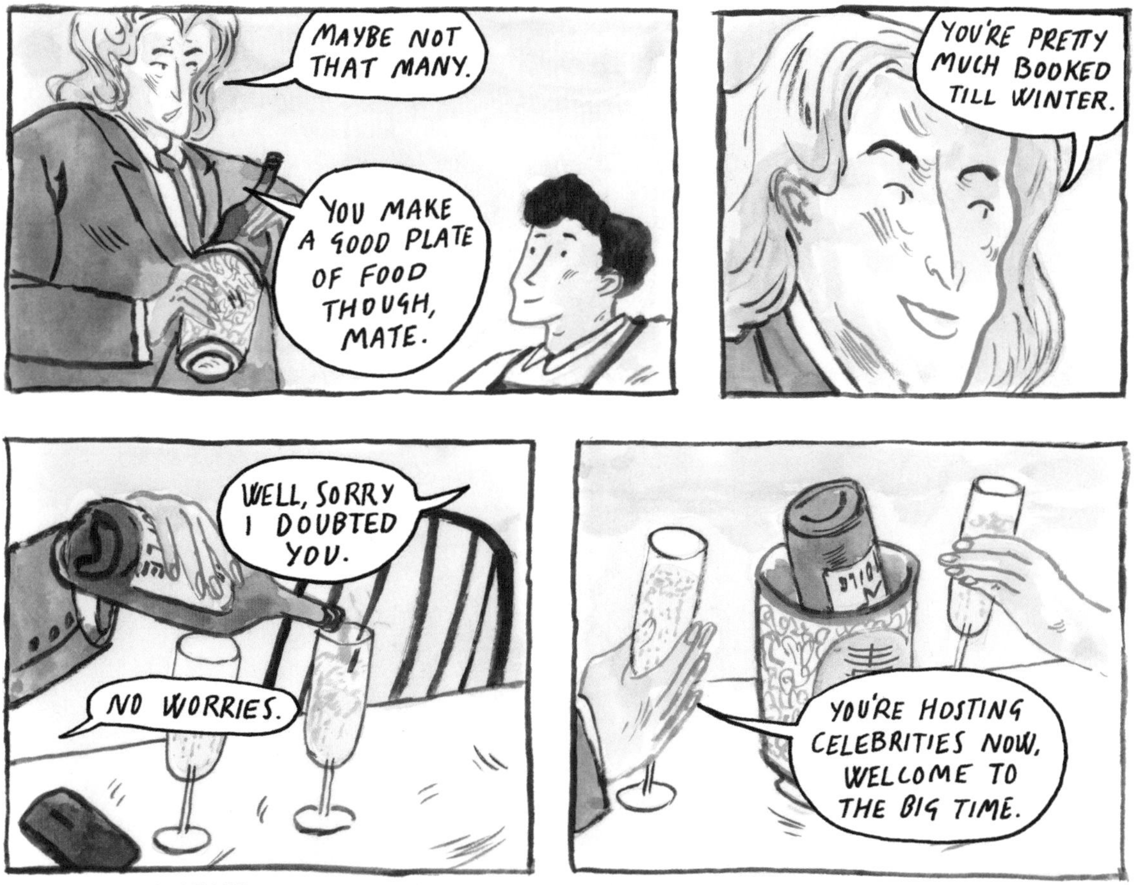
MAYBE NOT THAT MANY.
YOU MAKE A GOOD PLATE OF FOOD THOUGH, MATE.
YOU'RE PRETTY MUCH BOOKED TILL WINTER.
WELL, SORRY I DOUBTED YOU.
NO WORRIES.
YOU'RE HOSTING CELEBRITIES NOW, WELCOME TO THE BIG TIME.

MARCEL, TULIP REALISES, COULD BE HIS GUIDE INTO THE COVETED WORLD OF THE HAUTE-GOURMAND TASTE.

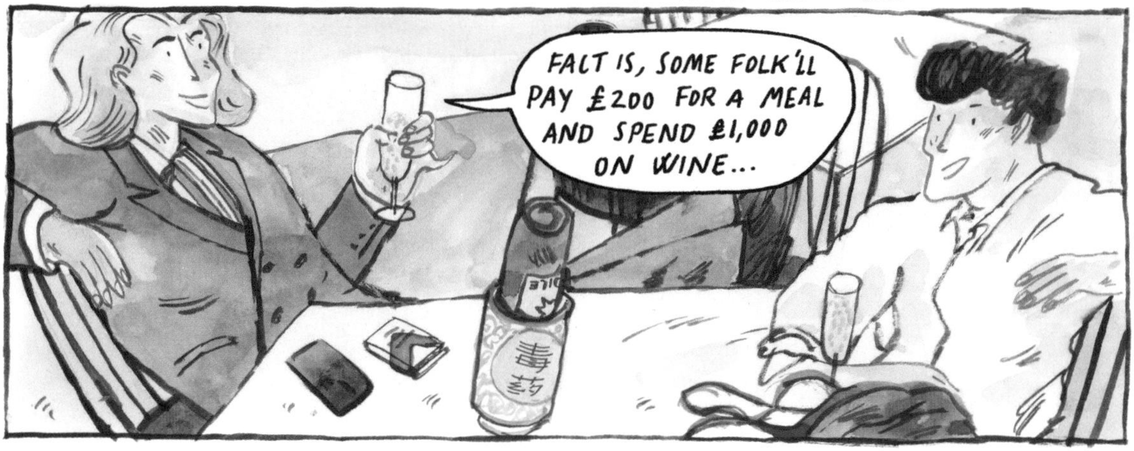
FACT IS, SOME FOLK'LL PAY £200 FOR A MEAL AND SPEND £1,000 ON WINE...

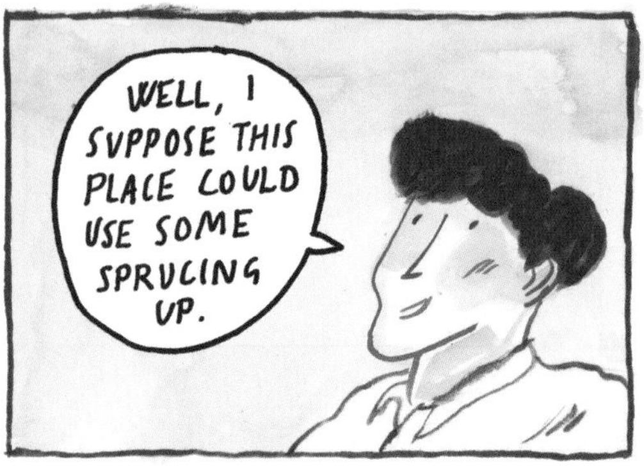
WELL, I SUPPOSE THIS PLACE COULD USE SOME SPRUCING UP.

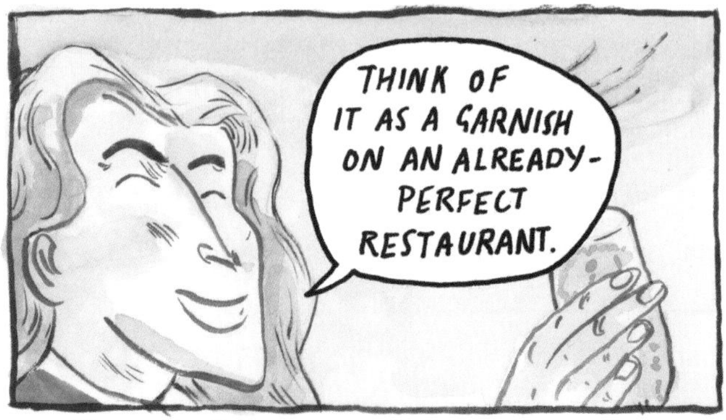
THINK OF IT AS A GARNISH ON AN ALREADY-PERFECT RESTAURANT.

MARCEL IS GIVEN A BUDGET AND SENT INTO TOWN, BUYING FINE WINES FOR THE CELLAR AND FINE ART FOR THE WALLS. HE HAS A KEEN ATTENTION TO DETAIL,

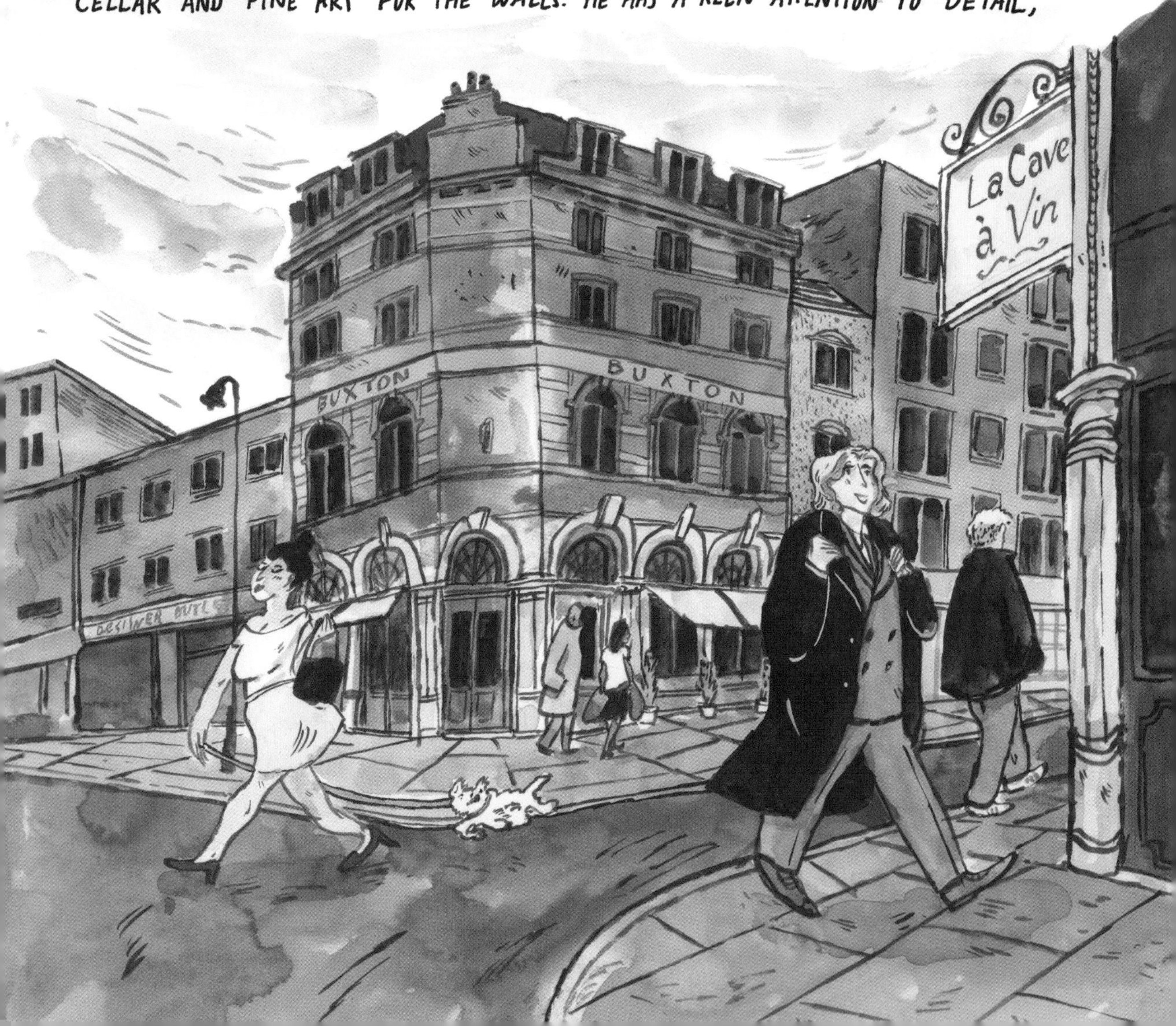
BUXTON
BUXTON
La Cave à Vin

WHETHER HE'S TASTING THE PERFECT BOURGOGNE,
ADMIRING A TASTEFUL ABSTRACT PAINTING,

OR METICULOUSLY FORGING A SUPPLIER'S SIGNATURE ON A FAKE
RECEIPT, SKIMMING A LITTLE OFF THE TOP OF HIS EXPENSES.

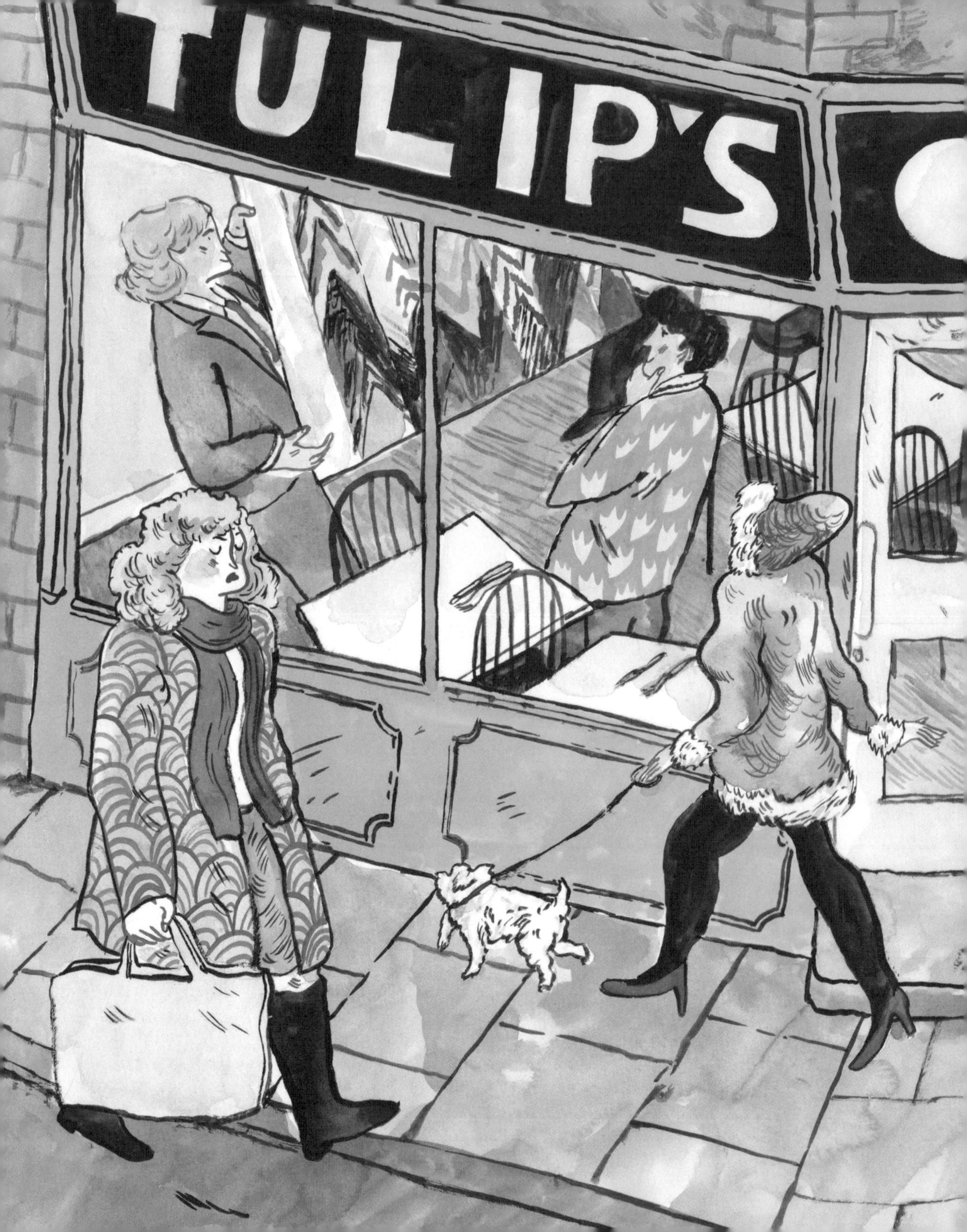
TULIP'S

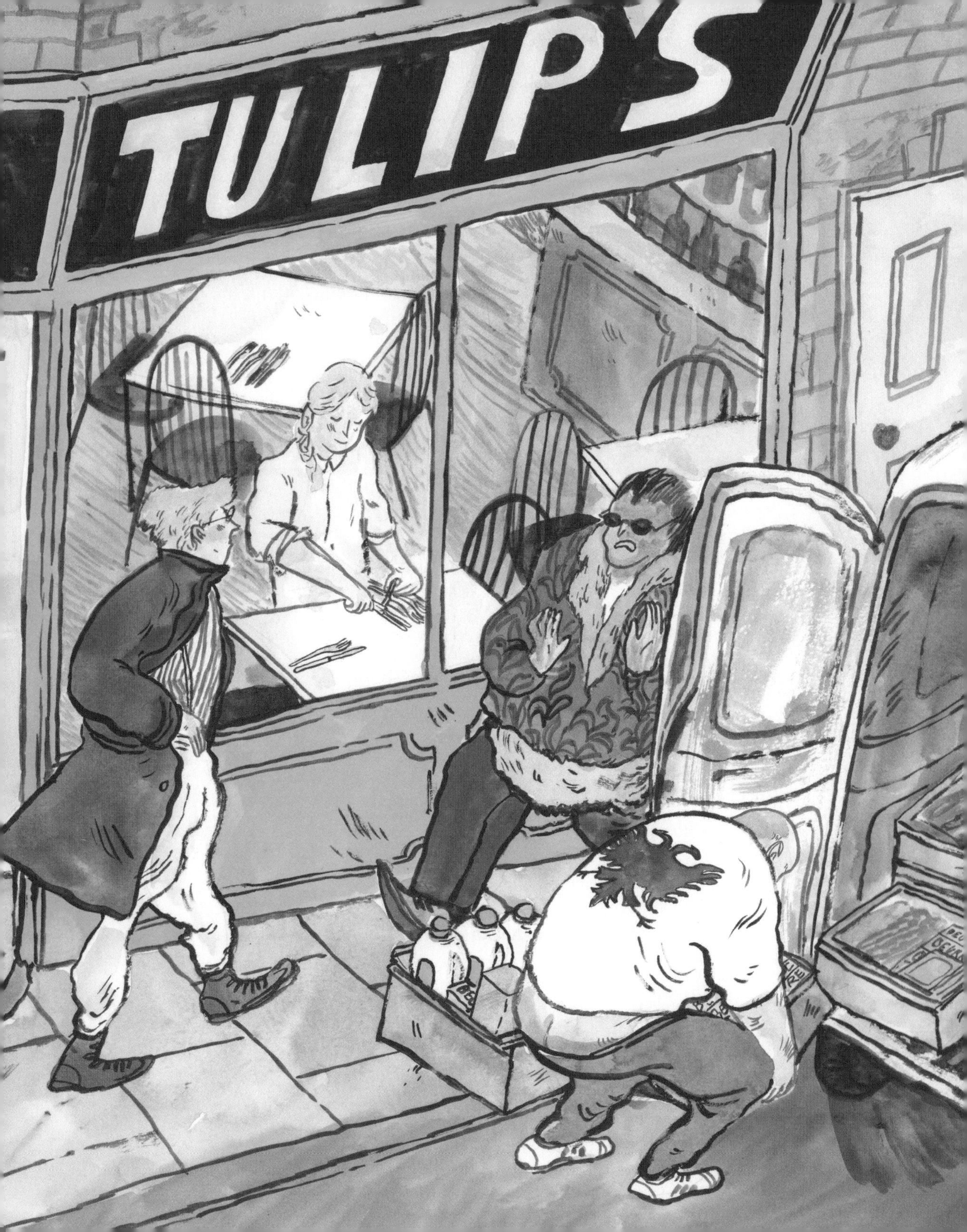
TULIP'S

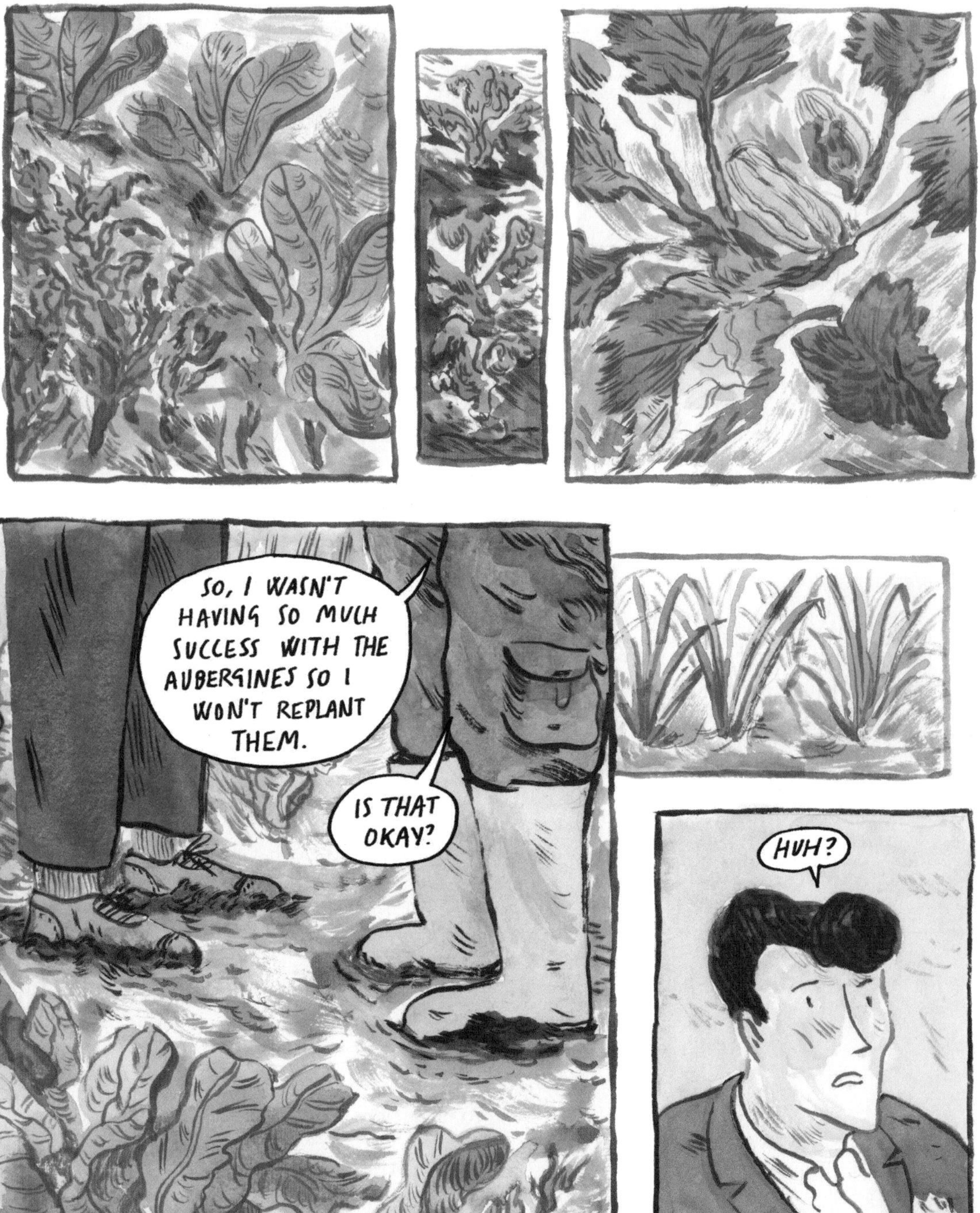
SO, I WASN'T HAVING SO MUCH SUCCESS WITH THE AUBERGINES SO I WON'T REPLANT THEM.
IS THAT OKAY?
HUH?

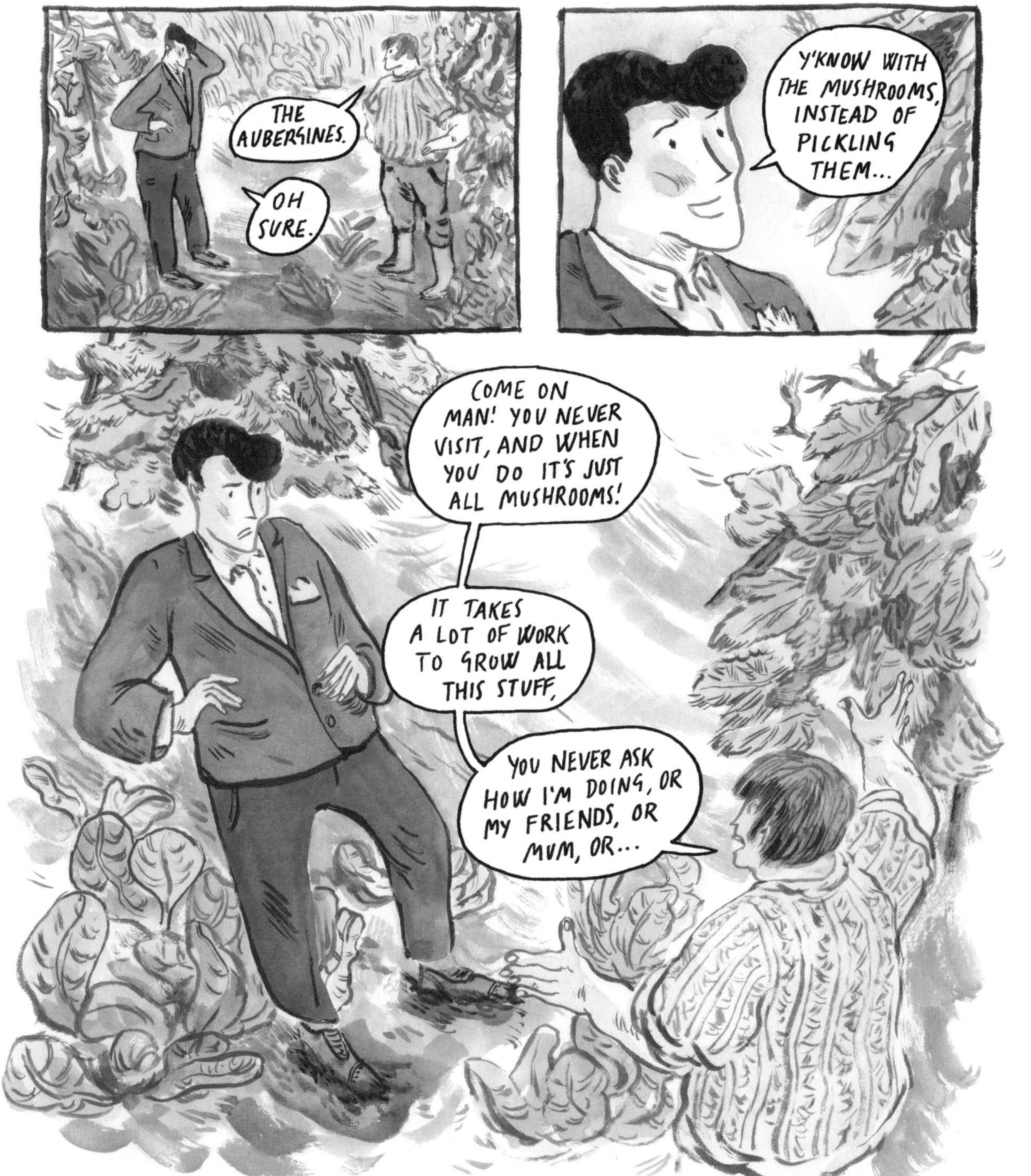
THE AUBERGINES.
OH SURE.
Y'KNOW WITH THE MUSHROOMS, INSTEAD OF PICKLING THEM...
COME ON MAN! YOU NEVER VISIT, AND WHEN YOU DO IT'S JUST ALL MUSHROOMS!
IT TAKES A LOT OF WORK TO GROW ALL THIS STUFF,
YOU NEVER ASK HOW I'M DOING, OR MY FRIENDS, OR MUM, OR...

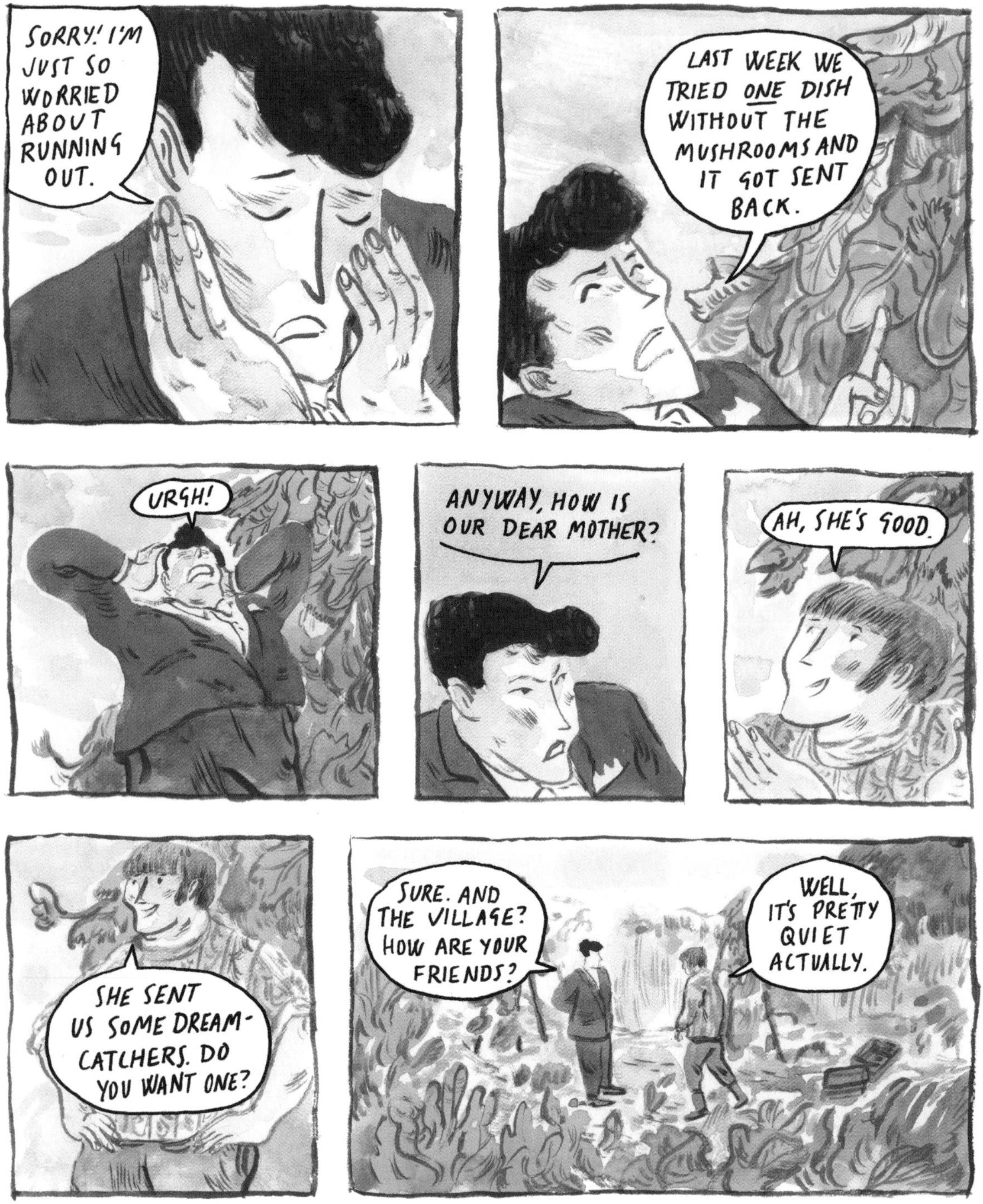
SORRY! I'M JUST SO WORRIED ABOUT RUNNING OUT.
LAST WEEK WE TRIED ONE DISH WITHOUT THE MUSHROOMS AND IT GOT SENT BACK.
URGH!
ANYWAY, HOW IS OUR DEAR MOTHER?
AH, SHE'S GOOD.
SHE SENT US SOME DREAM-CATCHERS. DO YOU WANT ONE?
SURE. AND THE VILLAGE? HOW ARE YOUR FRIENDS?
WELL, IT'S PRETTY QUIET ACTUALLY.

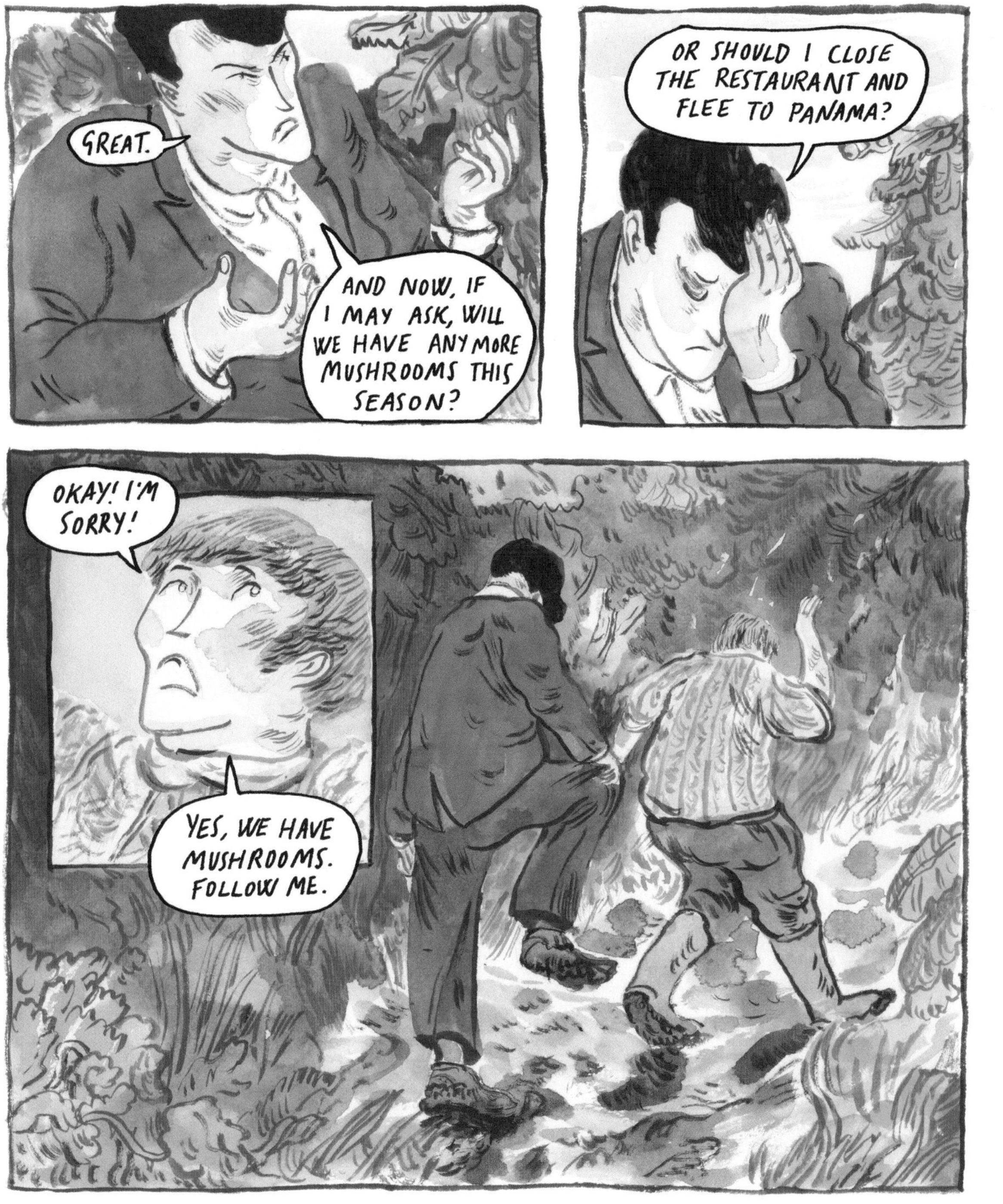
GREAT.
AND NOW, IF I MAY ASK, WILL WE HAVE ANYMORE MUSHROOMS THIS SEASON?
OR SHOULD I CLOSE THE RESTAURANT AND FLEE TO PANAMA?
OKAY! I'M SORRY!
YES, WE HAVE MUSHROOMS. FOLLOW ME.

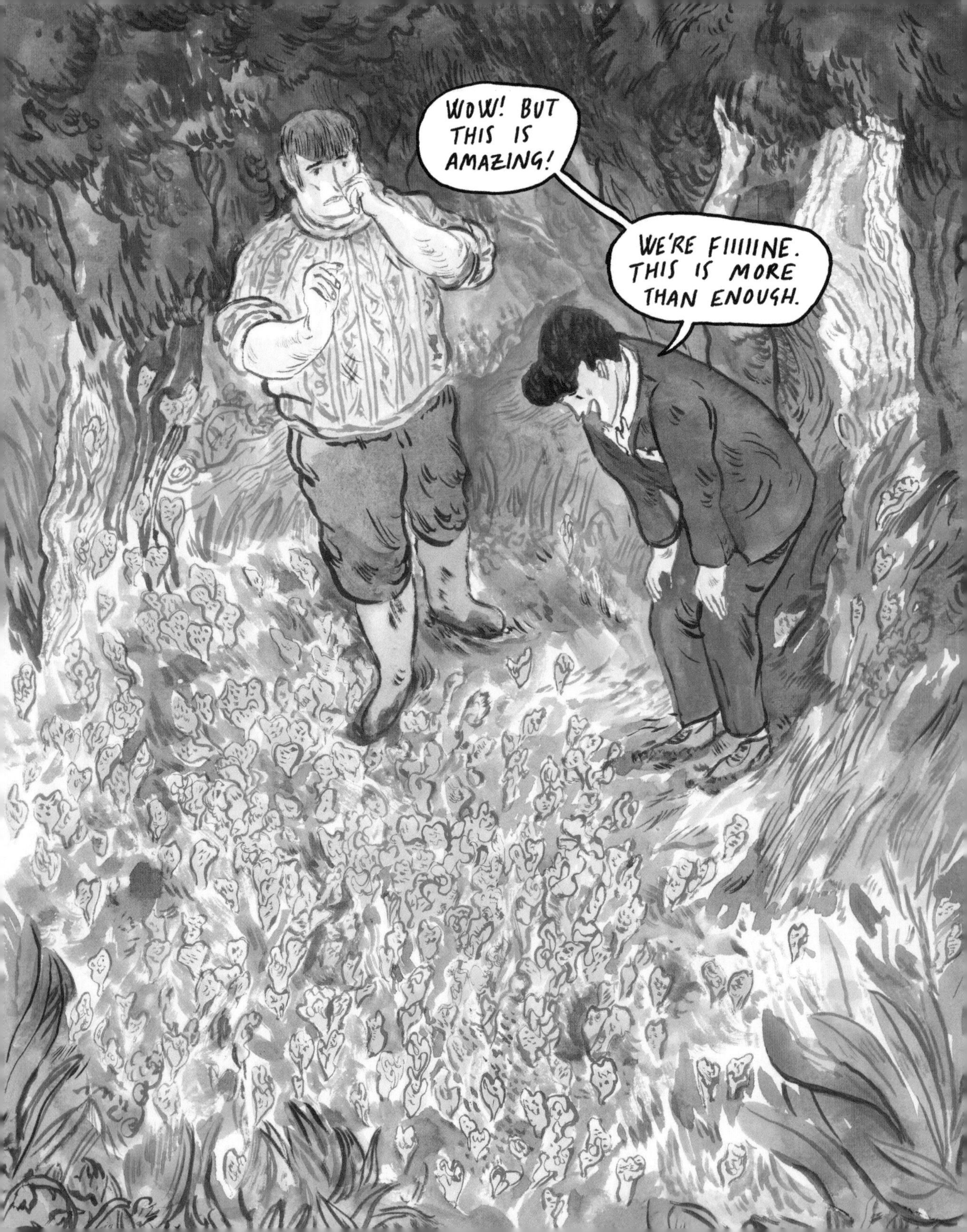
WOW! BUT THIS IS AMAZING!
WE'RE FIIIIINE. THIS IS MORE THAN ENOUGH.

THE THING IS... THIS MIGHT BE WHERE WE BURIED THAT GUY.
OH.
HOW "MIGHT BE" IS "MIGHT BE"?
I DON'T KNOW. IT WAS THE MIDDLE OF THE NIGHT WHEN WE BURIED HIM.
I'VE TRIED EVERYTHING TO MAKE THEM GROW. ALL SORTS OF FERTILISER AND COMPOST, IN SPECIAL BOXES IN POLYTUNNELS, IN THE HOUSE. I'VE BEEN TREATING THEM LIKE ORCHIDS! NO IDEA WHY THEY POPPED UP HERE SUDDENLY.

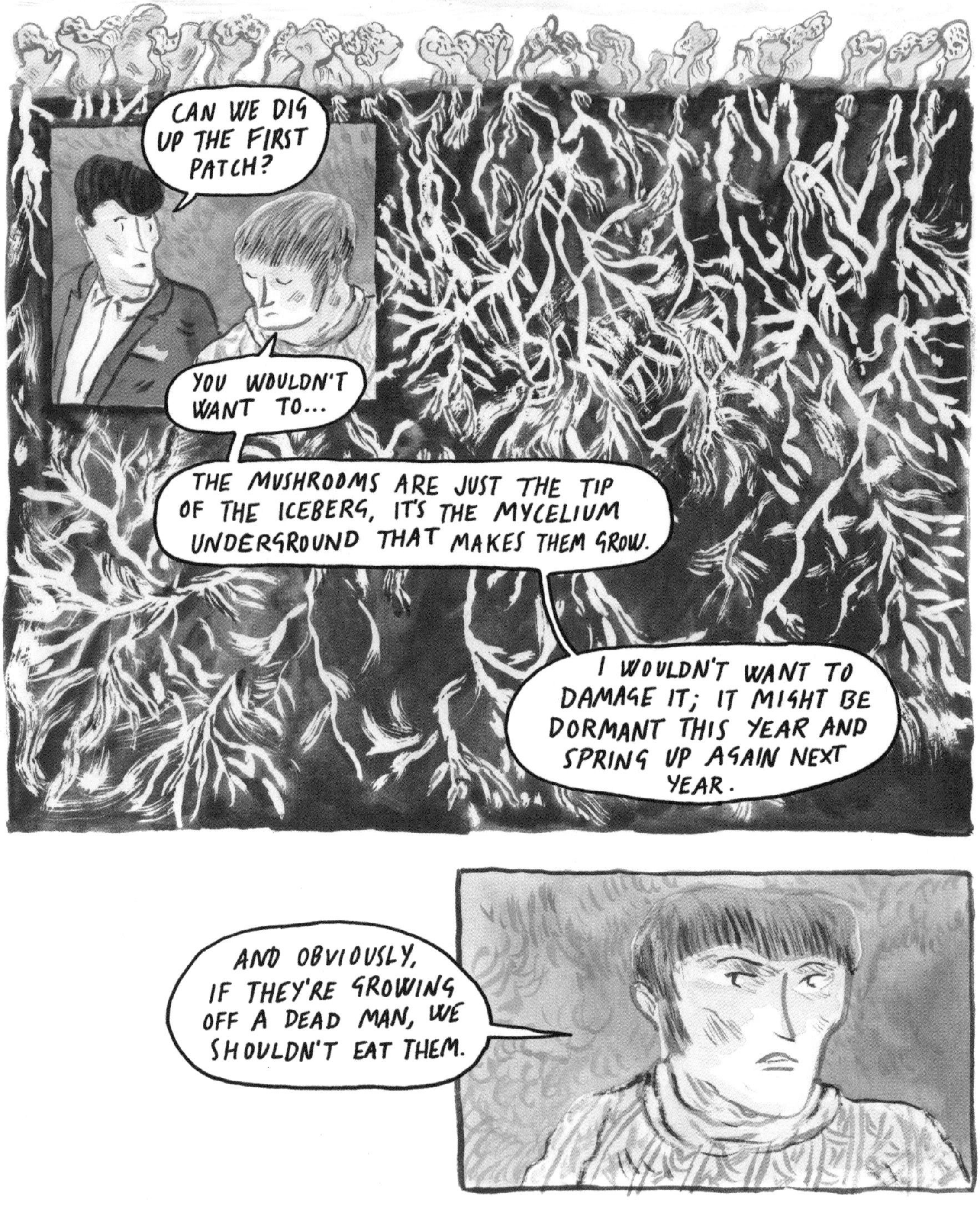
CAN WE DIG UP THE FIRST PATCH?
YOU WOULDN'T WANT TO...
THE MUSHROOMS ARE JUST THE TIP OF THE ICEBERG, IT'S THE MYCELIUM UNDERGROUND THAT MAKES THEM GROW.
I WOULDN'T WANT TO DAMAGE IT; IT MIGHT BE DORMANT THIS YEAR AND SPRING UP AGAIN NEXT YEAR.
AND OBVIOUSLY, IF THEY'RE GROWING OFF A DEAD MAN, WE SHOULDN'T EAT THEM.

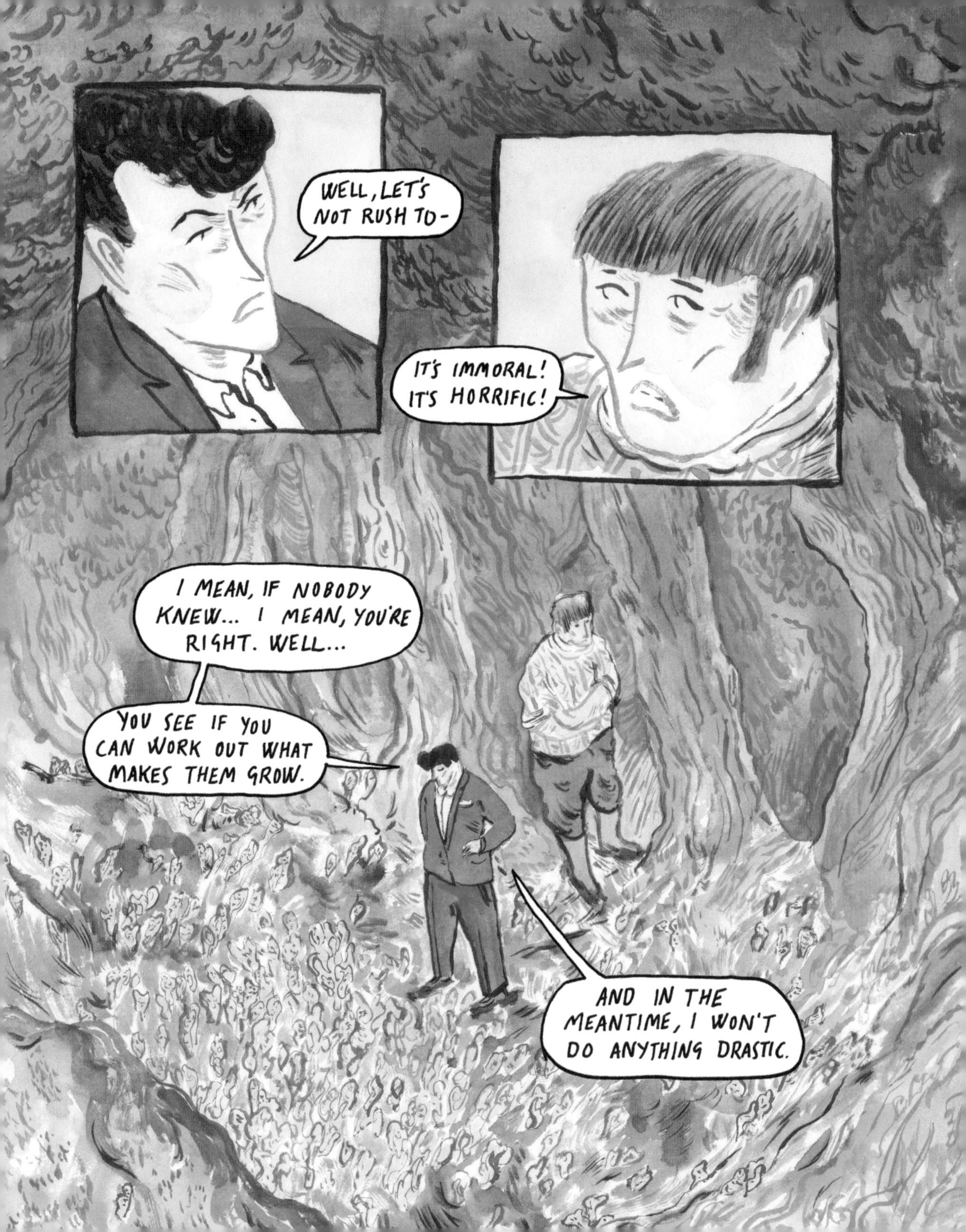
WELL, LET'S NOT RUSH TO-
IT'S IMMORAL! IT'S HORRIFIC!
I MEAN, IF NOBODY KNEW... I MEAN, YOU'RE RIGHT. WELL...
YOU SEE IF YOU CAN WORK OUT WHAT MAKES THEM GROW.
AND IN THE MEANTIME, I WON'T DO ANYTHING DRASTIC.

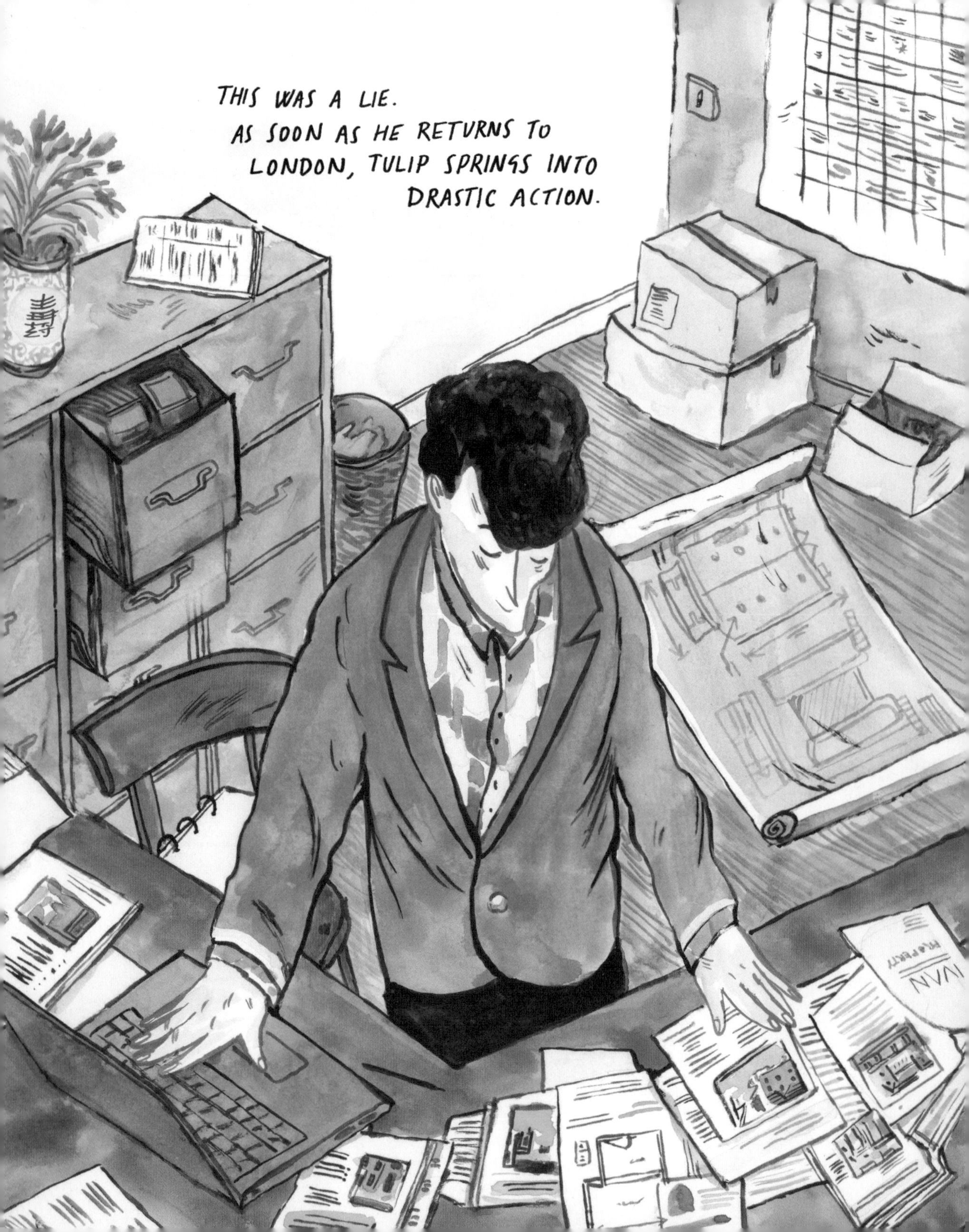
THIS WAS A LIE.
AS SOON AS HE RETURNS TO LONDON, TULIP SPRINGS INTO DRASTIC ACTION.
IVAN PROPERTY

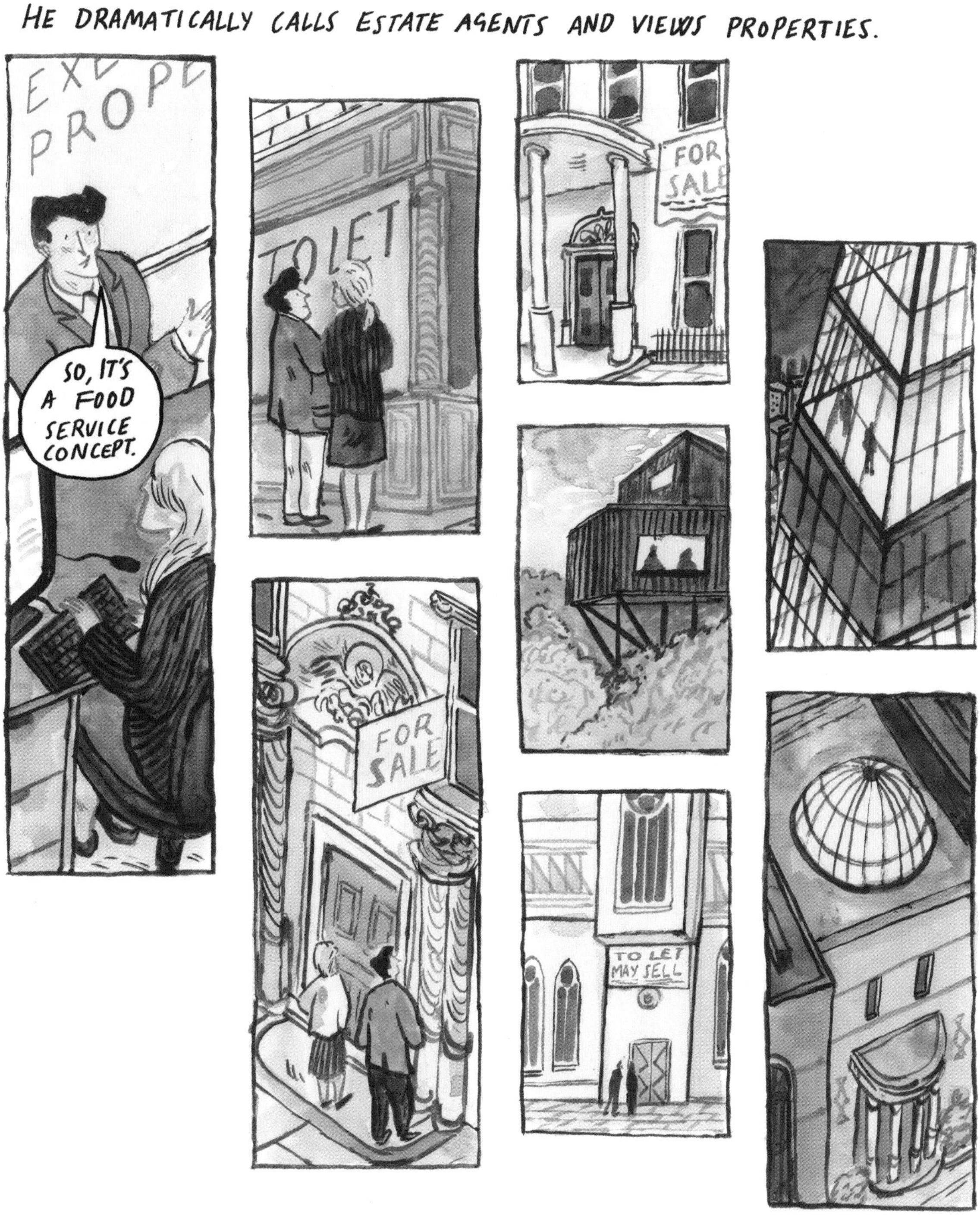
HE DRAMATICALLY CALLS ESTATE AGENTS AND VIEWS PROPERTIES.
SO, IT'S A FOOD SERVICE CONCEPT.
TO LET
FOR SALE
TO LET
MAY SELL

HE RECKLESSLY MAKES SPREADSHEETS. HE WILDLY SOLICITS INVESTORS.

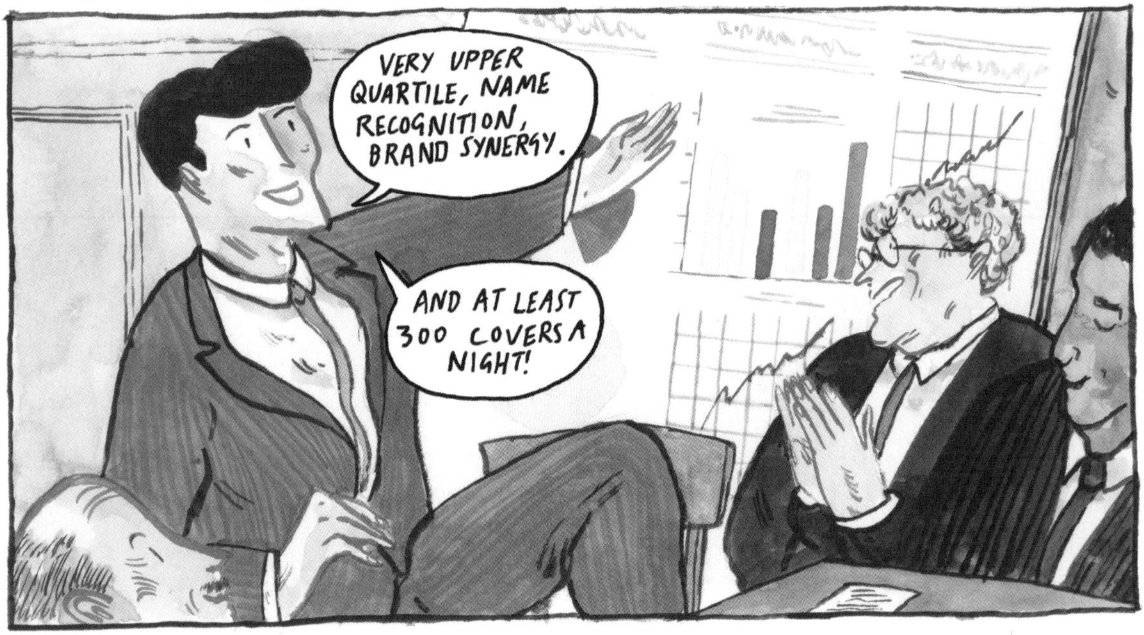
VERY UPPER QUARTILE, NAME RECOGNITION, BRAND SYNERGY.
AND AT LEAST 300 COVERS A NIGHT!

SINCE THE RESTAURANT OPENED, TULIP HAS CHARGED MORE AND MORE FOR THE MUSHROOMS, WHILE SERVING SIZES HAVE SHRUNK. THE NEW PATCH IS EVEN LARGER THAN THE FIRST, AND EVEN A QUICK CALCULATION AS TO ITS VALUE LEAVES TULIP REELING.

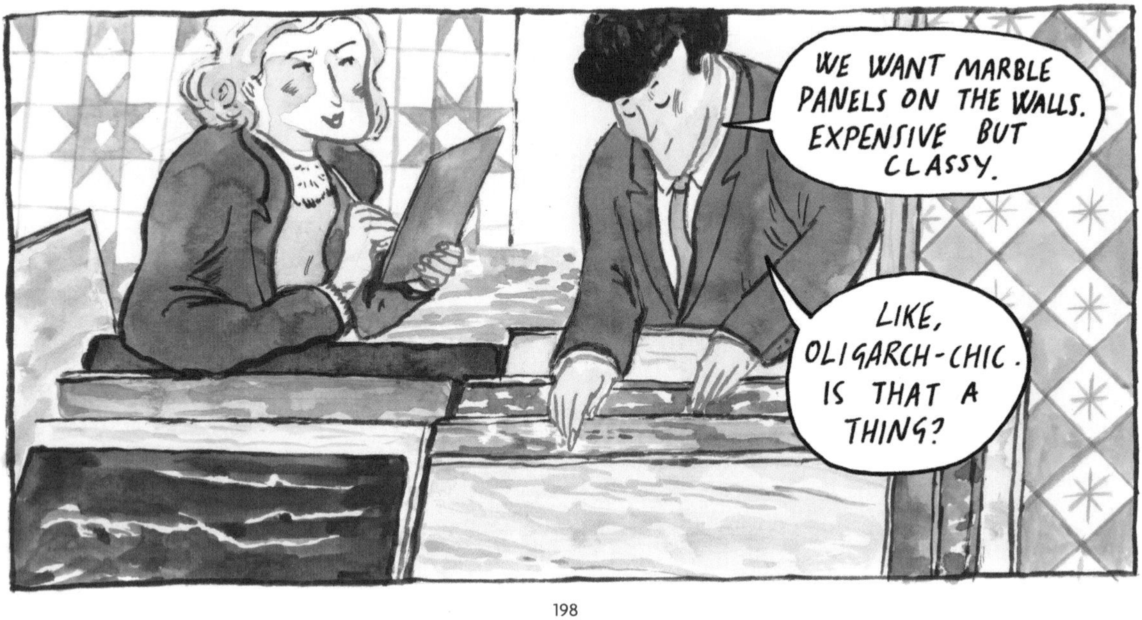
WE WANT MARBLE PANELS ON THE WALLS. EXPENSIVE BUT CLASSY.
LIKE, OLIGARCH-CHIC. IS THAT A THING?

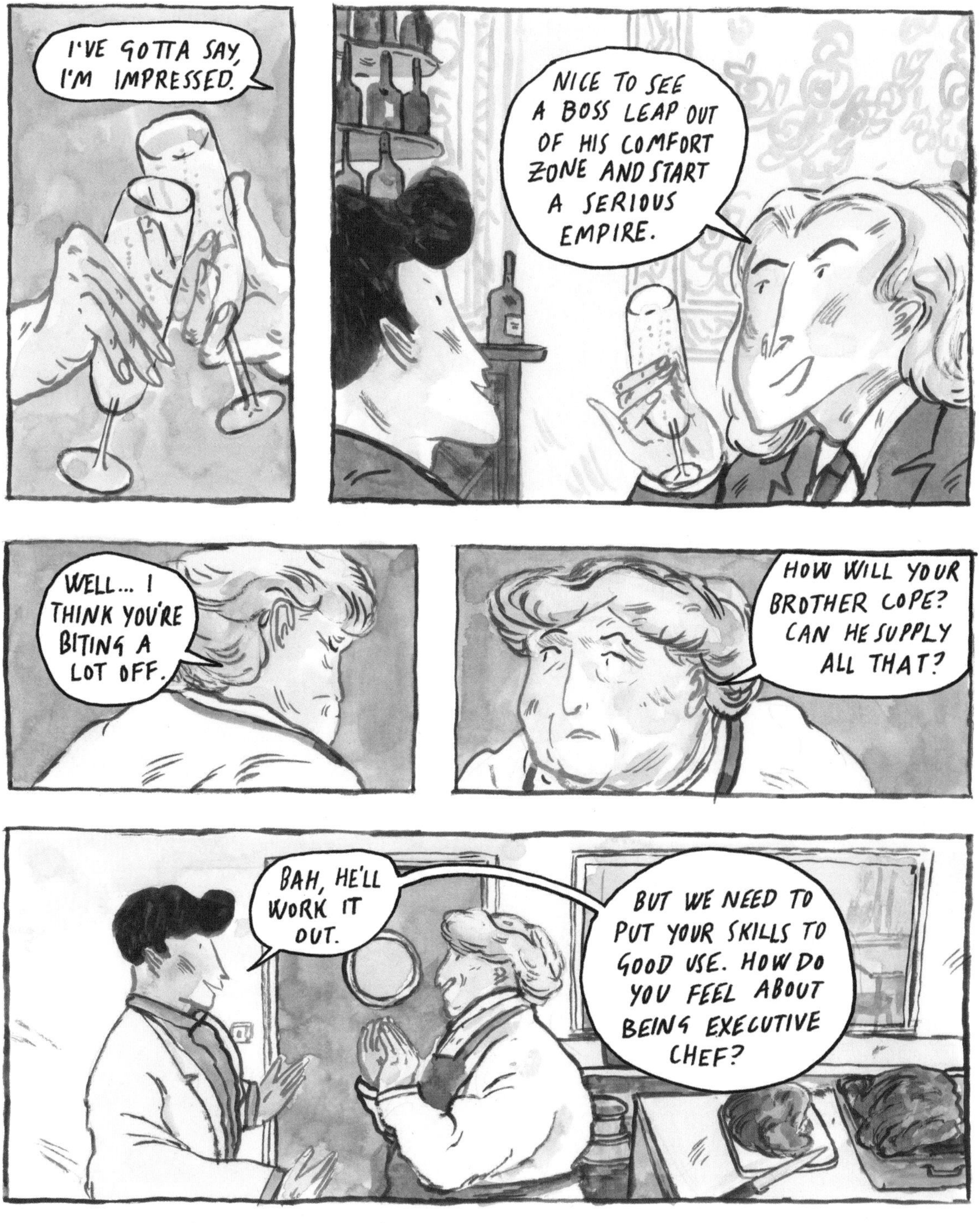
I'VE GOTTA SAY, I'M IMPRESSED.
NICE TO SEE A BOSS LEAP OUT OF HIS COMFORT ZONE AND START A SERIOUS EMPIRE.
WELL... I THINK YOU'RE BITING A LOT OFF.
HOW WILL YOUR BROTHER COPE? CAN HE SUPPLY ALL THAT?
BAH, HE'LL WORK IT OUT.
BUT WE NEED TO PUT YOUR SKILLS TO GOOD USE. HOW DO YOU FEEL ABOUT BEING EXECUTIVE CHEF?

BEFORE LONG, TULIP HAS SETTLED ON TWO NEW ESTABLISHMENTS: A LUXURIOUS GASTRONOMIC SHRINE IN SOUTH KENSINGTON, WHERE MABEL CAN PUSH THE BOUNDARIES OF HAUTE CUISINE.

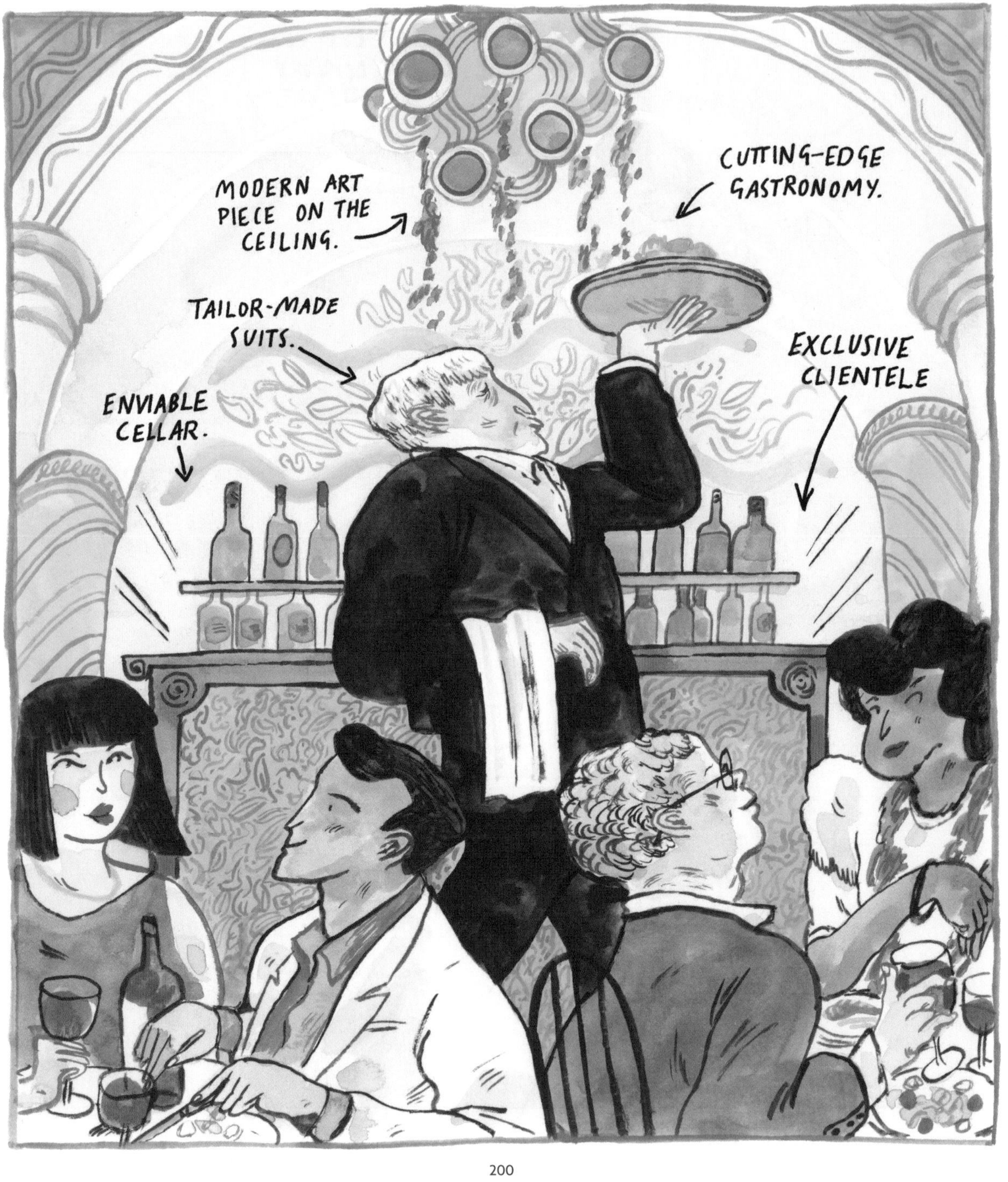
MODERN ART PIECE ON THE CEILING.
CUTTING-EDGE GASTRONOMY.
TAILOR-MADE SUITS.
EXCLUSIVE CLIENTELE
ENVIABLE CELLAR.

AND AN ENORMOUS PARTHENON OF CHIC DINING IN SOHO, UNDER MARCEL'S WATCHFUL EYE AS MAÎTRE D'.

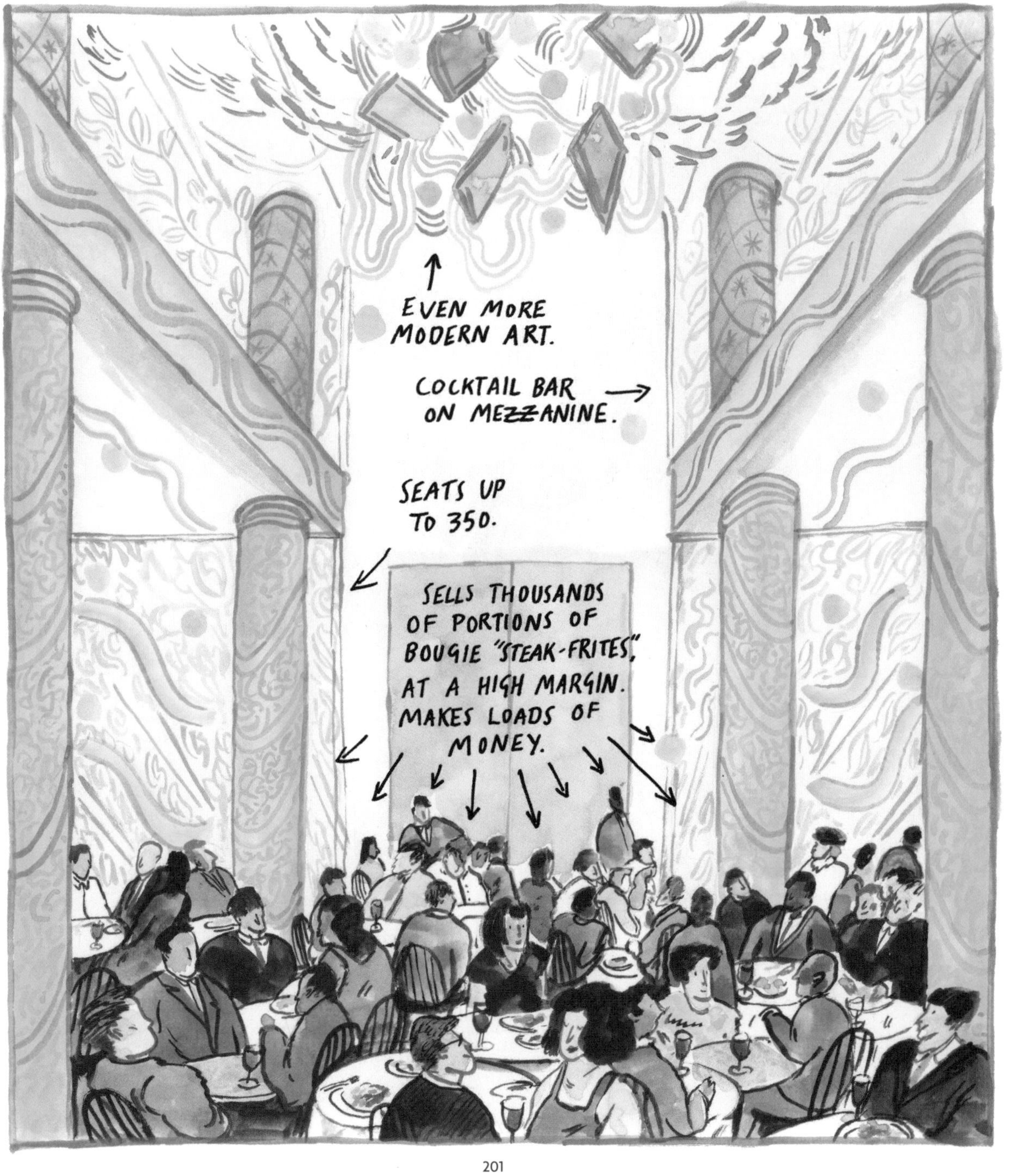
EVEN MORE MODERN ART.
COCKTAIL BAR ON MEZZANINE.
SEATS UP TO 350.
SELLS THOUSANDS OF PORTIONS OF BOUGIE "STEAK-FRITES", AT A HIGH MARGIN. MAKES LOADS OF MONEY.

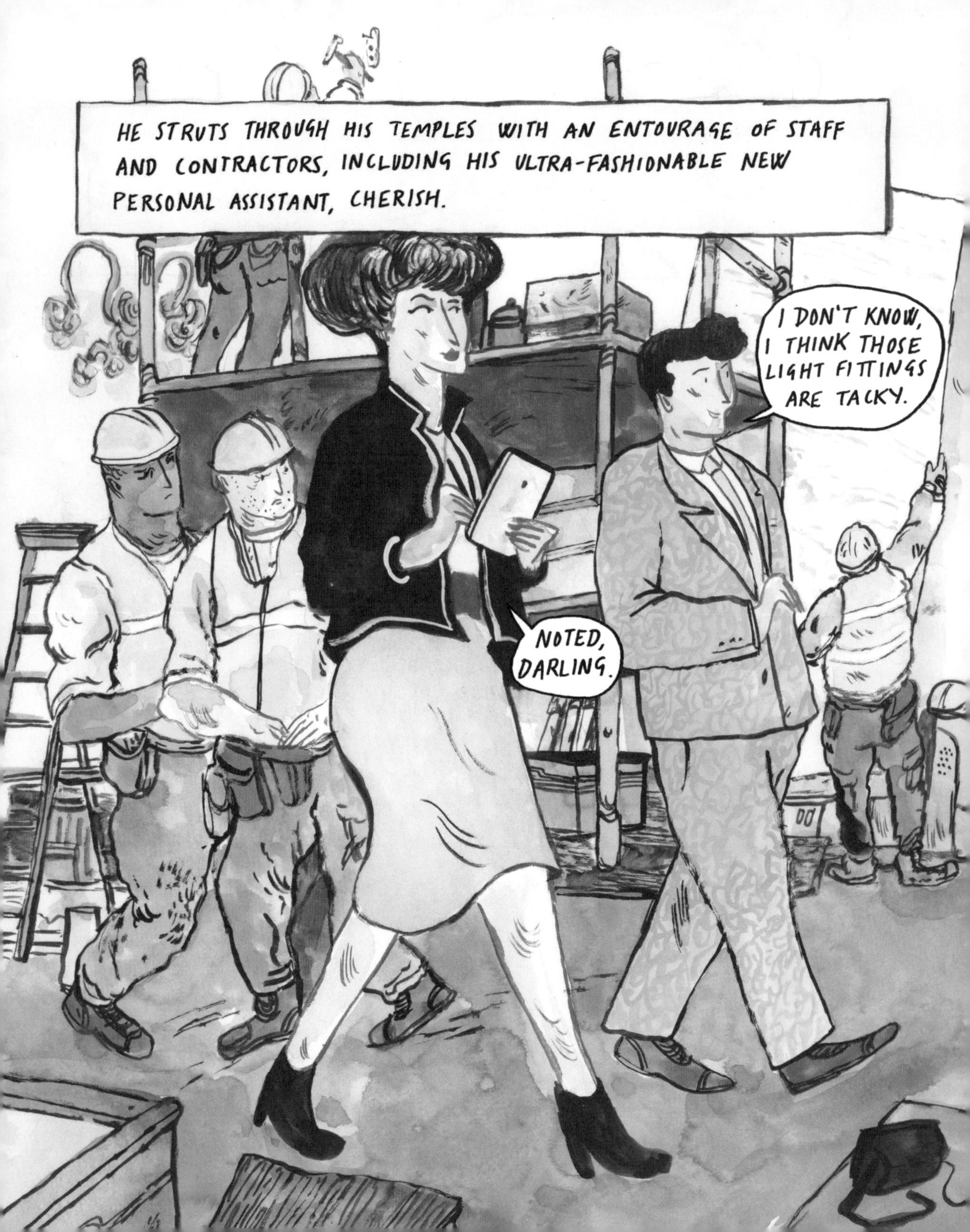
HE STRUTS THROUGH HIS TEMPLES WITH AN ENTOURAGE OF STAFF AND CONTRACTORS, INCLUDING HIS ULTRA-FASHIONABLE NEW PERSONAL ASSISTANT, CHERISH.
I DON'T KNOW, I THINK THOSE LIGHT FITTINGS ARE TACKY.
NOTED, DARLING.

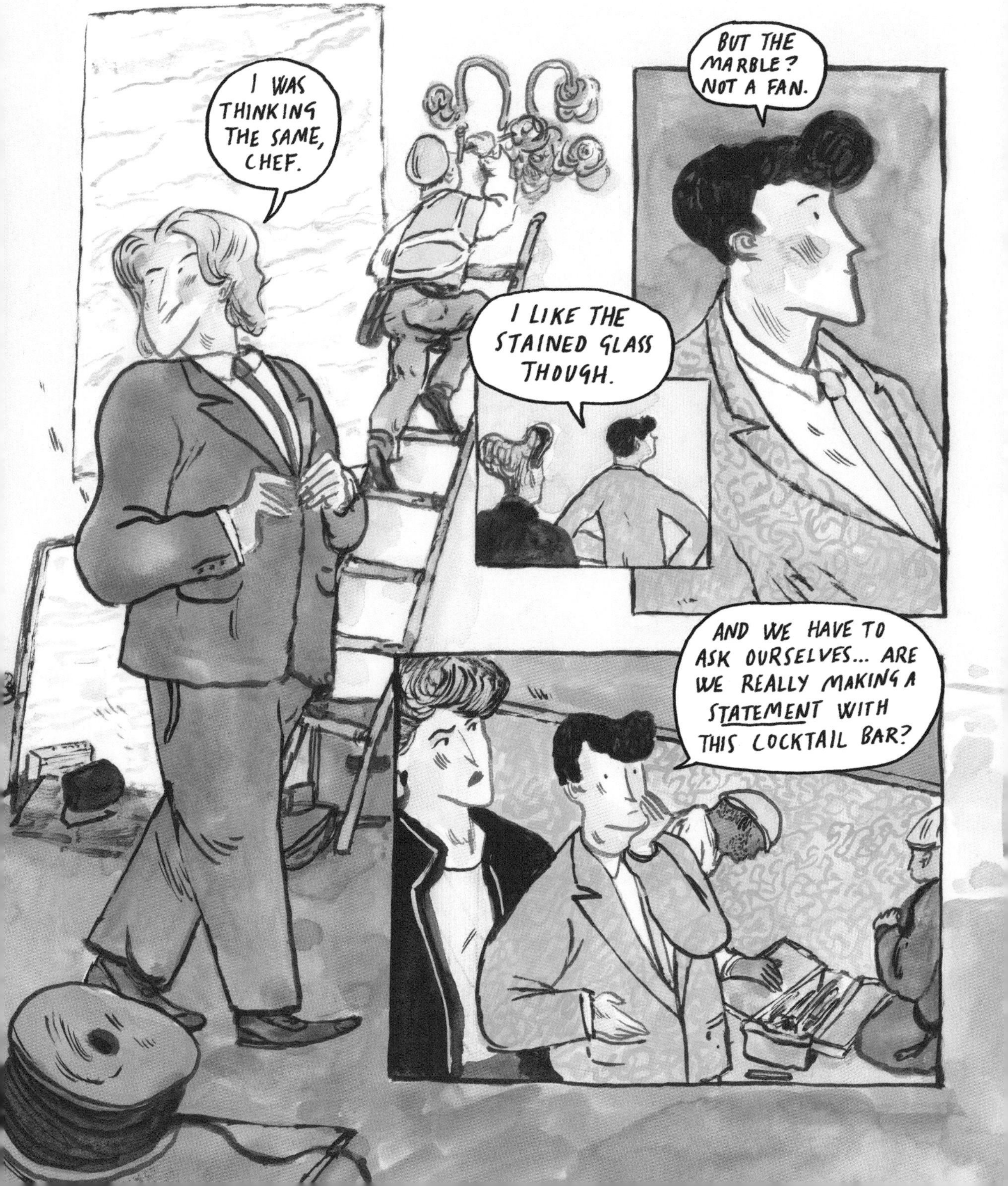
I WAS THINKING THE SAME, CHEF.
BUT THE MARBLE? NOT A FAN.
I LIKE THE STAINED GLASS THOUGH.
AND WE HAVE TO ASK OURSELVES... ARE WE REALLY MAKING A STATEMENT WITH THIS COCKTAIL BAR?

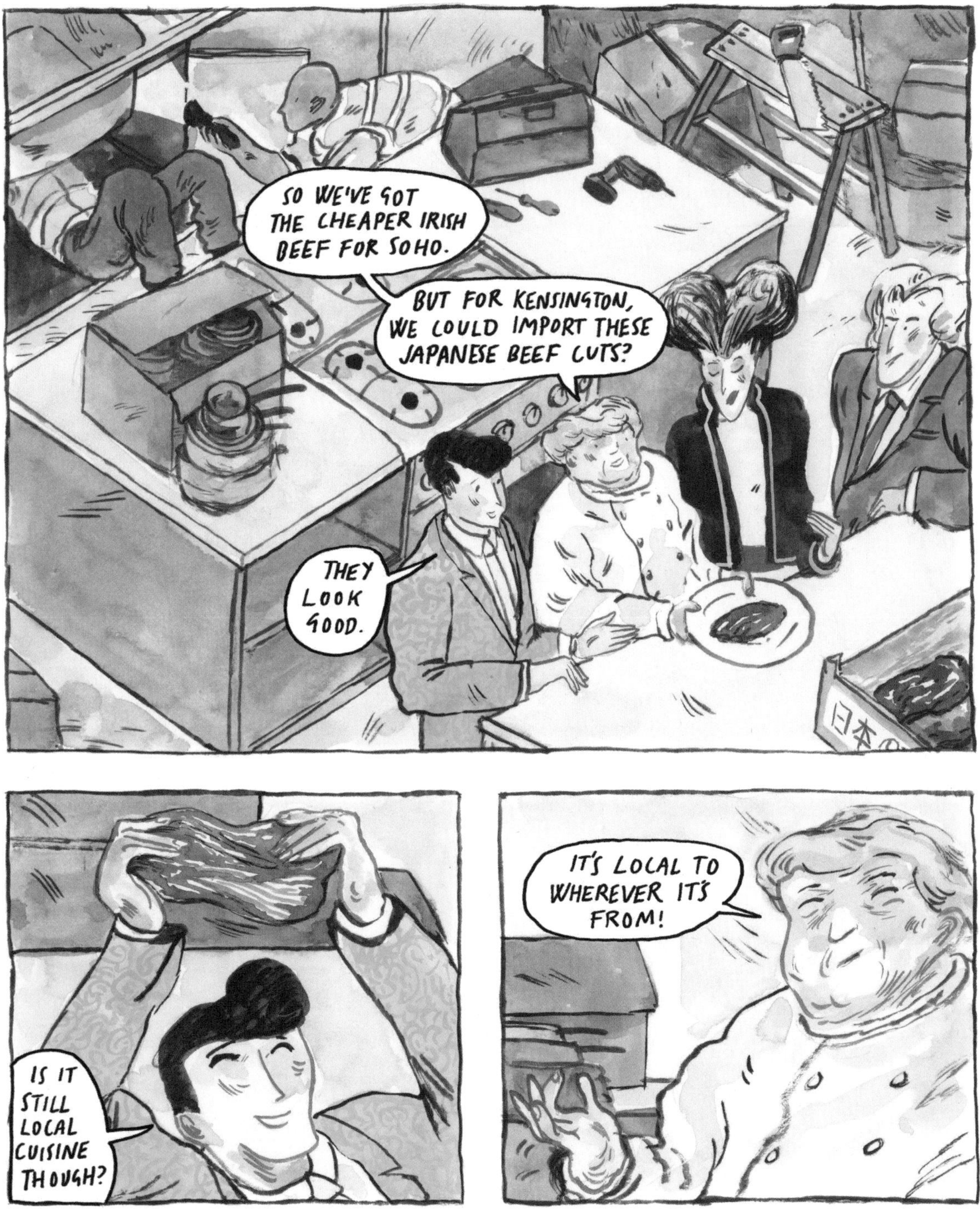
SO WE'VE GOT THE CHEAPER IRISH BEEF FOR SOHO.
BUT FOR KENSINGTON, WE COULD IMPORT THESE JAPANESE BEEF CUTS?
THEY LOOK GOOD.
IS IT STILL LOCAL CUISINE THOUGH?
IT'S LOCAL TO WHEREVER IT'S FROM!

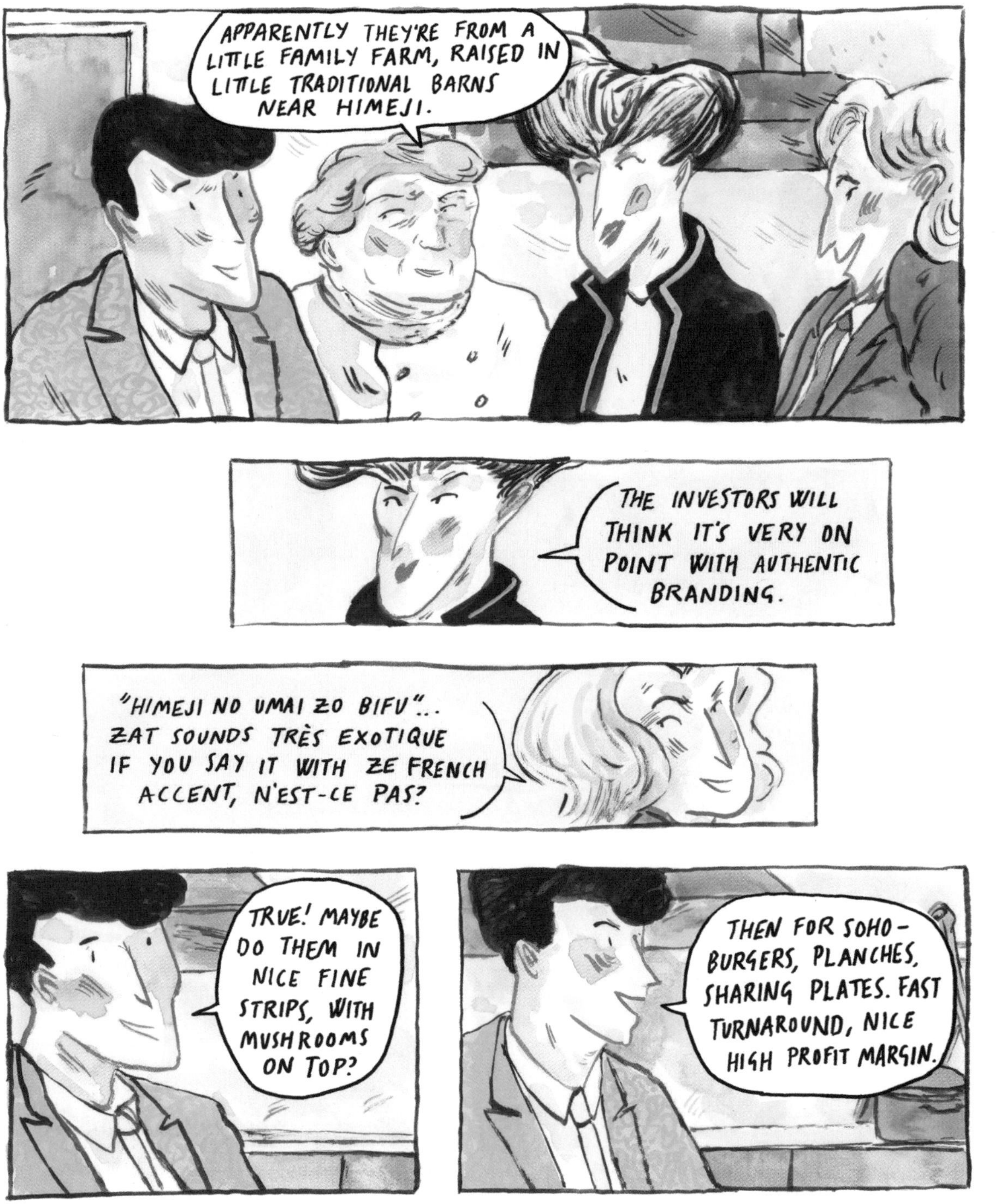
APPARENTLY THEY'RE FROM A LITTLE FAMILY FARM, RAISED IN LITTLE TRADITIONAL BARNS NEAR HIMEJI.
THE INVESTORS WILL THINK IT'S VERY ON POINT WITH AUTHENTIC BRANDING.
"HIMEJI NO UMAI ZO BIFU"... ZAT SOUNDS TRÈS EXOTIQUE IF YOU SAY IT WITH ZE FRENCH ACCENT, N'EST-CE PAS?
TRUE! MAYBE DO THEM IN NICE FINE STRIPS, WITH MUSHROOMS ON TOP?
THEN FOR SOHO-BURGERS, PLANCHES, SHARING PLATES. FAST TURNAROUND, NICE HIGH PROFIT MARGIN.

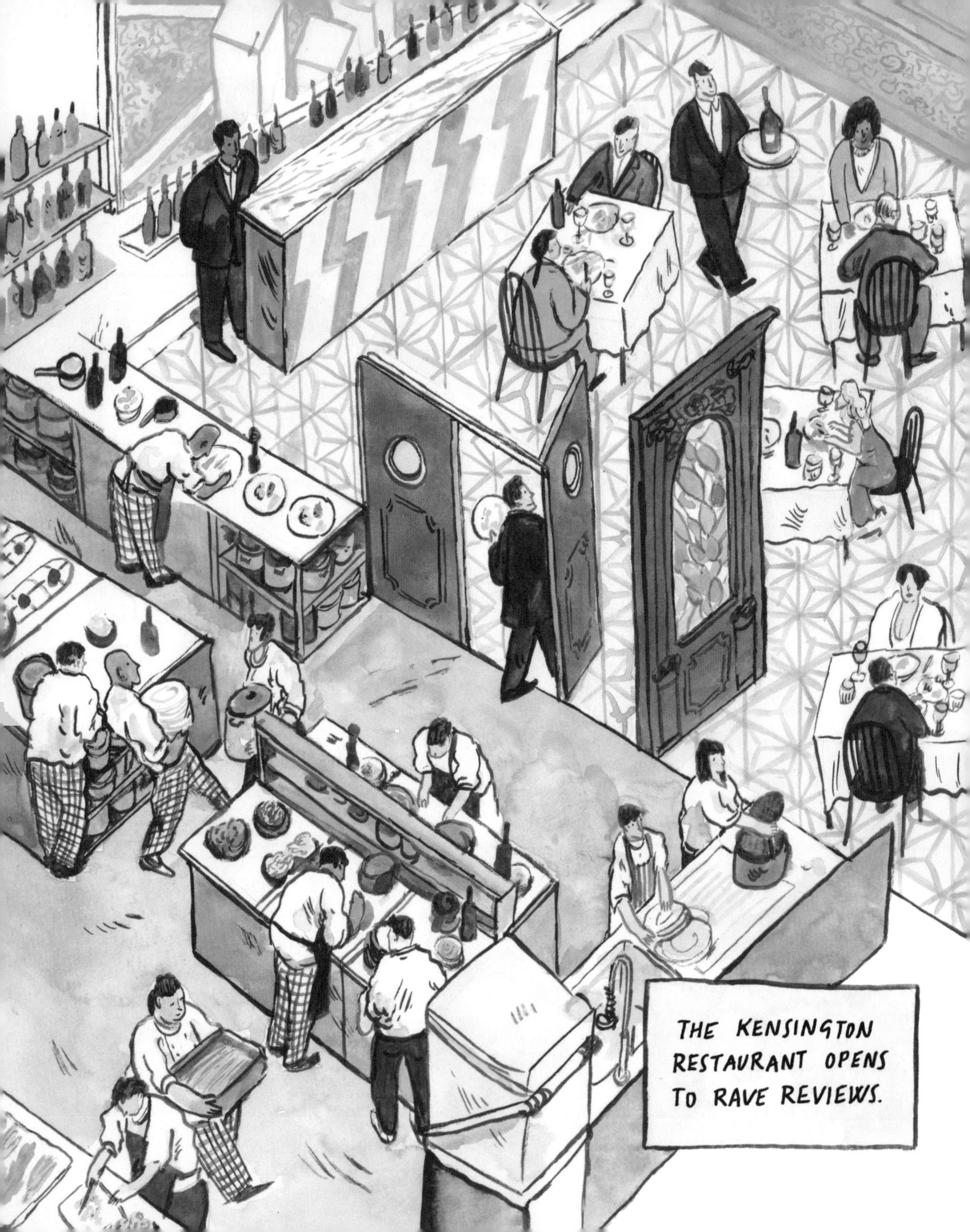
THE KENSINGTON RESTAURANT OPENS TO RAVE REVIEWS.

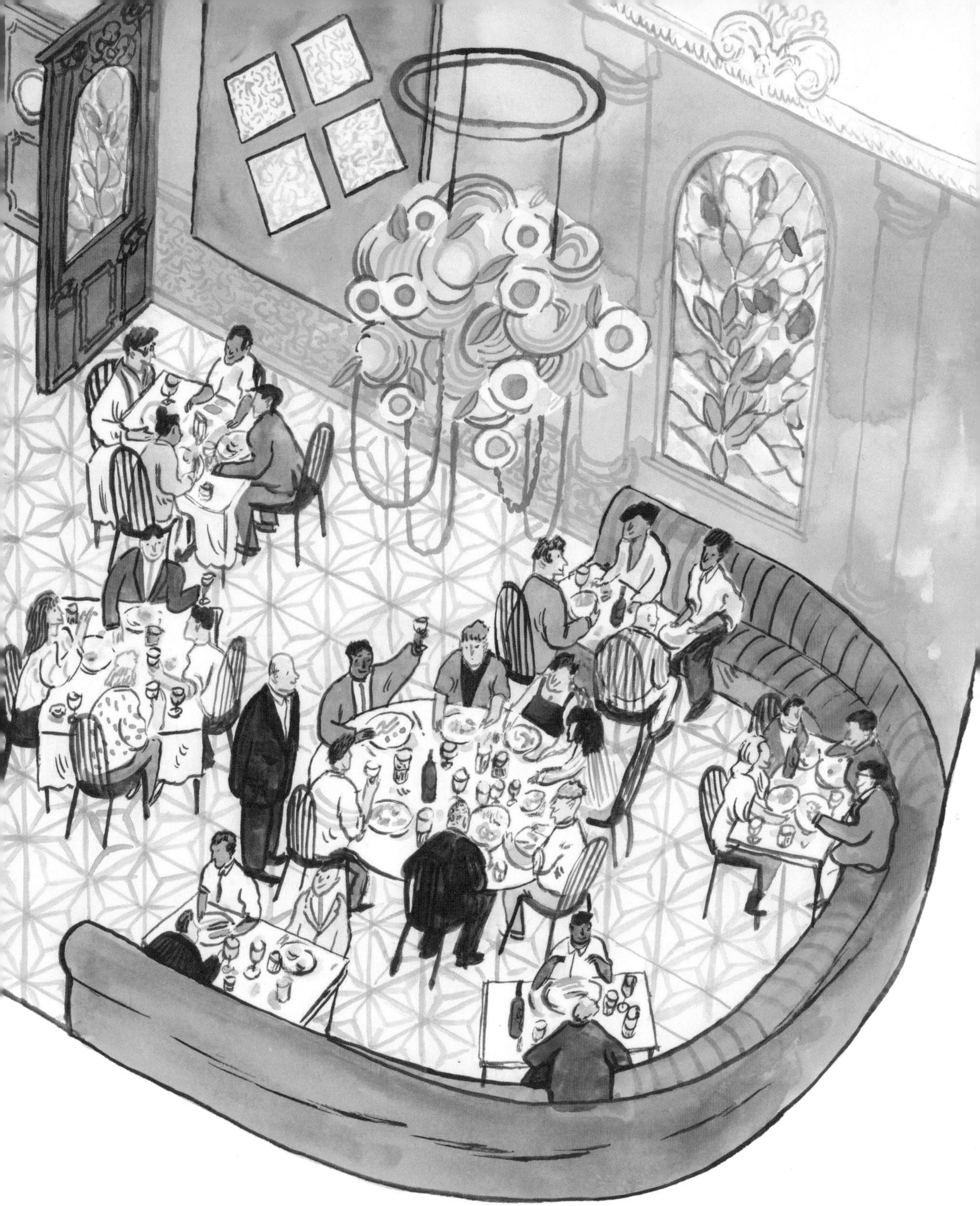

THE ERUDITE CROWDS ARE WOWED BY HIGH-CONCEPT COOKING, EXOTIC CUTS OF BEEF AND "ROWAN'S" "AUTHENTIC", "LOCAL" PRODUCE.

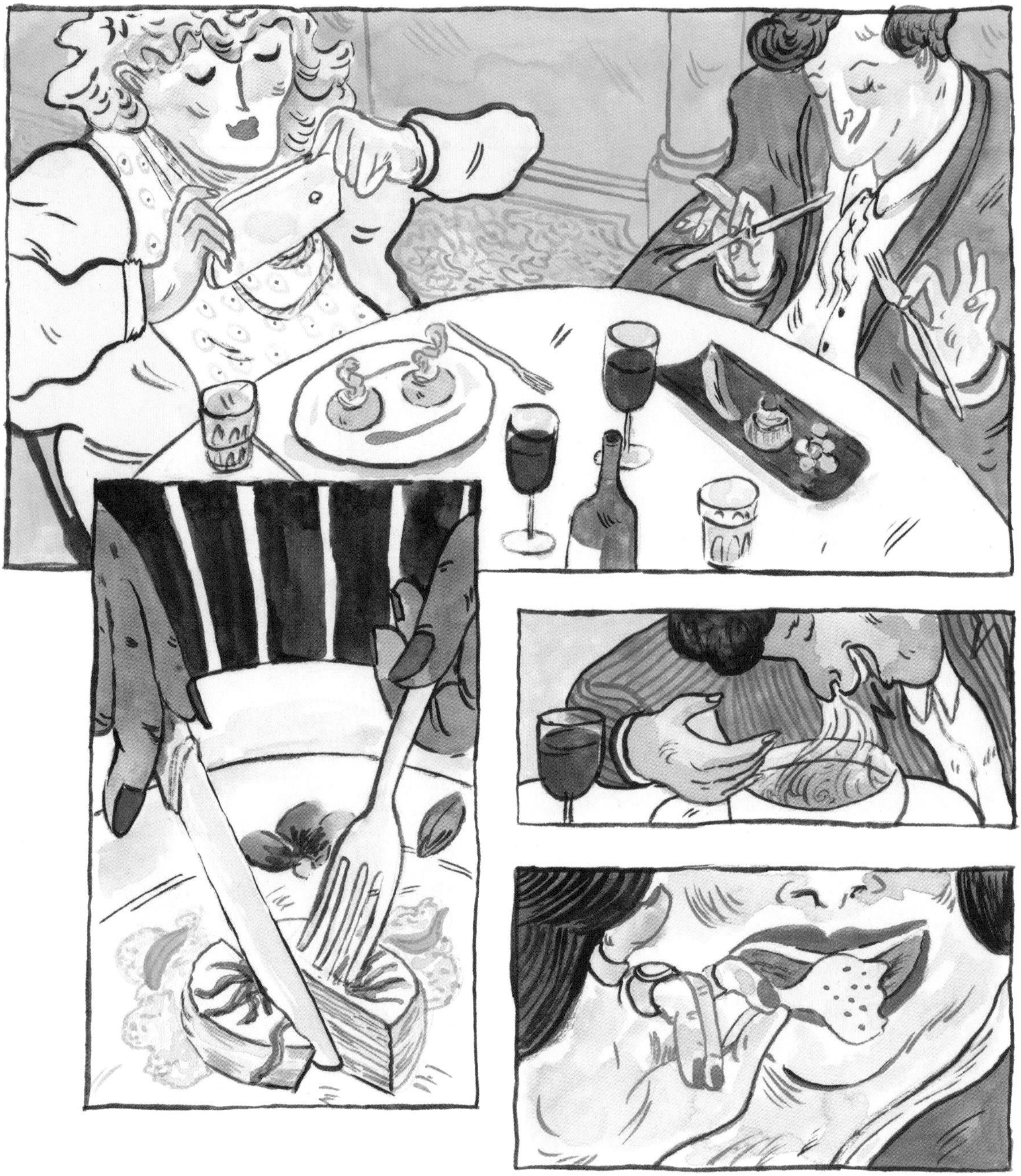

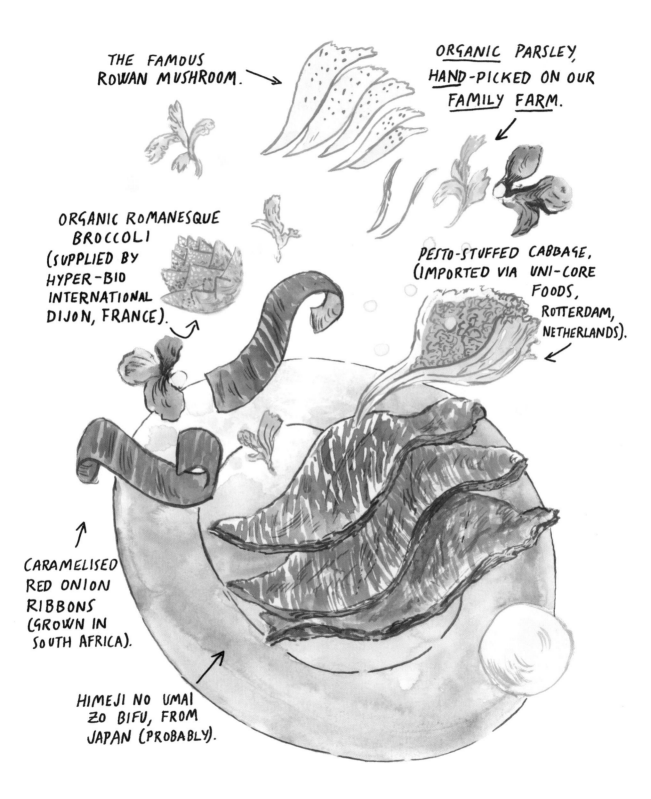

THE FAMOUS ROWAN MUSHROOM.

ORGANIC PARSLEY, HAND-PICKED ON OUR FAMILY FARM.

ORGANIC ROMANESQUE BROCCOLI (SUPPLIED BY HYPER-BIO INTERNATIONAL DIJON, FRANCE).

PESTO-STUFFED CABBAGE, (IMPORTED VIA UNI-CORE FOODS, ROTTERDAM, NETHERLANDS).

CARAMELISED RED ONION RIBBONS (GROWN IN SOUTH AFRICA).

HIMEJI NO UMAI ZO BIFU, FROM JAPAN (PROBABLY).

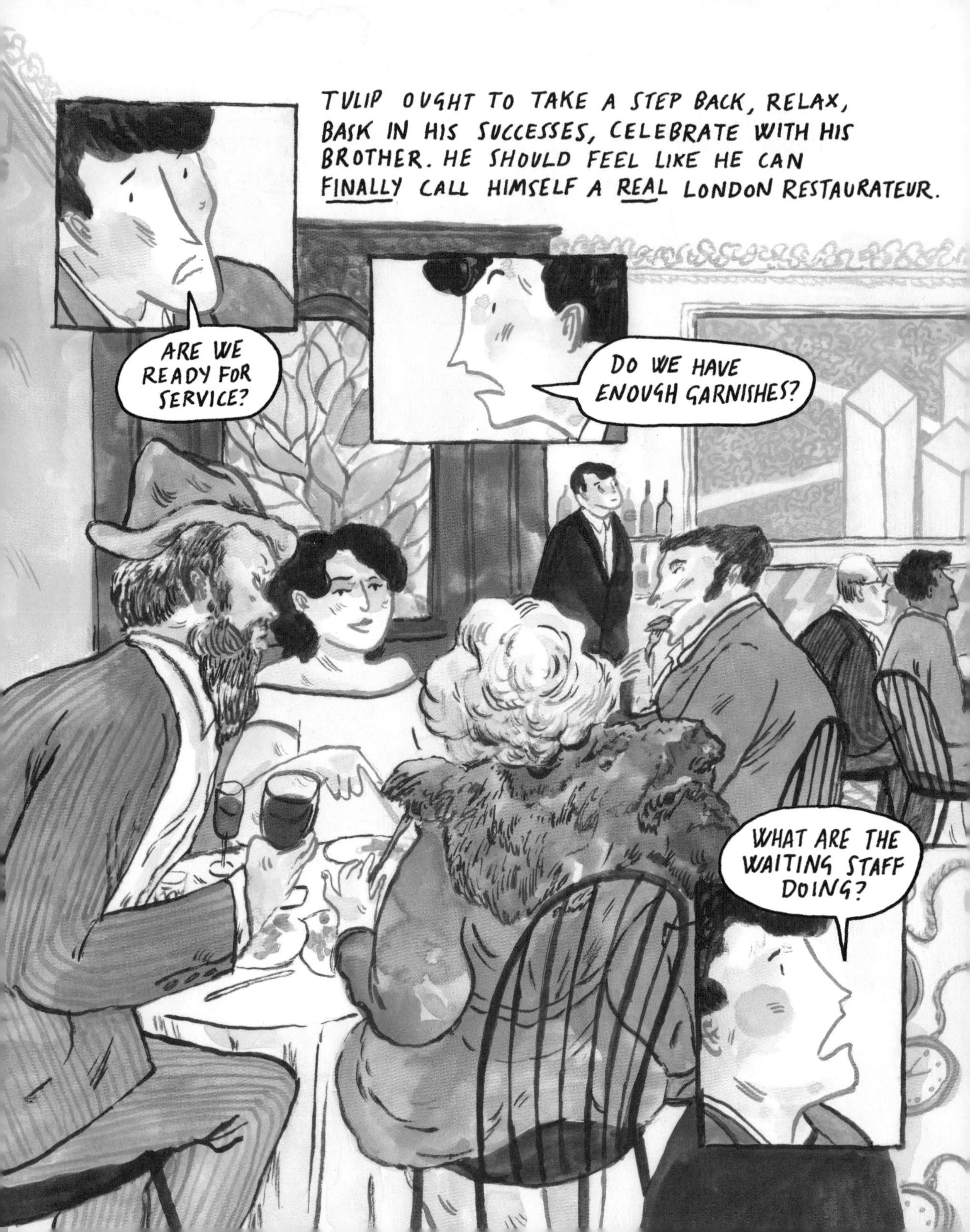
TULIP OUGHT TO TAKE A STEP BACK, RELAX, BASK IN HIS SUCCESSES, CELEBRATE WITH HIS BROTHER. HE SHOULD FEEL LIKE HE CAN FINALLY CALL HIMSELF A REAL LONDON RESTAURATEUR.
ARE WE READY FOR SERVICE?
DO WE HAVE ENOUGH GARNISHES?
WHAT ARE THE WAITING STAFF DOING?

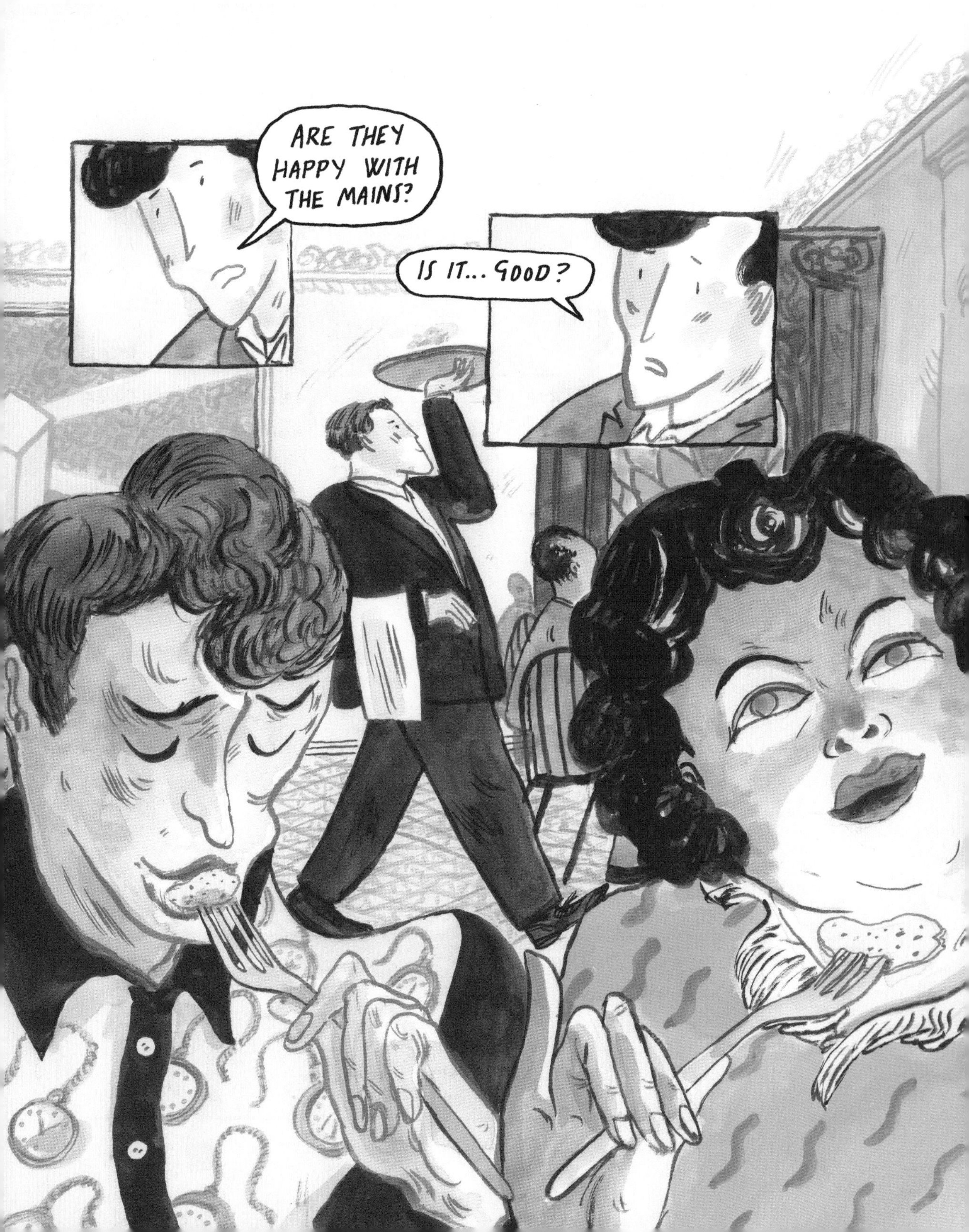
ARE THEY HAPPY WITH THE MAINS?
IS IT... GOOD?

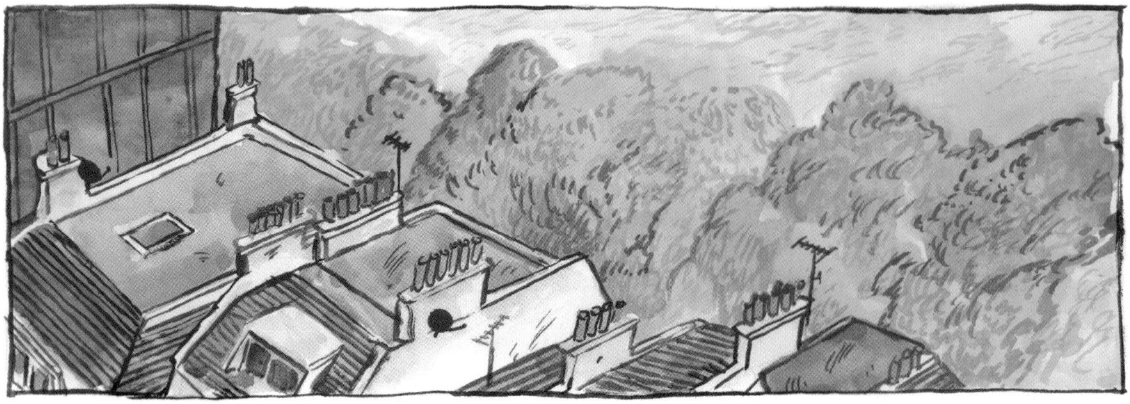

BUT WITH THE HANGOVER FROM THE OPENING NIGHT STILL SCALDING HIS BRAIN, THE HUNGER FOR SUCCESS IS ALREADY GNAWING AGAIN.

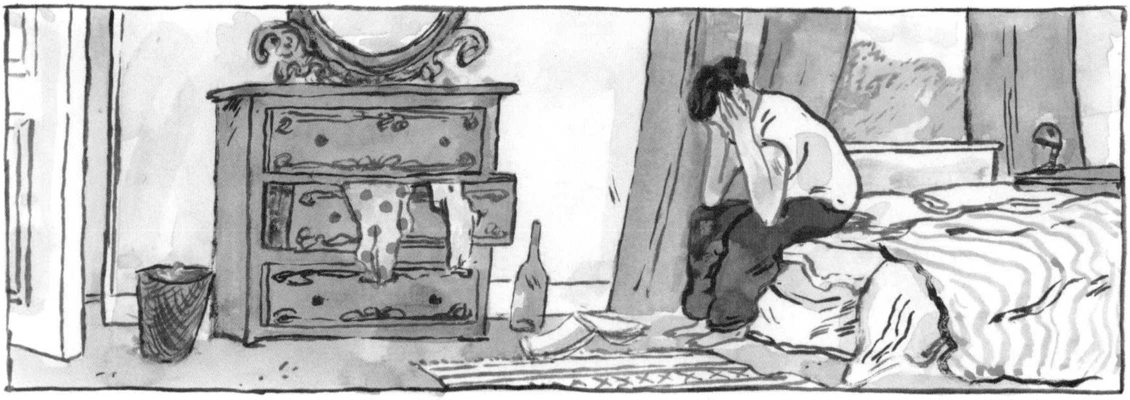

EVEN AS HE PEELS HIMSELF FROM BED IN THE NOONDAY SUN, HIS MIND RETURNS TO THE SOHO RESTAURANT.

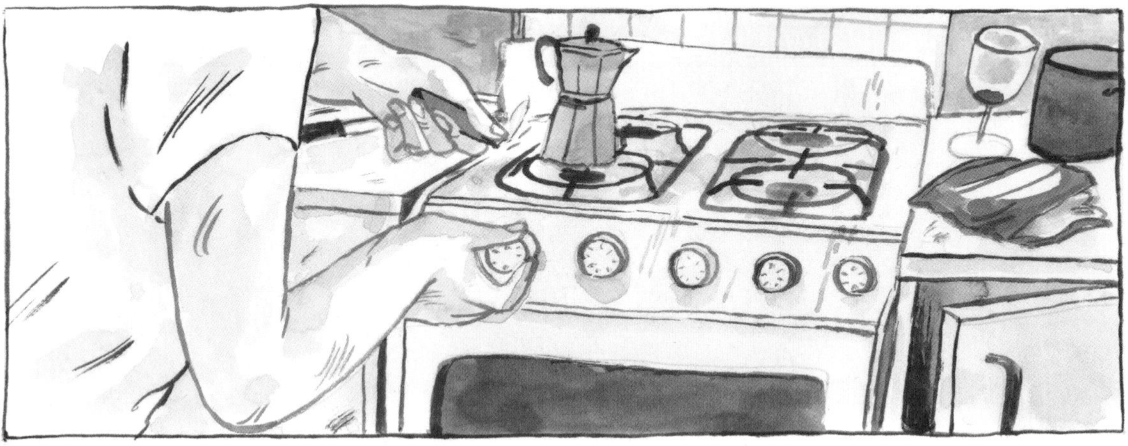

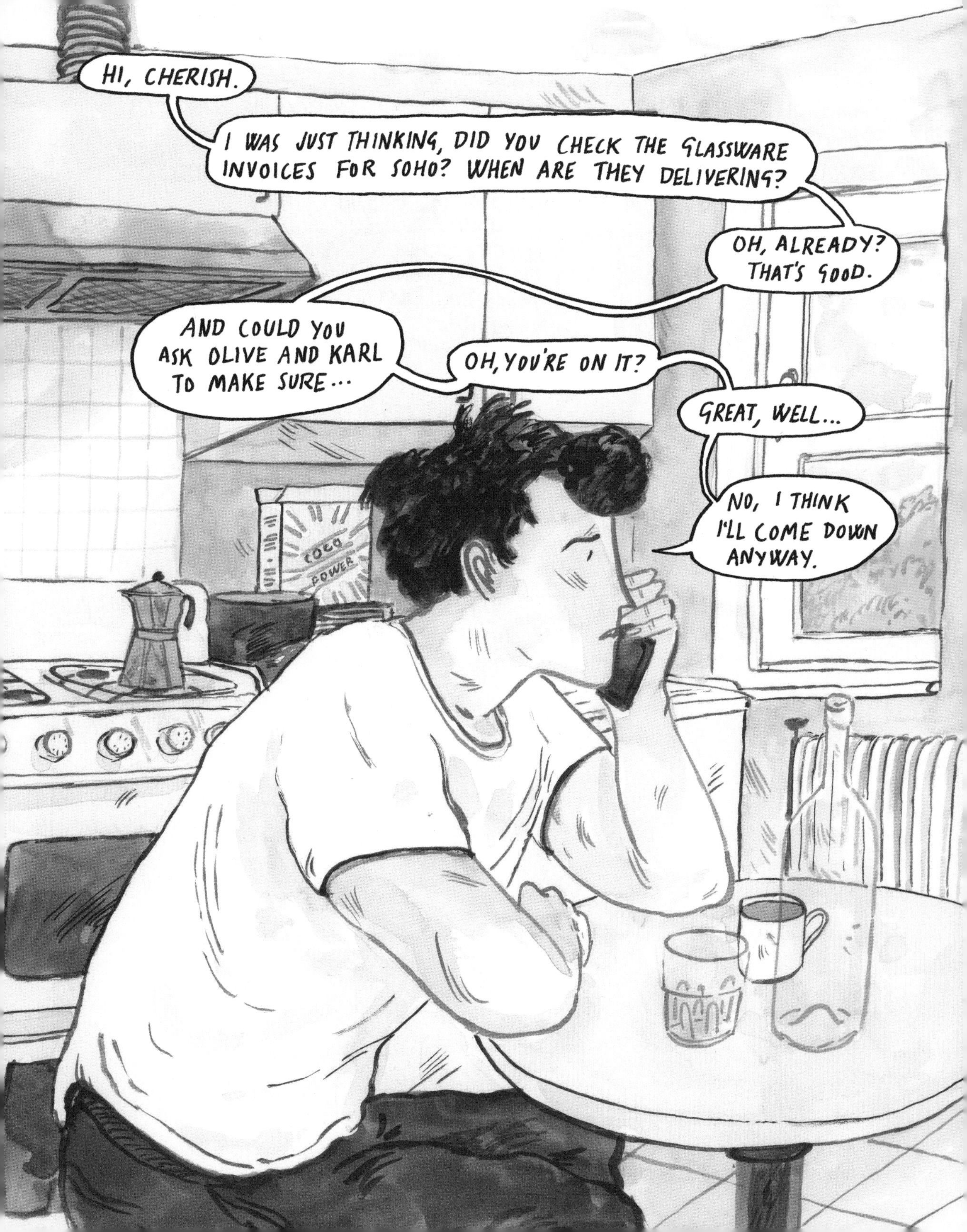
HI, CHERISH.
I WAS JUST THINKING, DID YOU CHECK THE GLASSWARE INVOICES FOR SOHO? WHEN ARE THEY DELIVERING?
OH, ALREADY? THAT'S GOOD.
AND COULD YOU ASK OLIVE AND KARL TO MAKE SURE...
OH, YOU'RE ON IT?
GREAT, WELL...
NO, I THINK I'LL COME DOWN ANYWAY.
COCO POWER

TULIP HAS SETTLED COMFORTABLY INTO THE WORLD OF LONDON'S GASTRONOMES. ALMOST EVERY NIGHT HE CAN BE FOUND PARADING WITH FELLOW CHEFS, FOOD CRITICS, SOCIALITES AND SYBARITES FROM THE WORLD OF FILM AND FASHION.

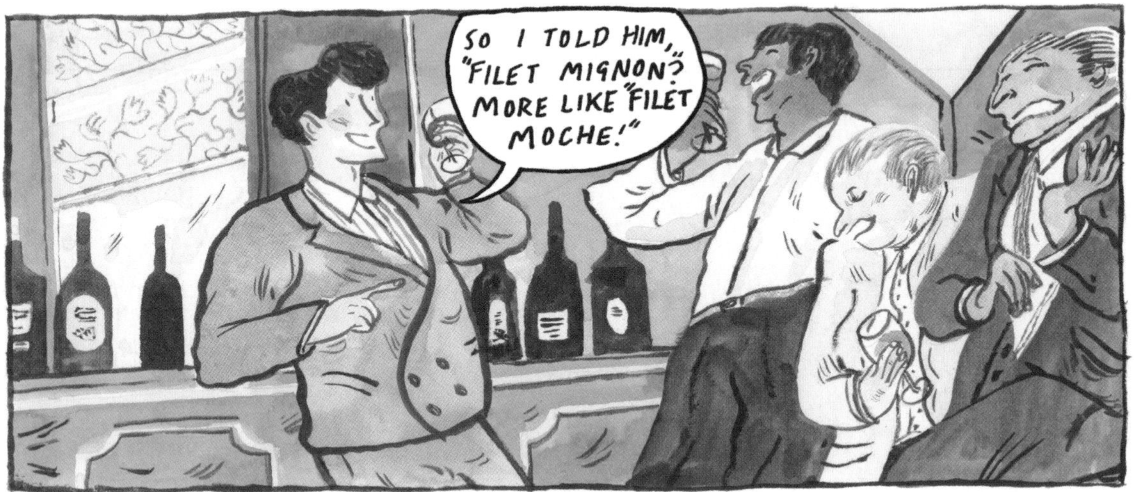
SO I TOLD HIM, "FILET MIGNON?" MORE LIKE "FILET MOCHE!"

APPEARING ONLY FLEETINGLY IN HIS OWN KITCHENS, HE INVARIABLY MAKES A SHOW OF PRESENTING DISHES TO HIS FAMOUS ACOLYTES.

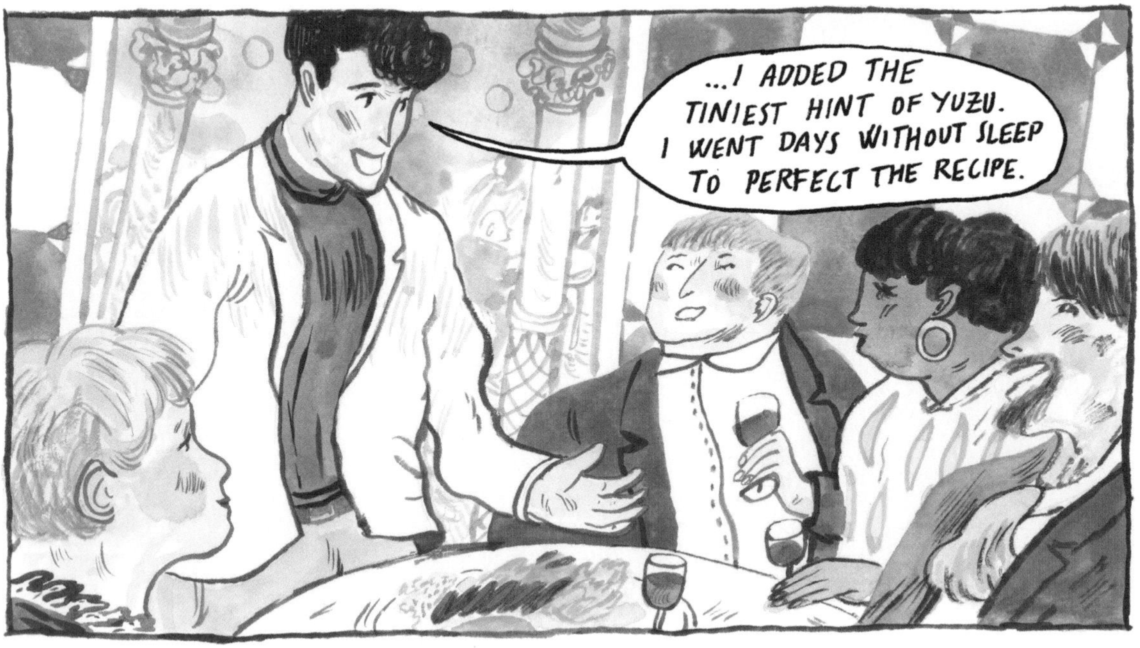
...I ADDED THE TINIEST HINT OF YUZU. I WENT DAYS WITHOUT SLEEP TO PERFECT THE RECIPE.

UNENDINGLY, THE MUSHROOMS WORK THEIR MAGIC, AND GUESTS WALTZ OUT OF THE RESTAURANT WITH AN INVIGORATED GLOW.

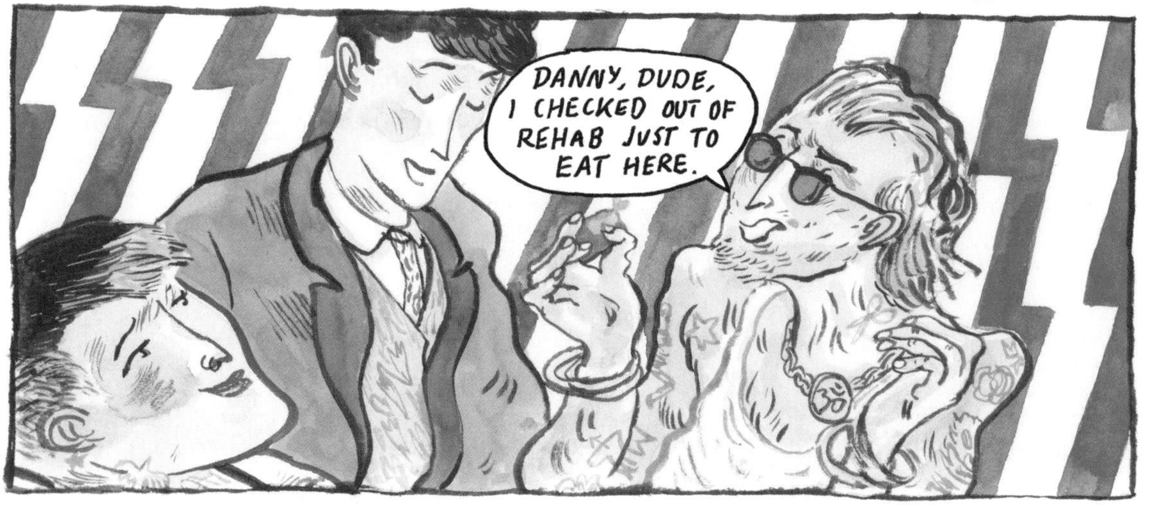
DANNY, DUDE, I CHECKED OUT OF REHAB JUST TO EAT HERE.

THE PRESS LOVES NOTHING MORE THAN A RAGS-TO-RICHES STORY.

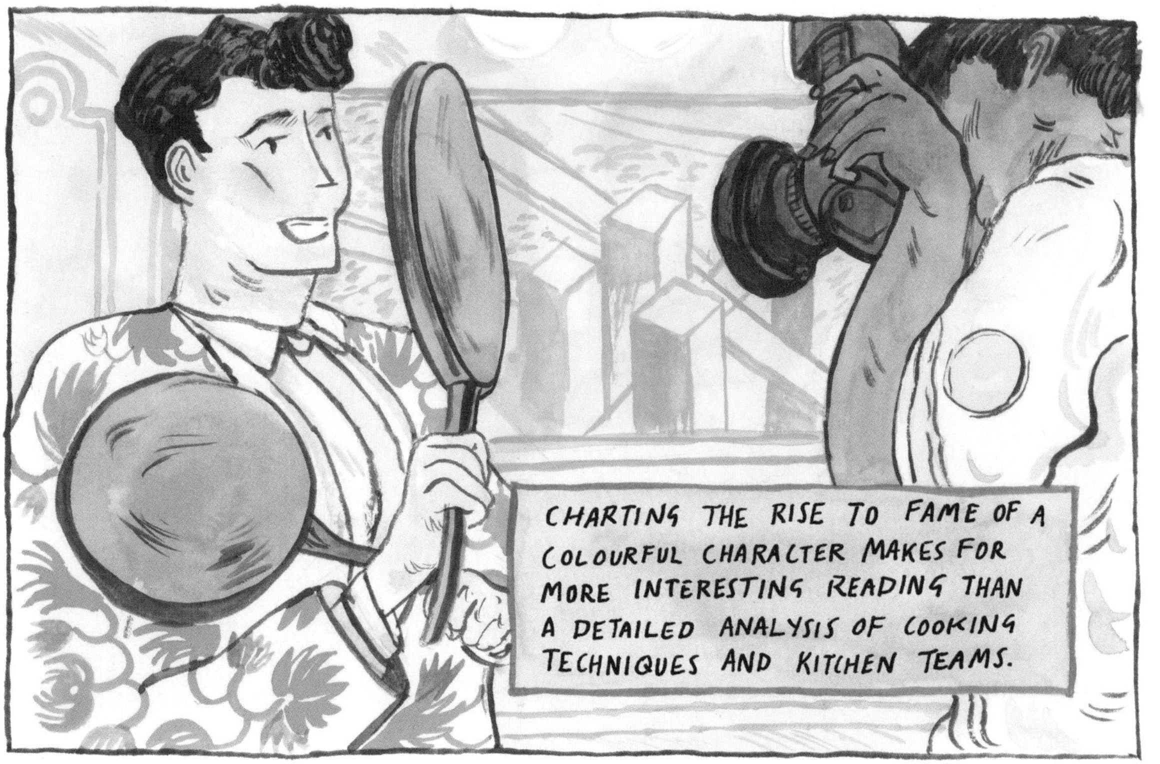
CHARTING THE RISE TO FAME OF A COLOURFUL CHARACTER MAKES FOR MORE INTERESTING READING THAN A DETAILED ANALYSIS OF COOKING TECHNIQUES AND KITCHEN TEAMS.

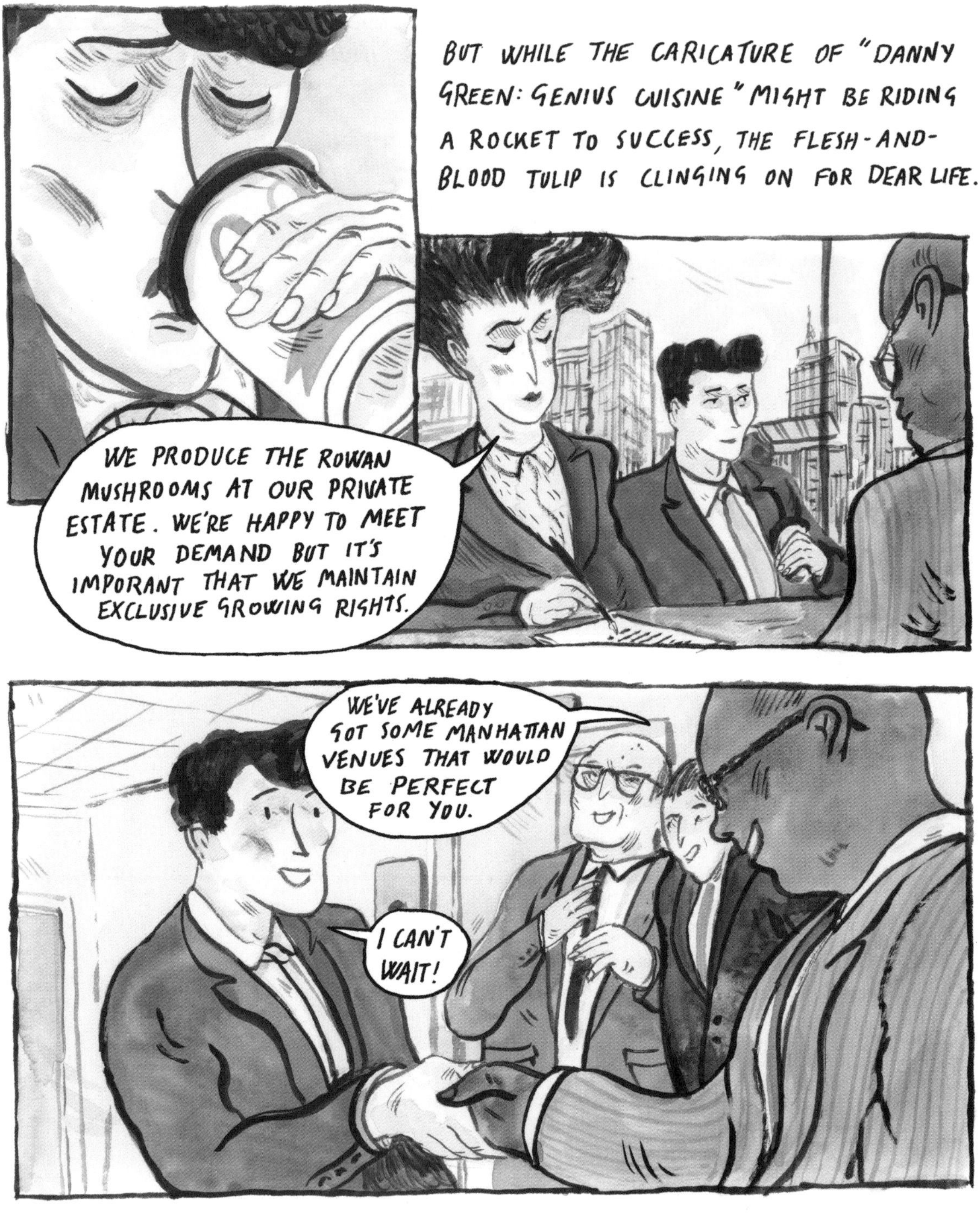
BUT WHILE THE CARICATURE OF "DANNY GREEN: GENIUS CUISINE" MIGHT BE RIDING A ROCKET TO SUCCESS, THE FLESH-AND-BLOOD TULIP IS CLINGING ON FOR DEAR LIFE.
WE PRODUCE THE ROWAN MUSHROOMS AT OUR PRIVATE ESTATE. WE'RE HAPPY TO MEET YOUR DEMAND BUT IT'S IMPORANT THAT WE MAINTAIN EXCLUSIVE GROWING RIGHTS.
WE'VE ALREADY GOT SOME MANHATTAN VENUES THAT WOULD BE PERFECT FOR YOU.
I CAN'T WAIT!

IN A WAY, THINKS TULIP, THESE RICH INVESTORS ARE ACTUALLY INFLICTING AN ACT OF CRUELTY ON HIM.

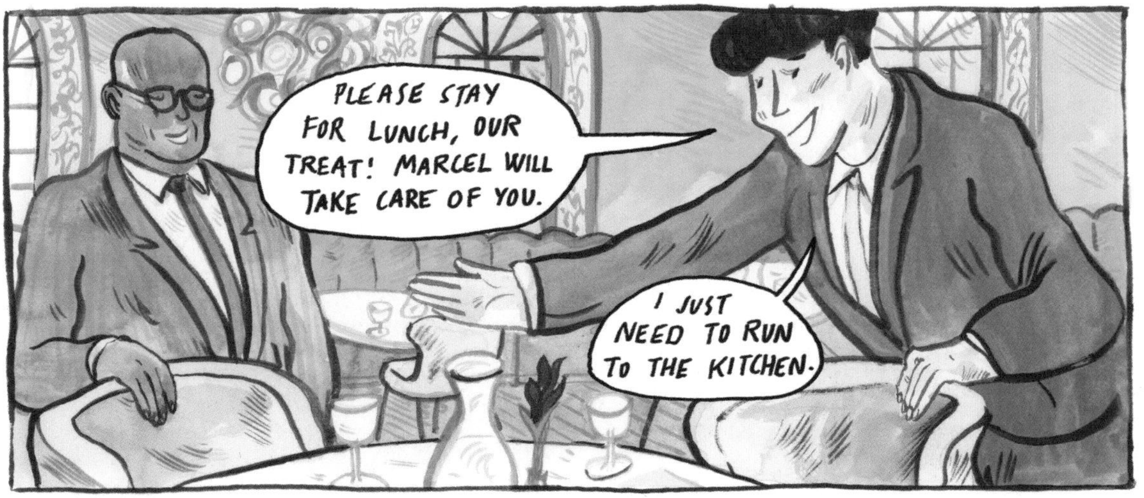
PLEASE STAY FOR LUNCH, OUR TREAT! MARCEL WILL TAKE CARE OF YOU.
I JUST NEED TO RUN TO THE KITCHEN.

IN THEIR INCESSANT EFFORTS TO OFFER HIM VAST SUMS OF MONEY FOR INCREASINGLY TINY NUMBERS OF MUSHROOMS, THEY'RE FORCING HIM TO ADMIT THAT NO MATTER HOW MANY TIMES HE RECOUNTS THEM, HE HAS NO WAY OF KNOWING IF THE MUSHROOMS WILL KEEP GROWING BACK.

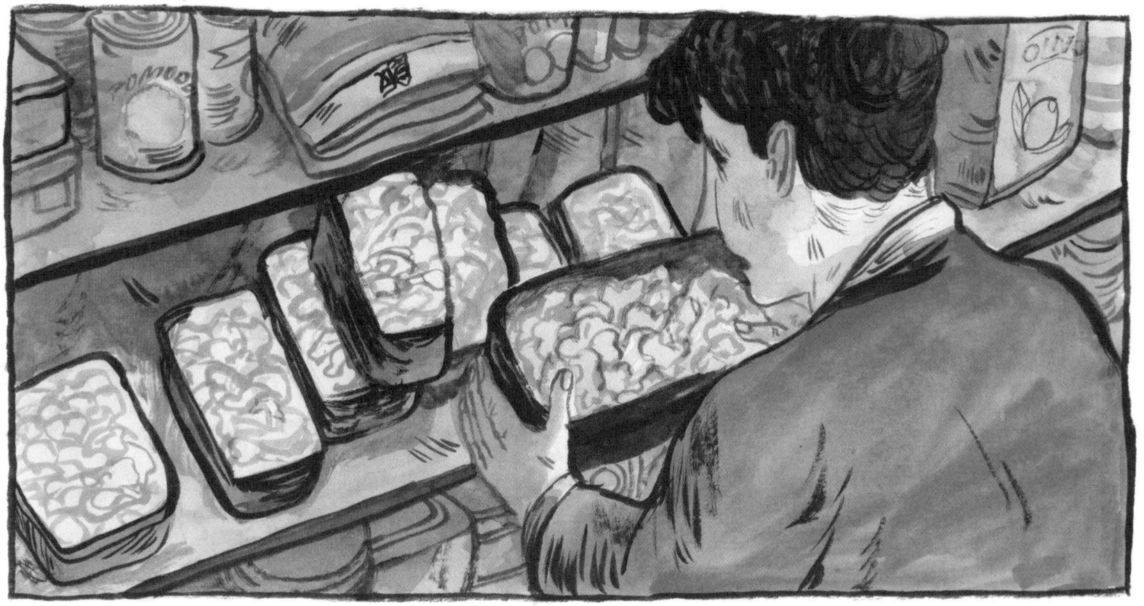

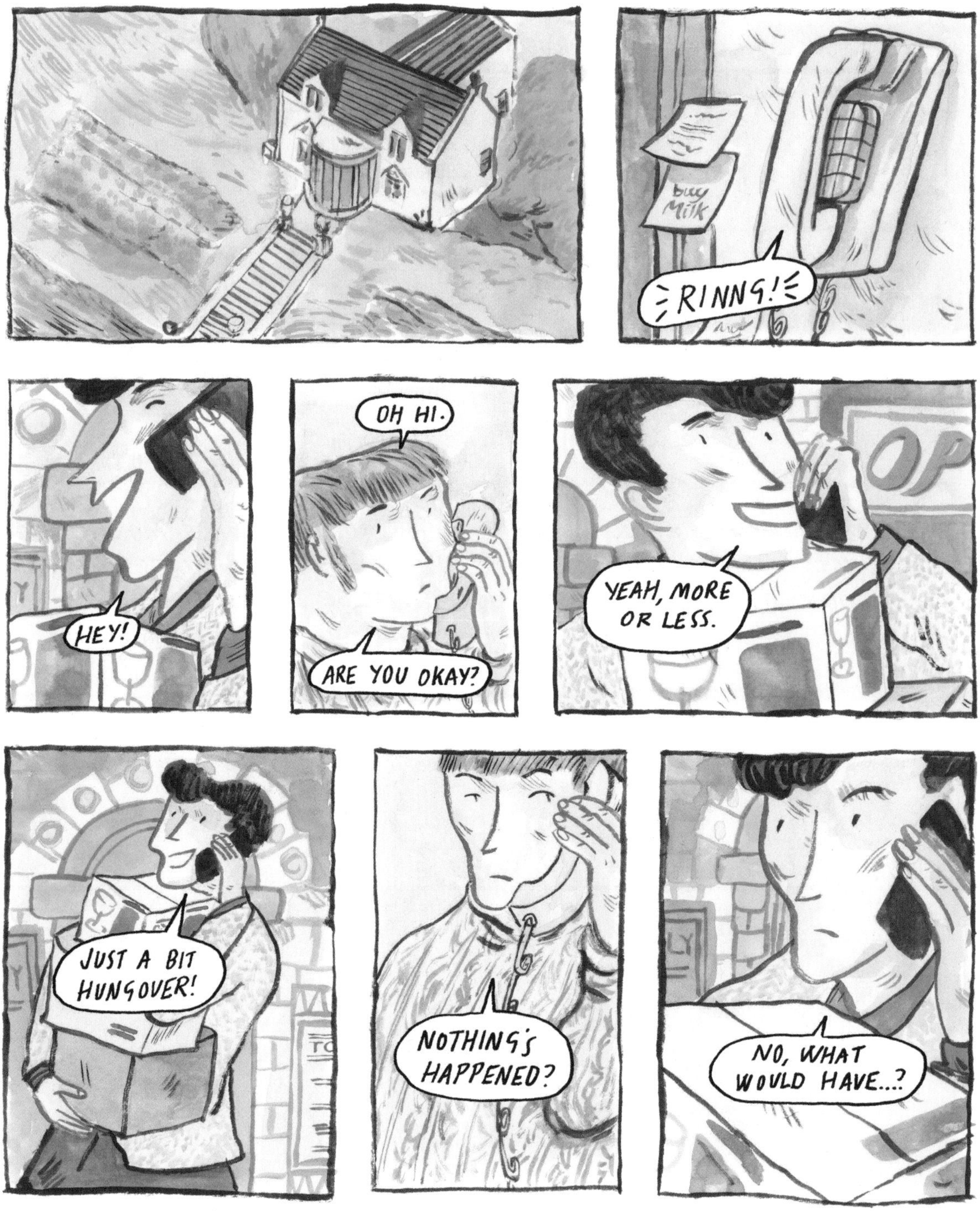
buy Milk
RINNG!
HEY!
OH HI.
ARE YOU OKAY?
YEAH, MORE OR LESS.
JUST A BIT HUNGOVER!
NOTHING'S HAPPENED?
NO, WHAT WOULD HAVE...?

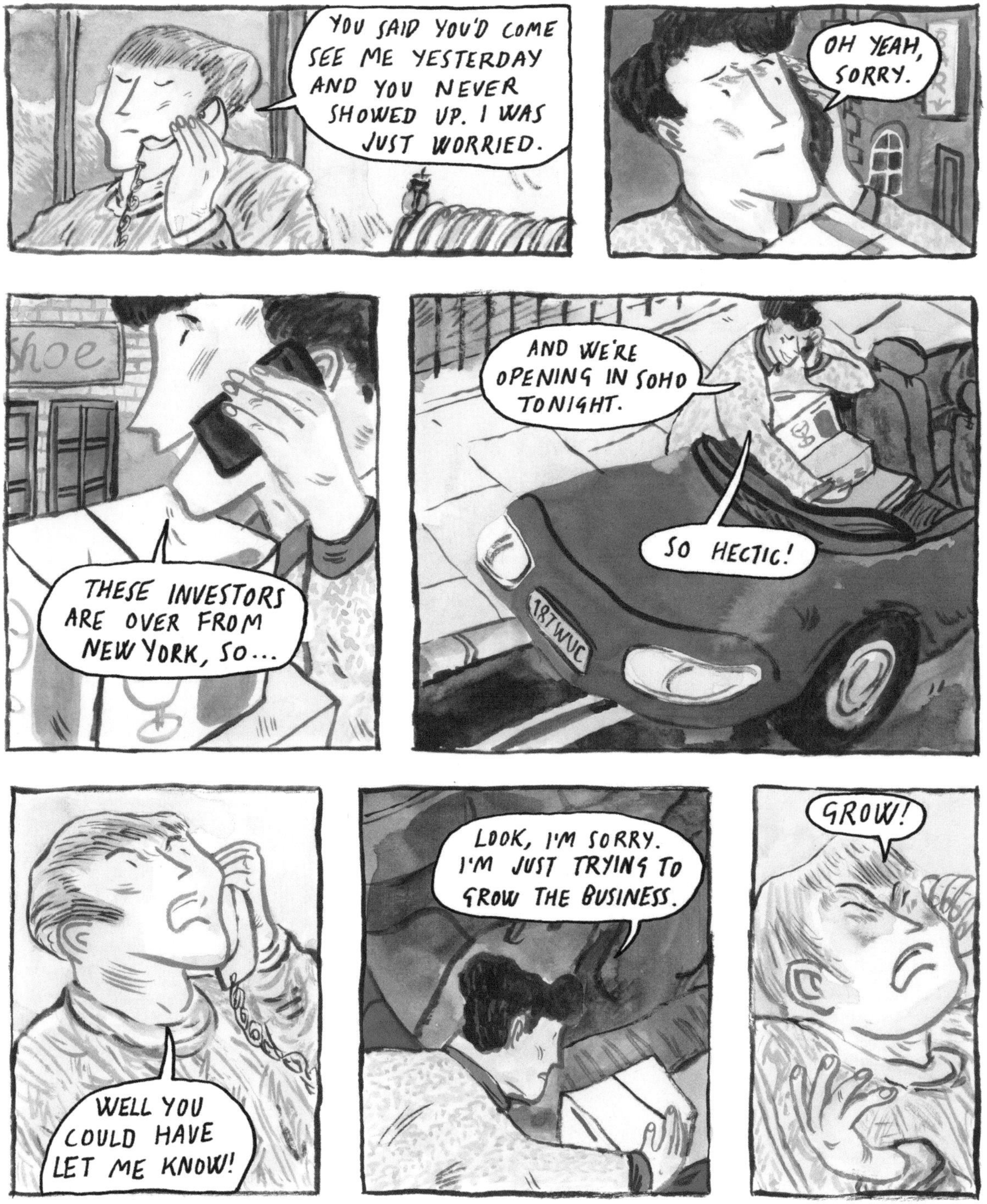
YOU SAID YOU'D COME SEE ME YESTERDAY AND YOU NEVER SHOWED UP. I WAS JUST WORRIED.
OH YEAH, SORRY.
shoe
THESE INVESTORS ARE OVER FROM NEW YORK, SO...
AND WE'RE OPENING IN SOHO TONIGHT.
SO HECTIC!
187 WUC
WELL YOU COULD HAVE LET ME KNOW!
LOOK, I'M SORRY. I'M JUST TRYING TO GROW THE BUSINESS.
GROW!

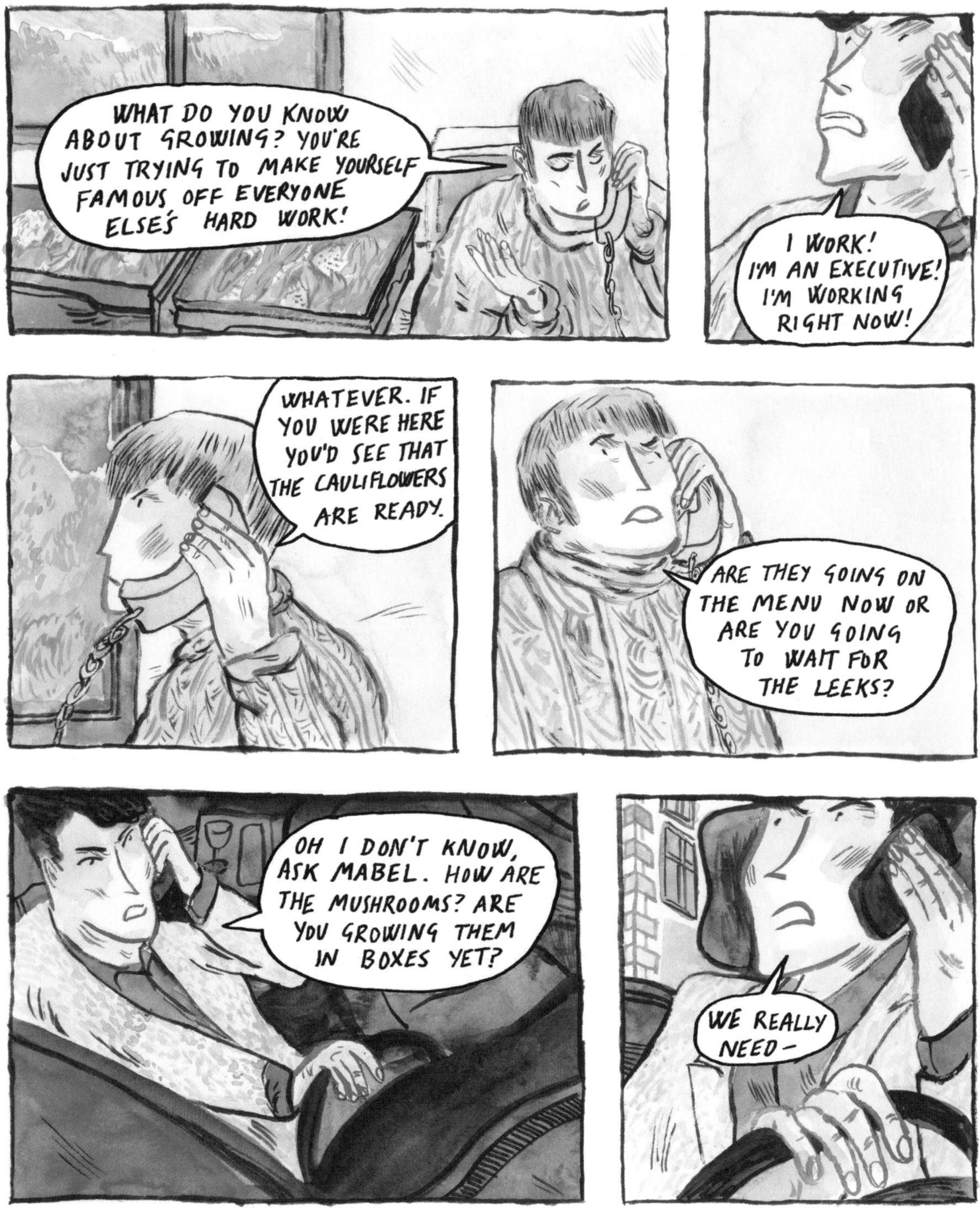
WHAT DO YOU KNOW ABOUT GROWING? YOU'RE JUST TRYING TO MAKE YOURSELF FAMOUS OFF EVERYONE ELSE'S HARD WORK!
I WORK! I'M AN EXECUTIVE! I'M WORKING RIGHT NOW!
WHATEVER. IF YOU WERE HERE YOU'D SEE THAT THE CAULIFLOWERS ARE READY.
ARE THEY GOING ON THE MENU NOW OR ARE YOU GOING TO WAIT FOR THE LEEKS?
OH I DON'T KNOW, ASK MABEL. HOW ARE THE MUSHROOMS? ARE YOU GROWING THEM IN BOXES YET?
WE REALLY NEED—

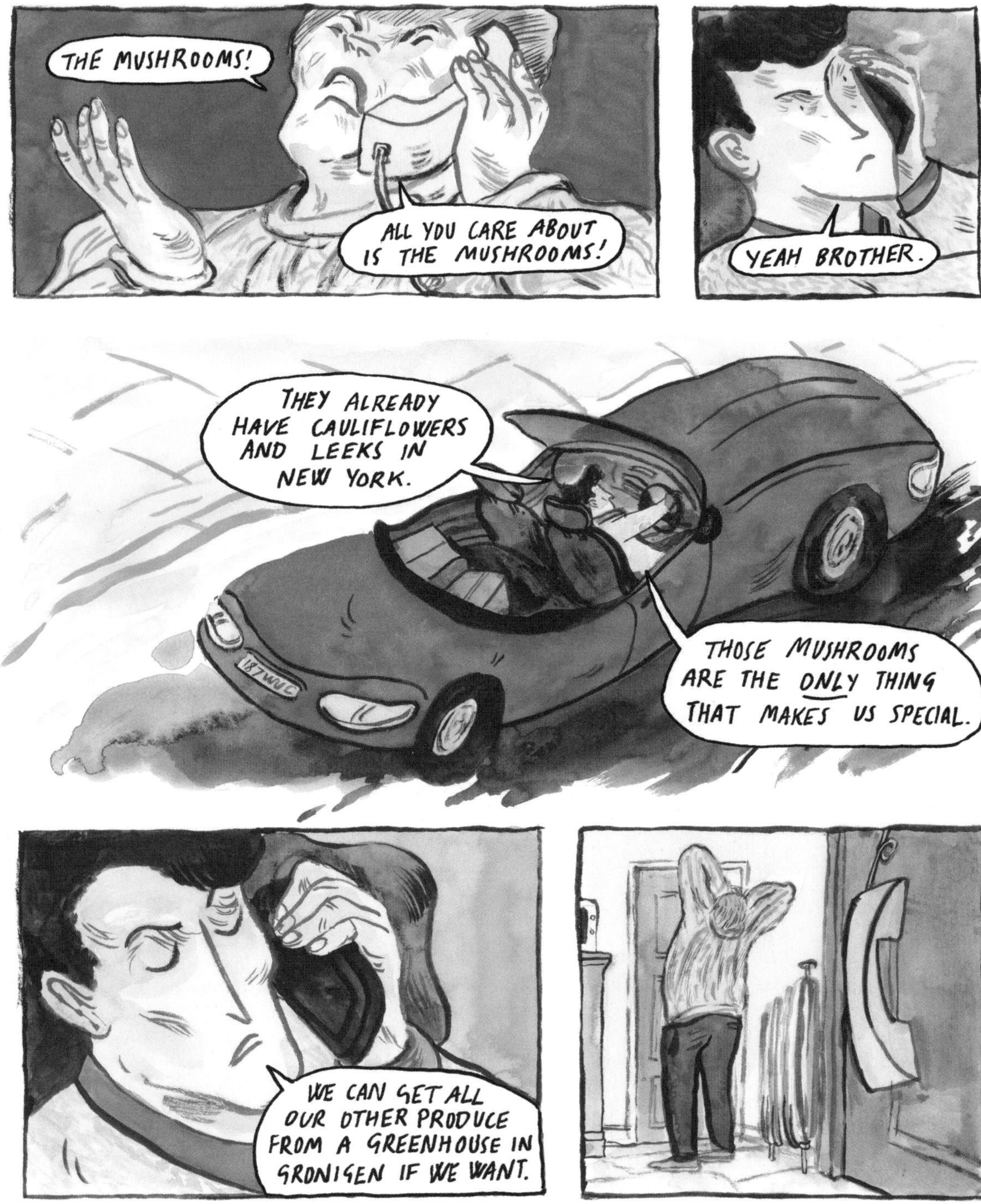
THE MUSHROOMS!
ALL YOU CARE ABOUT IS THE MUSHROOMS!
YEAH BROTHER.
THEY ALREADY HAVE CAULIFLOWERS AND LEEKS IN NEW YORK.
THOSE MUSHROOMS ARE THE ONLY THING THAT MAKES US SPECIAL.
WE CAN GET ALL OUR OTHER PRODUCE FROM A GREENHOUSE IN GRONIGEN IF WE WANT.

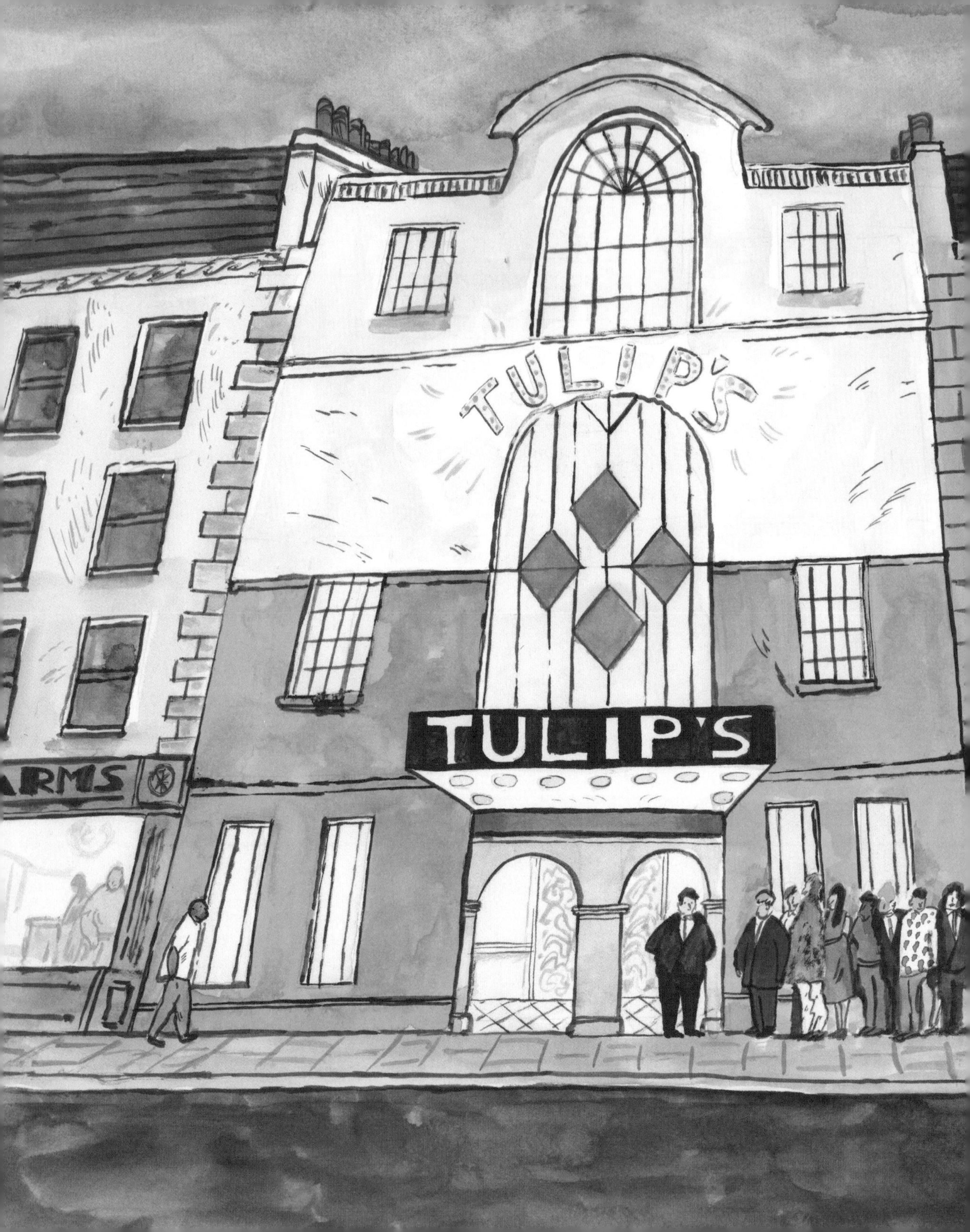
TULIP'S
TULIP'S
ARMS

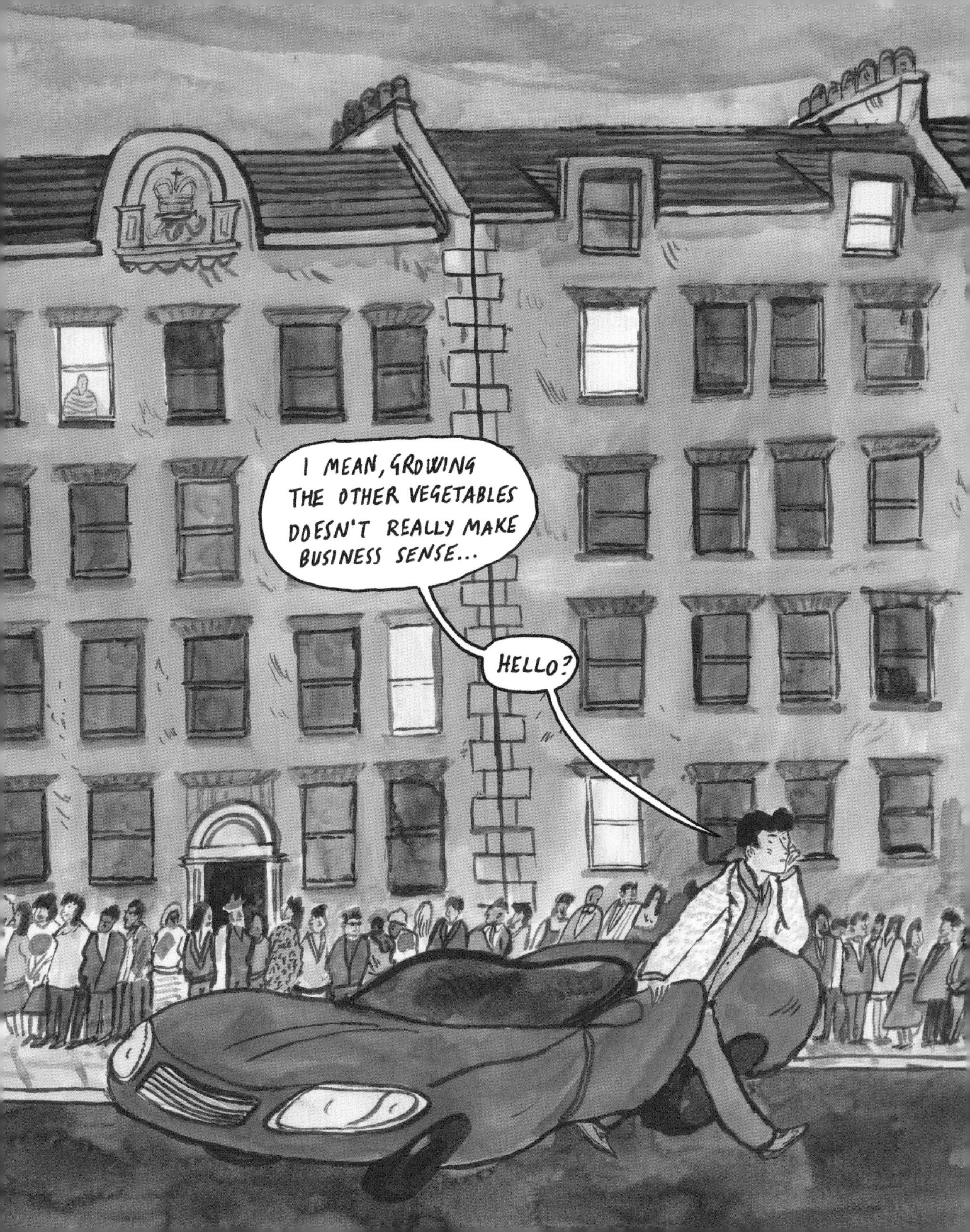
I MEAN, GROWING THE OTHER VEGETABLES DOESN'T REALLY MAKE BUSINESS SENSE...
HELLO?

EVEN AS HIS SOHO RESTAURANT OPENS, HE'S DISTRACTED WITH PLANS FOR A FOURTH OUTLET IN LONDON'S FINANCIAL DISTRICT, AN "ON-BRAND FAST FOOD EXPERIENCE" TO FEED MORE MOUTHS WITH CHEAPER INGREDIENTS AT A HIGHER MARGIN.

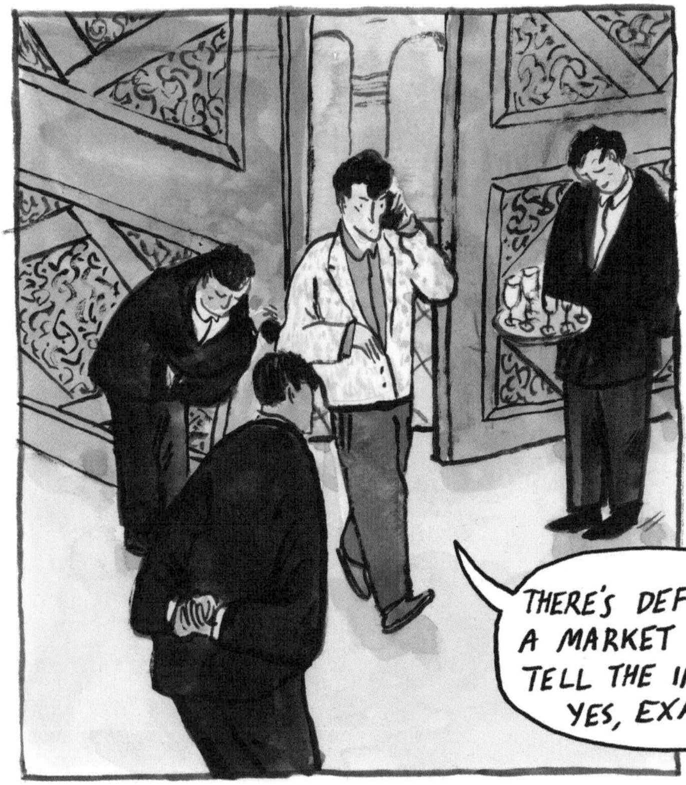
THERE'S DEFINITELY A MARKET OPENING. TELL THE INVESTORS, YES, EXACTLY.

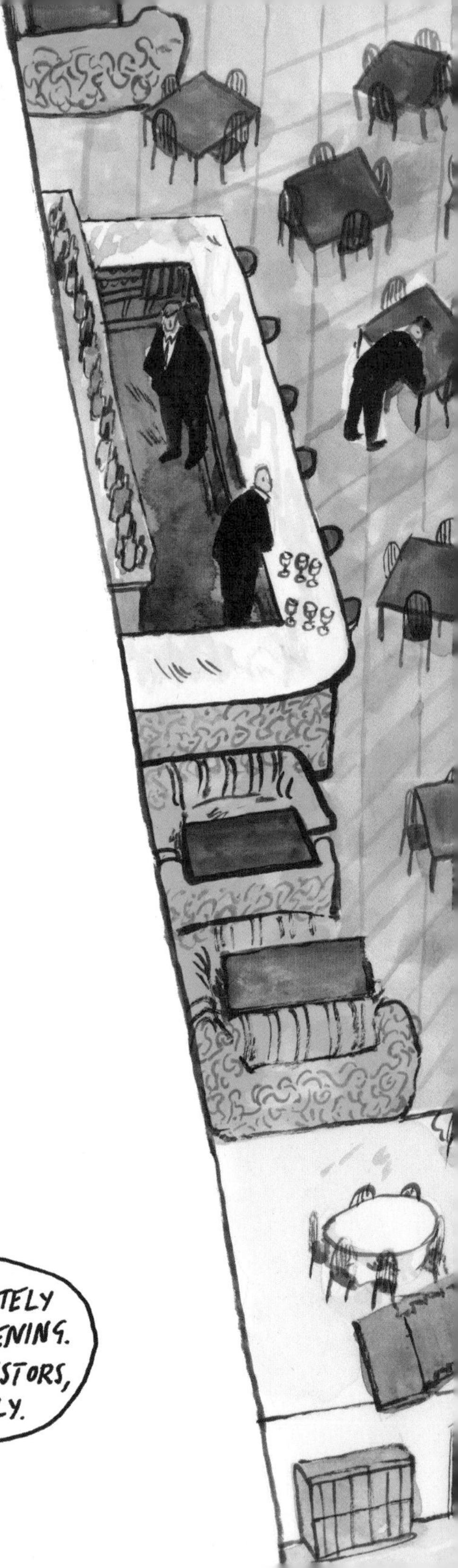

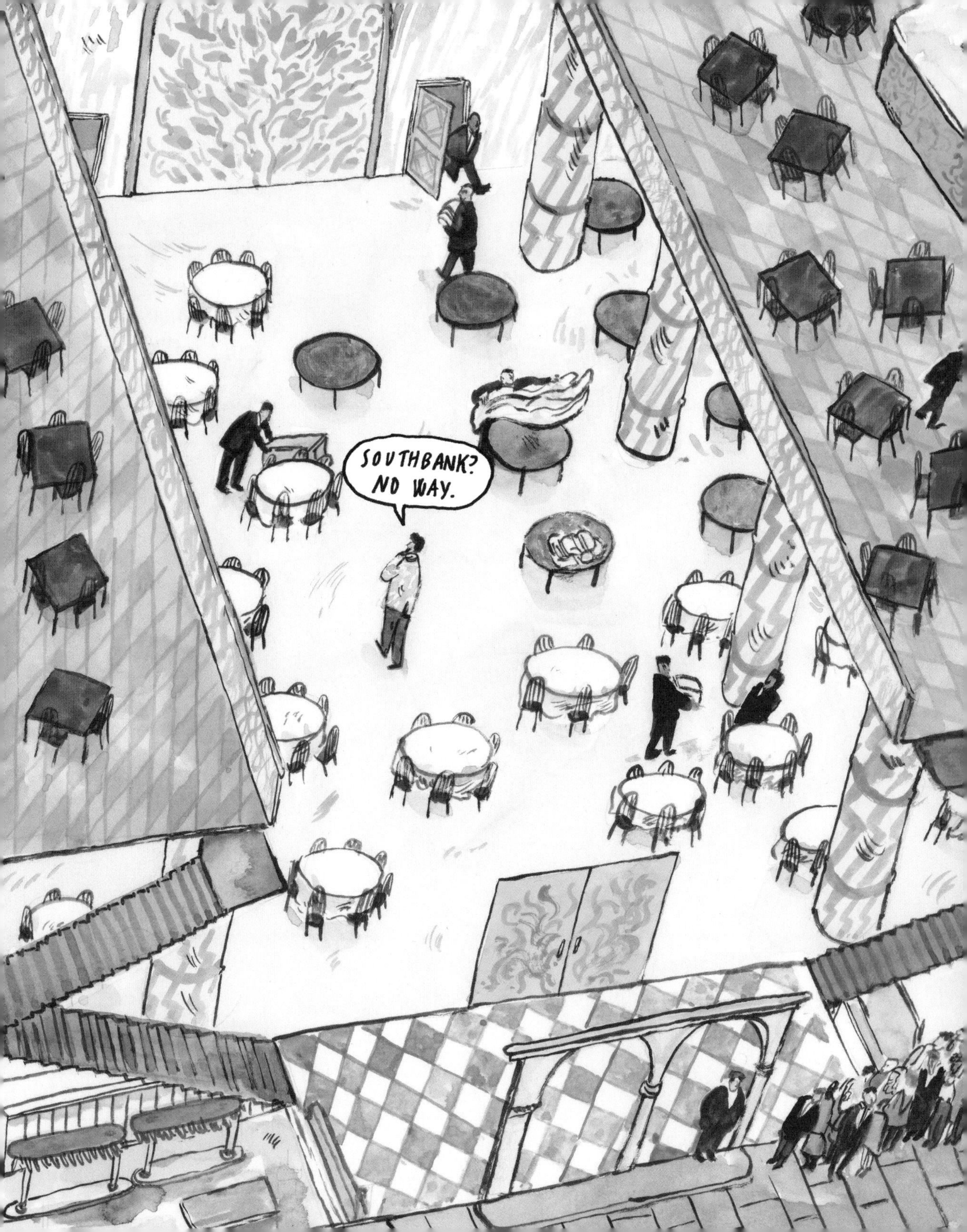
SOUTHBANK? NO WAY.

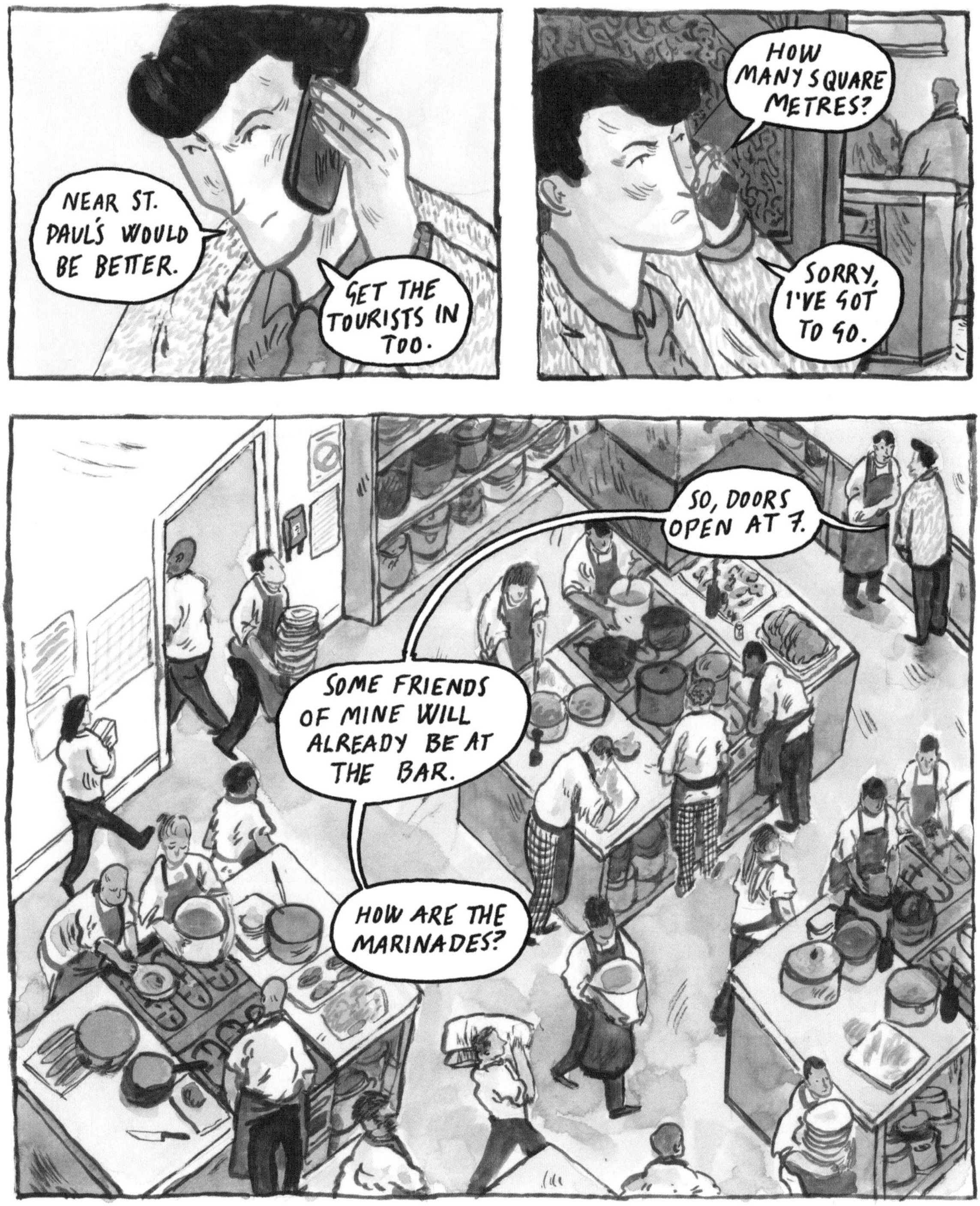
NEAR ST. PAUL'S WOULD BE BETTER.
GET THE TOURISTS IN TOO.
HOW MANY SQUARE METRES?
SORRY, I'VE GOT TO GO.
SO, DOORS OPEN AT 7.
SOME FRIENDS OF MINE WILL ALREADY BE AT THE BAR.
HOW ARE THE MARINADES?

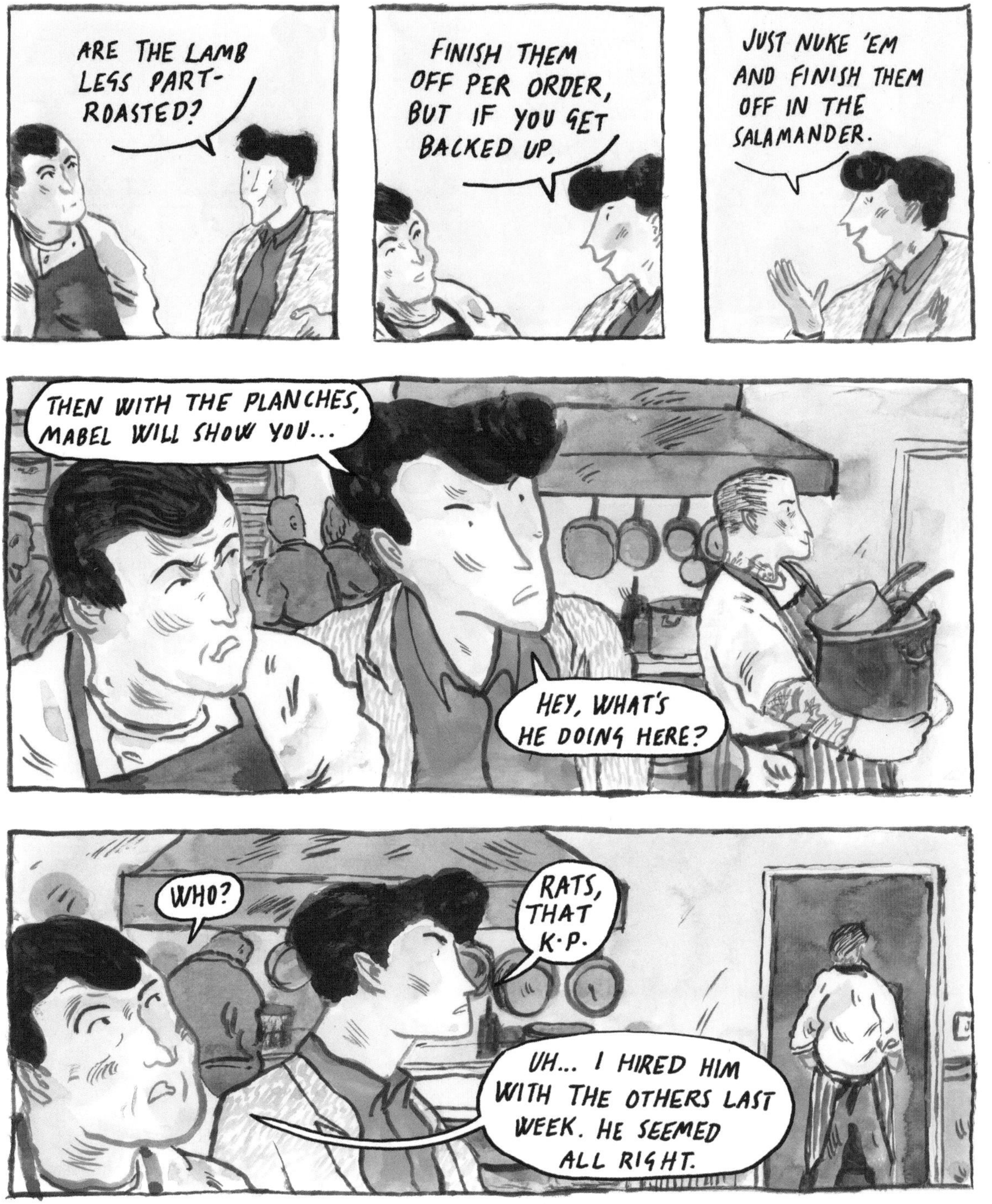
ARE THE LAMB LEGS PART-ROASTED?
FINISH THEM OFF PER ORDER, BUT IF YOU GET BACKED UP,
JUST NUKE 'EM AND FINISH THEM OFF IN THE SALAMANDER.
THEN WITH THE PLANCHES, MABEL WILL SHOW YOU...
HEY, WHAT'S HE DOING HERE?
WHO?
RATS, THAT K·P.
UH... I HIRED HIM WITH THE OTHERS LAST WEEK. HE SEEMED ALL RIGHT.

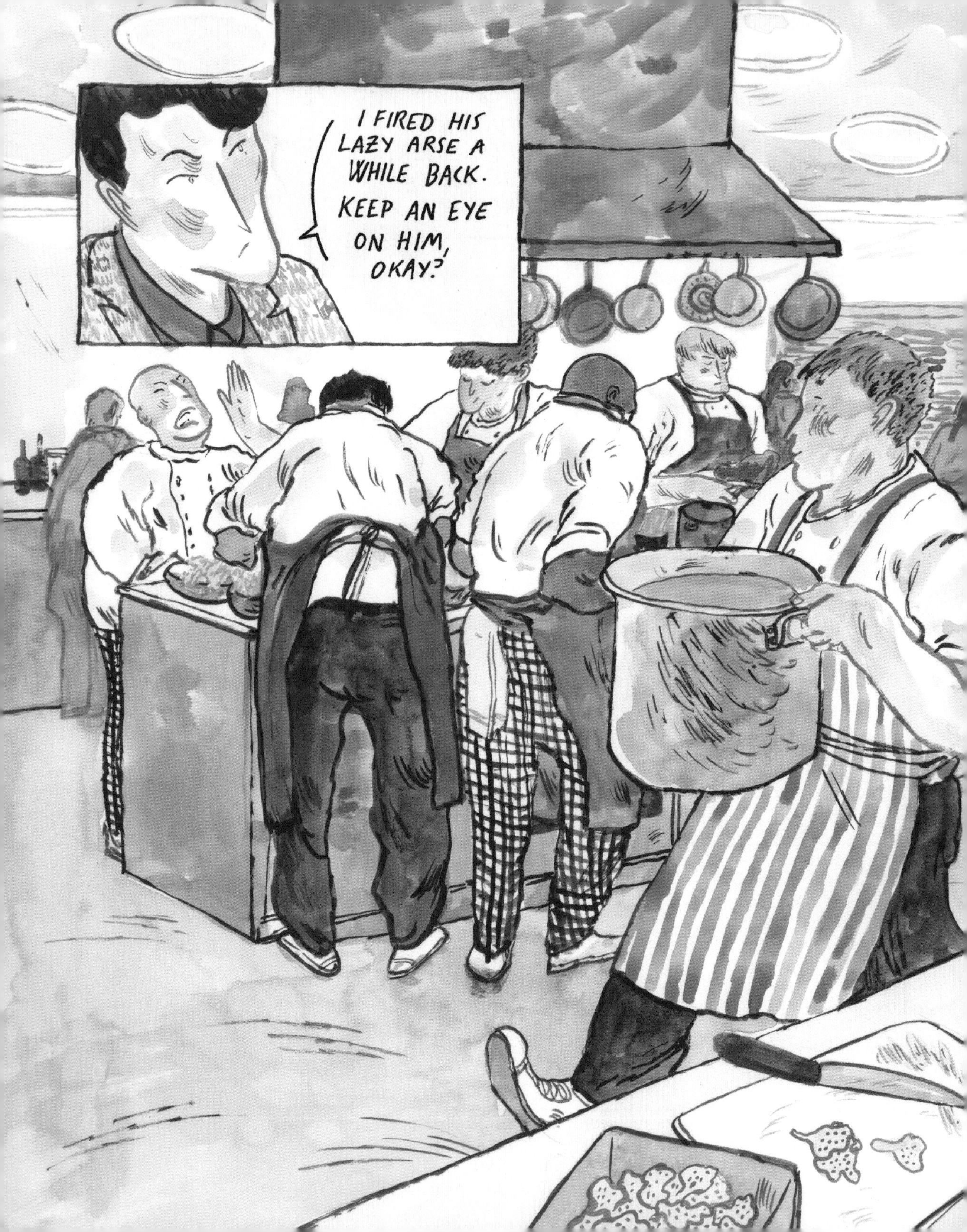
I FIRED HIS LAZY ARSE A WHILE BACK. KEEP AN EYE ON HIM, OKAY?

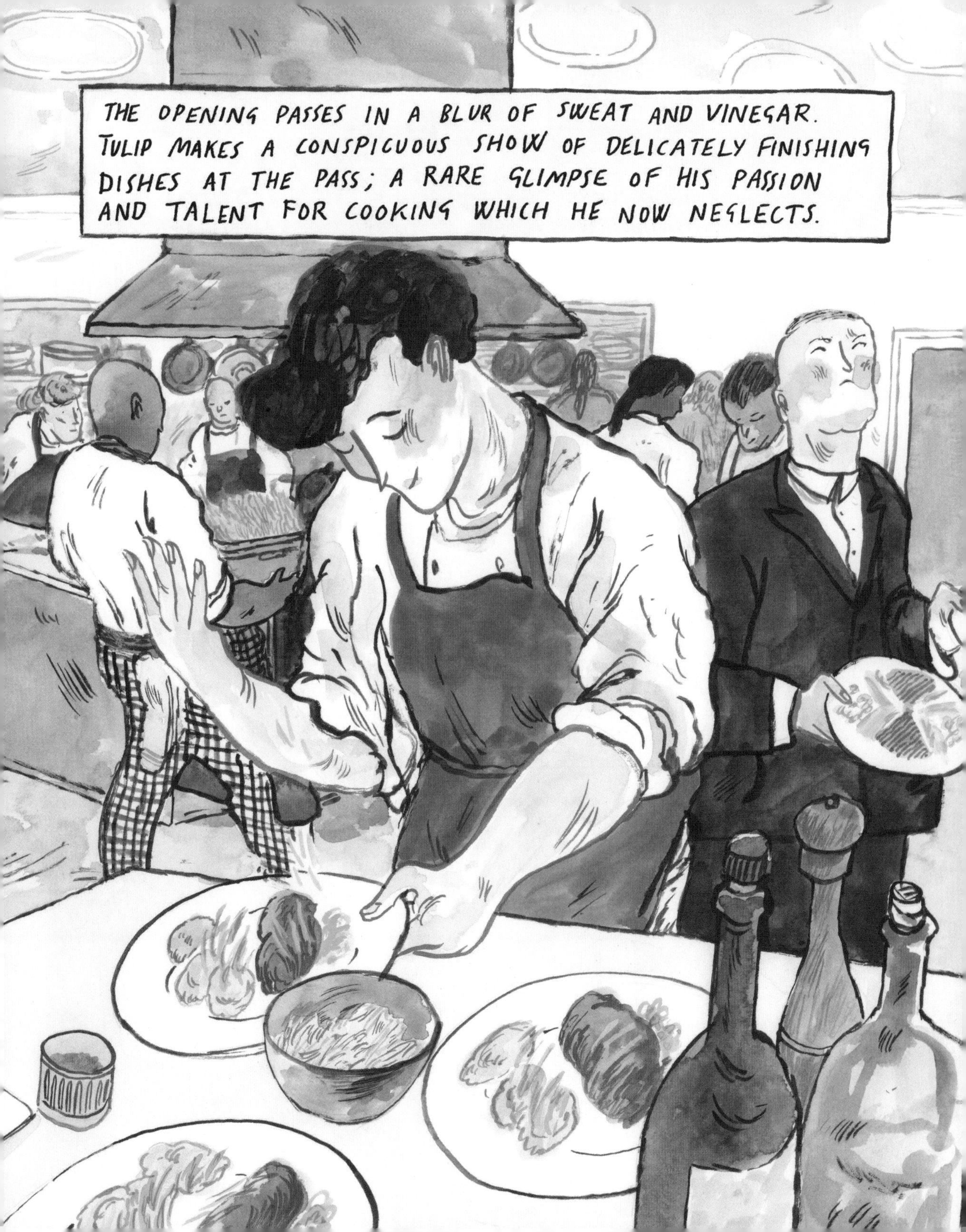
THE OPENING PASSES IN A BLUR OF SWEAT AND VINEGAR. TULIP MAKES A CONSPICUOUS SHOW OF DELICATELY FINISHING DISHES AT THE PASS; A RARE GLIMPSE OF HIS PASSION AND TALENT FOR COOKING WHICH HE NOW NEGLECTS.

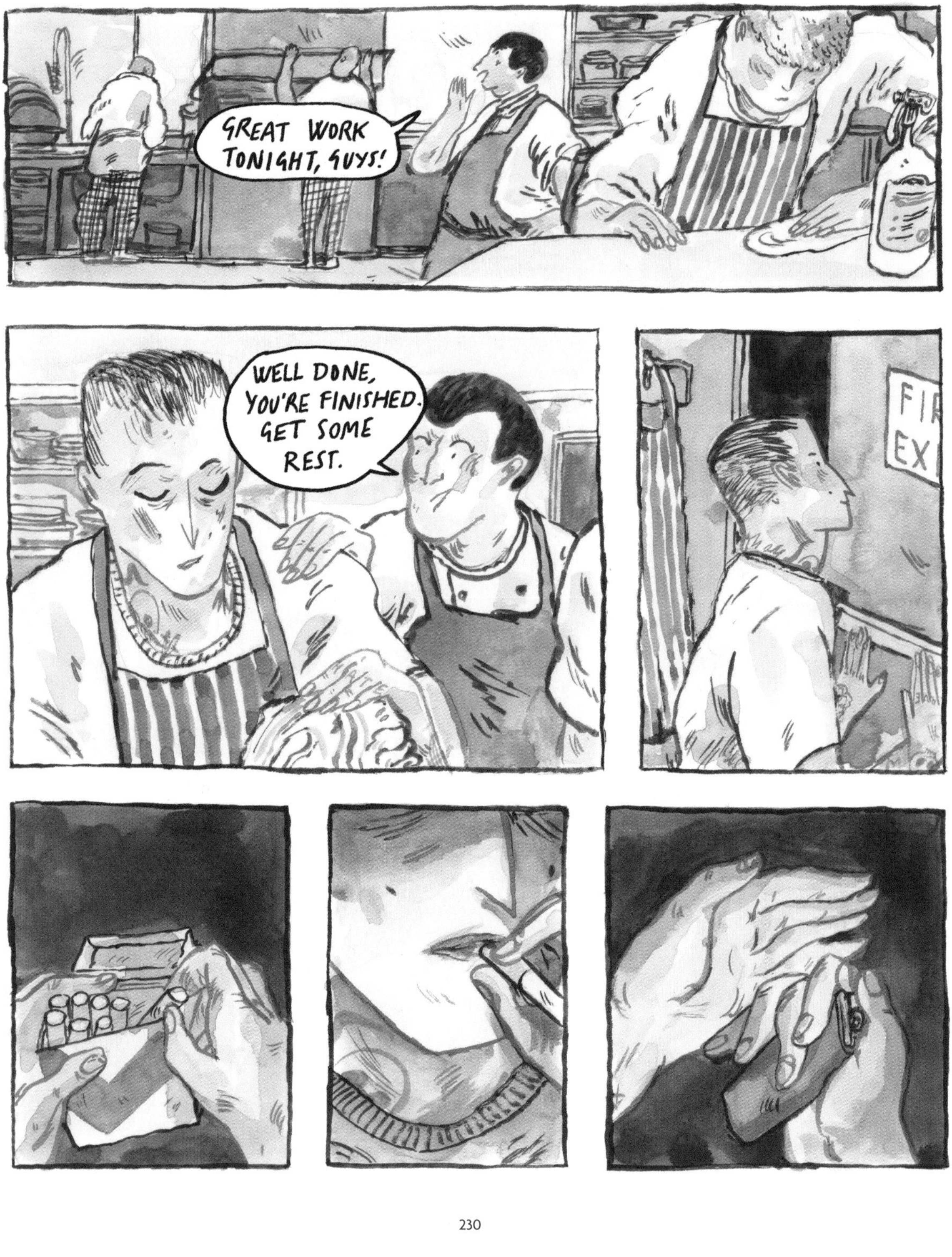
GREAT WORK TONIGHT, GUYS!
WELL DONE, YOU'RE FINISHED. GET SOME REST.
FIRE EXIT

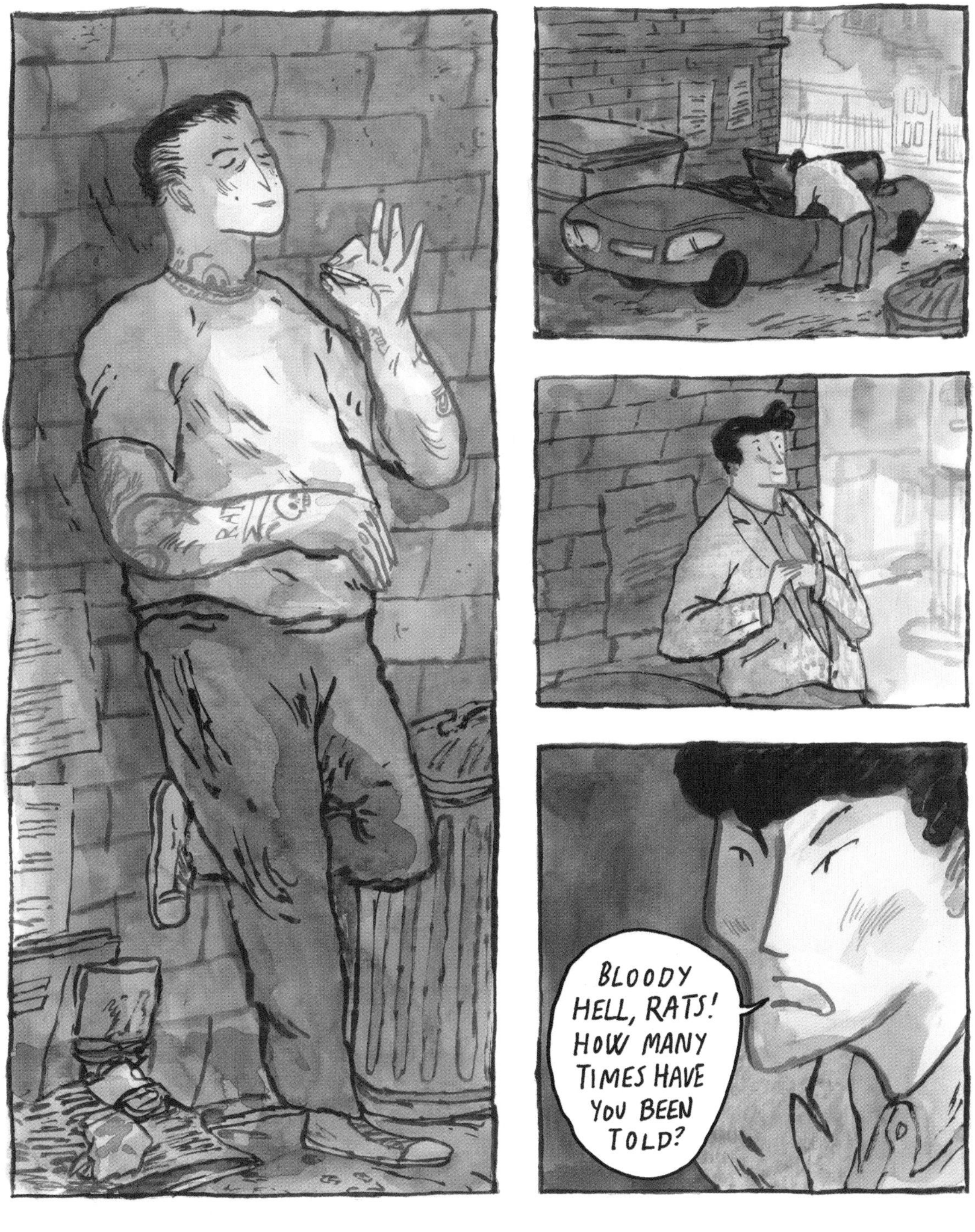
RAT
RATS
BLOODY HELL, RATS! HOW MANY TIMES HAVE YOU BEEN TOLD?

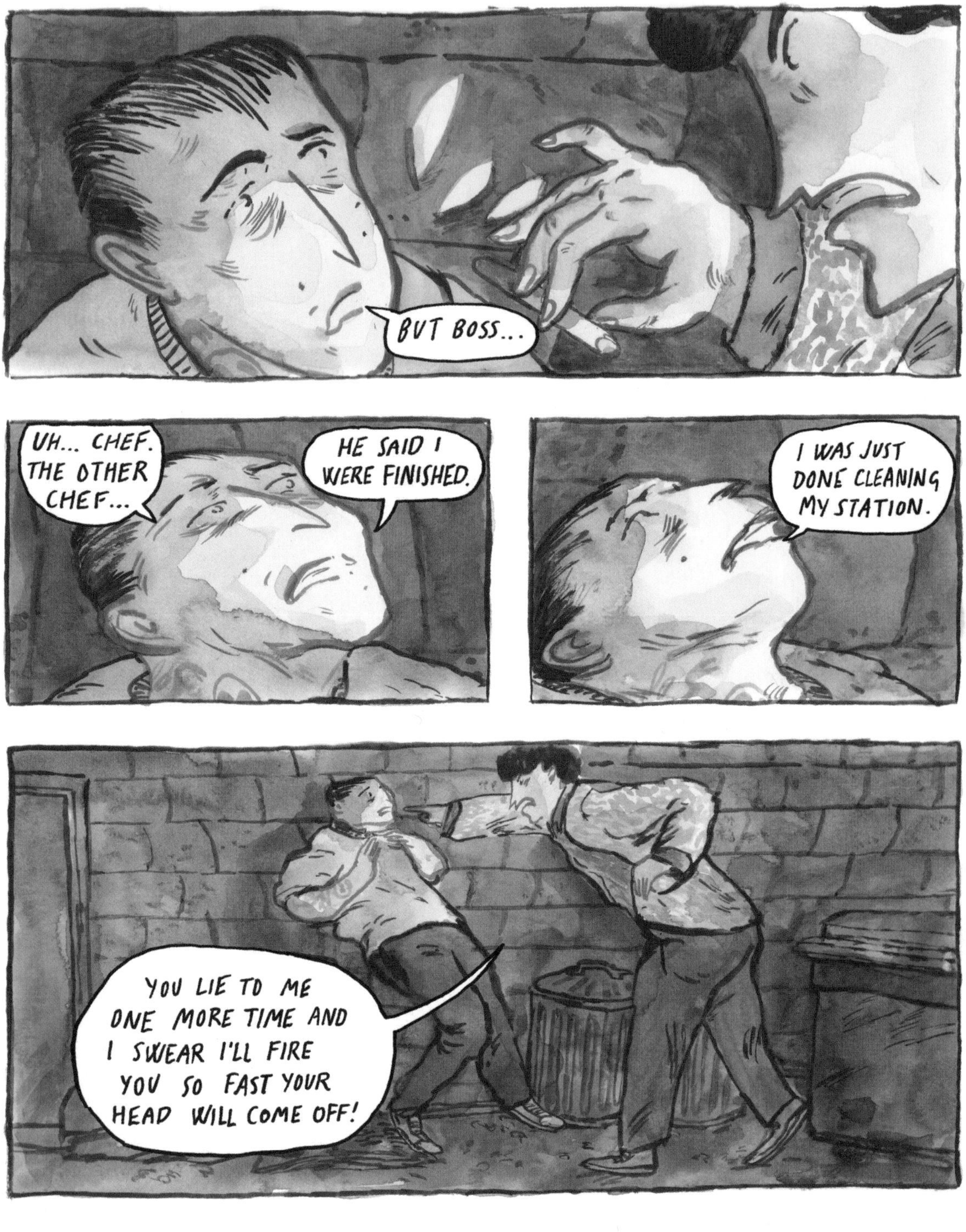
BUT BOSS...
UH... CHEF. THE OTHER CHEF...
HE SAID I WERE FINISHED.
I WAS JUST DONE CLEANING MY STATION.
YOU LIE TO ME ONE MORE TIME AND I SWEAR I'LL FIRE YOU SO FAST YOUR HEAD WILL COME OFF!

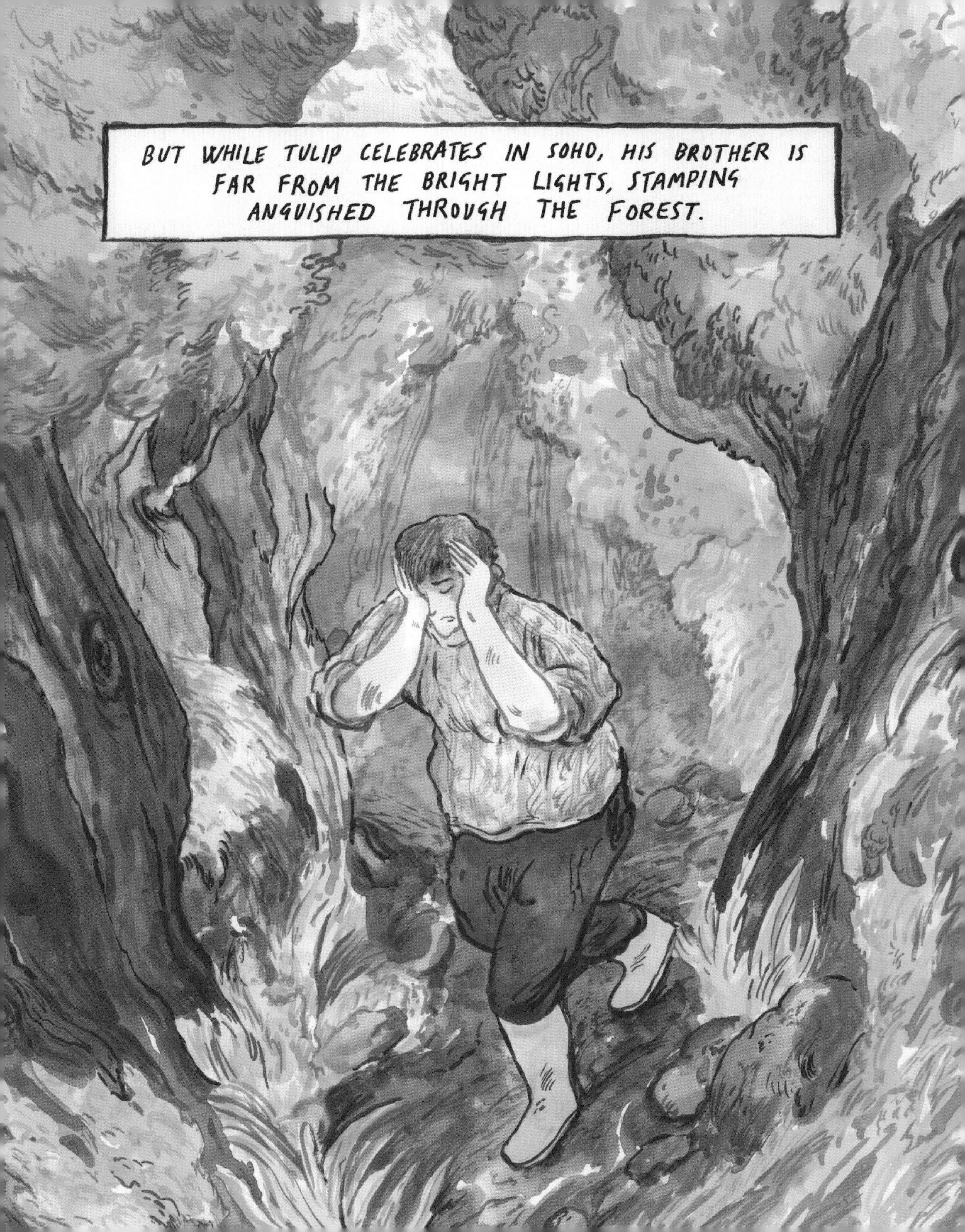
BUT WHILE TULIP CELEBRATES IN SOHO, HIS BROTHER IS FAR FROM THE BRIGHT LIGHTS, STAMPING ANGUISHED THROUGH THE FOREST.

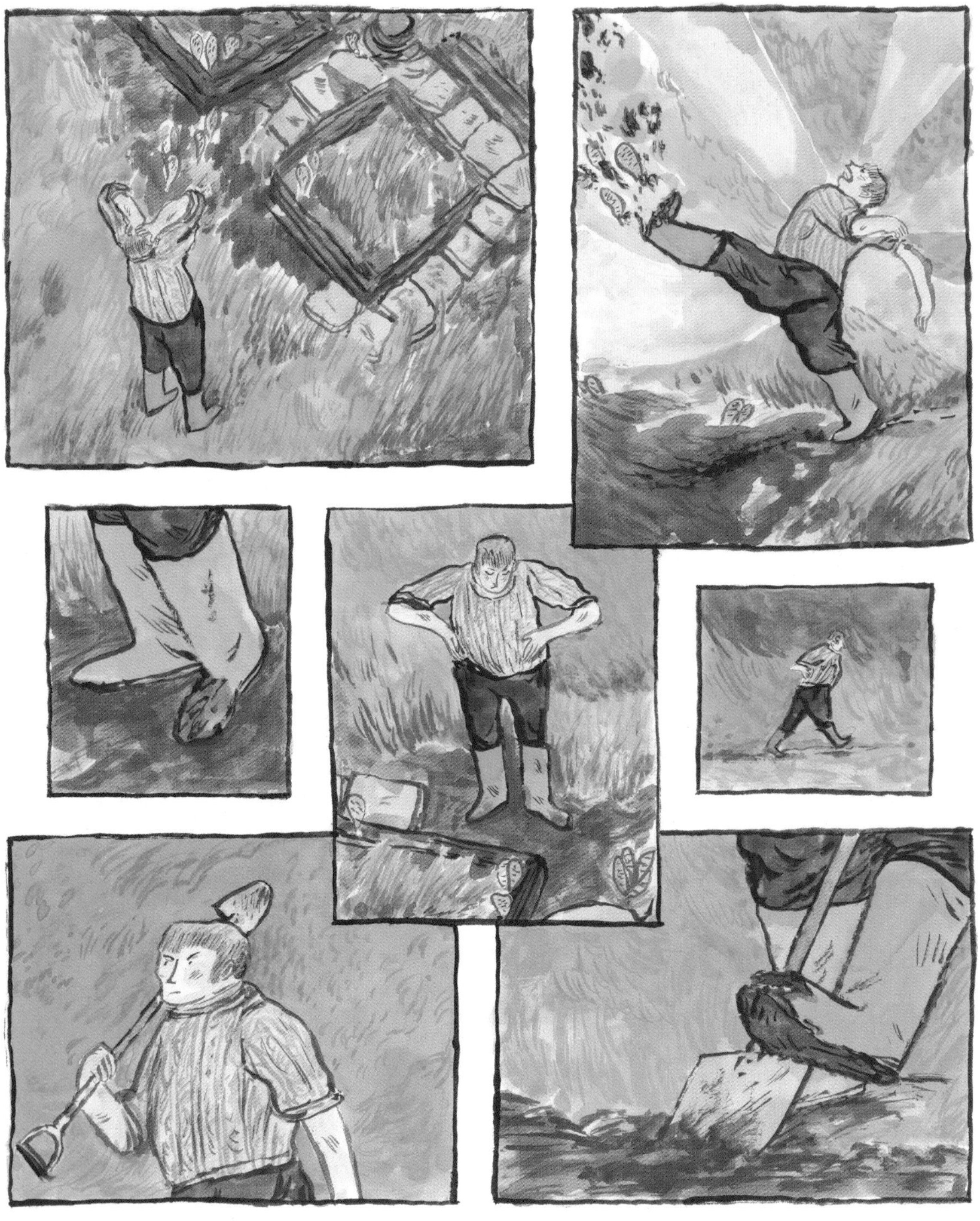

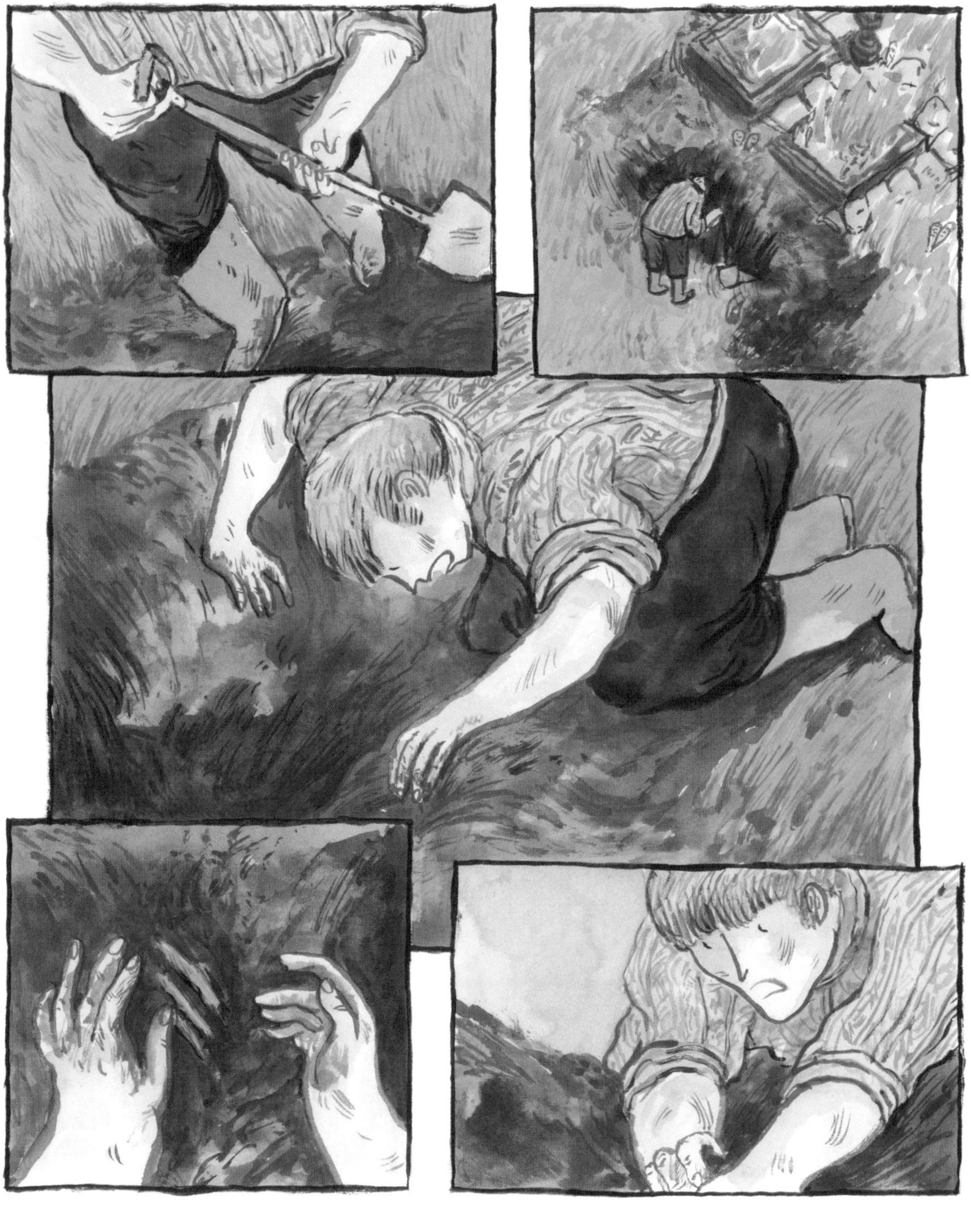

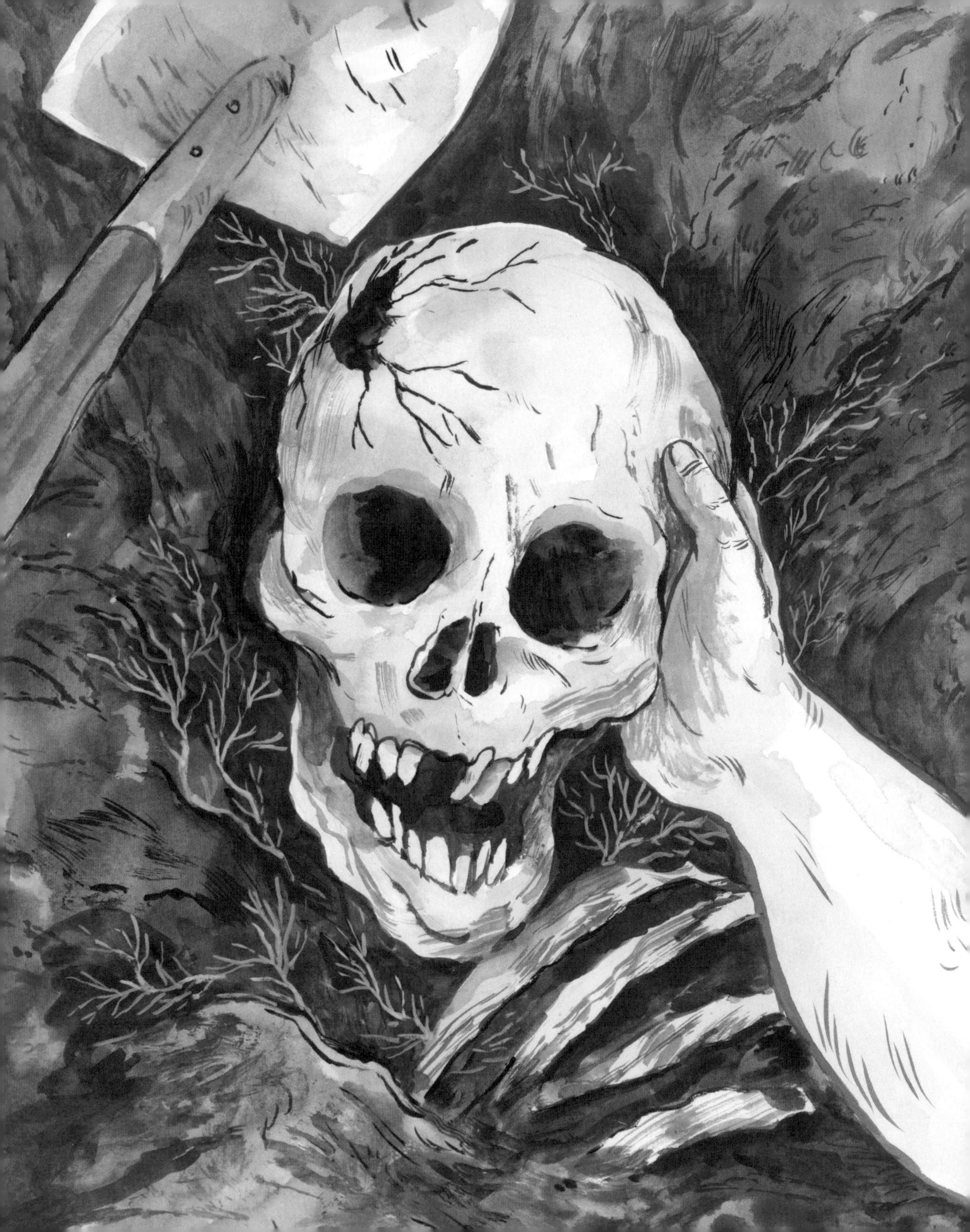

ROWAN IS FLOODED WITH A HEAVY MIXTURE OF NUMBING DREAD AND ACIDIC PANIC.

HE STRIKES OUT WITH HIS SPADE, DIGGING AT RANDOM.

HE HACKS AT EVERY PATCH OF SOIL IN THE GARDEN THAT HASN'T ALREADY BEEN TURNED OVER BY HIS PLOUGH.

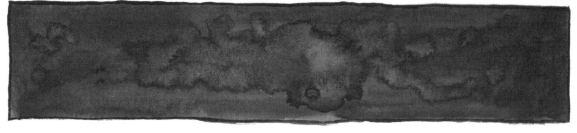

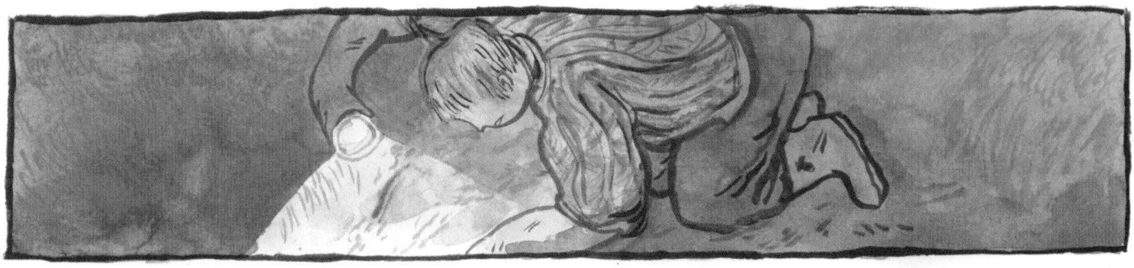

HE WORKS THROUGHOUT THE NIGHT. AS THE SUN RISES, HE HAS FOUND NOTHING.

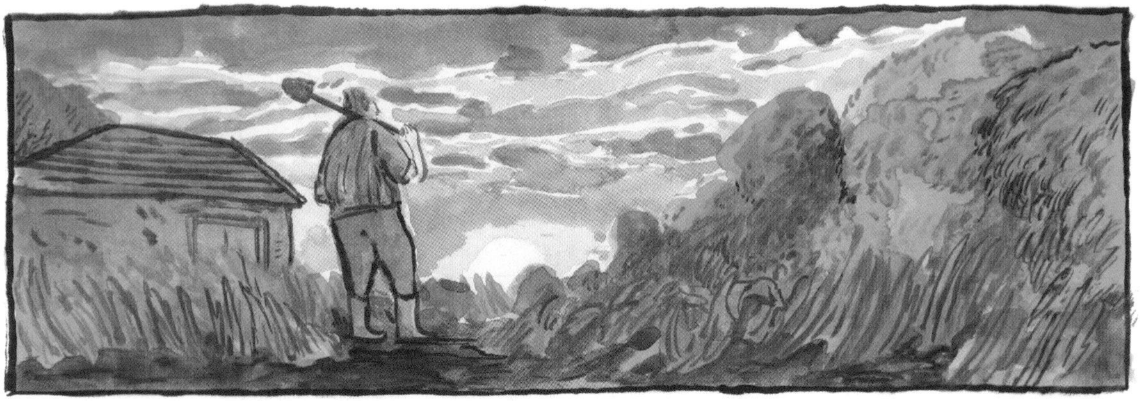

WHATEVER HAPPENED TO HIS AUNT, SHE'S NOT BURIED HERE.

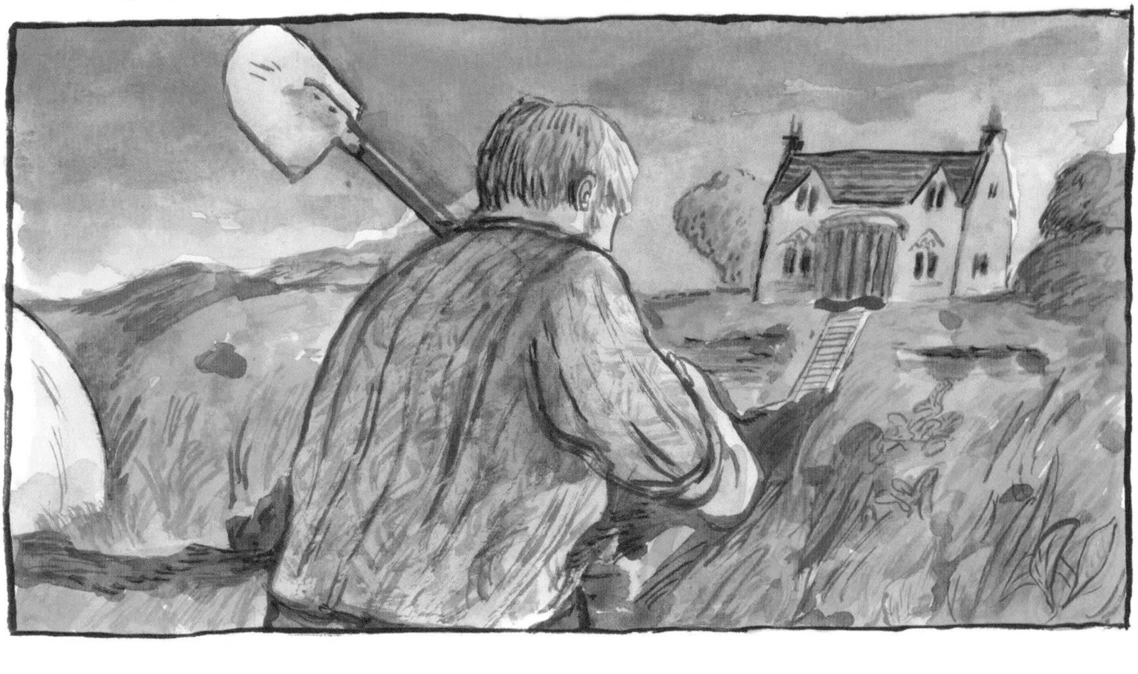

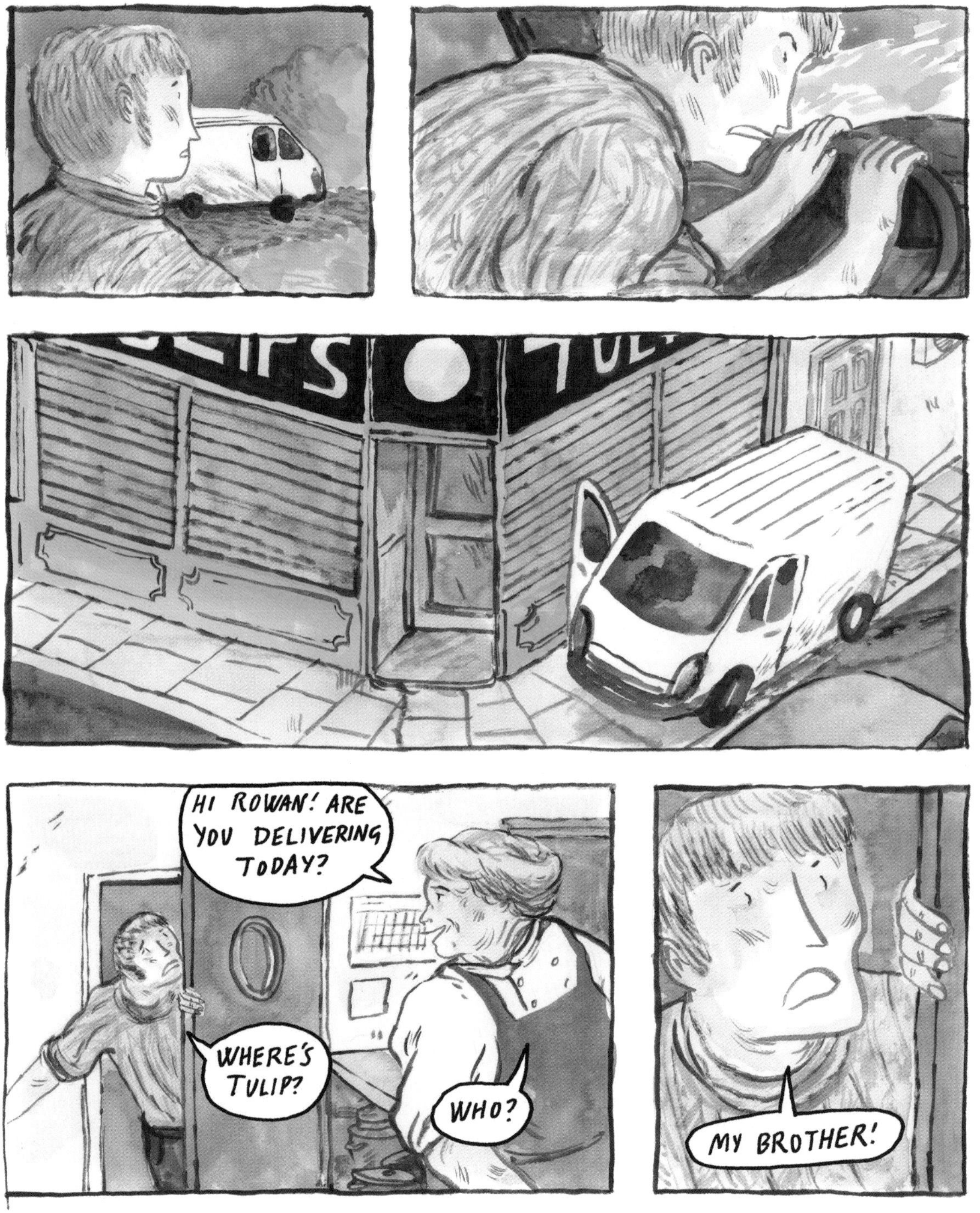
HI ROWAN! ARE YOU DELIVERING TODAY?
WHERE'S TULIP?
WHO?
MY BROTHER!

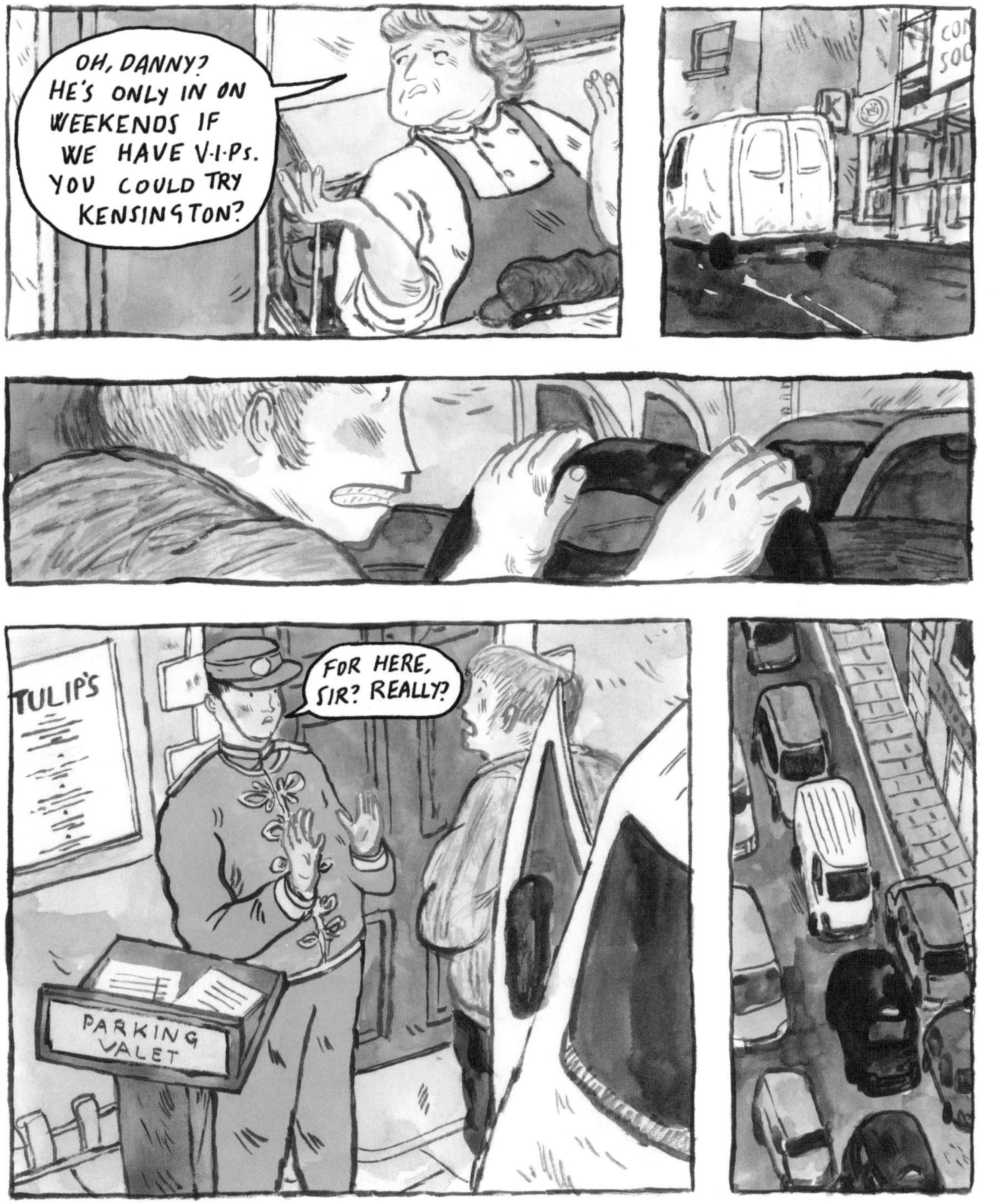
OH, DANNY? HE'S ONLY IN ON WEEKENDS IF WE HAVE V.I.Ps. YOU COULD TRY KENSINGTON?
TULIP'S
FOR HERE, SIR? REALLY?
PARKING VALET

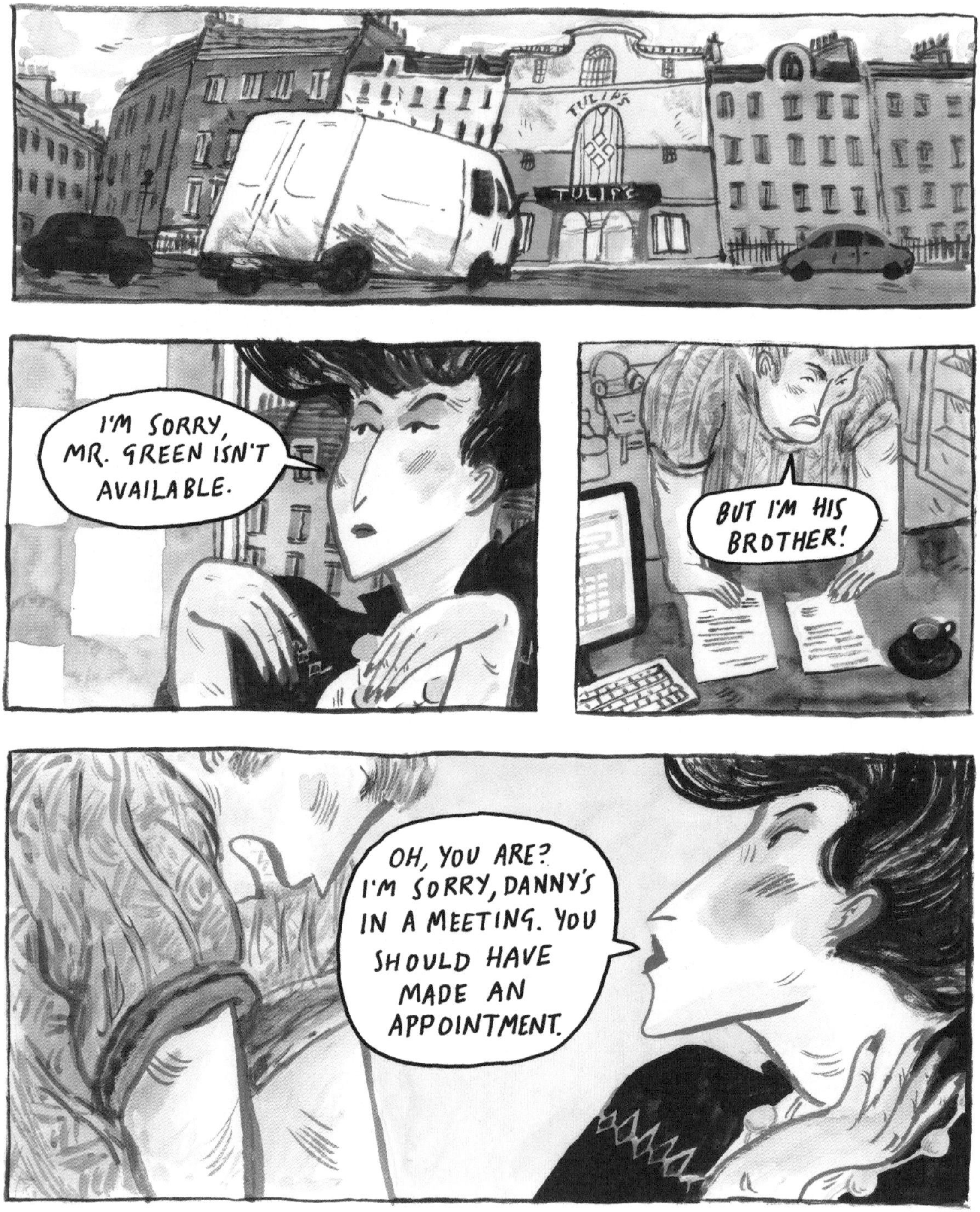
TULIPS
TULIPS
I'M SORRY, MR. GREEN ISN'T AVAILABLE.
BUT I'M HIS BROTHER!
OH, YOU ARE? I'M SORRY, DANNY'S IN A MEETING. YOU SHOULD HAVE MADE AN APPOINTMENT.

PROWLING IN SLEEPLESS AGONY, ROWAN TURNS HIS ATTENTION TO THE HOUSE. FOR THE FIRST TIME, HE SEES IT AS MORE THAN A SERIES OF DARK ROOMS FOR STORING ONIONS AND MUSHROOMS.

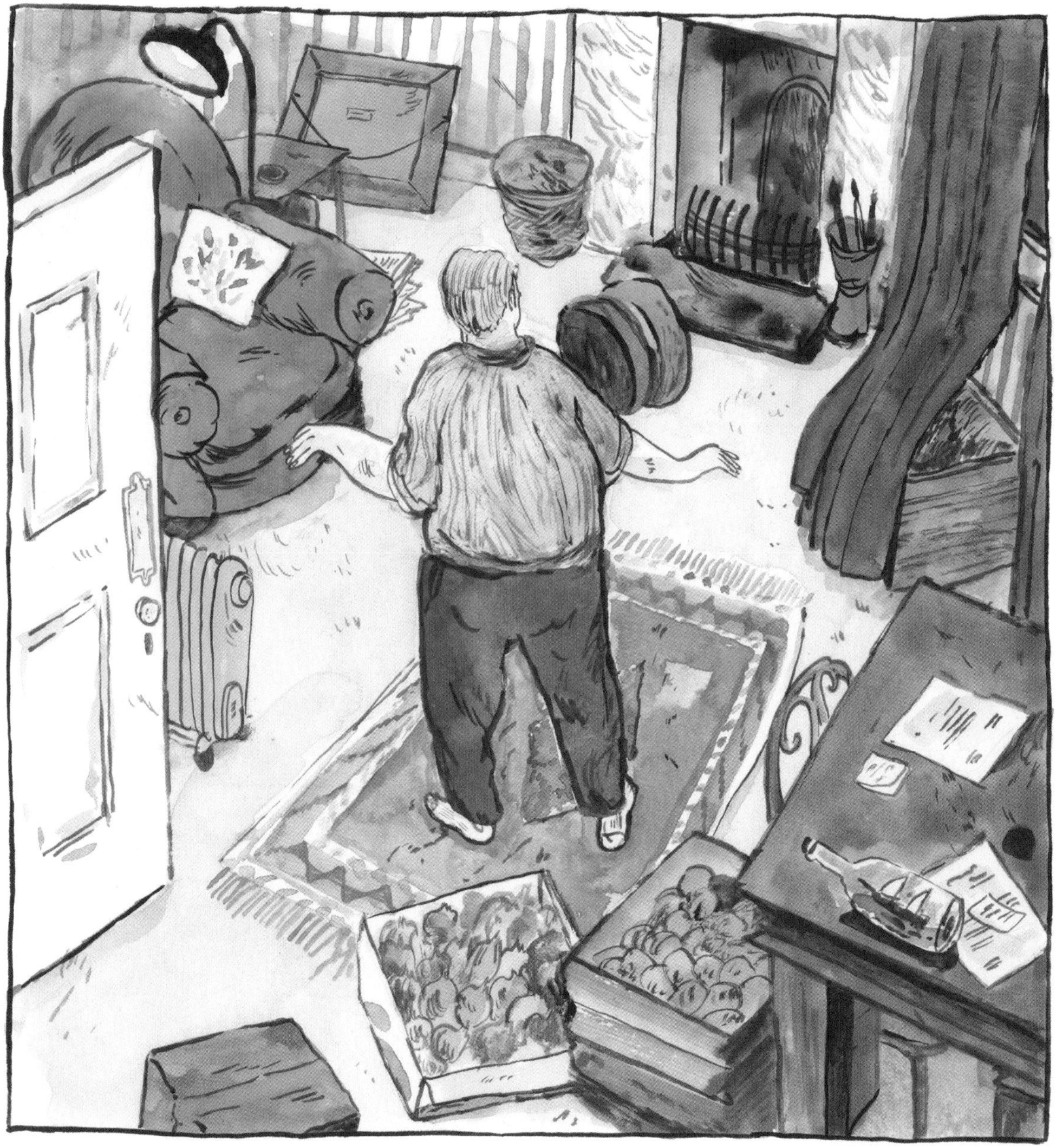

THROUGH THE DUST, THE LIVES OF THE FORMER OWNERS BECOME CLEAR.

SEPARATE BEDROOMS.
SEPARATE BATHROOMS.

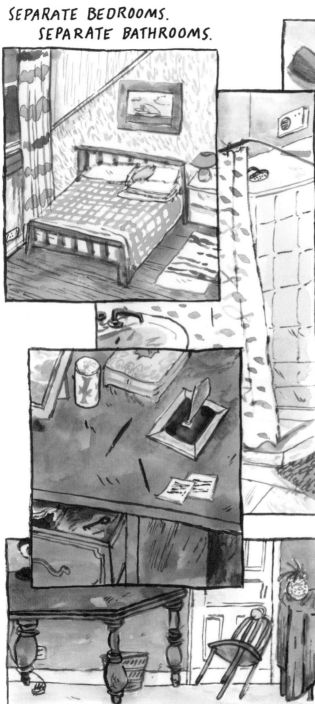

EVEN SPACES FOR LEISURE,
T·V·S, SOFAS, DESKS, ARE
ALL IN SEPARATE ROOMS.

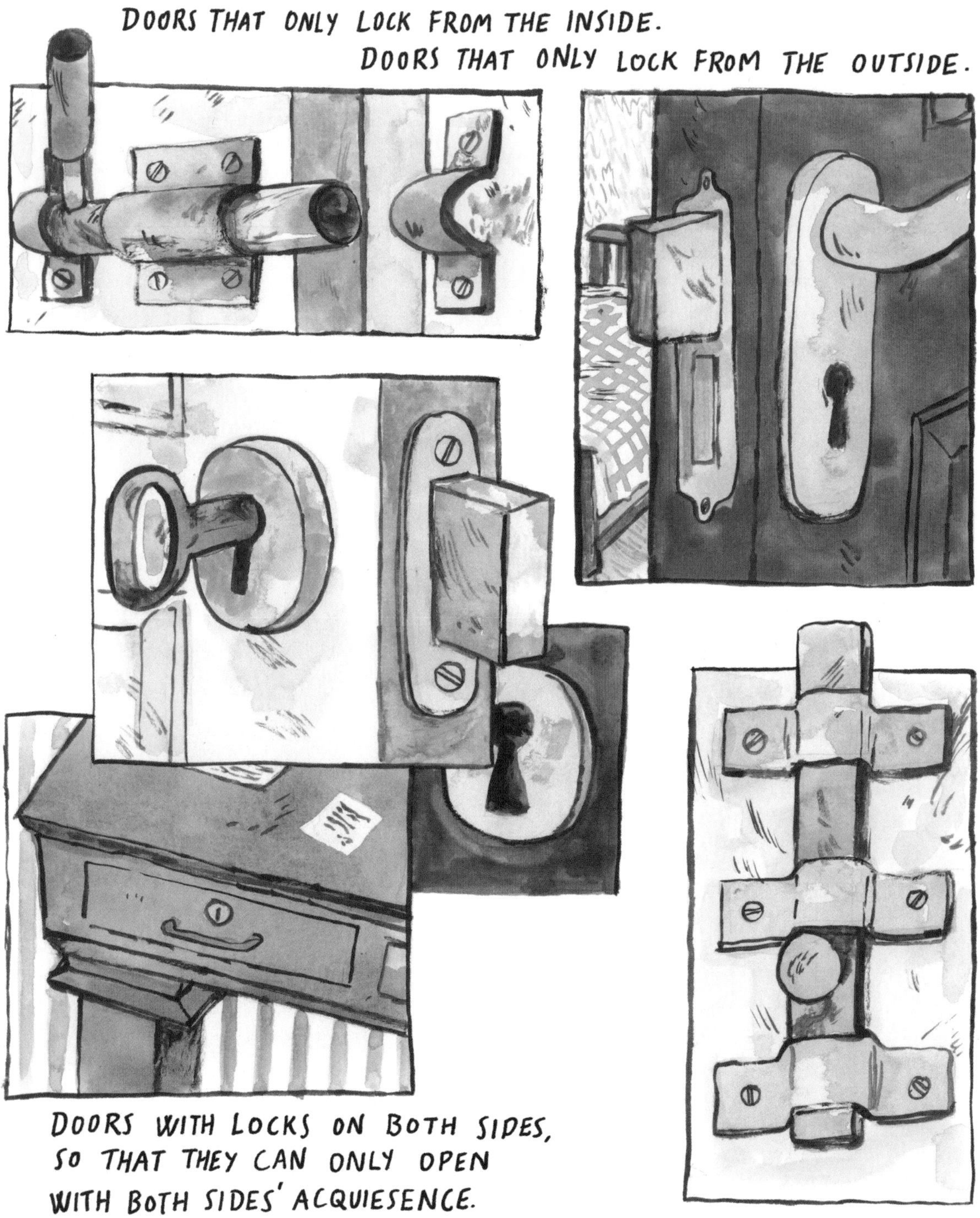
DOORS THAT ONLY LOCK FROM THE INSIDE.
DOORS THAT ONLY LOCK FROM THE OUTSIDE.
DOORS WITH LOCKS ON BOTH SIDES, SO THAT THEY CAN ONLY OPEN WITH BOTH SIDES' ACQUIESENCE.

THE ONLY TRACES OF FORAY BETWEEN THE TWO SIDES ARE PASSIVE-AGRESSIVE NOTES, SCATTERED ON DESKS, STUCK TO CUPBOARDS, FILLING WASTE-PAPER BASKETS.

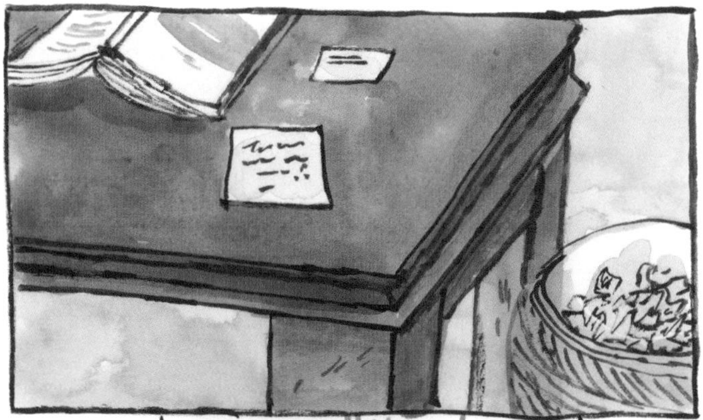

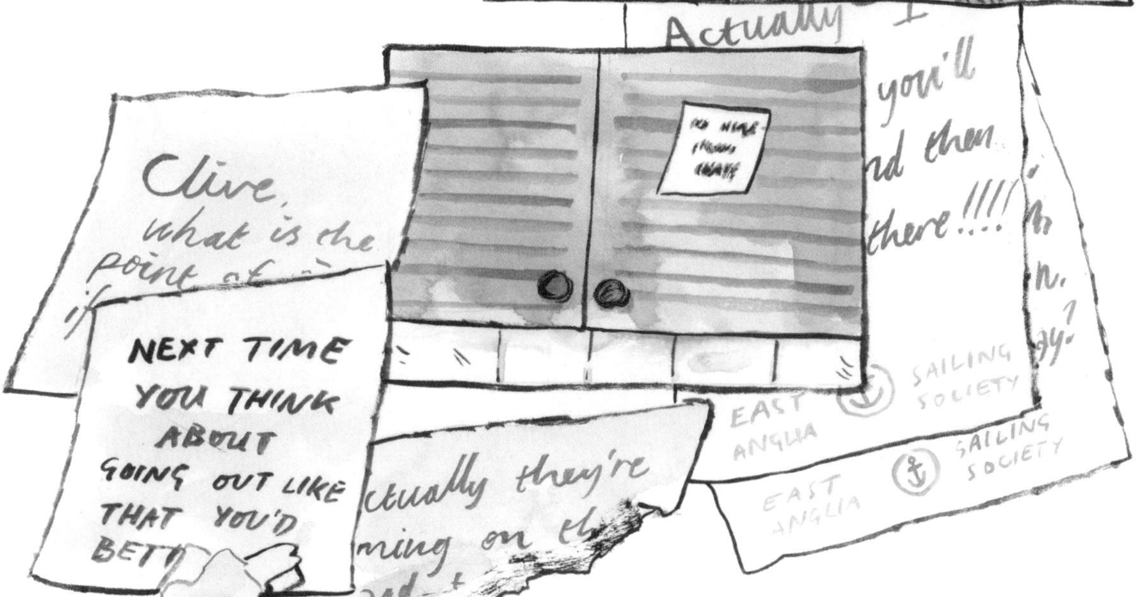
Actually I
you'll
nd then
there!!!!
Clive,
what is the
point of
NEXT TIME YOU THINK ABOUT GOING OUT LIKE THAT YOU'D BETT
ctually they're
ming on th
EAST ANGLIA
SAILING SOCIETY
EAST ANGLIA
SAILING SOCIETY

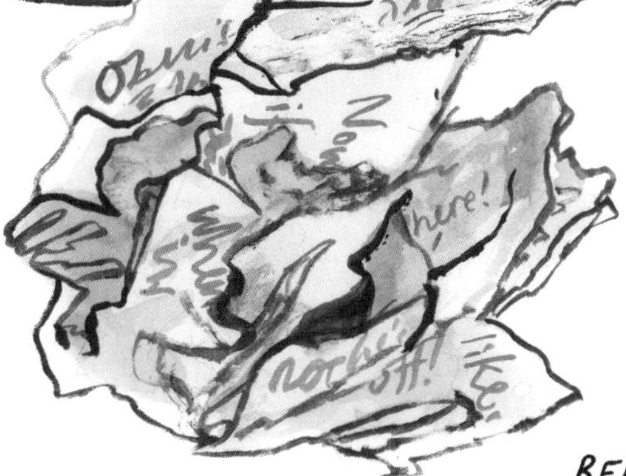
here!

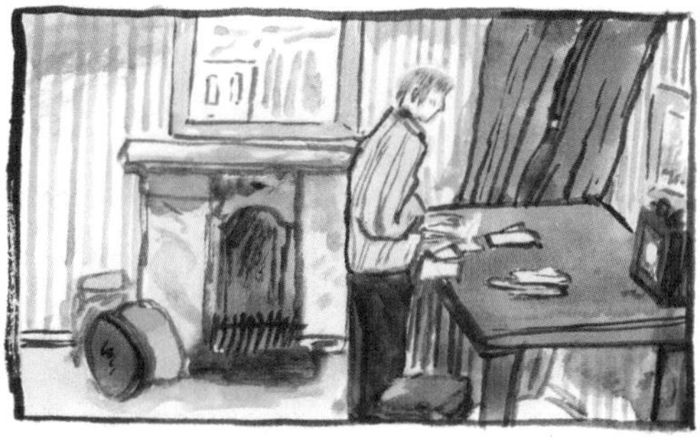

BEHIND THE SMILING HOLIDAY PHOTOS, THE COUPLE LOATHED EACH OTHER.

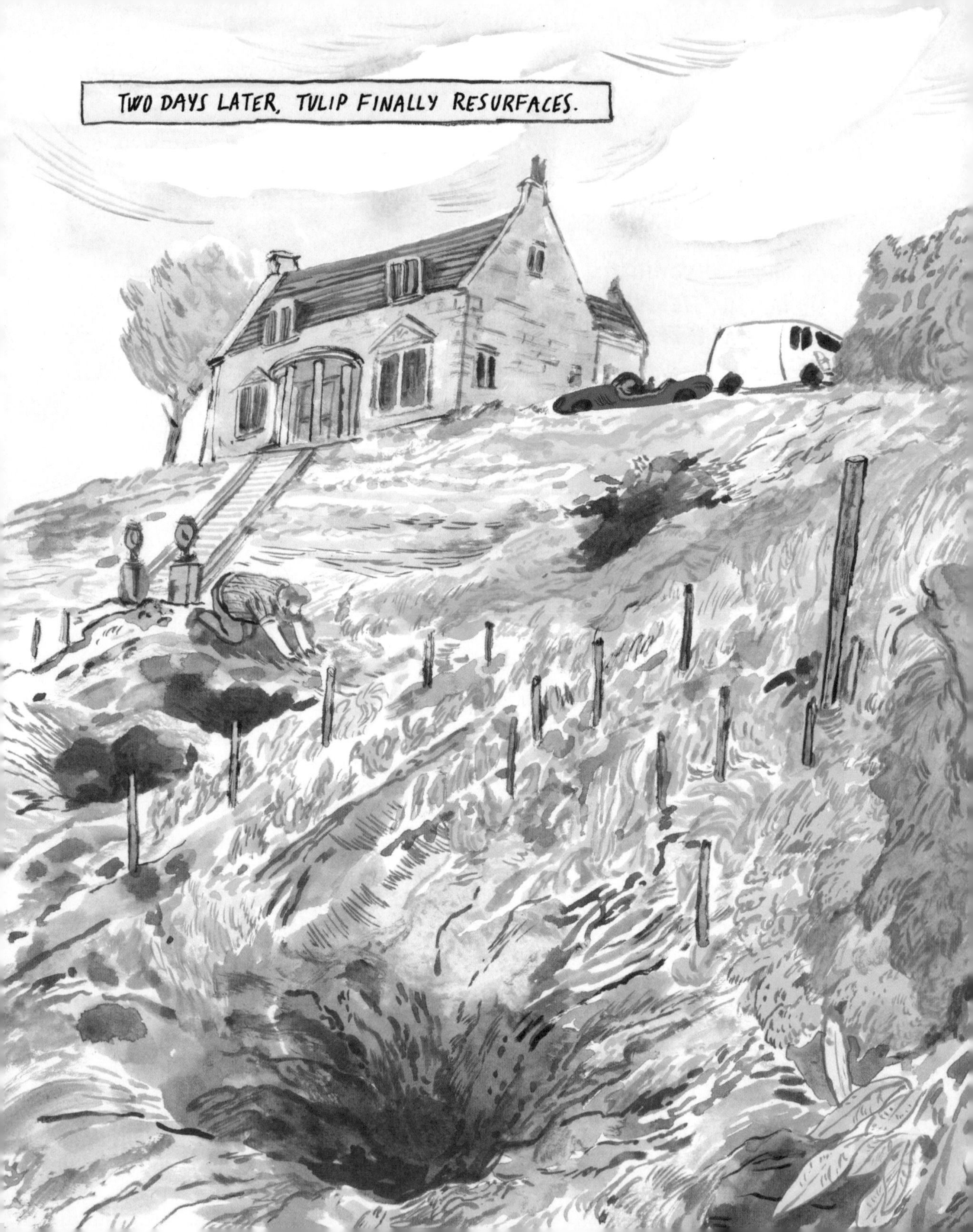
TWO DAYS LATER, TULIP FINALLY RESURFACES.

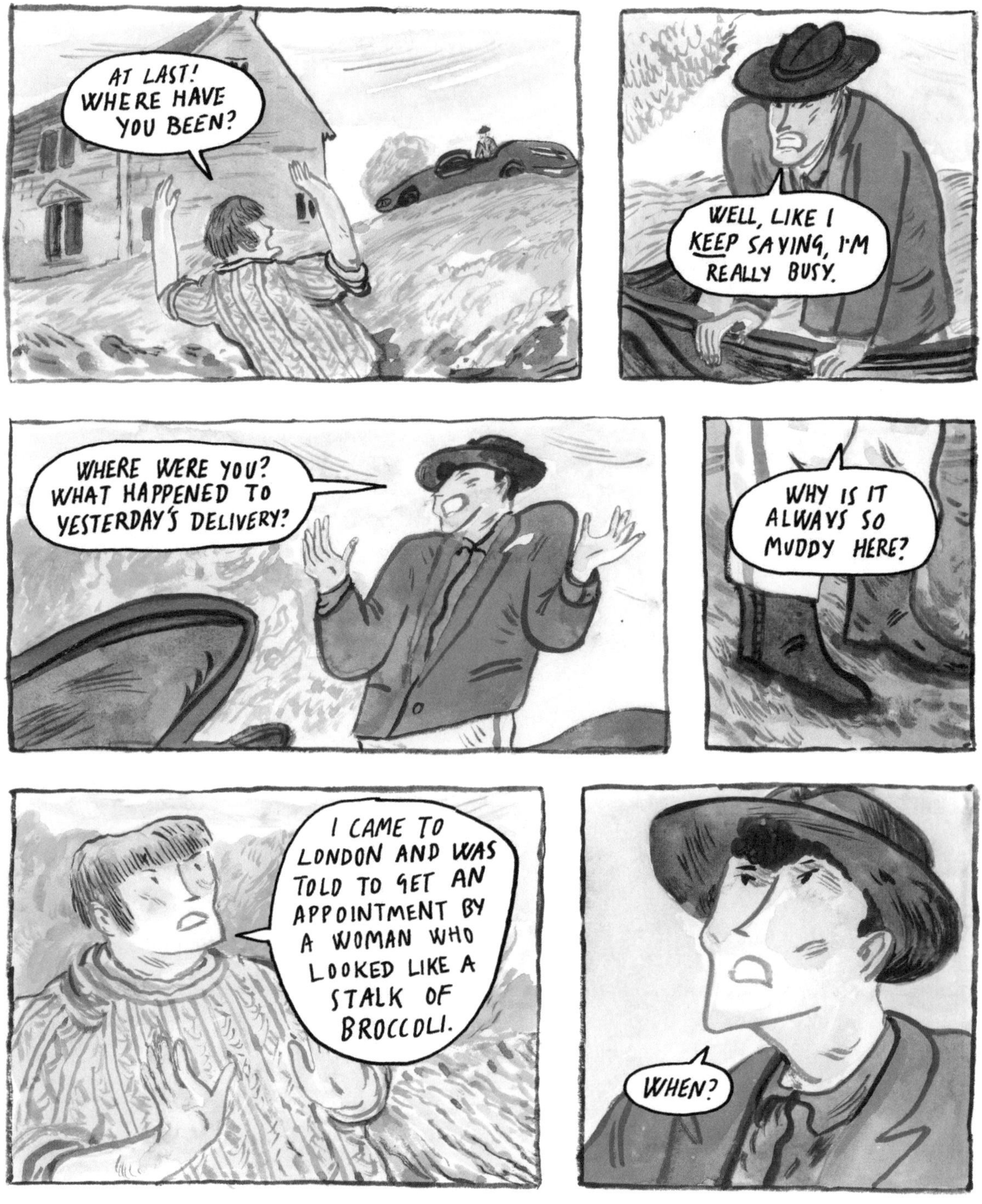
AT LAST! WHERE HAVE YOU BEEN?
WELL, LIKE I KEEP SAYING, I'M REALLY BUSY.
WHERE WERE YOU? WHAT HAPPENED TO YESTERDAY'S DELIVERY?
WHY IS IT ALWAYS SO MUDDY HERE?
I CAME TO LONDON AND WAS TOLD TO GET AN APPOINTMENT BY A WOMAN WHO LOOKED LIKE A STALK OF BROCCOLI.
WHEN?

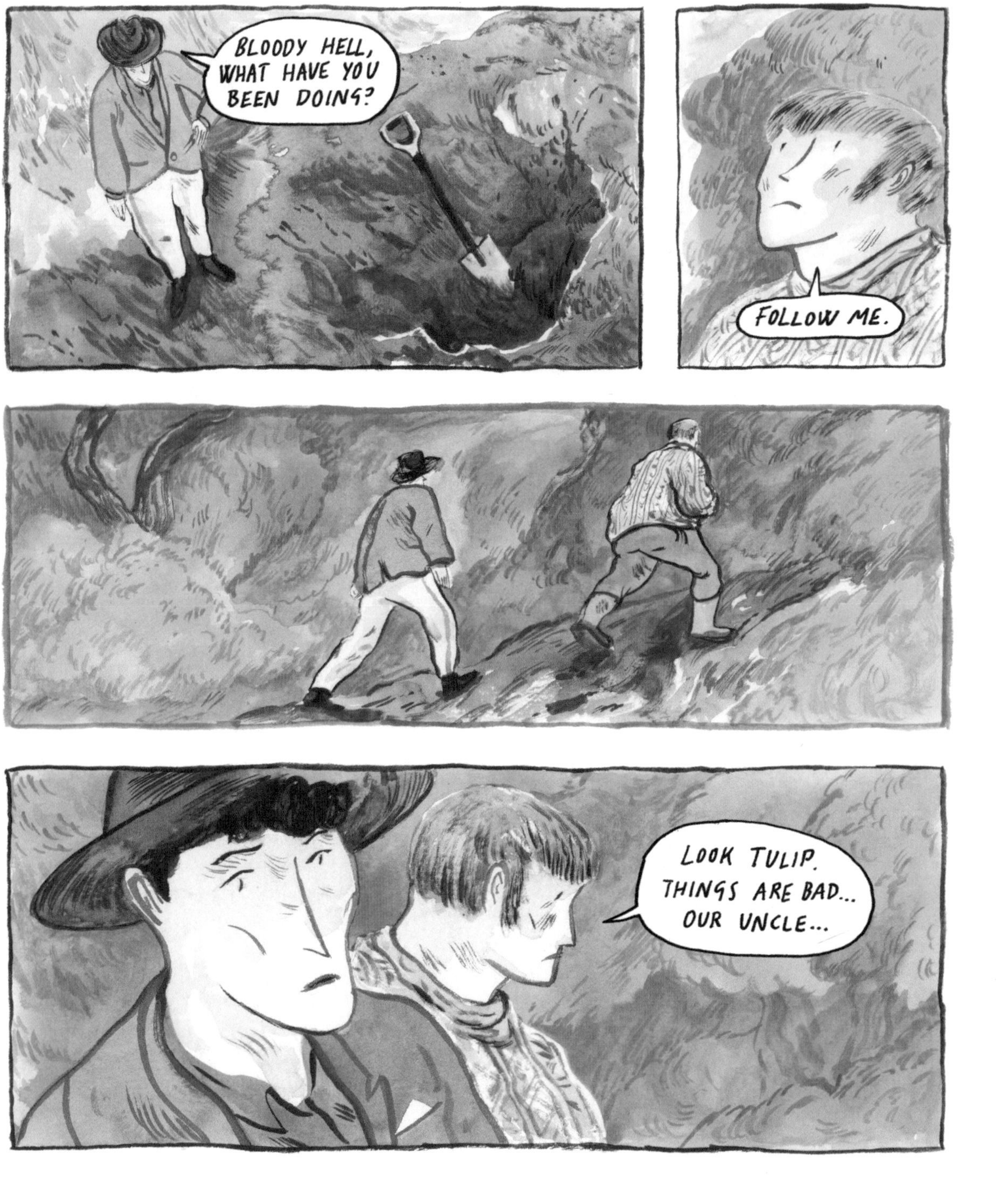
BLOODY HELL, WHAT HAVE YOU BEEN DOING?
FOLLOW ME.
LOOK TULIP. THINGS ARE BAD... OUR UNCLE...

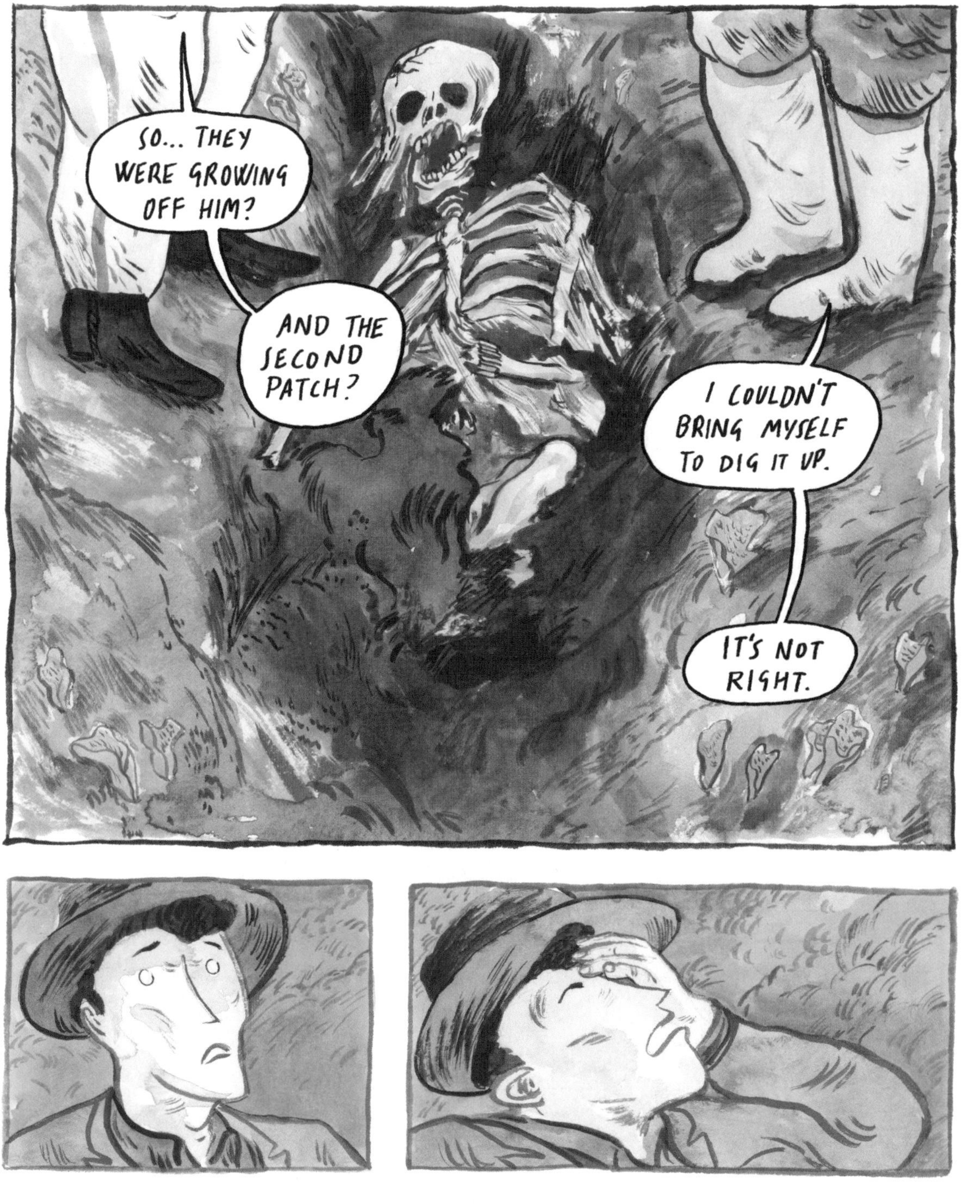
SO... THEY WERE GROWING OFF HIM?
AND THE SECOND PATCH?
I COULDN'T BRING MYSELF TO DIG IT UP.
IT'S NOT RIGHT.

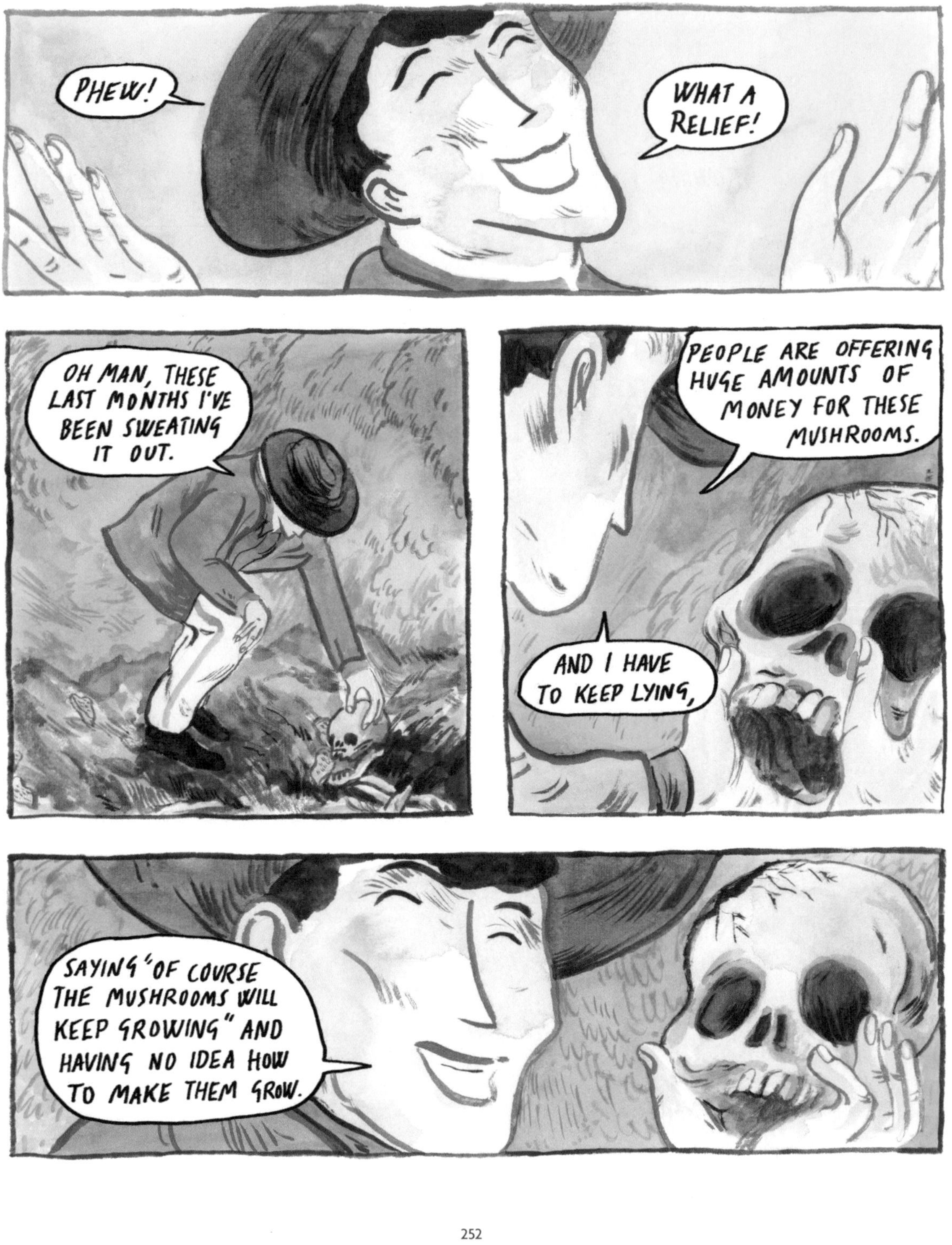
PHEW!
WHAT A RELIEF!
OH MAN, THESE LAST MONTHS I'VE BEEN SWEATING IT OUT.
PEOPLE ARE OFFERING HUGE AMOUNTS OF MONEY FOR THESE MUSHROOMS.
AND I HAVE TO KEEP LYING,
SAYING "OF COURSE THE MUSHROOMS WILL KEEP GROWING" AND HAVING NO IDEA HOW TO MAKE THEM GROW.

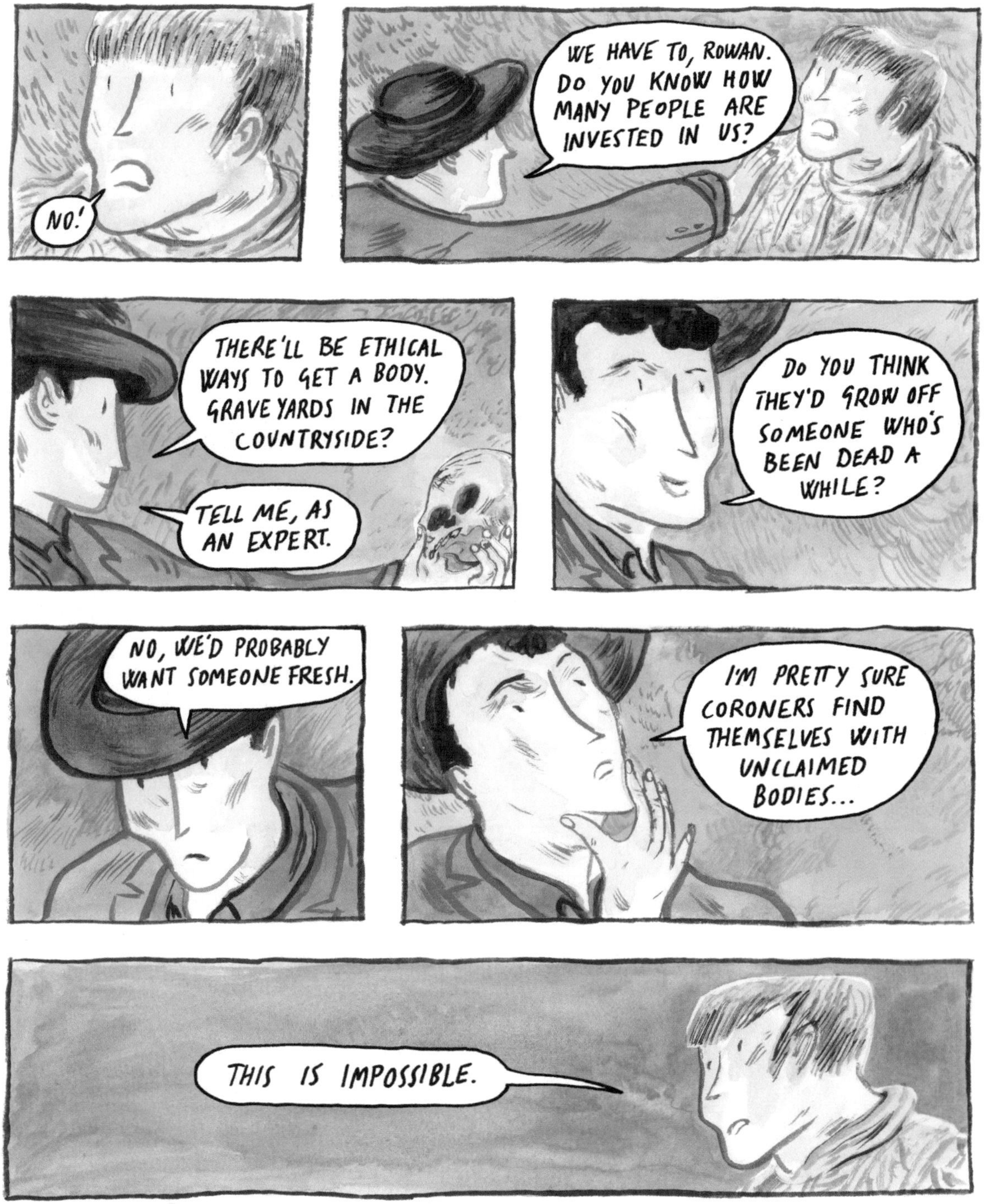

NO!
WE HAVE TO, ROWAN. DO YOU KNOW HOW MANY PEOPLE ARE INVESTED IN US?
THERE'LL BE ETHICAL WAYS TO GET A BODY. GRAVE YARDS IN THE COUNTRYSIDE?
TELL ME, AS AN EXPERT.
DO YOU THINK THEY'D GROW OFF SOMEONE WHO'S BEEN DEAD A WHILE?
NO, WE'D PROBABLY WANT SOMEONE FRESH.
I'M PRETTY SURE CORONERS FIND THEMSELVES WITH UNCLAIMED BODIES...
THIS IS IMPOSSIBLE.

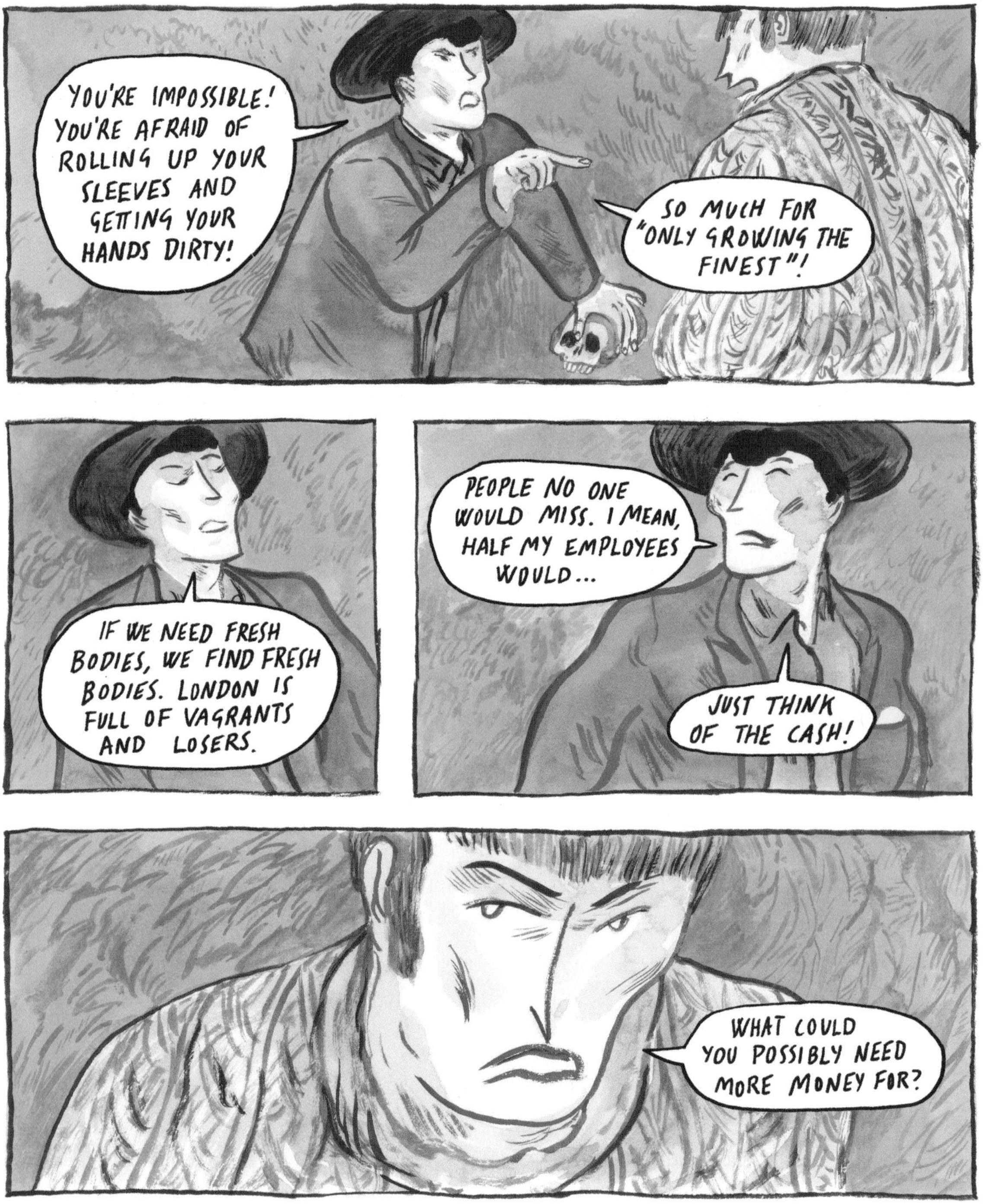
YOU'RE IMPOSSIBLE! YOU'RE AFRAID OF ROLLING UP YOUR SLEEVES AND GETTING YOUR HANDS DIRTY!
SO MUCH FOR "ONLY GROWING THE FINEST"!
IF WE NEED FRESH BODIES, WE FIND FRESH BODIES. LONDON IS FULL OF VAGRANTS AND LOSERS.
PEOPLE NO ONE WOULD MISS. I MEAN, HALF MY EMPLOYEES WOULD...
JUST THINK OF THE CASH!
WHAT COULD YOU POSSIBLY NEED MORE MONEY FOR?

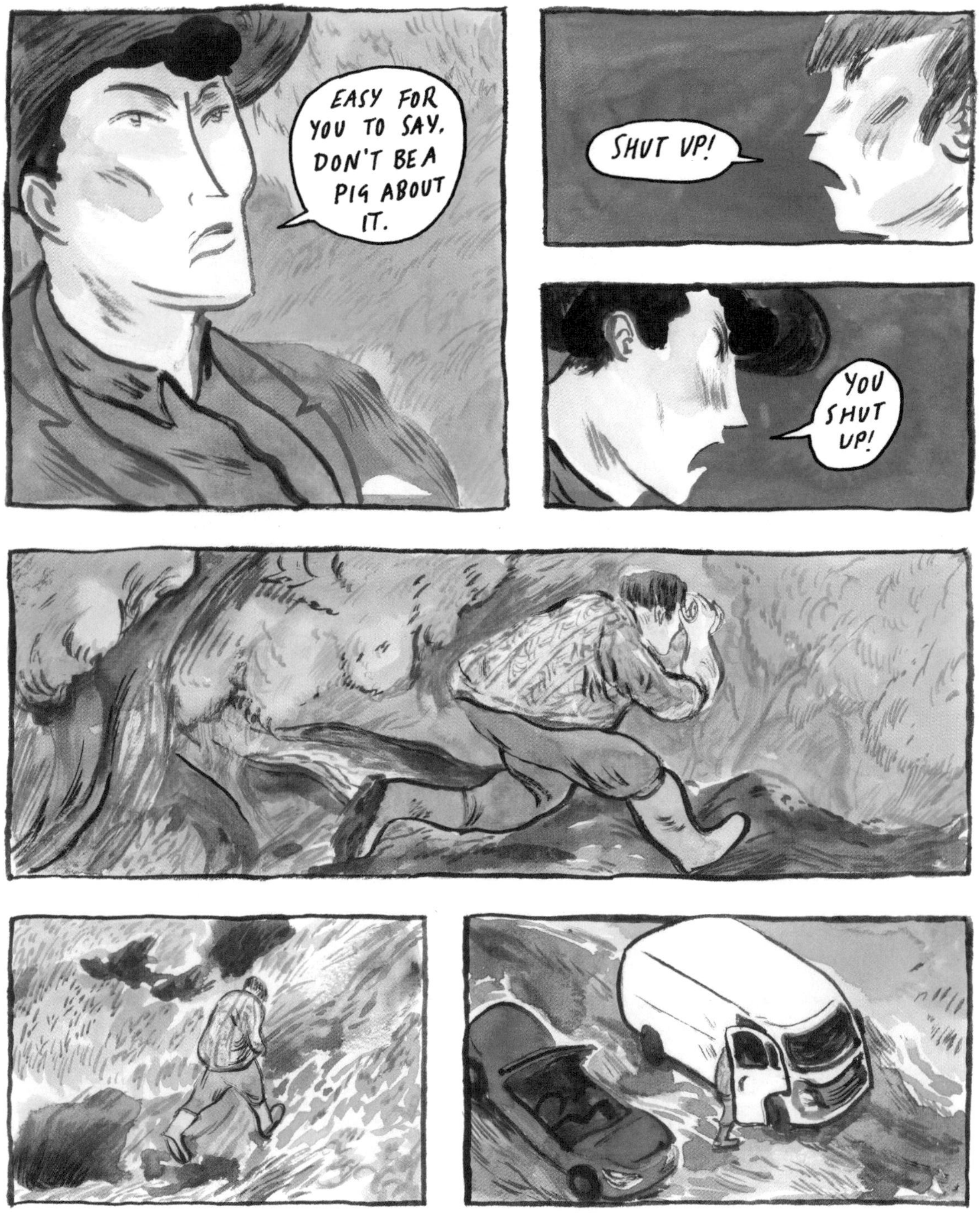
EASY FOR YOU TO SAY. DON'T BE A PIG ABOUT IT.
SHUT UP!
YOU SHUT UP!

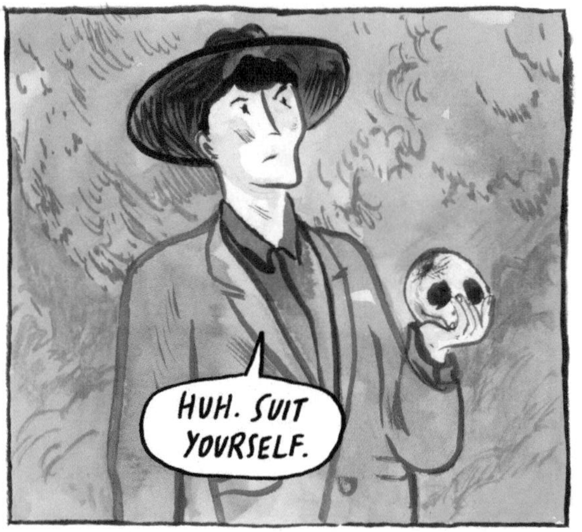
HUH. SUIT YOURSELF.

TULIP WATCHES HIS BROTHER DISAPPEAR, BAFFLED.

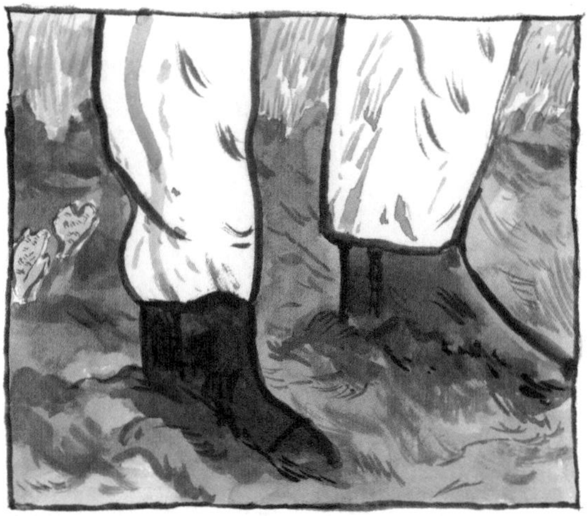

THEN LOOKS WITH RESIGNATION AT HIS MUDDY SHOES.

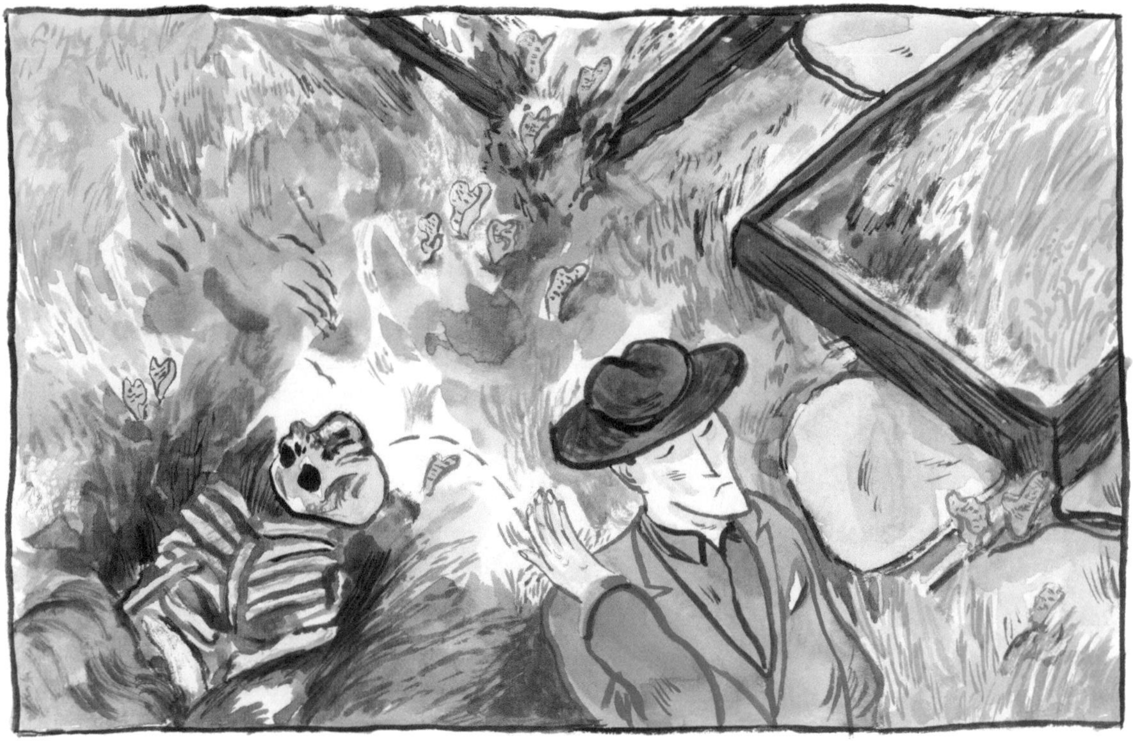

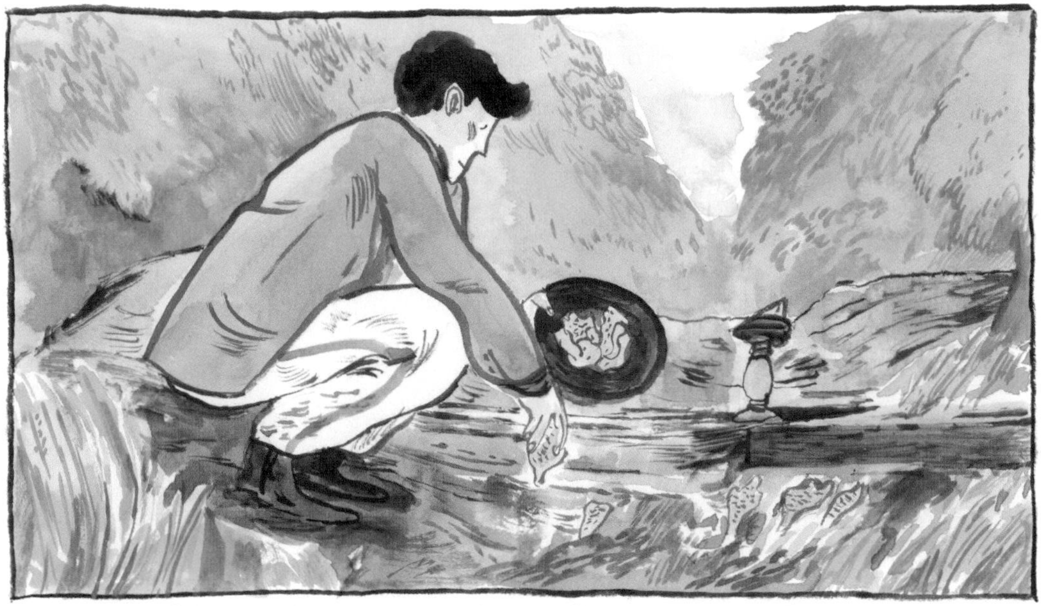

ROWAN BEGINS THE LONG JOURNEY NORTH. HIS MOTHER WAS RIGHT ABOUT THE MAINLAND. NOW HE NEEDS HER ISLAND, HER COMFORT, HER SECURITY MORE THAN EVER.

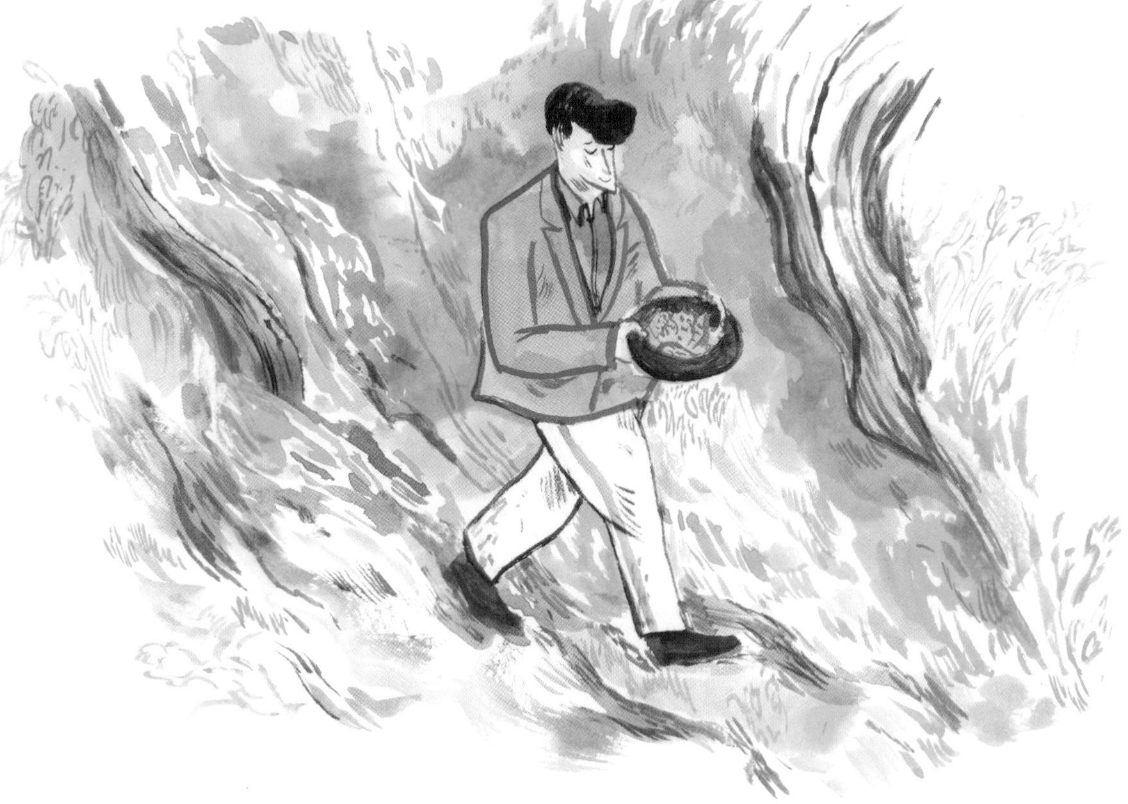

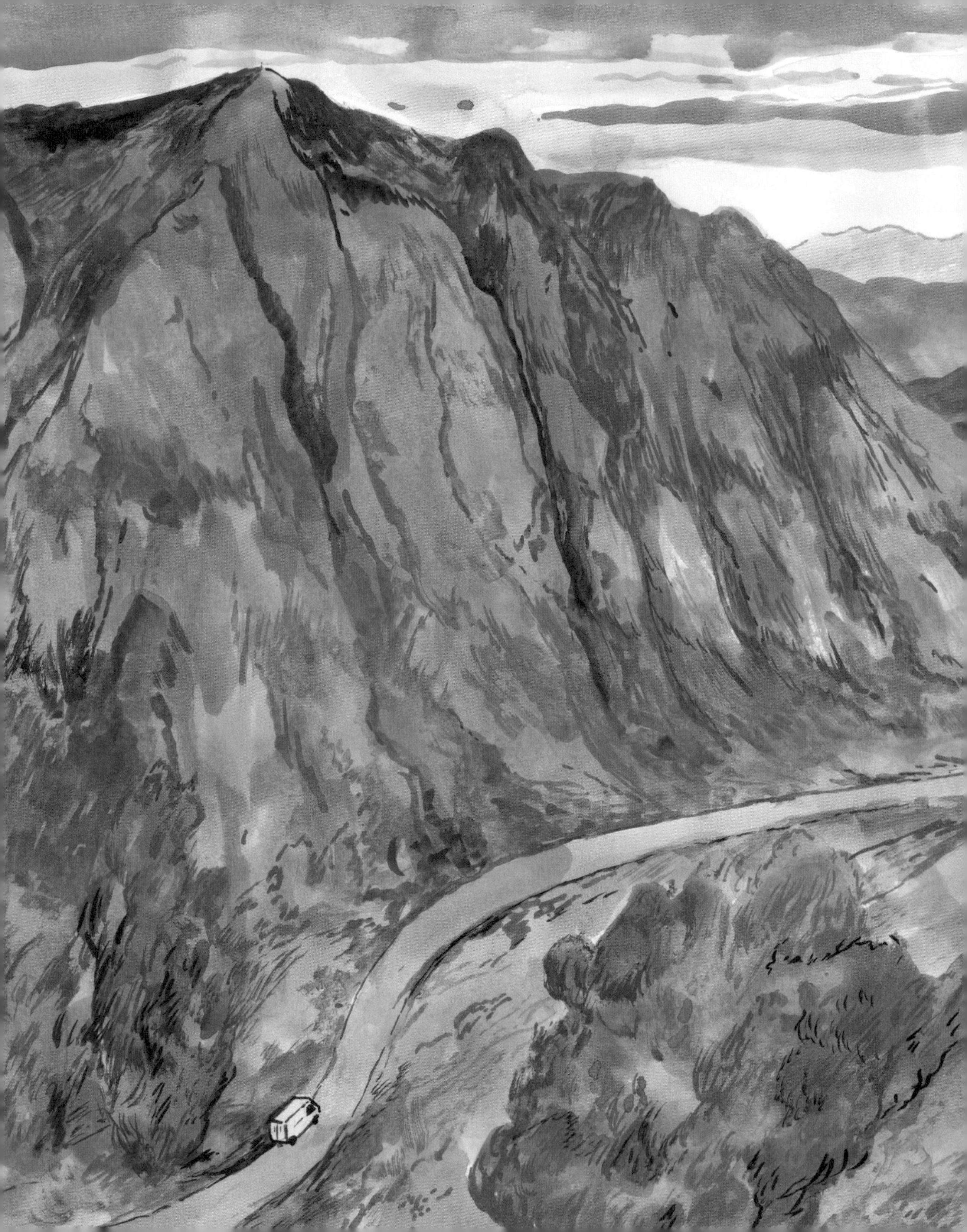

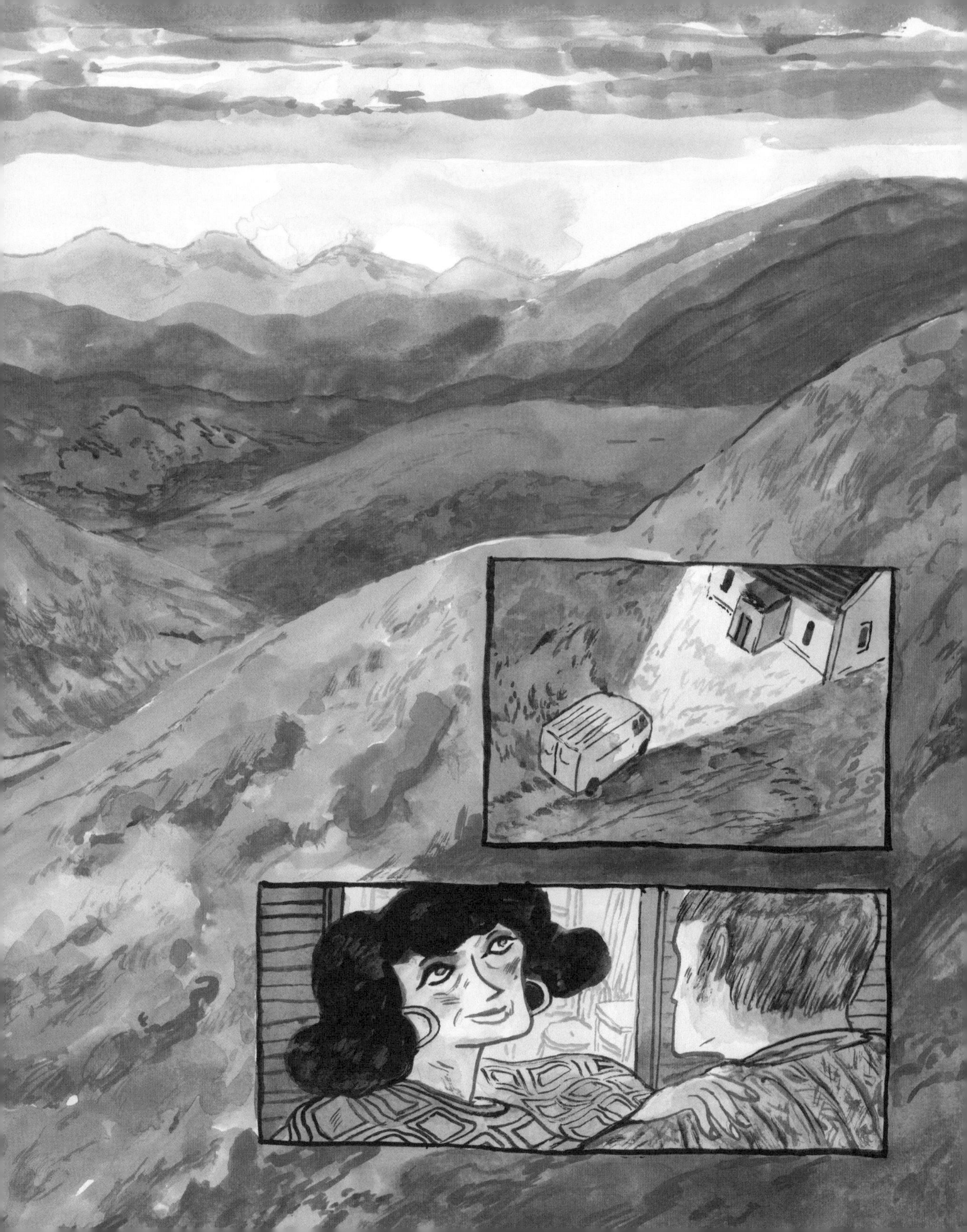

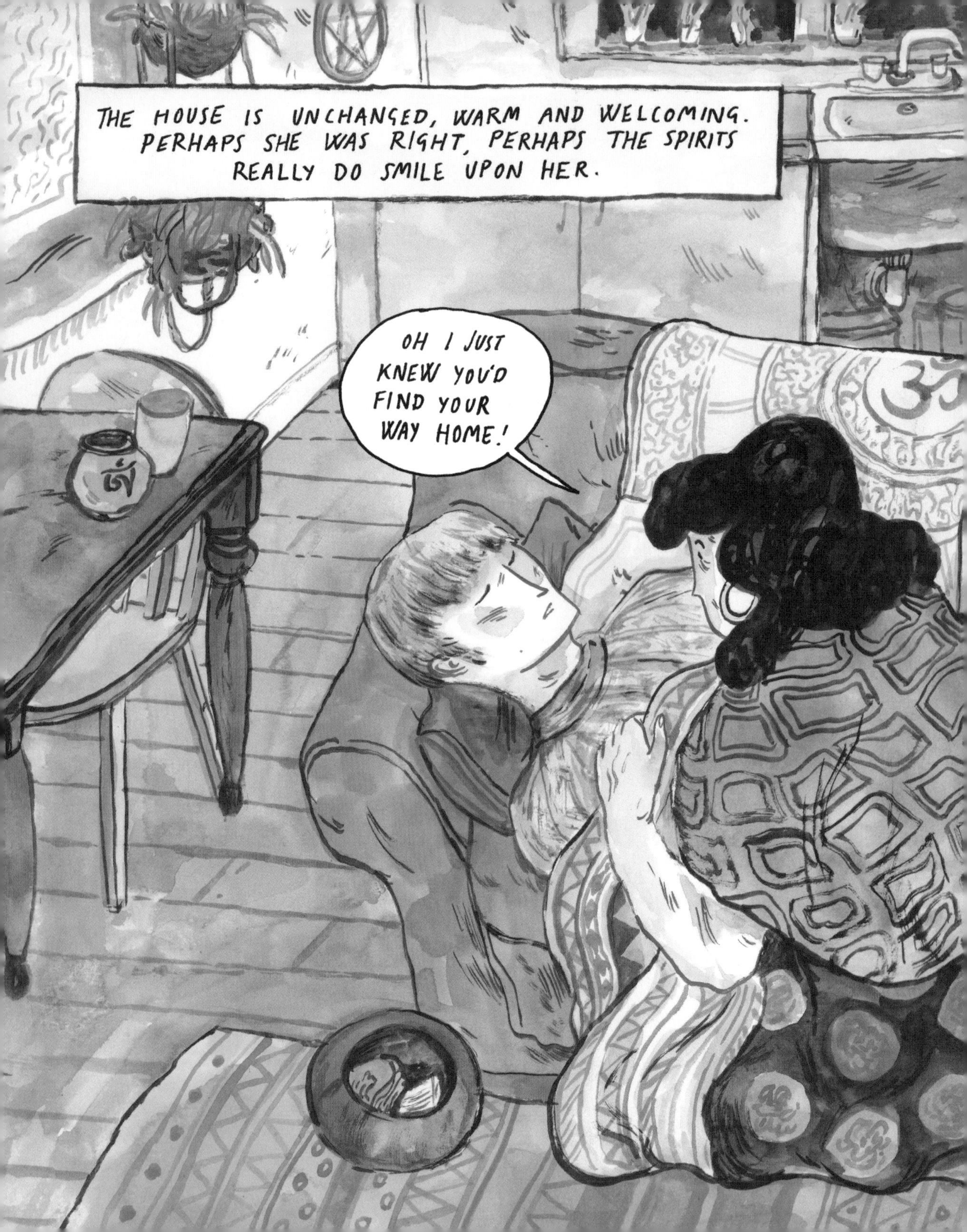
THE HOUSE IS UNCHANGED, WARM AND WELCOMING. PERHAPS SHE WAS RIGHT, PERHAPS THE SPIRITS REALLY DO SMILE UPON HER.
OH I JUST KNEW YOU'D FIND YOUR WAY HOME!

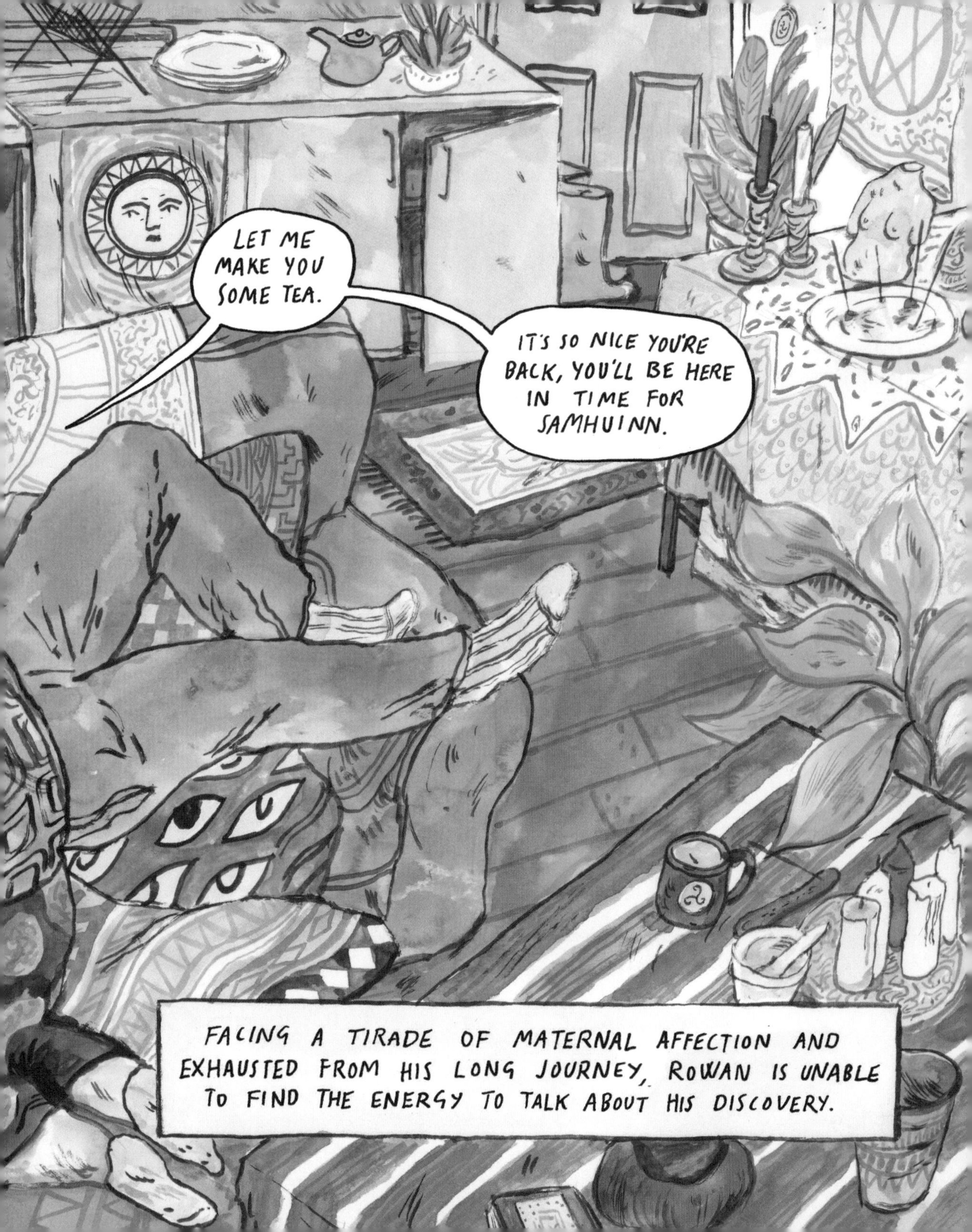
LET ME MAKE YOU SOME TEA.
IT'S SO NICE YOU'RE BACK, YOU'LL BE HERE IN TIME FOR SAMHUINN.
FACING A TIRADE OF MATERNAL AFFECTION AND EXHAUSTED FROM HIS LONG JOURNEY, ROWAN IS UNABLE TO FIND THE ENERGY TO TALK ABOUT HIS DISCOVERY.

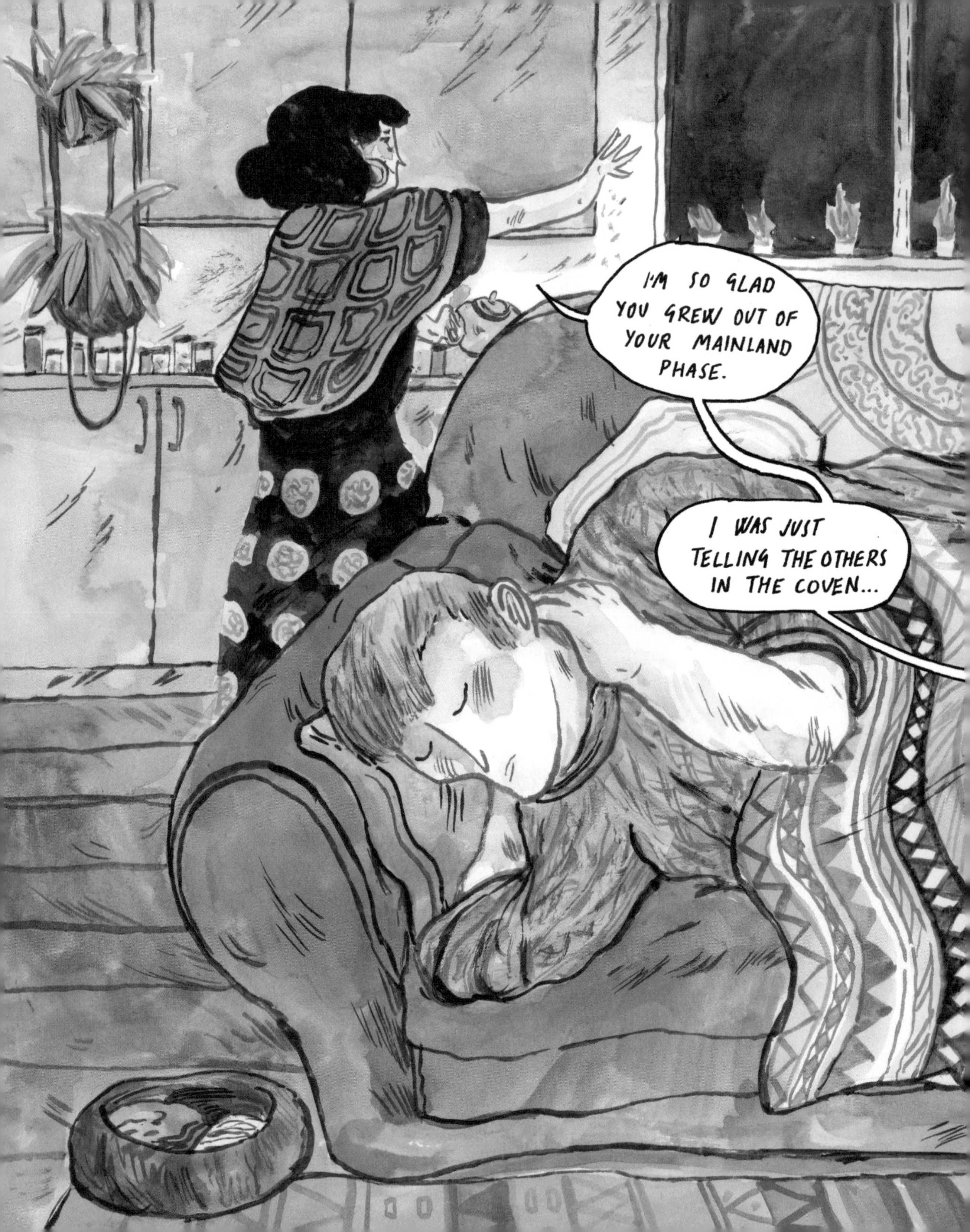
I'M SO GLAD YOU GREW OUT OF YOUR MAINLAND PHASE.
I WAS JUST TELLING THE OTHERS IN THE COVEN...

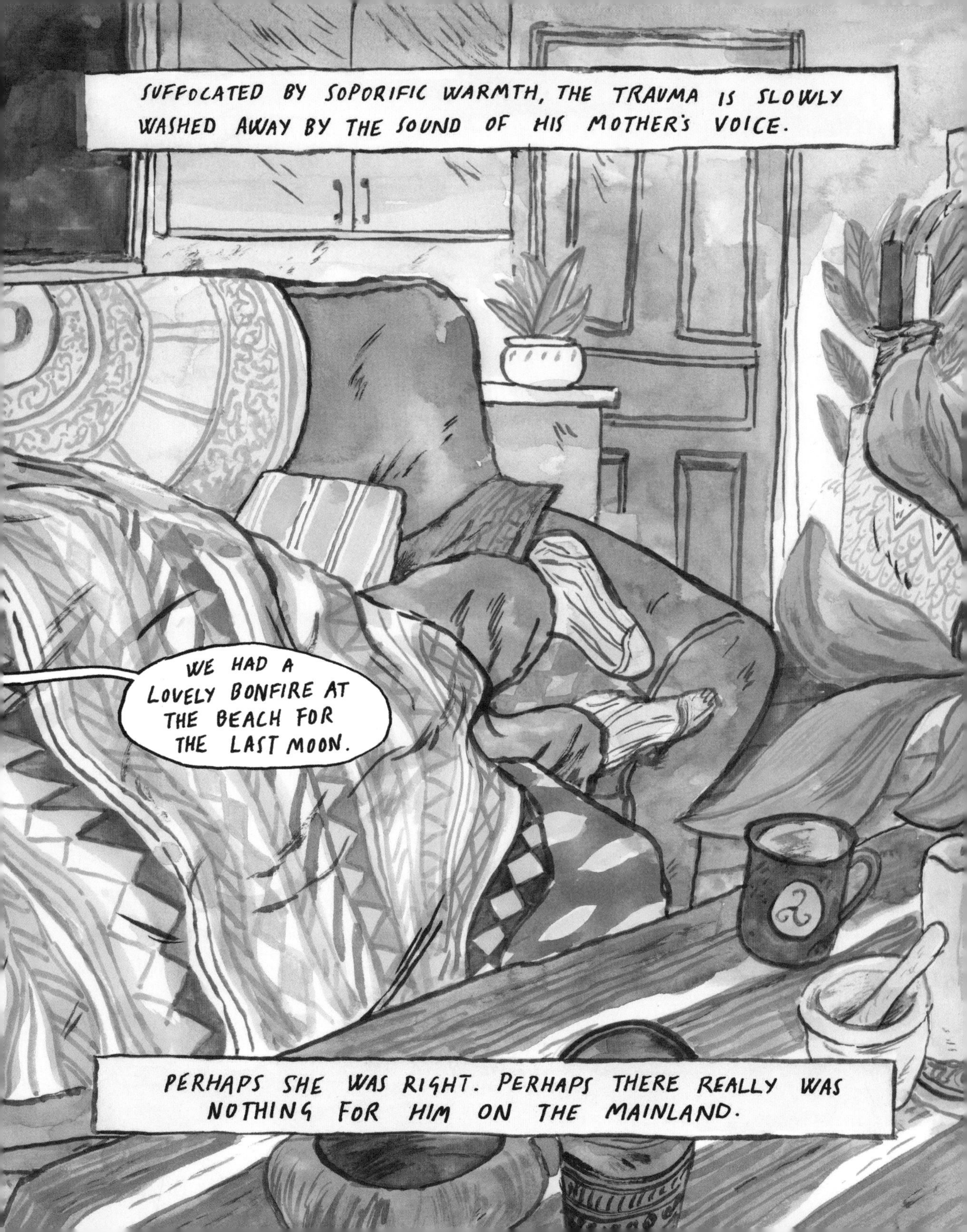
SUFFOCATED BY SOPORIFIC WARMTH, THE TRAUMA IS SLOWLY WASHED AWAY BY THE SOUND OF HIS MOTHER'S VOICE.
WE HAD A LOVELY BONFIRE AT THE BEACH FOR THE LAST MOON.
PERHAPS SHE WAS RIGHT. PERHAPS THERE REALLY WAS NOTHING FOR HIM ON THE MAINLAND.

HER MURMURING OVERWHELMS HIM. SHE IS RIGHT. THE ENERGY REALLY IS THERE, PUSHING HIM, GENTLY RETURNING HIM TO HIS RIGHTFUL PLACE IN THE COSMOS.
...AND THERE'S PLENTY OF NEWS. THEY CHANGED THE FERRY TIMES AGAIN.
AND IAN AND PRIMOSE GOT MARRIED. OH, AND ROSEMARY IS PREGNANT AGAIN. HER SHINGLES CAME BACK TOO...

BUT I MADE HER A BOX OF FENNEL AND CAMOMILE INFUSIONS, THAT'LL HELP.
SHE'D BE RIGHT AS RAIN IF SHE STOPPED TAKING THOSE HORRID CHEMICAL MEDECINES.

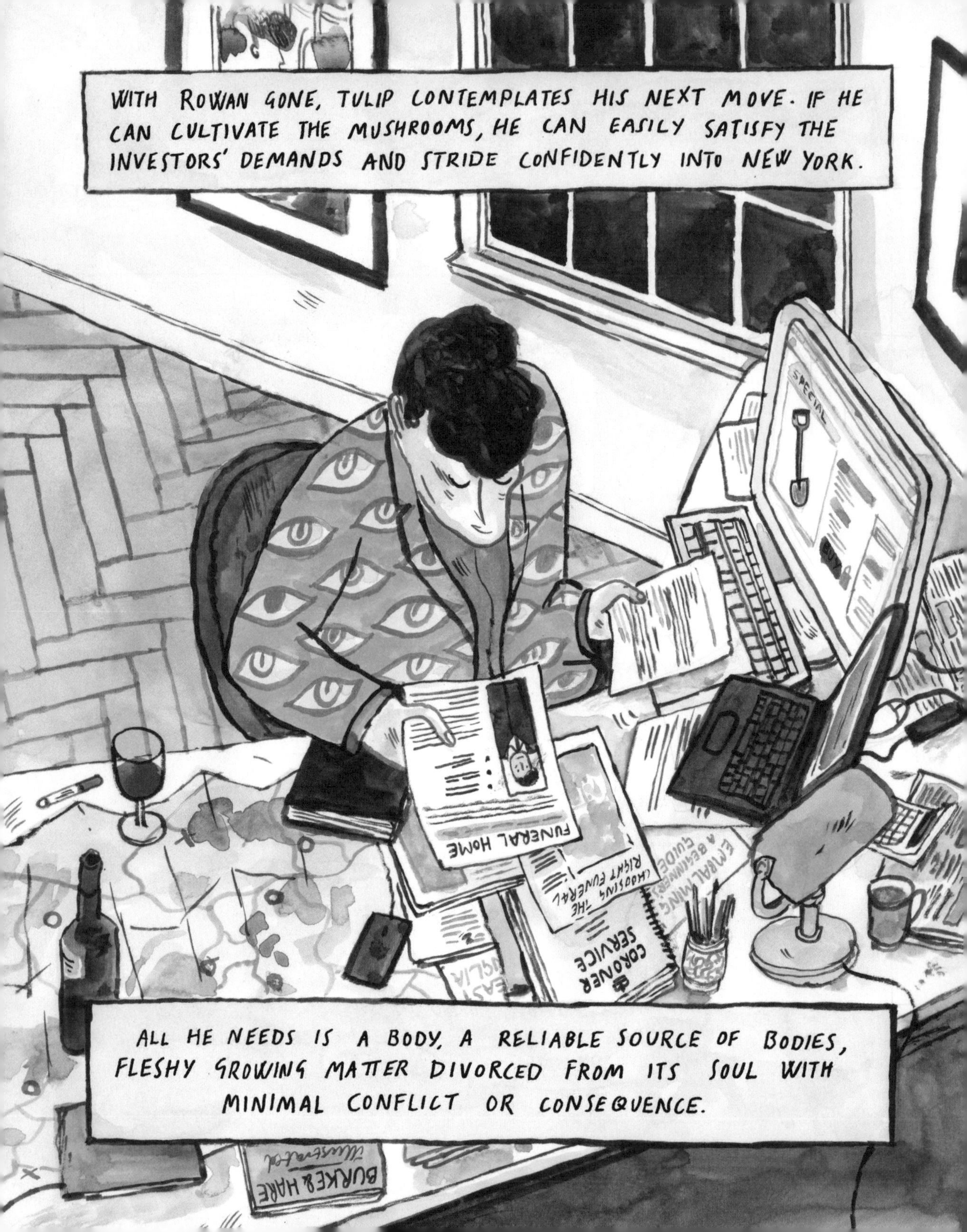
WITH ROWAN GONE, TULIP CONTEMPLATES HIS NEXT MOVE. IF HE CAN CULTIVATE THE MUSHROOMS, HE CAN EASILY SATISFY THE INVESTORS' DEMANDS AND STRIDE CONFIDENTLY INTO NEW YORK.
SPECIAL
BUY
FUNERAL HOME
CHOOSING THE RIGHT FUNERAL
EMBALMING A BEGINNER'S GUIDE
CORONER SERVICE
ALL HE NEEDS IS A BODY, A RELIABLE SOURCE OF BODIES, FLESHY GROWING MATTER DIVORCED FROM ITS SOUL WITH MINIMAL CONFLICT OR CONSEQUENCE.
BURKE & HARE
Illustrated

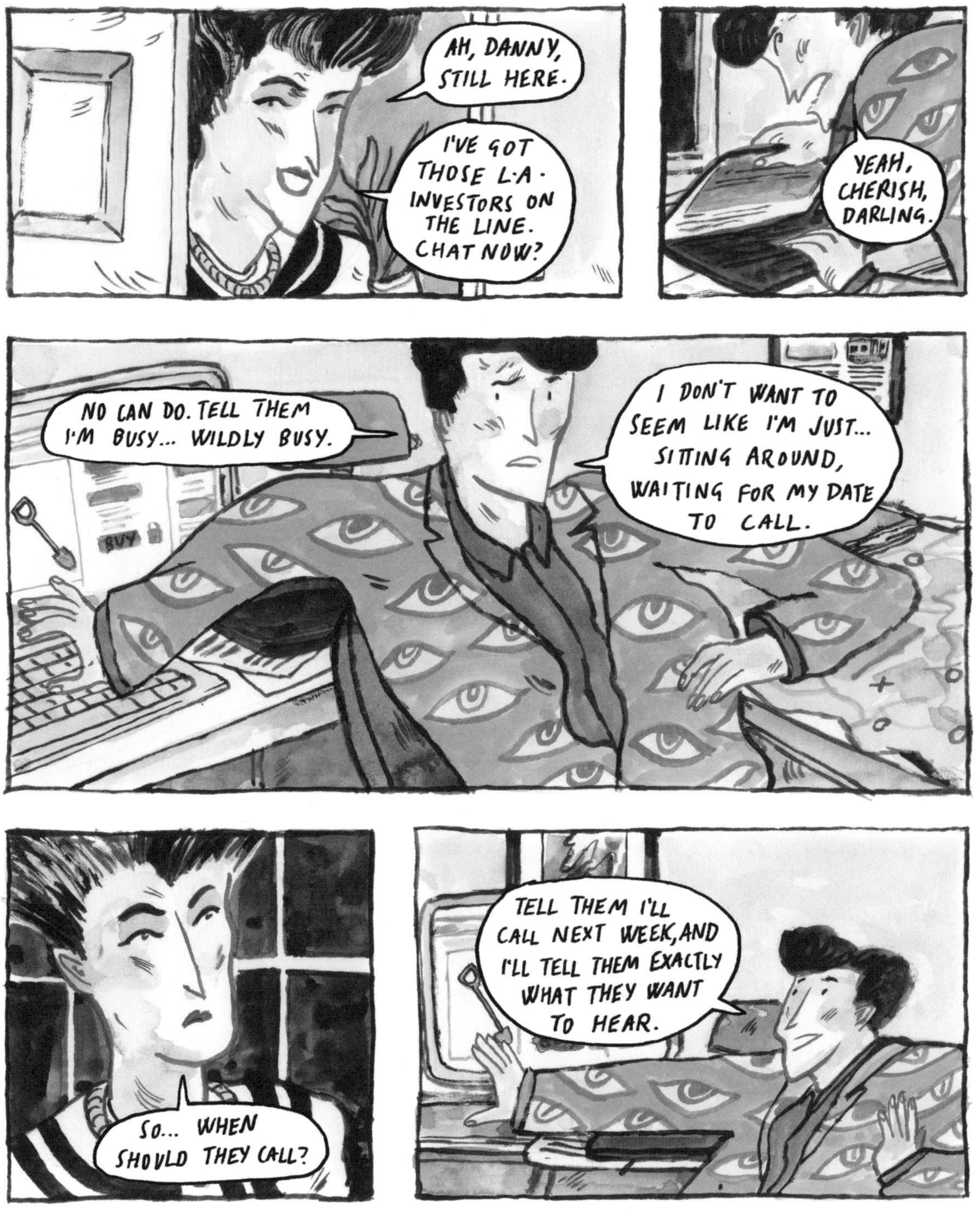
AH, DANNY, STILL HERE.
I'VE GOT THOSE L.A. INVESTORS ON THE LINE. CHAT NOW?
YEAH, CHERISH, DARLING.
NO CAN DO. TELL THEM I'M BUSY... WILDLY BUSY.
I DON'T WANT TO SEEM LIKE I'M JUST... SITTING AROUND, WAITING FOR MY DATE TO CALL.
BUY
SO... WHEN SHOULD THEY CALL?
TELL THEM I'LL CALL NEXT WEEK, AND I'LL TELL THEM EXACTLY WHAT THEY WANT TO HEAR.

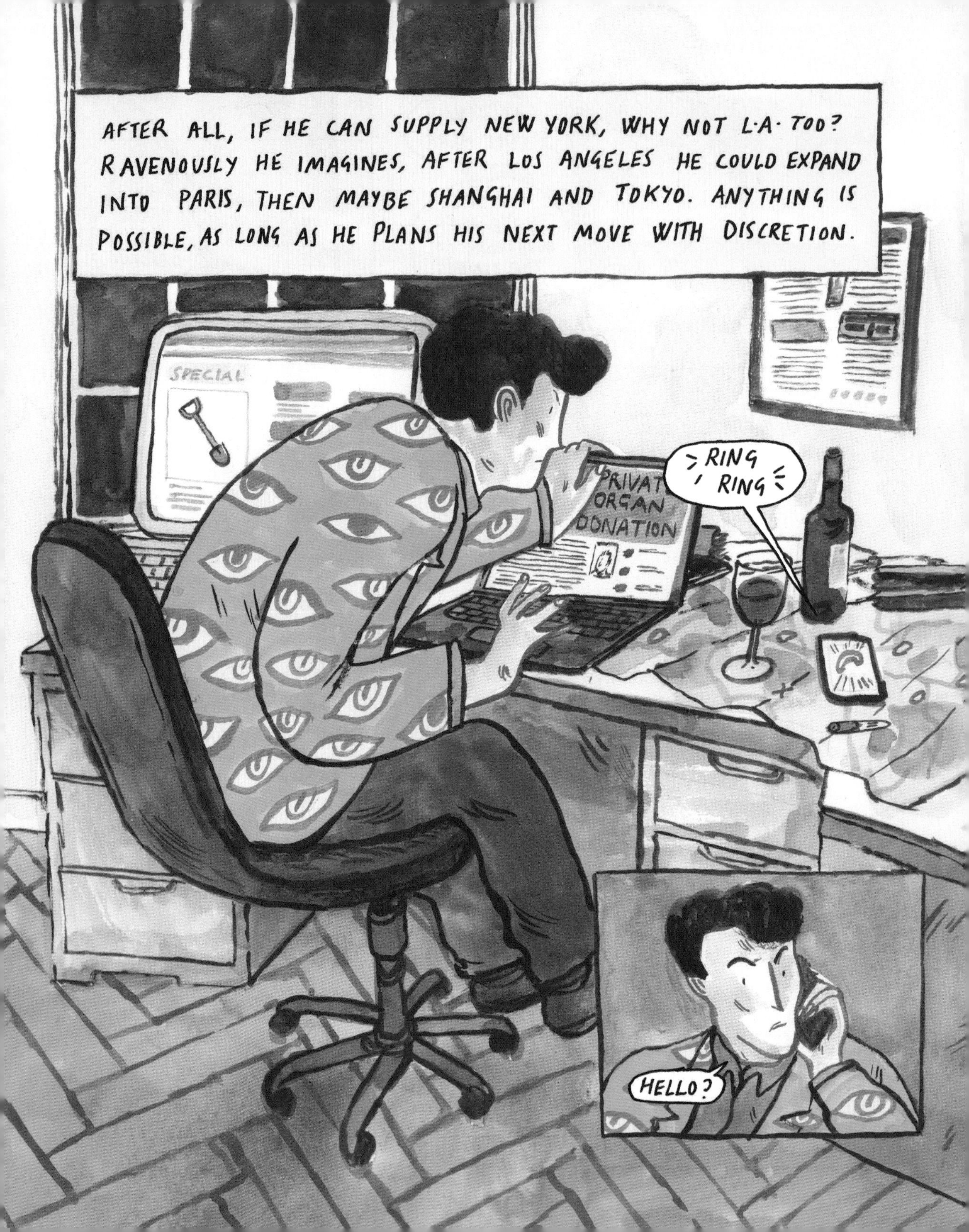
AFTER ALL, IF HE CAN SUPPLY NEW YORK, WHY NOT L.A. TOO? RAVENOUSLY HE IMAGINES, AFTER LOS ANGELES HE COULD EXPAND INTO PARIS, THEN MAYBE SHANGHAI AND TOKYO. ANYTHING IS POSSIBLE, AS LONG AS HE PLANS HIS NEXT MOVE WITH DISCRETION.
SPECIAL
PRIVAT ORGAN DONATION
RING RING
HELLO?

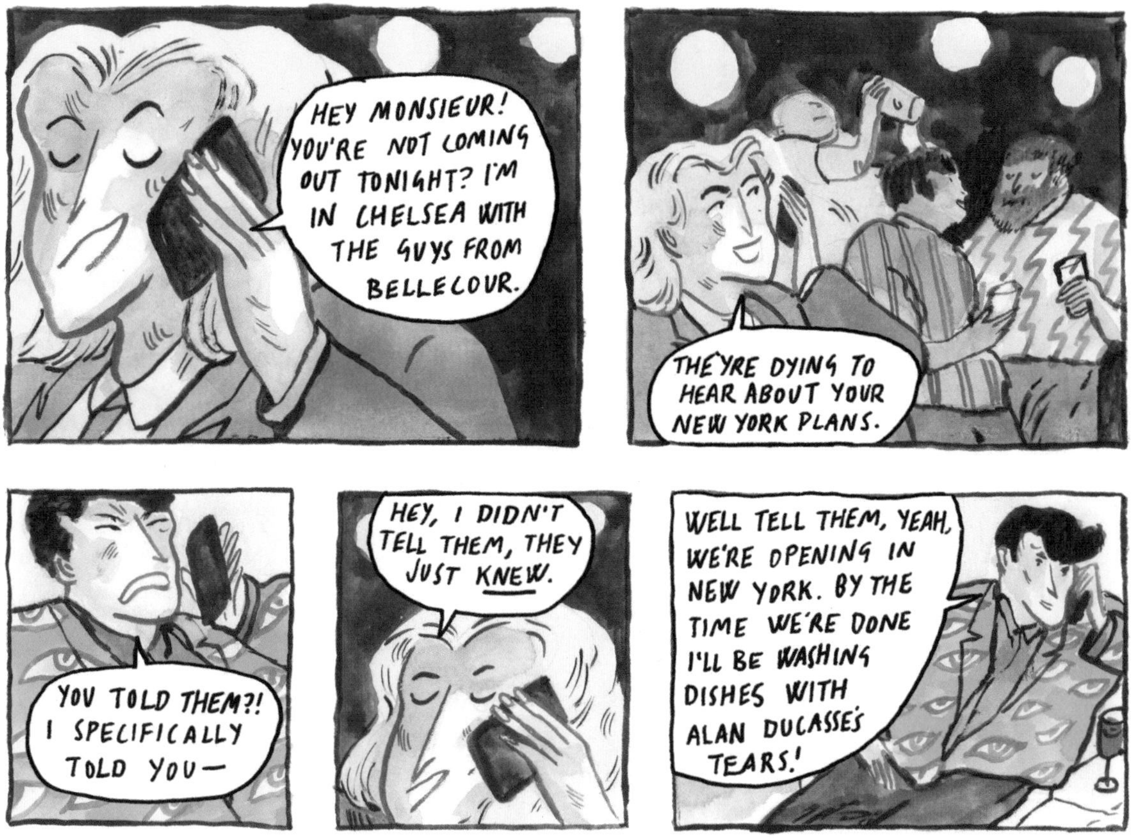
HEY MONSIEUR! YOU'RE NOT COMING OUT TONIGHT? I'M IN CHELSEA WITH THE GUYS FROM BELLECOUR.
THEY'RE DYING TO HEAR ABOUT YOUR NEW YORK PLANS.
YOU TOLD THEM?! I SPECIFICALLY TOLD YOU—
HEY, I DIDN'T TELL THEM, THEY JUST KNEW.
WELL TELL THEM, YEAH, WE'RE OPENING IN NEW YORK. BY THE TIME WE'RE DONE I'LL BE WASHING DISHES WITH ALAN DUCASSE'S TEARS!

... WITH DISCRETION. HE EMPLOYS OVER A HUNDRED PEOPLE NOW. COULD ANY OF THEM BE TRUSTED TO BURY A BODY WITHOUT BRAGGING ABOUT IT IN A BAR AFTERWARDS? MABEL? TOO BUSY. CHERISH? TOO SQUEAMISH. MARCEL? TULIP SHUDDERS AT THE THOUGHT OF TRUSTING HIM WITH SOMETHING SO SECRET. THERE IS ONLY ONE PERSON HE CAN TRUST, ABSOLUTELY, FOREVER.

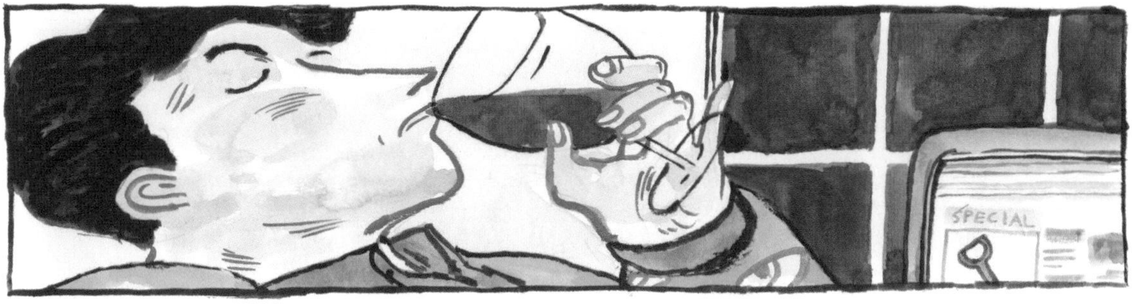
SPECIAL

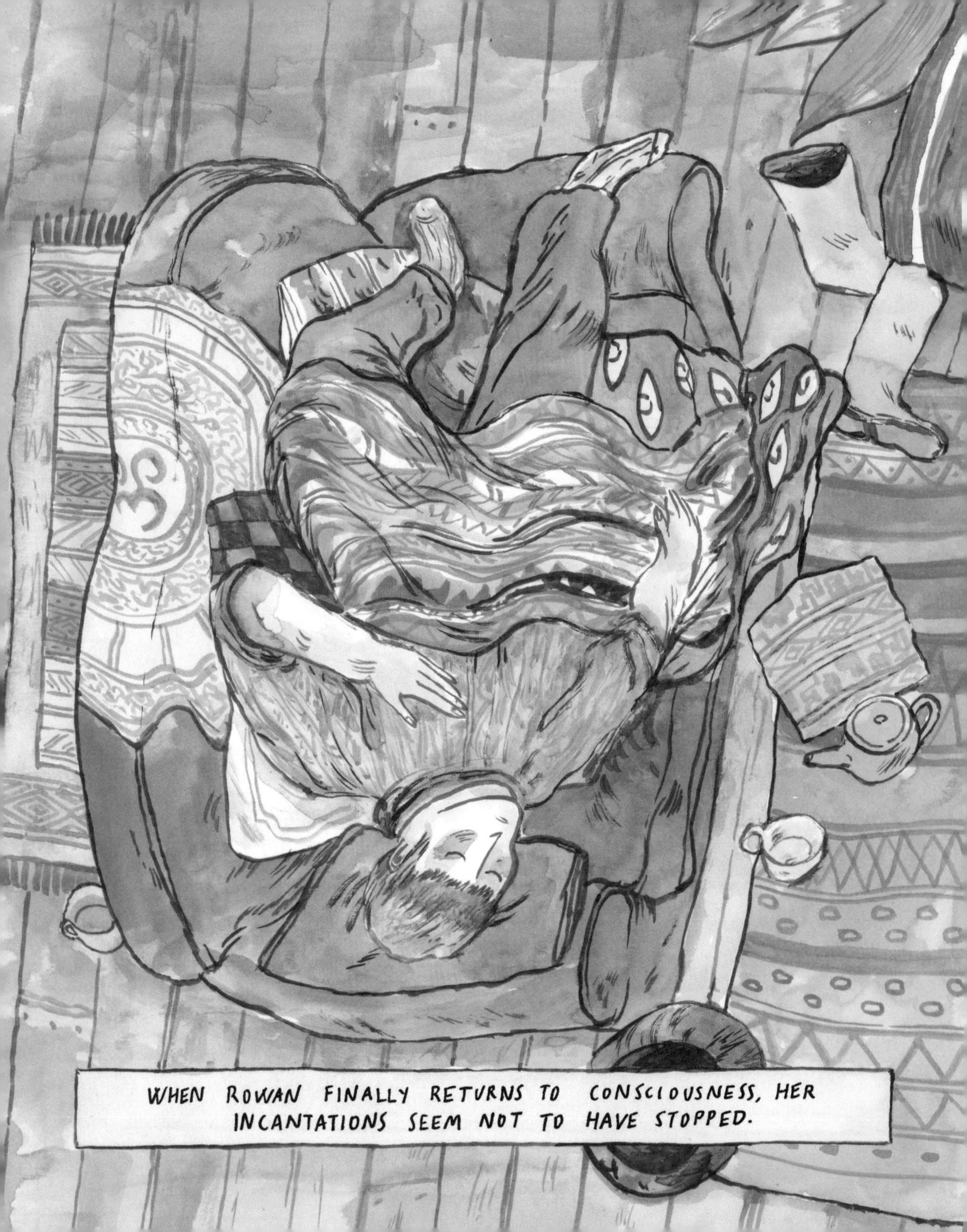

WHEN ROWAN FINALLY RETURNS TO CONSCIOUSNESS, HER INCANTATIONS SEEM NOT TO HAVE STOPPED.

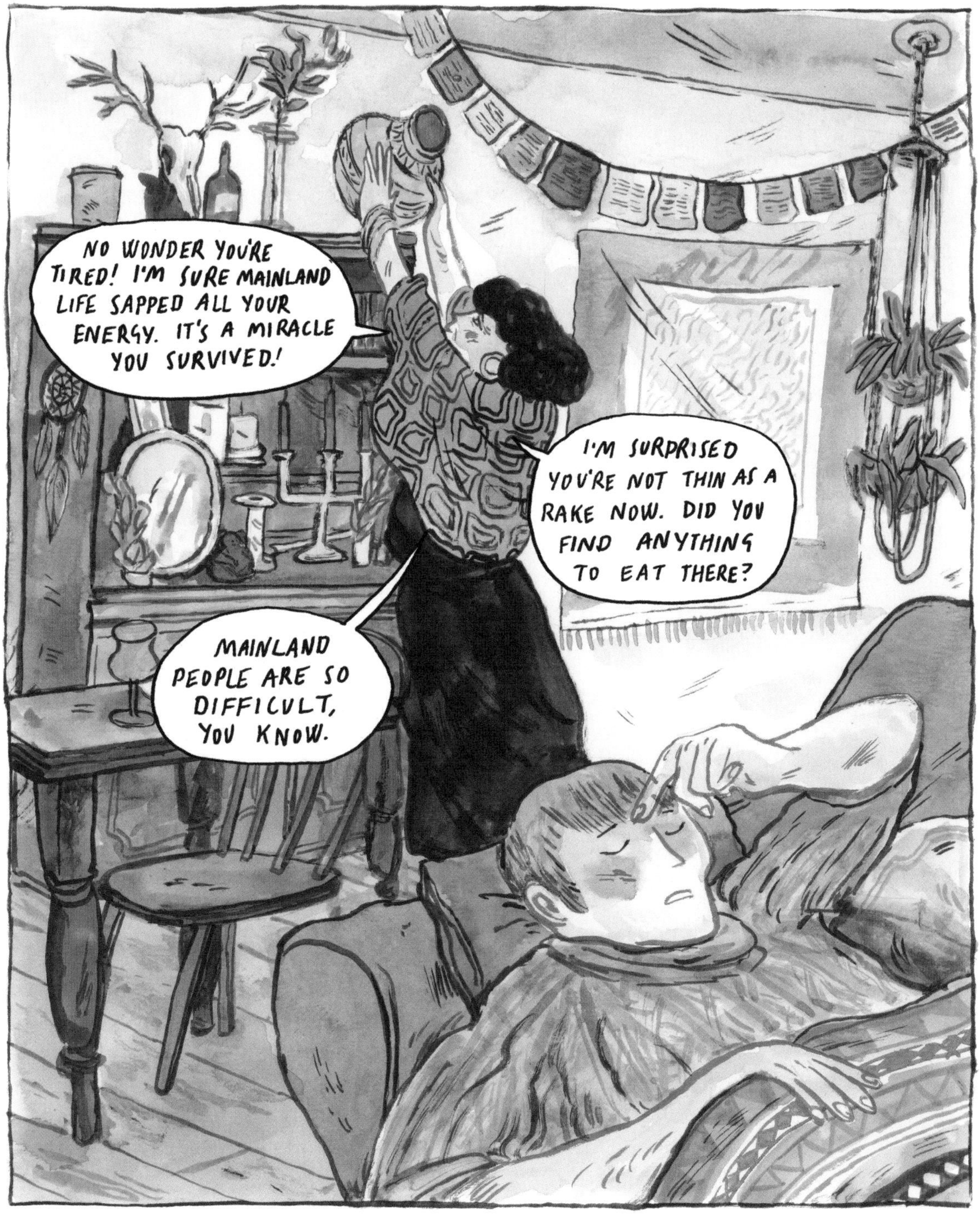
NO WONDER YOU'RE TIRED! I'M SURE MAINLAND LIFE SAPPED ALL YOUR ENERGY. IT'S A MIRACLE YOU SURVIVED!
I'M SURPRISED YOU'RE NOT THIN AS A RAKE NOW. DID YOU FIND ANYTHING TO EAT THERE?
MAINLAND PEOPLE ARE SO DIFFICULT, YOU KNOW.

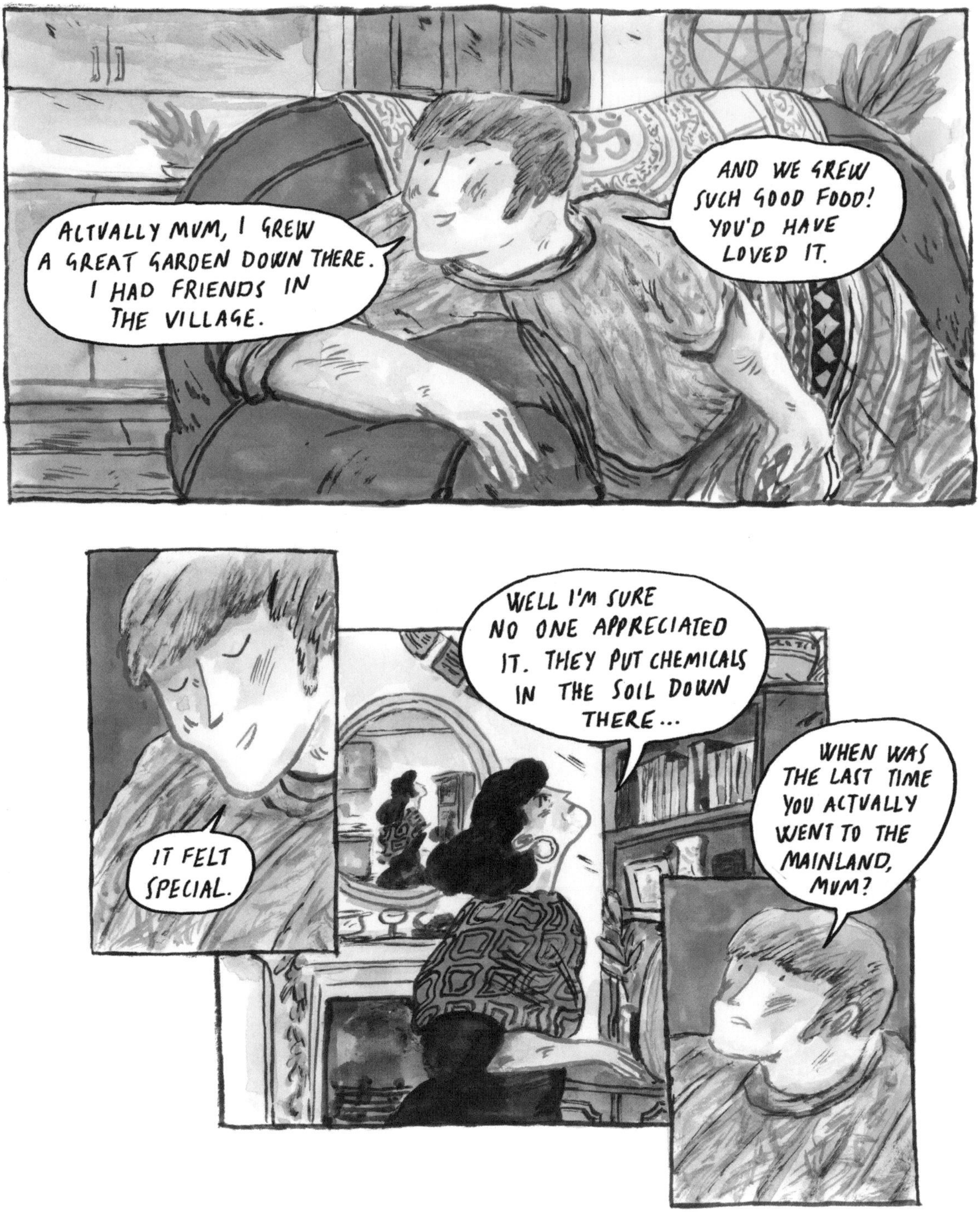
ACTUALLY MUM, I GREW A GREAT GARDEN DOWN THERE. I HAD FRIENDS IN THE VILLAGE.
AND WE GREW SUCH GOOD FOOD! YOU'D HAVE LOVED IT.
IT FELT SPECIAL.
WELL I'M SURE NO ONE APPRECIATED IT. THEY PUT CHEMICALS IN THE SOIL DOWN THERE...
WHEN WAS THE LAST TIME YOU ACTUALLY WENT TO THE MAINLAND, MUM?

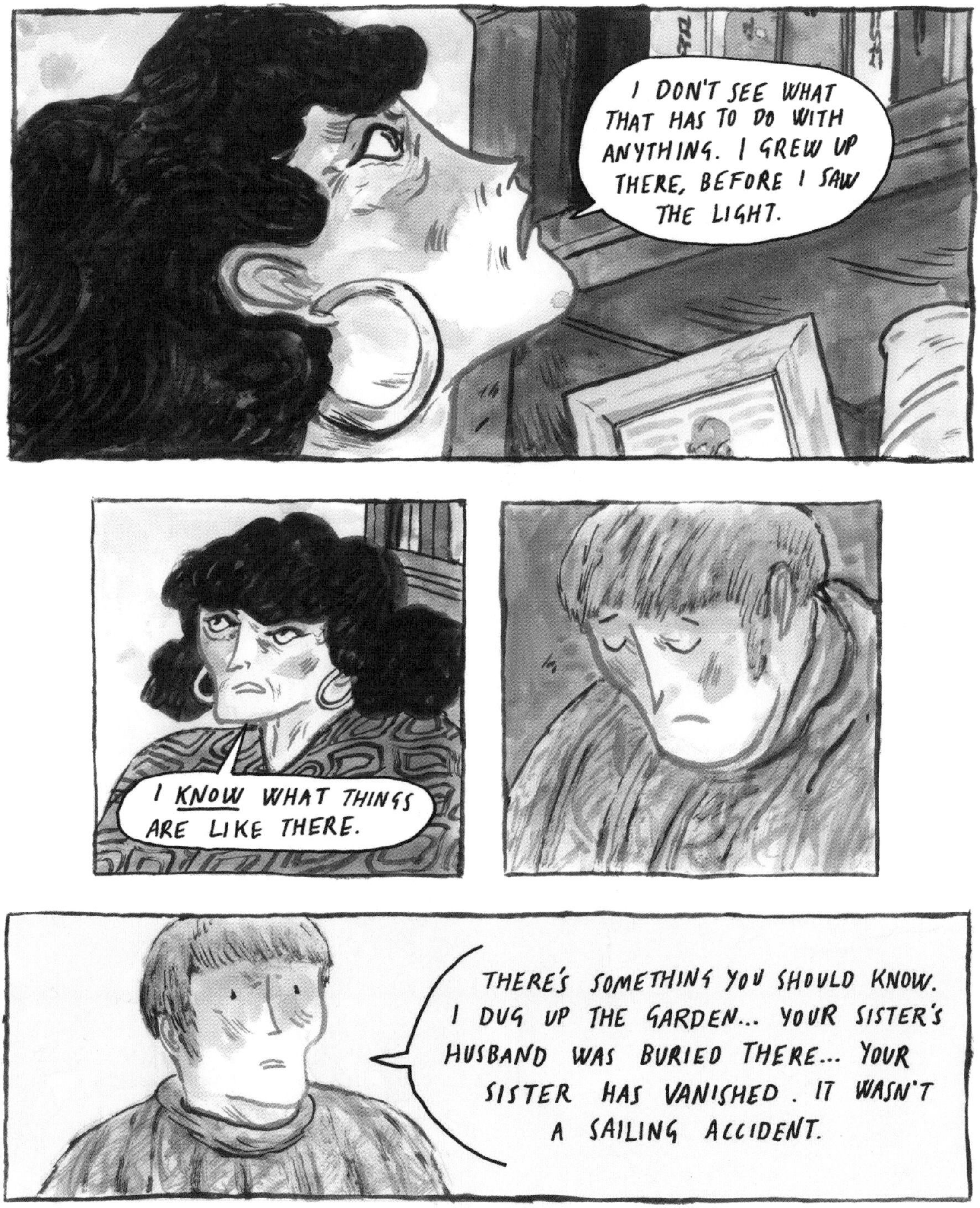
I DON'T SEE WHAT THAT HAS TO DO WITH ANYTHING. I GREW UP THERE, BEFORE I SAW THE LIGHT.
I KNOW WHAT THINGS ARE LIKE THERE.
THERE'S SOMETHING YOU SHOULD KNOW. I DUG UP THE GARDEN... YOUR SISTER'S HUSBAND WAS BURIED THERE... YOUR SISTER HAS VANISHED. IT WASN'T A SAILING ACCIDENT.

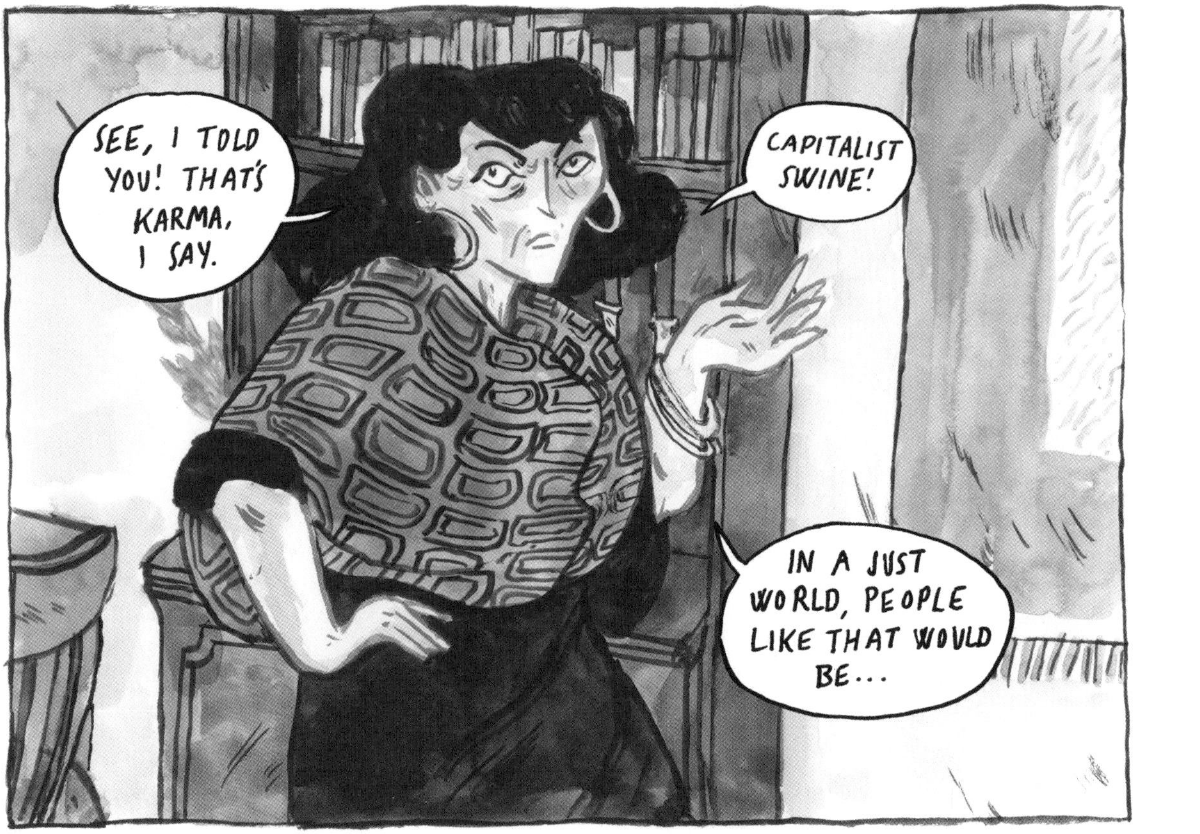
SEE, I TOLD YOU! THAT'S KARMA, I SAY.
CAPITALIST SWINE!
IN A JUST WORLD, PEOPLE LIKE THAT WOULD BE...

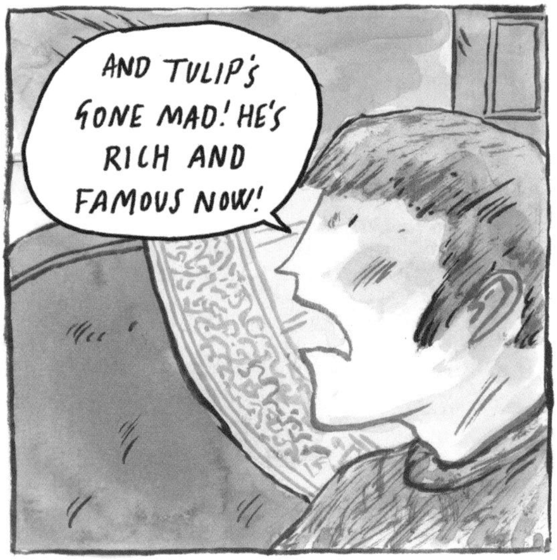
AND TULIP'S GONE MAD! HE'S RICH AND FAMOUS NOW!

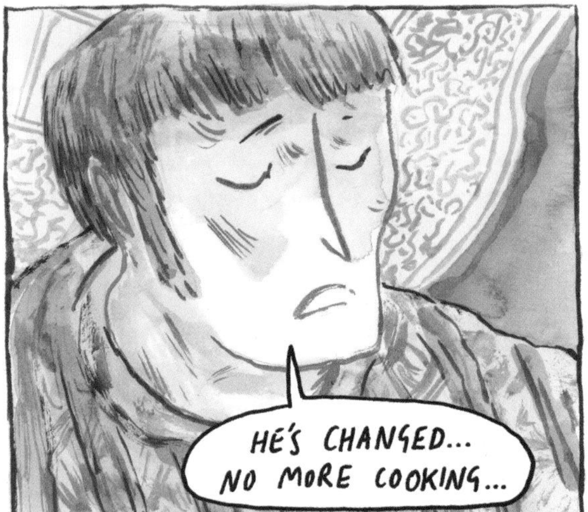
HE'S CHANGED... NO MORE COOKING...

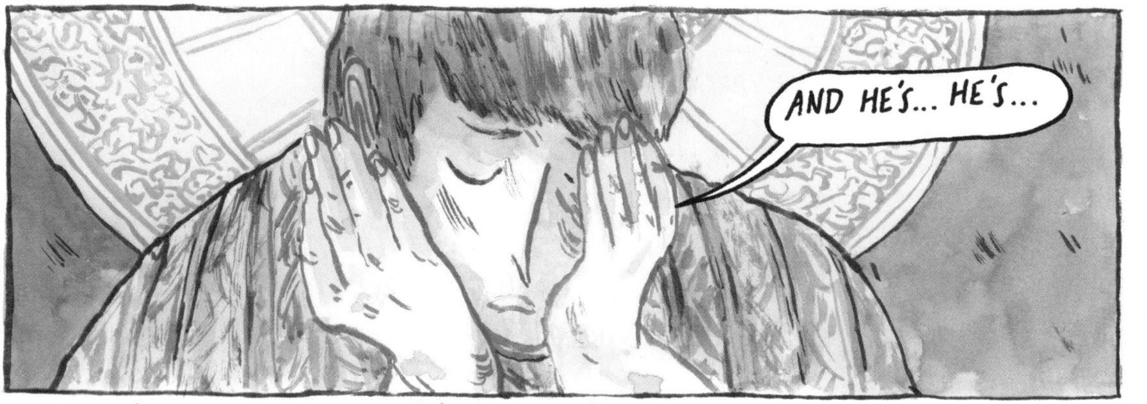
AND HE'S... HE'S...

ROWAN COULD HARDLY BRING HIMSELF TO SAY IT. HOW COULD HE EXPLAIN, THE MUSHROOMS, THE SIGHT OF THE SKELETON, THE DEEP, VIOLENT DESIRE AND EXCITEMENT IN TULIP'S EYES?

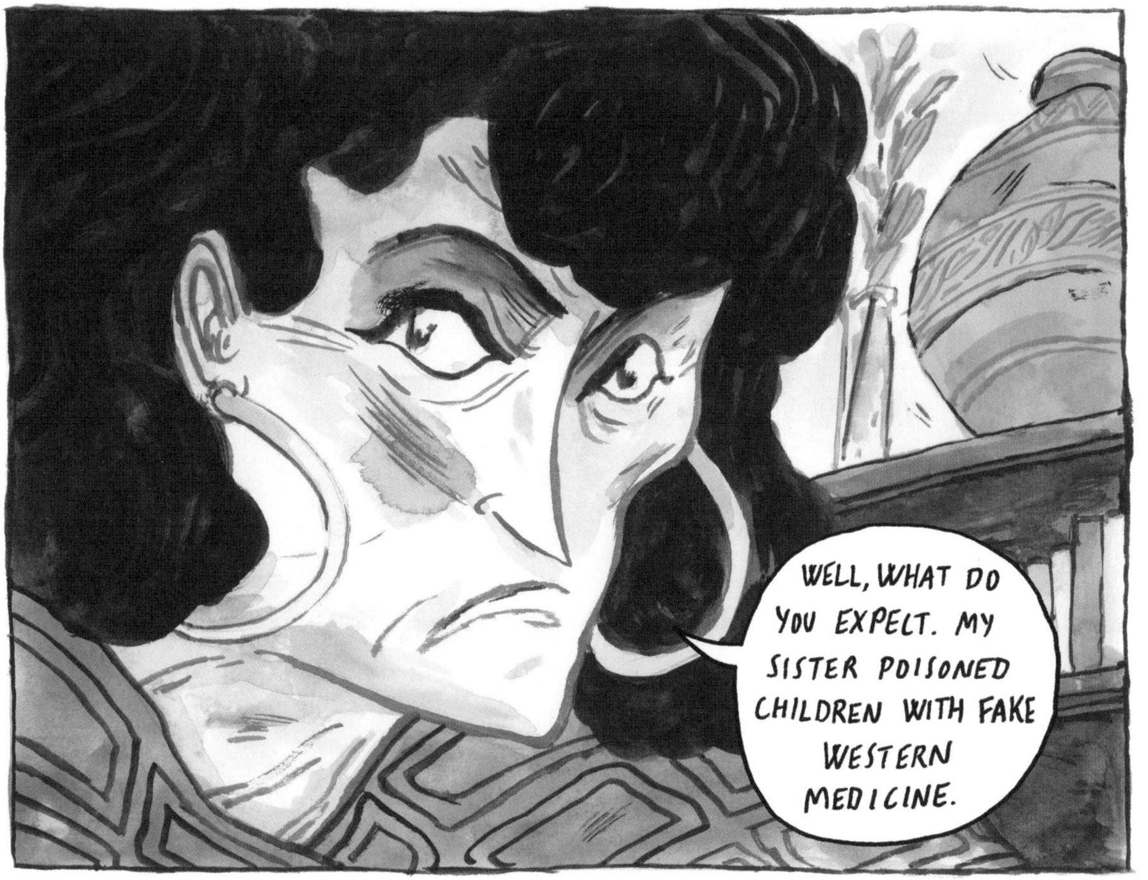
WELL, WHAT DO YOU EXPECT. MY SISTER POISONED CHILDREN WITH FAKE WESTERN MEDICINE.

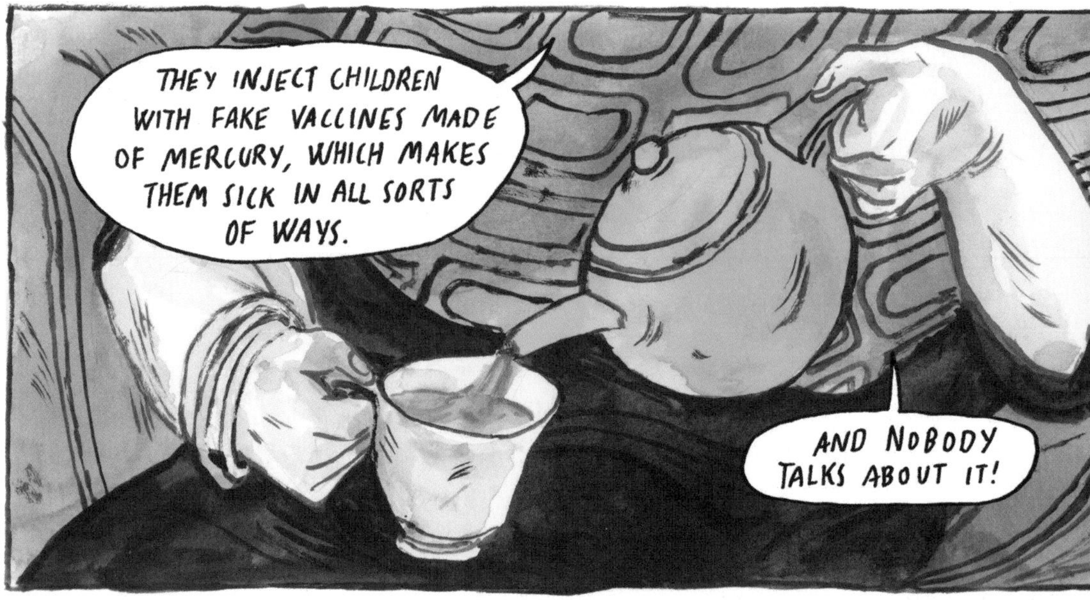
THEY INJECT CHILDREN WITH FAKE VACCINES MADE OF MERCURY, WHICH MAKES THEM SICK IN ALL SORTS OF WAYS.
AND NOBODY TALKS ABOUT IT!

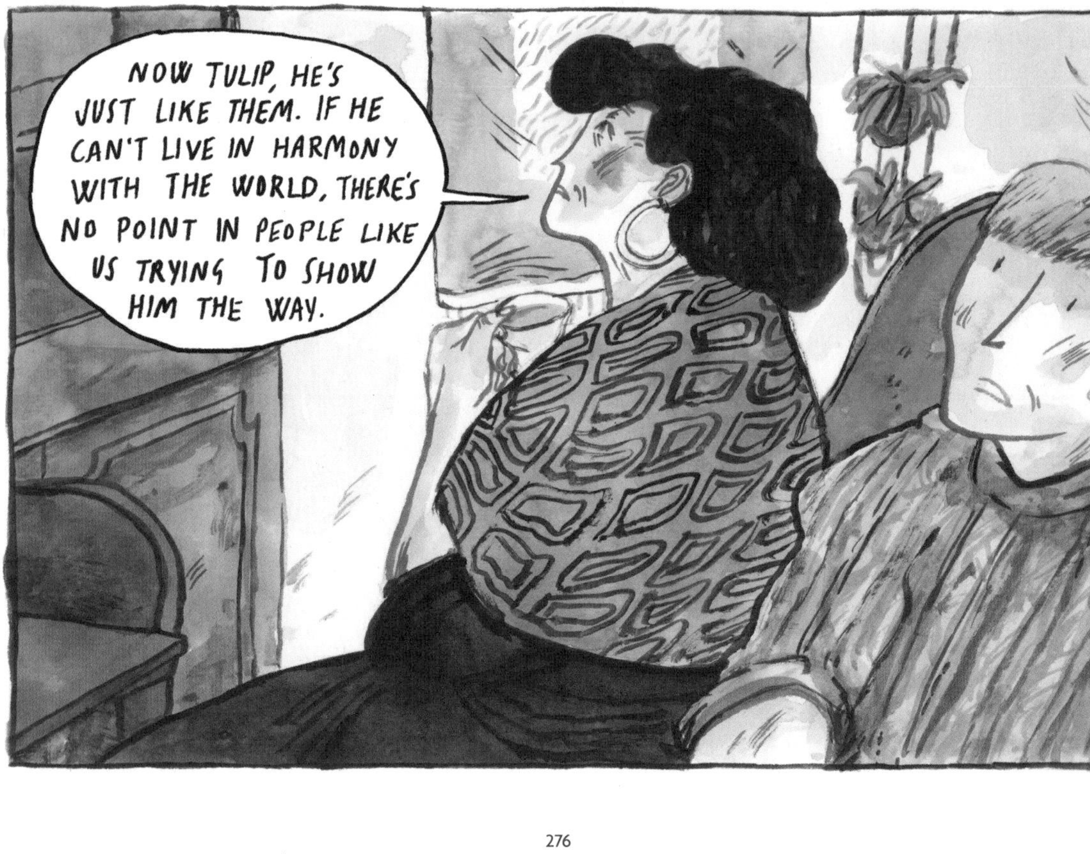
NOW TULIP, HE'S JUST LIKE THEM. IF HE CAN'T LIVE IN HARMONY WITH THE WORLD, THERE'S NO POINT IN PEOPLE LIKE US TRYING TO SHOW HIM THE WAY.

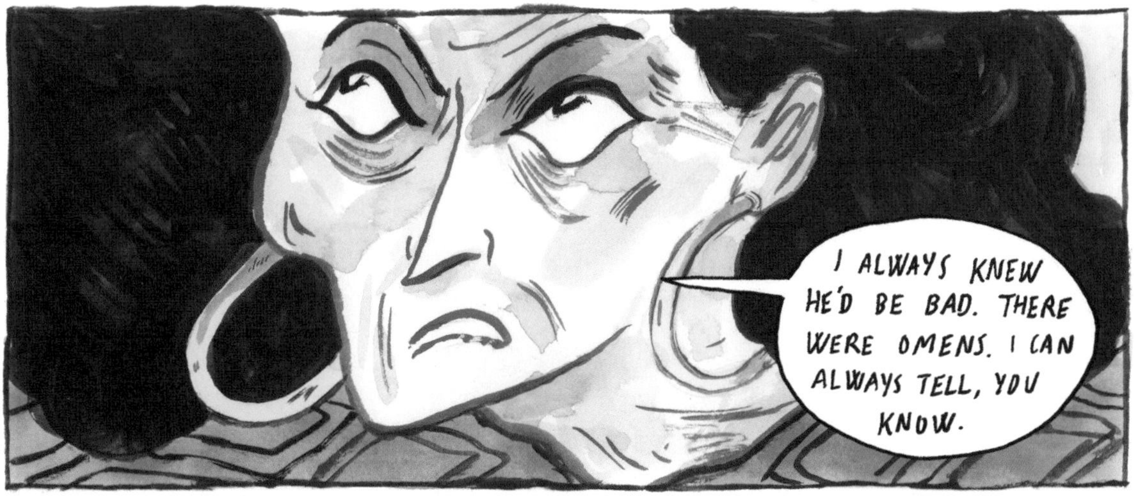
I ALWAYS KNEW HE'D BE BAD. THERE WERE OMENS. I CAN ALWAYS TELL, YOU KNOW.

ROWAN IS HORRIFIED. FOR THE FIRST TIME, HE SEES BEYOND HER PRETENSE OF ENLIGHTENMENT, HER IDEALS OF HEALTH AND WISDOM. HE SEES A BITTER CORE, A ROT BEHIND THE FAÇADE OF CARING AND NURTURING, AN ACRID DESIRE TO CONTROL.

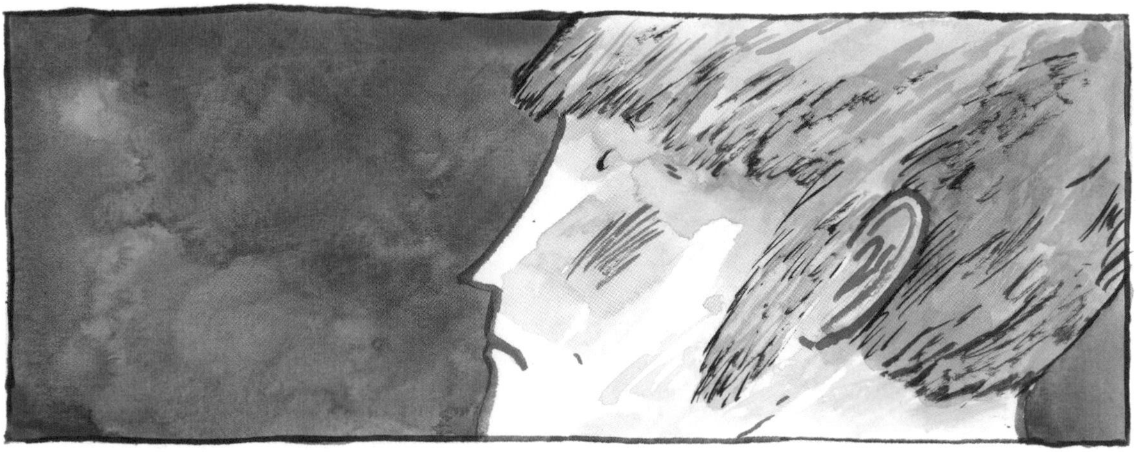

A WOMAN WHO ABANDONED HER FRIENDS AND FAMILY, WHO ISOLATED HERSELF ON A REMOTE ISLAND, WHO, WITH FURY AND PARANOIA, DAMNED ANYTHING THAT DIDN'T CONFORM TO HER NARROW, UNCOMPROMISING, JOYLESS VIEW OF THE WORLD.

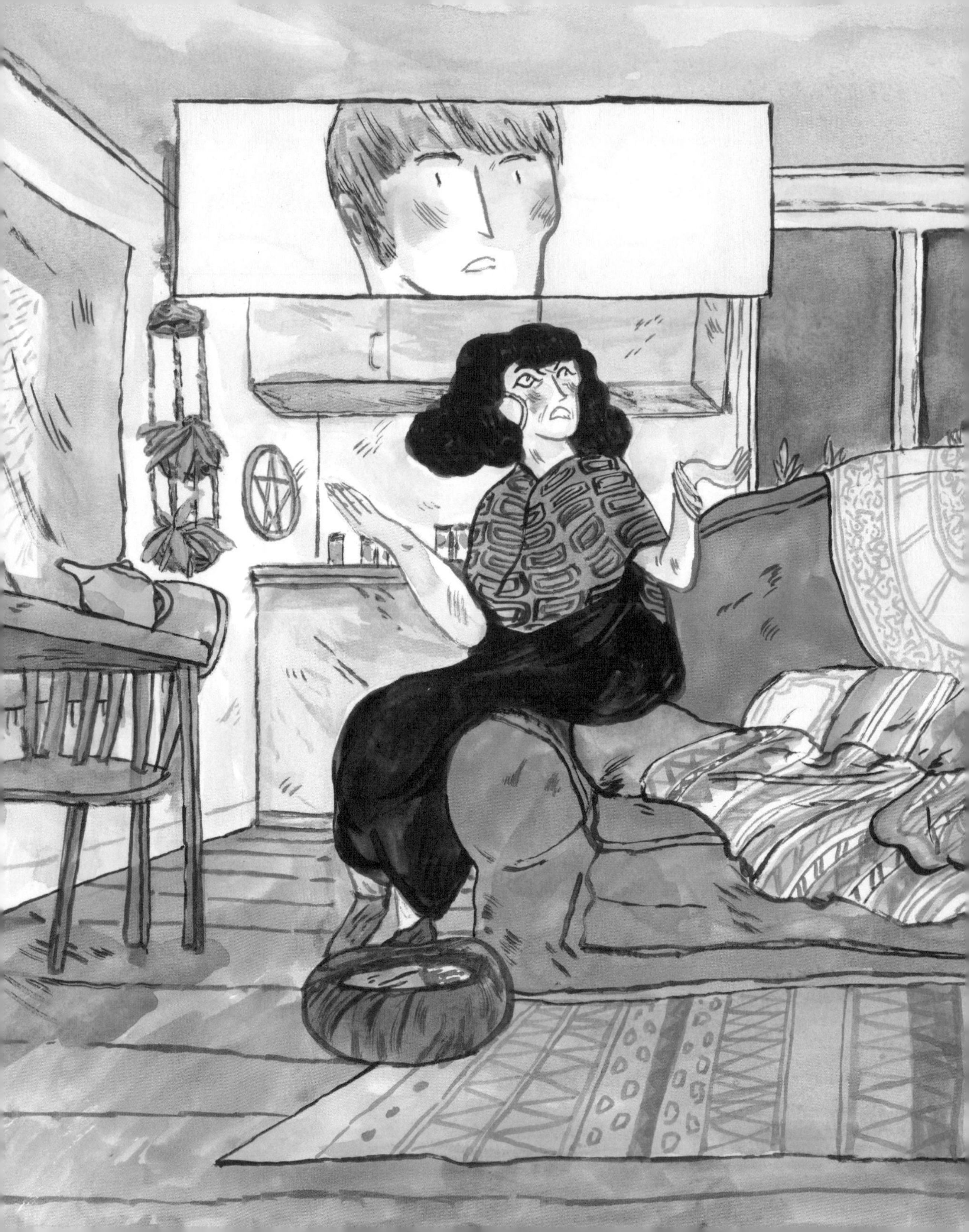

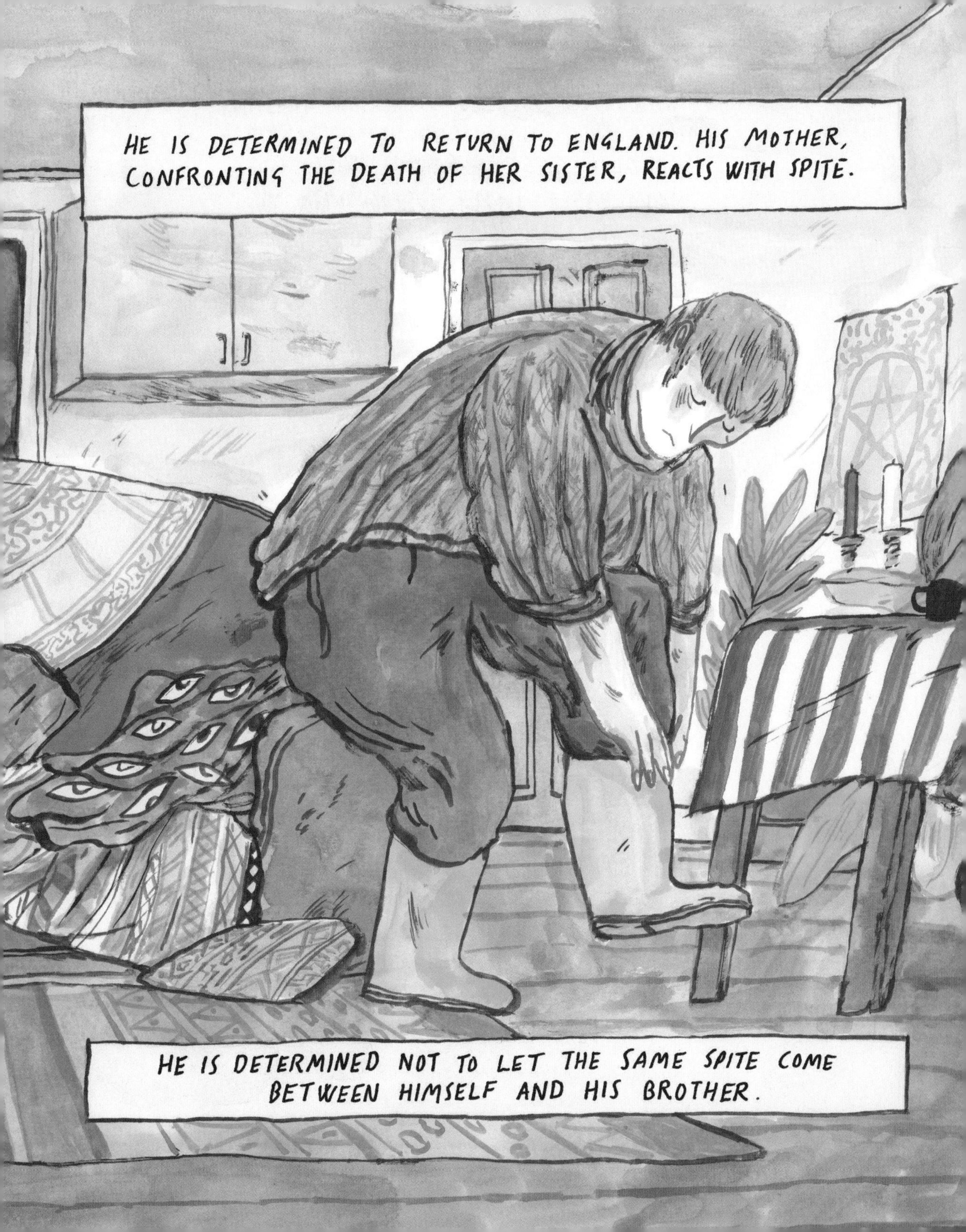
HE IS DETERMINED TO RETURN TO ENGLAND. HIS MOTHER, CONFRONTING THE DEATH OF HER SISTER, REACTS WITH SPITE.
HE IS DETERMINED NOT TO LET THE SAME SPITE COME BETWEEN HIMSELF AND HIS BROTHER.

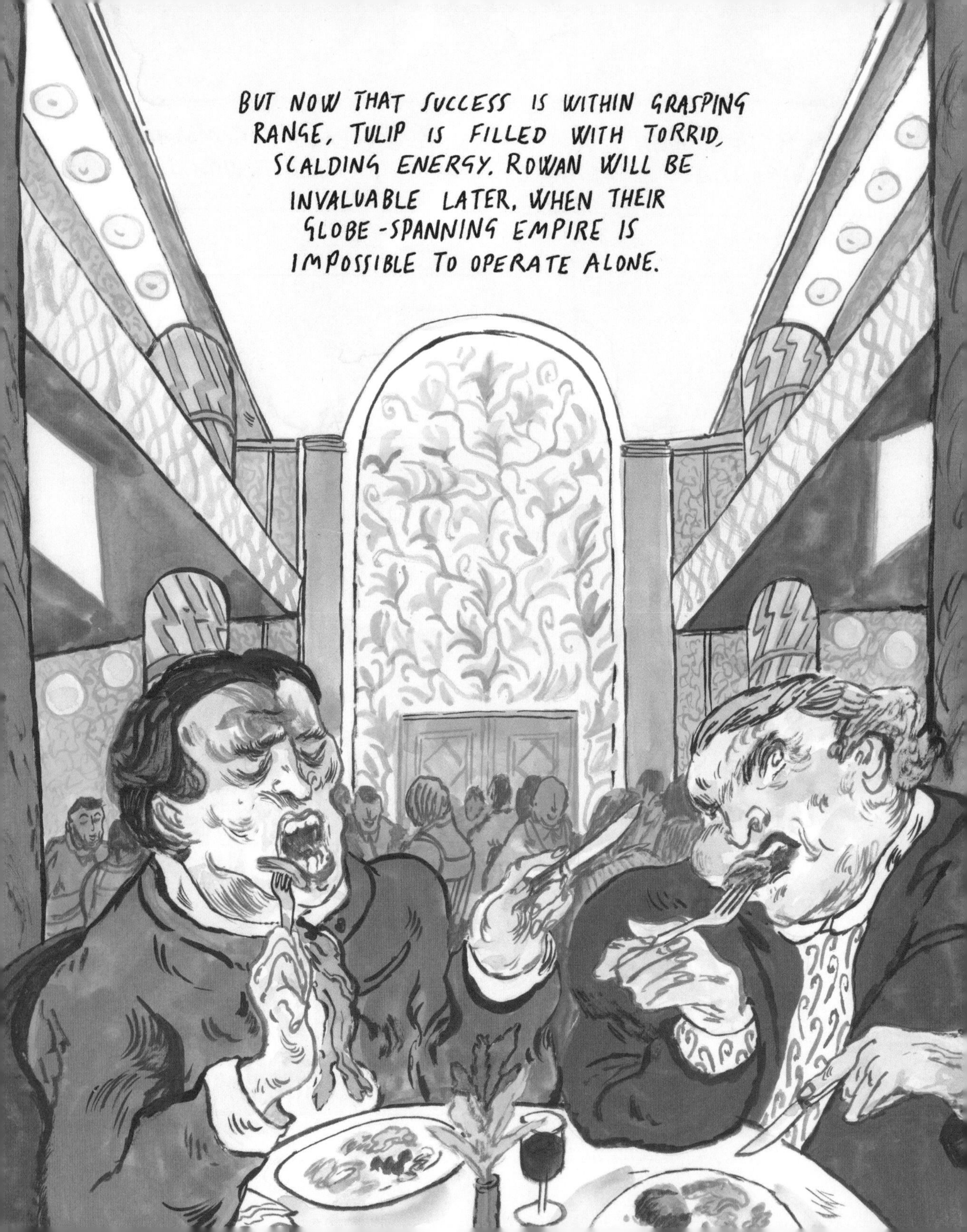
BUT NOW THAT SUCCESS IS WITHIN GRASPING RANGE, TULIP IS FILLED WITH TORRID, SCALDING ENERGY. ROWAN WILL BE INVALUABLE LATER, WHEN THEIR GLOBE-SPANNING EMPIRE IS IMPOSSIBLE TO OPERATE ALONE.

BUT FOR NOW, TULIP MUST SOW THE FIRST SEEDS. NO MOMENT CAN BE WASTED.

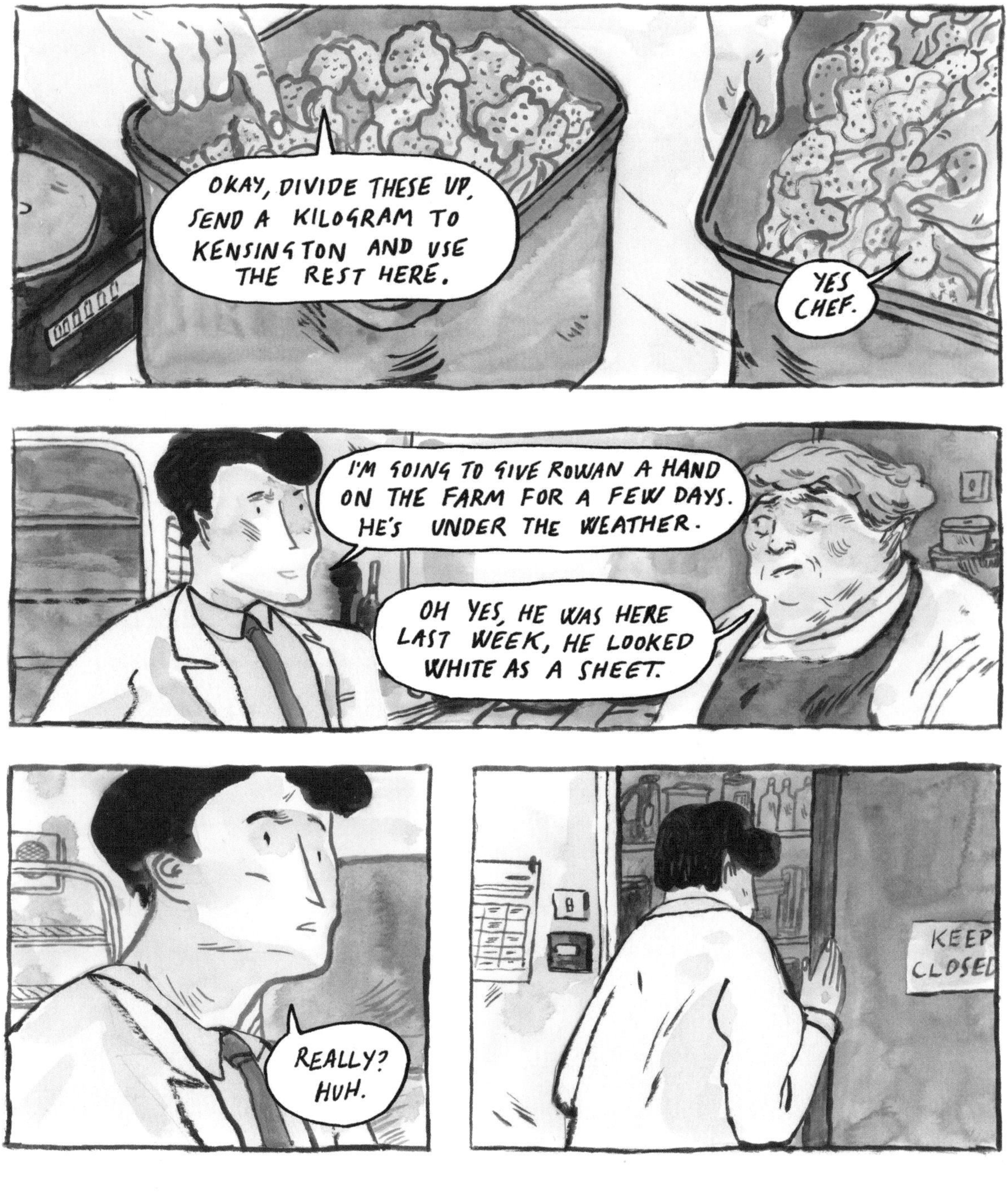
OKAY, DIVIDE THESE UP, SEND A KILOGRAM TO KENSINGTON AND USE THE REST HERE.
YES CHEF.
I'M GOING TO GIVE ROWAN A HAND ON THE FARM FOR A FEW DAYS. HE'S UNDER THE WEATHER.
OH YES, HE WAS HERE LAST WEEK, HE LOOKED WHITE AS A SHEET.
REALLY? HUH.
KEEP CLOSED

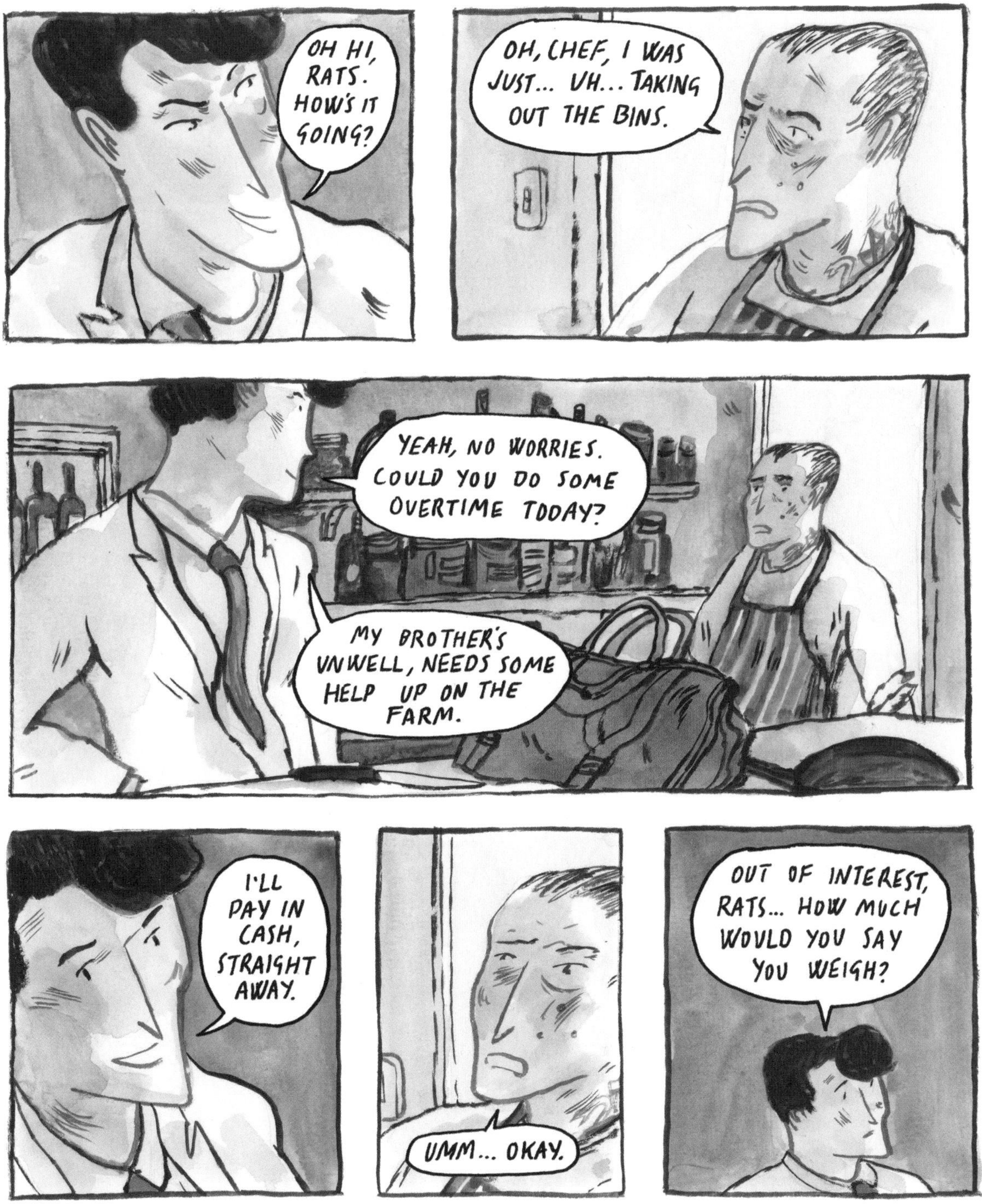
OH HI, RATS. HOW'S IT GOING?
OH, CHEF, I WAS JUST... UH... TAKING OUT THE BINS.
YEAH, NO WORRIES. COULD YOU DO SOME OVERTIME TODAY?
MY BROTHER'S UNWELL, NEEDS SOME HELP UP ON THE FARM.
I'LL PAY IN CASH, STRAIGHT AWAY.
UMM... OKAY.
OUT OF INTEREST, RATS... HOW MUCH WOULD YOU SAY YOU WEIGH?

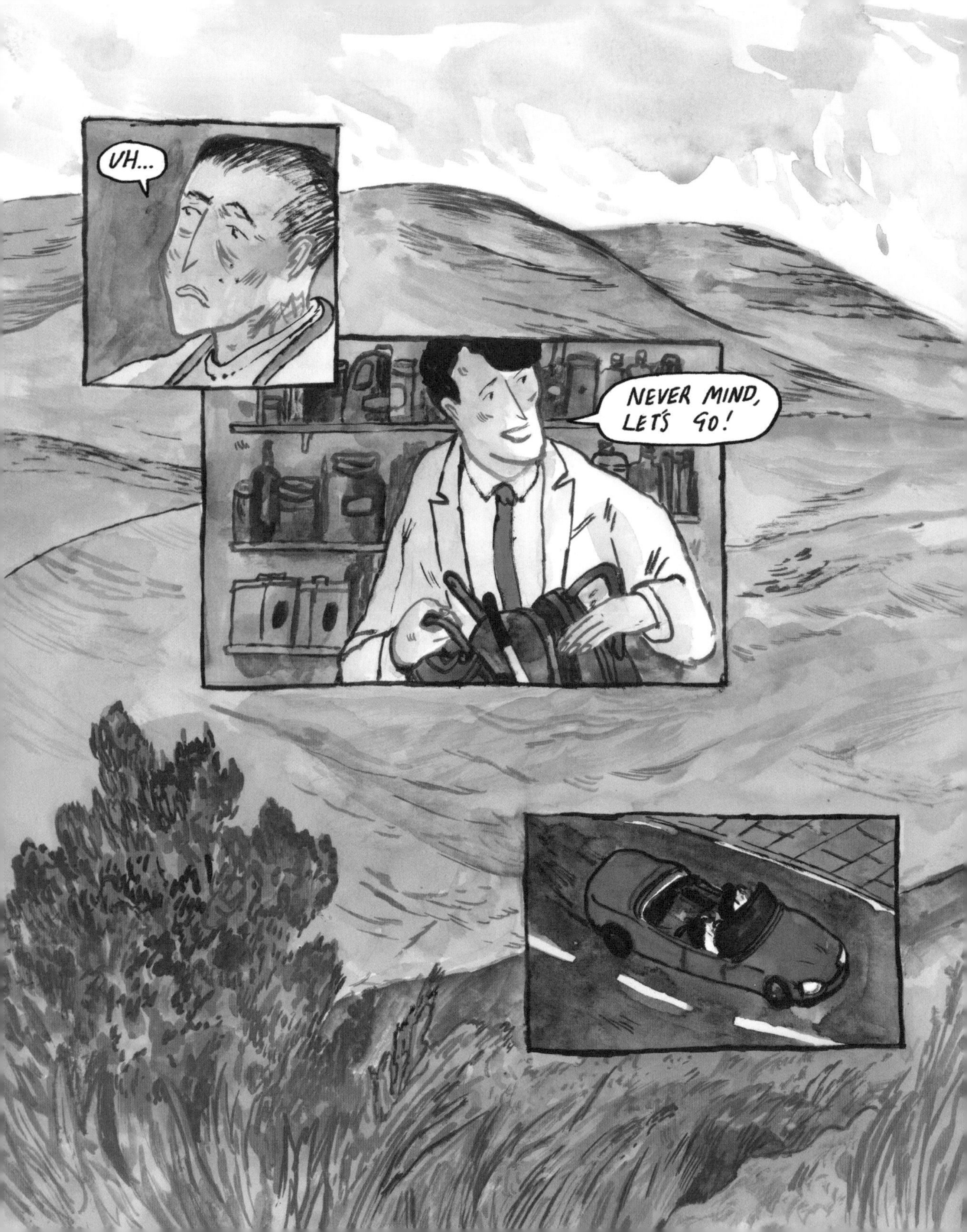
UH...
NEVER MIND, LET'S GO!

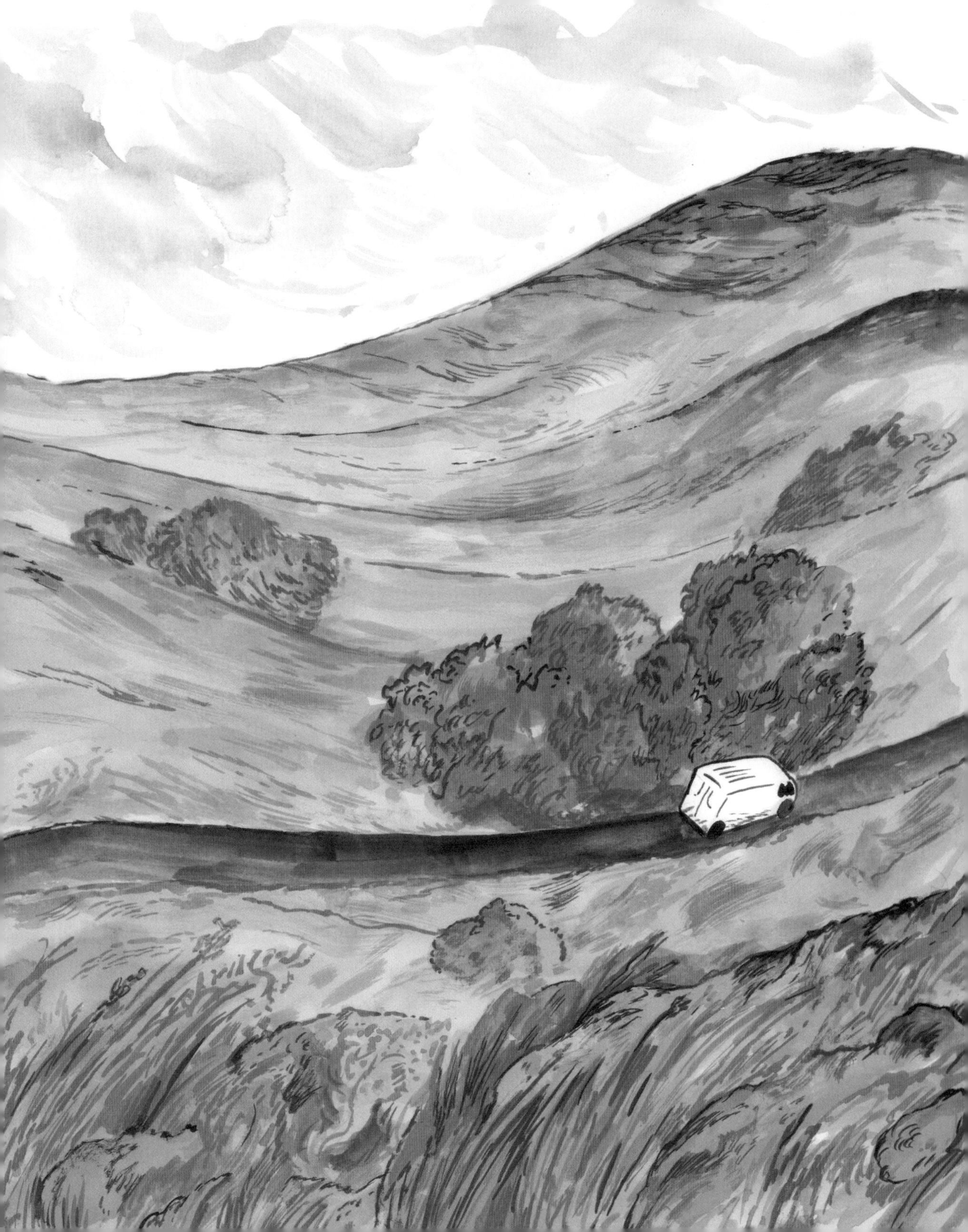

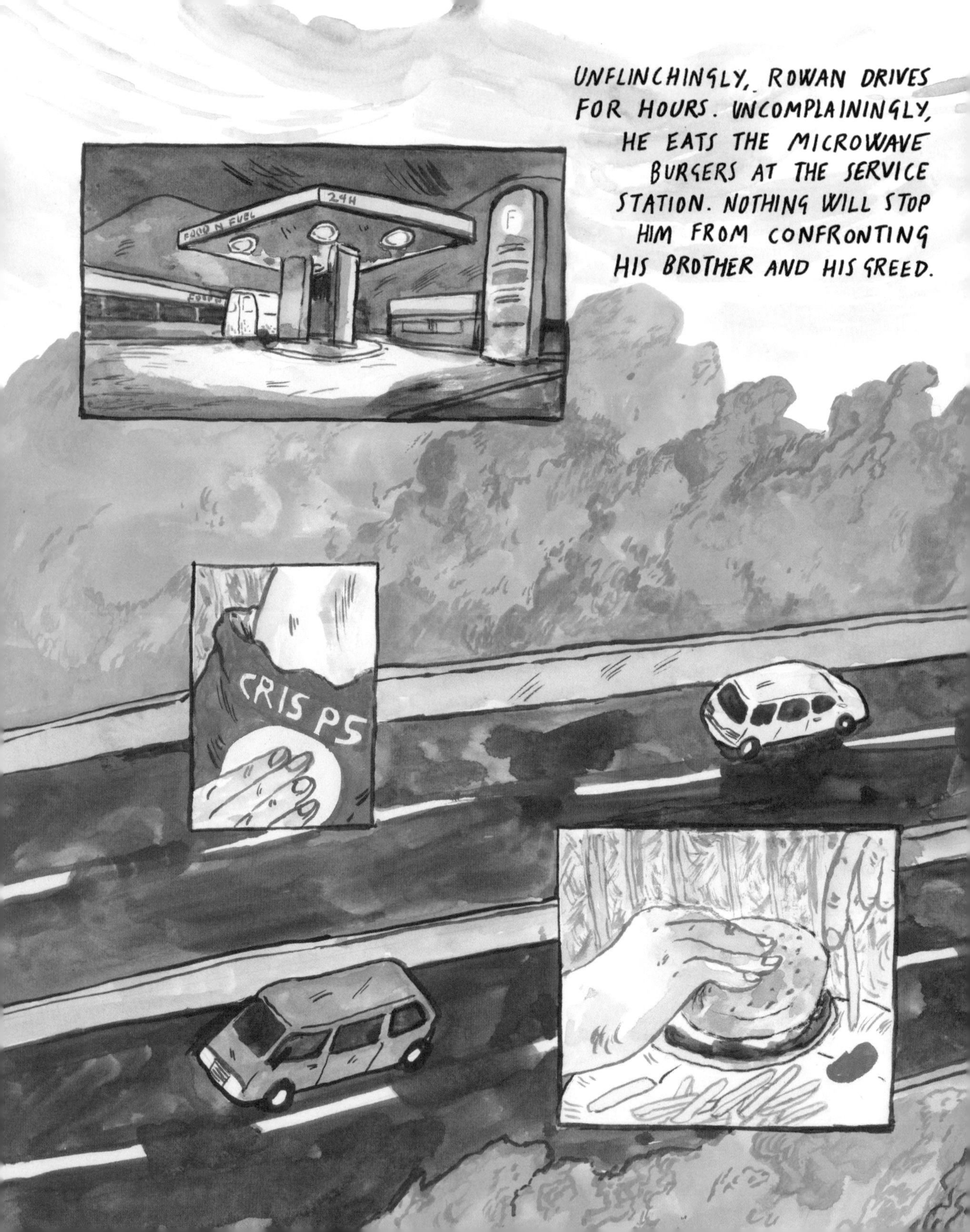
UNFLINCHINGLY, ROWAN DRIVES FOR HOURS. UNCOMPLAININGLY, HE EATS THE MICROWAVE BURGERS AT THE SERVICE STATION. NOTHING WILL STOP HIM FROM CONFRONTING HIS BROTHER AND HIS GREED.
FOOD N FUEL
24H
F
CRISPS

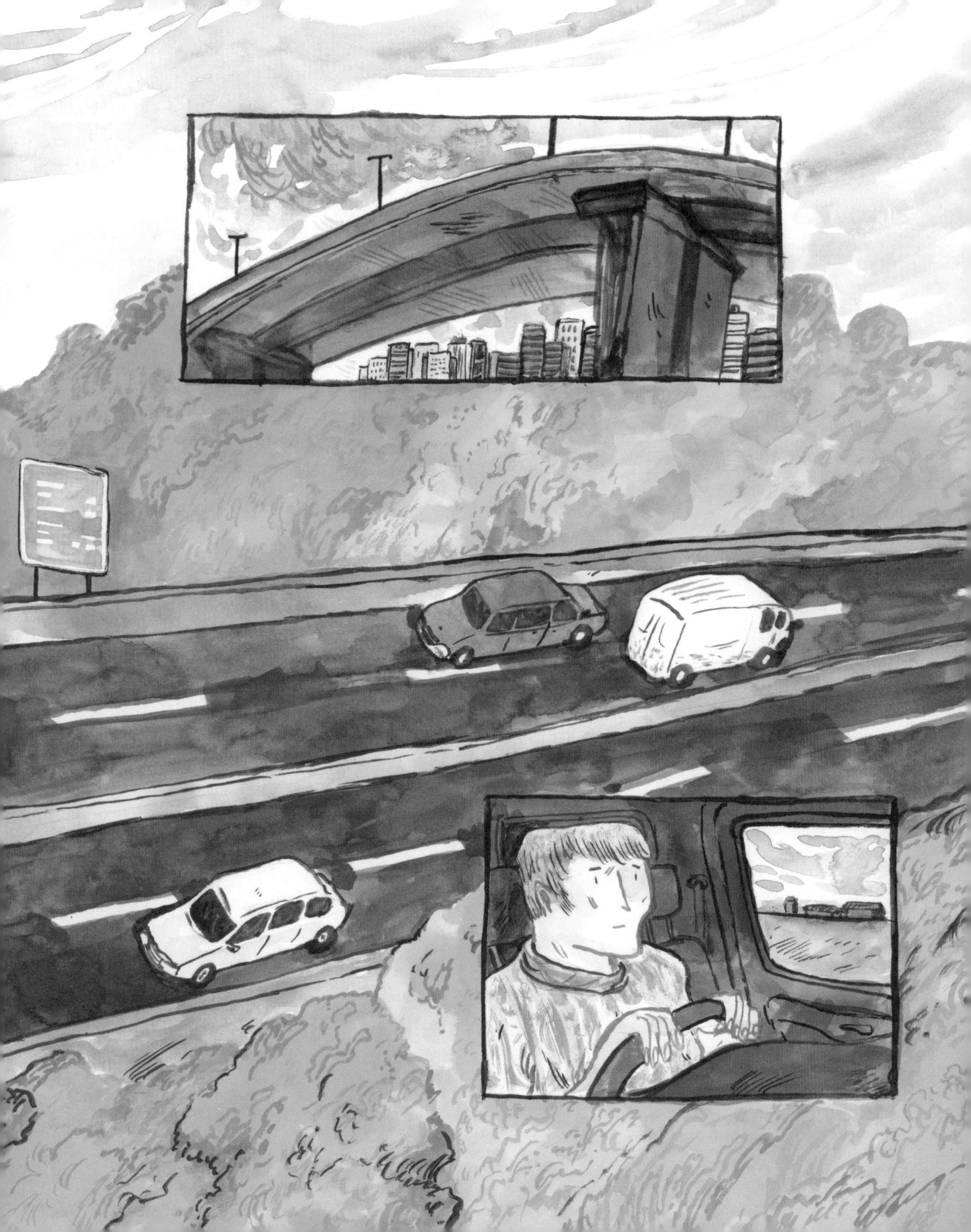

ALREADY, AMONGST THE DISTURBED SOIL, FRESH SHOOTS ARE APPEARING. THE CROPS STRETCH TOWARDS THE SUN. ROWAN IS ENVELOPED BY THEIR HEADY SCENT. NOTHING COULD BE MORE INSPIRING THAN THIS. HE STRETCHES OUT HIS OWN BODY AND TAKES GRATEFUL GULPS OF FRESH AIR.

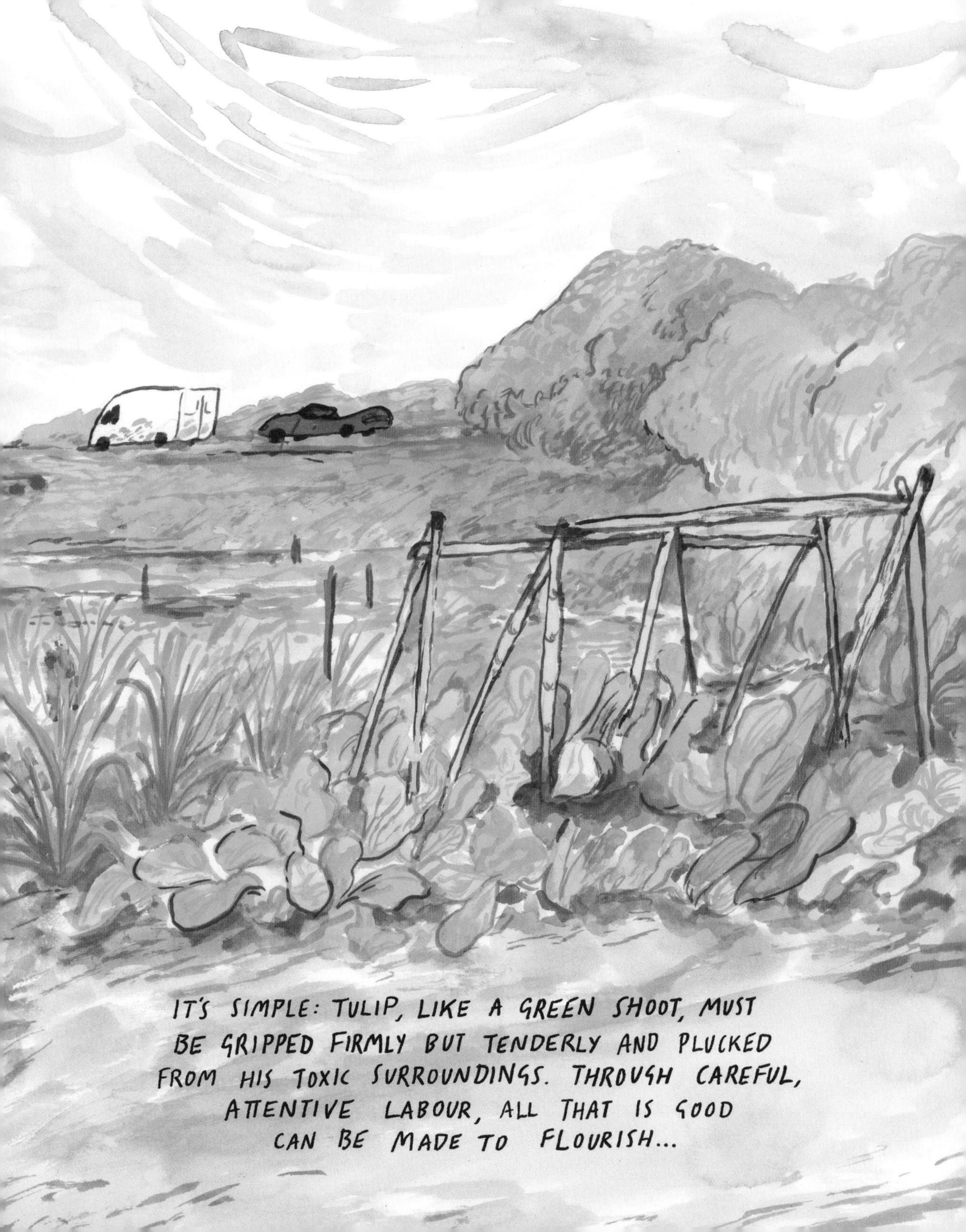
IT'S SIMPLE: TULIP, LIKE A GREEN SHOOT, MUST BE GRIPPED FIRMLY BUT TENDERLY AND PLUCKED FROM HIS TOXIC SURROUNDINGS. THROUGH CAREFUL, ATTENTIVE LABOUR, ALL THAT IS GOOD CAN BE MADE TO FLOURISH...

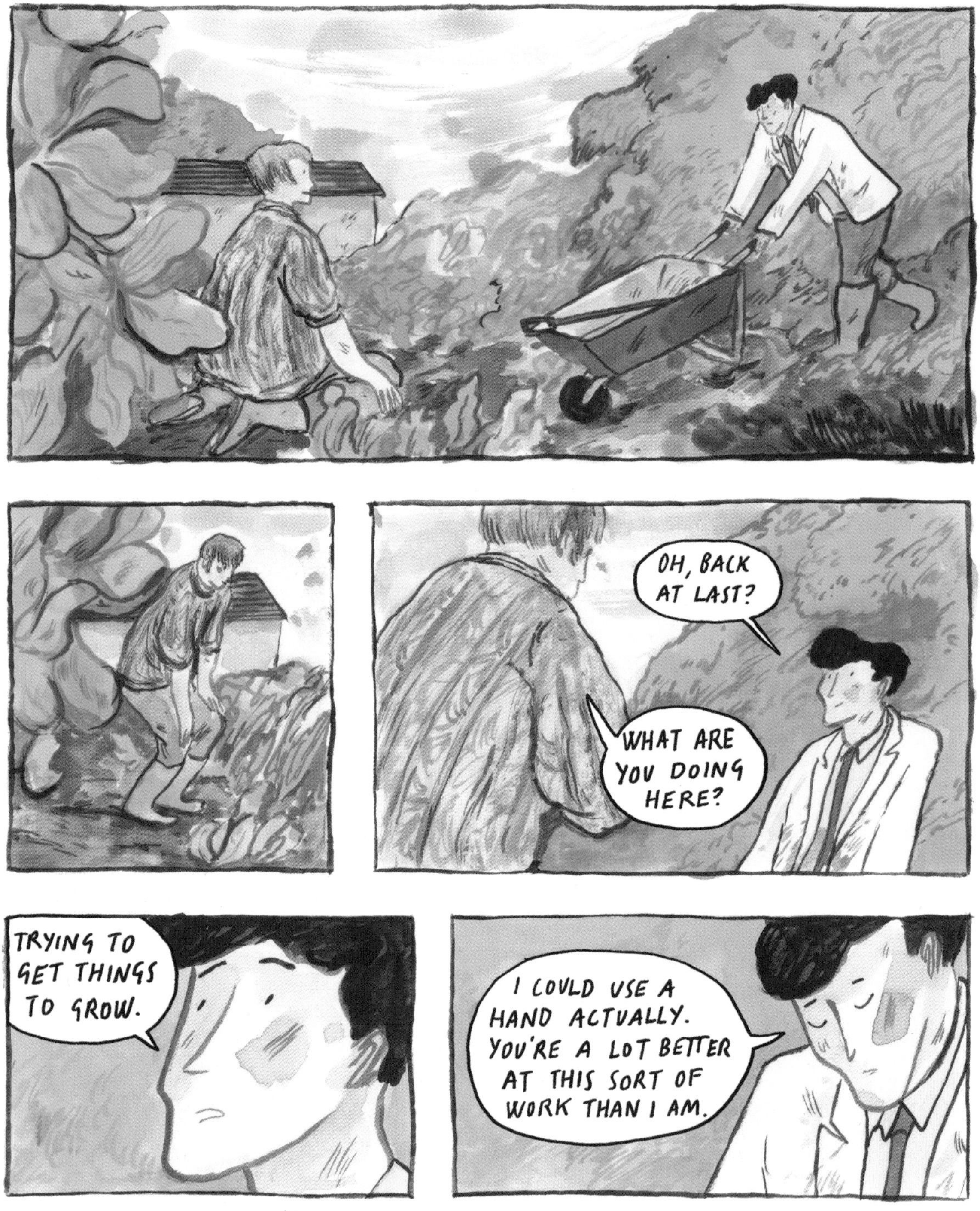
OH, BACK AT LAST?
WHAT ARE YOU DOING HERE?
TRYING TO GET THINGS TO GROW.
I COULD USE A HAND ACTUALLY. YOU'RE A LOT BETTER AT THIS SORT OF WORK THAN I AM.

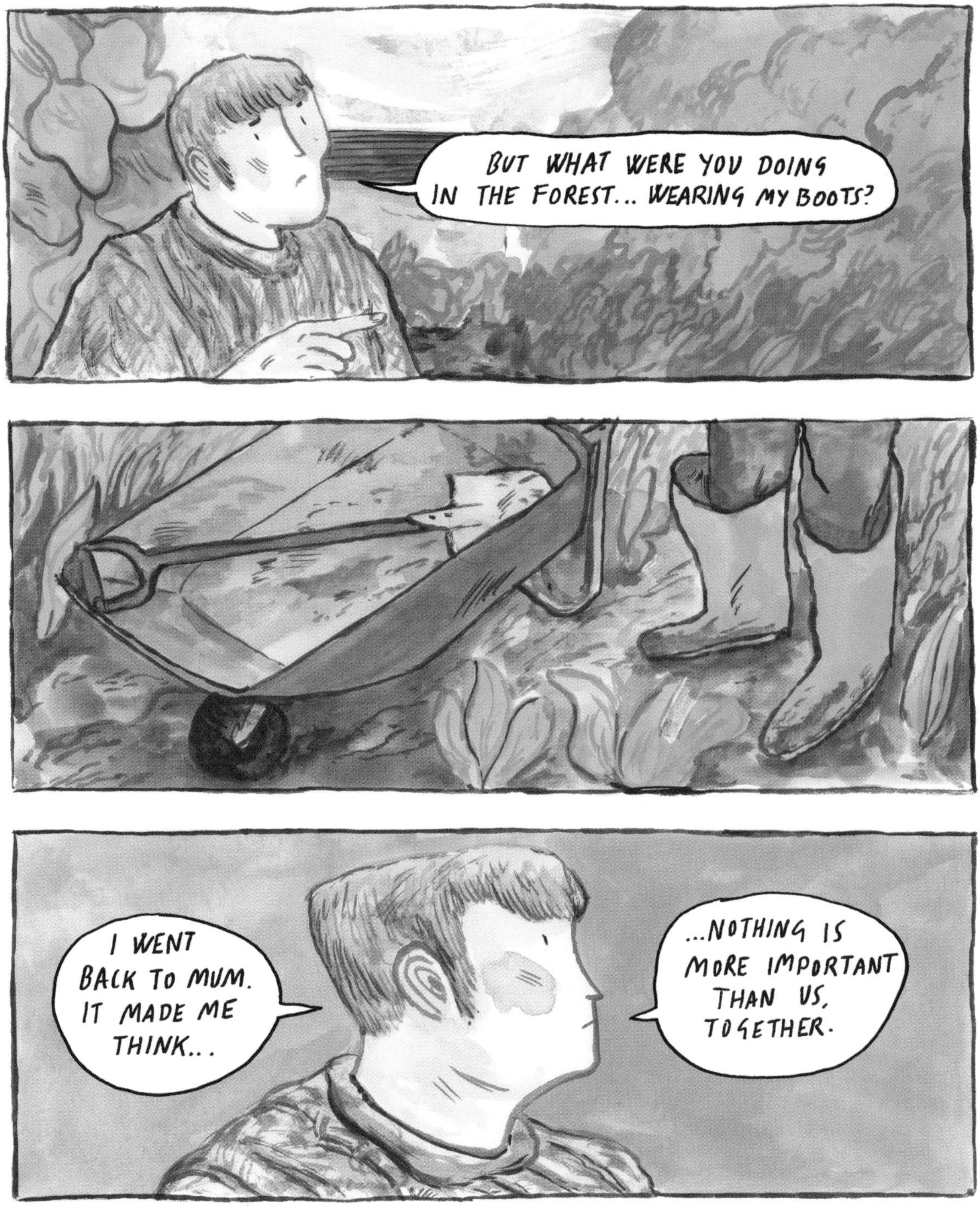
BUT WHAT WERE YOU DOING IN THE FOREST... WEARING MY BOOTS?
I WENT BACK TO MUM. IT MADE ME THINK...
...NOTHING IS MORE IMPORTANT THAN US, TOGETHER.

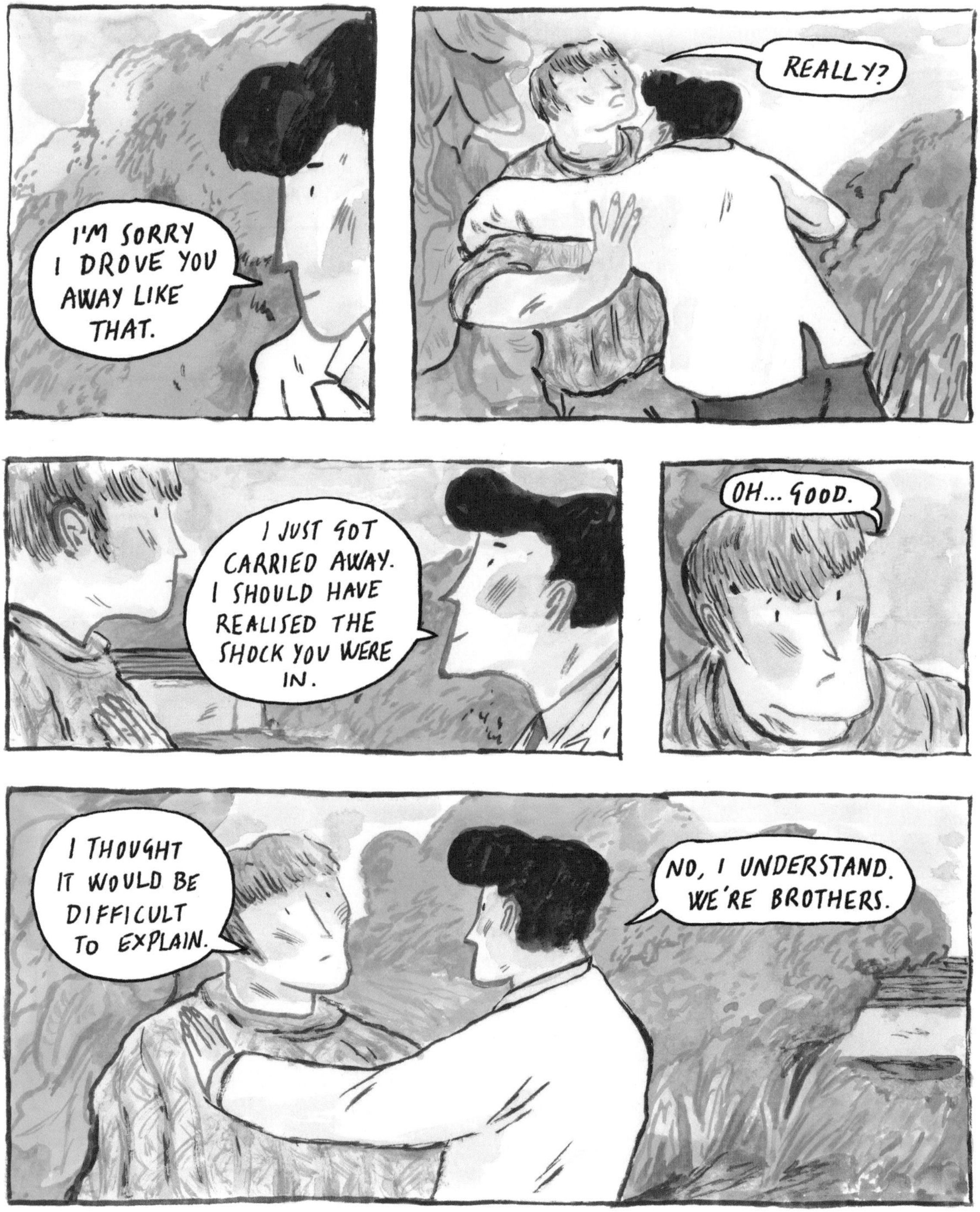
I'M SORRY I DROVE YOU AWAY LIKE THAT.
REALLY?
I JUST GOT CARRIED AWAY. I SHOULD HAVE REALISED THE SHOCK YOU WERE IN.
OH... GOOD.
I THOUGHT IT WOULD BE DIFFICULT TO EXPLAIN.
NO, I UNDERSTAND. WE'RE BROTHERS.

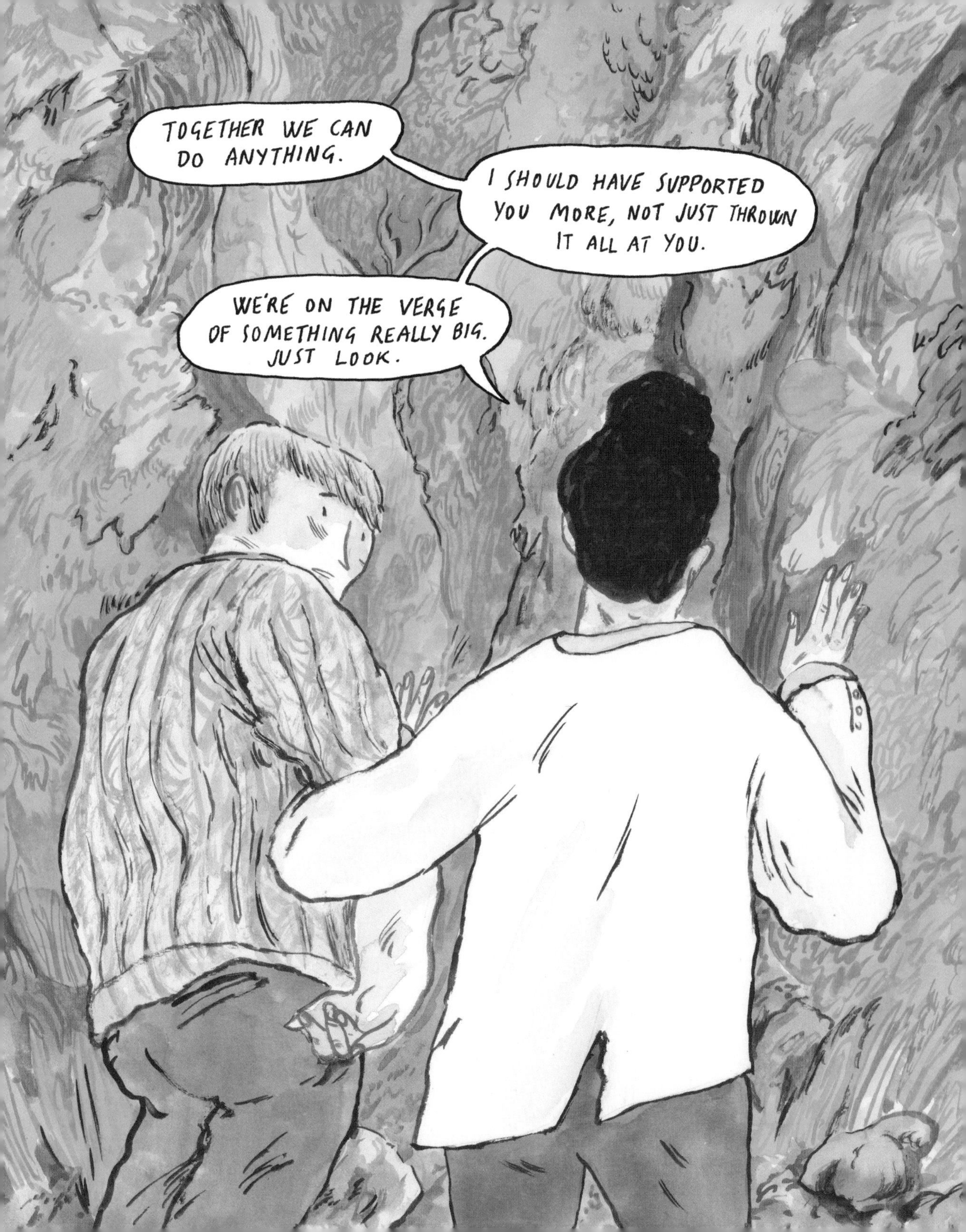
TOGETHER WE CAN DO ANYTHING.
I SHOULD HAVE SUPPORTED YOU MORE, NOT JUST THROWN IT ALL AT YOU.
WE'RE ON THE VERGE OF SOMETHING REALLY BIG. JUST LOOK.

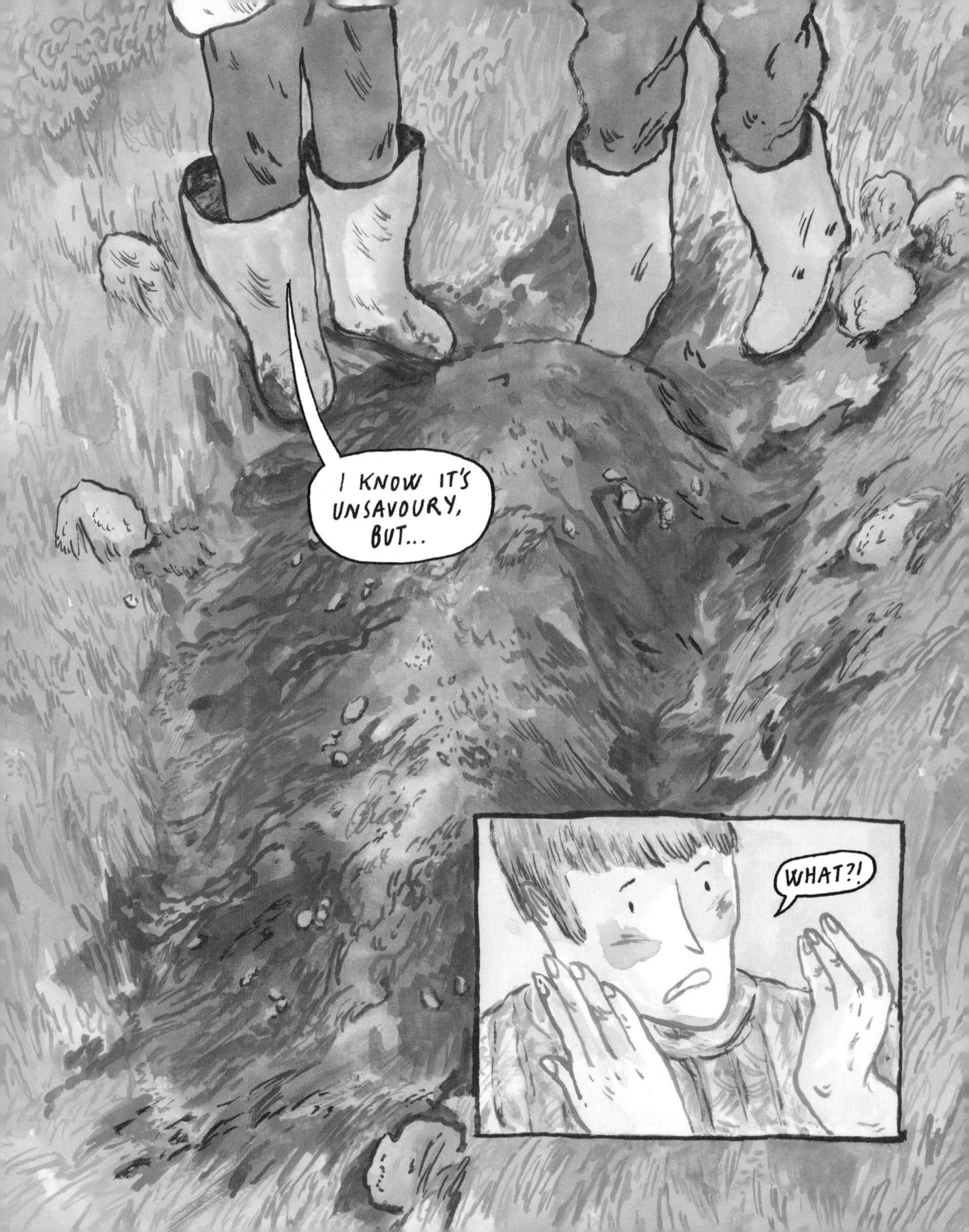
I KNOW IT'S UNSAVOURY, BUT...
WHAT?!

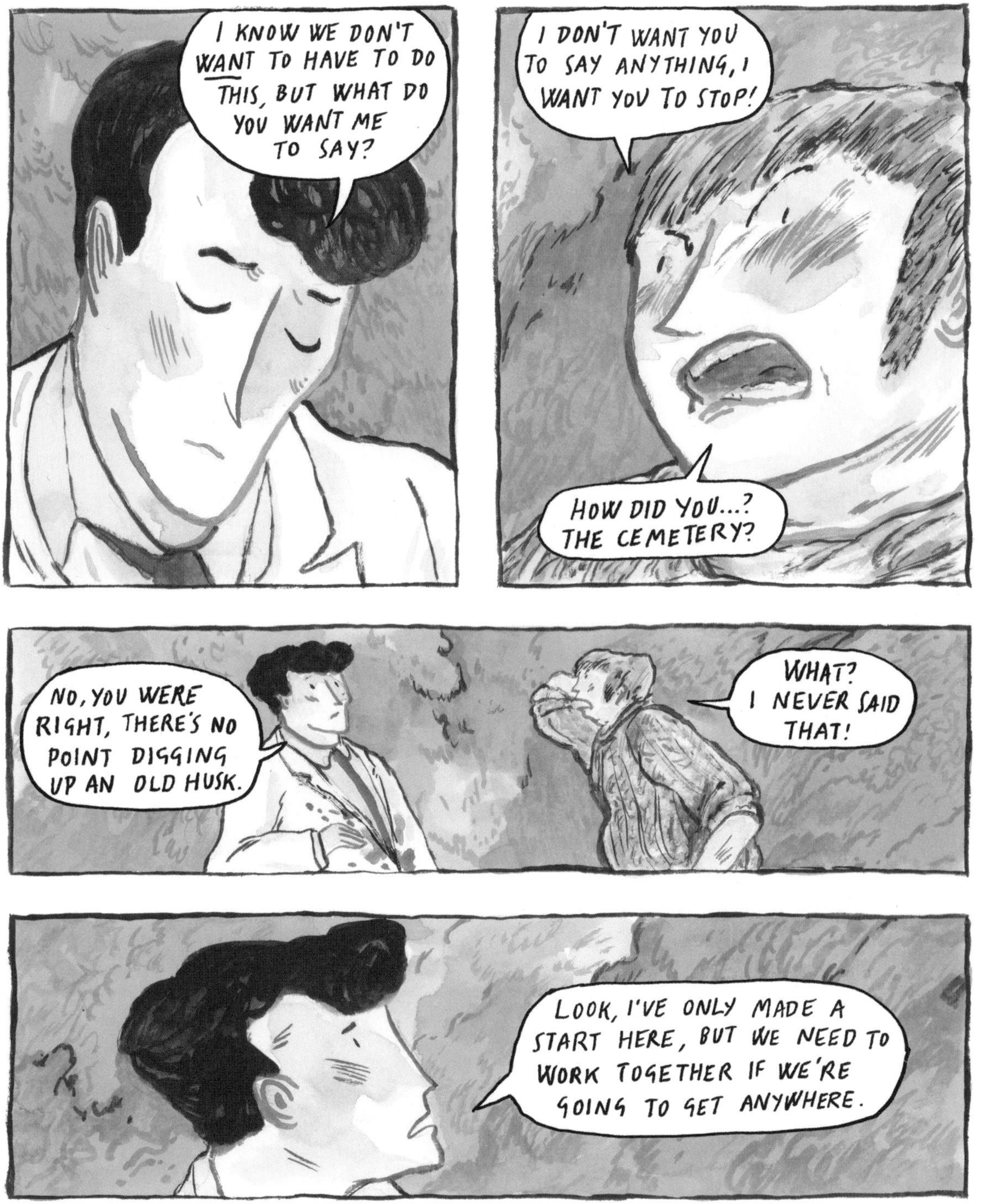
I KNOW WE DON'T WANT TO HAVE TO DO THIS, BUT WHAT DO YOU WANT ME TO SAY?
I DON'T WANT YOU TO SAY ANYTHING, I WANT YOU TO STOP!
HOW DID YOU...? THE CEMETERY?
NO, YOU WERE RIGHT, THERE'S NO POINT DIGGING UP AN OLD HUSK.
WHAT? I NEVER SAID THAT!
LOOK, I'VE ONLY MADE A START HERE, BUT WE NEED TO WORK TOGETHER IF WE'RE GOING TO GET ANYWHERE.

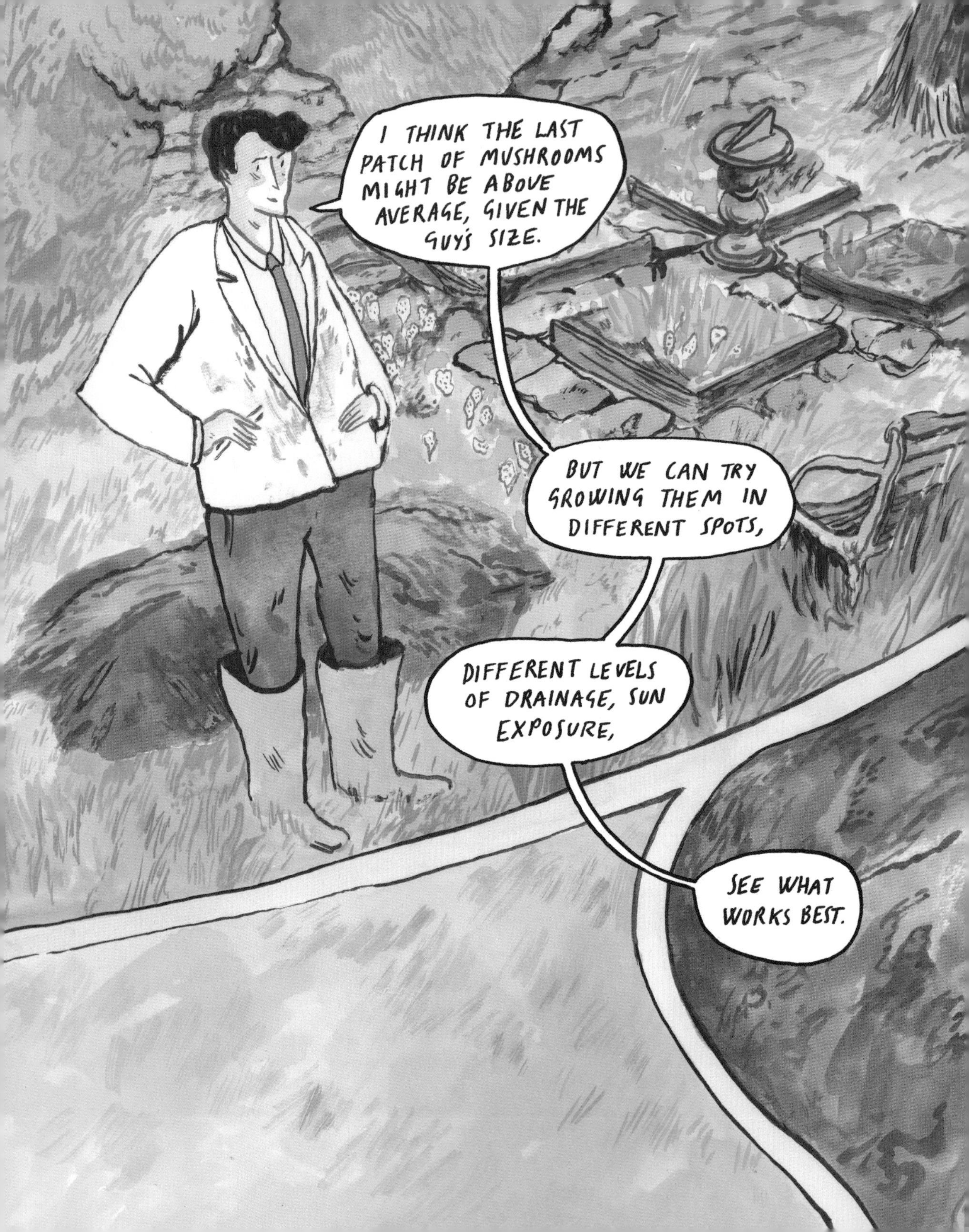
I THINK THE LAST PATCH OF MUSHROOMS MIGHT BE ABOVE AVERAGE, GIVEN THE GUY'S SIZE.
BUT WE CAN TRY GROWING THEM IN DIFFERENT SPOTS,
DIFFERENT LEVELS OF DRAINAGE, SUN EXPOSURE,
SEE WHAT WORKS BEST.

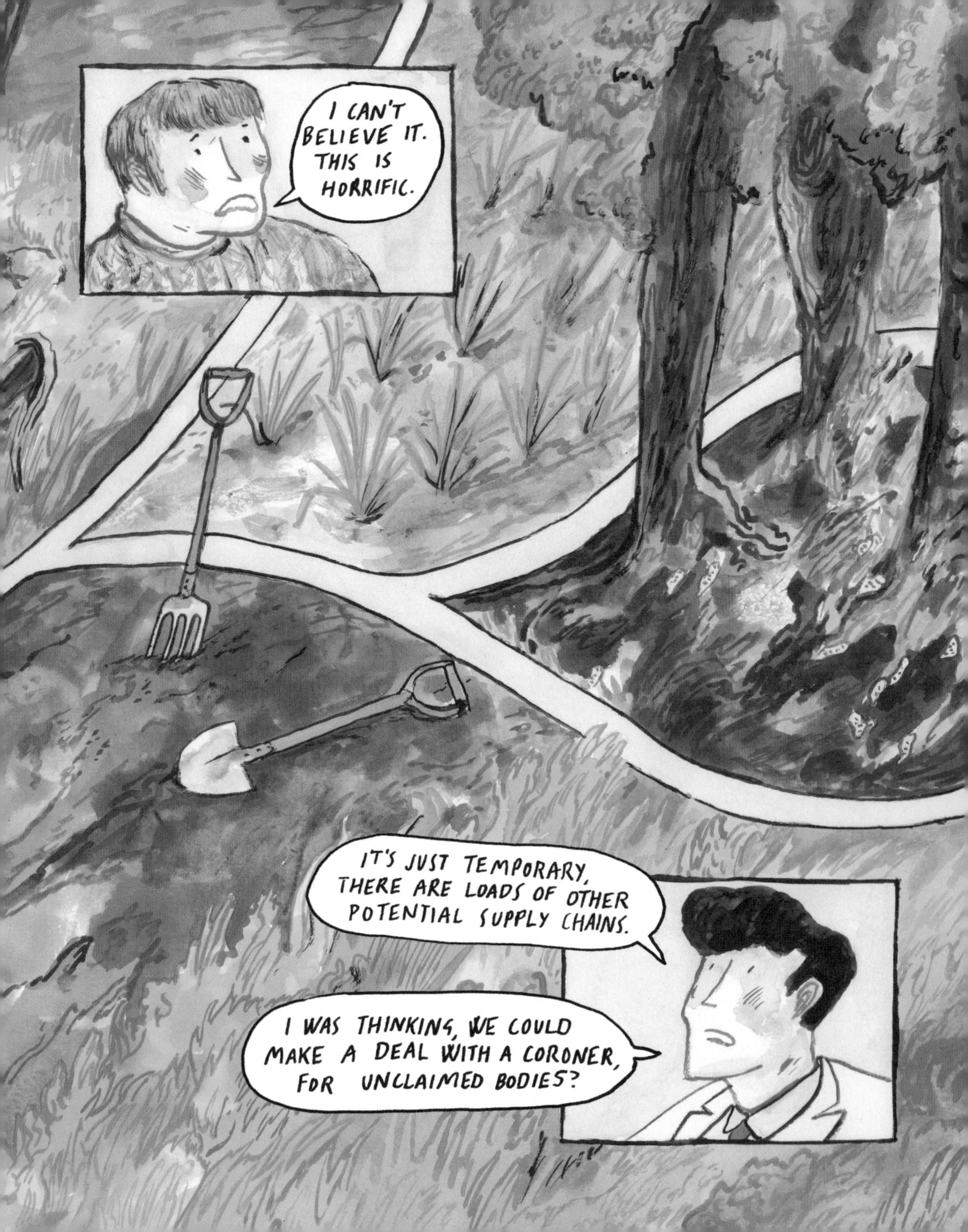
I CAN'T BELIEVE IT. THIS IS HORRIFIC.
IT'S JUST TEMPORARY, THERE ARE LOADS OF OTHER POTENTIAL SUPPLY CHAINS.
I WAS THINKING, WE COULD MAKE A DEAL WITH A CORONER, FOR UNCLAIMED BODIES?

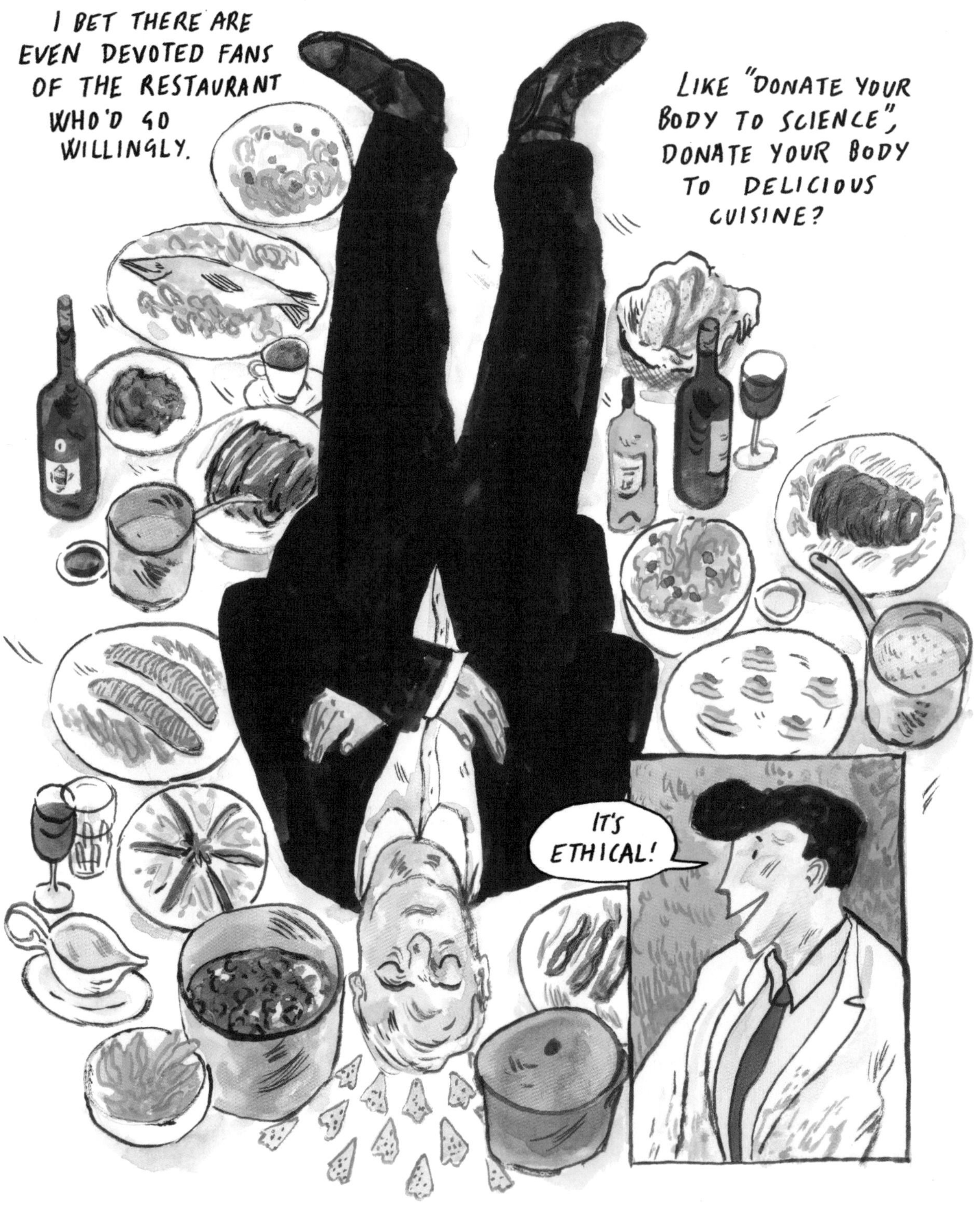
I BET THERE ARE EVEN DEVOTED FANS OF THE RESTAURANT WHO'D GO WILLINGLY.
LIKE "DONATE YOUR BODY TO SCIENCE", DONATE YOUR BODY TO DELICIOUS CUISINE?
IT'S ETHICAL!

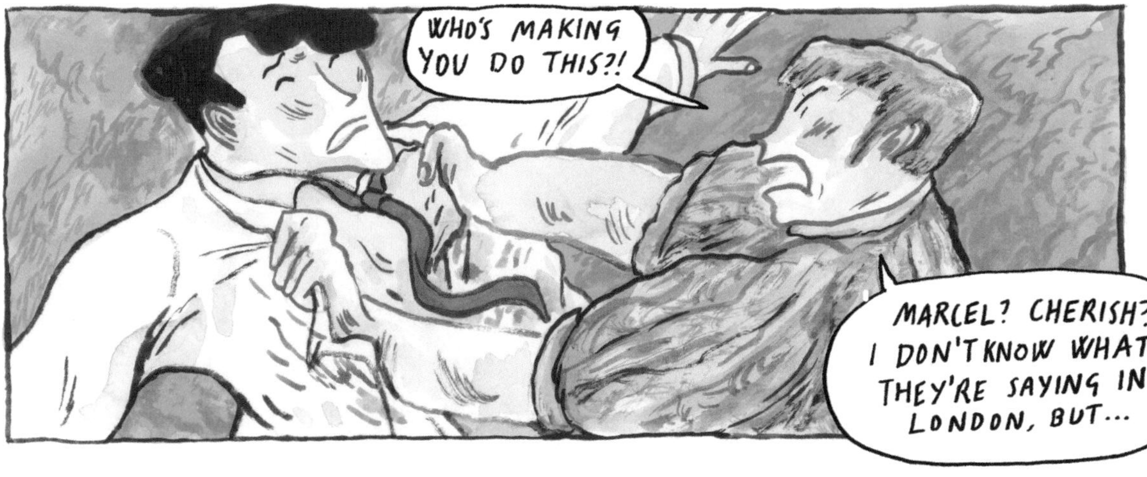
WHO'S MAKING YOU DO THIS?!
MARCEL? CHERISH? I DON'T KNOW WHAT THEY'RE SAYING IN LONDON, BUT...

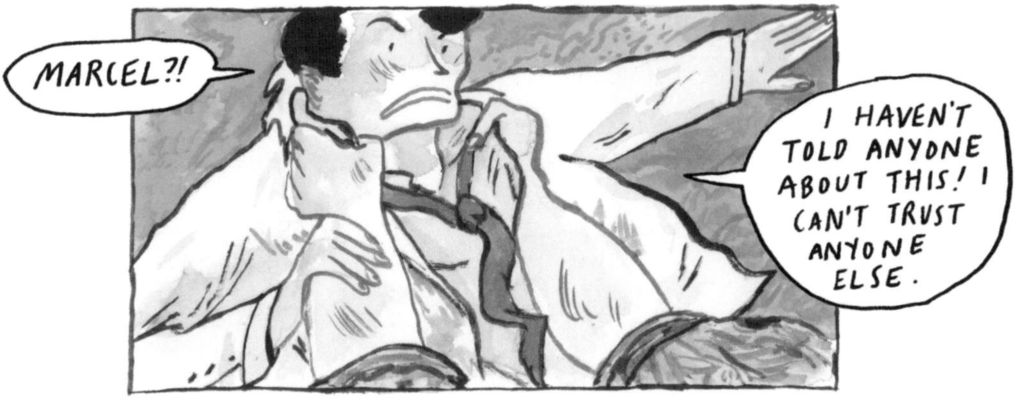
MARCEL?!
I HAVEN'T TOLD ANYONE ABOUT THIS! I CAN'T TRUST ANYONE ELSE.

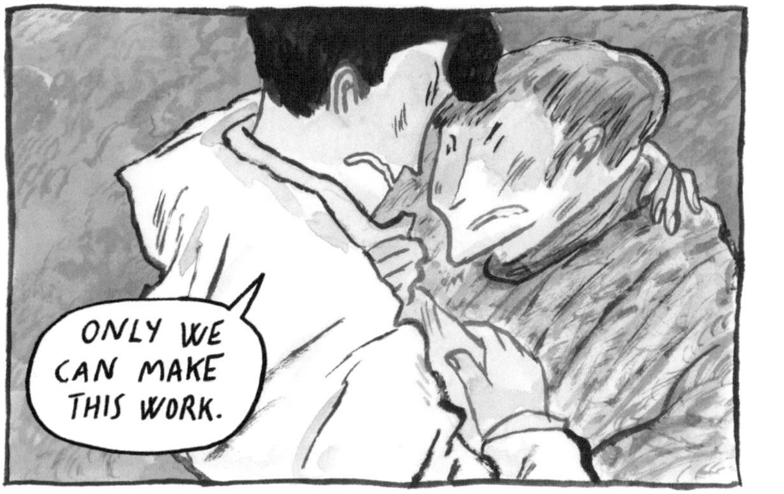
ONLY WE CAN MAKE THIS WORK.

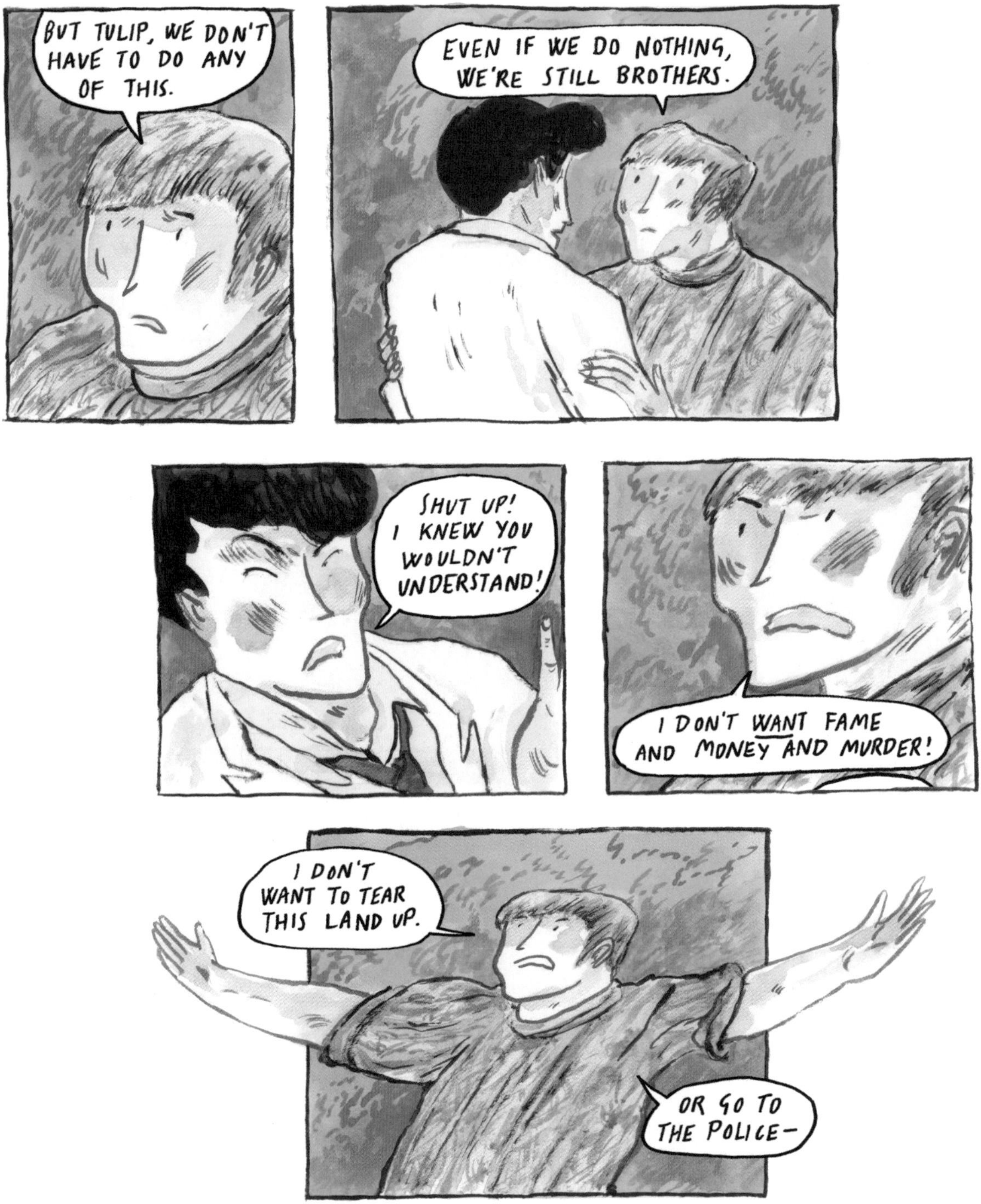
BUT TULIP, WE DON'T HAVE TO DO ANY OF THIS.
EVEN IF WE DO NOTHING, WE'RE STILL BROTHERS.
SHUT UP! I KNEW YOU WOULDN'T UNDERSTAND!
I DON'T WANT FAME AND MONEY AND MURDER!
I DON'T WANT TO TEAR THIS LAND UP.
OR GO TO THE POLICE-

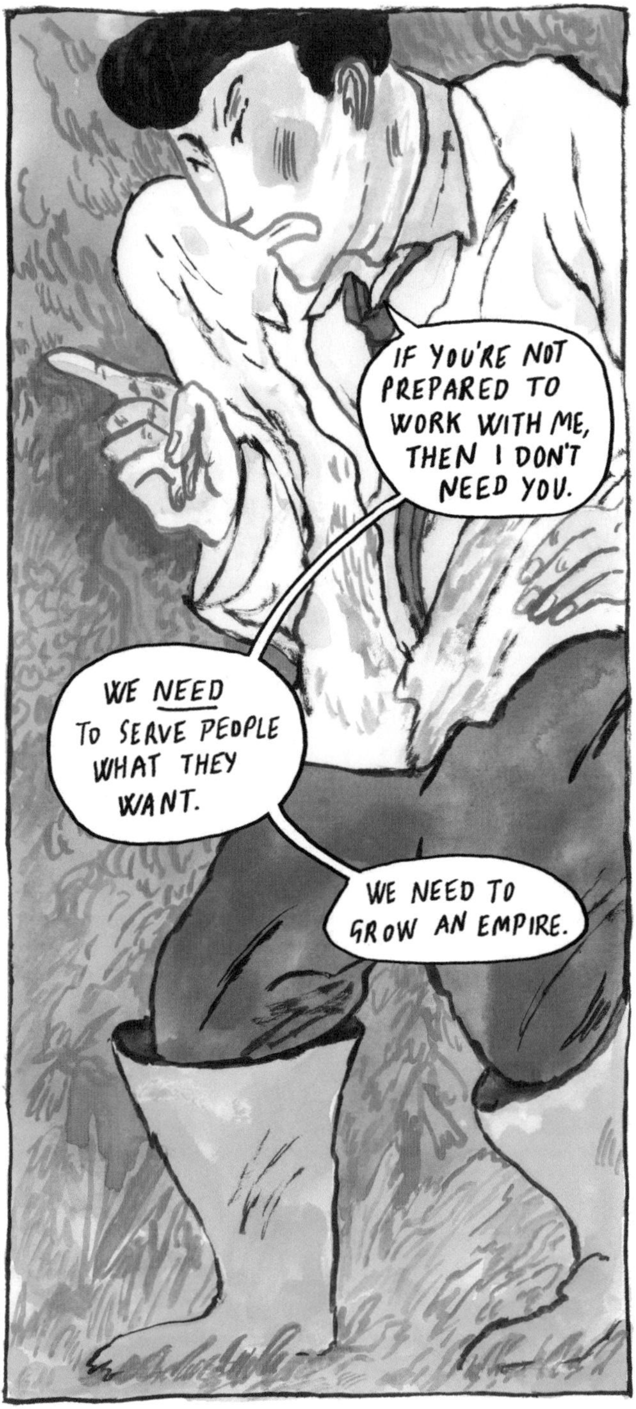
IF YOU'RE NOT PREPARED TO WORK WITH ME, THEN I DON'T NEED YOU.
WE NEED TO SERVE PEOPLE WHAT THEY WANT.
WE NEED TO GROW AN EMPIRE.

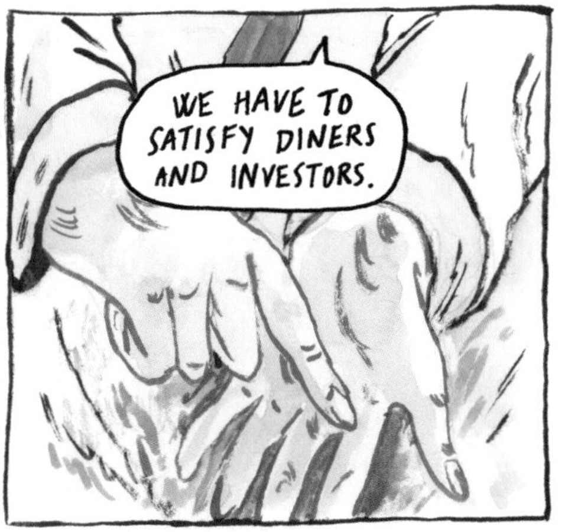
WE HAVE TO SATISFY DINERS AND INVESTORS.

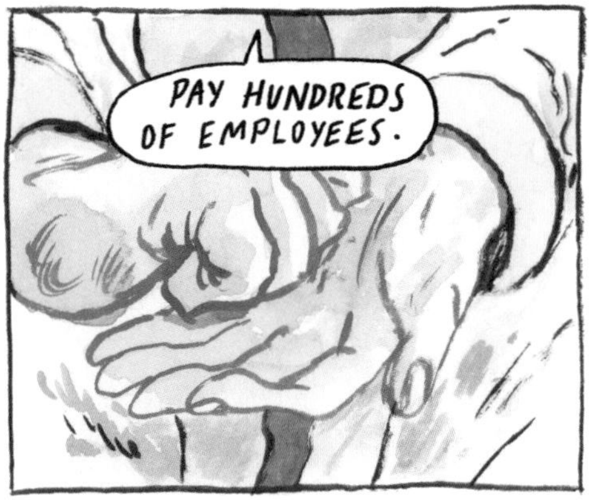
PAY HUNDREDS OF EMPLOYEES.

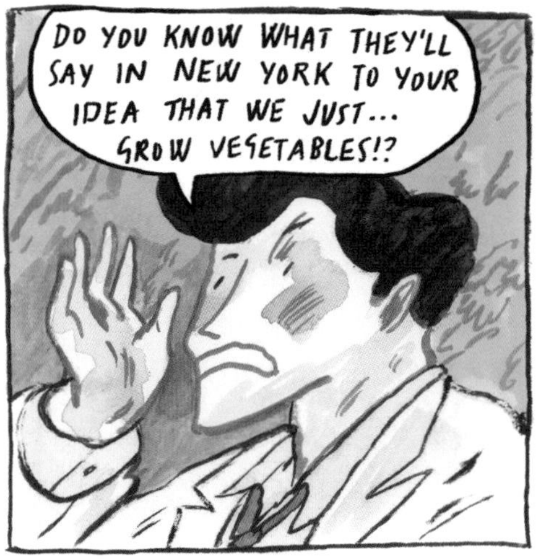
DO YOU KNOW WHAT THEY'LL SAY IN NEW YORK TO YOUR IDEA THAT WE JUST... GROW VEGETABLES!?

IF YOU DON'T LIKE IT, YOU CAN SOP IT UP ON THE ISLAND WITH MUM!
NO.
I'M PUTTING A STOP TO IT.

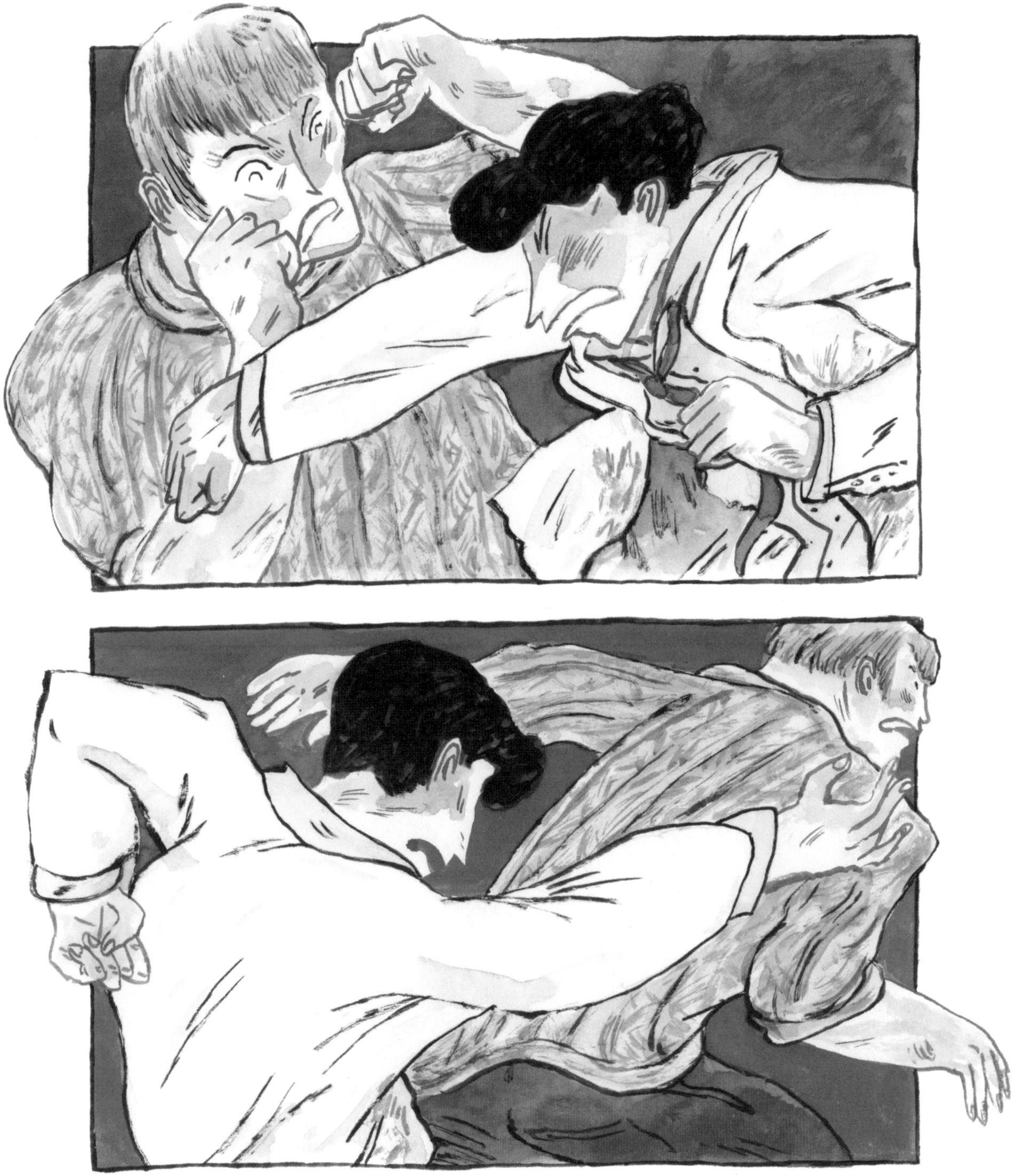

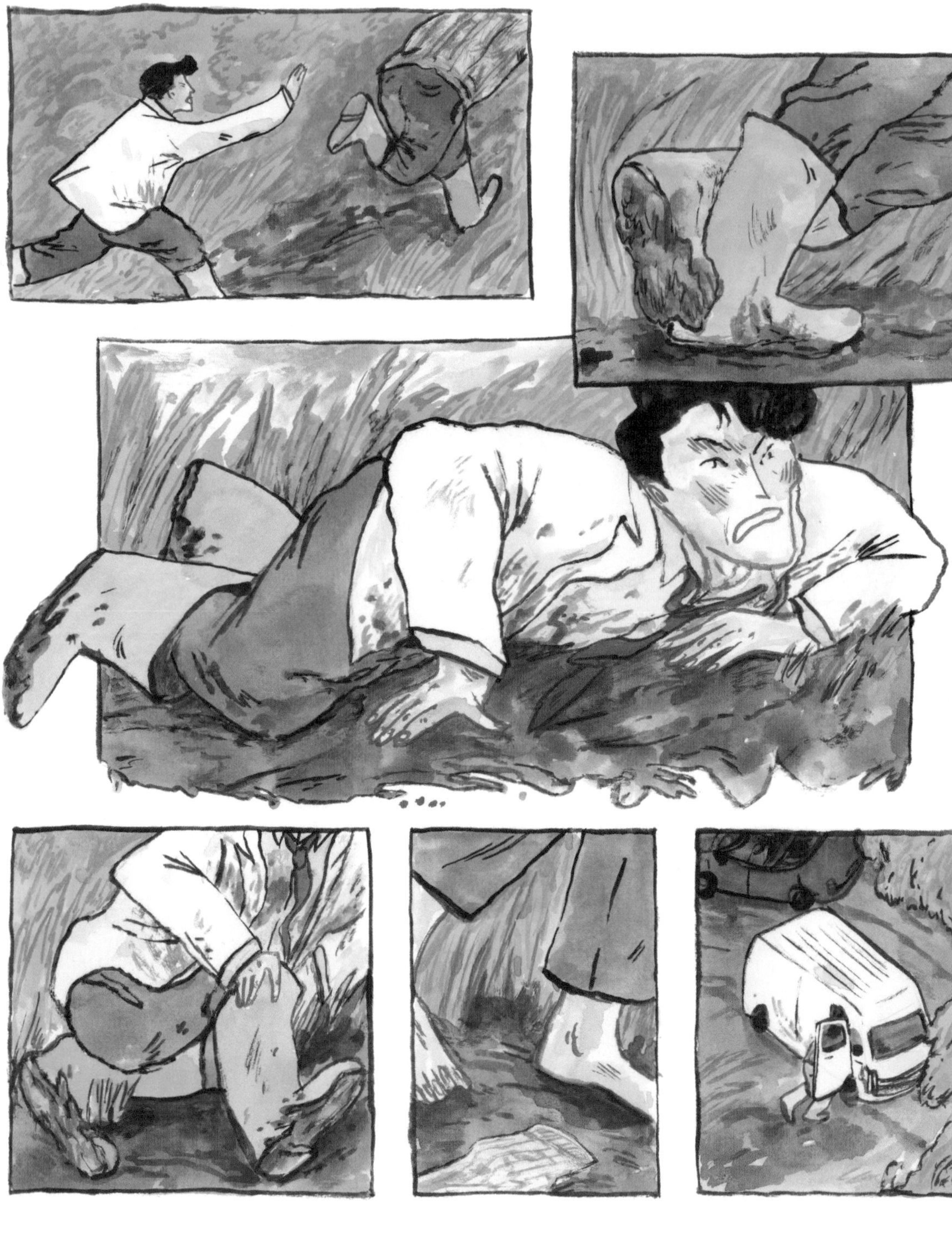

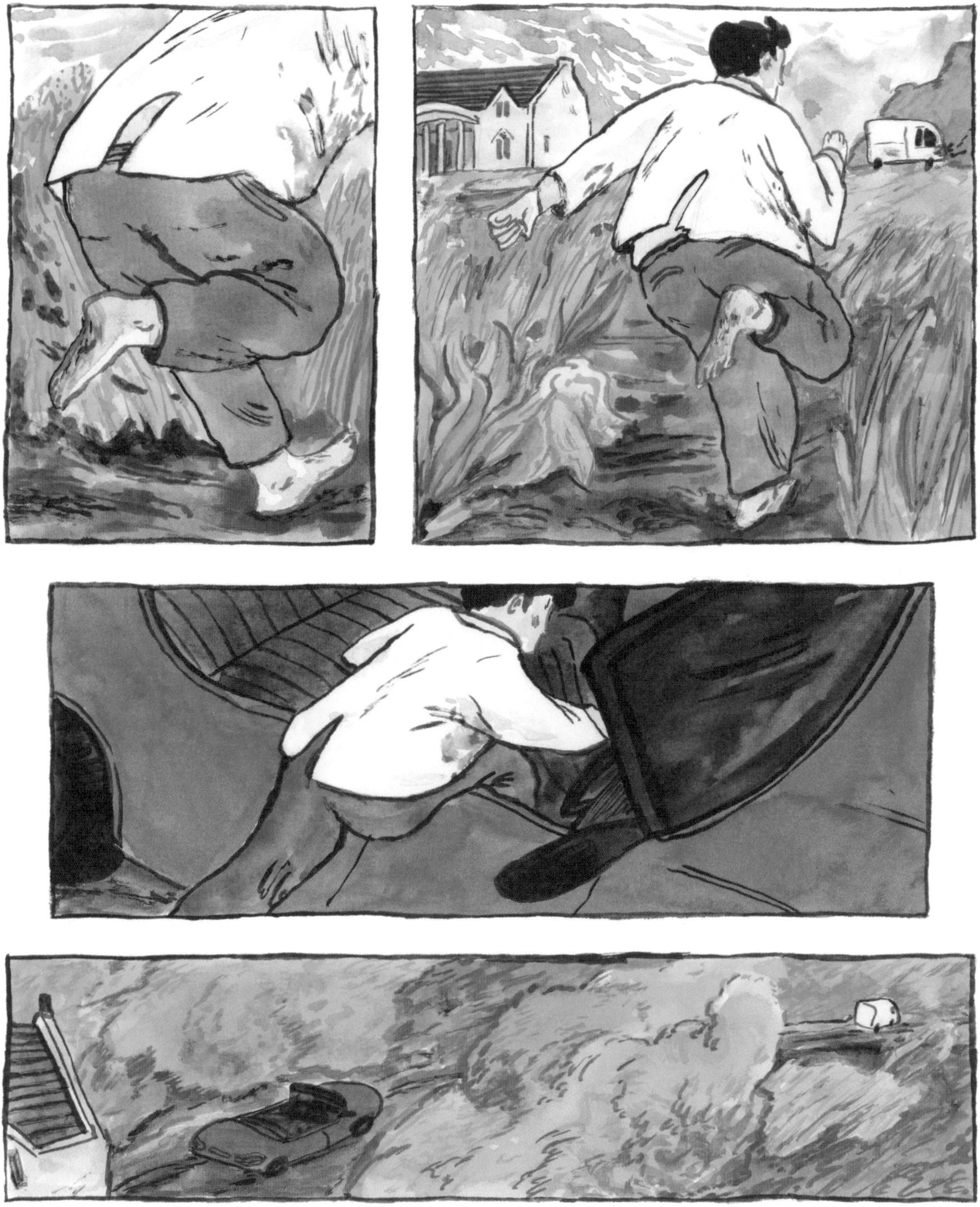

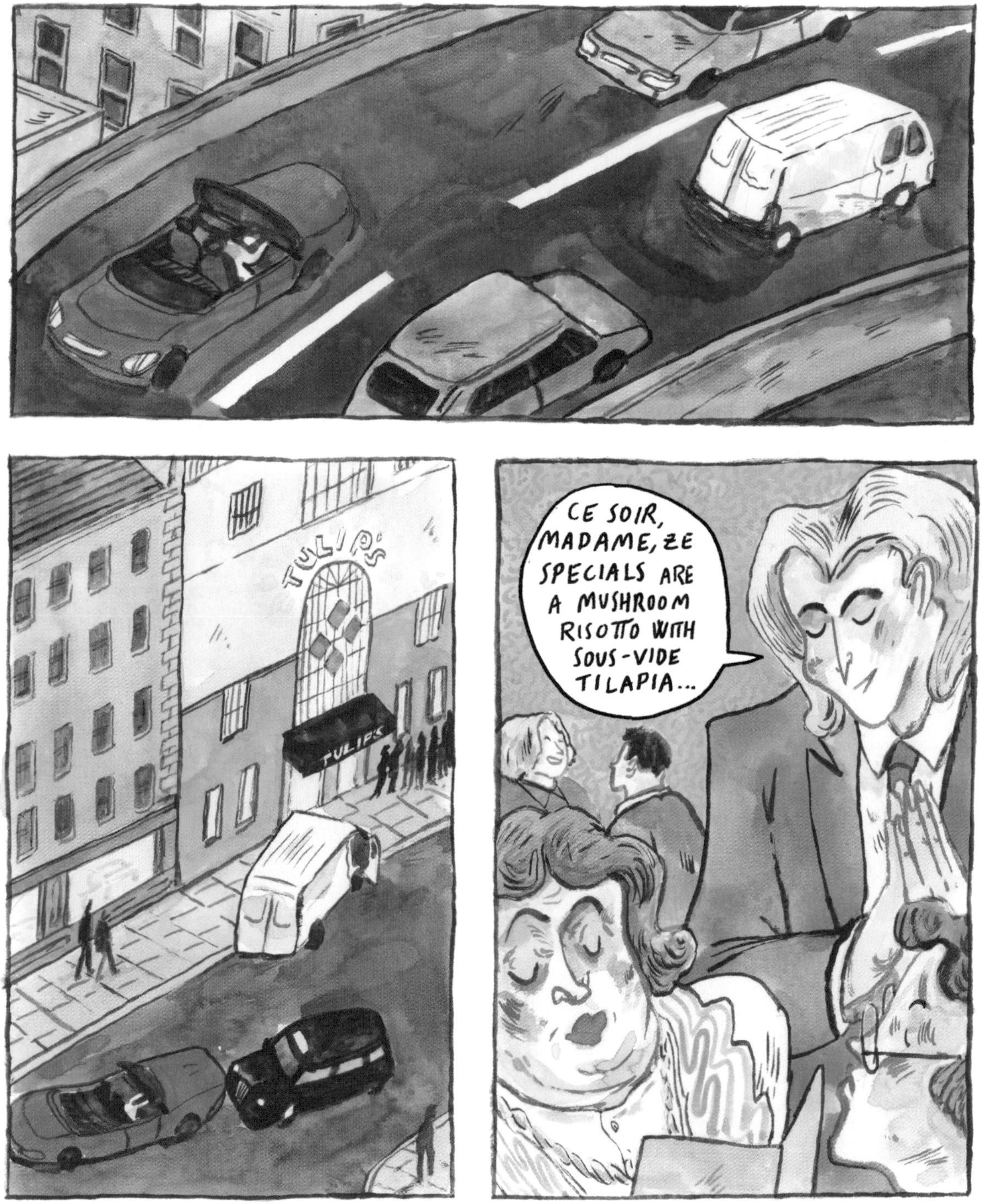
TULIPS
TULIPS
CE SOIR, MADAME, ZE SPECIALS ARE A MUSHROOM RISOTTO WITH SOUS-VIDE TILAPIA...

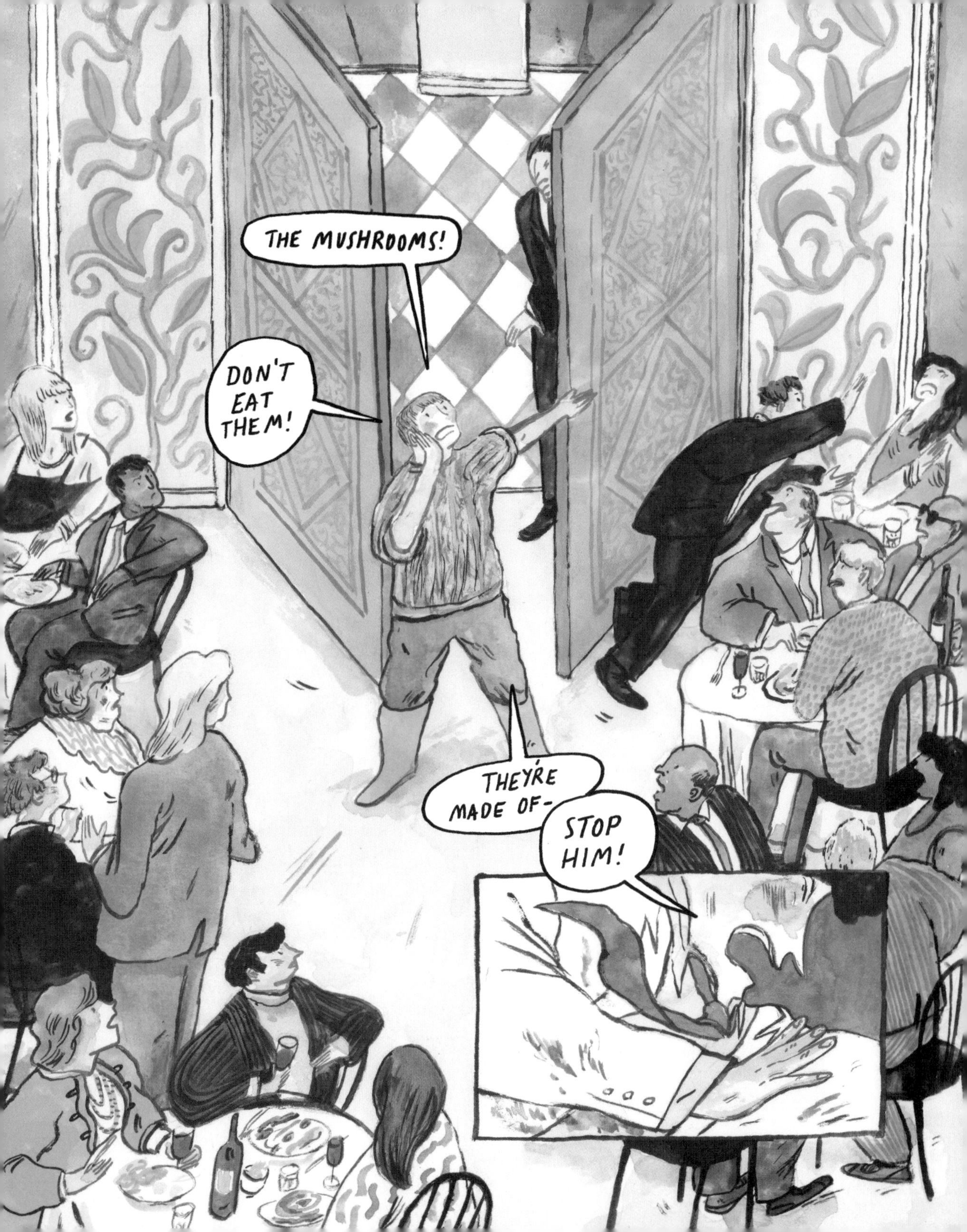
THE MUSHROOMS!
DON'T EAT THEM!
THEY'RE MADE OF-
STOP HIM!

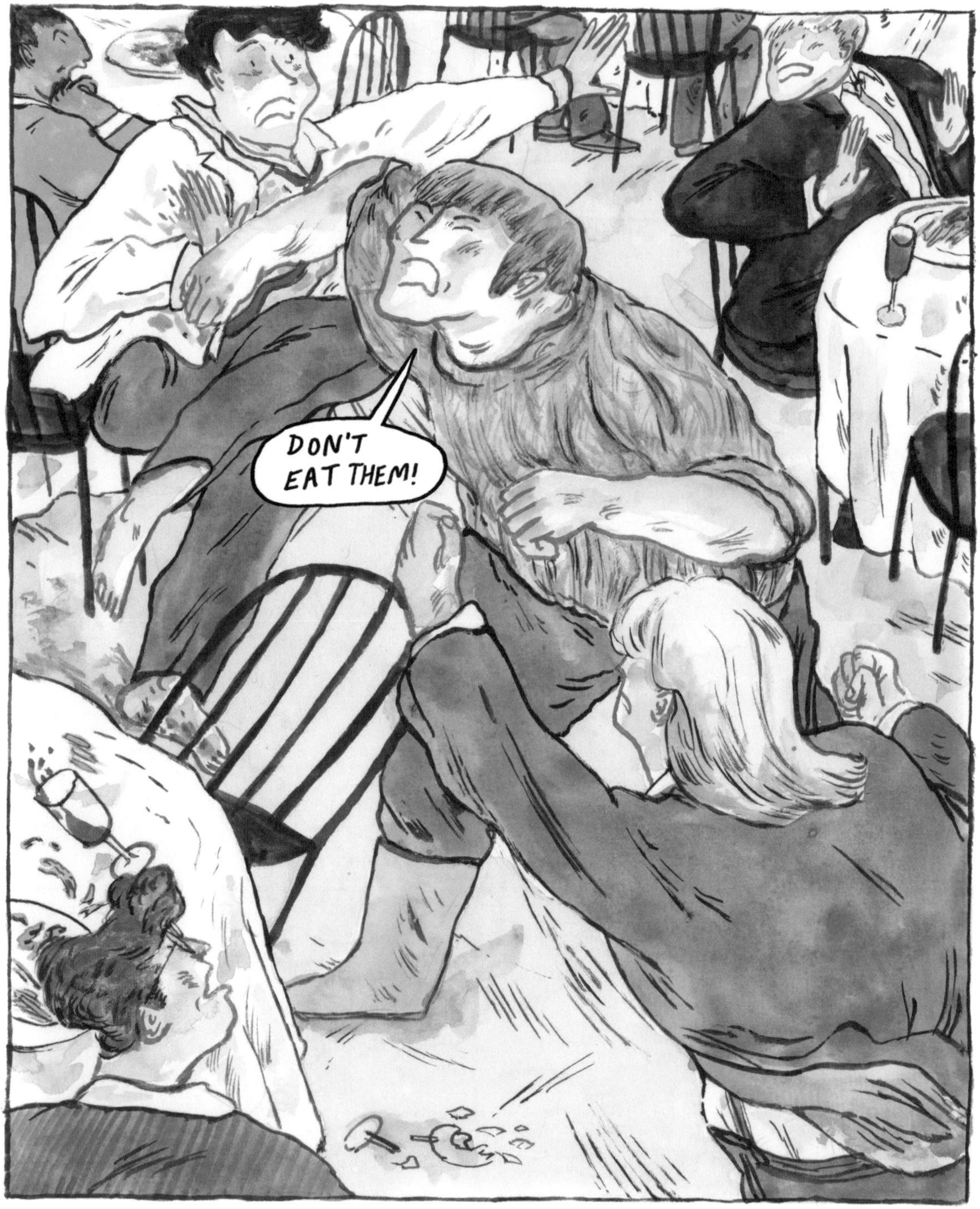
DON'T EAT THEM!

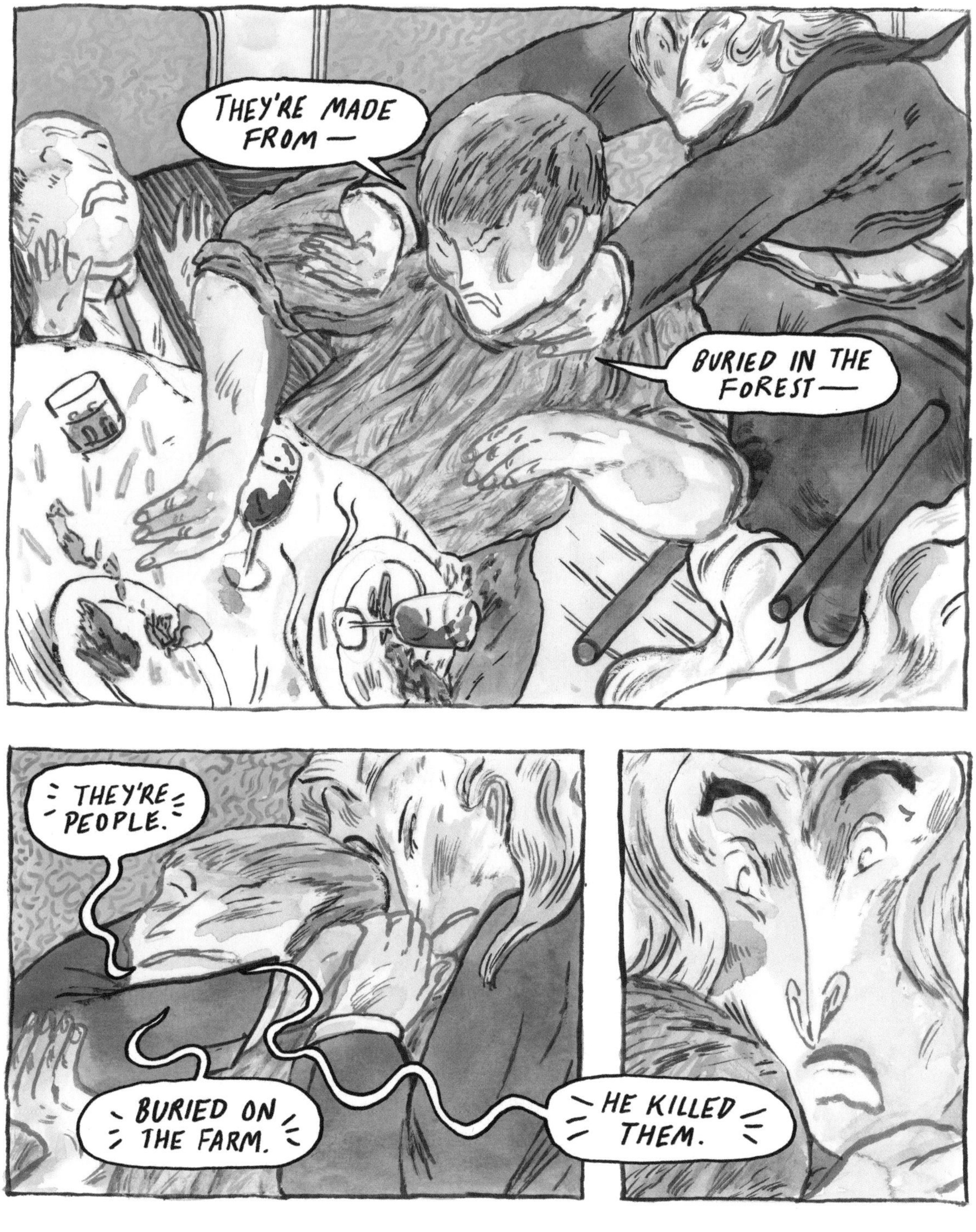
THEY'RE MADE FROM—
BURIED IN THE FOREST—
THEY'RE PEOPLE.
BURIED ON THE FARM.
HE KILLED THEM.

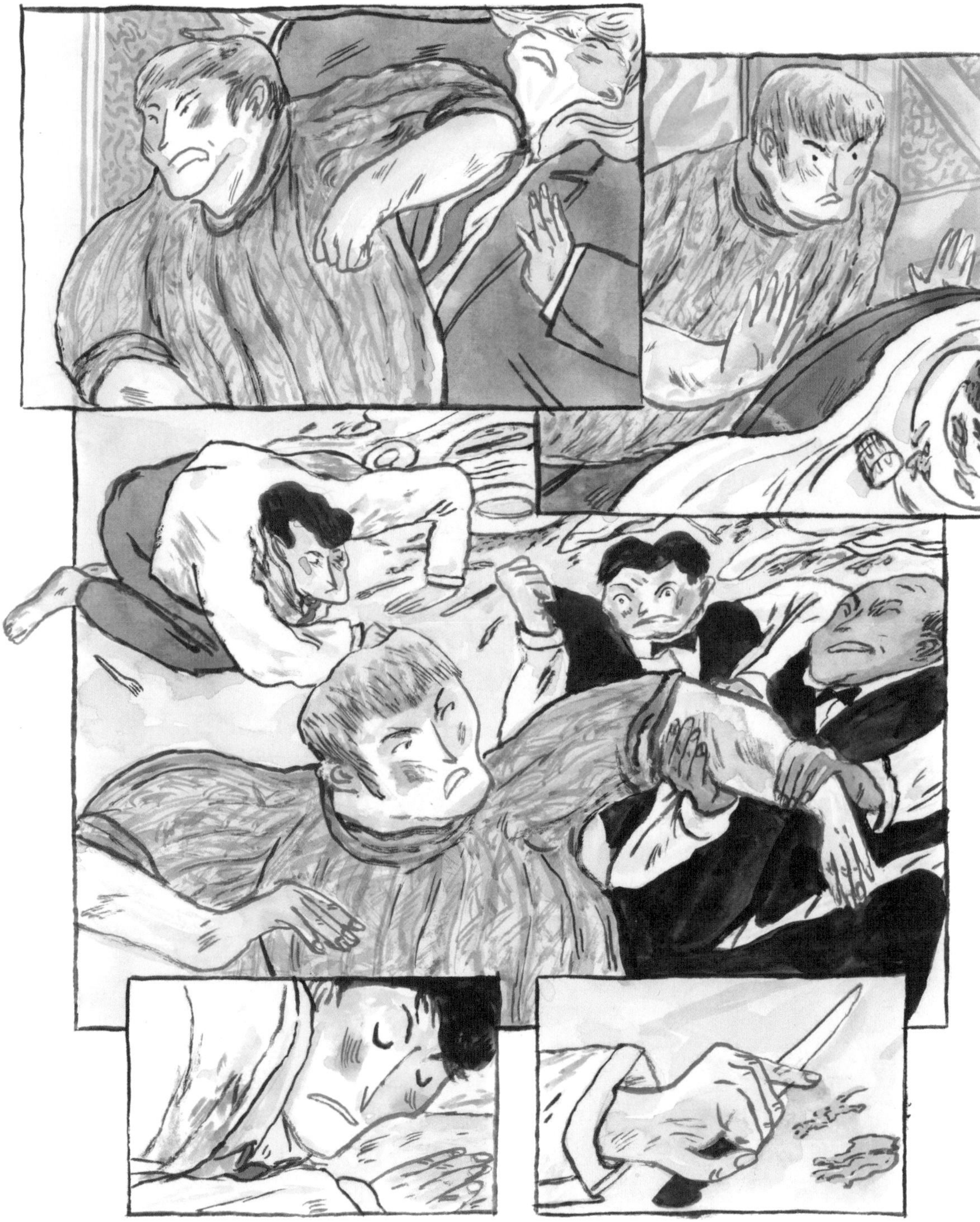

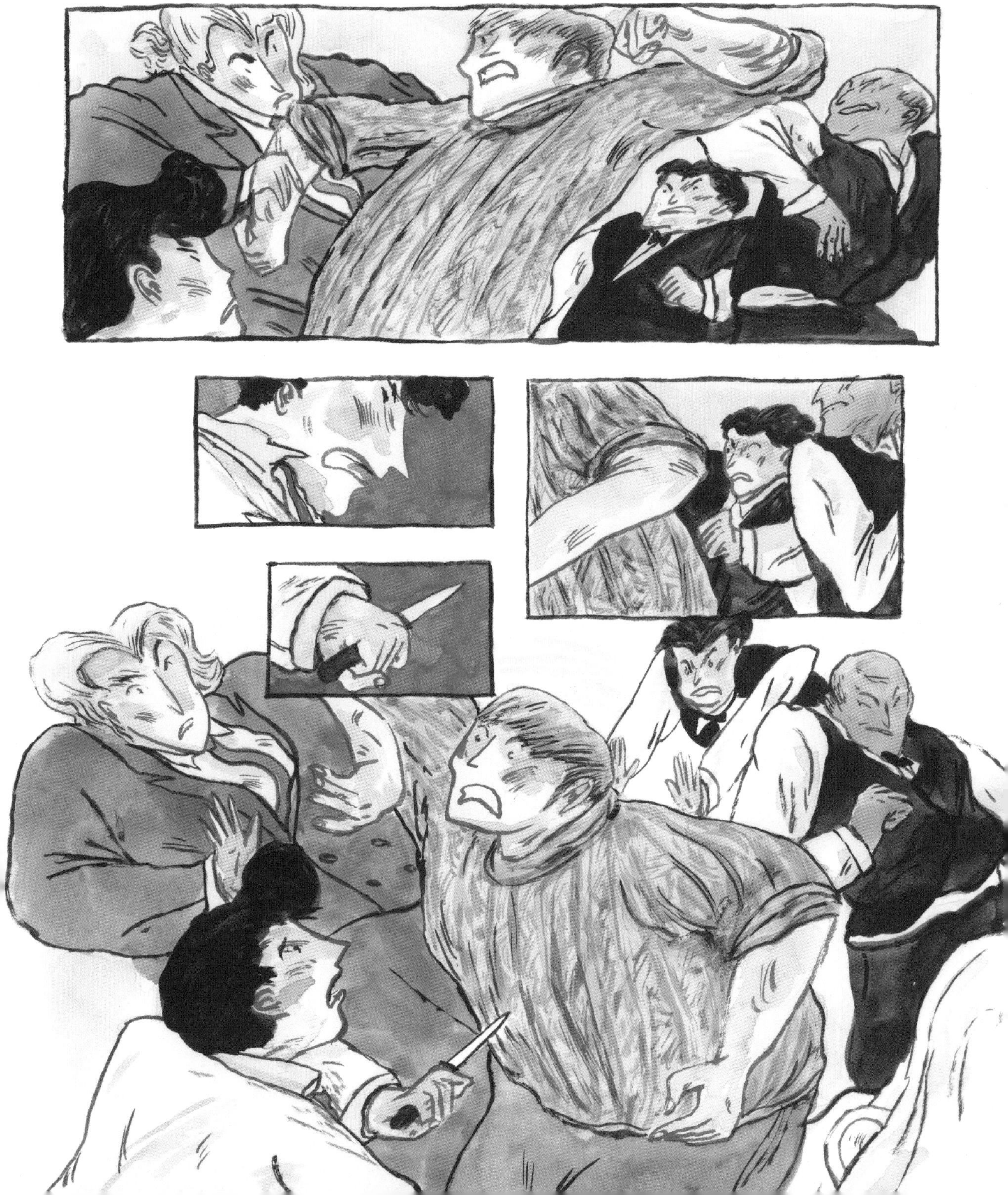

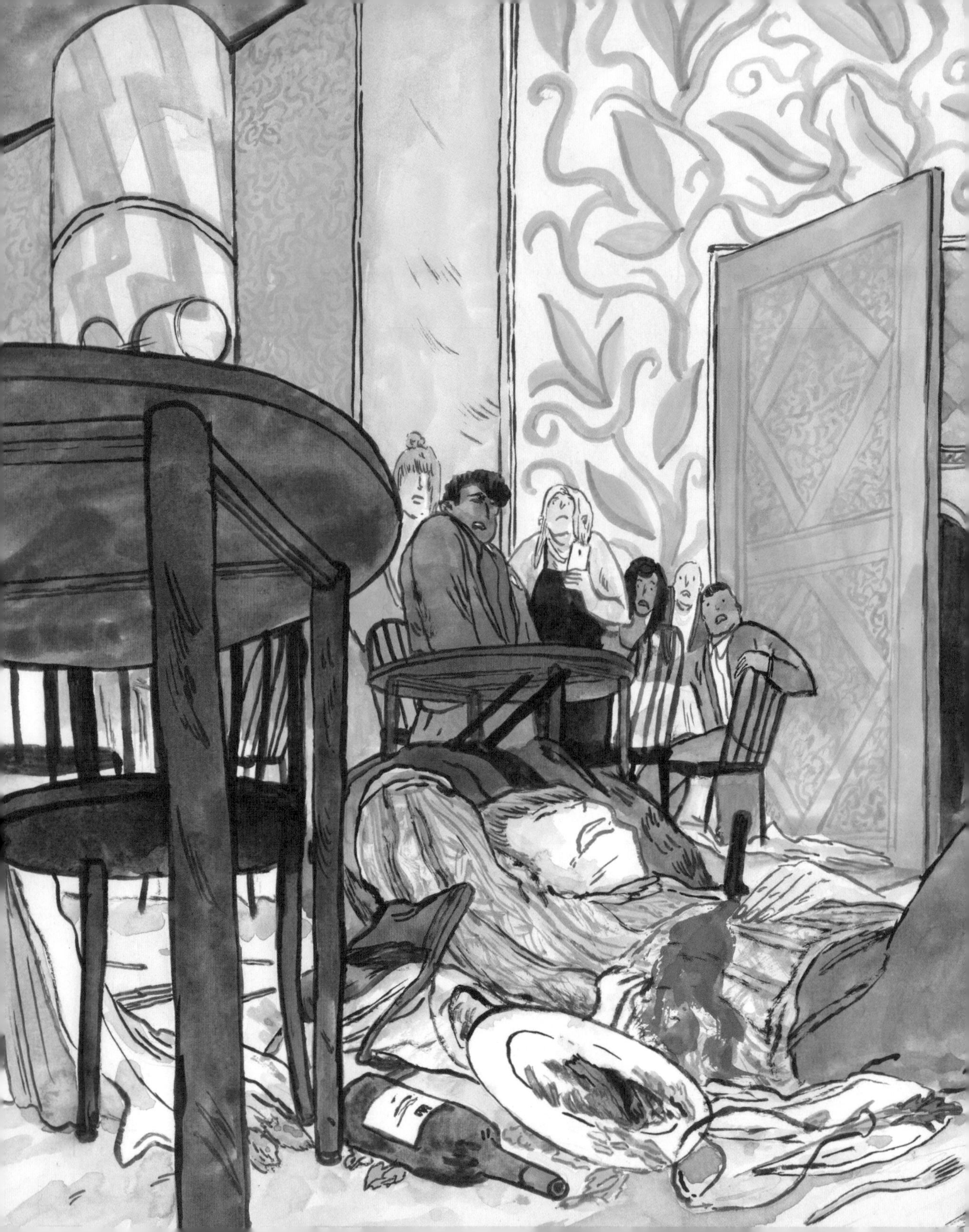

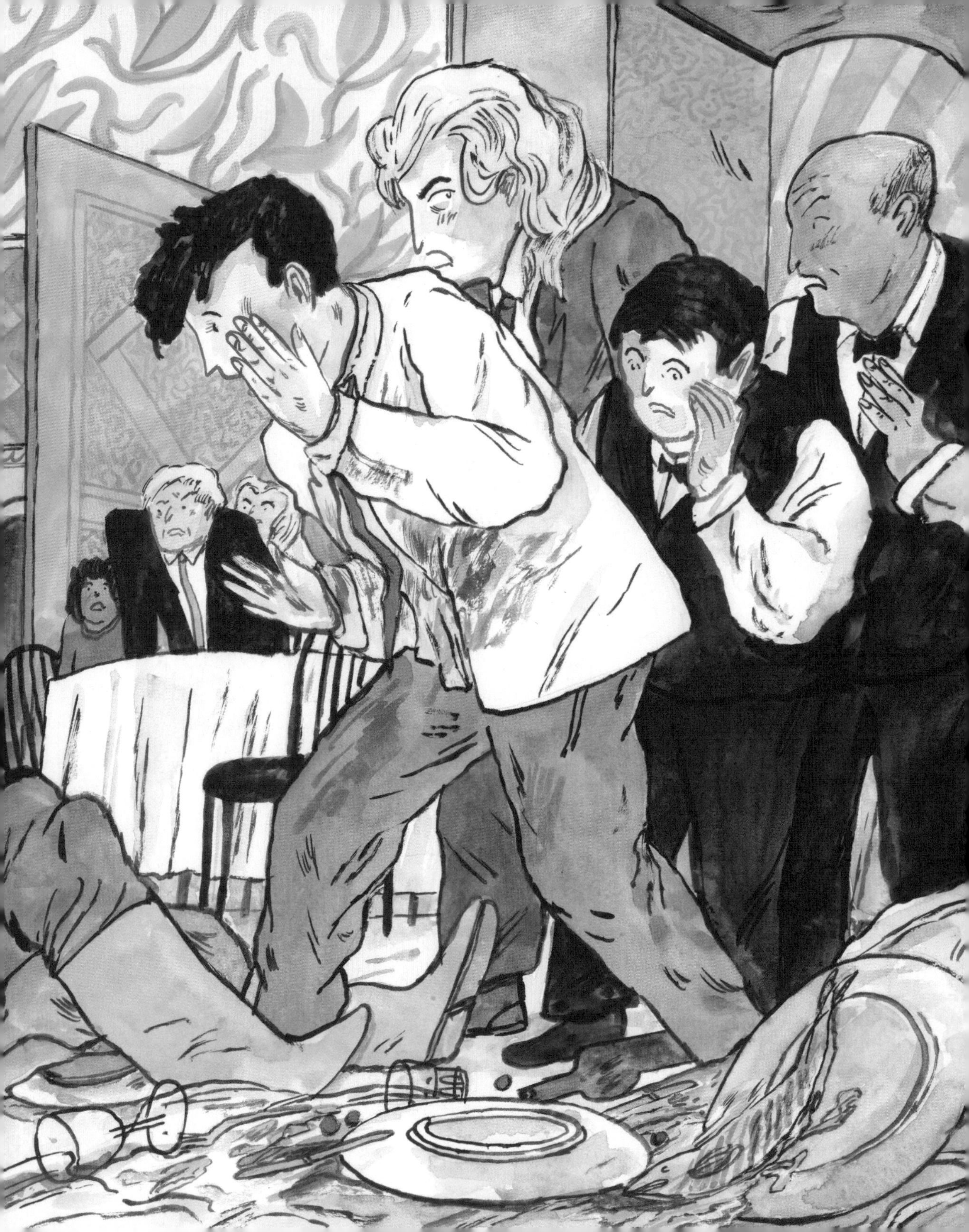

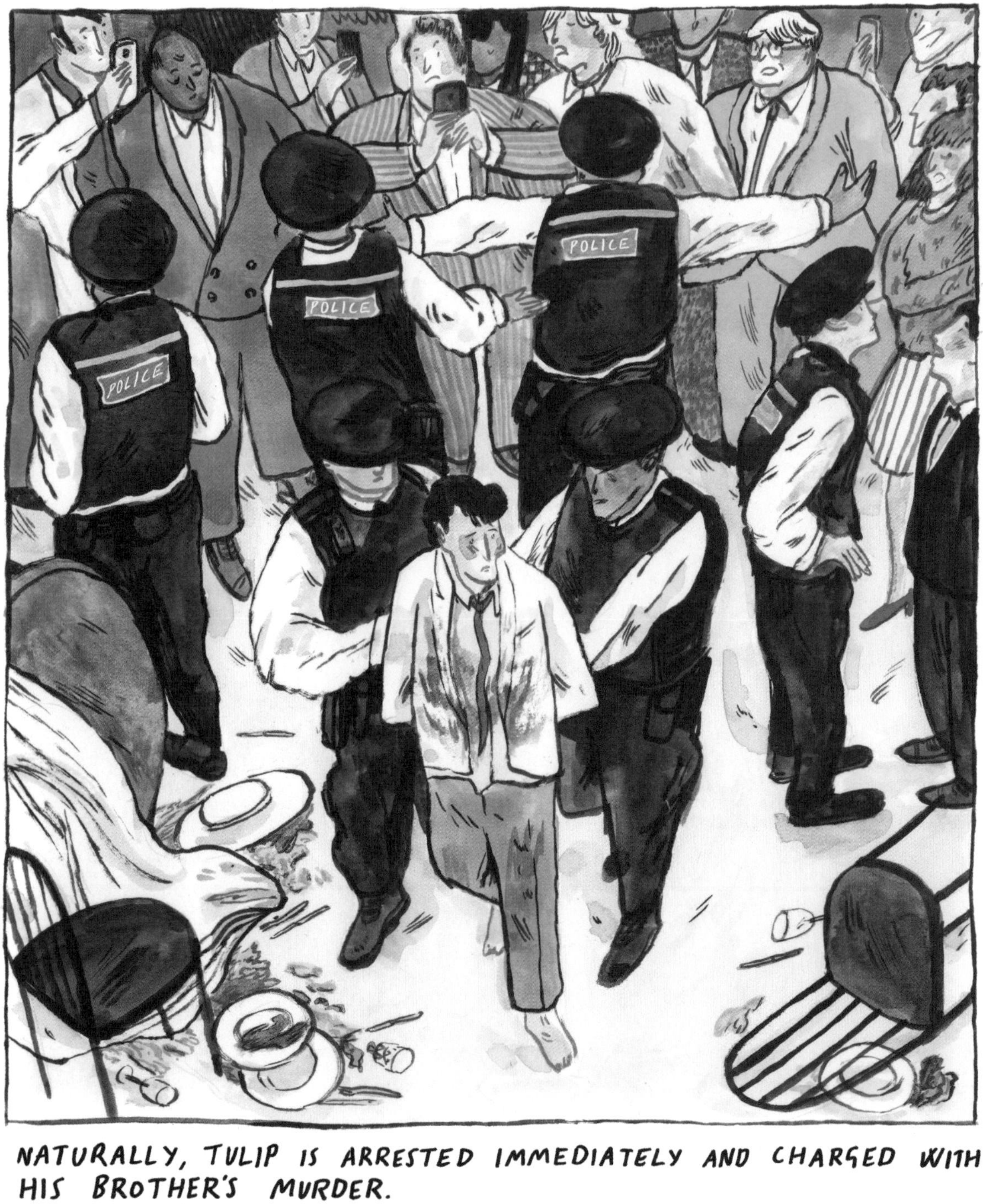
POLICE
POLICE
POLICE

NATURALLY, TULIP IS ARRESTED IMMEDIATELY AND CHARGED WITH HIS BROTHER'S MURDER.

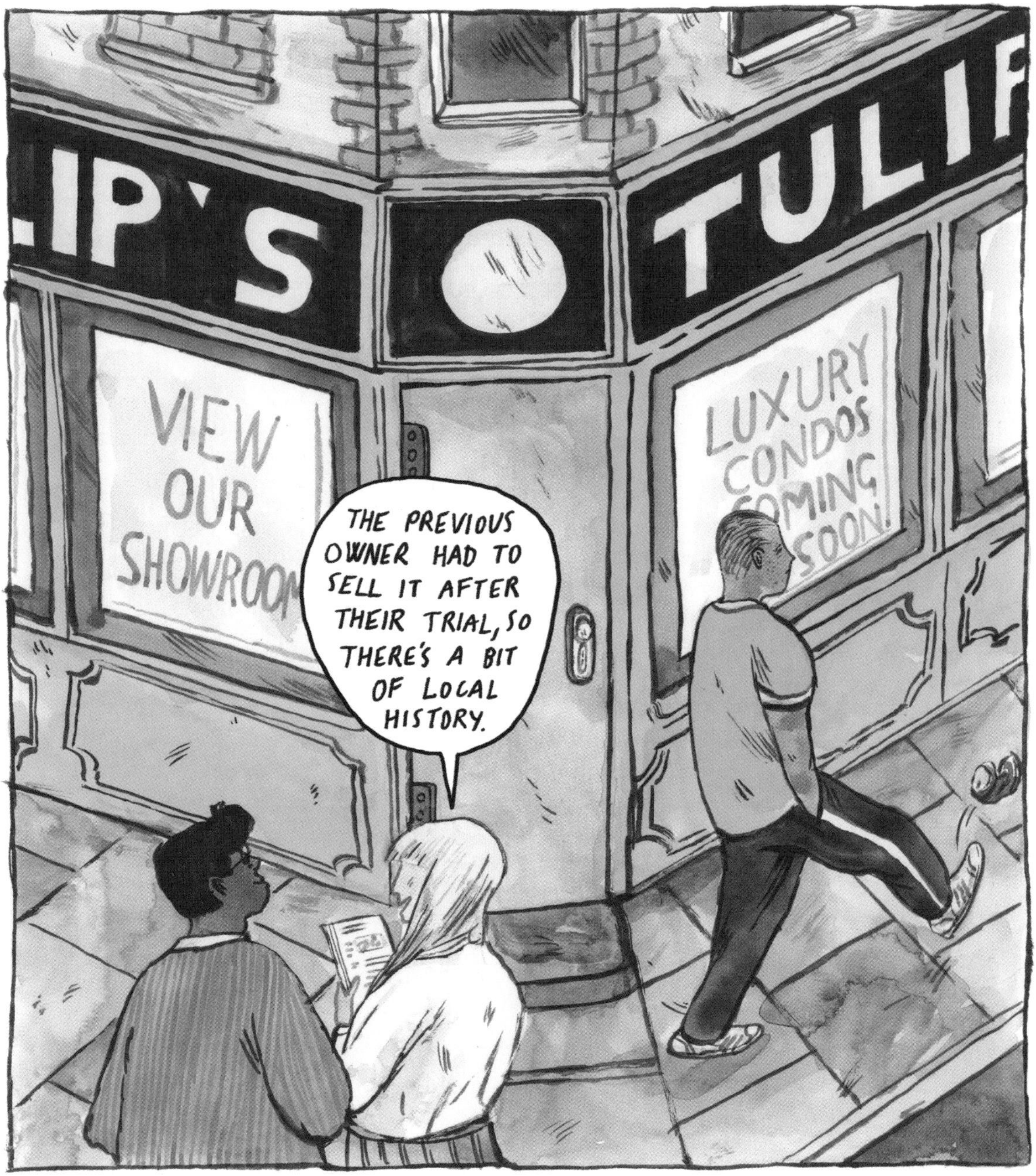
LIP'S
TULIP
VIEW OUR SHOWROOM
LUXURY CONDOS COMING SOON!
THE PREVIOUS OWNER HAD TO SELL IT AFTER THEIR TRIAL, SO THERE'S A BIT OF LOCAL HISTORY.

IF THE SCANDAL WASN'T ENOUGH TO DISSUADE DINERS, THE SHOCKED INVESTORS PULL OUT AND THE NEW YORK PARTNERS SUE FOR DAMAGES. THE RESTAURANTS CLOSE.

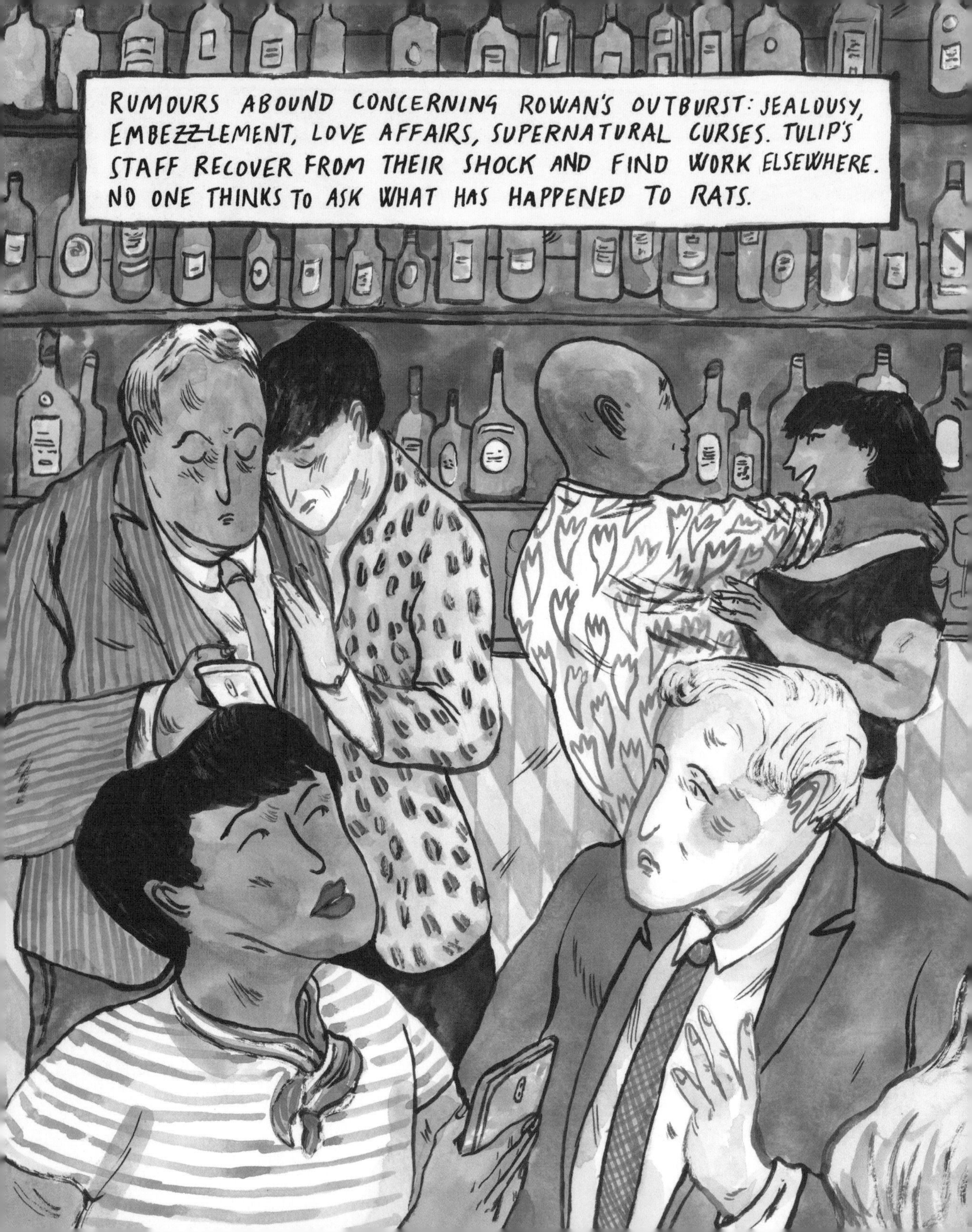
RUMOURS ABOUND CONCERNING ROWAN'S OUTBURST: JEALOUSY, EMBEZZLEMENT, LOVE AFFAIRS, SUPERNATURAL CURSES. TULIP'S STAFF RECOVER FROM THEIR SHOCK AND FIND WORK ELSEWHERE. NO ONE THINKS TO ASK WHAT HAS HAPPENED TO RATS.

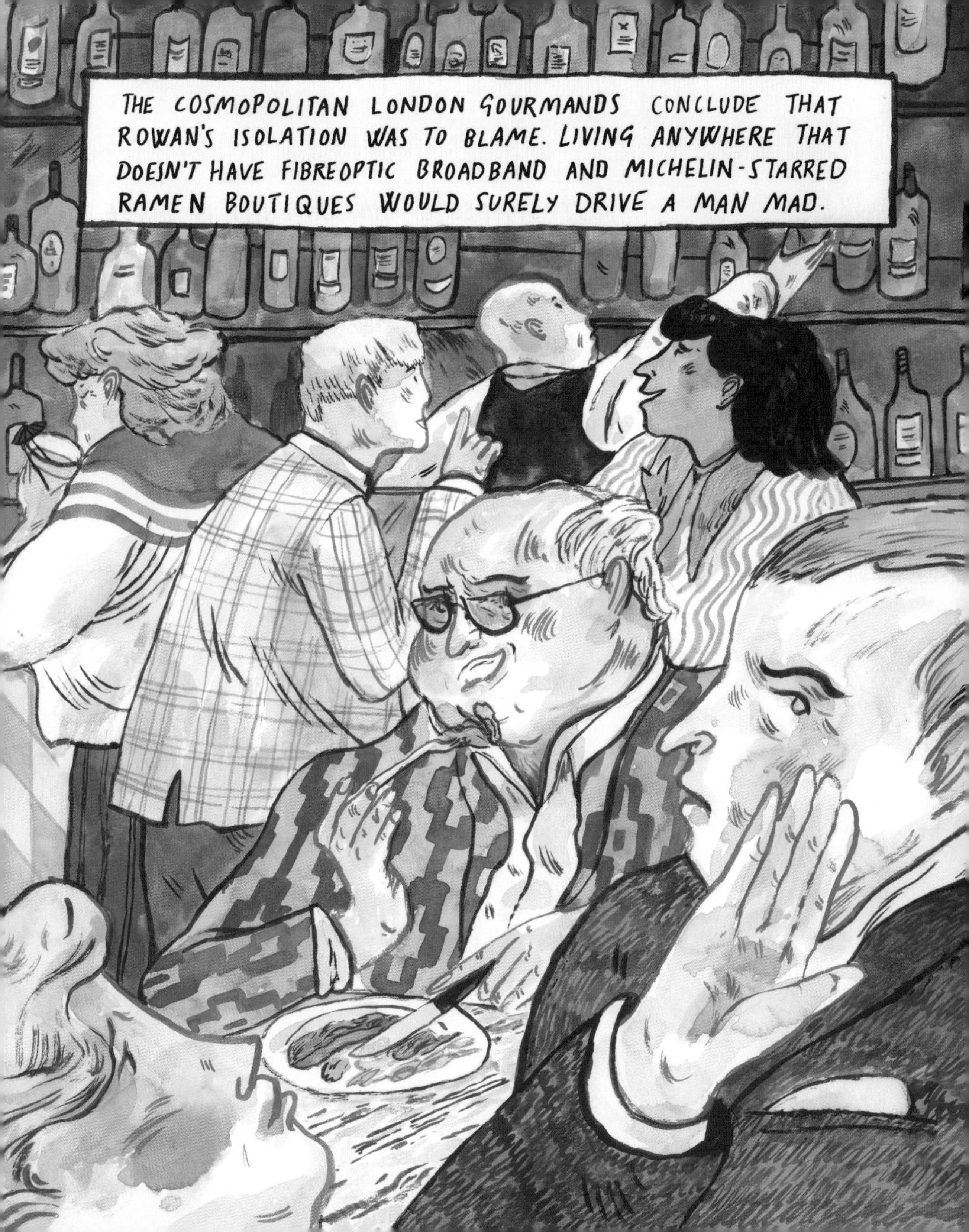
THE COSMOPOLITAN LONDON GOURMANDS CONCLUDE THAT ROWAN'S ISOLATION WAS TO BLAME. LIVING ANYWHERE THAT DOESN'T HAVE FIBREOPTIC BROADBAND AND MICHELIN-STARRED RAMEN BOUTIQUES WOULD SURELY DRIVE A MAN MAD.

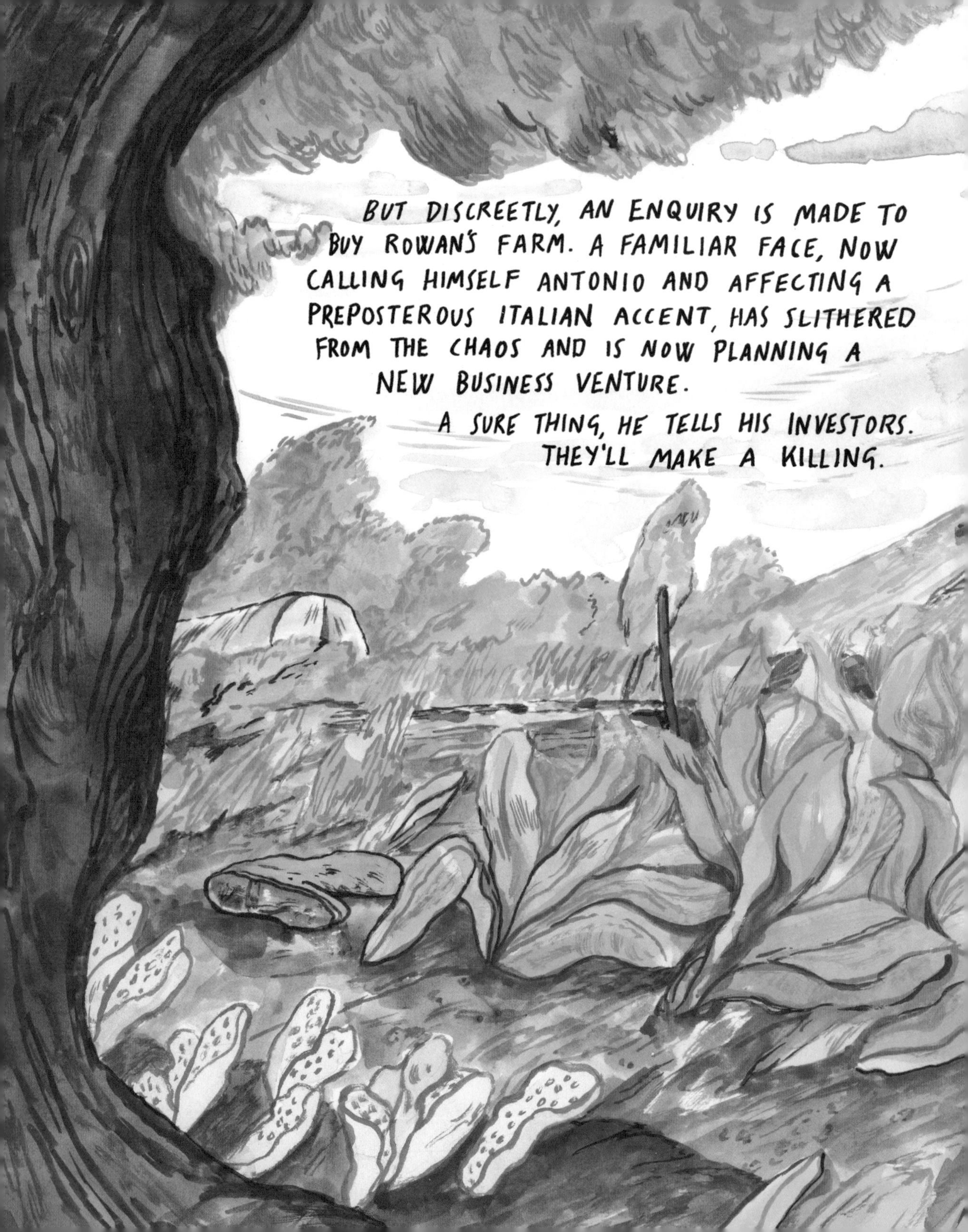
BUT DISCREETLY, AN ENQUIRY IS MADE TO BUY ROWAN'S FARM. A FAMILIAR FACE, NOW CALLING HIMSELF ANTONIO AND AFFECTING A PREPOSTEROUS ITALIAN ACCENT, HAS SLITHERED FROM THE CHAOS AND IS NOW PLANNING A NEW BUSINESS VENTURE.
A SURE THING, HE TELLS HIS INVESTORS. THEY'LL MAKE A KILLING.

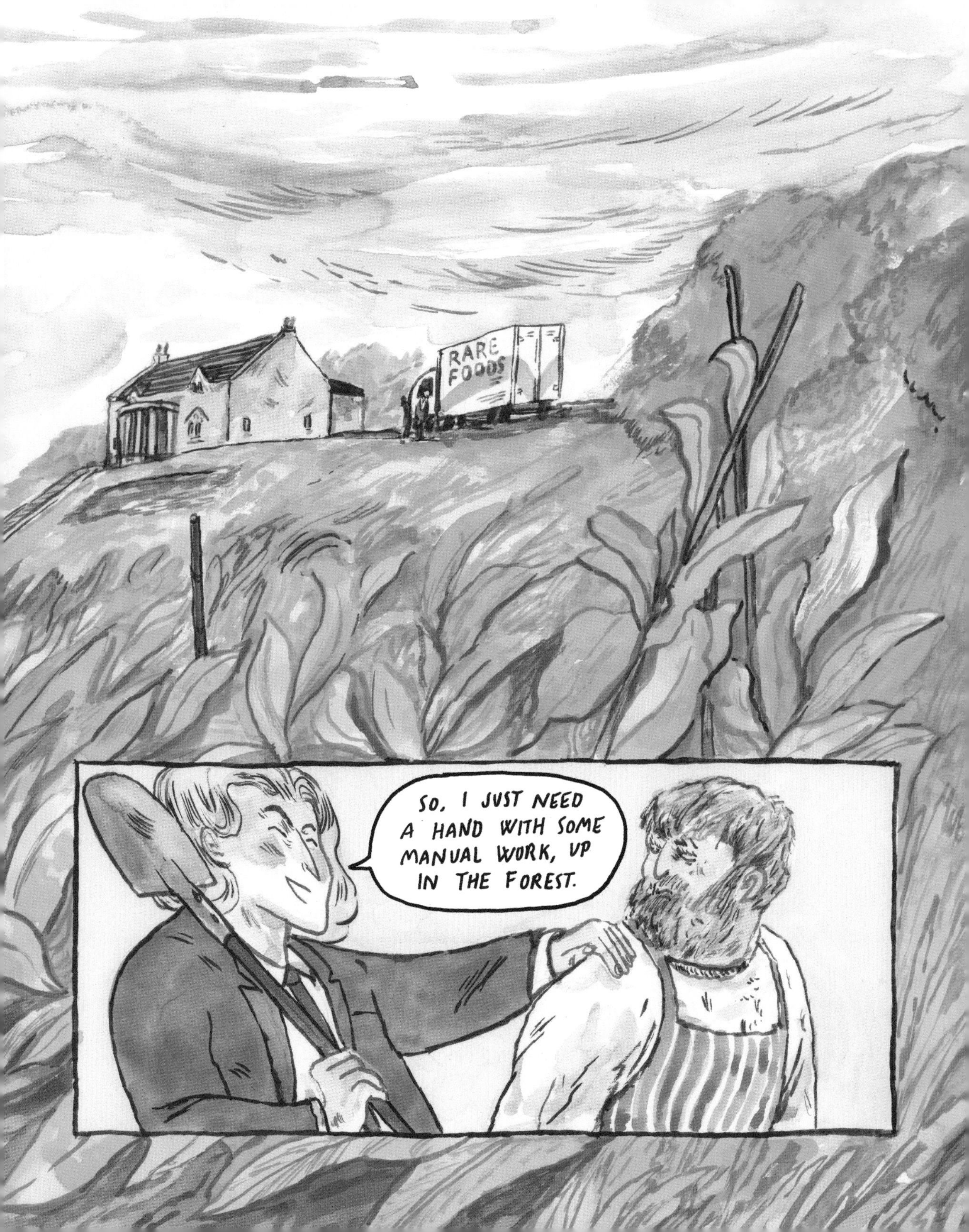
RARE FOODS
SO, I JUST NEED A HAND WITH SOME MANUAL WORK, UP IN THE FOREST.

This book would not have been possible without the support of the following people: Aarik Persaud of Cormack's Seafood and Val Buchanan of Buchanan Bistro, for their insights into the restaurant world; my sister Megan Albon, for her extensive knowledge of market gardening; and to my wife Cat O'Neil, for her love, encouragement, and morbid imagination.